THE FIRST WORLD WAR

TRILOGY

JOSEPH A. ALTSHELER

CONTENTS

THE GUNS OF EUROPE

THE FOREST OF SWORDS

THE HOSTS OF THE AIR

THE GUNS OF EUROPE

1

THE SISTINE MADONNA

JOHN TURNED a little to the left, going nearer to the window, where he could gain a better view of the Madonna, which he had heard so often was the most famous picture in the world. He was no technical judge of painting--he was far too young for such knowledge--but he always considered the effect of the whole upon himself, and he was satisfied with that method, feeling perhaps that he gained more from it than if he had been able to tear the master-work to pieces, merely in order to see how Raphael had made it.

"Note well, John, that this is the Sistine Madonna," began William Anson in his didactic, tutorial tone. "Observe the wonderful expression upon the face of the Holy Mother. Look now at the cherubs gazing up into the blue vault, in which the Madonna like an angel is poised. Behold the sublime artist's mastery of every detail. There are those who hold that the Madonna della Sedia at Florence is its equal in beauty and greatness, but I do not agree with them. To me the Sistine Madonna is always first. Centuries ago, even, its full worth was appreciated. It brought a great price at----"

The rest of his speech trailed off into nothingness. John had impatiently moved further away, and had deliberately closed his ear also to any dying sounds of oratory that might reach him. He had his own method of seeing the wonders of the Old World. He was interested or he was not. It was to him a state of mind, atmospheric in a way. He liked to breathe it in, and the rattle of a guide or tutor's lecture nearly always broke the spell.

Anxious that Mr. Anson should not have any further chance to mar his pleasure he moved yet closer to the great window from which came nearly all the light that fell upon the Sistine Madonna. There he stood almost in the center of the beams and gazed upon the illumined face, which spoke only of peace upon earth and good will. He was moved deeply, although there was no sign of it in his quiet eyes. He did not object to emotion and to its vivid expression in others, but his shy nature, feeling the need of a defensive armor, rejected it for himself.

It was a brighter day than the changeful climate of Dresden and the valley of the Elbe usually offered. The sunshine came in a great golden bar through the window and glowed over the wonderful painting which had stood the test of time and the critics. He had liked the good, gray city sitting beside its fine river. It had seemed friendly and kind to him, having in it the quality of home, something almost American in its simplicity and lack of caste.

They had arrived as soon as the doors were opened, and but few people were yet in the room. John came from his mood of exaltation and glanced at the others, every one in turn. Two women, evidently teachers, stood squarely in front of the picture and looked alternately at the Madonna and one of the red volumes that mark the advance of the American hosts in Europe. A man with a thick, black beard, evidently a Russian, moved incessantly back and forth, his feet keeping up a light shuffle on the floor. John wondered why some northern races should be so emotional and others so reserved. He had ceased to think that climate ruled expression.

A stout German frau stood gazing in apparent stolidity. Yet she was not so stolid as she seemed, because John caught a beam of appreciation in her eye. Presently she turned and went out, doubtless returning to some task of the thrifty housewife in this very city of Dresden. John thought her emblematic of Germany, homely herself, but with the undying love of the beautiful shown so freely in her fine cities, and in the parks, gardens and fountains more numerous than in an other country.

Her place was taken by an officer in a uniform, subdued in color, but martial. He was a tall, stiff man, and as he walked with a tread akin to the goosestep his feet clanked upon the floor. He wore a helmet, the cloth cover over the spike, but John noticed that he did not take off the helmet in the presence of the Sistine Madonna. He moved to a place in front of the picture, brushing against the sisterhood of the red book, and making no apology. There he stood, indifferent to those about him, holding himself as one superior, dominant by force, the lord by right of rank over inferior beings.

John's heart swelled with a sense of resentment and hostility. He knew perfectly well that the stranger was a Prussian officer--a strong man too, both in mind and body. He stood upright, more than six feet tall, his wide shoulders thrown well back, his large head set upon a powerful neck. Reddish hair showed beneath the edges of the helmet, and the blue eyes that gazed at the picture were dominant and masterful. He was about thirty, just at the age when those who are strong have tested their minds against other men in the real arena of life and find them good. The heavy, protruding jaw and the compressed lips made upon John the impression of power.

The picture grew somewhat dim. One of those rapid changes to which Dresden is subject occurred. The sunshine faded and a grayness as of twilight filtered into the room. The glances of the young American and the Prussian officer turned away from the Madonna at the same time and met.

John was conscious that the blue eyes were piercing into him, but he had abundant courage and resolution and he gave back the look with a firmness and steadiness, equal to the Prussian's own. The cold steel of that glance rested upon him only for a few moments. It passed on, dissected in an instant the two teachers with the red guide book, and then the man walking, to the window, looked out at the gray walls of the city.

John had not lowered his eyes before the intrusive gaze, but he felt now as if he had been subjected to an electric current. He was at once angry and indignant, but, resolving to throw it off, he shrugged his shoulders a little, and turned to his older friend who was supposed to be comrade and teacher at the same time.

Mr. Anson, the didactic strain, strong in him, recovered his importance, and began to talk again. He did not confine himself any longer to the Sistine Madonna, but talked of other pictures in the famous gallery, the wonderful art of Rubens and Jordaens, although it seemed to John's normal mind that they had devoted themselves chiefly to studies in fat. But the longest lecture must come to an end, and as the inevitable crowd gathered before the Madonna William Anson was forced by courtesy into silence. The Prussian had already gone, still wearing his defiant helmet, his sword swinging stiffly from his belt, his heavy boots clanking on the floor.

"Did you notice that officer?" asked John.

"I gave him a casual glance. He is not different from the others. You see them everywhere in Germany."

"He seemed typical to me. I don't recall another man who has impressed me so much. To me he personified the great German military organization which we are all so sure is invincible."

"And it *is* invincible. Nothing like the German army has ever before stood on this planet. A great race, strong in both body and mind, has devoted itself for half a century to learning everything that is to be learned about war. It's a magnificent machine, smooth, powerful, tremendous, unconquerable, and for that very reason neither you nor I, John, will ever see a war of the first magnitude in Europe. It would be too destructive. The nations would shrink back, appalled. Besides, the tide is the other way. Remember all those ministers who came over with us on the boat to attend the peace conference at Constance."

John accepted readily all that Mr. Anson said, and the significance of the Prussian, due he was sure to his own imagination, passed quickly from his mind. But he was tired of pictures. He had found that he could assimilate only a certain quantity, and after that all the rest, even be they Raphael, Murillo and Rubens, became a mere blur.

"Let's go out and walk on the terraces over the river," he said.

"But many other famous pictures are here. We can't afford to go back to America, and admit that we haven't seen some of the masterpieces of the Dresden gallery."

John laughed.

"No, we can't," he said, "because if we do ignore a single one that's the very one all our friends will tell us we should certainly have seen. But my eyes are growing tired, there's a congestion in the back of my head, and these polished floors have stiffened my ankles. Besides, we've plenty of time, and we can come back as often as we wish."

"I suppose then that we must go," said Mr. Anson, reluctantly. "But one should make the most of the opportunities for culture, vouchsafed to him."

John made no reply. He had heard that note so often. Mr. Anson was tremendous on "culture", and John thought it all right for him and others like him, but he preferred his own methods for himself. He led the way from the gallery and the older man followed reluctantly.

The sun, having gone behind the clouds, stayed there and Dresden was still gray, but John liked it best in its sober colors. Then the homely touch, the friendly feeling in the air were stronger. These people were much like his own. Many of them could have passed for Americans, and they welcomed as brethren those who came from beyond the Atlantic.

He looked from the Bruhl Terraces over the Elbe--a fine river too he thought it--the galleries, the palaces, the opera house, the hotels, and all the good gray city, beloved of English and Americans as well as Germans.

"What is that buzzing and whirring, John?" asked Mr. Anson suddenly.

"Look up! Always look up, when you hear that sound, and you will see the answer to your question written in the skies! There it goes! It's passing over the portion of the city beyond the river."

The long black shape of the Zeppelin dirigible was outlined clearly, as it moved off swiftly toward the southwest. It did not seem to diminish in size, as it left the city, but hung huge and somber against the sky, its whirr and buzz still audible.

"An interesting toy," said Mr. Anson.

"If a toy, it's certainly a gigantic one," said John.

"Tremendous in size, but a toy nevertheless."

"We're going up in it you know."

"Are you still bent upon that wild flight?"

"Why there's no danger. Herr Simmering, the proprietor of our hotel, chartered a dirigible last week, and took up all the guests who were willing to pay and go. I've talked to some of them and they say it was a wonderful experience. You remember that he's chartered another for next week, and you promised me we could go."

"Yes, I promised, but I thought at the time that something would surely happen to prevent it."

"Indian promises! I won't let you back out now!"

William Anson sighed. His was a sober mind. He liked the solid earth for his travels, and he would fain leave the air to others. The daring of young John Scott, for whom he felt in a measure responsible, often alarmed him, but John concealed under his quiet face and manner an immense fund of resolution.

"Suppose we go to the hotel," Mr. Anson said. "The air is rather keen and I'm growing hungry."

"First call in the dining-car," said John, "and I come."

"I notice that you're always eager for the table, although you shirk the pictures and statues, now and then."

"It's merely the necessity of nature, Mr. Anson. The paint and marble will do any time."

William Anson smiled. He liked his young comrade, all the more so perhaps because they were so different. John supplied the daring and adventurous spirit that he lacked, and the youth had enough for two.

"I wonder if any new people have come," said John, as they walked down the steps from the terrace. "Don't think I'm weak on culture, Mr. Anson, but it's always interesting to me to go back to the hotel, see what fresh types have appeared, and guess from what countries they have come."

"The refuge of a lazy mind which is unwilling to cope with its opportunities for learning and progress. John, I feel sometimes that you are almost hopeless. You have a frivolous strain that you ought to get rid of as soon as you can."

"Well, sir, I had to laugh at those fat Venuses of Rubens and Jordaens.

They may be art, but I never thought that Venus weighed three hundred pounds. I know those two painters had to advertise all through the Low Countries, before they could get models fat enough."

"Stop, John! Is nothing sacred to you?"

"A lady can be too fat to be sacred."

Mr. Anson shook his head. He always stood impressed, and perhaps a little awed before centuries of culture, and he failed to understand how any one could challenge the accepted past. John's Philistine spirit, which he deemed all the more irregular in one so young pained him at times. Yet it was more assumed than real with young Scott.

They reached their hotel and passed into the dining-room, where both did full justice to the good German food. John did not fail to make his usual inspection of guests, but he started a little, when he saw the Prussian officer of the gallery, alone at a table by a window overlooking the Elbe. It was one of the pleasantest views in Europe, but John knew very well that the man was thinking little of it. His jaw had not lost is pugnacious thrust, and he snapped his orders to the waiter as if he were rebuking a recruit.

Nobody had told John that he was a Prussian, but the young American knew it nevertheless, and he knew him to be a product, out of the very heart of that iron military system, before which the whole world stood afraid, buttressed as it was by tremendous victories over France, and a state of readiness known to be without an equal.

Herr Simmering, fat, bland and bald, was bending over them, asking them solicitously if all was right. John always liked this bit of personal attention from the European hotel proprietors. It established a friendly feeling. It showed that one was not lost among the swarm of guests, and here in Germany it invariably made his heart warm to the civilians.

"Can you tell us, Herr Simmering," he asked, "who is the officer alone in the alcove by the window?"

Herr Gustav Adolph Simmering, the soul of blandness and courtesy, stiffened in an instant. With the asking of that simple question he seemed to breathe a new and surcharged air. He lost his expansiveness in the presence of the German army or any representative of it. Lowering his voice he replied:

"A captain attached in some capacity to the General Staff in Berlin.

Rudolf von Boehlen is his name. It is said that he has high connections, a distant cousin of the von Moltkes, in much favor, too, with the Emperor."

"Do Prussian officers have to come here and tell the Saxons what to do?"

The good Herr Simmering spread out his hands in horror. These simple Americans surely asked strange and intrusive questions. One could forgive them only because they were so open, so much like innocent children, and, unlike those disagreeable English, quarreled so little about their bills.

"I know no more," he replied. "Here in Germany we never ask why an officer comes and goes. We trust implicitly in the Emperor and his advisers who have guarded us so well, and we do not wish to learn the higher secrets of state. We know that such knowledge is not for us."

Dignified and slow, as became an important landlord, he nevertheless went away with enough haste to indicate clearly to John that he wished to avoid any more questions about the Prussian officer. John was annoyed. He felt a touch of shame for Herr Simmering.

"I wish the Germans wouldn't stand in such tremendous awe of their own army," he said. "They seem to regard it as some mysterious and omnipotent force which is always right."

"Don't forget their education and training, John. The great German empire has risen upon the victories of 1870, and if ever war between them should come again Germany could smash France as easily as she did then."

"I could never become reconciled to the spectacle of an empire treading a republic into the earth."

Mr. Anson smiled. He had dined well, and he was at peace with the earth.

"Names mean little," he said indulgently.

John did not reply, but his under jaw thrust forward in a pugnacious manner, startlingly like that of the Prussian. The officer, although no word had passed between them, nor even a glance of real hostility had aroused a stubborn antagonism, increased by the obvious awe of Herr Simmering and the deference paid to him by the whole establishment of the hotel.

He saw Captain von Boehlen go out, and drawn by a vague resolve

he excused himself, abandoning Mr. Anson who was still trifling pleasantly with the fruit, and also left the dining-room. He saw the captain
receive his helmet from an obsequious waiter, put it on his head and
walk into the parlor, his heavy boots as usual clanking upon the
polished floor. In the final analysis it was this very act of keeping his
helmet on, no matter where he was, that repelled young Scott and
aroused his keen enmity.

John went to the smoking-room. Von Boehlen lingered a moment or
two in the parlor, and then took his way also down the narrow passage to
the smoking-room. It was perhaps a part of the American's vague plan
that he should decide suddenly to go by the same way to the parlor.
Hence it was inevitable that they should meet if Captain von Boehlen
kept his course--an invariable one with him--in the very center of the
hall. John liked the center of the hall, too, particularly on that day. He
was tall and strong and he knew that he would have the advantage of
readiness, which everybody said was the cardinal virtue of the Prussian
army.

Just before they reached the point of contact the Prussian started
back with a muttered oath of surprise and annoyance. His hand flew to
the hilt of his sword, and then came away again. John watching him
closely was sure that hand and hilt would not have parted company so
readily had it been a German civilian who was claiming with Captain
Rudolf von Boehlen an equal share of the way.

But John saw the angry flash in the eyes of the Prussian die suddenly
like a light put out by a puff of wind, and the compressed line of the lips
relax. He knew that it was not the result of innate feeling, but of a mental
effort made by von Boehlen, and he surmised that the fact of his being a
foreigner had all to do with it. Yet he waited for the other to apologize
first.

"Pardon," said the captain, "it is somewhat dark here, and as I was
absorbed in thought. I did not notice you."

His English was excellent and his manner polite enough. John could
do nothing less than respond in kind.

"It was perhaps my fault more than yours," he said.

The face of Captain von Boehlen relaxed yet further into a smile.

"You are an American," he said, "a member of an amiable race, our welcome guests in Europe. What could our hotels and museums do without you?"

When he smiled he showed splendid white teeth, sharp and powerful. His manner, too, had become compelling. John could not now deny its charm. Perhaps his first estimate of Captain von Boehlen had been wrong.

"It is true that we come in shoals," he responded. "Sometimes I'm not sure whether we're welcome to the general population."

"Oh, yes, you are. The Americans are the spoiled children of Europe."

"At least we are the children of Europe. The people on both sides of the Atlantic are apt to forget that. We're transplanted Europeans. The Indians are the only people of the original American stock."

"But you are not Europeans. One can always tell the difference. You speak English, but you are not English. I should never take an American for an Englishman."

"But our basis is British. Despite all the infusions of other bloods, and they've been large, Great Britain is our mother country. I feel it myself."

Von Boehlen smiled tranquilly.

"Great Britain has always been your chief enemy," he said. "You have been at war with her twice, and in your civil war, when you were in dire straits her predominant classes not only wished for your destruction, but did what they could to achieve it."

"Old deeds," said John. "The bad things of fifty or a hundred years ago are dead and buried."

But the Prussian would not have it so. Germany, he said, was the chief friend of America. Their peoples, he insisted, were united not only by a tie of blood, but by points of view, similar in so many important cases. He seemed for some inscrutable reason anxious to convince one as young as his listener, and he employed a smoothness of speech and a charm of manner that John in the morning in the gallery would have thought impossible in one so stiff and haughty. The spell that this man was able to cast increased, and yet he was always conscious of a pitiless strength behind it.

John presently found himself telling his name, how he was traveling with William Anson, older than himself, and in a way both a comrade and a tutor, how he expected to meet his uncle, James Pomeroy, a United

States Senator, in Vienna, and his intention of returning to America early in the autumn to finish his course at the university.

"I should like to see that America of yours," said von Boehlen, after he had told something of himself, "but I fear it is not to be this year."

"You stay in Dresden long?" asked John.

"No, I leave tonight, but we may meet again, and then you can tell me more of that far western world, so vast and so interesting, but of which we Europeans really know so little."

John noticed that he did not tell where he was going. But he surmised that Prussian army officers usually kept their destination to themselves. His talk with von Boehlen had impressed him more than ever with the size, speed and overwhelming power of the German army machine. It was not possible for anything to stand before it, and the mystery that clothed it around imparted to it a superhuman quality.

But he brushed away such thoughts. The sun was shining again. It danced in a myriad golden beams over the Elbe, it clothed in warmth the kindly city, and von Boehlen, with a politeness that was now unimpeachable rose to tell him good-bye. He acknowledged to himself that he felt a little flattered by the man's attention, and his courtesy was equal to that of the Prussian. Then the officer, dropping his hand to the hilt of his sword, apparently a favorite gesture, stalked away.

It was John's first impulse to tell Mr. Anson of his talk with von Boehlen, but he obeyed his second and kept it to himself. Even after he was gone the feeling that some motive was behind the Prussian's blandness remained.

A letter came that afternoon from his uncle, the Senator. He was in Vienna, and he wished his nephew and Mr. Anson to join him there, cutting short their stay in Dresden. They could come by the way of Prague, and a day or two spent in that old Bohemian city would repay them. John showed the letter to Mr. Anson, who agreed with him that a wish from the Senator was in reality a command, and should be obeyed promptly.

John, although he liked Dresden, had but one regret. He could not go up in the Zeppelin dirigible and he hastened to tell Herr Simmering that his entry was withdrawn.

"I'll have to cut out the dirigible," he said in his colloquial tongue. "Perhaps you can find somebody to take my place."

"Perhaps," said the landlord, "and on the other hand it may be that the dirigible will not go up for me.

"Why? I thought you had chartered it for a second trip."

Herr Simmering compressed his lips. John saw that, under impulse, he had said more than he intended. It was an objection of his to Germany--this constant secrecy and mystery that seemed to him not only useless but against the natural flow of human nature.

"Are all the Zeppelins confiscated by the government?" he asked, speaking wholly at random.

Herr Simmering started. Fat and smooth, he shot a single, menacing glance at the young American. But, in a moment, he was smiling again and John had not noticed.

"Our government never tells its plans," he said. "Mr. Anson says that you leave tomorrow for Prague."

"Yes," said John curiously, "and I can almost infer from your tone, Herr Simmering, that you will be glad to see us go."

But Herr Simmering protested earnestly that he never liked to lose paying guests, above all those delightful Americans, who had so much appreciation and who made so little trouble. The German soul and the American soul were akin.

"Well, we do like your country and your people," said John. "That's the reason we come here so much."

In the evening, while Mr. Anson was absorbed in the latest English newspapers which had just come in, John went out for a walk. His favorite method of seeing a European city was to stroll the streets, and using his own phrase to "soak" it in.

He passed now down the street which led by the very edge of the Elbe, and watched the long freight boats go by, lowering their smoke-stacks as they went under the bridges. The night was cloudy, and the city behind him became dusky in the mists and darkness. Dresden was strangely quiet, too, but he soon forgot it, as he moved back into the past.

The past, not the details, but the dim forgotten life, always made a powerful appeal to John. He had read that Dresden began with a little fishing village, and now he was trying to imagine the tawny men of a thousand years ago, in their rude canoes, casting their nets and lines in the river which flowed so darkly before him. But the mood did not endure long. He strolled presently upon the terraces and then back toward the king's palace, drawn there by a great shouting.

As he approached the building he became conscious that an event of interest was occurring. A huge crowd had gathered, and the youth of it was demonstrating with energy, cheering and breaking soon into national songs.

John pressed into the edge of the crowd, eager to know what it was all about, but not yet able to see over the heads of the close ranks in front of him. "What is it? What is it?" he asked of several, but they merely shrugged their shoulders, unable to understand English.

John was angry at himself once more for knowing nothing of German. The whole life of a nation flowed past him, and all of it was mysterious, merely because he did not have that little trick of tongue. He caught sight at last of a man in an automobile that moved very slowly in the heart of the crowd, the people fairly pressed against the body of the machine. It was obvious that the stranger furnished the occasion for the cheering and the songs, and John repeated his questions, hoping that he would ultimately encounter some one in this benighted multitude who understood English.

His hope was not in vain. A man told him that it was the King of Saxony returning to his capital and palace. John then drew away in some distaste. He did not see why the whole population of a city, even though they were monarchists, should go wild over the coming home of a sovereign. Doubtless the King of Saxony, who was not so young, had come home thousands of times before, and there must be something servile in a people who made such an old story an occasion for a sort of worship.

He pushed his way out of the crowd and returned to the terrace. But the noise of the shouting and the singing reached him there. Now it was mostly singing, and it showed uncommon fervor. John shrugged his shoulders. He liked such an unreasonable display less than ever, and walked far along the river, until no sound from the crowd reached him.

When he returned toward the hotel everybody had gone, save a few policemen, and John hoped that the king was not only in his palace, but

was sound asleep. It must be a great tax upon Saxon energy to demon-
strate so heavily every time he came back to the palace, perhaps from
nothing more than a drive. He found that Mr. Anson, having exhausted
the newspapers, had gone to his room, and pleasantly weary in both
body and mind, he sought his own bed.

2

THE THUNDERBOLT

JOHN AND MR. ANSON ate breakfast not long after daylight, as they expected to take an early train for Prague. They sat by a window in a small dining-room, overlooking pleasant gardens, and the Elbe, flowing just beyond the stretch of grass and flowers. The weather of the fickle valley had decided once again to be good. The young sunshine gilded the surface of the river and touched the gray buildings with gold. John was reluctant to leave it, but he had the anticipation, too, of fresh conquests, of new cities to be seen and explored.

"We'll be in Prague tonight," he said, "and it will be something very different, a place much more medieval than any we have yet visited."

"That's so," said Mr. Anson, and he trailed off into a long historical account of Prague, which would serve the double purpose of instructing John, and of exhibiting his own learning. The waiter, who could speak English, and with whom John, being young, did not hesitate to talk at times, was bent over, pouring coffee at his elbow.

"Pardon me, sir, but where did you say you were going?" he asked almost in a whisper.

"To Prague?"

"I shouldn't go there, sir, if I were you."

"Why not?"

"You'll run into a war."

"What do you mean, Albrecht?"

But Albrecht was already on the way to the kitchen, and he was so long in returning that John dismissed his words as merely the idle talk of a waiter who wished to entertain Herr Simmering's American guests. But when they went to an agency, according to their custom, to buy the railway tickets to Prague they were informed that it would be better for them not to go to the Czech capital. Both were astonished.

"Why shouldn't we go to Prague?" asked Mr. Anson with some indignation. "I've never heard that the Czechs object to the presence of Americans."

"They don't," replied the agent blandly. "You can go to Prague without any trouble, but I don't think you could leave it for a long time."

"And why not. Who would wish to hold us in Prague?"

"Nobody in particular. But there would be no passenger trains during the mobilization."

The eyes of John and Mr. Anson opened wider.

"Mobilization. What mobilization?" asked the elder.

"For the war that Austria-Hungary is going to make on Servia. The various army corps of Bohemia will be mobilized first."

"A war!" exclaimed Mr. Anson, "and not a word about it beforehand! Why this is a thunderbolt!"

John was thoughtful. The agent had made an amazing statement. It was, in truth a thunderbolt, as Mr. Anson had said, and it came out of a perfectly clear sky. He suddenly remembered little things, meaning nothing at the time, but acquiring significance now, the curious actions of Captain von Boehlen, the extraordinary demonstration at the return of the Saxon king to his palace, and the warning words of the waiter. He felt anew their loss in not knowing the language of the country and he gave voice to it.

"If we'd been able to speak German we might have had some hint of this," he said.

"We'll learn German, and be ready for it the next time we come," said Mr. Anson. "Now, John, in view of what we've heard, it would be unwise to go to Prague. Have you anything else in mind?"

"Let's go straight to Vienna. It's a great capital, and it has so much railroad communication that we could certainly get out of it, when we want to do so. Besides, I'm bound to see the Danube."

"And your uncle, the Senator, is there. Well, we'll chance it and go to Vienna. Can we get a train straight through to that city?"

"One leaves in an hour and is due at nine tonight," replied the agent to whom he had addressed the question.

They bought the tickets, and when the Vienna express left the station the two with their baggage were aboard it. John was by the window of their compartment, watching the beautiful country. He loved rivers and lakes and hills and mountains more than either ancient or modern cities, and as they sped along the valley of the Elbe, often at the very edge of the river, his mind and his eyes were content. His absorption in what was flitting by the window kept him for some time from noticing what was passing in the train. A low, but impatient exclamation from Mr. Anson first drew his attention.

"I never saw such crowding before in a European train," said he. "This compartment is marked for six, and already nine people have squeezed into it."

"That's so," said John, "and there are men sitting on their valises in the corridors. An enormously large proportion of them are officers, and I've noticed that great crowds are gathered at every station we pass. The Austrians seem to get a lot of excitement out of a war with a little country like Servia, in which the odds in their favor are at least twenty to one."

"The Austrians are a polite, agreeable, but volatile race," said Mr. Anson. "They are brave, but in war they are usually beaten. Napoleon made his early reputation out of the Austrians. They are--wait a minute, John, and I will read you more about them from this excellent book on Austria that I bought in Dresden."

"Excuse me this time; won't you, sir. We're coming to another station, and the crowd is bigger than ever. I want to see if they cheer us more than they did at the one a few miles back."

When they were beyond the town John turned his attention to the occupants of the compartment who had now increased to ten. They did not differ from ordinary travelers, but his attention was held longest by a young man, not much above his own age. He was handsome and blonde with a fine open face, and John put him down as a Viennese. He knew that the Viennese, although fellow Germans, were much unlike the Berliners, their souls being more akin to those of the French.

He could not remember at what station the young man had boarded the train, but it was evident that he was already weary, as his head rested heavily against the cushion and his eyelids drooped. "A good fellow, I'm sure," said John to himself. "I'd like to know him. I hope he's going on to Vienna with us."

They were well across the Austrian border now, and an officer came through the train, asking for passports. Luckily, John and Mr. Anson had provided themselves with such documents, not because they believed them of any value, but, as John said, they always ran true to form, and if any official paper were offered they meant to have their share of it. Now they found these documents, considered worthless hitherto, very useful. The Austrian officer smiled when he looked at them.

"Amerikanischer," he said, showing his large, even white teeth. "I haf a cousin leeving in New York."

"I've no doubt he's a fine fellow," said John, as the officer passed on, "and I wish I knew him. I believe it's true, Mr. Anson, that we Americans are the spoiled children of the world."

"It's so, John, although I object to the adjective, 'spoiled' and it's so because we're far away, and mind our own business. Of course a democracy like ours does many foolish things, and often we make ourselves look ridiculous, but remember John, that we're an honest, straightforward people, and it's foreign to all our nature to tread on the weak or cower before the strong."

John thought little of the words then, Mr. Anson preached so much--although he was to remember them later--because his attention was diverted to the young stranger whom the officer was now asking for his passport. The youth--he was little more than such--raised his head languidly from the cushion and without wholly lifting his weary lids produced his passport from the inside pocket of his coat. John could not keep from seeing the name on it, "August Wilhelm Kempner."

"Ah, from Vienna," said the examining officer, "and your occupation is described here as that of a painter."

"Yes," said the weary youth, "but I fear that it is no occupation at all in times like these."

As he spoke in German John did not understand him, but he knew that he was making some sort of explanation. He also saw that the officer was satisfied, as, smiling with the courtesy common to the Austrians, he passed into the corridor, and entered the next compartment. John, by and by, spoke to young Kempner, using good French--he remembered that many Austrians understood French--and the young man promptly replied but in broken and fragmentary French.

The two managed to carry on a more or less connected conversation, in which several people in the compartment joined freely with scraps of English, French and German, helping out one another, as best they could, and forming a friendly group. It seemed to John that something of the ordinary stiffness prevailing among strangers was relaxed. All of them, men and women, were moved by an unusual emotion and he readily attributed it to the war, although a great state like Austria-Hungary should not become unduly excited over a struggle with a little one like Servia.

But he let Mr. Anson do most of the talking for America, and by and by began to watch through the window again. The green of the rich country rested both eye and brain, and, a war between Austria-Hungary and Servia was not such a tremendous affair. There was always trouble down in that Balkan region. Trouble there, was far less remarkable than the absence of it. As for himself he wanted to see the Danube, which these careless Viennese persisted in calling the Donau, and the fine old capital which had twice turned back the Turks, but not Napoleon.

He soon saw that they would reach Vienna long after the destined time. The stops at every station were long and the waiting crowds thickened. "I did not know so many people were anxious to see our entry into the capital," said John.

"They are numerous, but not more so than we deserve," replied Mr. Anson in the same vein.

It was midnight when they reached Vienna. John bade farewell to Kempner, his companion of the journey to whom he had been strongly attracted, and after the slight customs examination drove away with Mr. Anson to a modest hotel.

It was so late and he was so tired that he thought he would sleep heavily. But sleep passed him by, and it was such a rare thing that John was troubled greatly. What was the matter with him? It could not be all those sounds of shouting and singing that were floating in at the open window! He had slept many a time at home, when the crowds were cheering continuously on election night.

The noise increased, although it was at least two in the morning. He had always heard that Vienna was a gay city, and never slept, but he had scarcely expected such an ebullient night life, and, his curiosity aroused, he rose and dressed.

From his seat at the window he heard the singing much more plainly, and far down the avenue he saw columns of marching men. He could not understand the words they sang, but he knew from the beat of the music that they were Austrian and German patriotic songs, and his curiosity increasing, he went down into the street, nodding to the dozing porter who stood at the door.

He found the streets thronged with a multitude constantly growing larger, and vivid with a pleased excitement. He had no doubt that it was the war with the little Balkan state that caused it all, and he could not refrain from silent criticism of a great nation which made so much ado over a struggle with a country that it outnumbered enormously. But he recalled that the Viennese were a gay, demonstrative people, and their excitement and light-heartedness were certainly infectious.

He was sorry again that he could not speak German, and then he was glad, when he saw young Kempner leaning against a closed window watching the parades. "I suppose that like me you couldn't sleep," he said in French.

Kempner started. He had not seen John's approach, and, for the moment, John almost thought that the look he gave him was not one of welcome. But it passed swiftly. Then he stretched out his hand and replied.

"No, I couldn't. If you who come from across the sea wish to witness the enthusiasm of my countrymen how much more would it appeal to me?"

"Has anything definite happened?"

"Yes, Austria-Hungary declared war on Servia today. It had to come. As our Viennese will tell you the Servians are a race of murderers. They murdered their own king, and now they have murdered our Archduke and Archduchess, heaping another sorrow upon the head of our aged emperor. We will finish them in a week."

John remembered some words of Burke about no one being able to indict a whole nation, and he was about to quote them, but second thought kept him silent. He must not argue with a people, perhaps justly infuriated about what was no business of his. He remained with Kempner, but sensitive and quick to receive impressions he soon concluded that the young Austrian wished to be alone. Perhaps he, too, was going to the war, and would soon have to tell his people good-by. That might account for his absent manner.

John, as soon as he conveniently could, gave an excuse and turned away. Kempner was polite, but did not seek to detain him. The American returned to his hotel, but at the first crossing looked back. He saw the form of Kempner disappearing into a narrow alley. "Taking a short cut home," said John to himself, "and it's what I ought to do, too. I've no business wandering about a strange city at such a time."

The same sleepy porter nodded to him, as he passed in and asked him no questions. Now slumber came quickly and he did not awake for breakfast, until Mr. Anson had pounded long and heavily on his door.

"Get up, John!" he cried. "Here's your uncle to see you, and you a sluggard, lying abed this late!"

John sprang up at the announcement of his uncle's presence. Sleep still lay heavy on his eyelids, and he was in a mental daze, but by the time he reached the door he had come out of it. They had not looked for his uncle the night before, owing to the lateness of the hour, although they were sure that he was stopping at the same hotel.

"Just a moment," he exclaimed, and without waiting to dress he opened the door, admitting the stalwart figure of the Senator, who hurried in to greet his favorite nephew.

"Jackie, my lad," he cried in a loud voice which had become oratorical from much use on the stump. "The sight of you is good for weak eyes. I'm always glad to see any American, any member of the finest race on God's earth, but I'm particularly glad to see you--they do say you look like me when I was a boy--although I'm bound to tell you that you're more than half asleep, on this your first morning in Vienna."

"I slipped out late to hear the shouting and singing and see the crowds, Uncle Jim. I haven't been in bed more than three or four hours. The city was so much awake that I had to stay awake, too."

"Well, don't you do it again. Always get your sleep, especially when you are on foreign travel. It's as hard work as political campaigning in the states, and that, Jackie, my boy, is no soft snap, as I ought to know, having done it more than thirty years."

Senator James Pomeroy, a western man, was something past sixty, of medium height, portly, partly bald, but heavy of mustache and with a short pointed beard. His eyes were gray, his face full, and he was of great physical strength. He was self-made and the job was no discredit to him. His nature was simple and open. America was the finest country, had the finest government and the finest people on earth, and the state of which he was the senior Senator was the choicest flower of the flowery flock.

"There was enough to keep a fellow awake," he said, "but I always sleep well. You must learn to do it, if you expect to achieve a success of life. When I was making my first campaign for the Lower House of our state, and I was barely old enough to be eligible, I lay awake and fretted over the votes that might be lacking to me when election came. I at last said to myself: 'Don't do it! Don't do it!' You may roll and you may tumble, but it won't win you a single vote. It's the smooth work you've done before that brings 'em in. Now, hustle on your clothes, Jackie, lad, and we'll have breakfast, not one of these thin continental affairs, but a real breakfast, if I have to go in the kitchen myself and seize it."

"What about this war, Uncle Jim?"

"A small affair, soon over. We came very near having one, too, with Mexico, but luckily we've got a president who doesn't play to the gallery, and he sat hard on the war-maniacs. I think I was of some little assistance to him myself in that crisis. But, my boy, Europe is the pet home of war scares. They're always coming across the Atlantic by mail and wire. 'War clouds in the Balkans!' 'Eastern question sets Europe by the ears!' 'France plots to get back Alsace-Lorraine and Germany arms!' 'German Kaiser warns Austrian Kaiser against Triple Entente!' Bang! Boom! everybody going to war in the next five minutes--but they don't. You'll find 'em all a half hour later in the cafés, eating and drinking. Europe can't fight, because there isn't time between meals. They eat five times a day here, and they eat long at a time. How could they possibly sandwich in a war. I'm sixty-two years old, and as far back as I can remember European war clouds have been passing like little summer clouds, and they will continue to pass long after you're an old man, Jackie. I make that statement deliberately, and I challenge successful contradiction."

He expanded his great chest, and looked around with an air of defiance. It was his favorite oratorical manner, now grown into a habit. But no one challenged him, and they went to a bountiful breakfast, for which the Senator paid willingly, demanding no greater return than the attention of the others while he talked.

Later in the day the three drove together in the grounds of Schönbrunn, and John's thoughts passed for a while to the great Corsican who had slept there, and who had led his army to victory over this the haughtiest of European monarchies, and perhaps for that reason the weakest. The tremendous convulsion upon which Napoleon had ridden to such dazzling heights seemed to him impossible: it was clearly impossible according to all the rules of logic, and yet it had occurred. That was the most startling period in the history of the modern world, and, forgetting what was about him, he tried to evoke it from the past.

He was recalled to the present by their driver, an eager Austrian, who asked them in broken English if they wished to see the old emperor arrive home from Ischl. He pointed with his whip to an open space, adjoining the Schönbrunn grounds, where people were already gathering.

"Of course, my good man," replied Senator Pomeroy in oratorical tones. "We will go to see the emperor, but only as an object of curiosity. Far be it from me to pay any homage to the representative of a decayed system. I look on, merely as a free American citizen, no better and no worse than the millions whom I strive to the best of my ability to represent in our National legislative halls. Get us in as close as you can, driver."

John was frankly eager. He disliked the military monarchies as much as the Senator did, but he wanted to see the old emperor at whom fate had shot so many cruel arrows. His carriage was to come down a certain street from the railway station, and their skillful driver maneuvered them to the very edge of it. The crowd was immense, and it was electric with excitement. It was no ordinary occasion and all the emotions of the excitable Viennese had been aroused.

As far as John could see the multitude ran, and the packed heads seemed to rise and fall like waves of the sea. Troops in magnificent uniforms of the most vivid colors were everywhere. The day itself seemed to be ablaze with their gorgeousness. If John had been asked to define the chief difference between Europe and America he would have replied that it was a matter of uniforms.

The crowd which seemed already to fill every space nevertheless grew larger, and waves of emotion ran through it. John did not think they could be defined in any other way. At home people differed in their opinions, every man to his own, but here they appeared to receive them from somebody higher up, and the crowd always swayed together, to this point or that, according to the directing power.

He had never before seen so much emotional excitement. Vienna's thrill, so obvious the night before, had carried over into the day, increasing as it went along, and it was a happy intoxication, infectious in its nature. He began to feel it in his own veins, although his judgment told him that it was no business of his. Yet the brilliant uniforms, the shimmer of steel, the vast shifting crowd of eager faces, the deep and unbroken murmur of anticipation would have moved an older and dryer mind.

Anticipatory shouts arose. They were in German, but John knew that they meant: "He comes!" Nevertheless "he," which was the Emperor, did not yet come, and the crowd thickened and thickened. He saw the people stretching along leafy avenues, and in the distance they were wedged into a solid mass, faces and figures running together, until they presented the complete likeness of the waving sea.

"A strange sight and highly interesting," said the Senator oratorically. "It must take generations of education to teach a people to make a symbol of one man. And yet if we could get at the reality we'd surely find him a poor and broken creature."

"Man doesn't always grow according to his nature, he's shaped by continual pressure," said Mr. Anson.

John scarcely heard either of them, because he saw far down the avenue that the waves of the human sea were rolling higher than before. An increasing volume of sound also came from that solid sheet of faces, and it seemed to part slightly in the center, as if a sword had been thrust between. Carriages, automobiles and the flame of uniforms appeared in the cut. A roar like thunder arose from two hundred thousand people.

John knew that the Emperor, in truth, was now coming. Such a spontaneous outburst could be for nothing else, and, in spite of every effort of the will, his own excitement increased. He leaned forward for a better view and just in front of their carriage he saw a slender upright figure that looked familiar. A second glance told him that it was Kempner.

"Oh, Kempner!" he called, full of friendly feeling. "Come here with us. You can see better!"

Kempner glanced up, and John distinctly saw a shadow come over his face. Then he looked at them as one looks at strangers with a blank, uncomprehending gaze, and the next instant slipped with extraordinary agility into some crevice of the crowd and disappeared.

John flushed. Kempner's conduct was both rude and strange. He glanced at his uncle and Mr. Anson, but they, absorbed in the coming of the Emperor, had neither seen nor heard, and he was glad. His own attention now turned to the event of the moment, because the mighty roar was increasing in volume and coming nearer, and down the opening lane a carriage followed by others was speeding. Along either side of the lane the soldiers were packed so closely that they formed a living wall, but John, standing up in their own carriage, saw over their heads.

He saw an old, old man in splendid uniform, sitting by the side of an impassive officer also in a splendid uniform. The old man's cheeks were sunken, and the heavy-lidded eyes stared straight before him. He sat erect, but whether it was his own strength or the arrangement of the seat John could not tell. His hand flew up, forward, then down, and up forward and down again in automatic salute.

He was so near presently that it was only a spear's length over the heads of the soldiers. Then John saw how truly old he was, and suddenly his heart revolted. Why should this old, old man, broken by appalling sorrows, be dragged out to have wars made in his name? The schemers and plotters, whoever they were might let him rest in peace.

The carriage flashed on, and behind it came the others as fast. They would not linger, to give a chance for bombs and knives. In an instant the emperor was gone through the gates of Schönbrunn, and first the soldiers and then the roaring crowd closed in behind.

The Senator gave the order, and their carriage drove slowly away, the three discussing what they had seen while the happy driver exulted over the glorious show, so dear to the heart of a Viennese. But John once more thought the excitement was not warranted by a little war with a little country like Servia.

They devoted three or four days to Vienna, a capital, they had often heard, as gay as Paris, and certainly splendid in appearance, but pleasure seemed to hang fire. There was a cloud over the city, the cheering and singing parades went on all through the nights, but at times in the day the spirits of men seemed to droop.

John told himself over and over again that this heavy change in the atmosphere was not justified by the size of Servia. The three of them once more and often bewailed their lack of German. People talked all around them and they heard nothing. Austrians who hitherto had a fair knowledge of English forgot it entirely, when they were asked questions.

The Senator in the privacy of their rooms thundered and thundered. He hated all this secrecy. He wondered what those men were doing at Schönbrunn in the name of the old Emperor. As for himself he liked the arena of public life in the United States, where you rolled up your sleeves--such was his metaphor--and told what you were for and what you were against, without fear or favor. Democracies did wrong or rather foolish things, but in them it was impossible for a few military leaders, hid in a palace, to play with the lives of hundreds of thousands.

John, although saying nothing, agreed with him fully. The last three or four days had depressed him in a manner unusual in one so young. His silent rebuff by Kempner had hurt his spirit to an extent far beyond the nature of the incident, and, realizing it, he wondered why. He kept a sharp watch in the streets for the young Austrian, but he did not see him again.

At last there came a time when the greatest of all thunderbolts fell. It was the simple hand of a waiter that caused it to fall. The others had finished their coffee and rolls at breakfast and had gone out, leaving John alone at the table.

"What is the matter with Vienna?" he said casually to the waiter, who he knew could speak English.

The man hesitated, then he leaned over and said in a fearful whisper:

"It's not a little war. It's not just a war with Servia which we can finish in a week, but it's to be such a war as the world has never seen."

John started, looked up at the man. His face was intensely earnest. How should one in his humble calling have news of such import? And yet at Dresden he had been warned by another waiter, and warned truly.

"Are you sure?" he asked.

"Yes, sir, they're all going into it. Europe will be covered with armies!"

"When?"

"In a few hours! Now, sir! Oh, I can't say any more!"

He hurried away, leaving John convinced that he told the truth. It was stunning, appalling, unbelievable, impossible, but he believed it nevertheless. There were underground channels of communication and true news might come by the way of the kitchen as well as the palace. He was absolutely convinced that he had heard a fact. Now he knew the cause of that heaviness and depression in the atmosphere. Well the clouds might gather, when such a thunderbolt as a general war was going to fall!

He immediately hunted up his uncle and Mr. Anson who had not yet left the hotel, and told them what he had heard. Conviction seized them also.

"It's come at last, this European war! after a thousand false alarms, it's come!" said the Senator, "and my boy, Vienna is no place for three honest Americans who do not work in the dark. I say it, and I say it without fear of contradiction, that it behooves us to flee westward with all the speed we can."

"You won't hear any contradiction from me," said Mr. Anson. "Vienna is a fine city, but nothing becomes it more than our leaving it. Which way do we go?"

"There's a train in two hours for Salzburg and Munich," suggested John.

"Hurried packing," said the Senator, "but we can do it. Get ready the baggage you two and I'll pay the bills. We'll go to Salzburg and sleep there tonight, and tomorrow we'll reach Munich. The more I think about this the less I like it. Why didn't we read all those signs earlier! I suppose it's because we'd heard the false cry of wolf so many dozens of times."

John and Mr. Anson made all speed with the baggage while the Senator paid the bills, and, as they drove in their cab to the station, the three felt more than ever the need of haste. The clouds seemed to be shutting down completely on Vienna. John felt that it was hard to breathe, but he knew it was the effect of the imagination. He was oppressed by a sense of an impending and appalling catastrophe, something more tremendous than anything that the world had yet experienced. He had an impression that he had come to the end of an era, and the impression was all the more powerful because it had been made so suddenly.

They passed through an excited station filled with a swirling crowd, and secured places on a train, they scarcely knew how. Here people sat and stood upon one another, and, as the train sped westward, they knew that the storm was bursting with terrific violence. The nervous people around them no longer restrained themselves. Europe was to be swept with fire and sword, but above all the Germans and Austrians were going to smash up France. They dwelt most upon that. The French and the French Republic must go. There was no longer a place for them in the world.

To John's modest wish that France would not come into it they gave a stare and frown of disapproval. France had to come in, she must come in, the two German powers would see that she was smitten down as a nation was never overwhelmed before. Oh, no, Britain would do nothing. Of course she wouldn't. She'd stay behind her barrier of the sea, and, perhaps, at the last when the spoils of war were to be snatched from the exhausted combatants, she'd step in and snatch them. No, they needn't consider Britain, and Germany and Austria could easily dispose of France and Russia.

Much of this was said in English and French to the three travelers and John's heart sickened. Poor France! Why should she be smashed up! Why should the French nation be exterminated? He did not forget that France was a republic like his own country. She had been beaten once by Germany--and the victor's terms were hard--and whatever her faults had been that was enough. He did not like Frenchmen personally any better than Germans, but at that moment his sympathies went to the French and he felt a great pity for France.

The train crept along, and, after double the usual time, they reached Salzburg, where they passed an uneasy night, and, the next day, boarded another train which was to cross the German border and take them to Munich. It, too, was packed with an excited mass of humanity, and as John passed along the corridor he saw Kempner in one of the compartments.

Remembering his previous rebuffs he intended to take no notice, but the young Austrian nodded at him and smiled.

"I see that you flee," he said in his broken French, "and you do well to flee. Europe is aflame."

"That's so," said John, "and, since it's no fire of ours, we Americans mean to be on the Atlantic foam, as soon as we can."

As there was a vacant seat in the compartment and Kempner seemed very friendly now, John sat down to talk a little. He longed occasionally for companionship of his own age, and his heart warmed again to the young Austrian.

"I see that you're running, too," said John.

"Yes," smiled Kempner. "I'm a man of peace, a painter, or rather I would be one, and as my heart is a little weak I'm not drawn for military service. I'm on my way to Munich, where I mean to study the galleries."

"I'm going to Munich, too," said John. "So we can travel together."

"Then if we expect to reach Munich we'd better jump out now. Quick!"

"What for?"

"It seems that this is the Austrian border, and trains are not crossing it now, owing to the mobilization. A German train has come to meet us. Look, most of the passengers have transferred already!"

John saw his uncle and Mr. Anson standing on the steps of the German train and looking about vainly for him. There had been no announcement of the change, and, annoyed, he ran down the corridor and sprang to the ground, closely followed by Kempner.

"Passporten! passporten!" shouted some one, putting a strong hand on his arm.

John saw his uncle and Mr. Anson going into the German train, evidently thinking that he was inside, and his alarm increased.

"Amerikanischer! Amerikanischer!" he said to the Austrian officer, who was holding his arm and demanding his passport. The officer shook his head and spoke voluble German. John did not understand it, but he knew that the man at such a time would insist upon seeing his passport. Kempner just behind him was in the same bad case.

The whistle of departure sounded from the train, and John, in despair, tore at the passport in an inside pocket. He saw that the officer would never be able to read it in time, and he endeavored to snatch himself from the detaining grasp. But the Austrian hung on firmly.

As he fairly thrust the document in the face of the official he saw the wheels of the coaches moving.

"I'll come on the next train!" he shouted to the air.

The officer looked over the passport deliberately and handed it back. The train was several hundred yards down the track.

"Now, yours," he said to Kempner, and the young man passed it to him.

"August Wilhelm Kempner," said the officer, and then he added, looking the young man squarely in the eye: "I happen to know August William Kempner who lives in Vienna and he bears no resemblance to you. How do you happen to have his passport?"

"That I won't explain to you," said the false Kempner, and suddenly he struck him a stunning blow on the temple with his clenched fist.

The officer, strong though he was, went down unconscious.

"Run! Run! Follow me!" exclaimed the young man. "They'll think you were my comrade and it may mean your death!"

His action had been so violent, and he spoke with such vehemence that John was mentally overborne. Driven by a powerful impulse he followed the flying man.

Kempner, for so John still called him, darted into a narrow street not wider than an alley, leading between two low houses. He had had no opportunity hitherto to observe the border place in which they had stopped. It was small, but like many of the old European towns it was very closely built, and some of its streets were scarcely wide enough for two abreast.

The fugitives ran swiftly. Kempner evidently knew the place, as he sprang in and out with amazing agility, and the sounds of pursuit died in a minute or two. Then he darted between two buildings that almost touched, entered a small churchyard in the rear of a Gothic church and threw himself down behind a great tombstone. And even as he did so he pulled John down beside him.

As they lay close, still trembling from exertion and excitement, Kempner said to John, and now he spoke in perfect French:

"Since I got you into this trouble I think it my duty to get you out of it again if I can. Of course the people of the town saw us running, and I rushed through that narrow passage in order to evade their sight."

His tone had a dry and quaint touch of humor and John, despite his exhaustion and alarm, could not keep from replying in a similar vein.

"If I don't owe you thanks for the first statement I do at least for the second. I don't know German, and so I couldn't understand what you and that Austrian officer said, but I fancy your name is not Kempner."

"No. It's not, and I'm not an Austrian. I'm a Frenchman, for which I return thanks to the good God. Not that Americans are not great and noble people, but it's a fortunate thing that so many of us are satisfied with our birth."

"I was thinking so when you announced with such pride that you were a Frenchman."

The other laughed softly.

"A fair hit," he said, "and I laid myself open to it."

"Now since you're not August William Kempner, and are not an Austrian, will you kindly tell me your name and your nation, as in any event I am no enemy of yours and will betray you to nobody."

"My race, as you might infer from the beauty and purity with which I speak my native language, is French, and my name, which I no longer have a motive in concealing from you, is Philip Lannes. I'm a collateral descendant of Napoleon's great marshal, Lannes, and I'm willing to boast of it."

"Occupation--I will risk another inference--is something like that of a spy."

The Frenchman looked keenly at the American and again laughed lightly.

"You're not far wrong," he said. "It was the passport of another man that I carried, and I happened to meet an official who knew better. It was mere chance that you were with me at the time and would have been taken for my comrade. Didn't you know that a great war was going to burst?"

"I've just learned it."

"And one of the objects of those who are making the war is to smash my country, France. How could one serve her better than by learning the preparations and forces against her? Oh, I've been among the Austrians and I've been watching them! They've made some terrible mistakes. But then the Austrians always make mistakes. There's an old saying that what the Austrian crown loses by war it wins back by marriage. But I don't think royal marriages count for so much in these days. Lie close! I think I hear soldiers in the alley!"

John hugged the earth in the shadow of the great tombstone.

3

T HE REFUGE

JOHN SCOTT, in those moments of hiding and physical exhaustion, had little time to think, yet he was dimly conscious that he, an American who meant to meddle in the business of nobody, had fallen into a most extraordinary situation. By a sudden mischance he had lost in a few moments his uncle and the man who was at once his comrade and tutor, and now he had been running for his life with a stranger.

Yet he obeyed the warning words of Lannes and fairly tried to burrow into the earth. The name, Lannes, had exerted at once a great influence over him. The career of Napoleon had fascinated him, and of all his marshals the brave and democratic Lannes had appealed to him most. And now he was hiding with one who had in his veins kindred blood of this great and gallant figure.

Despite his anxiety John turned a little and looked at the young Frenchman who lay beside him. Lannes was but a year or two older than the American. Tall, slender, narrow of waist, and broad of chest and shoulders he seemed built for both agility and strength. He was fair of hair and gray of eye. But those gray eyes were his most remarkable feature. They were intensely bright, and the light in them seemed to shift and change, but no matter what the change might be they were always gay and merry. John surmised that he was one of the few, who by a radiant presence, are born to be a source of joy to the world, and time was to confirm him in his opinion.

"Luckily the big tombs of dead and forgotten Germans rise on either side of us," whispered Lannes, "and the chances are good that we won't be discovered, but we must keep on lying close. We're on the German side in this town and the Germans will look longer than the Austrians. They're at the end of the alley now, not thirty feet away."

John heard them marching. The thump, thump of solid German feet was plainly audible. It was a sound that he was to hear again, and again, and never forget, that heavy thump, thump of the marching German feet, a great military empire going forward to crush or be crushed. Even in those moments he was impressed less by his sense of personal danger than by his feeling that a nation was on the march.

"They've turned," said Lannes, and John heard the thump, thump of the feet passing away. But he and the young Frenchman lay still, until the last echo had died. Then Lannes sat up and peeped over the edge of one of the tombs.

"They'll search elsewhere," he said, "but they won't come here again. We'll have to be cautious, however, as they'll never stop, until they've gone all through the town. Trust the Germans for that. Now aren't you glad I brought you among the tombs? Could we have found a better hiding place?"

His manner was so gay and light-hearted that John found it infectious. Yet, he was resolved not to yield entirely. He had been dragged or pushed into too desperate a quandary.

"Suppose they don't find us now, what then?" he asked. "It may be all right for you, but as for me, my uncle and my friend are on the way to Munich, and I'm marooned in a land, the language of which I don't understand."

"But you're with me!"

"So I am, but you're a stranger. You belong to a country with which Germany is at war or going to war. You're a spy, and if you're caught, which is highly probable, you'll be hanged or shot, and because I'm with you they'll do the same to me."

Lannes plucked a grass stem and chewed it thoughtfully, although his eyes at no time lost their cheerful twinkle.

"I do seem to have plunged you into a whole lake of trouble," he said at length. "I'll admit that my own neck is in the halter, and it behooves me to escape as soon as I can, but don't think I'll ever neglect you. I mean to see that you get to Munich and rejoin your friends."

"How?"

"It's a secret for the present, confined to me. But trust me! can't you?"

His speech had glided from French into English so good that it was colloquial, and of the vernacular. Now he looked directly into John's eyes, and John, looking back, saw only truth in their gray smiling depths. There are some things that we feel, instinctively, and with overwhelming power, and he knew that the young Frenchman would be as true as steel. He held out his hand and said:

"I believe every word you say. I'll ask no questions, but wait for what happens."

Lannes took the outstretched hand and gave it a grasp of extraordinary power. The joyous lights in his wonderful gray eyes shifted and changed with extraordinary rapidity.

"I like you, John Scott, you Yankee," he said. "You and I will be the best of friends and for life. Thus does the great American republic, which is you, pledge eternal friendship with France, the great European republic, which is me."

"You put it well, and now what are we going to do?"

"Graveyards are good places, my old--my old, being as you know, a translation of *mon vieux*, a term of friendship, becoming to you because of your grave demeanor--but it's not well to stay in them too long. You've noticed doubtless that the skies are darkening over the spur of the Alps toward Salzburg?"

"And what then?"

"It means that we must seek quarters for the night, and night is always friendly to fugitives. I promised that I'd take you to your friends in Munich--I can't do it in an hour or even in two, although I'll lead you to food and a bed, which are not to be despised. But we must wait a little longer."

"Until night comes fully?"

"Truly, until it's complete night. And, fortunately for you, it will be very dark, as I see plenty of clouds sailing in this direction from the mountains."

John, who was lying on his back, looked toward the south, and saw that the crests of the peaks and ridges were already dim with somber masses floating northward and westward. The air was growing cooler, and, in a half hour, the ancient churchyard was sure to be veiled in darkness. For the present Philip and he relapsed into silence, and John's thoughts traveled anxiously toward his uncle and Mr. Anson. What would they think had become of him? He knew that the Senator who was very fond of him would be alarmed greatly, and it was a bad time in Europe for any one to be missing.

But there was stern stuff in John Scott, and knowing that they must wait he put anxiety from him as much as he could and waited.

The heavy clouds, although they did not give forth rain, swept up, and brought black darkness with them. The white tombstones became pale, and the town beyond was invisible. Lannes rose and stretched himself deliberately, limb by limb.

"Are you willing, John Scott?" he asked, "to follow me and ask no questions?"

"Yes, Philip Lannes, I am."

"Well, then, John--I think I'll call you that because you and I are friends, and you may say Philip, too, which will save time--I'm going to lead you to temporary safety and comfort. I'll tell you, too, enough to assuage your curiosity. There's a little Huguenot quarter to this town. Louis Quatorze, as you know, drove many good people out of France. Some went to your own new land, but the majority settled in the surrounding countries. They've intermarried chiefly with themselves, and, after more than two hundred years on foreign soil, many of them still have French hearts in French bodies."

"Lead on then. I think I'd like to meet these good Huguenots. I'm growing tremendously hungry, Philip."

"Hunger is frequent in a great war. You'll grow used to it."

His manner took away any sting that his words might have contained. John could yet see those wonderful gray eyes shining through the twilight, and his heart warmed anew to the young Frenchman. If he were to be cast away in this strange German town Lannes was just the comrade whom he would have chosen.

"We're resurrected," continued Lannes, "and we'll leave our graveyard. May it be a long time before I enter another! And yet with a world going to war who can tell?"

But the touch of gravity was only for an instant. The joyous note quickly returned to his voice.

"Keep by my side," he said, "and walk in the most careless manner, as if you were a native of the town. If anybody asks question let me make all the replies. God gave me one special gift, and it was an easy tongue. It's not work for me to talk. I like to do it."

"And I like to hear you," said John.

"Which leaves us both satisfied. Now, it's lucky for us that our old European towns are so very old. In the Middle Ages they built with narrow streets, and all sorts of alleys and passages. Leading from the cemetery is just the sort of passage that you and I need at this time. Ah, here it is, and luckily it's empty!"

They had crossed the narrow street beyond the cemetery, and were looking into a dark tunnel between two low stone houses. No one was in sight. Lannes stepped without hesitation into the tunnel.

"Keep with me," he said, repeating his injunction, "and we'll soon be under shelter."

His manner was so cheerful, so confident that John instinctively believed him, and walked boldly by his side into the well of darkness. But as his eyes grew used to it he made out the walls crumbling with age and dripping with damp. Then the sound of heavy feet came thundering down the passage.

"Some one leading a horse," whispered Lannes. "There's a stable on our right. It's nothing. Seem not to notice as you pass."

The thunder of the feet, magnified in the confined space, increased, and presently John saw a boy leading one of those huge-footed horses, used for draft in Europe. The animal stepped slowly and heavily, and the boy was half asleep. John and Philip, hovering in the shadow of the wall, passed him so lightly that doubtless he was not conscious of their presence.

The Frenchman turned into a tributary alley, narrower and darker than the other, and Lannes knocked at a heavy oaken doorway, before which a small lantern cast a dim light. John had good eyes, and accustomed to the heavy shadows, he saw fairly well.

He concealed an imaginative temperament under a quiet manner, and he was now really back in the Middle Ages. It must have been at least four or five hundred years since people lived up little alleys like this. And the door with its heavy iron bands, the shuttered window above it, and the dim lantern that lighted the passage could belong only to long ago. The house and its neighbors seemed to have been built as much for defense as for habitation.

Lannes knocked again, and then John heard inside the soft tread of feet, and the lifting of heavy bars. It was another mediæval touch, and he swung yet further back into the past. The door was opened slightly and the face of an elderly woman appeared at the crevice.

"It's Philip Lannes with a friend, Mother Krochburg," said the young Frenchman in a whisper, "and friend as you've often been to me I never needed the friendship of you and your house more than I do now."

She said something in German and opened the door wider. Lannes and John pressed in, and she instantly closed it behind them, putting the heavy bars in place. They stood in complete darkness, but they heard her moving about, and presently she lighted a small lamp which did not dispel the shadows beyond the range of a few feet.

But as she stood in the center of the beams the woman was outlined clearly for John. She was at least sixty, but she was tall and strong, and bore herself like a grenadier. She was looking at Lannes, and John had never beheld a gaze of more intense, burning curiosity.

"Well?" she said, and to John's surprise she now spoke in French. Lannes gave back her gaze with one fully as concentrated and burning.

"Angelique Krochburg, wife of Paul Krochburg, descendant of the Krochburgs, rightly called the Crochevilles," he said, drawing himself up and speaking with wonderful distinctness, "it has come at last."

"The war! The great war!" she said in a sharp whisper. John noticed that her strong figure trembled.

"Yes, the great war!" returned Lannes with dramatic intensity. "Germany declares war today on Russia. I know it. No matter how I know it, but I know it. She will make war on France tomorrow, and it will be the first object of her princes and military caste to destroy our republic. They reckon that with the aid of Austria they will rule the whole continent, and that in time the tread of their victorious armies will be heard all over the world."

The woman drew a breath so deep and sharp that it made a hissing sound between her teeth. John saw the lamp in her hand trembling.

"Then Philip Lannes," she said, "which is it to be--the peoples or the kings?"

Lannes drew himself up again--John recognized the dramatic quality in him--and replied in words that he shot forth like bullets:

"The peoples. Armies can be defeated, but nations cannot be put down. Our Napoleon, despite his matchless genius, found it so in his later empire. And they have reckoned ill at Berlin and Vienna. The world in alarm at military domination will be against them. They say the English won't fight and will keep out. But Mother Krochburg or Crocheville--I prefer the sound of Crocheville--we French know better. A thousand years of our history say that the English will fight. We have Agincourt and Cressy and Poitiers and La Belle Alliance to say that they will fight. And now they will fight again, but on our side. The bravest of our ancient enemies will stand with us, brothers in arms, shoulder to shoulder against an arrogant foe!"

"Do you know this, Philip Lannes, or is it some dream of that hopeful brain of yours?"

"It's not a dream. I know it. It hasn't been long since I was among the English. They will have to join us. The German threat will force them to it. Blinded by their own narrow teachings the generals at Berlin and Vienna cannot see the storm they've let loose. Ah, Madame Crocheville, it's more than two hundred years since any of your people have lived in France, but you are as true a Frenchwoman as if your feet had never pressed any but French soil!"

"There is truth in that wild head of yours."

"And the time of France and the French is coming. The republic has restored us. The terrible year of 1870 will be avenged. French valor and skill will bloom again!"

John had stood on one side, while they talked or rather allowed their emotions to shoot forth in words. But he was watching them intently, bent slightly forward, and, like Parsifal, he had never moved by the breadth of a single hair. The woman now glanced toward him.

"He can be trusted?" she asked Lannes.

"Absolutely. His head is in the German noose. He must do as we bid or that noose will close."

The gay ring had returned to Lannes' voice and a faint smile crossed the face of Madame Crocheville.

"It's the best of securities," she said, and John, compelled to acknowledge its truth, bowed.

"Who are pursuing you," she asked.

"Nobody at present," replied Lannes. "I'd have passed the border safely, but a pig of an Austrian officer happened to know the man whose passport I have. It was one chance in a thousand, and it went against me. My friend here is an American, and, as he was dragged into it, we must save him."

"It's likely that you need both food and rest as well as concealment."

"We do, and thank you for what we know we are going to receive."

She smiled again faintly. John surmised that she had a warm place in her heart for Lannes. Who would not? He was as light-hearted now as if he had come to a ball and not to a refuge. His eyes moved about the room and he seemed pleased with all he saw.

"Food and a little of the good wine that I've found here before would be indeed most welcome," he said, "and I speak for my new American friend as well as myself."

"Come!" she said briefly, and the two followed, as she led the way into a passage not more than wide enough for one, and then up a stone stairway into a room ventilated by only a single narrow window.

"Wait here," she said. She closed the door and John heard the huge German key turning in the lock. But the slit of a window was open, and he saw in the room two beds, a table, two chairs and some other furniture. The ceiling was low and sloping and John knew that they were directly under the eaves.

Lannes threw himself into one of the chairs and drew several mighty breaths.

"We're locked in, John," he said, "but it's for our good. Nobody can get at us, while Madame Crocheville holds the key, and she'll hold it. More than two hundred years on German soil, and still French, heart and soul. There must be something great and true in France, when she can inspire such far-flung devotion. That isn't a bad place, John. As the French general said in the Crimea, *'J'y suis, j'y reste'* and I'm resting now."

"She knows all about you, I take it?"

"Of course. I've been here before, often. That little window looks out into a tiny court, and you'd probably be amazed at the amount of luxury to be found in this place. This old Europe of ours is often far better than it looks."

"I didn't see the man of the house."

"Oh, yes you did. Frau Krochburg or Madame Crocheville, if you wish secretly to call her so, is very much the man of the house. There is a Herr Krochburg, but he won't come in our way now. Madame will do everything for us at present. I've touched a spark of fire to her soul, and it has blazed up. Those Huguenots of long ago were really republicans, and it's republican France now, for the success of which she prays with every breath she draws."

"She's locked us in pretty securely. I heard that big German key turn."

"To keep others from getting at us. Not to keep us from getting out. Now, I hear it turning again, and I'll wager that she's coming back with something that will rejoice us to the core."

The door opened and Madame Crocheville walked into the room, bearing a large tray which she placed upon a chair until she could close and lock the door again. Then she bore it to the table and John looked at it with great longing. He was young, he was healthy and he had a digestion beyond criticism.

"I told you so," exclaimed Lannes triumphantly, "and look, Madame Crocheville has brought us her best--a bottle of the light, white wine made in this very district, and good! You can dismiss your American scruples--it's very mild--filet of beef, tender, too, baked potatoes, salad, bread and butter and cheese. It is truly fit for a king. Madame Crocheville, two young and starving souls, thank you."

A smile lighted up her stern, almost masculine features. Then her face, in truth, looked feminine and tender.

"You're wild and reckless, but you're a good boy, Philip Lannes," she said, "and I know that you'd willingly lay down your life for the France that I've never seen, but which I love. You say again that the great war is at hand."

"It has come. In a few days four hundred million people will be in it, and I know that France will come out of it with all her ancient glory and estate."

"I hope and pray so," she said fervently, and then she left them.

The two ate and drank with wonderfully keen appetites, but they did not forget their manners. John noticed that Philip was extremely fastidious at the table, and he liked him the better for it. And the food was wonderfully good. John felt new life and strength flowing into his veins.

"I suppose we stay here tonight," he said.

"Yes it would be dangerous for us to leave so soon. Madame Crocheville will take good care of us tonight and tomorrow, and tomorrow night we'll leave."

"I don't see just how we'll go," said John. "There are German troops in this town, as we know, and even if we could get out of it, where then would we be. I want to go to Munich, and you, I take it, want to reach France. We can't go by land and we can't go by water. How then can we go?"

"No, we can't go by either land or water, but we'll go in another way. Yes, we'll surely do it. This filet is certainly good. Take another piece. You haven't tasted the tomato salad yet, and it's fine. No, I won't tell you how we're going, because in every affair of life there's always a possible slip. You just wait upon the event, and learn patience. Patience is a wonderful quality to have, I ought to know. I've seen how much it does for others, and how often I've suffered from the lack of it."

"I'll wait, because I have to. You're right about the filet. It's good. I think I'll take some more of it."

"You can't have it. Pig of an American, it would be your third piece."

"But it would be your third, too!"

"I know it, but I saw its merits first. So, I get a discoverer's third as a reward. Feel a lot better, don't you, John?"

"I feel like a general now. Where did you learn such good, every-day English."

"Studied it ten years at school, and then I lived two years in that great, splendid unkempt country of yours. Mind your step! Good-by, little girl, good-by! We must get the men higher up! Tariff for Revenue only! Hurrah for the Goddess of Liberty! Our glorious American eagle bathes one wing in Lake Superior and the other in the Gulf of Mexico! Our foreign commerce would be larger if it were not for our grape-juice diplomacy! Now for the Maxixe and the Hesitation all at the same time!"

He sprang from his chair and whirled and jerked about the room in a kind of wild Apache dance. John laughed until his eyes grew wet.

"You've been there," he said, as Lannes sat down again, panting. "You've proved it, and I no longer wonder at your fine colloquial English."

"I like your country and I like you Americans," said Lannes seriously. "You are the favorite children of the world, and I say children purposely, because you are children. You think you are terribly wicked, but you're not wicked at all. You're mere amateurs in vice compared with the hoary and sinful nations of Europe. We're more quiet about it, but we practice tricks that you never dream of. We've made you think you're dollar-worshipers, but while the dollars are dropping through your fingers, John, we're hanging on to the francs, and marks, and shillings, and rubles and gulden and pesos and kronen with a grasp that death itself often fails to break."

John did not know whether to be pleased or displeased, but finally concluded to be pleased.

"Perhaps you're telling the truth," he said.

"I know I am. But here comes Madame Crocheville for the dishes. She will also say: 'Good night my wild and reckless but gallant Philip, and the same to you young American stranger.'"

"How do you know?"

"Never mind how I know. I know."

Madame Crocheville came in and she looked at the two with satisfaction. Their appearance had improved greatly under the ministrations of her good food and drink. She put the dishes on her tray and went to the door. When she had turned the key she looked back and said:

"Good night, my wild and reckless but gallant Philip, and the same to you, young American stranger."

Then she went out, closed the door, and the two heard the big key turning again in the lock. The young Frenchman looked at the young American and smiled in content.

"How did you know so exactly?" asked John.

"Just call it an uncommonly accurate guess. Now, I think I'll put out the lamp. The light from the window is sufficient for us, and we don't want to take any unnecessary risk."

He blew out the light, but John went to the window, and looked out on the tiny court or place, on the far side of which ran a street so narrow that it would have been called an alley at home.

He could not see much owing to the thick darkness, and it had begun to rain also. The air was chill and heavy with damp. John shivered. Fate had played him a weird trick by causing him to lose his train, but she had atoned for it partly by giving him this brave young Frenchman as a comrade. It was wonderfully snug and comfortable in the house of Madame Crocheville, called by her fellow townsmen and townswomen Frau Krochburg.

"I'm glad it's not a part of your plan for us to escape tonight, Philip," he said.

"And what's the cause of your gladness."

"It's raining, and it's as cold as winter. I like this place, and I think I'll go to bed."

"A good plan. Everything is ready for us."

There was a little adjoining room, in which they found water, towels and could make all the other preparations for the night, and John, feeling a sudden great weariness, made ready. When he was in bed he saw Lannes still at the window.

"Better crawl in, too, Philip," he called. "This is a fine bed, and I fancy the other is just as good."

"I'll join you in slumber land soon. Good night."

John closed his eyes, and in a few minutes he was sleeping soundly. He was first to awake the next morning, and he saw that it was a gray day. The rain had ceased, but there was no one in the little court or street beyond. Philip slept soundly, and, as it was early, John did not awake him. But he rose and dressed shortly before Madame Crocheville came with breakfast.

"You have slept well, I hope," she said.

"Never better," replied Lannes for them both.

"I hear from others that which you told me last night. Germany has declared war upon Russia, and the mightiest of the German armies marches today against France. Philip! Philip! Poor France will be crushed!"

"Not so, Madame! France is not ready and the German armies will go far toward Paris, but France, the republic, will not fall. I am young, but I have heard, and I have seen. French valor is French valor still, and Germany is creating for herself a ring of foes."

"You make me believe! You make me believe, Philip, in spite of myself," she said.

"We shall see what we shall see," said Lannes with confidence.

The day passed and they did not seek to stir from the room. Madame Crocheville brought them food, but talked little. Time was very heavy. John did not dare to go much to the window, for fear of being seen. The night at last came again, and to their great joy it was dark without either moon or stars.

"Now we'll go," said Lannes.

"I'm ready," said John, although he did not have the remotest idea how they were going.

T HE THRILLING ESCAPE

MADAME CROCHEVILLE BROUGHT THEM SUPPER, and they ate with strong appetites. John was all courage and anticipation. He was chafing over his compulsory day and night in one room, despite its comfort and safety, and he was ready for any risk. He wanted to reach his uncle and Mr. Anson, knowing how great must be their anxiety. Lannes was as eager to be away, for other reasons.

"Don't make the risks too great," said Madame Crocheville, as she paused with the tray of empty dishes.

"We will not," replied Lannes earnestly. "It is not a time for folly."

He went out with Madame, leaving John alone in the room, but he returned in two or three minutes, and thrust an automatic pistol in the young American's hand.

"Put this in your pocket," he said, "and here's a little bag of cartridges that you can drop into another pocket."

"But it's not my war," said John, "I don't want to shoot at anybody."

"No, it's not your war, but it's forcing itself upon you, and you may have to shoot. You'll be wise to take what I offer you."

Then John took them, and an hour later they stole out of the house, carrying with them the earnest hopes of Madame Crocheville. The house, doubtless, had other inmates, but she was the only one whom John had seen, and her competency gave the impression that no other was needed.

"We're going out into the country," said Lannes.

"Show the way."

"Don't you feel any curiosity about it?"

"A lot, but, remember I promised to ask no questions." Lannes laughed.

"So you did," he said, "and I knew that you were a man who'd keep your word, as you're doing. We're going to leave this town and the country about it, but I'll say nothing about the way it's to be done. There's some danger, though, and I'm armed just as you are."

"I'm not afraid of a little danger."

"I knew you were not. Here we are in the passage again, and it's as dark as a well. Mind your step, and, when we come out into the broader street, walk as if you had lived here all your life. But the town is half deserted. All the younger men have gone away to the war."

They came into the street and walked carelessly along, passing only an occasional old man or woman. The wonderful German mobilization, like a net, through which nothing slipped, was going on, and the youthful strength of the town was already departing toward the French border.

"No notice of us will be taken until we come to the outskirts," said Lannes, "but there they have sentinels whom we must pass."

It was on the tip of John's tongue to ask how, but he refrained. He was willing to put his trust in this young Frenchman who was proving himself so trustworthy, and he continued in silence by his side. It did not take them long to reach the area of scattered houses. Walking swiftly among them they entered a vegetable garden, and John saw beyond the metals of a railway track, a bridge, and two soldiers, gun on shoulder, guarding it.

"We're going to pass under that bridge," said Lannes.

Now John could not refrain from asking how.

"It crosses a canal and not a river," said Lannes. "It's an old disused canal, with but little water in it, and we'll go down its bed. Come on, John."

The canal flowed at the foot of the garden, and they lowered themselves into the bed, where they found a muddy footing, between the water and the bank, which rose four or five feet.

"We'll bend over and hug the bank," said Lannes. "In the darkness we may be able to go under the bridge, unseen by the two sentinels. At any rate we must chance it. If they fire on us the odds are at least twenty to one against our being hit. So, don't use the automatic unless the need is desperate."

A chill ran along John's spine. He had never fired at anybody, and nobody had ever fired at him. A week ago he was a peaceful tourist, never dreaming of bullets, and now he was fairly hurled into the middle of a gigantic war. But he was one who accepted facts, and, steadying himself for anything, he followed Lannes who, bent almost double, was walking rapidly.

They were within twenty yards of the bridge now, and John distinctly saw the two sentinels. They were stout Bavarian lads, with heavy, unthinking faces, but he knew that, taught in the stern German school, they would fire without hesitation on Lannes and himself. He devoutly hoped they would not be seen, and it was not alone their own safety of which he was thinking, but he did not want to use the automatic on those kindly Bavarian boys.

As they came within the shadow of the bridge they bent lower and went much more slowly. Strange thrills, the product of excitement and not of fear, ran down John's back. This was no play, no game of make-believe, he was running for his life, and a world which had been all peace a few days ago was now all war. It was impossible, but it was happening and it was true. He could not comprehend it all at once, and he was angry at himself because he could not. These emotions went fleeting by, even at the moment, when they passed under the bridge.

They paused directly beneath the superstructure, and hugged the bank. John could see the two sentinels above, one at either end. Lannes and he had come thus far in safety, but beyond the bridge the shadows were not so deep, and the banks of the canal were lower.

"I think that luck has favored us," whispered Lannes.

"I hope it will continue to do so."

"It will. It usually goes one way for a little while. Come!"

They passed from the shelter of the bridge and ran down the old canal. Luck favored them for forty or fifty yards, and then one of the sentinels caught a glimpse of John's figure. Hastily raising his gun he fired.

John felt a rush of air past his face, and heard the thud of the bullet as it buried itself in the soft bank. A cold chill ran down his spine, but he said nothing. Lannes and he increased their speed. The sentinels did not fire again. Perhaps they thought imagination had been tricked by a shadow.

A hundred yards farther on, and the canal passed through woods, where it was so dark that one could not see far. Lannes climbed the bank and threw himself down among the trees. John imitated him.

"Are you hit?" asked Lannes.

"No, but I felt the wind from the bullet."

"Then you've had your baptism of war, and as it was a German bullet that was seeking you you're one of us now."

John was silent.

Both lay a while on the grass in the dense shadow of the trees, until their panting passed into regular breathing. The darkness did not decrease, and no sound came from the fields. It was evident that they had not been followed. John felt that all his strength had returned, but he waited patiently for Lannes to lead the way.

The Frenchman rose presently and went to the edge of the grove.

"The coast is clear," he said, "and we might as well depart. Come, Monsieur John. You've shown great power over your curiosity, and I'll ask you to show it a little longer. But I'll say this much. You can barely make out a line of hills across those fields. Well, they are five or six miles away and we're going toward them at a leisurely but fairly rapid pace."

"All right. Show the way. I think I'm in good shape for a canter of several miles."

They walked steadily more than an hour, and the night lightened somewhat. As they approached the hills John saw that they were high, rough, and covered with dark green foliage. It was possible that Lannes was seeking a refuge among them, but reflection indicated that it was not probable. There could be no secure hiding place in a country so thickly populated, and in a region so far away from France. Lannes must have something else in view.

When they came to the first slope Lannes led boldly upward, although he followed no path. The trees were larger than one usually sees in Europe, and there was some undergrowth. At a point two or three hundred feet up they stopped and looked back. They saw nothing. The town was completely hidden by the night. John had a strong feeling of silence, loneliness and awe. He would have insisted upon knowing where Lannes was leading him, but the young Frenchman had shown himself wholly trustworthy.

The way continued upward. Lannes was following no path, but he advanced with certainty. The night lightened somewhat. A few stars came out, and an edge of the moon showed, but the town was now shut off from sight by the foliage on the hills, and they seemed absolutely alone in the world.

John knew that they were not likely to see houses, owing to the habit the rural people had on the continent of living in villages, but they might pass the hut of a stray woodcutter or charcoal burner. He had no mind to be taken back to the town and his hand slipped down to the butt of the automatic.

"You've plenty of courage, John," said Lannes, "and you've a very steady nerve, too. Courage and steady nerve don't always go together. You'll need both."

"For our escape?"

"Yes. It's scarcely possible to walk out of Germany because the borders are guarded everywhere. The land is closed to us, nor can we go by water either. As an American they might have passed you on, if you had not become so strongly identified with me, but borrowing one of your English expressions we are now tarred with the same brush. But, as I told you before, we shall leave Germany nevertheless."

John's curiosity was intense, but pride still kept him from asking any questions. In silence he followed Lannes, who was traveling upward. The region now became utterly dreary, steep, stony and rain-washed.

Not even the thrifty European peasant could have drawn any part of a living from those blasted rocks.

They came at last to the crest of the hills, or rather low mountains, and passed into a depression which looked to John like some age-old crater. Then he heard Lannes draw a deep breath, almost a sigh, and he knew it was caused by relief of the mind rather than of the body.

"Well, we're here," said Lannes, sitting down at the stony edge of the crater.

"Yes, we're here," said John, also sitting down, "and being here, where are we?"

Lannes laughed. It was a pleased and friendly laugh, and John recognized it as such.

"Wait until we draw about a hundred long breaths apiece," said Lannes, "and then we'll have action."

"Suits me. That was a big climb."

As they rested, John looked down with renewed interest at the crater. He saw that the center of it was quite level, and evidently the soil on that spot was rich, as it was covered with thick long grass. Nearer by, among the stones, lay faggots, and also smaller pieces of wood.

"John," said Lannes, at the end of a few minutes, "you'll help me with these billets, won't you?"

"Of course. What do you want to do?"

"To build a fire. Aren't you cold?"

"I hadn't thought about it. I'm not likely to notice either heat or cold at such a time."

Lannes laughed. It was a low laugh of satisfaction, but wholly without irony.

"You're not cold," he said, "nor am I, and if we were we wouldn't build a fire to keep us warm. But we're going to build one."

They laid the faggots and smaller pieces together, and then cut off dry splinters with their clasp knives. Lannes set fire to the splinters with a match, and the two stood away. The blaze spread rapidly, and soon crackled and burned at a merry rate, sending up high flames.

"Aren't you afraid the fire will warn some one?" asked John.

"I hope so," was the startling reply.

Lannes threw on more wood. He seemed anxious that the flames should rise higher. They obeyed his wish, shooting upward, and sending streams of sparks far above. Then he stepped back, and, sitting down on a stone, began to look into the skies, not a stray glance, but a long, unbroken anxious gaze.

The heavens were yet brightening. More stars sprang out, the segment of the moon broadened and shone like burnished silver. The last cloud was gone, leaving the skies a vast vault of dusky blue. And Lannes never took his eyes from the great arch, although they traveled from horizon to horizon, searching, searching, searching everywhere.

The young Frenchman's action and manner had an indescribable effect upon John. A warning thrill ran down his back, and there was a strange, creeping sensation at the roots of his hair. Without knowing why, he, too, began to gaze steadily into the skies. The little town from which they had escaped and the possibility of the wandering woodcutter or charcoal burner passed from his mind. His whole soul was in his eyes as he stared into the heavens, looking for he knew not what.

The gaze of Lannes turned chiefly toward a range of mountains, to the south, visible only because of the height on which they stood. Anxiety, hope, belief and disbelief appeared on his face, but he never moved from his seat, nor spoke a word. Meanwhile the flames leaped high and crackled, making the only sound heard in all that desolation and loneliness.

How long they sat there, watching the skies John never knew, but the time seemed hours, and throughout it Lannes did not once take his gaze from above. Now and then, he drew a sharp breath, as if a hope had failed, but, in a moment or two, hope came back to his eyes, and they still searched.

John suddenly felt a great thrill again run down his spine, and the roots of his hair quivered. He was looking toward the mountains in the south, and he believed that he saw a black dot hanging in the air above them. Then another dot seemed to hang beside it. So much looking could make one see things that were not, and he rubbed his eyes. But there hung the dots, and they were growing larger.

John looked long and he could not now doubt. The black dots grew steadily. They were apparently side by side, and they came fast toward the hill on which Lannes and he stood. He glanced at his comrade. He had never before seen a face express so much relief and exultation.

"They come! they come!" said Lannes, "I knew they would!"

John looked back. The black dots were much nearer, and he began to make out dim shapes. Now, he knew. The full truth burst upon him. They were aeroplanes, and he knew that Lannes had summoned them out of the black ether with his fire. He felt the great thrill along his spine again. It was magic; nothing less. Flights in the air were yet too novel to allow of any other feeling.

"They're coming to us!" said John.

"Yes," said Lannes, pride showing in his tone. "I called them and they came. I told you, John, that we'd escape, neither by land, nor by water, but that we would escape. And so we will. We go by air, John. The heavens open and receive us."

He rose and stretched out his arms, as if to meet the coming black shapes. The dramatic instinct in him was strong, and John could well pardon it as he saw that his emotion was extraordinary.

"The heavens open a path for us!" he cried.

The two aeroplanes were now circling over their own hill, and John could discern human shapes in them. They began to descend gently, as the operators skillfully handled the steering rudders.

"Well done! well done!" said Lannes to himself rather than to John. "They couldn't be managed better."

Presently the machines began to loop and make spirals, and then both sank gently upon the grassy turf in the center of the glade. A man stepped forth from the seat in each machine and saluted Lannes, as if he were a commander. Lannes returned the salute promptly and gracefully.

"We saw the fiery signal, lieutenant," said one of the men in French, as he took off his great glasses, "and we came as fast as we could."

"I knew that you would do so, Castelneau," said Lannes, "and I knew that Méry would be as prompt."

The two aviators bowed with evident gratification, and Castelneau said:

"We are proud of praise that comes from the most daring and skillful airman in France, which means in this case the world. We thank you, Lieutenant Lannes."

Lannes blushed and said: "You overrate me, Castelneau."

John glanced at him. And, so this youth with the easy manner and the wonderful eyes was the greatest of all flying men! John's own mind was not mechanical, but his glance became a gaze of admiration. What a mighty achievement it was to cleave the air like a bird, and leave the whole solid earth beneath. One, in fact, did leave the world and hang in space. For the moment, he thought more of the wonder than of its bearing upon his own fortunes.

He glanced down at the machines resting on the grass. Their motors were still throbbing, and in the dimness they looked like the rocs of Arabian mythology, resting after a gigantic flight. In truth, everything had taken on for John an aspect of unreality. These men were unreal, Lannes and he were unreal, and it was an unreal world, in which nothing but unrealities moved.

"My new friend is an American," said Lannes, "and he's to be trusted, since his own life as well as ours is at stake. Monsieur John Scott, Messieurs Gaston Castelneau and August Méry. John, these are two skillful and valued members of the French flying corps. I want you to shake hands with brave men."

John gladly shook their gloved hands.

"Castelneau, and you, Méry, listen," said Lannes, and again his voice took on that dramatic ring, while his figure seemed to swell in both size and stature. "It is here! It has come, and the whole world will shake beneath its tread!"

"The war!" they exclaimed with one voice.

"Aye the war! The great war! the world war! The planet-shaking war! Germany declared war today on Russia and tomorrow she declares war on France! Never mind how I know! I know, and that's enough! The strength and weight of a Germany that has devoted its best mind and energy for nearly half a century to preparation for war will be hurled at once upon our poor France! We are to be the first and chief victim!"

"It will not be so!" said Castelneau and Méry together.

"No, I think not. Republican France of 1914 is not Imperial France of 1870. There I think Imperial Germany has made her great mistake. And we have friends, as Imperial France had not! But every son of France must be prepared to shed his blood in her defense!"

Castelneau and Méry bowed gravely. John could tell little about them, except they were short, thick men, apparently very strong. They wore caps, resembling those of a naval officer, heavy, powerful glasses, and baggy clothing, thick and warm. John saw that they paid Lannes great deference, and he remembered the words of Castelneau that the young Frenchman was the greatest airman in France. And he had a vague impression, too, that France led in flying.

"Can France win against Germany, my lieutenant?" asked Méry, who had not spoken hitherto. "The Germans outnumber us now in the proportion of seven to four, and from a time long before we were born they've thought war, dreamed war, and planned war."

"We'll not have to fight Germany, single handed, my good Méry," replied Lannes. "We'll have friends, good friends, powerful friends. And, now, I suppose that you have extra clothing with you?"

"Enough for two, sir. Your friend goes with you?"

"He does unless he wishes to remain here and be shot as a spy by the Germans."

Lannes did not glance at John as he spoke, but it was a calculated remark, and it met with an instant response.

"I'll go with you in the machine," he said.

And yet it took great courage to make the resolve. The three Frenchmen were practised aviators. They traveled in the air as John would have traveled on the water. He had never been in a flying machine in his life, and his mind did not turn to mechanics.

"We must not waste time in delay," said Lannes. "Mr. Scott and I will go in the first machine, and we will start straight for France. John, I promised to take you to Munich, but I can't do it now. I'll carry you to France. Then you may cross over to Switzerland, and communicate with your people in Munich. It's the best that can be done."

"I know," said John, "and I appreciate the effort you're making for me. Nor would I be in your way at a time when you may be able to do so much for your country."

"Then we go at once. Castelneau, we take the *Arrow*."

He pointed to the smaller of the machines.

"Yes, my lieutenant," said Castelneau, "it is the better for a long flight."

"I thought so. Now, Castelneau, you and Méry return to the hidden station in the mountains, while Mr. Scott and I take flight for France. John, here are your clothes."

John hastily put on the heavy garments, which seemed to him to be made of some kind of oilskin, thrust his hands into heavy gloves, and put on the protecting glasses. But as he did it his pulses were beating hard. The earth on which he now stood looked very good and very solid, and the moonlit ether above him was nothing but air, thin, impalpable air, through which his body would cleave, if he fell, with lightning speed. For a moment or two he was afraid, horribly afraid, but he resolutely put the feeling down.

Lannes was also clothed anew, looking like a great baggy animal, but he was rapid and skillful. John saw at once that the praise of Castelneau was justified.

"Here is your seat, John," said Lannes, "and mine is here. All you'll have to do is to sit still, watch the road and enjoy the scenery. We'll give her a shove, and then you jump in."

There was some room on the grass for the preliminary maneuver, and the four shoved the machine forward and upward. Then Philip and John, quickly releasing their grasp, sprang into their seats.

Lannes' eyes behind the heavy glasses were flashing, and the blood was flying through his veins. The daring strain, the utter defiance of death which appears so often in French blood was up and leaping. He was like a medieval knight, riding to a tournament, confident of victory, only Philip Lannes was not any conqueror of narrow lists, the vast space in which the whole universe swings was his field of triumph. His hand sought the steering rudder, and the machine, under the impulse of the strong push it had received, rose into the air.

John's sensation as he left the earth for the very first time in his life was akin to seasickness. The machine seemed to him to be dipping and gliding, and the throbbing of the motor was like the hum of a ship's machinery in his ear. For a few moments he would have given anything he had to be back on that glorious solid earth. But again he put down the feeling of fear.

He turned his head for a last look at Castelneau and Méry, and, to his amazement, he could barely make them out standing by the other machine, which looked like some great, vague bird poised on the grass. Directly below him he saw the tops of trees, and at that moment they looked to his excited fancy like rows of glittering spear points, poised to receive him.

"Look up! Look up!" said the sharp voice of Lannes in his ear. "It's always the fault of beginners to look down and see what they've left."

His tone was more than sharp, it was peremptory, commanding. John glanced at him and saw his steady hand on the rudder, and his figure loose and swinging easily like that of a sailor poised on a rolling deck. He knew that Lannes' manner was for his own good, and now he looked straight up at those heavens, into which they were ascending.

The motor throbbed, and John knew that the machine was ascending, rising, but not at a sharp angle. The dizzy feeling began to depart, and he longed to look down again, but did not do so. Instead he kept his eyes upward, his gaze fixed on the dusky blue heavens, which now looked so wide and chill. He knew that the little distance they had come from the earth was nothing to the infinity of the void, but by some mental change the stars seemed to have come much nearer, and to have grown hugely in size. There they danced in space, vast and cold.

The machine dipped a little and rose again. John dared another glance at Lannes, who was swaying easily in his seat, feeling all the exaltation of a confident rider who has a swift horse beneath him.

"I'm better now," said John above the purring of the motor.

Lannes laughed deep down in his throat, and with unction.

"Getting your air-legs, so to speak," he said. "You're learning fast. But don't look down at the ground, at least not yet. By and by you'll feel the thrill, which to me is like nothing else on earth--or rather above it. You've noticed, haven't you, that it's growing colder?"

"Not yet. I suppose the excitement has made my blood flow faster than usual, and that keeps me warm."

"It won't much longer. We're up pretty high now, and we're flying fast toward that beautiful country of mine. Can't you feel the wind rushing like a hurricane past your ears?"

"Yes, I do, and in the last minute or two it's acquired an edge of ice."

"And that edge will soon grow sharper. We're going higher."

John felt the upward swoop of the plane. The sensation that a ship gives a passenger when it dips after a swell returned, but it quickly passed. With it went all fear, and instead came a sort of unreasoning exhilaration, born of a strange new tincture in his blood. His ears were pounding and his heart had a more rapid beat. He hoped that Lannes would go yet higher. Yes, his comrade was right. He did feel the wind rushing past, and heard it, too. It was a pleasant sound, telling of trackless miles through the ether, falling fast behind them.

Those moments were filled for him with a new kind of exaltation. Despite the cold heights the blood still flowed, warm, in his veins. The intangible sky was coming nearer and its dusky blue of the night was deepening. The great, friendly stars looked down, meeting his upturned gaze, and still danced before him.

Now, he dared to stare down for the second time, and his heart took a great leap. Far beneath him, somber and dark, rolled the planet on which he had once lived. He had left war and the hate of nations behind. Here was peace, the steady throb of the motor in his ear was soothing music.

"I see that you've got your air-balance, John," said Philip, "you learn fast. I think that Castelneau and Méry would approve of you. Since you've learned to look down now with steady eyes take these glasses."

He handed him a pair of powerful glasses that he took from under the seat, and John, putting them to his eyes turned them downward. It gave him a strange tingling sensation that he from some unknown point in space should look at the earth as a distant and foreign planet.

But the effect of the glasses was wonderful. The earth sprang forth in the moonlight. He saw forests, fields, villages, and the silver ribbon of a river. But all were racing by, and that, even more than the wind rushing past, gave him an idea of the speed at which they were going. He took a long, long look and then returned the glasses.

"It's tremendous," he said. "I confess that at first I felt both fear and physical ill. But I am getting over it, and I feel instead the thrill of swift motion."

"It's because we have a perfect piece of track."

"There's no track in the air!"

"Oh, yes, there is. If you'd thought a moment you'd have known it, though I'll admit it's a shifting one. When you stand on the ground and turn your eyes upward all the sky looks alike. But it's far from it. It's full of all kinds of winds, currents and strata, pockets, of which all aviators stand in deadly fear, mists, vapors, clouds of every degree of thickness and complexion, and then you have thunder and lightning, just as you do on land and sea. It's these shifting elements that make the navigation of the air so dangerous, John. The whole question would be solved, if there was nothing but stationary air, growing thinner in exact proportion as we rise. But such a condition of aerial peace could not be reached unless we could go up fifty miles, where there is no air, and that we'll never be able to do."

"How high are we now?"

"About three thousand feet. Draw that collar more closely about your neck. You may not feel cold, because of the new fire in your blood, but you are cold, nevertheless. Now, see those whitish streams below us. They're little clouds, vapor mostly, they don't contain rain. You've read the 'Arabian Nights,' haven't you, John?"

"Yes, and I know just the comparison you're thinking of."

"What is it, then? See if you're right."

"The roc, great, fabled bird, flying through the air with those old Arabs perched on its back."

"Right! He guessed right the very first time. That's one of your Americanisms, isn't it? Oh, I know a lot of your choicest expressions. Hit it up lively! That's what we're doing. He's full of pep! That's what we are; aren't we, John? Come across with a double play! And we're doing that, too."

"I don't know that your baseball metaphor is exactly right, Philip, but your heart is certainly in the proper place. When do we get to France?"

"Don't talk about that yet, because it's impossible to approximate. This smooth track will not go on forever. It's lasted longer than usual already. Then, we'll have to eat, later on. There's food here in a tiny locker that you can't see, but it may be better for us to drop down to the earth when we eat. Besides, while we're sailing through the sky, I'd like to observe as much as I can of this German mobilization and take the news of it to France. That, of course, leaves you out of consideration, John, but I'm bound to do it."

"Don't regard me. I've no right to ask anything of you. I'm a guest or a prisoner, and in either capacity it behooves me to take what comes to me."

"But I got you into it, and so I feel obligations, but, heavy as they are, they're not heavy enough to keep me from seeing what I can see. I told you that we were going toward France, but we're not taking the direct course. I mean to fly over the ancient city of Nuremburg, and then over Frankfort-on-the-Main. Look out, now, John, we're going to drop fast!"

The machine descended rapidly in a series of wide spirals, until it was within seven or eight hundred feet of the earth.

"Look down now," said Lannes, "and without the glasses you can see a town."

But he had taken the glasses himself, and while he held one hand on the steering rudder he made a long and attentive examination of the place, and of low works about it, which he knew contained emplacements for cannon.

"It's a fortified town and a center for mobilization," he said. "All day long the recruits have been pouring in here, responding to the call. They receive their uniforms, arms and ammunition at that big barracks on the hill, and tomorrow they take the trains to join the giant army which will be hurled on my France."

John heard a sigh. Lannes was afraid after all that the mighty German war machine, the like of which the world had never seen before would crush everything.

"It will be hard to stop that army," he could not keep from saying.

"So it will. The Germans have prepared for war. The French have not. John, John, I wish I knew the secrets of our foes! For more than forty years they've been using their best minds and best energies for this. We don't even know their weapons. I've heard strange tales of monster cannon that the Krupps have sent out of Essen, and of new explosives of unimagined power, I don't know whether to believe these tales or not. But I do know that the Germans will be ready to the last cartridge."

"But something in the machine may go wrong, Phil."

"That's our hope. We've got to smash some of the wheels, or rods or levers. If we compel them to change their plan they won't have time to organize a perfect new one."

"The old simile of the watch, I suppose. It'll run a hundred years if all the works are kept right. But if a single one of them goes wrong it's done forever."

"It's as you say. Sit steady, now. We're going to take another upward swoop. I've seen enough of that town and its forts, and I don't want to linger so close to the earth that they'll see us."

The machine rose like a mighty bird, but shortly after it reached the top of its flight John felt a slight jerk. It was a sudden movement of Lannes' hand on the steering rudder that had caused it.

"John," he said, and the voice shook a little, "take the glasses. Look off there in the northwest, and see if you can't make out a black object hanging in the sky?"

John took the glasses and put them to his eyes.

5

THE FIGHT IN THE BLUE

JOHN TURNED his glasses toward the northwest, where cloud wrack hung. At first he could see nothing, as the dark blue sky was obscured by the darker mists and vapors, but he presently discovered in the very midst of them an object that looked jet black. It was moving, and slowly it took the shape of an aeroplane. He wondered at the keenness of Lannes' vision, when he was able to pick out so distant an object with the naked eye.

"What do you make of it?" asked Lannes.

"It's an aeroplane, or some other kind of flying machine."

"And which way do you think it's going?"

"The same way that we are. No, it seems to be nearer now."

"Likely it's running parallel with us in a sense; that is we two are moving down the sides of a triangle, and if we continue long enough we'd meet at the point."

"Perhaps it's Castelneau and Méry in the other plane?"

"Impossible! They would certainly stay on the mountains far behind us. They would never disobey orders. We're back into a bank of fine air now and the machine almost sails itself. Let me have the glasses a moment."

But he looked many moments. Then he calmly put the glasses away in the tiny locker and said:

"It's not a French machine, John, and it's not a friend's. It's a German Taube, and it's flying very fast. I think the man in it has seen us, which is unfortunate."

"And there's another!" exclaimed John in excitement. "Look! He's been hidden by that long, trailing sheet of vapor off toward the north. See it's close to the other one."

"Aye, so it is! And they are friends, twin foes of ours! Two Taubes, but only one man in each, while there are two in this tight little machine! They have certainly seen us, because they're bending in rapidly toward us now!"

"What do you intend to do? Meet them and fight?"

"Not unless we have to do it. I've news for France which is worth more than my life, or yours either for that matter--or more than my honor or yours. No, John, we'll run for it with all our might, and the *Arrow* is one of the prettiest and sweetest little racers in all the heavens!"

Lannes' hand pressed upon the steering rudder, and the machine, curving from its western course, turned toward the south. The motor throbbed faster and louder and John became conscious almost at once that their speed was increasing. Although the heavy cap was drawn down over his ears he heard the wind whistling as it rushed past, and it was growing much colder. In spite of himself he shivered, and he was sure it was the cold, not fear.

John's nature was sensitive and highly intellectual, but his heart was brave and his will powerful. He remembered that while two planes were in pursuit only one man was in each pursuer while there were two in the pursued. His gloved hand slipped down to the butt of the automatic.

He had no idea how fast they were going, but he knew the speed must be terrific. He grew colder and colder. He wondered how Lannes, taut and strained, bent over the steering rudder, could stand it, but he recalled the words of Castelneau that he was the best flying man in the world.

Lannes, in truth, felt neither stiffness nor cold, then. The strain of daring in the French nature which the Anglo-Saxon would call recklessness responded fully and joyfully to the situation. Not in vain, while yet so young, was he a king of the air. Every pulse in him thrilled with the keen and extraordinary delight that comes only from danger, and the belief in victory over it. His hand touched the rudder as the fingers of a pianist touches the keys of a piano, and in either case it was the soul of an artist at work.

Oh, it was a beautiful machine, the *Arrow*, strong, sinuous, graceful! Sure like the darting bird! It answered the lightest pressure of his hand upon the rudder, and he drew from it harmonies of motion that were true music to him.

But while the hand on the rudder did its work his eyes swept the heavens with a questing gaze. Had he been alone in the *Arrow* he could have left the German Taubes far behind, but the extra weight of the passenger was a terrible burden for so light and delicate a machine. Yet he was glad John was with him. Already Lannes had a deep liking for the young American whose nature was so unlike his own.

That questing gaze lingered longest on the southern heavens. One who flees on the land must pick his way and so must one who flees through the skies. Now, the mind of the flying man was keyed to the finest pitch. He thought of the currents of air, the mists, the vapors, and, above all, of those deadly pockets which could send them in an instant crashing to the earth far below. No engineer with his hand at the throttle of a locomotive was ever more watchful and cautious.

John, too, was looking into the south, where he saw a loom of cloud and haze. It appeared that the heavens had drawn a barrier across their way, and he saw that Lannes was turning the *Arrow* again toward the west, as if he were seeking a way around that barrier.

Then he looked back. The Taubes, beyond a doubt, were nearer, and were flying in a swift true line.

"Are they gaining?" asked Lannes, who kept his eyes on the "country" ahead, seeking to choose a way.

"Considerably. They have been flying close together, but now they're separating somewhat; at least it seems so, although my eyes are tricky in an element so new to me."

"They're probably right in this instance. It's their obvious course. It's impossible for us to fly perfectly straight, and whenever we curve one or the other of their machines will gain on us. I've heard that a troop of lions will adopt this method in pursuing an antelope, and that it's infallible."

"Which means that we can't escape?"

"There's a difference. The antelope can't fight back, but we can. Don't forget the automatic I gave you."

"I haven't. Not for a second."

"But it won't come to that yet, and may not at all. See, how those clouds and vapors are stretching. They hem us in on the south, and now they're curving around in our front on the west, too. We can't lose the Taubes, John, here on this lower level, as we're not more than two thousand, perhaps not more than fifteen hundred feet above the earth, but we may be able to do it higher up. Steady, now! We're going to rise fast!"

The machine tilted up at an angle that made John gasp, but he quickly recovered himself and resisted a desperate inclination to grasp anything he could reach and hold on with all his might. He knew that the strap passed about his body held him so firmly that he could not fall out. Still, it shortened his breath and made his pulses bound, rather than beat.

Up! up they went into the thinner air, the nose of the *Arrow* again turned toward the south. Lannes did not look back. His mind and soul were absorbed in the flight of his machine, and his heart throbbed with exaltation as he knew that it was flying beautifully. But he called upon John to note the pursuers.

"They're curving up, too," said John. "They're very steady, and I think they're still gaining."

"Daring men! Yes, the Germans have good flyers, and we'll have a hard time in shaking them off. Still, we may lose them among the clouds."

"I think they're rising at a sharper angle than we are."

"Trying to get above us! Ah, I know what that means! Why did I not think of it at first? We must not permit it! Never for a moment!"

"Why not?"

But Lannes did not reply. Apparently he had not heard him, and

John did not repeat the question.

"Watch! John! Watch!" said Lannes, "and tell me every movement of theirs!"

"You can depend on me!"

The nose of the *Arrow* was still tilted upward, and John knew that they had come to a great height, as the cold struck to his very bones. The air also was darker and damper, and he saw that they were in the region of mists of vapors. Mentally he already used terms of land as terms of the air. Before them lay banks of cloud which were the same as mountains.

"One Taube is directly behind us and it seems to me a little higher," he announced. "The other has cut off to the right and also a little higher, if I see right."

"Then we must rise fast! We can't let them get above us!"

The nose of the *Arrow* tilted up yet farther, and shot into colder and darker regions. John saw mists and vapors below, but the earth was invisible. He was truly hanging between a planet and the stars, and this was the void, dark and thin, cold and infinite.

"Steady again!" said Lannes. "We're going to descend for a while."

The nose of the *Arrow* dropped down many degrees, and then they seemed to John to slide through space, although they slid like lightning. The air felt damper and thicker, and the area of vision contracted fast. They had plunged into a bank of vapor, and search as he would with both eye and glass he could see no sign of the Taubes.

"We've lost them for the time at least," he said.

"I hoped for it," said Lannes. "That's why I made for this area of vapor. It's exactly like a ship escaping in a fog from a fleet--only we haven't escaped yet."

"Why not?"

"We can't hang in here. If we do they'll explore for us, and if we go on and through it they'll follow. Yet we can hope for a gain. Isn't it a beautiful machine, John, and hasn't it behaved nobly?"

He patted the *Arrow* as a man would a horse that had saved his life with its speed.

"We'll go slowly here, John. Have you got good ears?"

"Yes. Why?"

"Then uncover them and listen. In case one of the Taubes draws near you can hear its humming and throbbing. My hearing may be deadened a little for the time by my tension in sailing the *Arrow*, so you're our reliance."

John listened intently, and in a few minutes the sound they feared came to his ears.

"I hear it," he said suddenly, "and as sure as we live it's directly over our heads!"

"Then we must mount at once!"

Up shot the *Arrow*, and passing through the vapor it flew again with nothing above it but the clear, cold stars. John looked down, but his vision was lost in the mass of floating mist. He exulted. They had lost the Taubes! But joy lasted only a moment. Out from the bank shot a dark shape. It was one of the machines, and in two minutes the other appeared.

"They've come through the mist, too, and they see us," he said to Lannes. "They seem to be trying to rise above us."

"I thought it would be their plan, if we didn't lose 'em. We've got to make another dash. We're pointing toward Switzerland, now, John, and maybe if we have luck we can descend in a neutral country. But I don't want to do it! I tell you I don't want to do it!"

He spoke with uncommon energy, but relapsed afterward into complete silence. The humming of the motor increased, and the icy wind rushed past John's ears in a perfect hurricane. He drew his cap down further and sank his neck and ears deeper in his collar. Nevertheless he thought he would freeze. The fingers that still clasped the butt of the automatic felt stiff and bloodless.

"What are they doing now, John?"

"They are gaining again--Ah, and there's a change!"

"What's that change?"

"One machine seems to have dropped a little lower than we are, while the other is rising higher."

"And that has come, too! I expected it. This, John, is what you might call an attempt to surround us. I'm surprised that they didn't attempt it sooner. Watch the Taube that's rising. Watch it all the time, and tell me everything it does!"

He spoke with the most intense energy and earnestness, and John knew that he had some great fear in regard to the upper Taube. So, he never took his eyes from it, and he noted that it was not only rising fast, but that its gain was perceptible. As it was his first flight it did not occur to him in those moments of excitement that his own weight was holding back the *Arrow*, and Lannes had been willing to risk death rather than tell him.

"They're coming very fast," he said to Lannes, "and the upper machine seems to be the swifter of the two."

"Naturally. That's the reason why it's now the upper one. Is it above us yet?"

"No, but in fifteen minutes more it will be, at the present rate of speed."

"About how much higher above us do you think it is?"

"A thousand feet maybe, but I never calculated distances of this kind before."

"Likely it's near enough. Let me know when it's about to come directly over us, and on your life don't fail!"

John watched with all his eyes. He saw the hovering shape, and he caught a glimpse of the arm of the man who steered. But it became to his fancy a great bird which, with its comrade below, pursued them. That name, Taube, the dove, called so from its shape, was very unfitting.

While he was watching he saw the Taube swoop down at least five hundred feet, and at the same time make a burst of speed forward.

"It will be over us! almost directly! within a minute!" he shouted to Lannes.

The *Arrow* swerved to on side with such suddenness that John reeled hard against his seat, despite the strap that held him. At the same moment he caught a glimpse of some small object shooting past the *Arrow*.

"What was it? what was it?" he cried.

"A bomb," replied Lannes. "That was the reason why I didn't want either of the Taubes to get above us. I was sure they had bombs, and if one of them fell upon us, well, nobody would ever find our pieces. Hold hard now, we're going to do a lot of zigzagging, because that fellow probably has more bombs, where the one he just dropped came from."

John's interest in what followed was, in a measure, scientific. He realized afterward that he should have been terribly frightened. In fact, he felt more fear later on, but at that moment the emotions that produce fear were atrophied. The extraordinary nature of his situation caused instead wonder and keen anticipation.

The *Arrow* shot to the right and then to the left. It dipped, and it rose, and then it darted on a level line toward the south.

John wondered afterwards that the delicate fabric was not torn to pieces, but Lannes was not a supreme flying man for nothing. Every movement was part of a plan, executed with skill and precision. Once more his hand played upon the rudder, as the fingers of a great pianist play upon the keys.

"Is the fellow directly above us yet, John?" he asked.

"Not at this moment, but I think he must have been several times. He has dropped at least three more bombs."

"Then his supply is probably getting small, and he'll be extremely careful with what's left. It's no easy task, John, to drop a bomb from a height, and hit a small target, moving as swiftly as the *Arrow*. Let him alone for the present, and look out for the fellow below. See what he is doing."

John looked down quickly. He had almost forgotten the existence of the second Taube, and he was surprised to find it beneath them and close at hand. The dark, hooded face of the man in the seat looked up at them. As well as John could judge he was using the superior speed of his Taube to keep up with the *Arrow*, and, at the same time, to rise slowly until they approached the point of contact. His apprehensions were quickly transferred from the upper to the lower Taube.

"The second machine is under us and rising," he said.

"And the second attack is likely to come from that point. Well, he can't drop bombs on us. That's sure, and we can meet him on his own ground or rather in his air. John, did you ever shoot at a man?"

"Never!"

"You're going to do it very soon. The automatic I gave you is a powerful weapon, and when the fellow rises enough you must shoot over the side at him. Take good aim and have no compunction, because he'll be shooting at us. But you've the advantage. You're free, while he has to steer his Taube and fire at the same time."

John drew the big automatic. He felt a shiver of reluctance, but only one. He and Lannes were in desperate case, and he would be fighting for the lives of both.

Clutching the powerful weapon in a firm hand he looked down again. The Taube had come much nearer, and he heard suddenly a crack sharp and clear in the thin air of the heights. A bullet sang by his ear. The man in the lower machine had a pistol or perhaps a rifle--John had not seen him raise any weapon.

Lannes glanced at John, whose face had hardened, but he said nothing. John pulled the trigger of the big automatic, and he saw the Taube waver for a moment, and then come on as steadily as ever.

"I don't think I hit him," he said, "but I believe the bullet flattened on his machine."

"You're getting close. Give him another. There went his second. I felt its wind past my face."

John pulled the trigger again, but marksmanship at such an immense height, between two small machines, flying at great speed was almost impossible. Bullet after bullet flew, but nobody was hit, although several bullets struck upon the *Arrow* and the Taube, doing no serious harm, however.

"I'm doing my best," said John.

"I know it," said Lannes. "I notice that your hand is steady. You'll get him."

John looked down, seeking aim for his fifth bullet, when he suddenly heard an appalling crash, and the Taube, a flying mass of splinters, disappeared in a flash from view. It had happened so quickly that he was stunned. The machine had been and then it was not. He looked at Lannes.

"The fellow above us dropped another bomb," said Lannes in a voice that shook a little. "It missed us and hit his comrade, who was almost beneath."

"What a death!" said John, aghast for a little while. Then he pulled himself together and looked up at the other Taube. It was hovering almost over them like a sinister shadow. As John looked something flashed from it, and a heavy bullet sang past.

"He has a rifle! Give him what's left in the automatic!" shouted Lannes.

John fired and he knew that his bullet had struck one of the exposed arms, because a moment later a drop of blood fell almost on his face.

"You've winged him," said Lannes. "Look how the Taube wobbles! You must have given him a bad wound in the arm. He'll have all he can do now to save himself. Good-bye to the pursuit. Luck and your skill, John, have saved us."

John, feeling faint, leaned against the seat.

"I think I'm air-sick," he said.

"It'll pass soon, but you're tremendously lucky. It's not often a fellow gets into a battle in the air the first time he goes up. See what's become of the Taube."

"It's descending fast. I can see the man struggling with it. I hope he'll reach the ground all right."

"He did his best to kill us both."

"I know, but I hope he'll get down, anyway."

"He will. He's regained control of his machine, but he can use only one arm. The other hangs limp. And now for a glorious flight in this brave little *Arrow* of ours."

"Will you return to our original course?"

"I think we'd better not. The German flying men are out, and we might have another fight, from which we would not emerge as well as we have from this. No one must ever underestimate the Germans. They're organized to the last detail in every department. I, a Frenchman, willingly say this. I'll make our flight more southerly. We'll come down in Switzerland. I'd like to go on to France, but we must make a descent soon. We're both cold and overstrained, and it won't be a real violation of neutrality just to touch Switzerland once."

The *Arrow* now sank to a much lower level, and that planet, which they had left came again into view. It was not much more than a dark shadow, save for the sheen of high mountains in the south, but John was glad to see it again. It was like the return of an old friend. It was the fine Earth, not one of the great planets, but the only planet he knew.

He felt a great weakness, but they had descended so much that the intense cold was going away. The thicker and warmer air lulled him, and he sank into a sort of stupor from which he soon roused himself with anger. He considered it a disgrace to him that he should sleep, while Lannes still picked their way through the currents, and pockets and flaws of the heavens.

"You might sleep if you feel like it," said Lannes. "You did all the fighting, and I ought to do all the flying, especially as it's my business and I've had lots of experience. Go ahead, old man. It'll be all the better for us if you get back your strength."

Under Lannes' urging John leaned back a little more in his seat, and closed his eyes. It was true that he was horribly tired, and his will seemed to have weakened, too. Flying was new to him, and now the collapse after so much tension and excitement had come. In a few minutes he slept, but the *Arrow* sailed swiftly on, mile after mile.

John's sleep was sound, but not long. When he awoke it was still night, although the dark bore a suspicious tint of silver in the east. The physical and mental weakness had departed, but he was singularly cold and stiff. When he sought to move, something firm and unyielding about his waist restrained him.

His eyes opened slowly and he looked around. On three sides space met his vision, just dusky blue sky with floating banks and wisps of vapor. But far off to the south, rising like mighty battlements, he saw a dim line of mountains clad in snow. Then it all came back to him. He was aloft in the *Arrow*, the first time that he had ever awakened in the void between the stars and his own planet.

There was Lannes at the rudder, looking a little bent and shrunken now, but his hand was as delicate and true as ever. The machine hummed softly and steadily in his ears, like the string of a violin.

"Philip!" he cried in strong self-reproach, "show me how, and I'll sail the *Arrow* for a while and you can rest."

Lannes shook his head and smiled.

"You're an apt student," he said, "but you couldn't learn enough in one lesson, at least not for our purpose. Besides, I'll have plenty of rest soon. We're going to land in an hour. Behold your first sunrise, seen from a point a mile above the earth!"

He swept his free hand toward the east, where the suspicion of silver had become a certainty. In the infinity of space a mile was nothing, but all the changes were swift and amazingly vivid to John. The silver deepened, turned to blue, and then orange, gold and red sprang out, terrace after terrace, intense and glowing.

Then the sun came up, so burning bright that John was forced to turn his eyes away.

"Fine, isn't it?" said Lannes appreciatively. "It's good to see the sunrise from a new point, and we're up pretty high now, John. We must be, as I said, nearly a mile above the earth."

"Why do we keep so high?"

"Partly to escape observation, and partly because we're making for a cleft in the mountain straight ahead of us, and about on our own level. In that cleft, which is not really a cleft, but a valley, we'll make our landing. It's practically inaccessible, except by the road we're taking, and our road isn't crowded yet with tourists. Look how the light is growing! See, the new sun is gilding all the mountains now with gold! Even the snow is turned to gold!"

His own wonderful eyes were shining at the tremendous prospect, outspread before them, peak on peak, ridge on ridge, vast masses of green on the lower slopes, and now and then the silver glitter of a lake. The eyes of him who had been so stark and terrible in the battle were now like those of a painter before the greatest picture of the greatest master.

"The Alps!" exclaimed John.

"Aye, the Alps! Hundreds of thousands of you Americans have come all the way across the sea to see them, but few of you have ever looked down on them in the glow of the morning from such a height as this, and you are probably the only one who has ever done so, after an all-night fight and flight for life."

"Which makes them look all the better, Philip. It's been a wonderful night and flight as you call it, but I'll be glad to feel the solid mountain under my feet. Besides, you need rest, and you need it badly. Don't try to deny it."

"I won't, because what you say is true, John. My eyes are blurred, and my arms grow unsteady. In that valley to which we are going nobody can reach us but by way of the air, but, as you and I know, the air has our enemies. Do you see any black specks, John?"

"Not one. I never saw a more beautiful morning. It's all silver, and rose and gold, and it's not desecrated anywhere by a single German flying machine."

"Try the glasses for a longer look."

John swept the whole horizon with the glasses, save where the mountains cut in, and reported the same result.

"The heavens are clear of enemies," he said.

"Then in fifteen minutes the *Arrow* will be resting on the grass, and we'll be resting with it. Slowly, now! slowly! Doesn't the machine obey beautifully?"

They sailed over a river, a precipice of stone, rising a sheer two thousand feet, above pines and waterfalls, and then the *Arrow* came softly to rest in a lovely valley, which birds alone could reach before man took wings unto himself.

The humming of the motor ceased, and the machine itself seemed fairly to snuggle in the grass, as if it relaxed completely after long and arduous toil. It was in truth a live thing to John for the time, a third human being in that tremendous flight. He pulled off his gloves and with his stiffened fingers stroked the smooth sides of the *Arrow*.

"Good old boy," he said, "you certainly did all that any plane could do."

"I'm glad you've decided the sex of flying machines," said Lannes, smiling faintly. "Boats are ladies, but the *Arrow* must be a gentleman since you call it 'old boy.'"

"Yes, it's a gentleman, and of the first class, too. It's earned its rest just as you have, Philip."

"Don't talk nonsense, John. Why, flying has become my trade, and I've had a tremendously interesting time."

John in common with other Americans had heard much about the "degenerate French" and the "decadent Latins." But Lannes certainly gave the lie to the charge. If he had looked for a simile for him in the animal kingdom he would have compared him with the smooth and sinuous tiger, all grace, and all power. Danger was the breath of life to him, and a mile above the earth, with only a delicate frame work holding him in the air he was as easy and confident as one who treads solid land.

John unbuckled the strap which had held him in the *Arrow*, stepped out and fell full length upon the grass. His knees, stiff from such a long position in one attitude, had given way beneath him. Lannes, laughing, climbed out gingerly and began to stretch his muscles.

"You've something to learn yet about dismounting from your airy steed," he said. "You're not hurt, are you?"

"Not a bit," replied John, sitting up and rubbing his knees. "The grass saved me. Ah, now I can stand! And now I can move the rusty hinges that used to be knees! And as sure as you and I live, Philip, I can walk too!"

He flexed and tensed his muscles. It was a strange sight, that of the young American and the young Frenchman capering and dancing about in a cleft of the Alps, a mile above the valley below. Soon they ceased, lay down on the grass and luxuriated. The heavy suits for flying that they had worn over their ordinary clothing kept them warm even at that height.

"We'll rest until our nerves relax," said Lannes, "and then we'll eat."

"Eat! Eat what?"

"What people usually eat. Good food. You don't suppose I embark in the ship of the air like the Arrow for a long flight without provisioning for it. Look at me."

John did look and saw him take from that tiny locker in the *Arrow* a small bottle, two tin cups, and two packages, one containing crackers, and the other thin strips of dried beef.

"Here," he said, shaking the bottle, "is the light red wine of France. We'd both rather have coffee, but it's impossible, so we'll take the wine which is absolutely harmless. We'll get other good food elsewhere."

He put the food on a little mound of turf between them, and they ate with hunger, but reserve. Neither, although they were on the point of starvation would show the ways of an animal in the presence of the other. So, their breakfast lasted some time, and John had never known food to taste better. When they finished Lannes went back to the locker in the Arrow.

"John," he said, "here are more cartridges. Reload your automatic, and keep watch, though nothing more formidable than the lammergeyer is ever likely to come here. Now, I'll sleep."

He rolled under the lee of a bank, and in two minutes was sleeping soundly.

6

BOVE THE STORM

JOHN HAD SLEPT WELL in the Arrow, and that fact coupled with his extraordinary situation kept him wide-awake. It was true that he had returned from the dizzy heights of the air, but he was still on the dizzy side of a mountain.

He stood up and tensed and flexed his muscles until he was sure of his physical self. He remembered the weakness in his knees that had sent him down like a little child, and he was so ashamed of himself that he was resolved it should not happen again.

Then he walked to the edge of the little valley which in the far distance had looked like a cleft in the side of the mountain. It was rimmed in by a line of stunted pines, and holding to a pine with each hand he looked over. He saw that sheer stone wall which he had beheld first from above when he was in the Arrow, and far below was the ripple of silvery white that he knew to be the river. To the north lay rolling hills and green country melting under the horizon, the old Europe that men had cultivated for twenty centuries and that was now about to be trodden to pieces by the iron heel of tremendous war.

John understood it. It seemed at the moment that his mind expanding to such an extent could comprehend the vastness of it all, the kingdoms and republics, the famous and beautiful old cities, and the millions of men who did not hate one another involved in a huge whirlpool of destruction. And yet, expand as his mind did, it could not fully comprehend the crime of those who had launched such a thunderbolt of death.

His eyes turned toward the south. It was perhaps not correct to call that little nest in which the Arrow lay a valley. It was a pocket rather, since the cliffs, unscalable by man rose a full half mile above it, and far beyond glimmering faintly in the sunshine he saw the crest of peaks clad in eternal snow.

Truly his view of the Alps was one of which he had never dreamed, and Lannes was right in saying that no man had ever before come into that valley or pocket, unless he had taken wings unto himself as they had done. They were secure where they were, except from danger that could come through the air.

He took the glasses, an uncommonly powerful pair from the locker and examined every corner of the heavens that he could reach. But he saw none of those ominous, black dots, only little white clouds shot with gold from the morning sun, floating peacefully under the blue arch, and now and then some wide-winged bird floating, aslant, from peak to peak. There was peace, peace everywhere, and he went back from the dizzy edge of the precipice to the side of the Arrow. Lannes still slept heavily, and John appreciated his great need of it, knowing how frightful his strain must have been during that long night.

He felt that he was wholly in Lannes' hands, and he did not know the young Frenchman's plans. He might wish to get away early, but John resolved to let him sleep. Whatever they undertook and wherever they went strength and steadiness must be of the utmost importance, and Lannes alone could take them on their flight.

John leaned against a little hillock and watched the country that rolled northward. For the first time in hours he thought of his uncle and Mr.

Anson. And yet he was so filled with wonder at his own translation into another element that he did not worry greatly about them. They would hear of him soon, he felt sure, and in a time of such vast anxiety and fear for half a world brief apprehension about a single person amounted to but little.

He dozed a short while, and then awoke with a start and an effort of the will. Lannes still slept like one dead. He felt that the young Frenchman and the *Arrow* were in his care, and he must fail in nothing. He stood up and walked about in the pocket, shaking the dregs of sleep from his brain. The sun doubled in size from that height, was sweeping toward the zenith. The radiant sky contained nothing but those tiny clouds floating like white sails on a sea of perfect blue. The gold on the snow of the far peaks deepened. He was suffused with the beauty of it, and, for a little space the world war and the frightful calamities it would bring fled quite away.

Lannes awoke about noon, stood up, stretched his limbs and sighed with deep content. He cast a questing glance at the heavens, and then turned a satisfied look on John.

"No enemy in sight," he said, "and I have slept well. Yea, more, I tell you, Yankee that you are, that I have slept magnificently. It was a glorious bed on that grass under the edge of the cliff, and since I may return some day I'll remember it as one of the finest inns in Europe. Have you seen anything while I slept, Monsieur Jean the Scott?"

"Only the peaks, the hills, the blue sky and three or four big birds which I was unable to classify."

"Let their classification go. When we classify now we classify nothing less than armies. Do you think the *Arrow* has had sufficient rest?"

"A plenty. It's a staunch little flying machine."

"Then we'll start again, and I think we'll have an easy trip, save for the currents which are numerous and varied in high mountains."

"What country are we in now?"

"A corner of Switzerland, and I mean for us to descend at a neat little hamlet I've visited before. They don't know war has begun yet, and we can get there provisions and everything else we need."

They launched the Arrow, and once more took flight, now into the maze of mountains. Their good craft frequently rocked and swayed like a ship at sea and John remembered Lannes' words about the currents.

Reason told him that intervening peaks and ridges would make them break into all forms of irregularity, and he was glad when they hovered over a valley and began to descend.

He saw about half a mile below them a small Swiss village, built on both sides of a foaming little river, and, using the glasses as they dropped down, he also saw the whole population standing in the streets, their heads craned back, staring into the skies. The effect was curious, that of the world turned upside down.

"The place has four or five hundred inhabitants, and it is a good village," said Lannes. "I have been here four times before, and they know me. Also they trust me, though through no merit of mine. They have seen flying machines often enough to know that they are not demons or monsters, but not often enough to lose their curiosity concerning them. We shall descend in the midst of an audience, inquisitive but friendly."

"Which you like."

Lannes laughed.

"You judge me right," he said. "I do love the dramatic. Maybe that's one reason why I'm so fond of flying. What could appeal to the soul more than swimming through the air, held up on nothing, with a planet revolving at your feet? Why a man who is not thrilled by it has no soul at all! And how grand it is to swoop over a village, and then settle down in it softly and peacefully like some magnificent bird, folding its wings and dropping to the ground! Isn't it far more poetical than the arrival of a train which comes in with a clang, a rattle, and smoke and soot?"

John laughed in his turn.

"You do put it well for yourself, Philip," he said, "but suppose our machine broke a wing or something else vital. A mile or a half mile would be a long drop."

"But you'd have such a nice clean death. There would never be a doubt about its completeness."

"No, never a doubt. Have you picked your port?"

"'Port' is a good enough place. We'll land on that little park, squarely in the center of the population."

"You're truly in love with the dramatic. You want an audience whenever it's safe."

"I admit it. There is something about the old Roman triumph that would have made a mighty appeal to me. Think of a general, young, brilliant, garlanded, coming into Rome along the Appian Way, with the chariots before him, the captive princes behind him, miles of beautiful young girls covered with roses, on either side, and then the noble villas, and the patricians looking down from the porticoes, the roar of Rome's thunderous million acclaiming him, and then the Capitoline with the grave and reverend senators, and the vestals and the pontifex maximus, and all the honors for the victory which his brain and courage have won for the state."

"I'm not so sure that I'd like it, Philip."

"'De gustibus non disputandum,' as somebody wrote, John. Well, here we are, settling down gently in the place something or other, and just as I told you all the people are around it, with their eyes and mouths wide open."

The aeroplane settled softly upon the grass amid great and sincere cheers, and John looked about curiously. He had returned to the world from space, a space inhabited only by Lannes, himself and the two Germans, one of whom was now dead. That pocket in the mountain had not counted. It was like a bird's nest in a tree, and this was the solid, planetary world, upon which he had once dwelled.

An elderly man of fine appearance, and with a long brown beard, reaching almost to his waist, stepped forward. Lannes lifted the cap and glasses that hid his head and face and greeted him in French.

"It is I, Philip Victor Auguste Lannes, Heir Schankhorst," he said politely. "You will remember me because I've dropped out of the skies into your village before. The young gentleman with me is one of those strange creatures called Yankees, who come from far across the ocean, and who earn money by the sweat of their brows in order that we may take it from them."

There was such a mellow tone in his voice, and the friendly gleam in his eyes was so wonderful that neither Herr Schankhorst nor his people could resist him. It seemed that most of them understood French as they raised another cheer, and crowded around the two men of the sky, plainly showing their admiration. None mentioned the war, and it was clear that the news of it had not yet penetrated to that remote valley in the high mountains. Lannes introduced John by his right name and description to Herr Schankhorst who was the burgomaster and then, still followed by the admiring crowd, they hurried away to the little inn, two stalwart youths being first detailed to keep watch over the Arrow.

"They're proud of their trust and they'll guard it as they would their lives," said Lannes in English to John. "Meanwhile we'll have dinner in this inn, which I know from experience to be the best, and we'll have the burgomaster and the Protestant clergyman to dine with us. This is German-speaking Switzerland, but these people fear the Germans and they don't fear us. So, we're welcome."

The inn was small, but the food and drink were of the best. John was well supplied with gold, and he did not hesitate to spend it for the burgomaster, the Lutheran clergyman, Lannes and himself.

"No you can't pay your share," he said to Lannes, "because you haven't any share. Remember, I've been a free passenger in the Arrow, which belongs to you, and it's my time to settle the bill."

"Have your way," said Lannes.

They had been speaking in English, and Lannes politely explained to their guests that his comrade was an obstinate Yankee, a member of a nation, noted for its stubborness, but the most delightful of people when you let them have their way, which after all was a way that generally harmed nobody.

The burgomaster and the clergyman smiled benevolently upon John and John smiled back. He had noticed already that Americans were popular among the great masses of the people in Europe. It was only those interested in the upholding of the classes who frowned upon them and who tried to write or talk them down. He was keen enough too, despite his youth, to deduce the reasons for it.

Here in this little town he was looked upon with favor because he was from America, and soon he was busy answering questions by the burgomaster and clergyman about his own land.

They made no reference to any war or approaching war, and he surmised that they had no thought of such a tremendous catastrophe-- Lannes informed him later that they had neither telegraph nor telephone--and John following the cue of his comrade made no reference to it. They ate with sharp appetites, but an end had to come at last. Then

Lannes went out into the town to buy his supplies, leaving John to entertain the guests.

John felt deeply that little period of rest and kindly simplicity and the time was soon to come, when he would look back upon it as the greenest of green spots in the desert.

Lannes returned in an hour and announced that they were ready for another flight. They went back to the *Arrow* which the stalwart youths were still guarding, proud of their trust.

"Must you really go?" said the burgomaster to Lannes. "Why not stay with us until tomorrow? Look, the clouds are gathering on the mountains. There may be a storm. Better bide with us till the morrow."

"We thank you from the bottom of our hearts for your kindness," said Lannes, as he and John took their seats, "and under any other circumstances we would stay, but Herr Schankhorst there is a call for us, a call that is sounding all over Europe, a call louder than any that was ever heard before on this old continent."

Lannes raising his voice spoke in clear, loud tones, and he had the impressive manner that he knew so well how to assume. The crowd, eager and expectant, pressed nearer, all about the Arrow. John saw that the dramatic instinct, always alive within his partner, had sparkled into flame.

"And there is reason for this call," continued Lannes, raising his voice yet further, until the most distant were sure to hear every syllable. "The trumpet is sounding throughout Europe. You may well thank the good God that you dwell here in your little valley, and that all around you the mountains rise a mile above you. There were many trumpets when the great Napoleon rode forth to war, but there are more now."

A gasp arose from the crowd, and John saw faces whiten.

"All Europe is at war," continued Lannes. "The nations march forth against one another and the continent shakes with the tread of twenty million soldiers. But stay here behind your mountain walls, and the storm will pass you by. Now push!"

Twenty youths shoved the *Arrow* with all their might and the plane rising gracefully in the air, soared far above the village. John looked down and again he saw the whole population with heads craned back and eyes turned upward, but he knew now that they were swayed by new and powerful emotions.

"Lannes," he said, "I never saw such an actor as you are."

"But think of the opportunity! How could I overlook such a chance! They knew absolutely nothing of the war, did not dream of it, and here was I with the chance to tell them the whole tremendous truth, and then to shoot suddenly up into the air far beyond their hearing. It was the artistic finish that appealed to me as much as the announcement. Tell your great news and then disappear or become silent. Don't linger over it, or you will mar the effect."

"We're leaving the valley out of sight, and I judge by the sun that our course is northwesterly."

"Right my brave aviator, but I don't think you'll be able to use the sun much longer for reckoning. The worthy burgomaster was right. Look behind you and see how the clouds are gathering!"

John gazed at the vast mass of the Alps, stretching their tremendous rampart across the very heart of Europe. The *Arrow* had gone higher, and deep down in the south he saw the ridges and sharp peaks stretching on apparently to infinity. But it was a wild and desolate world. Even as he looked the far edges dropped away in the gloom of advancing clouds. The gray of the horizon became black and sinister.

But he looked on, his gaze held by the sublimity of the mountains and the powerful spell, cast by an historic imagination. He was not only gazing upon the heart of Europe, but upon the heart of great history. There, where that long black line led through the clefts the army of Hannibal was passing. He shut his eyes and he saw the dark Carthaginian with his deep eyes, his curly perfumed beard, a scarlet robe wrapped around him, its ends dropping upon his horse, his brothers and the captains riding just behind him, and behind them the Carthaginian sacred band, the Spaniards, the Gauls, the Celts, the wild Numidians shivering on their barebacked horses, the monstrous elephants, the women, and all the strange and heterogeneous elements which the fire and genius of the great leader fused into an army unconquerable by the bravest and best soldiers of antiquity, a great man holding a great nation at bay for half a life time.

Mind and eye ran down the long line of the ages. He saw Goths and

Vandals, Germans and Gauls pouring through the passes upon Italy, and then almost in his own time he saw that other, the equal of Hannibal, almost exactly the same age, leading another army over the mighty mountains into the rich plains below. He watched the short figure of Napoleon, and behind him the invincible French youth, born of the republic, dragging their cannon through the snow to victory.

"Open your eyes, John, are you going to sleep?"

"I was never further from sleep, and my eyes were so wide open that I saw more than I ever did before in my life."

"And what did you see, my wise John?"

"I saw generals and nations crossing the mountains down there. I saw through a space of many centuries, and the last I saw was your Napoleon leading his troops over the Great St. Bernard to Marengo."

Lannes' eyes flamed like stars.

"And the great marshal whose name I bear was there with him," he said. "It was near Marengo that he won his Dukedom of Montebello. Napoleon cannot come back, but victory may perch again on the banners of France."

John understood him. He knew how Frenchmen must have writhed through all the years over Gravelotte and Sedan and Metz. He knew how deeply they must have felt the taunt that they were degenerate, and the prediction of their enemies that they would soon sink to the state of a second class power. He knew how Americans would have felt in their place, and, while he had never believed the sneers, he knew they had been made so often that some Frenchmen themselves had begun to believe them. He understood fully, and the ties that were knitting him so strongly to Lannes increased and strengthened.

"They were really republicans who won the victories of Napoleon," he said, "and you have been a republic again for forty-four years. Republics give life and strength."

"I think they do, and so does a liberal monarchy like that of England. Freedom makes the mind grow. Well, I hope we've grown so much that with help we'll be able to whip Germany. What's become of the Alps, John?"

"The clouds have taken 'em."

There was nothing now in the south but a vast bank of gray, and presently John felt drops of rain on his face. Besides, it was growing much colder. He did not know much about flying, but he was quite sure that in the midst of a great storm of wind and rain they would be in acute danger. He looked anxiously at Lannes, who said reassuringly:

"We'll go above it, John. It's one of the advantages of flying. On earth you can't escape a storm, but here we mount so high that it passes beneath us. After you get used to flying you'll wonder why people trust themselves on such a dangerous place as the earth."

John caught the twinkle in his eye, but he was learning fast, and his own heart thrilled too as they swung upward, rising higher and higher, until the thin air made the blood beat heavily in his temples. At last he looked down again. The earth had vanished. Vast clouds of gray and black floated between, and to John's startled eyes they took on all the aspects of the sea. Here the great swells rolled and tumbled, and off far in the north stretched a vast smooth surface of tranquility. But beneath him he saw flashes of light, and heard the heavy mutter as of giant guns. High above, the air was thin, cold and motionless.

A troubled world rolled directly under them, and the scene that he beheld was indescribably grand and awful. The clouds were in conjunction, and thunder and lightning played as if monstrous armies had crashed together. But here they sailed steadily on a motionless sea of air. He shared the keen pleasure that Lannes so often felt. The *Arrow* suddenly became a haven of safety, a peaceful haven away from strife.

"Aren't you glad you're not down there?" asked Lannes.

"Aye, truly."

"The winds that blow about the world, and the clouds that float where the winds take them appear to be having a terrible commotion, but we are safe spectators. Monsieur Jean the Scott, I wonder if the time will ever come when we'll have a flying machine that can manufacture its own air to sail in. Then it could rise to any height."

"Phil, you're dreaming!"

"I know I am but I'm not dreaming any more than you were just now when you saw Napoleon and his army crossing the Alps. Besides who can forecast the achievements of science? Why, man who was nothing but a savage yesterday is just getting a start in the world! Who can tell what he'll be doing a million years from now? Think of going on, and on in the void, and maybe arriving on Venus or Mars!"

"In that case we'll find out whether that Mars canal story is true or not."

Lannes laughed.

"I come back to earth," he said, "or rather I come back to a point a safe distance above it. How's our storm making out?"

"It seems to be moving westward."

"And we're flying fast toward the north. We'll soon part company with the storm, and then we'll drop lower. But John, you must take the glasses and watch the skies all the time."

"Which means that we'll fly near the French border, and that I've got to be on the lookout for the Taubes and the dirigibles."

"And he guessed right the very first time. That's more of your American slang. Yes, John, the hosts of the air are abroad, and we must not have another encounter with the Germans. Before night we'll be approaching the battle lines, and the air will be full of scouts. Perhaps it will be better to do the rest of our traveling at night. We might drop down in a wood somewhere, and wait for the twilight."

"That's true Philip, but there's one question I'd like to ask you."

"Go ahead."

"Just how do you classify me? I belong to America, which has nothing to do with your gigantic war, and yet here I am scouting through the air with you, and exposed to just as much danger as you are."

"I don't think I could have answered that question about classification yesterday, John, but I can without hesitation today. You're an Ally. And you're an Ally because you can't help it. Germany represents autocracy and France democracy. So does England who is going to help us. You've risked your life over and over again with me, a Frenchman, one who would look upon the defeat of the German empire as almost the millennium. You may like the German people, but all your principles, all your heart-beats are on our side. When we get to some convenient place you'll write to your uncle and friend at Munich that you've joined England and France in the fight against German militarism. Oh, you needn't protest! It's true. I know you. You're quiet and scholarly, but your soul is the soul of adventure. I've seen how you responded to the thrill of the Arrow, how you're responding at this very moment I know with absolute certainty, Monsieur Jean the Scott, that you'll be fighting on the side of England and France. So you'd better make up your mind to stick to me, until we reach the French army."

John was silent a moment or two. Then he reached out and grasped Lannes' free hand.

"I was thinking of doing the things you predict," he said, "and to keep you from being a false prophet, Phil, old man, I'll do them."

Lannes returned his strong grasp.

"But if the English come into the war on your side," continued John, "I think I'll join them. Not that I'm overwhelmingly in love with the English, but they speak our American language, or at least variations of it. In the heat of battle I might forget the French word for, retreat, but never the English."

Lannes smiled.

"You won't be running, old fellow," he said. "You're right of course to join the English since they're close kin to you, but I have a feeling, John Scott, that you and I will see much of each other before this war is over."

"It may be so. I'm beginning to think, Phil, that lots of things we don't dream about happen to us. I certainly never expected a week ago to be in the middle of a great war."

"And you expected least of all, Monsieur Jean the Scott, to be sailing smoothly along in the air far above the clouds, and with a terrific storm raging below."

"No, I didn't. If a man had predicted that for me I should have said he was insane. But I think, Phil, the storm is leaving us or we've left it. That big ball of darkness giving out thunder and fire is moving fast toward the west."

"So it is, and there's clear air beneath us. And the Alps are reappearing in the south."

"Right you are, Philip. I can see a half dozen peaks, and there is another, and now another. See, their white heads coming out of the mists and vapors, whole groups of them now!"

"Don't they look from here like a friendly lot of old fellows, John, standing there and nodding their snowy pates to one another, just as they've done for the last million years or more!"

"You hit the nail on the head, Phil. Understand that? It's one of our phrases meaning that you've told the exact truth. There goes that wicked storm, farther and farther to the west. Soon the horizon will swallow it up."

"And then it will go on toward Central France. I hope it won't damage the vineyards. But what a fool I am to be talking about storms of weather, when the German storm of steel is about to sweep over us!"

"You don't talk very hopefully, when you speak of a German invasion at once."

"But I am hopeful. I expect the invasion because we are not ready. They accuse us French of planning a surprise attack upon Germany. What nonsense, when we're not even prepared to defend ourselves! The first sound of this war will show who was getting ready to attack. But John we'll drive back that invasion, we and our allies. I repeat to you that the French of 1914 are not the French of 1870. The Third Republic will command the same valor and devotion that served the First. But here I am talking like an old politician. Get the glasses, John, and look at our field of battle, the heavens. It's all in the light now, and we can't afford another encounter with the Taubes."

John took a long look. The passage of the storm had purified the air which was now of dazzling clearness, a deep, silky blue, with a sun of pure red gold that seemed to hang wonderfully near. Lannes permitted the *Arrow* to drop lower and lower, until the earth itself sprang up into the light.

John saw again the green hills, the blue lakes and the streams, neat villages and splendid country houses. It was his planet, and he was glad to come once more where he could see it.

"It was fine up there above the clouds," he said to Lannes, "but after all I've got a very kindly feeling for the earth. It's like meeting an old friend again."

"Comes of use and habit, I suppose if we lived on Venus or Mars we'd have the same kind of attachment. But like you, John, I'm glad to see the earth again. The scenery is more varied than it is up in the heavens. What do you see through the glasses, John? Don't miss anything if it's there. It's too important."

"I see in the north just under the horizon four black specks. It's too far away for me to tell anything about 'em, but they move just as those two Taubes did before their shape became clear."

"More Taubes. That's certain. And it's time for us to get away. We're almost on the border John and the German aeroplanes and dirigibles are sure to have gathered."

"There's a forest a little to the right of us. Suppose we go down there."

Lannes examined the forest.

"It seems fairly large," he said, "and I think it will make a good covert. But whether good or bad we must drop into it. The German airships are abroad and we can take no chances."

The *Arrow* descended with increased speed. John still used the glasses, and he searched every nook of the forest, which like most of those of Europe had little undergrowth. It contained no houses at all, but he picked out an open space near the center, large enough for the landing of the Arrow, which he pointed out to Lannes.

"I suppose you'd call it a respectable forest," said John. "I see some trees which are at least a foot through, near the ground. Luckily it's summer yet and the foliage is thick. If I were one of you Europeans I'd never boast about my trees."

"Some day I'm going to run over to that America of yours, and see whether all you tell me about it is true. Steady now, John, I'm about to make the landing, and it's my pride to land more gently every time than I did the time before."

They slid down softly and alighted on the grass. Lannes' triumph was complete, and his wonderful eyes sparkled.

"The best I've done yet," he said, "but not the best I will do. John, what time is it?"

"Half-past five."

"With our long evenings that makes considerable daylight yet. Suppose you take your automatic, and examine the woods a little. I'd go with you, but I'm afraid to leave the *Arrow* here alone. Leave the glasses with me though."

John, after regaining his land legs, walked away among the woods, which evidently had been tended with care like a park, bearing little resemblance, as he somewhat scornfully reminded himself to the mighty forests of his own country. Still, these Europeans, he reflected were doing the best they could.

The region was hilly and he soon lost sight of Lannes, but he threshed up the wood, thoroughly. There was no sign of occupancy. He did not know whether it lay in Germany or France, but it was evident that all the foresters were gone. A clear brook ran through a corner of it, and he knelt and drank. Then he went back to Lannes who was sitting placidly beside the Arrow.

"Nothing doing," said John in the terse phrase of his own country. "At imminent risk from the huge wild animals that inhabit it I've searched all this vast forest of yours. I've forded a river three feet wide, and six inches deep, I've climbed steep mountains, twenty feet high, I've gone to the uttermost rim of the forest, a full half-mile away on every side, and I beg to report to you, General, that the wilderness contains no human being, not a sign of any save ourselves. Strain my eyes as I would I could not find man anywhere."

Lannes smiled.

"You've done well as far as you've gone," he said.

"I could go no farther."

"You said you saw no sign of man."

"None whatever."

"But I do."

"Impossible!"

"Not impossible at all. Why don't you look up?"

John instantly gazed into the heavens, and he was startled at the sight he beheld. The population of the air had increased suddenly and to a wonderful extent. A score of aeroplanes were outlined clearly against the sky, and as he looked the distant drumming noise that he had heard in Dresden came again to his ears. A monstrous black figure cut across his vision and soon sailed directly overhead.

"A Zeppelin!" he said.

"A huge fellow," said Lannes. "The aeroplanes are German too, or there would soon be trouble between them and the Zeppelin."

"Should we take to flight?"

"No, it's too late. Besides, I think we're safe here. The foliage is so dense that they're not likely to see us. This forest must lie in Germany, and I judge that the heads of their armies have already passed to the west of us. The planes may be scouting to see whether French cavalry is in their rear. Do you hear that? I say, John, do you hear that?"

From a far point in the west came a low sound which swelled gradually into a crash like thunder. In a few moments came another, and then another and then many. They could see no smoke, no fire, and the very distance lent majesty to the sound.

John knew well what it was, the thudding of great guns, greater than any that had been fired before by man on land. Lannes turned ashy-pale.

"It's the cannon, the German cannon!" he said, "and that sound comes from France. The Kaiser's armies are already over the border, marching on Paris. Oh, John! John! all the time that I was predicting it I was hoping that it wouldn't come true, couldn't come true! You Americans can't understand! In your new country you don't have age-old passions and hates and wrongs and revenges burning you up!"

"I do understand. It must be a serious battle though. All the planes are now flying westward, and there goes the Zeppelin too."

"Which leaves us safe for the present. Besides, the twilight is coming."

7

T HE ZEPPELIN

THE BRILLIANT SUNLIGHT faded into gray, but the European twilight lingers, and it was long before night came. John and Lannes stood beside the Arrow, and for a while neither spoke. They were listening to the thunder of the great guns and they were trying to imagine how the battle was swaying over the distant and darkening fields. The last of the air scouts had disappeared in the dusk.

"The sound doesn't seem to move," said Lannes, "and our men must be holding their own for the present. Still, it's hard to tell about the location of sound."

"How far away do you think it is?"

"Many miles. We only hear the giant cannon. Beneath it there must be a terrible crash of guns and rifles. I've heard, John, that the Germans have seventeen-inch howitzers, firing shells weighing more than two thousand pounds, and France furnishes the finest roads in the world for them to move on."

He spoke with bitterness, but in an instant or two he changed his tone and said:

"At any rate we haven't made a god out of war, and that's why we haven't seventeen-inch cannon. Perhaps by not setting up such a god we've gained something else--republican fire and spirit that nothing can overcome."

The twilight now deepened and the darkness increased fast in the wood, but the deep thunder on the western horizon did not cease. John thought he saw flashes of fire from the giant cannon, but he was not sure. It might be sheaves of rays shot off by the sunken sun, or, again, it might be his imagination, always vivid, but stimulated to the last degree by the amazing scenes through which he was passing.

After a while, although the throb of the great guns still came complete darkness enveloped the grove. It seemed now to John that the sound had moved farther westward, but Lannes had just shown such keen emotion that he would not say the Germans were pushing their way farther into France. However, Lannes himself noticed it. Presently he said:

"The battle goes against us, but you may be sure of one thing, Monsieur Jean the Scott, we were heavily outnumbered and the German artillery must have been in caliber as four to our one."

"I've no doubt it's so," said John with abundant sympathy.

"The fire seems to be dying. Probably the night is too dark for the combat to go on. What do you think we ought to do, John?"

"You're the airman, Phil. I'm only a raw beginner."

"But a beginner who has learned fast. I think the sound of that battle in France has weakened my nerve for the moment, and I want your advice. I ask for it again."

"Then suppose we stay where we are. This isn't a bad little forest, as forests go in Europe, and in the night, at least, it's pretty dark. The enemy is all around us, and in the air over our heads. Suppose we sleep here beside the Arrow."

"That's a good sound Yankee head of yours, John. Just as you think, it would be dangerous for us to run either on land or in the air, and so we'll stay here and take the chances. I secured two blankets at the village, and each will have one. You go to sleep, John, and I'll take the first watch."

"No, I'll take the first. You need rest more than I do. You've been sailing the Arrow, and, besides, your nerves have been tried harder by the echo of that battle. Just for a little while I mean to boss. 'Boss,' I'll explain to you, means in our American idiom a commander, a Napoleon. Now, stop talking, wrap yourself in your blanket and go to sleep."

"I obey. But keep your automatic handy."

He fell asleep almost instantly, and John, lying near with his own blanket about him, kept watch over him and the Arrow. He did not feel sleepy at all. His nerves had been keyed to too high a pitch for rest to come yet. His situation and the scenes through which he had passed were so extraordinary that certain faculties seemed to have become blunted. Although surrounded by many dangers all sensation of fear was gone.

The blanket was sufficient protection even against the cool European night, and he had found a soft and comfortable place on the turf. The wood was silent, save for the rustle of a stray breeze among the leaves. Far in the night he heard twice the faint boom of the giant cannon deep down on the western horizon. For all he knew the sounds may have come from a point twenty miles away.

He walked a little distance from the Arrow, and listened intently. But after the two shots the west was silent. The earth settled back into gloom and darkness. He returned to the *Arrow* and found that Lannes was still sleeping heavily, his face pale from exertion and from the painful emotions that he had felt.

John was sorry for him, sorry from the bottom of his heart. Love of country was almost universal, and it must be almost death to a man, whose native land, having been trodden deep once, was about to be trodden again by the same foe.

He went once more to the little stream and took another drink. He sat by its banks a few minutes, and listened to its faint trickle, a pleasant soothing sound, like the almost unheard sigh of the wind. Then he returned to his usual place near the Arrow.

Dead stillness reigned in the grove. There was no wind and the leaves ceased to rustle. Not another note came from the battle of the nations beyond the western horizon. The *Arrow* and its master both lay at peace on the turf. The stillness, the heavy quiet oppressed John. He had been in the woods at night many times at home, but there one heard the croaking of frogs at the water's edge, the buzzing of insects, and now and then the cry of night birds, but here in this degenerate forest nothing stirred, and the air was absolutely pulseless.

Time began to lengthen. He looked at his watch, but it was not yet midnight, and Lannes was still motionless and sleeping. He had resolved, as most of the strain had fallen upon his comrade, to let him sleep far beyond his allotted half, and he walked about again, but soundlessly, in order to keep his faculties awake and keen.

The night had been dark. Many clouds were floating between him and the moon. He looked up at them, and it seemed incredible now that beyond them human beings could float above the thunder and lightning, and look up at the peaceful moon and stars. Yet he had been there, not in any wild dash of a few minutes, but in a great flight which swept over nights and days.

His early thoughts were true. A long era had ended, and now one, charged with wonders and marvels, had begun. This mighty war was the signal of the change, and it would not be confined to the physical world. The mind and soul would undergo like changes. People would never look at things in the same way. There had been such mental revolutions in the long past, and it was not against nature for another to come now.

John was thoughtful, perhaps beyond his years, but he had been subjected to tremendous emotions. The unparalleled convulsion of the old world was enough to make even the foolish think. Event and surmise passed and repassed through his mind, while he walked up and down in the wood. Hours crept slowly by, the clouds drifted away, and the moon came out in a gush of silver. The stars, great and small, danced in a sky that was always blue, beyond the veil.

He came back for the third time to the brook. He was thirsty that night, but before he knelt down to drink he paused and every muscle suddenly became rigid. He was like one of those early borderers in his own land who had heard a sinister sound in the thicket. It was little, a slight ring of steel, but every nerve in John was alive on the instant.

Still obeying the instincts of ancestors, he knelt down among the trees. His vivid fancy might be at work once more! And then it might not! The ringing of steel on steel came again, then a second time and nearer. He slid noiselessly forward, and lay with his ear to the earth. Now he heard other sounds, and among them one clear note, the steady tread of hoofs.

Cavalry were approaching the grove, but which? German or French? John knew that he ought to go and awake Lannes at once, but old inherited instincts, suddenly leaping into power, held him. By some marvelous mental process he reverted to a period generations ago. His curiosity was great, and his confidence in his powers absolute.

He dragged himself twenty or thirty yards along the edge of the brook toward the tread of hoofs, and soon he heard them with great distinctness. Mingled with the sound was the jingling of bits and the occasional impact of a steel lance-head upon another. John believed now that they were Germans and he began to creep away from the brook, toward which the troop was coming directly. It was not possible to estimate well from sound, but he thought they numbered at least five hundred.

He was back thirty yards from the brook, lying flat in the grass, when the heads of horses and men emerged from the shadows. The helmets showed him at once that they were the Uhlans, and without the helmets the face of the leader alone was sufficient to tell him that the Prussian horsemen had ridden into the wood.

The one who rode first with his helmet thrown back a little was Rudolf von Boehlen, the man with whom John had talked at Dresden, and who had made such an impression upon him. He had known the scholarly Prussian, the industrial Prussian, and the simple good-natured Prussian of the soil, but here was the Prussian to whom the first god was Mars, with the Kaiser as his prophet. It was he, and such as he, who ruled the industrious and kindly German people, teaching them that might was right, and that they always possessed both.

John saw through the eyes of both fact and fancy. Von Boehlen was a figure of power. Mind and body were now at the work for which they had been trained, and to which the nature of their owner turned them.

Despite his size and weight he sat his horse with lightness and grace, and his cold blue eyes searched the forest for victims rather than foes. John saw in him the product of ceaseless and ruthless training, helped by nature.

But von Boehlen, keen as his eyes were, did not see the figure of the watcher prone in the grass. He let his horse drink at the brook, and others rode up by his side, until there was a long line of horses with their heads bent down to the stream. It occurred to John then that their only purpose in entering the wood was to water their animals. He saw von Boehlen take a map from his pocket, and study it while the horse drank. He was not surprised at the act. He had no doubt that the brook, tiny though it might be, was marked on the map. He had heard that the Germans foresaw everything, attended to the last detail, and now he was seeing a proof of it. How was it possible to beat them!

He did not consider the danger great, as he listened to the long lapping and gurgling sound, made by so many horses drinking. It was likely that the whole troop would ride away in a few minutes, and only a possible chance would take them in the direction where the *Arrow* and Lannes lay. But the trees grew thickly in the circle about them, and that chance was infinitely small.

The Uhlans, under the lead of von Boehlen, turned presently, and rode back through the edge of the wood into a field, but they went no farther. John, following a safe distance, saw them unsaddle on the grass and make their camp. Then he hurried back to Lannes and awoke him gently.

"What! what is it?" exclaimed Lannes. "The Germans in Paris! The capital fallen, you say!"

"No! No! Not so loud! Come out of your dreams! Paris is all right, but there are Uhlans just beyond the edge of the wood, and some scouts of theirs may come tramping here."

Lannes was thoroughly awake in another instant.

"You did not wake me when my time came, John," he said.

"I didn't because you needed the rest more than I did."

"Where did you say the Uhlans were?"

"In a field at the eastern edge of the wood. They are Prussians led by an officer, von Boehlen, whom I saw at Dresden before the war began. They rode into the wood to water their horses, but now they've gone back to make a camp."

"You've certainly watched well, John, and now I suppose we must run again. They follow us in the air and they follow us on the ground. This is a bad trap, John. Suppose you go to von Boehlen, tell him who you are, how you were kidnapped in a way, and throw yourself on his mercy. You'll be safe. The Germans want the friendship of the Americans."

"And desert you at such a time? Philip Lannes, you're not worthy to bear the name of the great Marshal!"

Lannes laughed in an embarrassed manner.

"It was merely an offer," he said. "I didn't expect you to accept it."

"You knew I wouldn't. Come, think quick, and tell us what we're going to do!"

"You fit fast into your new role of what you call boss, Monsieur Jean the Scott!"

"And I mean to be boss for the next five minutes. Then you will have decided how we're going to escape and you'll resume your place."

"As I said we won't abandon the Arrow, so our passage will be through the air. John, I mean that we shall run the gantlet. We'll pass their air fleet and reach our own."

He spoke in low tones, but they contained the ring of daring. John responded. With the ending of the era, the changing of the world, he had changed, too. Shy and sensitive the spirit of adventure flamed up in him. Those flights in the air had touched him with the magic of achievements, impossible, but which yet had been done.

"Suppose we launch the *Arrow* at once," he said. "I'm ready to try anything with you."

"I knew that, too. One thing in our favor is the number of clouds hanging low in the west, where their air fleet is. It's likely that most of the planes and dirigibles have gone to the ground, but they'll keep enough above to watch. The clouds may enable us to slip by."

"If I had my way I'd wrap myself in the thickest and blackest of the clouds and float westward with it."

"We'll have to go slowly to keep down the drumming of the motor. Now a big push and a long push. So! There! Now we're rising!"

The Arrow, the strength and delicacy of which justified all of Lannes' pride, rose like a feather, and floated gracefully above the trees, where it hung poised for a few minutes. Then, as they were not able to see anything, Lannes took it a few hundred yards higher. There they caught the gleam of steel beyond the wood, and looked down on the camp of Uhlans.

With the aid of the glasses they saw most of the men asleep on the ground, but twenty on horseback kept watch about the field.

"One look is enough," said Lannes. "I hope I'll never see 'em again."

"Maybe not, but there are millions of Germans."

"That's the worst of it. Millions of 'em and all armed and ready. John, I've chosen our road. We'll go north by west, and I think we'd better rise high. During the night the German machines are likely to hang low, and we may be able to pass over 'em without detection. What do you think of those clouds?"

"They're not drifting much. They may hide us as a fog hides a ship at sea."

The *Arrow* began to soar. The Uhlans and the grove soon faded away, and they rode among the clouds. John's watch showed that it was about three o'clock in the morning. He no longer felt the chill of the air in those upper regions. Excitement and suspense made his blood leap, warm, through his veins.

Lannes, after his long sleep, was stronger and keener than ever. His hand on the steering rudder knew no uncertainty, and always he peered through the clouds for a sign of the foe, who, he knew well, was to be dreaded so much. John, glasses at eye, sought the same enemy.

But they heard and saw nothing, save the sights and sounds of the elements. A cold, wet wind flew across their faces, and the planet below once more turned in space, invisible to eye.

"One could almost think," said John, "that we don't turn with it, that we hang here in the void, while it whirls about, independent of us."

"I wish that were so," said Lannes with a laugh. "Then we could stay where we are, while it turned around enough beneath us to take the Germans far away. But don't you hear a faint buzzing there to the west, John?"

"Yes, I was just about to speak of it, and I know the sound, too. It's one of the big Zeppelins."

"Then it's likely to be much below. I judge from the presence of the trees that, we must be somewhere near the German outposts."

"I wish that we dared to descend enough to see."

"But we don't dare, Monsieur Jean the Scott. We'd drop into a nest of hornets."

"Better slow down then. Their scouting planes must be somewhere near."

"Good advice again. Oh, you're learning fast. And meanwhile you're committing yourself more and more deeply to our cause."

"I've already committed myself deeply enough. I've told you that your prediction about my joining a British force is true."

"But you'll have to stay with us French until the British come. John, is it my imagination or do I hear that buzzing below us again?"

"You really hear it, and I do, too. It's a big Zeppelin beyond a doubt, and therefore we must not be far from a German base. You know they have to build huge sheds in which to keep the Zeppelins."

"No doubt they have such a station near enough on their side of the border. But, John, I'm going to have a look at that air-elephant. In all this thick darkness they'd never know what we are. Are you ready for it?"

"Ready and anxious."

The *Arrow* dropped down toward the buzzing sound, which rapidly grew louder. John had heard that a silencer had been invented for Zeppelins, but either it was a mistake or they apprehended a hostile presence so little that they did not care to use it.

He was rapidly becoming inured to extreme danger, but his heart throbbed nevertheless, and he felt the chill of the high damp air. At the suggestion of Lannes, who called him the eyes of the ship, he retained the glasses, and, with them, sought continually to pierce the heavy masses of cloud. He could not yet see anything, but the heavy buzzing noise, much like the rattling of a train, increased steadily. The Zeppelin could not be very far beneath them now.

John felt a sudden rush of wind near him and a dark object swung by. Lannes swiftly changed their own course, and darted almost at a right angle in the darkness.

"A Taube?" whispered John.

"Yes, one of the armored kind. Two men were in it, and most likely they carried rifles. They're on watch despite the night. Maybe they fear some of our own planes, which must be not many miles in front. Oh, France, is not sleeping, John! Don't think that! We are not prepared as the Germans were, but we've the tools, and we know how to use them."

He corrected the course of the *Arrow* and again dropped down slowly toward the Zeppelin. John's eyes, used to the darkness, caught a glimpse of Lannes' face, and he was surprised. He had never before seen one express such terrible resolution. Some dim idea of his purpose entered the American's mind, but he did not yet realize it fully.

But his sense of the weird, of acting in elements, hitherto unknown to man, grew. The Arrow, smooth, sleek and dangerous as death, was feeling its way in the darkness among a swarm of enemies. Its very safety lay in the fact that it was one among many, and, wrapped in the dark, the others could not tell its real character, fifty feet away.

John could truthfully say to himself afterwards that he did not feel fear at that time. He was so absorbed, so much overwhelmed by the excitement, the novelty and the cloud of darkness hiding all these actors in the heavens that no room was left in him for fear.

Lower and lower they dropped. The Zeppelin, evidently not far above the earth, was moving slowly.

John was reminded irresistibly of an enormous whale lounging in the depths of the ocean, which here was made up of heavy clouds. In another minute by the aid of the powerful glasses he made out two captive balloons, and a little farther westward three aeroplanes flying about like sentinels pacing their beats. He also saw beneath them lights which he knew to be the fires of a great camp, but he could not see the men and the cannon.

"The German camp is beneath us," he said.

"I thought you'd find it there," returned Lannes bitterly. "It's where our own camp ought to be, but our men were defeated in that battle which we heard, and here the Germans are."

John did not see him this time, but the look of pitiless resolve in the eyes of the young Frenchman deepened. That the Germans should come upon the soil of France and drive the French before them overwhelmed him with an agony that left no room for mercy.

"There goes another of the Taubes," he whispered, as a shadow flitted to the right "They're cruising about in lively fashion. If anybody hails us don't answer. I'll turn away in the darkness, pretending that we haven't heard."

The hail came almost as he spoke, but the Arrow veered to one side again at an angle, and then, after a few minutes, came back to a point, where it hovered directly over the Zeppelin and not far away. John saw beneath them now the huge shape, ploughing along slowly through the heavy bank of air. It loomed, in the darkness, a form, monstrous and incredible.

"Are we just over the thing, John?" asked Lannes.

"Exactly. Look down and you can see."

"I see."

Then his arm flashed out, and he hurled something downward with all the concentrated force of hate. There came a stunning crash mingled with rending and tearing sounds and frightened cries, and then the monstrous shape was gone. The place where it had hung in the heavens was empty and silent.

John's heart missed a dozen beats. His jaw fell and he stared at Lannes.

"Yes, I intended it from the first," said Lannes, "and I haven't a single compunction. I got that bomb, and three others in the Swiss village when I left you at the inn. I did not tell you of them because--well, because, I thought it better to keep the secret to myself. It's war. The men in that Zeppelin came to destroy our towns and to kill our men."

"I'm not accusing you. I suppose, as you say, it's war. But hadn't we better get away from here as fast as we can?"

"We're doing it now. While we were talking I was steering the *Arrow* westward. Hark, do you hear those shots!"

"I hear them. It can't be that they're firing at random in the air, as they would be more likely to hit one another than a slim and single little shape like the Arrow."

"They're signaling. Of course they're organized, and they're probably trying to draw all the planes to one spot, after which they'll spread out and seek us. But they won't find us. Ah, my sleek Arrow! my lovely little Arrow, so fast and true! You've done your duty tonight and more! We've run the gantlet, John! We're through their air fleet, and we've left a trail of fire! They won't forget this night!"

John sat silent, while Lannes exulted. Meanwhile the Arrow, piercing the low clouds, rushed westward, unpursued.

8

THE FRENCH DEFENSE

THEY FLEW on in the darkness, and both remained silent. John at first had felt resentment against Lannes, but he reflected that this was war, and it was no worse to kill with a bomb in the air than with a shell on land. It was hard, however, to convince oneself that destruction and death were sovereigns in Europe.

After a long time Lannes pointed to the east, where a thin gray was showing.

"The sun will soon be up," he said, "and it will drive the last cloud before it. We're going to have a fine day. Look down at this, our France, Monsieur Jean the Scott, and see what a beautiful land it is! Can you wonder that we don't want the armed feet of the Germans to tread it down?"

The darkness was shredding away so fast that John got a clear view. He was surprised, too, to find how low they were flying. They were not more than a hundred yards above the tops of the trees, and the glorious country was all that Lannes had claimed for it.

He saw woods heavy in foliage, fields checkered in green and brown, white roads, neat villages and farm houses, and the spires of churches. It seemed impossible that war should come upon such a land. This word "impossible" was often recurring to John. It was impossible that all Europe should go to war and yet the impossible was happening. The world would not allow twenty million men to spring at one another's throats, and yet they were doing it.

Lannes suddenly uttered a deep "Ah!" and pointed with a long forefinger.

"Our camp," he said. "On the hill about five miles to the left. The planes have seen us. Three are coming to meet us."

John saw the camp distinctly through the glasses, a long intrenched position on a low, broad hill, many guns in front and many horses in the rear, with the banners of France floating over the works.

"We'll be there soon," said Lannes joyfully. "Here, John, wave this!"

He took a small French flag from the locker and John waved it with vigor. The fastest of the planes was soon beside them and Lannes called out gayly:

"The Arrow, Philip Lannes at the rudder, and John Scott, an American, who is going to fight with us, as passenger and comrade!"

Thus they flew into the republican camp, and a great crowd came forward to meet them. Lannes stepped out of the Arrow, saluted an officer in the uniform of a captain, and asked:

"What corps is this?"

"That of General Avillon."

"Then, sir, would you be so good as to conduct me to his headquarters? I have been in both Berlin and Vienna in disguise, and on service for our government. I have information and minute maps."

"Come with me at once," said the officer eagerly.

"I ask you to make my comrade comfortable while I am gone. He is an American, John Scott, whom an accident threw with me. He is the bravest of the brave and he's going to serve with us."

Lannes was dramatic and impressive. Again he was the center of a scene that he loved, and, as always, he made the most of it. John reddened at his high praise, and would have withdrawn farther into the crowd, but enthusiastic young officers about him would not let him. "Vive l'Américain!" they shouted and patted him on the shoulders.

Lannes went at once with the captain, and John was left with his new friends. Friends, in truth they were, and their enthusiasm grew as he told of their extraordinary flight, their battle with the Taubes, and the destruction of the Zeppelin by Lannes. Then their applause became thunder, and, seeing it in the distance and the perspective, John became more reconciled to the throwing of the bomb. War was killing and one could not change it.

While they heard his story and cheered him the French did not neglect his comfort. Young officers, many of whom were mere boys, insisted upon entertaining this guest from the air. It was so early that they had not yet had their own breakfasts, and while different groups fought for him he finally sat down beside a fire with a dozen lieutenants of about his own age.

The food was abundant and good, and, as he ate and drank, he was compelled to tell their story over again.

"I'm glad Lannes got that monster, the Zeppelin," said one of the young lieutenants. "God knows we've had little enough success so far. They say we were ready for war, and had planned to strike. But it was the Germans who struck. That proves who had done the planning. They say that our officers were in Belgium, making ready for the French army to march through that country, and yet when the Germans pushed into Belgium they found no French. The accusation refutes itself."

"Are the Germans in Belgium?" asked John, astonished.

"With a great army, and England has declared herself. She is sending a force to our help. You will not lack for comrades who speak your own tongue."

"We thought we heard last night the sounds of a battle."

"You thought right. It was we who were fighting it, and we were defeated. We were driven back many miles, but we were not beaten, man to man. With even numbers we could have held them, but they were three or four to one, and they have monster cannon which far outrange ours."

"It was one of those giant guns I heard, because we heard nothing else. Are the Germans coming forward for another attack?"

"We don't know. Our aeroplanes report no movement in their camp, but the sun has scarcely risen yet. Still we all think they'll come. We know it's their plan to make a gigantic rush on Paris. Our spies report that their most frequent boast is: 'Ten days to France and twenty days to Paris.' Well, the first part of it is more than fulfilled."

Silence and sadness fell over the group of brave young men. John's heart was filled with sympathy for them. His nature was one that invariably took the part of invaded against invaders, and the invaders had already struck a mighty blow. But it was he, as yet a stranger among them, who restored cheerfulness.

"I've been with one Frenchman through adventures and dangers, of which I never dreamed," he said. "Never once did his hand or eye waver. I know that there are hundreds of thousands of Frenchmen like him, and such men can't fail."

"Thank you," one of them said simply. "We Frenchmen of the Third Republic shall try to fight as well as the Frenchmen of the First Republic, and we'll pray that our allies, the English, may come soon."

John was silent. He knew even better than they how necessary was the arrival of the English. He had been in Germany and he had seen something of the mobilization. He knew that the planet had never before borne anything comparable to the German war machine which was already rolling forward upon France and Belgium. Would the invaded, even with the help of England, be able to stop it?

The breakfast finished, he lay down in one of the tents on a blanket, and, despite the noises of the camp, soon slept. But he was awakened by Lannes two or three hours later.

"I've found a way for you to send telegrams through Switzerland, and then to Munich, telling your people where you are and what you are going to do," he said, "and now I'm going to leave you for a while. I'm going on another scout in the Arrow, but I go alone. You, I take it, will do your fighting now on land. But, John Scott, I've been proud to know you and to have had such a flight with you. I don't suppose that any other beginner has ever had such a lively start as yours, but you've gone through it like a veteran. I want to shake your hand."

He pulled off his aviator's glove, and the two hands met in a powerful clasp. Then his dramatic instinct keenly alive he turned and sprang into the waiting Arrow. The young officers gave it a long push, and, rising lightly and gracefully, it soared over the army, far up into the blazing sunlight. Its strange navigator waved one hand to those below, and then the Arrow, true to its name, shot away toward the north.

"There goes the bravest man I ever saw," said John. "Give him air to float in, and I believe he'd try for the sun."

"All those flying men are brave," said a young officer, "but Lannes is the bravest of them all, as he is also the most skillful. As a scout he is worth ten thousand men to us."

"I must look for those English of whom he spoke," said John, "I have trespassed upon your courtesy here long enough. I wish to join them and serve with you."

"They're not all English by any means. Fully half of them are your own countrymen, Americans. The English and Americans quarrel much among themselves, but they unite against any foe. My own name is Creville, Louis Creville, and I'll take you to this company, The Strangers, as with pride they call themselves."

Creville led the way, and John followed toward another wing of the French force. The young American observed the French soldiers closely. They did not look either so stalwart or so trim as the Germans. Their long blue coats, and baggy red trousers had a curious effect. The color scheme seemed to John more fitted to a circus than to an army, but they were lively, active men, their faces gay and their eyes full of intelligence. He knew from his history that they had looked just the same way and had acted just the same way when they followed the victorious banners of Napoleon into nearly every capital of Europe.

"We're almost at the camp of the Strangers," said Captain Creville. "None could ever mistake it, because their debate this morning upon their respective merits is uncommonly spirited. Listen!"

"I tell you, Wharton, you Yankees have no discipline. By Gad, sir, your lack of it is startling."

"We don't need it, Carstairs, because we were always able to lick you English without it."

"Lick us, you boasters! Where did you ever lick us?"

"Wherever we were able to find you."

"My histories tell me that you never looked for us much."

"But those histories were written by Englishmen. I'll lay you a good five-dollar bill against one of your shilling-short pounds that I beat you into Berlin."

"As a prisoner, yes. I've no doubt of it."

"Gentlemen," said Creville, as he took a step forward, and looked into a little dip, "I bring you a new comrade."

Within the dip lay at least two hundred youths and young men. Nearly all were fair, and they were unmistakably Americans and English. The two who had been carrying on the violent controversy were stretched flat on the grass almost at the feet of Creville. But they sat up, when they heard him, and John saw that they were uncommonly handsome and athletic, their age about his own. They stepped forward at once, and extended to John the hand of fellowship. Captain Creville made the introductions.

"He wishes to enlist with you," he said.

"He'll be welcome, I know," said the Englishman, Carstairs. "Our commander, Captain Colton, is not here at this moment, but we expect him in a half hour. How did you arrive, Mr. Scott?"

"He dropped down," replied Creville for John. "Dropped down. I don't understand you, Captain?"

Creville pointed straight up into the heavens.

"He came like the bird," he said. "He sailed through the air, seeking his nest. As soon as he saw us he said: 'Here is the perfect place; here I can dwell with the kindest and best people in the world; and down he swooped at once.'"

"I suppose you mean that he's an airman and that he came in a flying machine," said the American, Wharton. "Carstairs will arrive at that conclusion, too, if you give him time, but being an Englishman, time he must have."

"But when I arrive at the conclusion it will be right," said Carstairs.

"It's true that Mr. Scott came by machine," said Captain Creville, who was now speaking in excellent English. "He arrived with our great young aviator, Philip Lannes, and he has had many and thrilling adventures, of which he will tell you later. I suppose you will take your part in these English and American controversies, Mr. Scott, but your new captain will have nothing to do with them."

"Is he an Englishman or an American?"

"You can decide that for yourself. He was born in England. His mother was American and his father English. He was taken to America when he was three years old, and was educated there, but, after finishing at Harvard, he spent a year at Oxford. It seemed to all of us that his appointment as captain of this troop was most happy. The English are sure that he's English, the American know that he's American, he himself says nothing, and so all are happy. Ah, here he comes now, ahead of time!"

Daniel Coulton, a tall fair young man with a fine, open face, entered the dip, and Captain Creville at once turned John over to him.

"We're glad to have you, Mr. Scott," said Colton, "but the service will be hard and full of danger."

"I expect it, sir."

"These young men are serving France for love, and nearly all of them are privates. Carstairs and Wharton are in the ranks and you'll have to take a place with them."

"I accept gladly, sir."

"The right spirit. Wharton, you and Carstairs get him a uniform and arms, and he'll stay with you until further orders."

Then Captain Coulton hurried away. Captain Creville bowed and also withdrew.

"Come on, Scott," said Carstairs. "We've an extra uniform, and it'll just about fit you. A rifle, cartridges and all your other arms are ready, too."

John was equipped promptly, and then many introductions followed. It was a little Anglo-American island in the midst of a French sea, and they gave a joyous welcome to a new face. John noticed that many of them bore slight wounds, and he soon learned that several others, hurt badly, lay in an improvised hospital at the rear.

"The Germans are pressing us hard," said Wharton. "They whipped us yesterday afternoon, and they're sure to come for us again today. There's Captain Colton now standing on the earthwork, watching through his glasses. In my opinion something's doing."

Nearly all the Strangers went forward. From a hillock, John with his two new friends looked toward the forest, miles in their front. The forest itself was merely a blind mass of green, but overhead swung aeroplanes and captive balloons.

"Look up!" said Carstairs.

John saw a half dozen aeroplanes hovering some distance in front of their own lines.

"I think they're signaling," said Carstairs. "One of those monster guns must be getting ready to disgorge itself."

"The forty-two centimeter?" said John.

"Yes, and I'm right, too. I saw a flash in the forest, and here comes the little messenger!"

There was a roar and a crash so tremendous that John was almost shaken from his feet. An enormous shell burst near the earthworks, sending forth a perfect cloud of shrapnel and steel fragments. It resembled the explosion of a volcano, and as his ears recovered their power after the shock John heard the cries of many wounded.

"I think this force carries only one such gun with it," said Carstairs, "and it will be some time before they can fire it again. We have nothing to equal it, but the French seventy-five millimeter is an awful weapon. The gunners can time them so the shells burst only fifteen or twenty feet from the ground, and then they rain death. I think it likely that we have out now a flanking force that will get within range."

"There's cover to the right," said Warton, "if the French batteries advance at all, it will be that way."

They were ordered to stand to their arms, but it did not keep them from watching, as at present there was nothing for them to do. A second shot came presently from the forty-two centimeter, but the shell burst too far away to do any harm. John and his comrades turned their attention back to the right, where a line of woods ran.

Ten minutes more of waiting and they saw a succession of flashes among the trees. The French field guns far in advance of the main force were at work.

"Well done," said Carstairs. "The French artillery is fine, Scott. I believe their medium guns can beat any others of the same class in the world. Look how those woods flame with their fire! It scares me to go up in the air, but I'd like to be in one of those aeroplanes, where I could see the effect of the cannonade."

"There goes 'Busy Bertha' again," said Wharton.

"What's 'Busy Bertha'?" asked John.

"Oh, it's merely a nickname we've given to the Krupp monster. The French started it, I believe, but it's spread to the Strangers. It's aimed at our field guns this time! There the shell has burst in the forest! I wish I knew what it had done!"

"Not much, I judge," said Carstairs, "because the French guns are replying with as much fervor as ever. The woods are fairly blazing with their fire!"

[Illustration] "A second shot came presently from the forty-two centimeter."

"And yonder," said John, "are the Uhlans. Look at that mass of steel on the far edge of the plain!"

An immense force of German cavalry was issuing from the forest directly in their front, and was forming in a long line. The distance was great, but the August sunshine was so clear that all objects were magnified and made more vivid. The three clearly saw the great mass of German horsemen defiling toward the French right. Captain Colton of the Strangers reappeared and stood near them, watching through a pair of powerful glasses. John knew that he was anxious, and, although his experience of war was only three or four days old, he well knew the reason why.

"I've glasses myself," said Carstairs, who was holding a pair to his eyes. "Take a look, Scott."

John accepted them eagerly. They were strong, and the German cavalry seemed to come very near. Then he saw how numerous they were. They must be thousands and thousands, and the front files, which had wheeled, were already disappearing in the forest on the French right. In America most forests would have been impracticable for cavalry, but it was not likely to be so here, where there was little or no undergrowth.

John turned the glasses back to the point in the woods where the French field guns were posted. There he saw rapid flashes and the steady rolling crash continued. Evidently the seventy-five millimeter French cannon were all that was claimed for them. But he knew that the German cavalry must now be protected largely by the forest, and his heart beat heavily with apprehension for the French guns and their gunners.

"There goes 'Busy Bertha' again!" exclaimed Wharton.

John remembered nothing clearly for the next minute or two. There was a vast rushing sound, a crash of thunder, and, although he was not touched, he was thrown from his feet. He sprang up, dazed, cleared his eyes and looked around. The monstrous shell, weighing more than a ton, had burst almost in the heart of the French army, killing or wounding at least three hundred men, and spreading awe among the others. Nothing so capable of destruction and made by man had ever before been seen in the history of the world. And the shot had come from a point at least ten miles away, where the giant lay invisible.

The glasses had not been hurt in the fall and he handed them back to Carstairs. No harm had been done among the Strangers, although he was not the only one who had been thrown to the ground. But they were bold hearts and they jested among themselves.

"I hope they won't aim that pop-gun so well again," said Wharton.

"After all, Scott," said Carstairs, "you were perhaps safer with Lannes a half mile up in the air. The forty-two centimeter couldn't reach you there."

"Maybe not," said John, "but I'm one of the Strangers now, and I'll take my chances with them. I'm most alarmed about the Uhlans who have gone into the woods on our right."

"To cut off our field guns, of course. And look! Here comes the German army in our front to support their flanking movement!"

The fire in the wood increased in intensity, and John saw a great body of French troops advancing to the support of their artillery. Evidently the French leader meant to maintain his fire there and also to protect his field guns against capture.

"I told you, Wharton," said Carstairs, "that the Germans would give us no rest, that they would advance at once to a new battle."

"You didn't have to tell it to me. I knew it as well as any Englishman could possibly know it, perhaps better, but I'm modest, and I didn't talk about it."

"If you only kept your ignorance as well as your knowledge to your-self, Wharton, you'd have a greater reputation for wisdom. Look out!"

A shell that failed to explode in the air struck near. Carstairs threw himself upon Wharton, and, at the imminent risk of his own life, dragged him down just in time, as the shell burst and threw fragments over their heads.

"Thanks, Carstairs," said Wharton. "Your first name is Percy, but you don't act like a Percy."

"Expect the same from you, old fellow, when the time comes."

"I'll do my best."

John was absorbed now in the tremendous panorama of war, carried on with all the mighty machines of death that man had invented. A heavy German force appeared on their left also. It was yet distant, but it was nearer than the great mass in the center. Untrained as he was he knew nevertheless that the Germans, with their greatly superior numbers, were seeking to envelop the French. But the defensive guns on the right in the wood were maintaining a swift and terrible fire. They were pouring showers of shrapnel not only on the Uhlans, but upon the gray masses of infantry crossed the wide intervening fields.

The Strangers were now drawn up by one of the earthworks, but it would be a long time before they went into action. That heaving gray sea of Germans could not come within range of the rifles for an hour yet. Meantime the artillery would carry on the battle over a space of miles. While he waited he could look on and see it all.

More and more guns were coming into action. Batteries were sent off to the left to meet the second German flanking force there, and soon the heaviest of the French cannon in the center were able to reach the advancing enemy directly in their front.

The scene became tremendous and full of awe. There was little smoke, but along two vast semi-circles, one convex, and the other concave, flashes ran like continuous lightning, while the whole earth grumbled and roared. The air seemed surcharged with death, and John suddenly found it hot in his lungs as he breathed.

Through the roar of the guns he heard all the time the malicious shrieking of the shrapnel. It was falling among the defenders, killing and wounding hundreds, and John knew that the storm beat also on the great gray circle that was ever coming nearer. Now and then a crash, louder than all the rest, came from the forty-two centimeter, and whenever the shell struck true it tore everything about it to pieces, no matter how strong.

The thunder of the guns was so steady and so near one note that the Strangers could talk almost in an ordinary tone.

"It's our guns on the right that are in the most danger," said John.

"Correct," said Wharton. "The Uhlans are trying to cut them off, because those guns are doing great damage. Take the glasses again, and you can see their shells tearing through the German lines."

"I don't know that I want to see."

"Oh, look! This is war, and you'll have to get used to it!"

Then John looked and he saw that the German lines were not unbroken, as they had seemed to the naked eye. The shrapnel were tearing through them, making great holes, but the massive German columns never faltered for an instant. The gaps in their ranks were filled up, and they came on at an even pace, resolved to capture or destroy the French force. And they carried with them the memories of Gravelotte, Sedan and Metz. They would do as well as the men of old von Moltke had done.

John felt a thrill of admiration. The great military monarchy had built its machine well. It seemed at the moment resistless. It was made of steel rather than human flesh and blood, and it would roll over everything. Nothing had yet stopped that mighty concave curve of gray, although more and more French cannon were coming into action, and from right to left, and from left to right, they showered it with unceasing death.

But the German artillery, far more numerous and powerful than the French, were supporting their infantry. Shells were poured fast upon the hasty earthworks. Hundreds and hundreds of the defenders fell. The roar was now so stupendous that John could scarcely hear, and the air, before golden in the sunshine, turned a livid fiery hue.

All the Strangers were now formed in one of the trenches, and then wisely knelt low. John heard the shrieking, whining noise incessantly over his head, and it made his blood run cold. Instinctively he pressed hard against the side of his trench, but his curiosity was so keen that from time to time he raised his head above the edge to see how the battle fared directly in front. The gray Germans were much nearer, marching with the solid tread that seemed able to carry them across the world, while their gigantic artillery on the flanks and in the intervals flamed and roared without ceasing.

John knew that the loss among the French must be great, and he knew, too, that when the huge machine struck them they would be shattered. He wondered that the French leader did not order the retreat, but while he was wondering a trumpet suddenly sounded a shrill clear note audible amid the roar of the great guns, and he saw Captain Colton beckon to the Strangers.

John knew they were going into battle, but he felt relief because their long waiting was over. His senses had become dulled to danger. He felt the surge and sweep of tremendous conflict, and relief came with action.

As they stood up he obtained a better view of the field. The Germans were yet nearer now, and, seen through the blazing light of the cannon, they were magnified and increased. Although yet too distant in the center, the flanks were near enough to open fire with the rifles, and their crash in scores of thousands was added to the tremendous roar of the cannon fire.

Captain Colton beckoned again to the Strangers, and joining a heavy infantry force they crept out toward the right, and then among the trees. John divined at once their mission. They were to support and save the French field batteries which had gone into the wood and which had done so much damage to the German army.

They could not mistake their destination. The flash and crash came from a point directly in front of them, and the whole forest was lighted up by the blaze of the guns. Farther to their right John heard the heavy tramp of horsemen in thousands. There he knew were the Uhlans, circling to cut off the French guns.

The wood opened out, leaving wide clear spaces, and then John saw the countless helmets of the Uhlans, as they charged with a deep-throated German roar. It seemed that they were to be ridden into the earth, but he found himself kneeling with the others and firing his rifle as fast as he could pull trigger into the charging mass.

John felt like a man sending bullet after bullet into some huge wild beast, seeking to devour. For the moment the Uhlans were blended into one mass, a single entity. He had a vision of the wild faces of men, of the huge red eyes of horse, and of their open slavering mouths, disclosing rows of cruel white teeth. It was those white teeth that he saw clearest, and often he fired at the horses rather than their riders.

Nearer came the Uhlans. The earth resounded with their tread. The cruel white teeth of the horses flashed almost in John's face. He began to have a horrible fear that they could not stop these ruthless horsemen, but the French relieving force had brought with it light guns, which were now pushed up, opening almost point blank on the Uhlans.

The hail of steel drove directly in the faces of horses and men, and they reeled back. Men might stand such a fire, but horses could not. They bolted from it by hundreds, knocked down and trampled upon one another, creating a vast turmoil and confusion among the Germans.

John was conscious that he had sprung to his feet, and was advancing again with his comrades directly upon the Uhlans. They were still reloading and firing as fast as they could, and the light artillery, between the spaces, was cutting a perfect harvest of death. As the Uhlans were driven back out of the open and among the trees their difficulties increased. It was impossible to fall into any kind of formation and charge such a formidable infantry defended by guns.

The riflemen pressed closer and closer and poured upon them such a deadly fire that after many vain efforts to hold their ground the trumpets sounded the recall, and all those who were able to ride retreated.

The French set up a tremendous cheer and swept forward to meet their field guns which were slowly retiring, sending heavy volleys into the German masses as they withdrew. Yet their escape was a narrow one. Without the sortie from the fort they would certainly have been cut off by the Uhlans.

John found himself shouting in triumph with the French. He shared their feelings now because their danger had been his danger, and he was fast becoming the same in spirit.

"Just in time!" shouted Wharton in his ear. "See how the Germans come on, and come without ending!"

The great German mass in the open was now almost abreast of them. Their numbers seemed endless. Their huge cannon filled the air with projectiles which poured upon the French earthworks, and, captive balloons and aeroplanes hanging over them, directed their fire. The sight, magnificent in some aspects, was terrible nevertheless, and for a moment or two John was appalled.

"We've got to get back quick as we can," shouted Carstairs, "or they'll be on us, too!"

"Right! old man!" shouted Wharton, agreeing with him for once.

They were already retiring, and the field artillery was going with them. But the deadly seventy-five millimeter guns were not idle, although they were withdrawing. They sent shell after shell, which hung low over the German ranks, and then burst in a whirlwind of steel fragments and splinters. Death was showered upon the gray masses, but they never flinched, coming on steadily, with the deep German cheer, swelling now and then into thunder.

The battle was so near that the Strangers could no longer hear one another, although they shouted. Their company luckily had suffered little, but now the bullets began to search their ranks, and brave young Americans and brave young Englishmen gave up their lives under an alien flag.

John was conscious of neither elation nor despair. The excitement was too great. His heart hammered heavily against its walls, and the red mist before him deepened until it became a blazing glare. Then the rush of hoofs came again. The Uhlans had reformed and made a second charge. The riflemen beat it off, and, still protecting the guns, joined the main French force.

But it was evident there that the French must retreat again. The powerful artillery of the Germans had cut their defenses to pieces. The earth was torn by the great shells as if mining machinery had been at work, and the ground was covered with dead and wounded. Valor against numbers and long preparation was unavailing.

"If we don't go we're lost," shouted Carstairs.

"And if we go today we can come back and fight another day!" said Wharton.

The French leader gathered together his army, beaten for a second time, and slowly retired across the hills. The French character here showed itself entirely different from what popular belief had made it. John saw no signs of panic. The battered brigades closed up and withdrew, turning a steady and resolute face to the enemy. Their deadly artillery continually swept the front of the advancing Germans, and at intervals their riflemen sent back withering volleys.

John's excitement did not abate. Again he loaded and fired his rifle, until its barrel grew hot in his hand. The tumult was fierce and deafening beyond all description. He shouted to his comrades and his comrades shouted to him, but none could hear the sound of a human voice. The roar of the explosions was mingled without ceasing with the whining and shrieking of shrapnel and bullets.

Yet the retreating army defeated every attempt to close with it. The rifles and cannon mowed down the flankers to both right and left, and their powerful guns drove the pursuing center to a respectful distance. Toward night they came to a higher range of hills spreading to such a distance that they could not be flanked, and, turning there, they sat down, and waited, confident of their position.

9

THE RIDE OF THREE

THE BATTLE, including the fighting retreat, had lasted a long time and it had proved even to inexperienced John that the French force could not stand before the superior numbers of the Germans, and their tremendous equipment. And yet the French officers had shown much skill. They had inflicted great losses, they had drawn off all their artillery, and they had defeated every effort of their enemy to surround and destroy them.

John felt that not everything was lost as they sat down on the hills and began to fortify anew. There was no time for him to rest. He was only a private soldier, and, armed with a spade, he worked at a trench with all the strength and energy he could command. But his immediate friends of the Strangers were of no higher rank than himself and they were beside him engaged in the same task. "I'm only a new soldier," he said, "but it seems to me we did pretty well to get off with our army and our guns."

"So we did," said Carstairs. "I fancy the chief part of our occupation will be retreating until the British come up."

"There it goes," said Wharton. "Every Englishman has a fatal disease. You can never cure him of being an Englishman. If a million French and a hundred thousand English were to win a battle Carstairs would give all the credit of it to the hundred thousand English."

"I'd give it to 'em, because it belonged to 'em. Keep your fool Yankee head down, Wharton. Didn't you hear that shell whistle?"

"I heard it, and I heard a dozen others too," said John, who could not keep from shivering a little. "Why do they keep on bothering us, when we're now in too strong a position to be attacked, and the night too is at hand?"

"Oh, you'll get used to it," said Wharton. "They won't attack tonight, but they want to keep us disturbed, to create terror among us, and then we'll be easier, when they do come again."

"I don't hear the giant any more."

"You mean the forty-two centimeter. I fancy it's far in the rear. They have to have roads on which to drag it, and then, so they say, it has to be placed in a concrete bed before they can fire it."

"At any rate their fire is dying," said Carstairs, "and I'm jolly glad of it. I didn't get any sleep last night, and I want some tonight. I need it, after this back-breaking work."

Fortunately the trench was soon finished, and the long range firing ceased entirely. The night came on, hiding the two armies from each other, and fires sprang up in the French camp. Their light was ruddy and cheerful. Then came the glorious aroma of food, and, the Strangers called from their labors to the banquet, sat down and ate.

John had heard all his life what cooks the French were, but nothing that he had ever tasted before was like the food he ate and the coffee he drank that night. Incessant marching and fighting gave a savor that nothing else could impart.

While they still sat around the cooking fires they saw dim shapes in the heavens, and John, out of the depths of his experience, knew that they were the flying machines. Carstairs and Wharton saw him looking up.

"You may want to be there," said Wharton, "but I don't. I'd grow so giddy I'd jump right out of the machine. This sound and rolling earth suits me. I like its green grass, its rivers, its lakes and its mountains, and I don't want to go off, prospecting for other planets."

"It's lucky," said John, "that this army has flying machines of its own. If it didn't the Germans would be raining bombs upon us."

Carstairs shuddered.

"There's something heathenish and uncanny about it," he said. "Soldiers, by Jove, have to watch nowadays. If you're on the ship looking for an enemy of your size the little submarine down under the water may blow you to pieces, and if you're on the land holding your own against another army a little aeroplane away up in the sky may drop a bomb that will shatter you into seven million pieces."

"It's a hard world, Carstairs," said Wharton, "but I think discomfort rather than danger will come out of the sky tonight. The clouds are piling up and there'll be heavy rain. John, you little old flying man, won't that stop the Taubes?"

"They wouldn't venture much in a heavy rain, and I think we're safe from them, but you know that what their fliers can do ours can do too."

"That being the case I'll settle myself for rest and sleep. The French show us a lot of consideration as we've volunteered to fight for them, and there are tents for the Strangers. You're to have a place in ours."

John was grateful and said so. The strain of the last few days would have overpowered him, but luckily he was exceedingly strong and tenacious. Yet he was so tired that he could scarcely walk, and he was very very glad to go into the tent with Carstairs and Wharton. He received two blankets, and, putting one under him and the other over him, he lay near the open flap, where he could get a good view of much that was going on outside.

He soon saw that it was to be no storm of thunder and lightning, but a heavy soaking rain. The air too had turned colder, and he was grateful for the blankets. He was becoming inured to hardship so fast that they and the tent were as luxurious to him as a modern hotel would have seemed two weeks before.

Carstairs and Wharton, after a short combat in words, fell sound asleep, but John lingered a little. He saw the fires burning smokily, and French soldiers passing before the blaze. From where he lay he could also see far out upon the plain that lay before them. But everything there was veiled in heavy mists and low clouds. Although an army of perhaps a hundred thousand men was only a short distance away the night disclosed no trace of it.

The rain began to fall soon, coming down as John had foreseen in a strong, steady pour. The sound on the heavy canvas was so soothing that his nerves relaxed and he slept. He was awakened at an unearthly hour by the strong hand of Captain Colton pulling at his shoulder.

As soon as John realized that it was his commanding officer he sprang to his feet and saluted, although his eyes were yet heavy with sleep. It was still raining and the water poured from a heavy cape coat that Captain Colton wore over his uniform. Carstairs and Wharton were already on their feet.

"You three are chosen for a mission," said Captain Colton, "and I'll tell it to you as briefly as I can. We've received news tonight that another German force is coming from the northeast. If it gets upon our flank we're lost, but there is a French army, and perhaps an English force with it or near it to the west. If they can be brought up in time they will protect our flank and save us--and also themselves. But we must have trusty messengers. The flying machines can do little in the storm. So we fall back on the ancient agencies. Can you ride, Mr. Scott?"

"Yes sir."

"Then you three are to go at once. Other messengers will ride forth, but I should feel very proud, if it were the Strangers who brought help."

The little appeal was not lost on the three. He rapidly gave them instructions about the point, at which the second French force was supposed to be, and told them to ride for it as hard as they could, giving to them sealed despatches also. Their own army would be falling back meanwhile.

"Both Carstairs and Wharton know this region and the roads," he said to John, "and you keep with them. Are you ready?"

"Yes sir," answered the three together.

They stepped out into the rain, but forgetful of it. An orderly was holding three horses. In an instant, they were in the saddle and away. They passed through the lines and came out upon one of the splendid French roads, the three abreast. The rain was beating in their faces, but the orderly had tied cloaks to their saddles, and now they wrapped them about their bodies.

But John minded neither darkness, cold nor rain. Sensitive and quiet there was some quality in him that always responded to the call of high adventure. His mind was never keener, never more alert, and all his strength of body had returned. Wharton and Carstairs rode on either side of him, and he felt already as if they had been friends of years, knitted to him by a thousand dangers shared.

He looked back once at the intrenched camp, but the descent and curve of the road already hid it in the darkness. He saw nothing but the black outline of the hills, and low clouds floating across the whole horizon. Ahead was a blank. He was in one of the most thickly populated regions of the world, crowded with cities, but in the darkness and storm it looked like a wilderness.

Neither of his comrades spoke for a long time. He stole a look at his watch, and saw that it was three o'clock in the morning. They crossed two small rivers, foaming like torrents, and at the bridges reined into a walk, lest the hoof-beats be heard too far. But they did not meet any human being. Save for the road and the bridges the aspect of a wilderness was complete. John knew that numerous villages lay near, but in such a world war the people would put out their lights and keep close in their houses.

They turned after a while into a smaller road, leading more toward the north.

"The Uhlans may be in our rear," said Carstairs. "They seem to be everywhere, and we don't want to be cut off just at the beginning of our ride."

"Rein in," said Wharton. "I hear cavalry passing on the road we've just left."

"Speak of Uhlans, and they appear," whispered John.

They were Uhlans, no doubt. John recognized the helmets, but the men were riding back toward the armies. He and his two comrades kept their horses in the shadow of the bushes, and were in dread lest some movement of their animals betray them, but the droning of the rain was the only sound made. The Uhlans, about forty in number, rode on and the darkness swallowed them up.

"Since they've gone about their business we'd better go about ours," said Wharton.

"Those are the first wise words I've heard you speak in a half hour," said Carstairs.

"It's the first time I've spoken at all in a half hour," said Wharton.

"Which way do we go now?" asked John.

"Over a hill and far away," replied Carstairs. "To be more explicit we're coming to the hill now, and about daylight we'll reach a little village, where I think we'd better get food and news. You'll like the country, John, when it stops raining and the sunlight comes. Oh, it's a fair land, this land of France."

"I've seen enough of it to know that," said John. "Lead on, and I'll be glad to reach the next village. A wind has set up, and this rain cuts cruelly."

Carstairs rode in front, and for more than an hour they breasted the storm almost in silence. They climbed the hill, passed down the other side, crossed numerous brooks, and then saw reluctant daylight appearing through the rain.

John with the new caution that he had learned looked up. But the clouds were so heavy that he saw nothing there, not a dirigible, not a Taube, nor any form of aeroplane. Traveling, even on the business of an army, was still better on land.

"There's our village," said Wharton, pointing to a pleasant valley in which tiled roofs and the spire of a church showed.

"And there we'll be in fifteen minutes," said Carstairs. "I'm full of enthusiasm for the mission on which we ride as you two are also of course, but it will fairly overflow after I have a good warm breakfast."

Despite the earliness of the hour peasants were up and they watched with curiosity the three horsemen who approached. But enough of the uniform of the strangers showed, despite their cloaks, to indicate that they belonged to the French army, and they were welcome. An old man with a scythe, pointed toward an inn, and the three, increasing their speed, rode straight for it.

"I hope they'll have good coffee," said John.

"And fine bread," said Carstairs.

"And choice bacon," said Wharton.

"And plenty of eggs to go with the bacon," said John.

It was but a little village, forty or fifty houses, set among the hills, but in times of peace many people must have gone that way, because it had one of the best road inns that John had ever entered. They were early but the landlord soon had the flames going in a wide fire-place, before which the three stood, warming themselves and drying their clothes. And the heavy aromas arising promised that the coffee, bacon and all the rest would be everything they wished.

A boy held their horses near the main door which stood open that they might see. The three were a unit on this precaution. If by any possible chance their horses were lost their mission in all likelihood would be lost too. John, new recruit, nevertheless felt the full importance of watching. He stood with his back to the fire, where he could see the sturdy French boy, the reins of the three horses in his hands.

But he did not forget how good that fire felt. The great cape had not been able to protect him wholly from the rain, and, despite the excitement of their ride, he had become conscious that he was cold and wet. Now the grateful warmth penetrated to his bones, and vitality returned.

As he remained there, turning about a little before the fire but always keeping his eyes on the door, he saw the villagers come down in the rain and look in, some at the open door and some at the windows. None of them spoke, but all gazed intently at the three in French uniform who stood before the fire.

John knew why they had come and he was singularly moved by their silent, pathetic stare. They were hoping to hear good news, at least one little bit of it--these good French villagers whose soil was trodden again by an enemy who seemed invincible. Just as the breakfast was being laid upon the table the landlord said to them:

"Have you nothing for these brave people of ours, who, as you see, wait at the windows? They are the old men, the very young and the women. All the others are gone to the war. Yesterday we heard the sound of guns for a long time. Have you no success to report for France?"

The three shook their heads sadly and Wharton replied for them.

"Not yet," he said. "We belong to the French army engaged in the battle that you heard yesterday. But it was driven back again. The Germans come in overwhelming force, and we cannot withstand their numbers, but we were able to draw off with all our guns and leave them no prisoners."

The landlord said nothing in reply, but presently all those wistful and waiting faces disappeared. Then the breakfast was ready, and a fourth traveler, wet and cold as they had been, arrived. John saw him give the reins of his horse to the waiting boy before he came to the door, where he stood a moment, awaiting the landlord's welcome.

The stranger was in a French uniform, faded and dripping so much water that he must have been in the rain a long time. He was about thirty, medium in height, his face covered with much black beard, and John saw that he was staggering from weakness. But Monsieur Gaussin, the landlord, a man of kindly heart, had perceived that fact also, and he stepped forward quickly.

"Thank you for your arm, good host," said the stranger. "I am weak, but if I am so it is because I've ridden all night in the rain for France."

"A French soldier," said Monsieur Gaussin, opening wide his heart, "and you ride for France! Then you are not alone on such errands. Behold the three young men who are about to honor me by eating a breakfast, for which I shall take no pay."

Gaussin too was not without a touch of the dramatic instinct, and he proudly waved his arm, across which the white napkin lay, toward John, Carstairs and Wharton.

"When you have warmed and dried yourself a little and have drank a glass of this fine old liquor of mine," he said benignantly, "you shall join them."

"And we shall welcome you as a comrade," said Wharton. "We are not French--two Americans and one English--but we fight with the French and their cause is ours. My friends are Carstairs and Scott, and my own name is Wharton."

"And mine is Weber," said the man, "Fernand Weber, an Alsatian, hoping and praying that Alsace and all Alsatians may now be restored to France."

The good Monsieur Gaussin murmured sympathetically.

"But we must suffer and do much before we regain our lost provinces," Weber said.

"Will you not join us at the table?" asked Carstairs politely.

"Gladly, as soon as I have removed this wet coat," replied Weber.

As soon as he took off the outer garment they saw a stain of red across his left sleeve, and the good Monsieur Gaussin again murmured sympathetically.

"It's nothing," laughed Weber. "The Uhlans are abroad, as you may have discovered for yourself. They ride over the whole country, and in the night I was chased by them. The bullet creased my arm, but I carry the emergency bandage. One, two, three, I made it fast, and here we are."

There was something attractive in his manner, his frankness, and the light way in which he dismissed his adventure. The hearts of the three warmed toward one who rode perilously for France as they were doing.

"Come," said John, "you must be starving to death. We certainly are, and if I'm kept any longer from this heavenly coffee there'll be a rebellion."

Annette, the neat maid who was serving them smiled, and Monsieur Gaussin smiled also. But Weber did not keep them waiting. He slid into the fourth chair that had been placed, and, for a little space, gastronomy of the most harmonious kind prevailed.

"From which direction do you come?" asked Carstairs.

"North," replied Weber flashing a smile from gray eyes.

John thought his eyes good, but all the lower part of his face was concealed by the beard.

"I hope you're doing better there than we are on the east," said Carstairs.

"Have you, then, had bad luck?" asked Weber.

"I'd scarcely blame any part of it on luck. Jove, but it's just a plain case of the other side being ready, while we are not."

"And you ride then for help?"

"Something of that kind, although of course we couldn't tell anybody where we are going."

"And I shall not dream of asking you. I know a soldier's duty too well. I ride on an errand myself, but I shall not refuse to tell you anything because you are not going to ask me."

All four laughed. John liked Weber better and better. He saw that he was a cheerful man, with a touch of humor, and he heartened the other three mightily.

Weber told that the French were now well ahead with their preparations, the English were beginning to stir and presently the Germans would find the armies before them much more powerful.

"On what road did you receive your wound?" asked John. "You won't mind telling us this, I hope, because that will be a good road for us to avoid."

"The Uhlans may have passed on," replied Weber, shrugging his shoulders, "but it was the road from the north. I encountered them about fifteen miles from here. It was so dark that I couldn't see very well, but I don't think they numbered more than half a dozen."

"We were going on that road," said Carstairs rising, "but perhaps we'd better take the western one for the present. We have to hurry. Good-by, Mr. Weber, we're glad we met you, and we hope that transfer of the title deeds of Alsace real estate will take place."

Weber's gray eyes beamed.

"It's good of another race to help us," he said. All three shook hands with him, said friendly farewells to the benignant Monsieur Gaussin and the neat Annette, and hurried to their horses.

"A good fellow that Weber," said Carstairs as they swung into their saddles. "I hope we'll swing Alsace and Lorraine too, back into France for him."

"If it's done," said Wharton, "England will claim that she did it."

"A perfectly justifiable claim."

Wharton turned upon John a look of despair.

"Can you ever change a single idea of theirs?" he asked. "They're quite sure they've done everything."

"There's one race," said John, "to whom they yield."

"I never heard of it."

"Oh yes, you have. When Sandy of the long red locks comes down from the high hills London capitulates at once. Don't you know, Wharton, that Great Britain and all her colonies are ruled by the Scotch?"

Carstairs broke into a hearty laugh.

"You have me there, Wharton," he said. "Certainly we're ruled by the Scotch. We have to let them do it or they'd make the country so disagreeable there'd be no living in it. Jove, but I wish I could hear the bagpipes now and see a hundred thousand of their red heads coming over the hills. It's such fine country around here that they'd never let the Germans have it."

"I like them too," said John. "They're brave men and they speak a sort of English."

Carstairs laughed.

"Don't criticize their English unless you want a fight," he said. "A man is often proudest of what he lacks."

"Just so, Carstairs, and I've often wondered too why so few of the English can speak their own language."

"Shut up, Scott! You've joined Wharton and two against one is not fair. Confound this rain! I wish it would stop! I'm getting wet and cold again. Here the road forks, and Weber said he came down from the north."

"And since he got a bullet in the arm the northern road is bad for us," said Wharton. "If you two agree we'll turn to the west."

"The west for us," said John and Carstairs together.

The country was hillier and more wooded than usual, but they saw little of it, as it was enveloped in a cloud of rain and mist. Nor did they meet any other travelers on the road, a fact which did not surprise them, as the whole region was now almost deserted by everybody save soldiers.

The high spirits they had accumulated at the inn were soon dissipated. It was impossible to remain gay, when one was sodden through and through. The rain came down, as if it meant to do so forever, and all the valleys were filled with mists and vapors. But the road clean and well paved led straight on, and Wharton and Carstairs seemed to know it well.

"Another inn would suit me," said John who was the first to speak in more than an hour. "I shouldn't want to stop because I know we haven't time for it, but I'd like to look in at the window, as I rode by, and see the fire blazing."

"You'll see nothing of that kind before one o'clock in the afternoon," said Carstairs. "Then we come to another neat little village, and another good inn. We'll have to stop there for our horses to feed, as we gave them nothing this morning. So you can do more than look at the window and see the blazing fire."

The road led now between high hedges, and they heard a report some distance to their right. Wharton who was in front suddenly pulled back his horse.

"What's the matter?" the other two exclaimed together.

"A bee stung me," replied Wharton grimly.

He held up his left hand. The blood was flowing from a thin red line across the back of it.

"A bullet did that!" exclaimed Carstairs.

A second report came, and John felt a rush of air past his face.

"Gallop, boys, gallop!" exclaimed Wharton. "Somebody has ambushed us, Uhlans, I suppose, and we've got to run!"

"They must be in the fields!" said Carstairs, as the three urged their horses at once to their utmost speed. Luckily, they had been coming at a slow pace and their mounts were strong.

John thought rapidly. The modern high-powered rifle carried far, and he judged by the faintness of the reports that the bullets had been fired from a point several hundred yards away. They had done under impulse the very thing they ought to do, and their present speed would soon leave the raiders behind.

The three rode neck and neck and as they galloped on two more bullets whistled near them.

"An ambush," said Carstairs coolly, "but we've rushed through it."

"Anyway, our luck is better than Weber's," said Wharton. "He was pinked in the arm and we're unhurt. At least I think so. How are you, Scott?"

"Well but scared."

"I believe the first statement, but not the second And you Carstairs."

"Well but annoyed."

"I believe both your statements."

"Is it your recollection that these hedges continue far, Carstairs?" asked Wharton.

"Five or six miles at least."

"That's mine too, but I hoped I was wrong. It gives those bushwackers an advantage. With the hedges right beside us we can't see well over them, but they on the hills at a distance can look down on us."

"You Yankees are sometimes right, Wharton, and this is one of the times. Those fellows, whoever they are, will probably get a few more shots at us. I'll lay you two to one they don't hit us."

"I never bet against my sympathies. Ping! didn't you hear it! There was a bullet, five seconds after you offered to bet."

"Yes, I know it. Here's the lock of hair it cut from my head."

He took the hair from his coat, where it had fallen, and let it flutter away. He did not show any alarm. Already it had become the pride of the three never to betray apprehension. John's face was like a mask, although his heart was beating hard. A whistle over his head showed that a bullet had passed there and he heard its plunk as it buried itself in a tree on the other side of the road.

He remembered with some consolation that the modern, small, high-powered rifle bullet, unless it killed, did not do so very much harm. It went through one so fast that it did not tear flesh or break bones, and the wounds it made were quick to heal.

Ping! Ping! and once more ping! They reached the crest of the hill and went swiftly down the other slope.

"I think we'll leave them behind here," said Carstairs. "We gain, as we've the open road, while they're obstructed in fields."

"I hope you're a true prophet, Carstairs," said Wharton. "I'm growing reconciled to an army shooting at me, but I would hate to be picked off by an ambushed sharpshooter."

Carstairs was a true prophet in this case. No more shots came and as they entered flat country with open fields, in which they could see every-thing they slowed to a walk, and not too soon, for the horses were breathing heavily, their mouths covered with foam. Then in order to spare their tired animals the three dismounted and walked a mile, leading them by the bridles.

"I'd never have thought the Uhlans were in the rear of our army," said Carstairs.

"I'm not at all surprised," said John.

"Why not?"

"Because I shall never be surprised at anything the Germans do. You English have fallen into the bad habit of thinking that what you haven't done nobody else does."

"I see," said Carstairs with a laugh. "Hit the poor old Britisher. You

Yankees are so used to it that you can't get out of the habit, even here and now, when you and I are allies."

"But it's the truth, the real vital truth," said John earnestly. "The Germans are ahead of you. They're like a medieval knight clad in steel and armed from head to foot, going out to fight a peasant in homespun. And you're the peasant in homespun, Carstairs."

"England is slow, I admit, but when she once takes hold she never lets go."

"Unless she takes hold, when there's something to take hold of it's no use."

"Stop quarreling with him, Scott," said Wharton. "That's my job, and you can't take it from me. I've set two tasks for myself, one to defeat the German army and one to change Carstairs, and I tell you confidentially, John, that I think the defeat of the German army will prove the easier of the two."

"Look how those banks of fog are rolling up," said Carstairs. "The rain is decreasing, but in a quarter of an hour we won't be able to see a thing twenty yards away."

"We shall welcome the fog," said John, who was beginning to feel now that he was on equal terms with the other two.

"So, we should," said Carstairs, "but does fog conduct sound well?"

"I don't know," replied John. "Why?"

"Because I think I hear a noise a long distance to the right. It has a rolling, grinding quality, but that doesn't help me to tell what makes it."

The three stopped, and with all their senses alert listened. Both John and Wharton heard the sound, but they were unable to tell its nature. The fog meanwhile was closing in, heavy and almost impenetrable.

"I think," said John, "we ought to see what it is. The thing is projecting itself squarely across our path. We've got a mission, but the more news we take the better."

Wharton and Carstairs agreed with him, and finding a low place in the hedge that ran beside the road they forced their way through it. They were remounted now, and the rest had made the horses fit for either a fight or a race.

They rode across the field and then through a belt of open forest, but the fog was so dense they were compelled to keep close together lest they lose one another. The rolling sound increased and now other notes came with it. A little farther and they saw dim lights in the fog.

"An army," whispered Carstairs, "and the torch-bearers are showing the way through the fog. Now what kind of an army is it?"

"German of course," said Wharton. "We know well enough that no French force is near here. It's a part of the flood that's bearing down on France and Belgium."

"There are more trees here to the right," said John. "Let's enter them and get a better view. Even if we were seen we could escape anybody in this fog."

"Good idea," said Carstairs. "I'm as anxious as you to know more. This fair land of France is bearing strange fruit now."

Keeping a wary eye for Uhlans who must be somewhere near they rode with all the courage of youth into a clump of trees that grew upon a hillock close to the road. There, in the shelter of the foliage, they looked down upon what was passing.

"Busy Bertha!" said Wharton.

John beheld a giant cannon, one of the mighty howitzers which he had treated as a fable, a soldier's idle dream, until he had heard it booming in the night. But here was another drawn by a powerful motor. Its monster mouth was turned up at an angle toward the sky, and in the fog lighted only by the torches the thing became alive to John, huge and misshapen, dragging itself over the ground, devouring human beings as it went, like the storied dragons of old.

He glanced at his comrades and saw that the monster had taken hold of them in the same way. They were regarding it with a kind of awe, and yet it was not alone. Its sinister shape merely predominated over every-thing else. It was preceded and followed by many other cannon, giants themselves, but overshadowed by the mammoth.

Motors drew most of the great guns, and there were thousands more carrying soldiers, arms and various kinds of equipment. Behind them came vast masses of gray infantry, marching with the steady German tread. The heavy fog, which the torches lighted but dimly, magnified and distorted everything, and the sight was uncanny and terrifying.

John had the deepest respect for German arms. He knew the strong and tenacious German nature, and he had had some insight into the mighty preparations of the empire. Now he saw them rolling down every road upon France, and, for a little while he did not see how they could be beaten, not though all the world combined against them. The mammoth cannon moving slowly on through the fog typified their irresistible advance.

"I think we've seen enough," said Wharton. "We'd better be up and away."

"Too much for me," said Carstairs. "My eye what a gun!"

"It looks more like a dragon to me," said John.

They wheeled and rode away over the wet ground, which gave back but little sound of hoofs, and soon they were again on their own road, bearing to the west. They were very thoughtful, but their own risks of the morning from the hidden bullets were forgotten. The mind of every one of the three turned forward.

10

THE DRAGONS OF THE AIR

ABOUT MID-MORNING THE RAIN CEASED, the fog rose, and was soon scattered by a powerful sun. The beautiful country, fresh and green, reappeared. It was the fair land of France again and John rejoiced. His uniform dried fast upon him, and his spirits rose steadily. He saw the ruddy glow return to the cheeks of his comrades, and the horses seemed to grow stronger. The sky, washed by the rain, was a solid blue, and the air was crisp with the wine of life.

"It's good to breathe and live!" exclaimed Wharton joyously.

"You Yankees talk too much," said Carstairs.

"And you English talk at the wrong time."

"Generally we let our deeds talk for us."

"Then you don't say much."

John laughed. The pleasant way in which they quarreled always amused him.

"I promised not to take the side of either of you at any time," he said.

"You seem to be about evenly matched, and of course it wouldn't be fair for me in such a case to help my countryman."

"Two to one against us are about the odds we English like," said Carstairs.

"Boaster," said Wharton. "Position and army equal we could always whip you, man for man."

"Boaster yourself. Whenever we didn't whip you you'd always say that the position and arms were not equal."

"Stop long enough to look at those birds in the heavens," said John.

"Yes I see them," said Carstairs. "There are four but they're flying very high."

"No, they're five," said Wharton. "There's one on the left detached from the others."

"You're both wrong," said John, smiling from the depths of his superior knowledge. "They're not birds at all."

"Then what under the sun can they be?"

"Aeroplanes. Flying machines."

"Well you ought to know your kind of carriage. You've been up in one of them. Whose are they, I wonder?"

"I can't tell, they're so high, but I'd judge from the shape that they're the German Taubes."

Carstairs and Wharton looked grave.

"They're far over French territory," said Carstairs.

"So they are," said John, "but you're likely to see them much farther."

"I should think that if they went on they'd meet the French flyers," said Wharton, "and then there'd be some lively scenes up in the shining blue."

"They're ready to take the risks," said John. "I believe the Germans are willing to dare anything in this war. They think the world is against them and has resolved to crush them because the other nations are jealous. Their men higher up, the princes and the big military leaders have made them think so, and nothing on earth can ever shake them in the belief."

"You're probably right," said Wharton, "but our German birds seem to be gathering for something. Look how close together they hover now."

"And they're almost directly over our heads!" said John, a thrill of alarm shooting through him. "And see they're dropping down fast!"

"Which means?"

"Which means that they've seen us, that they've noted our French uniforms through powerful glasses, and that they're getting ready to swoop."

"Let 'em come!" said Wharton defiantly. "I never thought to take part in this kind of dove hunting, but if the Taubes will attack they must take the consequences."

He eased his rifle across his saddle bow. All three of them carried the modern, high-powered rifle which could kill at a tremendous range. Neither Wharton nor Carstairs yet felt any apprehension, but John knew better.

"Those are armored machines," he said, "and unless our bullets are very lucky indeed they'll glance off their steel sides."

"Armored flying machines!" exclaimed Carstairs. "I never heard of such things!"

"No, but you're hearing now. These Germans will teach you a lot! Why they even have Taubes that carry light machine guns."

"What ought we to do?"

John by reason of his brief experience in the air had suddenly become the leader, and the others recognized it.

"We must leave the road and make for those trees. They'll give us some protection!"

He pointed to a little grove two hundred yards away. The three sent their horses crashing through the hedge and galloped for it. Overhead the aeroplanes swooped lower and lower, like gigantic birds, darting at their prey.

It was John who came nearest to a full realization of their danger. His experience with Lannes had shown him the power of the flying machines and the skill and daring of the flying men. In the brief gallop toward the wood a succession of terrifying emotions flowed through his mind.

He remembered reading in some old book of primeval man and his constant menace from vast reptilian monsters clad in huge scales, as thick and hard as steel. It had never made much impression upon him. It was too far away and vague, but now it all came back with amazing detail and vividness.

He and his comrades were primeval men, and these swooping planes, shod with steel, were the ancient monsters seeking their prey. The air too was filled then with gigantic birds, enormous of beak and claw, from which man could find refuge only in caves or thick, tangled woods, and just such birds were seeking them now.

[Illustration] "Overhead the aeroplanes swooped lower and lower like gigantic birds."

But two hundred yards to the grove and yet it seemed two miles! His powerful imagination could already hear over his head the rush of the aeroplanes, like the swoop of monster wings, and he felt himself bending low in the saddle, lest his head be struck by an iron beak.

A rifle cracked in the air, and a bullet struck the ground between two of the horses. Then came a sinister burr-r-r and shots rained near them. It was a machine gun in one of the aeroplanes, flying so low now that the angle at which it was fired was not acute.

John was brave and his will was so strong that it had great control over his sensitive and imaginative mind. Yet he was never in his life more terrified. That vivid picture of primeval man fleeing with all his might from monsters of the air, grew more vivid every moment. He was fairly drenched in terror, as his dim ancestor must have been in like case, nor was he ashamed of it. He had one look each at his comrades, and their faces were ghastly white. He knew that his emotions were theirs too.

The bullets flew thicker, but aim is uncertain, when one is flying from a moving machine in the air, at speeding targets, and most of the bullets flew wide. Carstairs was grazed on the shoulder, and Wharton's horse was touched lightly on the flank, but gasping, both horses and riders, they plunged into the wood, reckless alike of trees and under-growth, desperately seeking safety from the winged terrors that pursued them.

It was fortunate for the three fugitives that it was not the ordinary European wood, trimmed and pruned like a park. It was heavy with foliage, and there was much undergrowth, in which the horse of Carstairs tripped and fell, throwing him. But he did not begrudge that, as the vines and bushes not only broke his fall, but meant safety.

"Since you're down Carstairs," said Wharton, "it's the duty of a comrade to join you."

He sprang off his own horse and stood, rifle in hand, among the bushes. John also dismounted, although in more leisurely fashion. His heart had ceased to beat so heavily when they entered the wood. The immediate anger of being snapped up by those giants of the air passed and the revulsion of feeling came. His pulses were still drumming in his ears, but he heard a louder throbbing above the trees. The angry and disappointed monsters were hovering there, still seeking their prey.

Bullets pattered on the leaves and twigs, but they went wide. The three horses shivered in terror, and the one that had been touched on the flank uttered a shrill neigh of distress. John took the lead.

"The undergrowth is thicker on our right," he said. "We must take our horse into it. They won't be able to get more than glimpses of us there."

"Right!" said Carstairs, "I think I can walk that far now. The strength is coming back into my knees, and I don't think they'll double under me. I don't mind telling you fellows that I was never before in my life so scared."

"Your confession is mine too," said Wharton.

They reached the new refuge without harm, although more shots were fired from the planes. The density of the bushes there was due to a small stream flowing through the wood, and while the horses were still exposed, in a measure, they found almost complete cover for themselves. The three lay down in the thicket and pointed upward the muzzles of their rifles.

The throbbing and droning over their heads had never ceased, and through the leaves they saw the armored planes hovering about not far above the tops of the trees. But the fugitives in their screen of leaf and thicket had become invisible.

"We'll have to chance it with our horses," whispered Wharton, "but for ourselves we may be able to give back as good as we send. Scott, are you a sharpshooter?"

"I'm a pretty good marksman, and I think I could hit one of those things if it should slow down."

"I suggest," said Carstairs, "that when one of us fires he immediately move away at least six or eight yards. Then they won't be able to locate us by the shots."

"Good for you old Britisher," said Wharton, "you do have moments of intelligence."

"Wharton, I'd like to say as much for you."

Both laughed but the laugh was uneasy and unnatural. It was merely the force of habit, compelling them to seek some sort of relief through words.

The planes had come together in a group for a few moments, but afterward they made a wide separation and flew about swiftly in irregular circles. John knew that it was meant to disturb the aim of those below, because the flying men had certainly seen that they carried rifles.

John crouched under a bush, and with the muzzle of his high-powered rifle turned upward, continually sought a target through the leaves. In those moments of danger and fierce anger he did not have left a single scruple against taking the life of man. They had hunted him remorselessly in a strange and terrific way. His first illusion that they were gigantic birds of prey remained, and he would be doing a service to the world, if he slew them.

A rifle cracked almost in his ear and Wharton uttered a little cry of disappointment.

"I heard the bullet thud on the metal side of that Taube," he said. "It isn't fair fighting us this way."

Then he and John, following the suggestion of Carstairs, promptly moved to another point in the bushes. Three bullets from the Taubes struck near the place they had just left. But John still watching had caught sight of a head and body, the two hands grasping a rifle projecting over the side of a Taube. Quick as a flash he fired, and with an aim that was literally as sure as death.

The man in the Taube heaved up, as if wrenched by an electric shock, then plunged head-foremost over the side and fell clear, his rifle dropping before him. John caught a swift vision of a falling figure sprawled out hideously, and then he heard the rending crash of twigs and branches followed by a heavy thump. His heart thrilled with horror. Those were human beings after all, up there in the air, and not primeval birds of prey.

"That one!" said Wharton. "Good shot, Scott!"

John's horror passed. He was still fighting for his life, and it was the men in the air who had attacked. He moved away again and by chance he came to the tiny brook, on which the bushes were strung like a thread. Lying flat on his face he drank, and he was astonished to find that he was so thirsty. Rising to his knees he glanced at his comrades and at the hovering aeroplanes. They had flown high out of the reach of bullets, and had drawn together as if for council. One of the horses rearing and threshing with fright had been killed by shots from the aeroplanes, but John did not notice it, until this moment. The other two tethered by their bridles to bushes had tried to break loose, but had failed. Now they were trembling all over, and were covered with perspiration. John felt sorry for them.

But the water had refreshed him wonderfully. He had not known before how hot and dry his throat had become. He invited his comrades to drink too, and they followed his example. Then they lay on their backs, and watched the council in the air. They could even hear the distant drumming of their motors. The machine, out of which John had shot the aviator, had carried two men, because there it was in the group with the others.

John's old and powerful feeling that he was at the end of one era and at the beginning of another, involving many new forces, returned with increased strength. To be besieged by enemies overhead was one of them, and, for the present at least, he saw no way of escape from the grove.

The sun was now in the zenith. The clouds, having gone away, made a clean sweep of it. There was not a fleck of dusk in the burning blue of the sky. The aeroplanes were outlined against it, as clearly as if they had been pictures in oil on canvas. The sun, great and golden, poured down fire, but it did not reach the three in the thicket.

"I wish I knew what those fellows were planning," said Carstairs. "At least they give us a rest, while they arrange for our destruction."

"But we're not destroyed yet, and you don't think it either, Carstairs," said Wharton. "Whatever I've said against you Britishers, I've never said you lacked courage."

"And if you had said it I'd have known that you didn't mean it."

Then the two shook hands in silence. Wharton closed his eyes and pretended to be asleep.

"What are they doing, John?" he asked presently.

"Still in council. A plane heavier than the others, evidently the one that has the machine gun is in the center. I judge therefore that it also carries the commander of the fleet."

"Acute reasoning. Wake me up when they seem to be starting anything. Meanwhile I can't be bothered, because a few aeroplanes choose to use our heavens."

He stretched himself, and breathed deeply and peacefully. But John knew well enough that he was not asleep. His rifle lay by his side, where it could be snatched up in a moment, and now and then his eyes opened to watch through the bushes the foe circling aloft. Carstairs also lay down bye and bye, but John remained sitting, the thick boughs of a bush covering him.

"Something has happened," he announced after awhile. "One of the planes, the smallest, I think is flying away toward the east."

The others sat up. The aeroplane, high in air, was going at tremendous speed. The others remained over the grove, swinging about lazily in circles, but too high for the rifles.

"Now, Carstairs," said Wharton, "you English pretend to omniscience. So, tell us at once what that means."

"If anybody had omniscience it would be we British of course, but I confess, Wharton, that this is beyond me. That aeroplane is certainly going fast. Now it's as big as my hand, now it's the size of an egg, now it's a dot and now it's gone."

"Perhaps it's seeking help," said John.

"I don't see why," said Wharton. "Enough are left to hold us in this grove. Their only difficulty is in getting at us. Even if they brought more the trees and the foliage would still be here to protect us."

"That's true," admitted John. "Then it may have been damaged by some of our bullets."

"But it left like a racer. I don't know how these machines are built, but I'd wager from the way it flew that not a wheel or spring or screw or rivet in it was damaged."

"The others are evidently waiting for it to come back."

"How do you make out that?"

"Because they merely float about beyond our reach and don't try anything against us. The day's passing, and if they didn't have some plan dependent on the machine that left, they'd be at work now trying to shoot us up."

Carstairs reached over and patted John on the head. "You talk sense, Scott," he said, "if it weren't for your accent you could pass for an Englishman."

"Then I'll see that he never changes his accent," said Wharton.

"I think I'll take a nap," said Carstairs, "and I really mean it. The grass and the bushes were heavy with rain when we came in here, although we didn't notice it, but the fine sun up there has dried everything now, and I've a good bed."

He lay very comfortably, with his head on a mound of turf, but he did not close his eyes. The lids were lowered but nevertheless he watched the heavens.

"Sorry for those poor horses of ours," he said. "One's killed and the other two, I suppose, will be scared to death before this thing's over."

"And then we'll have to walk," said Wharton.

"But we'll go on just the same."

"We can buy new horses, at the next village. No more walking for mine than I can help."

John was intently watching the eastern horizon. He was longing now for Lannes' powerful glasses. Nevertheless his eyesight was good, the best of the three, and presently the great pulse in his throat began to leap. But he did not say anything yet. He wanted to make sure. He waited a minute and then he said:

"A black dot has reappeared in the eastern sky. It's so tiny you couldn't see it unless you swept your eyes around the circle until they met it."

Carstairs sat up.

"Where?" he asked.

"Begin as I told you and sweep your eyes around the circle."

"Ah, I see it now! Or maybe it's just a mote in the dancing sunbeams."

"Oh no, it's not. Watch it grow. It's an aeroplane, and I'd wager everything against next to nothing that it's the one that left a little while ago. Whatever it went to do it's done."

"Upon my soul, I think you're right. It is growing as you say. Now the dot becomes a black spot as big as an egg, now it grows to the size of your hand, and now the shape of a flying machine, coming at terrific speed, emerges. The whole process of departure is reversed."

"And it's making straight for that overhanging group," said Wharton.

John watched the big birds of prey await the messenger, and again he longed intently for Lannes' powerful glasses. The returning machine was received by the others which formed a circle about it, and for some minutes they hung there in close company.

His nerves began to quiver again with excitement. He was sure that it was a menace. The small aeroplane would not have gone away on a mission without some excellent reason. Sure of his leafy covert he stood up, and watched the group which now circled almost exactly over their heads. Carstairs and Wharton stood beside him, and again they turned to him as the leader, now that it was an affair of the air.

"What do you make of it?" asked Carstairs, anxiously.

"It means harm, some new method of attack," said John, "but for the life of me I can't guess what it is."

"Then we've merely got to wait," said Wharton.

The three were standing close together, and a chill seemed to pass from one to another. That great danger threatened not one of the three doubted, and its mysterious character made it all the more formidable.

The aeroplanes drew apart a little and again circled about lazily. John began to have a hope that nothing would happen after all, when suddenly he saw a flash in the thickets and heard a stunning roar. A piece of metal whistled past his head, and leaves and twigs fell in a shower.

Acting partly from reason and partly from impulse he seized both Wharton and Carstairs and dragged them to the ground.

"A bomb!" he cried. "I had forgotten about bombs, although I've seen them used before. They had none with them and the little aeroplane went back to a hangar somewhere for a supply! They'll drop more and we'll be safer lying down!"

"You're right of course," said Wharton. "It's all as simple as day now. There goes the second!"

Came another flash and roar, but this time the bomb fell farther away, and the metal fragments flew high over their heads. A third followed with the same result, and they began to feel encouraged.

"Of course they have to drop them at random," said John, "and throwing down bombs from an aeroplane high in air is largely an affair of chance."

"Still," said Wharton, "I feel as if I would like to burrow in the earth, not merely for a foot or two, but for at least a hundred feet, where the biggest bomb ever made by the Germans couldn't reach me."

Carstairs uttered a cry of joy.

"What can you find to be glad about in a situation like this?" asked Wharton.

"I've been poking through the bushes and I find just beside us a deep gully."

"A trench made and ready for us! Come, we'll be the boys in the trenches!"

They passed through the bushes and dropped down in the gully which was in truth a great natural help to them. It was certain that in time a bomb would strike near, but unless it dropped directly on them they would be protected by their earthen walls from its flying fragments. And the odds were greatly against a bomb falling where they lay. The revulsion of feeling was so great that they became jovial.

"You've never agreed with me more than once or twice, Carstairs," said Wharton, "but I don't think you'll dispute it, when I say this is a fine, friendly little ravine."

"The finest I ever saw. I'm an expert in ravines. I made a specialty of 'em all through my boyhood, and I never saw another the equal of this."

"Now, they're guessing badly," said John, as a bomb burst in the far edge of the grove, some distances away.

"I wish we could find shelter for our horses," said Carstairs. "Those fellows in the air undoubtedly have glasses, and, not being able to see us, they may choose to demolish our remaining two beasts."

"There goes one now!" exclaimed John, as another bomb burst and a shrill neigh of pain followed.

A horse had been struck by two fragments, and wild with pain and terror it reared, struggled, finally broke its bridle, and galloped out into the fields, where it fell dead from loss of blood.

"Poor beast," muttered Carstairs, "I've always loved horses, and I'd like to get a little revenge."

"Maybe we can get it by waiting," said John, who was rapidly developing the qualities of leadership. "They can't possibly see us here in the gully which is lined thickly on either side with bushes."

"And you think if we lie quiet," said Wharton, "that they'll come down lower to see what damage they've done."

"That's my idea."

"You do seem to have a good head on you for a Yankee," said Carstairs.

They were silent a long time. Two more bombs were dropped but they did not strike near them. John heard the remaining horse straining at his bridle, and threshing among the bushes, but he did not succeed in breaking loose.

He was very comfortable among some leaves in the gully, but he was on his back, and he did not cease to watch the aeroplanes, drifting lazily between him and the heavens. It was hard to judge distances in the air, but he had watched them so long and so closely that they seemed to him after a while to be flying lower. Patient as the Germans were, they must see sometime or other whether their bombs had destroyed the fugitives in the grove.

"They're coming down toward the tops of the trees," he whispered. "Since they haven't heard from us for so long they've probably concluded that their bombs have finished us."

"They'll soon find out better," said Carstairs savagely. "That last horse they killed was mine, and the poor brute was torn horribly by pieces of the bomb."

John looked at him curiously.

"War is war," he said.

"I know it," replied Carstairs, "and that's why I shall be so particular to take good aim, when they drop within range. Confound it, I wish they didn't have those armored machines."

"Still they're bound to expose themselves now and then," said John, "or they can't see us."

They now knelt in the gully waiting for the Taubes, which were softly sinking lower and lower. All three were sharpshooters, and they had anger and the love of life to wing their aim.

"Suppose we pick our men," said John. "The heavy plane near the center of the group is undoubtedly the one that carries the machine gun, and so it's our most dangerous antagonist. It's not likely to have more than two men--otherwise the weight would be too great--one to steer and one to handle the gun."

"Excellent," said Carstairs. "You're undoubtedly the best marksman, Scott. Suppose when the machine tilts enough to give us aim you say: 'fire,' you taking the man at the rudder, while Wharton and I shoot at the one with the gun."

"All right, if you say so."

"Then it's agreed?"

"Agreed it is."

The muzzles of three rifles were now thrust through the bushes, ready to fire at an instant's notice. In those moments of intense excitement and with their own lives to save not one of the three had a single thought of mercy, Kindly in ordinary times war had taken complete possession of them for a space.

John concluded that the Germans were now sure of their success. It had been quiet so long in the grove that the fugitives must be dead. Moreover the afternoon was waning, and night would help the defenders, if they still lived. But he never took his eyes from the big aeroplane, floating easily like a great bird on lazy wing. Lower and lower it dropped and it came within easy range of the high-powered rifles. Now it slanted over on its side, still like a huge bird and the two men it carried came into view.

"Fire!" cried John, and there was one report as the three rifles cracked together. Never had bullets been sent with a more terrible aim. When the dead hand fell from the steering rudder the great machine turned quite over on its side. The two men and the machine gun were shot out, as if they had been hurled by a catapult, and crashed among the trees of the grove. The machine itself, still keeping its likeness to a huge bird, but wounded mortally, now fluttered about wildly for several minutes, and then fell with a tremendous crash among the trees. The other aeroplanes, obviously frightened by the fall of their leader, rapidly flew higher and out of range.

The three did not exult at first. Instead they were appalled.

"We certainly shot well!" said John at last.

"Oh I don't care!" said Carstairs, shaking himself, defiantly.

"They were after us, and we were bound to hit back!"

A bomb exploded in the woods, but they were not hurt. It stirred them to wrath again, and all their compunctions were gone. Instead, they began to feel a pride in their great sharpshooting.

"They've had enough of it for the present," said Wharton. "Look, the whole flock is mounting up and up, where our bullets can't reach 'em! Come down you rascals! Come down out of the sky and meet us face to face! We'll whip the whole lot of you!"

He stood at his full height and shook his rifle at the aeroplanes. John and Carstairs shared his feelings so thoroughly that they saw nothing odd.

"While they're so high," said John, "suppose we go and look at the fallen machine."

They found it among some trees, a part of the frame imbedded in the earth. It looked in its destruction a sinister and misshapen monster. The machine gun, broken beyond repair, lay beside it. They knew that two other shattered objects were somewhere near in the bushes, but they would not look for them.

"A great victory for the besieged," said Wharton, "but it leaves us still besieged."

"However the aspect of the field of battle is changing," said John.

"In what way?"

"The twilight is coming and the sky is our foe's field of battle."

The increase in their own chances became apparent at once. The obscurity of night would be like a blanket between them and the flying men, and its promise now was for speedy arrival. The glory of the sun had faded already in the east, and the sky was becoming gray toward the zenith.

"If that flock expects to achieve anything against us," said John, "they must set about it pretty soon. In an hour they will have to come close to the ground to see us, and I fancy we can then leave the grove."

"Yes," said Wharton, "it's up to them now. We can stand here waiting for them until the darkness comes. Now, they've begun to act!"

A bomb burst, but the obscuring twilight was so deceptive that it fell entirely outside the wood and exploded harmless in a field.

"Poor work," said Carstairs.

"As I told you it's exceedingly hard to be accurate, dropping bombs from a height," said John, "and the twilight makes it much more so."

Nevertheless the aeroplanes made a desperate trial, throwing at least a half dozen more bombs, some of which fell in the wood, but not near the three defenders, although the last horse fell a victim, being fairly blown to pieces.

Meanwhile the sun sank behind the earth's rim, and, to the great joy of the three, clouds again rolled along the horizon, showing that they would have a dark night, a vital fact to them. In their eagerness to strike while it was yet time the aeroplanes hovered very low, almost brushing the tops of the trees, exposing themselves to the fire of the three who after spending eighteen or twenty cartridges on them moved quickly to another part of the wood, lest an answering bomb should find them.

They did not know whether they had slain any one, but two of the planes flew away in slanting and jerky fashion like birds on crippled wings. The others remained over the grove, but rose to a much greater height.

"That was the last attack and we repelled it," said Carstairs, feeling the flush of victory. "Here is the night black and welcome."

The aeroplanes were now almost invisible. The darkness was thickening so fast that in the grove the three were compelled to remain close together, lest they lose one another. Under the western horizon low thunder muttered, and there was promise of more rain, but they did not care.

They resolved to leave the grove in a half hour, and now they felt deeply the death of their horses. But all three carried gold, and they would buy fresh mounts at the next village. Their regret at the loss was overcome by the feeling that they had been victorious in the encounter with the aeroplanes when at first the odds seemed all against them.

They waited patiently, while the night advanced, noting with pleasure that the mutter of thunder on the western horizon continued. Overhead two aeroplanes were circling, but they were barely visible in the dusk, and rescuing their blankets and some other articles that the horses had carried, the three, with their rifles ready, walked cautiously across the fields.

A hundred yards from the grove, and they looked up. The aeroplanes were still circling there. Wharton laughed.

"They probably think we haven't the nerve to leave the shelter of the trees," he said. "Let 'em watch till morning."

"And then they'll find that the birds have metaphorically but not literally flown away," said Carstairs, a tone of exultation showing in his voice also. "In this battle between the forces of the air and the forces of the earth the good old solid earth has won."

"But it may not always win," said John. "When I was up with Lannes, I saw what the aeroplane could do, and we are bound to admit that if it hadn't been for the grove they'd have got us."

"Right-o!" said Carstairs.

"True as Gospel," said Wharton.

"Do you know where the road is?" asked John. "Now that our horses are gone we've got to do some good walking."

"Here it is," said Carstairs. "Seven miles farther on is the little hamlet of Courville, where we can buy horses."

"Then walk, you terriers, walk!" said Wharton.

The three bending their heads walked side by side toward the hamlet of Courville, which they were destined never to reach.

11

T HE ARMORED CAR

THE THREE TALKED, because they were in the dark, and because they felt great joy over their escape. The clouds, after a while, floated away, and the thunder ceased to mutter. It seemed that the elements played with them, but, for the present, were in their favor. The walking itself was pleasant, as they were anxious to exercise their muscles after the long hard waiting in the grove.

But as the clouds went away and the stars came out, leaving a sky of blue, sown with stars, John could not keep from looking upward often. The aeroplanes and the daring men who flew them had made a tremendous impression upon him, and he constantly expected danger. But he saw none of those ominous black specks which could grow so fast into sinister shapes. He heard instead a faint rumbling ahead of them on the road to Courville, and he held up his hand as a warning.

"What is it?" asked Carstairs, as the three stopped.

"I don't know yet," replied John, "but the sound seems to be made by wheels."

"Perhaps a belated peasant driving home," said Wharton, as he listened.

"I don't think so. It appears to be a volume of sound, although it's as yet far away. I hear it better now. It's wheels and many of them."

"French reinforcements."

"Maybe, but more likely German. We've seen how ready the Germans are, and we know that they're spreading all over this region."

"Then it's safer for us out of the road than in it."

There was a hedge on either side of the road, but the three slipped easily through the one on the right, and stood in tall grass. The rumbling was steadily coming nearer, and John had no doubt it was made by Germans, perhaps some division seeking to get in the rear of the French forces with which he had fought.

There was a good moon and they saw well through the thin hedge. In ten minutes cyclers, riding six abreast, appeared on the crest of a low hill in the direction of Courville. The moonlight fell on their helmets and gray uniforms, showing, as John had expected, that they were Germans. Again he was beholding an example of the wonderful training and discipline, which had been continued for decades and which had put military achievement above everything else. Day and night the German hosts were advancing on France.

The cyclers, carrying their rifles before them, advanced in hundreds and hundreds, the files of six keeping perfectly even. Again the sight was unreal, productive of awe. Armies had never before gone to battle like this. The files close together, like a long, grayish-green serpent, moved swiftly along the road.

But it was not the wheels that had made the rumble. They instead gave out a light undulating sound, something like that of skaters on ice, and the three waited to see what was behind, as the rumbling grew louder.

The cyclers passed, then came the strong smell of gasoline, puffing sounds and the head of a great train of motor cars appeared. Most of the motors were filled with soldiers, others drew cannon and provision wagons. They were a full hour in passing, and at the rear were more than a hundred armored cars, also crowded with troops, some of them carrying machine guns also.

"I wish we were in one of those armored cars," said John, "then we wouldn't miss our horses."

"Well, why not get in one of them," said Carstairs.

"While we're about it why not wish for everything else that we can think of?"

"I mean exactly what I say. I didn't speak until I saw an opportunity. One of the cars seems to have something the matter with it and is drawing up by the side of the road not fifteen feet from us. The others have gone on, expecting it of course to catch up soon."

"Do you really mean what you suggest, Carstairs?" asked Wharton.

"I certainly do."

"Then what an Englishman suggests Yankees will perform."

"But with the help of the Englishman. Jove, what luck! There are only two men with the car. One is standing beside it, and the other is crawling under it. The machine is almost in the shadow of the hedge, and if we're smooth about it we can slip through, and be upon it, before we're seen."

"We must time ourselves. What's the plan?" asked Wharton.

"We'll assume when the man comes out from under the machine that he's fixed it. Then we'll make our rush, knock down the other fellow, jump into it and away. I'm an expert chauffeur, and I don't ask a better chance. Oh, fellows, what luck!"

"It's certainly favoring us," said Wharton, "and we must push it. It would be a crime to quit with such luck as this leading us on."

They slipped noiselessly through the hedge, and stood in its heavy shadow only a few feet from the car. They heard the man under it tapping with metal on metal. The other standing with his back to the three said a few words and the man replied.

"He says it's only a trifle, and it's all right now," whispered Carstairs, who understood German. "He's coming out from under the car. Now, fellows, for it!"

John struck the man standing beside the car with the butt of his rifle, but he did not make the blow hard--he could not bring himself to kill anybody in that manner. But the man fell senseless, and, just as his partner came from beneath it, the three leaped into the car, Carstairs threw on the speed, whirled about on air, it seemed to John, and left the German in the road, staring open-mouthed.

But the German recovered quickly and uttered a shout of alarm, drawing the attention of the armored motors, the rear files of which were not a hundred yards away.

"Down, you fellows!" cried Carstairs, who now took the lead. "Have your rifles ready to fire back, and enjoy what is going to be the greatest ride of your lives!"

Some wild spirit seemed to have taken hold of the Englishman. An expert driver, it may have been the touch of the wheel under his hand at such an exciting moment, and then it may have been the shots from the German cars that, in an instant, rattled upon the steel sides protecting the car.

"Hold fast, you fellows!" cried Carstairs, who bent low over the wheel, his flashing eyes now seeking to trace the road before them. "We are going to eat up the ground!"

The car gave its last dizzy lurch as it completed its circuit and shot ahead. John and Wharton had been thrown together, but they held on to their rifles and righted themselves. Then John noticed beside him the body and barrels of a machine gun, mounted and ready for use. He was the sharpshooter of the three and that gun appealed to him, as the car had appealed to Carstairs.

"Move over a little!" he shouted to Wharton.

"What are you going to do?"

"I'm going to fight that pursuing German army."

In an instant the machine gun began to crackle like a box of exploding crackers, sending back a hail of bullets which rattled upon the pursuing cars or found victims in them. But they, crouching down, were completely protected by the armor, and their careering machine made but a single target while they could fire into the pursuing mass.

Carstairs bent lower and lower. He had gone completely wild for the moment. Millions of sparks flew before his eyes. All the big and little pulses in his head and body were beating heavily. They had just scored two great triumphs. They had defeated the efforts of the masters of the air, and they had taken from their foe one of his most formidable weapons in which they might escape. His soul flamed with triumph, and that old familiar touch of the wheel filled him with the strength not of one giant, but of ten. He saw the road clearly now. There it lay ahead of them, long, white and sinuous, and he never doubted for a moment his ability to guide the armored car along in it at a mile a minute.

John in his turn was filled with the rage of battle. It was not often that one in his situation had a deadly machine gun at hand, ready to turn upon his enemies. While Wharton fed it from the great supply of ammunition in the car he turned a perfect stream of balls upon the pursuing motor, spraying it from side to side like a hose. Wharton looked up at his white strained face, in which his eyes burned like two coals of fire, and then he looked at the bent back and shoulders of Carstairs.

"Two madmen," he muttered. "A Britisher and a Yankee, mad at the same time and in the same place, and I'm their keeper! Good Lord, did a man ever before have such a job!"

Once he pulled John down a little as the machine guns in the pursuing car were getting the range, but behind the armored sheath of their car they were safe, for the present at least. Wharton regained his coolness and retained it. But he held to his belief that he rode a race with death, with one madman in front of him and another by his side.

Now and then the car took a frightful leap, and Wharton expected to land beneath it, but it always came down right, with Carstairs driving it faster and faster and Scott pouring balls from the machine gun and talking to it lovingly, as if it were a thing of life.

It was Wharton's grim thought that he was about to die soon, but that he would die gloriously. No common death for him, but one amid the crash of motors, machine guns and cannon. Meanwhile steel rained around them, but they were protected by the speed of their flight, and their armor. It was hard for the Germans to hit a fleeting target in a curving road, and the few balls or bullets that struck true fell harmless from the steel plates.

Wharton's own blood began to leap. The two with him in the car might be madmen, but they showed skill and vigor in their madness. The car sprang in the air, but it always came down safely. It whirled at times on a single wheel, but it would right itself, and go on at undiminished speed.

And the other madman at the gun did not neglect precautions. He kept himself well hidden behind the steel shield, and continued to spray the pursuing line from right to left and from left to right with a stream of projectiles.

On flew the car, down valleys and up slopes. It thundered across little ridges, and fled through strips of forest. Then Wharton amid their own roar heard the same deep steady rumble that had preceded the coming of the first German force. The sound was so similar he knew instinctively that it was made by a second detachment, advancing along the same road, but miles back. Their own headlong speed would carry them directly into it, and, as he saw it, they were completely trapped.

He leaned over, put a hand on the shoulder of Carstairs, and shouted in his ear:

"A second army of the enemy is in front, and we're going into it at the rate of a mile a minute!"

"Never mind!" Carstairs shouted back. "I know a little road not far ahead, leading off from this almost due westward. I'm going to take it, but it's a sharp turn. Hold tight you two!"

"For God's sake, Carstairs, slow up a little on the curve!"

But Carstairs made no answer. He did not even hear him now. He lay almost upon the wheel, and his eyes never left the track in front of him. He was the jockey riding his horse to victory in the greatest of all races.

Wharton ceased to feed the machine gun. The use for it had passed now. They were rapidly gaining on the pursuit, but the same speed was bringing them much nearer to the second force. He wondered if Carstairs really knew of that branch road, or if it were some wild idea flitting through his mad brain. As it was, he laid his rifle on the floor of the car, and commended his soul to God.

"Now!" suddenly shouted Carstairs, and it seemed to Wharton that they were whirling in a dizzy circle. Carstairs boasted afterwards that they made the curve on one wheel, but Wharton was quite sure that they made it on air.

They shot into a narrow road, not much more than a path leading through woods, and when Wharton looked back the pursuit was not in sight. They were now going almost at a right angle from either force, leaving both far behind, and Wharton suggested to Carstairs that he slow down--John had already ceased firing, because there was nothing to fire at. But his words were in vain. Carstairs would not yet come out of his frenzy. As John had talked to his gun he was now talking to his machine, bestowing upon it many adjectives of praise.

Wharton gave up the task as useless and sank back in his seat. He must let the fever spend itself. Besides he was gaining supreme confidence in the driving of Carstairs. The Englishman had shown such superb skill that Wharton was beginning to believe that he could drive the car a mile a minute anywhere save in a dense forest. So, he sank back in his seat, and relaxed mind and body.

They fled on over a road narrow but good. They passed lone farm houses sitting back in the fields, but Wharton had only a glimpse of them. A tile roof, a roar from the car and they were gone.

Yet the fever of Carstairs slowly burned itself out. They had long since been safe from any pursuit by the Germans in the main road, and now the young Englishman realized it. He took one hand from the wheel, and dashed back a lock of hair that had fallen over his brow. Then he slowed down quickly, and when they were going not more than seven or eight miles an hour he said like one coming out of an ecstasy.

"Don't the Germans build splendid cars?"

"And fine machine guns, too?" said John, in a high-pitched unnatural voice.

"Now here is where I take command," said Wharton firmly. "You two have been madmen, as mad as anybody can be, although it's true that your madness has saved us. But you've done your great deeds, sanity is returning, and you're in a state of exhaustion. Carstairs, give me the wheel at once. I'm not much of a driver, but I can take the car along safely at a rate of five miles an hour, which is all we need now."

Carstairs, the fires within him burned out wholly now, resigned the wheel to his comrade, and sank limply into a seat beside John.

"Now you two rest," said Wharton, sternly, "and if I hear a word out of either of you in the next hour I'll turn the machine gun on you."

They obeyed. Each was a picture of physical collapse. Wharton did not know much about automobiles. In the driver's seat he felt as if he were steering a liner, but in such case as his one readily takes risks, and he sent the machine along slowly and with fair success.

It was beginning to lighten somewhat, and he looked for a village.

They must have food, a fresh supply of gasoline, and news of their own army. They bore letters which they meant to deliver or die.

The same beautiful country, though less hilly, stretched before them. Many clear little streams flowed through the valleys, and here and there were groves free from undergrowth. Wharton believed that they were far toward the west, and near the British troops--if any had yet been landed in France.

"Are you two still in a convalescent stage?" he asked, glancing back.

"Getting along nicely, doctor, thank you, sir," said John. "I began to pick up just as soon as we left those German armies out of sight."

Then he turned to the comrade, sitting beside him.

"Carstairs, old man," he said, "I don't know what you are, at home, but here you're the greatest chauffeur that ever lived! I believe you could drive a car sixty miles an hour all day long on a single wheel!"

"Thanks, old man," said Carstairs, grasping his hand, "I didn't have time to look back, but I knew from the sounds that you were working a machine gun, as one was never worked before; fast enough by Jove to drive off a whole hostile army."

"You two have organized the greatest log rolling society in existence," said Wharton, "but you've been brave and good boys. Now let's take a look at this glorious car of ours which we had specially built for us in Germany."

The light in the east was increasing, and for the first time they made an examination of their capture. Despite the armor and presence of the machine gun it was upholstered in unusual style, with cushions and padded sides in dark green leather. There were many little lockers and fittings not to be found often in a car intended for war. On a tiny silver plate under the driver's seat a coat of arms was engraved. John, who was the first to catch sight of it, exclaimed:

"This car belongs to some duke or prince. Carstairs, you're a subject and not a citizen, and you ought to be up on all kinds of nobility worship. What coat of arms is this?"

"I don't know," replied Carstairs, "and I'm as free a man as you are, I'd have you to know."

"Breaking the treaty already," chuckled Wharton. "It doesn't matter whether we know the coat of arms or not. It's likely that the man standing in the road, the one whom John hit over the head with the gun was the duke or prince. Oh, if the Germans ever get you, Scott, they'll break you on the wheel for such an extreme case of *Majestätsbeleidigung!*"

"And if you pronounce that word again you'll break your jaw," said John. "Let's open all these lockers. We may find spoils of war."

It seemed a good suggestion, and taking the monkey wrench they broke open every locker. They found a pair of splendid field glasses, shaving materials, other articles of the toilet, and a tiny roll of fine tissue paper.

"I've an idea that we have something of value here," said John, as he held up the little roll. "It's in German, which I don't understand. Take it, Wharton."

There were six small sheets, and as Wharton translated them aloud and slowly they realized that in very truth they had made a precious capture. They contained neither address nor signature, but they notified the commander of the extreme German right wing that a British force would shortly appear near the Belgian border, on the extreme allied left, that it would be a small army, and that it could be crushed by a rapid, enveloping movement.

"The prince or duke whom you hit over the head, John," said Wharton, "was carrying this. He did not put it in his pocket, because he never dreamed of such a thing as the one that happened to him. But one thing is sure: our obligation to reach the allied force in the west is doubled and tripled. We three, obscure as we may be, may carry with us the fate of an army."

"He called us two madmen," said John, nudging Carstairs. "Now look at our good sober Wharton going mad with responsibility."

Wharton did not notice them. He was turning over and over the sheets of tissue paper, and his eyes glowed. His hands trembled, too, as he handled the precious document, but he did not let a single page fall.

"Glorious! splendid! magnificent!" he exclaimed. "By our capture, by our own courage and skill, and by ours alone we'll save the allied left wing from destruction."

The timeliness of their exploit, the wonderful chance had gone to Wharton's head. He forgot for the time his comrades, the motor, and the morning sun over the fields and the forest. He thought only of their arrival in the allied camp with those precious documents.

John and Carstairs exchanged glances again. They had come quite back to earth, but there could be no doubt that Wharton was taking an ascension.

"We'll treat him kindly," said Carstairs.

"Of course," said John. "Old friend of ours, you know. Been with us through the wars. But I want to tell you, Carstairs, and I hope I won't hurt your feelings, you being a monarchist, that I'm glad I hit that prince such a solid smash over the head. It will always be a pleasure to me to remember that I knocked out a royalty, and I hope he wasn't any mediatized prince either."

"Don't apologize to me. He was only a German prince, and they're so numerous they don't count British princes are the real thing."

"Stop talking foolishness you two!" exclaimed Wharton. "You ramble on, and we carry the fate of Europe in our hands! My God, we've wasted a quarter of an hour here talking! Carstairs, get back in the driver's seat, and I don't care how fast you drive! Scott, take your place at the machine gun, and shoot down anything that opposes us!"

"Mad! Quite mad!" John and Carstairs said together, but they obeyed with amazing promptness, and in a minute the car was spinning down the road at a great rate. But Wharton leaning forward and looking with red eyes in black rims, saw nothing they passed. He had instead a vision of the three arriving at some point far away with the prince's dispatches, and of English and French generals thanking those who had come in time to save them.

Carstairs drove with a steady hand, but he was his normal self now. He had seen that their supply of gasoline was sufficient to last a while, and he was content for the present with a moderate rate of speed. If they were pursued again then he could make another great burst, but he did not consider it likely that a third force of the foe would appear. They must be getting beyond the vanguard of the German invasion.

John sat beside Wharton. The machine gun was at rest, but he kept his rifle across his knee. Nevertheless he did not anticipate any further danger. He felt an immense satisfaction over their achievements, but the danger and strain had been so great that rest seemed the finest thing in the world. He hoped they would soon come to another of those neat French inns, where they would surely be welcome.

But Wharton was not thinking of inns and rest. He took out the dispatches and read them a second time. Then he folded them up triumphantly and put them back in his pocket again. His soul burned with ardor. Their fights with the aeroplanes and the armored cars were alike forgotten. They must get forward with the prince's dispatches.

The sun came over the slopes, and the day grew fast. John fell asleep in his seat with his rifle across his knees. He was aroused by the stopping of the car and the murmur of many voices. He sat upright and was wide awake all in a moment.

They had come to the village for which they had wished so ardently and they were surrounded by people who looked curiously at the car, the heavy dents in its armor, the machine gun, and, with the most curiosity of all, at the three occupants.

But their looks were friendly. The three in the car wore the French uniform, and while obviously they were not French, it was equally obvious that they were friends of France. John smiled at them and asked the burning question:

"Is there an inn here?"

They pointed across the street. There it was snug and unimpeach-able. Carstairs drove slowly to the front of it, and he and John meanwhile answered a torrent of questions. Yes, they had been in a fight with Germans, and, after seizing one of their armored cars, they had escaped in it. But it was true that the Germans were coming into France by all the main roads, and the people must be ready.

There were many exclamations of dismay, and the questions they asked John and Carstairs never ceased. But they said nothing to Whar-ton. His stern, absent expression did not invite confidences. He was looking over their heads at something far away, and he seemed merely to be going into the inn, because his comrades were doing so.

The three found the breakfast good as usual. Gasoline could be obtained. It was not for civilians, but as they were soldiers serving France they were able to buy a supply. The news that they desired was scarce, although there was a vast crop of rumors which many told as facts. John was learning that war was the mother of lies. He believed only what men had seen with their own eyes, and but little of that. It was incredible how people described in detail things they had witnessed, but which had never occurred.

Had a British army landed? It had. It had not. Where was it? It was in Belgium. It was in France. It was at the training camps in England. There was plenty of information, and one could choose whatever he liked best. John and Carstairs looked at each other in dismay. They had a car, but where were they to go. At least they carried dispatches for a British army which some of the French believed to be in France. But Wharton took no notice of the difficulty. He was silent, and preoccupied with their triumphant arrival that was coming.

John asked the most questions, and at last he found a woman whose words seemed to be based upon fact and not imagination. She had a cousin who was employed in the telegraph, and her cousin told her, that British troops had landed, that some of them at least had reached Paris, and then had gone north toward Belgium, the region of Mons or Charleroi, she believed. She spoke quietly and with much detail, and John believed that she had a mind able to tell the truth without exaggeration.

He held a brief conference with Carstairs, who had now replenished the gasoline, and who had also put stores of food in the car. Carstairs agreed with him that the statement was probably correct, and that at any rate they ought to govern themselves in accordance with it. They did not consult Wharton, who they knew was thinking only of the papers.

John took the wheel. Like Wharton he did not know much about driving, but it was a time when one had to do things. Carstairs soon fell asleep, but Wharton sat rigidly erect, staring before him.

John had felt the emotion of triumph strongly that morning, but now much of it was departing. The country was growing more beautiful than ever. He had never seen any outside his own to match it. This had the advantage of age and youth combined. Buildings were gray and soft with centuries, but the earth itself was fresh and eternal with youth. But he knew beyond any shred of doubt that it would soon be torn to pieces by the fighting millions.

There was no occasion for haste now, as they must feel the way, and they were beyond the German advance. While Carstairs slept and

Wharton stared ahead he examined the country. Once they passed near a town of considerable size, and he saw on a hill, in the center of it a great gray cathedral, its fine stonework glittering like tracery.

Then he saw the graybeards, the women, and the young boys and girls coming into the fields to work. All the men of fighting age were gone. He had seen the same in Germany, but it struck him anew with painful force, this turning of millions of workers upon one another, weapons in hand.

John stopped beside the fields once or twice and talked with the peasants. The old men could tell him nothing. They were stolid and stoical. Yes, there was war, but it was not any business of theirs to find where the armies were marching, and his heart went out more strongly than ever to the people, over whom military ambition and the folly of kings were driving the wheels of cannon.

It was well toward midday before he secured any real information. They encountered at the crossing of a brook a small French patrol under a lieutenant, an intelligent man, whom by lucky chance Carstairs had met two weeks before.

He told them that going at a moderate rate they could reach by the next morning a large French army which lay north and west. Some British troops--he did not know how many--had come up, and they were on the extreme left of the allied line. More were expected. In front of them were great masses of the Germans.

They gave him their own news, and then with mutual good wishes they drove on, Carstairs now at the wheel, and their pace increased. It was agreed that they should hasten much more, as soon as they were absolutely sure of the way. Wharton, for the first time, took part in the talk.

"When we have a definite point to aim at," he said, "we must take every risk and race for it. If we don't deliver these documents promptly to the generals we ought to be shot."

"We won't be shot for the lack of trying, Wharton," said John, "but if we go racing along the wrong road we'll be that much farther from our right direction."

"We ought to see more patrols soon," said Carstairs. "They'll surely be watching all through this region."

"Likely enough we'll find 'em in that wood ahead," said John, pointing to a long stretch of forest that clothed a group of hills. "It's just the place for 'em. From the top of that highest hill they can see for miles."

Carstairs increased their speed, and the car shot forward. It was a fine motor, John thought, and the bombardment it had received had not hurt it much. That German prince certainly knew how to select a car, and he had fortified it in a splendid manner.

John was smiling to himself again in satisfaction, as they dipped down the valley and entered the forest, which in that country they would certainly call a great one. Its shade was pleasant, too, as the beams of the sun were now vertical and hot.

"Nice region," said John approvingly. "See that old castle off there to the left."

An ancient castle, decayed and abandoned, crowned a little hill. Around it was a moat dry for generations, and one of the Norman towers had fallen down. It was a somber picture of lonely desolation.

"I suppose some fine old robber of a baron lived in that," said John, "and preyed upon the country, until he reached the hunting grounds of other robbers like himself."

"Deucedly draughty and uncomfortable they must have been," said Carstairs. "We've some of 'em in my country, but they must have been pretty hard living for my lord and my lady."

"I don't see that we have much advantage over those old fellows," said John thoughtfully. "They were little robbers, and here are all the countries of Europe trying to tear one another to pieces. After all, Carstairs, I'm beginning to think the Americans are the only really civilized people."

Carstairs grinned.

"You can't do it, Scott," he said, "you can't take Wharton's place. I'll argue with him about the merits of Briton and Yankee. It's his time-honored right, but I'll have no dispute with you."

Wharton smiled a stern assent.

"Then we'll let it go," said John, "but do you notice that this is a real forest. It must cover a half dozen square miles. I suppose that in your country they would call it the Royal Forest or by some such high-sounding name."

"Never you mind what we'd call it," rejoined Carstairs, "but whatever it is it's evident that something violent is going on within its shades! Listen!"

John started upright in his seat, as he heard the crackle of three or four shots so close together that they were almost in a volley, and then the sound of feet running swiftly. They stopped the machine, and a figure, stained, bleeding and desperate, emerged from the forest.

"A fugitive!" exclaimed John.

"But from what?" said Carstairs.

"The Germans, of course!" said Wharton.

The man, stained with blood, ragged and dirty came at great bounds, and before any one could put out a detaining hand he sprang into the car.

"Help, for God's sake!" he cried. "I'm a spy in the service of France, and the Uhlans are coming down through the wood after me!"

"Help you!" exclaimed Carstairs. "Of course we will! Any friend of France is a friend of ours!"

He bent low over the wheel once more in his old speeding attitude, and the car shot forward like an arrow.

12

THE ABANDONED CHÂTEAU

JOHN GLANCED BACK toward the point from which the shots had come, but it was already hidden by the curve of the hill. Moreover, the car was going so fast now that the Uhlans would be left as if standing still, and he turned his attention to the man who had crumpled at his very feet.

The stranger lay in a heap on the floor of the car, his breath coming in short gasps from sobbing lungs. There were red stains on the arms and right shoulder of his coat. John felt a great pity and dragged him into one of the seats. Then he uttered a cry of surprise. The features under their mask of blood and dirt were familiar.

"Weber!" he exclaimed.

Weber stared back.

"You, whom I met at the inn!" he said, "and your friends!"

"Yes, we're all here," said John cheerily. "This is indeed a singular chance!"

"A most fortunate one for me," said Weber, straightening himself, and endeavoring to arrange his clothing--it appeared that his pride was returning. "After this I shall think that Providence is watching over me. A man on foot seeking to escape has little chance against horsemen. I saw the automobile moving slowly and I sprang into it, intending to make the appeal which has been successful."

"Look who's here," said John to his comrades. "We've rescued Weber, the Alsatian, from the Uhlans. Battered a bit, but still in the ring and good for many another escape."

"So it is," said Carstairs, reaching back a hand. "We happened along just in time, Weber. It's a way we three have. I've no doubt that we'll rescue you at least a half dozen times more."

Weber grasped the proffered hand and shook it eagerly. Wharton bowed in a friendly manner, but he was still preoccupied. His hand rested on that point in his coat, beneath which the papers lay, and his thoughts were not with the fourth arrival in the car.

"Your wounds!" said John. "This is an automobile of princes, and for the present we are the princes. I've no doubt we can find in these lockers and drawers material of which to make bandages."

"They're slight. They don't matter," said Weber. "Pay no attention to them at a time like this. I know that you must be going toward the main French army, and time is of value. My strength is coming back now, and my courage, too. I will admit I was frightened. I thought my time had come. Perhaps that may seem a disgraceful confession, but it's true."

"Not disgraceful at all," said John sympathetically. "I haven't been a soldier more than a few days, but it's been long enough to teach me that brave men are often scared. What were you doing and how did you happen to come so near to being caught?"

"I've been inside the German lines. Oh, they're not so far away! And I was slipping out I had passed all, but a body of Uhlans, under a captain, von Boehlen, an uncommonly shrewd man. If I had been caught by him I would now be singing with the angels in Paradise."

He smiled faintly.

"I've met von Boehlen," said John, "and if he suspected you, you acted wisely to run with all your might. I saw him in Dresden on the eve of the war, and I've seen him since, though at some distance."

"We'll forget my narrow escape now," said Weber cheerfully.

"One can't remember such things long in these times."

"They're tremendous times."

"So tremendous that as soon as you've made one escape with your life you're due for another."

"You haven't heard of any Germans on this road?"

"No, but they're raiding far and wide, and von Boehlen will attempt anything."

"We've had uncommon luck so far, and I think it will continue. I see you're admiring our automobile. I wasn't jesting, when I told you it belonged to a prince."

"It's rather small for an armored car. They usually have seven or eight men in them."

"Yes, and it's fortunate for us that it's small. I told you luck was running our way. But as it is, it's a pretty heavy strain on the man at the wheel, although Carstairs there is an expert."

"I'm a pretty good chauffeur," said Weber, "and whenever Mr. Carstairs wishes it I'll relieve him at the wheel. Besides I know the country thoroughly, and I can take advantage of every short cut."

"I'll call on you soon," said Carstairs. "A lot of my enthusiasm for speeding has gone out of me. My arms ache all the time, but I'm good for another hour yet."

Weber did not insist. John understood why, as it was patent that he needed rest. He made himself comfortable in the seat, and the others left him in peace. The machine rolled on swiftly and smoothly. It was one of the beautiful roads so common in France, and John felt scarcely a jar. A full sun tinted the green country with gold.

The warmth was penetrating and soothing. John had lost so much sleep and the nervous drain had been so great that his eyelids became heavy. They came to a clear little brook, and decided to stop that all might have a drink. Weber used the chance also to bathe his face and hands and get rid entirely of blood, dirt and dust. He seemed then to John a rather handsome man, having the touch of the scholar in his face.

John walked about a little, stretching his arms, and thumping his chest in order to make himself more wakeful. But when he returned to the automobile, and sat down in the cushioned seat the old sleepiness returned. The effort to keep the eyelids from going down was painful. Carstairs in the driver's seat also yawned prodigiously.

"All my strength has returned now, and my nerve has come with it," said Weber. "Let me take the wheel. I see that you three are exhausted, as well you may be after such tremendous energy and so many dangers. I don't boast, when I say that I'm a good driver."

"Take the wheel, and welcome," said Carstairs, yawning prodigiously and retreating to a seat in the body of the car, beside John.

It was evident that Weber understood automobiles. He handled the wheel with a practised hand, and sent it forward with a skill and delicacy of touch equal to that of Carstairs.

"It is, indeed, a beautiful machine," he said. "Splendid work went into the making of it, and I can well believe as you do that it belonged to a prince."

John's sleepiness increased. The motion was so smooth and pleasant! And the absence of danger and strained effort lulled one to slumber. He fought it off, and then concluded that he was foolish. Why shouldn't he go to sleep? Carstairs was asleep already and Wharton, who felt such a tremendous weight of responsibility, was nodding. His eyelids fell. He raised them with a desperate effort, but they fell again and remained closed.

When John awoke a dimness over the western hills showed that the twilight was advancing. Through sleepy eyes he saw Weber's back as he bent a little over the wheel, steering steadily. The road now led through forest.

"Where are we, Weber?" he asked.

"Ah, awake are you," said the Alsatian, not looking back. "You saved my life, but it was most fortunate that you had the chance of doing it. Otherwise all of you would have perished from lack of sleep."

"Lack of sleep? What's that?" exclaimed Carstairs, waking up and hearing the last words. "Why, I'm always lacking sleep. I believe the greatest hardship of war is the way it deprives you of sleep. When I've helped take Berlin, Hamburg, Munich and other important German cities, and this war's over, I'm going back to England to sleep a month, and if anybody wakes me before the right time there'll be a merry civil war in that blessed isle."

Wharton, who had been somewhat uneasy in his sleep, woke up in turn, and his hand flew to his tightly buttoned coat. But he felt the papers safely there and his heart resumed its natural beat. Yet he was angry with himself. No man who carried perhaps the fate of a continent should ever close his eyes a moment.

"We're crossing a range of hills," said Weber, replying as soon as he could to John's question. "We've been making good time. We ought to strike the French line by midnight and then our journey will be over."

"And I'll be glad when we get there," said Carstairs. "I love automobiles, but I've had enough for the present even of such a fine machine as this. I judge that we slept well, Mr. Weber."

"I never saw two sleep better," replied Weber. "Mr. Wharton was a little troubled in his slumbers though."

"Oh, he's a very grave individual with great responsibilities," said Carstairs.

But he did not add anything about the dispatches.

"A little farther back," said Weber, "I saw a biplane. Although it was high in air I'm quite sure from its make that it was German."

"Scouting," said John. "It was pretty venturesome to come this far west."

"The Germans shun no risks," said Weber, gravely. "The biplane flew back toward the east. It did not alarm me greatly, but I saw another thing that did. Just before you awoke I noticed a gleam in the valley to the right, and I know that it was made by a sunbeam falling on the spiked helmet of a Uhlan."

The three stiffened with alarm, not so much for themselves as for their errand. Wharton's hand moved again toward the pocket, containing the papers, which had transformed him into a man with but a single thought.

"Uhlans here close to this road!" exclaimed John.

"Do you think it can be von Boehlen?"

"It may be. On the whole I think it probable," replied Weber. "Von Boehlen is a most daring man, and to scout along the skirts of the French army would be the most natural thing for him to do. I'm going to speed up a bit--that is, if you gentlemen agree that it's necessary."

"Of course," said John, and the machine sprang forward. He had taken the prince's glasses as his own share of the spoil. They were of great power, and now he searched the forest with them for their enemies. He soon found that Weber was right. He saw steel helmets on the right, and then he saw them on the left. They were surely Uhlans, and evidently they had seen the car.

He quickly put away the glasses and snatched up his rifle.

"You were right, Weber," he exclaimed. "They're German cavalry, and they've begun to pursue us. Faster! Faster! This machine can leave any horsemen behind!"

Weber turned back a despairing face.

"The car is doing its best!" he said. "Something has gone wrong with the machinery!"

He wrenched at the wheel, but he produced no such speed as that which Carstairs had got out of the car, when they were fleeing from the German automobiles. The two forces of Uhlans had now joined and were in the road galloping in swift pursuit. Many of them carried lances, which glittered in the late sun. The sight of the steel points made John shiver. It would be horrible to feel one of them in his back.

He turned to his machine gun. A touch of that old madness returned. The sight of the Uhlans had set his brain on fire.

"I'll teach you not to come too close, my fine lads," he said.

He aimed the gun and undertook to start the mechanism, but nothing moved. No shots came. He jerked at it widly, but it refused to budge. It was jammed, and it would take a long time to put it in order. His heart stood still and a cold perspiration came out on his face. How did it happen? Was it possible that he had left it in such a condition?

"What's the matter, John?" asked Wharton.

"The machine gun's jammed, and I can't fire a shot. The car seems to be breaking down, too. Don't you see that the Uhlans are gaining!"

"So, they are," said Wharton.

He and John snatched up their rifles and fired rapidly at the horsemen. Some of the bullets struck, but did not impede the pursuit. Carstairs pushed Weber out of the driver's seat, and seized the wheel himself. All his pride and confidence were aroused, and he did not have time to be polite. He could get the speed out of that machine and save them.

But it did not obey his hand. It staggered along like a tired man. Weber was right again. Something had gone wrong with the internal organism, and one could not stop to right it with pursuing Uhlans only a few hundred yards away.

"What shall we do?" exclaimed Weber. "Shall we jump for it and run? We may escape in the shelter of the forest?"

"Not yet," replied Carstairs firmly. "Not yet for three of us, though it may be best for you, since you'll be executed as a spy, when you're taken."

"If you don't go, I don't go either," said Weber. "We'll all stay together."

"Brave man!" said Carstairs admiringly. But he had time for no more words. He was wrenching at the machine as a rider for his life would pull at the mouth of a stubborn horse. Crippled as it was he managed to drag a little increase of speed from it. The Uhlans had dropped back somewhat and none of them fired. John believed that they refrained because they were sure of a capture. Wharton suddenly uttered a cry.

"A river," he exclaimed. "It's not more than five hundred yards ahead!"

His cry was echoed by Weber, but its tone was very different. The Alsatian's voice showed despair.

"I had forgotten," he exclaimed. "The river is too deep for fording, and the French have blown up the bridge! We're trapped!"

A deep flush came into the face of Carstairs. As in the case of John a touch of his first madness was returning. The three comrades were now wild together.

"Can you swim?" he shouted back to John.

"Yes!"

"And you?" to Wharton.

"Yes!"

"And you, too?" to Weber.

"Yes, fairly well; but what do you mean?"

"You wait two or three minutes and you'll see something. But when it's time to swim all of you be ready for it!"

A great shout came from the Uhlans, who had begun to gain again, and who could not now keep from seeing the river that cut off the fugitives. But Carstairs wrenched another pound or two of speed out of the automobile, and it shot forward.

"Stop! Stop for God's sake!" cried Weber. "You'll drown us all! It's better to jump out and take to the woods!"

"Never!" cried Carstairs, his daring flaming to the utmost. "We captured the automobile of a prince, and we'll not give it back again! Ah, the machine is returning to life! Look how much faster we're going! On, my beauty! Your last and greatest run is before you!"

The machine seemed to come out of its maimed and crippled condition, its strength flaring up for the last burst of speed. The jarring and jerking ceased and the road flew behind it.

The river came near at an astonishing rate, and John saw that it was wide and deep. He saw, too, the pillars of the ruined bridge, and he heard another cry from Weber, who started to spring out, but drew back.

Carstairs uttered a wild shout, and then the automobile, leaping far out into the stream, where the bridge had been, sank beneath the deep waters. John had prepared himself for the desperate stroke, and before the machine touched the surface he had sprung clear. Then he struck out desperately for the opposite bank, and his heart filled with gladness, when he saw Wharton and Carstairs swimming almost by his side.

They reached the shore before the Uhlans could come up, and darted into the shelter of the forest, where they threw themselves down on the ground and lay panting, every touch of wildness gone.

"Is Weber here?" asked John.

"No," replied Wharton, who felt of his papers again, and saw that they were wet, but safe.

"Did either of you see him?"

"Not after the auto made its jump."

"Then he must have been drowned. Poor fellow! But I'd rather be drowned than be executed as a spy."

It saddened them. They had learned to like Weber, and, having saved him once, they were sorry they could not save him twice. But one could not mourn long at such a time. The more daring of the Uhlans would certainly swim the river and continue the pursuit, and it was for the three to hide their trail as soon as possible. John rose first.

"Come, boys," he said. "Our clothes will dry faster while we're running."

"Put it that way if you like," said Carstairs. "At any rate I'm going to toddle."

They had lost their rifles, but they had their automatic pistols which might be of service in spite of their dips, but they wished to avoid the need of their use. They already heard the splashes as the Uhlans made their horses leap into the river, and they ran at their best speed through the forest, coming presently to a vineyard, which they crossed between the rows of vines, finding a high wire fence on the other side. As they darted between the strands they recognized that they could have no better barrier between them and pursuing horsemen.

Near them on the left was a large château, with a flower garden in front and a kitchen garden behind. They resisted the inevitable temptation of man to run to a roof for shelter and protection, and sped instead into the dense foliage and shrubbery that spread away toward the fields. There they threw themselves down again and panted for the breath that came so hardly through their exhausted lungs.

But they did not hear the sinister tread of the Uhlans, nor did they notice the presence of any human being, a fact which for the present failed to impress them, because the Uhlans filled their minds. Five minutes, ten, fifteen passed and still no sound.

"Perhaps they think we're drowned," whispered John. "They were not near enough to see us swim away from the automobile."

"I hope you're right, and maybe you are," said Wharton. "In any case I don't think they'll hunt for us long. We're not important enough for them to waste time on when they're so near the French lines."

"I'm going to stay where I am until I hear the tread of hoofs," said Carstairs. "I'm drying fast and it's comfortable lying here under the vines. You didn't lose those papers, when we were in the river; did you, Wharton?"

"They're safe in my pocket," replied Wharton, "and I had them wrapped up so thoroughly that they didn't have a chance to get wet."

"If the Uhlans don't find us in the next half hour," said John, "it's quite certain they won't find us at all. They won't spend more time than that on us."

Then they lay quite still, sheltered well under the vines. Their armored car, the car of the prince was now lying at the bottom of the river, but it had served them well. John was sure that they would find some other means of reaching the Franco-British army. He was fast learning that ways nearly always opened to daring and persistence.

The half hour passed, and no Uhlans appeared. They had crossed the river, as the splashes indicated, but, doubtless, finding no trail of the fugitives, they had believed them pinned under the car at the bottom of the river, and had gone away on some other more profitable quest.

But the three waited another half hour for the sake of precaution, and then came from under the vines. Twilight was now at hand, and they realized that they were physically weak after so much excitement and exertion.

"I might be able to limp along through the night," said Wharton, "but I doubt it."

"I know I can't," said Carstairs.

"Why try to go on?" said John. "Here's a house. Being in France it must be inhabited by French sympathizers. They'll shelter us and give us food."

"I think we'd better try it," said Carstairs.

"I agree with you," said Wharton, "but I think it strange that we've seen nobody attached to this place. So large a house and grounds must have at least twenty people about, and an affair like ours would certainly attract their attention. Yet, we see nobody."

"That's so," said John. "Suppose we wait a bit--it's darkening fast--and see what's happened."

They still stood among the vines, and, as the night was coming on and their clothing was only partially dried, they shivered with chill. The tile roof of the château, showing among the trees looked attractive. But no light appeared in any of the windows, and not a sound came from the house itself, nor any of the buildings about it.

The windows glittered like fire with the last rays of the sun, and then the darkness soon swept down, heavy and thick. The three holding their automatics, and shivering in the chill wind of the night, approached the silent château. John felt a little awe, too. Chance certainly was taking him into strange places, and he was devoutly glad that he had two good comrades by his side.

They passed out of the vineyard and entered the grounds, which were large, adorned with ancient trees, several statues, and a fountain, in which the water was still playing. The moonlight, coming out now, gave to the château an appearance of great age.

"I fancy that some old noble family lived here," he said. "It must have been quite a place once."

"Whoever they are, evidently they have no welcome for us," said Carstairs, "but I'm going in, anyhow. Whew, this wind cuts to the bone!"

"I'm just as cold as you are," said John, "and I'm just as much resolved as you are to find shelter here, whether I'm asked in or not. It may belong to a noble family, but I'm a nobleman myself, a king, one of a hundred million American kings."

"Then, king, you lead," said Carstairs. "It's your place. Go right up those steps."

A half dozen marble steps led to the great central door, and John walked up boldly, followed closely by the others. He lifted a huge brass knocker, and beat heavily with it again and again. No sound came back but its echo.

"Push, king," said Carstairs. "Any door will open to royalty. Besides your majesty has been insulted by the refusal to answer your summons."

John pushed hard, and the great door swung back slowly, quivering a little, but with the automatic in his hand, he walked into a hall, the other two at his shoulders. They closed the door behind them and stood there for a little space, accustoming their eyes to the dusk.

It was a long hall with tall windows, through which a faint light filtered. To the right was a stairway, on the first step of which was a figure, of complete medieval armor. Several faded pictures of ancient knights hung on the walls.

"It's old, very old," said Carstairs, "but its owners, whoever they are, have left with all their people. There's nobody to dispute our claim to lodgings, but did you ever see anything more lonesome?"

"There's a double door, leading into the interior of the house," said John. "Let's explore."

They entered a large apartment which John took to be the drawing-room. It was at once splendid and dignified, furnished in a style at least two centuries old. John liked it, and thought what it would be when it was filled with light and people.

A magnificent chandelier hung from the ceiling, and there were ornamented sconces about the walls, all containing many candles.

Evidently the owner of this château scorned such modern lights as gas and electricity.

"We might light a candle or two," said Carstairs. "Doubtless we can find matches about."

"No! No!" exclaimed Wharton. "I'm not at all sure that we're safe here from intrusion!"

"Think you're right," said Carstairs. "Let's explore further."

"Then I vote that we go downward," said John. "I've gathered from my reading that in the big European houses the kitchens are below stairs, and just now a kitchen will be much more welcome to me than a drawing-room."

True to John's reading the kitchen and storerooms were in the basement. Nothing had been disturbed, and they found ample food. Carstairs discovered a wine cellar, and he returned with a bottle of champagne.

"It's an old and famous vintage," he said, "and there'll be no harm in taking one."

"Here's a furnace in the cook-room," said John, "and billets of wood. Suppose we make a fire, and dry ourselves thoroughly while we eat and drink. It's too far down for the reflections of the flames to be seen outside."

The others promptly agreed with him. All wanted to get rid of the wet chill which struck so deeply into their bodies. A search disclosed matches, and John built the fire which was soon burning redly in the furnace. What a glorious warmth it threw out! It created them anew, and they realized that light and heat were the great vital elements of the world.

They drew a table before the fire, and put upon it the food and the bottle of champagne.

"We've been made welcome here after all," said John. "The souls of the absent owners have provided these things for us."

"That's dreamy sort of talk, John," said Wharton.

"Maybe, but I'll go further and say that the house itself invited us to come in. I've an idea that a house doesn't like to be abandoned and lonely. It prefers to be filled with people and to hear the sounds of voices and laughter. These old European houses which have sheltered generation after generation must be the happiest houses of all. I'd like to live in a house like this and I'd like for a house like this to like me. It would help life a lot for a house and its occupant to be satisfied with each other."

"We feel that way in England about our old country houses," said Carstairs, "and you'll come to it, too, in America, after a while."

"No doubt, but will you have a little more of this champagne? Only a half glass. I don't believe the owner, who must be a fine French gentleman, would ever begrudge it to us."

"Just a little. We're rather young for champagne, we three, but we've been doing men's work, and we've been through men's dangers. I wonder what they're doing along the Strand, tonight, John!"

"The same that they've been doing every night for the last hundred years. But you listen to me, Carstairs, old England will have to wake up. This war can't be won by dilettantes."

"Oh, she'll wake up. Don't you worry. It's not worth while to get excited."

"To take a serious view of a serious situation is not to grow excited. You Britishers often make me tired. To pretend indifference in the face of everything is obviously an affectation, and becomes more offensive than boasting."

"All right, I won't resent it. Here, John, take another piece of this cold ham. I didn't know they had such fine ham in France."

"They've a lot of splendid things in France," retorted John, in high, good humor, "and we'll find it out fast. I'm thinking the French soldiers will prove a good deal better than some people say they are, and this château is certainly fine. It must have been put here for our especial benefit."

"Now that we've eaten all we want and our clothing is dried thoroughly," said Carstairs, "I suggest that we put out the fire. There isn't much smoke, but it goes up that flue and escapes somewhere. Even in the night the Germans might see it."

"Good advice, Carstairs," said Wharton. "You're as intelligent sometimes as the Americans are all the time."

"Pleasant children you Americans."

"Some day we'll save the aged English from destruction."

"Meanwhile we'll wait."

They extinguished the fire, carefully put away all the dishes they had used, restored everything to its pristine neatness, and then the three yawned prodigiously.

"Bedrooms next," said Carstairs.

"Do you propose that we spend the night here," said Wharton.

"That's my idea. We're worn out. We've got to sleep, somewhere. No use breaking ourselves down, and we've found the château here waiting for us."

"What about the Germans?"

"We'll have to take our chances. War is nothing but a chain of chances, so far as your life is concerned."

The other two wanted to be persuaded, and they yielded readily, but John insisted upon one precaution.

"Old houses like this are likely to have isolated chambers," he said. "Some of them I suppose have their secret rooms, and if we can find such a place, lock the door on ourselves, and go to sleep in it we're not likely to wake up prisoners of the Germans."

Wharton and Carstairs approved of his suggestion, and they examined the house thoroughly. John concluded from the presence of all the furniture and the good order in which they found everything that the departure of its owners had been hasty, perhaps, too, with the expectation of a return on the morrow.

The room that they liked best they found on the third floor, not a secret chamber, but one that chance visitors to the house would not be likely to see. A narrow stairway starting near it led down through the rear of the house, and the door was fastened with a heavy lock in which the key remained.

It contained only some boxes, and John surmised that it was a store-room. But it seemed to suit their purpose admirably, and, bringing blankets from one of the bedrooms, they made their beds on the floor.

John was the last to go to sleep. The others were slumbering soundly before he lay down, but he stood a little while at the single window, looking out. The window was closed ordinarily with a heavy shutter, which was now sagging open. The boughs of a great tree waved almost against it.

The night was clear, but John saw nothing unusual outside. The château, and all its buildings and grounds were bathed in clear moon-light. The only sound was the soothing murmur of leaves before a light wind. It was hard to realize that a great war was sweeping Europe, and that they were in the thick of it.

But utter exhaustion claimed him, too, and soon three instead of two were sleeping soundly.

13

ON THE ROOF

JOHN WAS AWAKENED by the measured thud of heavy boots. It resembled the goosestep of the German army, and he turned over in order to stop the unpleasant dream. But it did not stop, and he sat up. Then it was louder, and it also had an echo.

His heart thumped wildly for a moment or two. The tread was inside the house, and it was made by many men. He slipped to the window, and his heart thumped more wildly than ever. The lawn was covered with German troops, most of them on horseback, the helmets of the Uhlans glittering in the moonlight. Officers stood on the steps at the main door, and at the edge of the vineyard were cannon.

John thought at first that they were lost. Then he remembered their precaution in securing an obscure and isolated room. The Germans might not trouble themselves about ransacking an abandoned house. At least there was hope.

He awoke his comrades in turn, first clasping his hands over their mouths lest they speak aloud.

"We have fellow guests," he said. "The Germans are sharing the house with us."

"Yes, I hear their boots on the steps," said Wharton. "What are we to do?"

John again resumed the leadership.

"Do nothing," he replied. "Do nothing as hard and continuously as we can. Our door is locked. It's natural that it should be so, only we must slip out the key, so it will appear that the owners having locked the door, took the key away with them. Then we'll lie quiet, and see what happens."

"It's the thing to do," said Carstairs, "because we can do nothing else. But I don't believe I can go to sleep, not to the chorus of German boots on the steps."

John slipped the big key from the lock and put it in a corner. Then he lay down again beside the other two. They could hear better with their ears to the floor. It was a solid and heavily built house in the European fashion. Nevertheless they heard the tread from many parts of it, and the sound of voices also.

"It's an invasion," whispered Carstairs. "They're all over the shop."

"Looks like it," said John, "but I've a notion that we're safe here unless they conclude to burn the house. The German advance is so rapid it doesn't seem likely to me they'll stay longer than tonight."

"Still I can't sleep."

John laughed to himself. He was becoming so thoroughly hardened to danger that the complaint of Carstairs amused him.

"They've got an affection for the top of the house," said Wharton, "You can hear them pounding through the upper rooms, and even on the roof."

"But nobody has tried our door yet," said Carstairs, "and it's a consoling thought."

They lay a long time, and heard the continual thump of feet about the place. It suggested at first the thought of plunder, but when John peeped out he did not see anybody bearing things from the house. He beheld instead a sight that caused him to summon the others. A young man had ridden up, and, as he dismounted, all the officers, several of whom were in the uniform of generals, paid him marked deference.

"It's a prince," whispered Carstairs. "It may be the Crown Prince himself, but I can't say, the light isn't good enough."

"And there are other princes behind him," said Wharton. "See the officers still kotowing. I didn't suspect that we had taken a room in a royal residence."

"I'd give a lot to know what they're about," said Carstairs. "Something big must be afoot."

"They're still moving about the house," said John. "We've got to wait. That's all."

They went back to their places on the floor, and waited as best they could, but they heard the sounds for a long time. After an interminable period they went back to the window and saw the prince and the cavalry riding away. The cannon too departed. A dozen Uhlans however remained posted on horseback about the house. The noises inside ceased.

"I can't make it out," whispered Carstairs. "Why should they go away and leave those Uhlans there guarding the house?"

"There must be something inside very precious to them," replied John.

"But what is it? Apparently the house itself is abandoned by all save ourselves."

"I don't know the answer, but my watch tells me it's far in the night. We've had our sleep and rest, and we must try to slip by the Uhlans and get away. Now's the time too."

"Right you are, John," said Wharton, as he felt once more of his precious pocket. "We can't linger, and risk being caught in a trap here."

"But I hear somebody still moving about the château," said Carstairs. "Wait a minute, boys."

He looked through the empty keyhole, and announced that he saw a faint light or the reflection of a light in the hall.

"Something's on foot," he said. "If their officers are sleeping here I should think they'd take the lower rooms, but it seems to me that they're fond of the top of the house, overfond of it."

John who was peeping out at the window once more announced that the Uhlans were still keeping a vigilant watch. They were riding slowly back and forth, and he had no doubt there were others in the rear of the château.

"But I repeat we mustn't linger," said Wharton. "Suppose we hold our automatics ready and slip out."

"Suits me," said John, and he cautiously unlocked the door. The three with their hands on their weapons stepped into the hall, where they noticed the faint glimmer of light, of which Carstairs had spoken. They stood there silently for a moment or two, pressing themselves against the wall, where they would be in the shadow.

"I think the light comes from above," said Carstairs. "You'll notice that the little stairway leads upward, apparently to the roof."

Wharton held up his hand, and the three were so still they scarcely breathed.

"Don't you hear it?" whispered Wharton. "That sound from the roof, the sputtering and crackling."

"I do hear it," said John, listening with all ears. "It's a faint sound, almost like the light crackling of fire. What does it mean Wharton?"

"The wireless."

"The wireless?"

"Yes, while we were sleeping the Germans were installing a wireless outfit on the roof, and it's talking. I tell you, boys, it's talking at a great rate, and it's saying something. You mayn't have noticed it, but the château stands on a hill, with a clear sweep, and our wireless here is having a big talk with distant stations. We've been sleeping, but the Germans never sleep."

"I suppose you know what you're talking about, Wharton, and you're sure it's a wireless outfit," said John.

"It's impossible for me to be wrong. I could never mistake the sound of the wireless for anything else."

"And it's there on the roof of this château, which belongs to us by right of occupancy, chattering away to German forces elsewhere!" said Carstairs in an indignant whisper.

"It's doing a lot more than chattering," said Wharton. "They wouldn't install a wireless on the roof of a house at this time of the night, merely for a little idle summer conversation. You saw that a prince and generals came here, and undoubtedly they ordered it done."

"Whatever they're talking about," said Carstairs, "it's not likely they're talking about us, so now is our chance to slip away."

"I'm not going to leave the château just now," said Wharton.

"Then what are you going to do?"

"I'd like to see the wireless on the roof and the man who is working it."

John glanced at Wharton. The light was very dim, but he noticed a spark in Wharton's eye, and he knew that something unusual was working in the back of his head.

"I think I'd like to have a look at the roof myself," he whispered.

"If you chaps are bent on going up there," said Carstairs, "I'm bound to go with you. But we'd better keep our automatics in our hands."

They emerged from the shadow of the wall, and reached the foot of the stairway that led to the roof. The door at the top was open, as the moonlight was shining down, and Wharton boldly led the way, walking on tiptoe, his automatic in his hand. At the open door John and Carstairs crowded up by his side, and three pairs of eyes peeped out at once.

They saw two men on the roof both with their backs turned to them. One was the operator of the wireless, sitting on a camp stool, working the instrument. The other, in an officer's uniform, was dictating messages. John surmised that they were talking with a station to the eastward, where some lofty ranges of hills ran.

But Wharton was the most deeply stirred of the three. The spark in his eye was enlarging and glowing more brilliant, and a great resolve had formed in his mind.

"There's nothing that we can do here," said Carstairs. "We'd better go at once."

"We're not going," said Wharton in a fierce whisper. "I can use the wireless, and that's just the instrument on which I wish to exercise my skill. I've heard enough to know they're not talking in code."

"Wharton, you are mad!" said John.

"If so, I'm mad in a good cause. Inside of ten minutes some German general will be hearing remarkable news from this station."

"I tell you again you're mad."

"And I tell you again I'm not. I'm a crack wireless operator and this is

my chance to prove it. I'm going up there. All who are afraid can
turn back."

"You know that if you're resolved to go mad we'll go mad with you.
What do you want us to do?"

"John, club your automatic, and hit that officer on the back of the
head with it. Hit hard. Don't kill him, but you must knock him unconscious at the first blow. Carstairs and I will choke all but a spark of life
out of the operator."

The three emerged from the stairway upon the flat portion of the
roof where the wireless plant had been installed not more than four or
five feet away. They made not the slightest sound as they stole forward,
but even had they made it the two Germans were so deeply absorbed in
their talk through the air that they would not have heard it.

John felt compunctions at striking an unsuspecting enemy from
behind, but their desperate need put strength in his blow. The officer fell
without a cry and lay motionless. At the same instant Wharton and
Carstairs seized the operator by the throat, and dragged him down. He
was a small spectacled man and he was only a child in the hands of two
powerful youths. In a minute or two and almost without noise they
bound him with strips of his own coat, and gagged him with a handkerchief. Then they stretched him out on the roof and turned to John's
victim.

The man lay on his face. His helmet had fallen off and rolled some
distance away, a ray of moonlight tipping the steel spike with silver. A
dark red stain appeared in his hair where the pistol butt had descended.

The figure was that of a powerful man, and the set of the shoulders
seemed familiar to John. He rolled him over, and disclosed the face of
von Boehlen. Again he felt compunction for that blow, not because he
liked the captain, but because he knew him.

"It's von Boehlen," he said, "and I hope I haven't killed him."

Carstairs inserted his hand under his head and felt of the wound.

"You haven't killed him," he said, "but you struck hard enough to
make him a bitter enemy. The skull isn't fractured at all, and he'll be
reviving in a few minutes. He's a powerful fellow, and we'd better truss
him up as we have his friend here."

While Carstairs and Wharton were binding and gagging von

Boehlen, John went to the railing about five feet in height that surrounded the central or flat part of the roof, the rest sloping away. The railing would hide what was passing there from the Uhlans below, but he wanted to take a look of precaution.

The men were riding up and down with their usual regularity and precision, watching every approach to the house, and making the ring of steel about it complete. This little wheel of the German machine was Working perfectly, guarding with invincible thoroughness against the expected, but taking no account of the unexpected. He came back to his comrades.

"All well below," he said.

Von Boehlen and the operator, the big man and the little man, were lying side by side. Von Boehlen's face was very pale, but his chest was beginning to rise and fall with some regularity. He would become conscious in three or four minutes. The operator was conscious already and he was staring at the three apparitions.

But Wharton was paying no attention to the captives. His soul fairly leaped within him as he took his seat at the instrument which was sputtering and flashing with unanswered questions.

"Is that the Château de Friant?" came the words flashing through the air.

"Yes this is the Château de Friant," replied Wharton, learning for the first time the name of the house, in which they had made themselves at home.

"Then why don't you answer? You broke off suddenly five minutes ago and we couldn't get another word from you."

"Something went wrong with the instrument, but it's all right now. Go ahead."

"Is Captain von Boehlen still there?"

"At my elbow."

"Take from his dictation the answers to the questions I ask you."

"At once, sir. He is ready to dictate."

"Have you seen anything of British troops, Captain von Boehlen?"

"I have sir. I saw them marching northward this afternoon."

"In what direction?"

"Toward Mons."

"What seemed to be their purpose?"

"To effect a junction with the main French army."

Wharton improvised rapidly. His whole soul was still alight. It had seldom been granted to one man, especially one so young as he to have two such opportunities, that of the papers, and that of the wireless, and he felt himself ready and equal to his task.

"Were they in large force?" came the question out of the dark.

"Larger than any of us expected."

"How many do you think?"

"About one hundred and fifty thousand men."

For two or three minutes no other question came, and Wharton laughed silently. "I've created a hostile force of a hundred and fifty thousand men," were his unuttered words, "and they don't like it."

"Is it possible for our advance column to get in between them and the French?" finally came the next question.

"It's too late," went back the winged answer. "The column would be destroyed."

"This is not in accordance with our earlier reports."

"No sir. But both the English and French have shown amazing activity. A French force of more than one hundred thousand men, of which we have had no report before, faces our right. It is prepared to strike our line just where it is thinnest."

Another silence, and Wharton's heart beat hard and fast. John standing near him, did not know what was being said through the dark, but he knew by the look on Wharton's strained face that it must be momentous. The wireless was silent, and now he heard the measured tread of horses' hoofs, as the Uhlans rode back and forth, guarding the wireless station against the coming of any foe.

Wharton listened intently at the receiver. Were they accepting all that he said? Why shouldn't they? He had given them no answer which they could know to be wrong.

"You are entirely sure of what you say?" came the question.

"Entirely sir. My Uhlans and I were able to ride under cover of a forest to a point within a few hundred yards of the enemy. We saw them in great masses."

"And their field artillery?"

"We were not able to count the guns, but they were very numerous."

"Then it seems that we can't drive a wedge between the English and the French."

"I fear that we can't sir."

"Send out a portion of the Uhlans under your best officers and report to me again at daylight."

"They shall go at once sir."

"Then good night. Captain von Boehlen. I congratulate you upon your energy and the great service that you have done."

"Thank you sir."

"We may call you again in the night."

"I shall be here sir."

"But I won't," said Wharton, as he stepped back and smashed the receiver with the butt of his automatic.

Then as he turned away he said:

"Boys, I've been talking with the Emperor himself maybe, and if not with some one very high in command. I'll tell you about it later, as we must waste no time in escaping from this château."

"I hope you told the Emperor that we are here, ready to defeat him," said John.

"I didn't tell him that exactly, but I told him or whoever it was something which may help us. Now, fellows, we must be off."

They crippled the instrument beyond hope of repair and started. As John turned toward the stairway, he glanced at von Boehlen. The Prussian had returned to consciousness and his eyes were wide open. They bent upon John such a look of anger and hatred that the young American shuddered. And yet, John felt von Boehlen had full cause for such feelings. Despite himself he believed that they owed him an apology, and stooping a little he said:

"It's been a cruel necessity, Captain von Boehlen. War is violence."

The Prussian's eyes glared back. A handkerchief in his mouth kept him from speaking, but his eyes said enough.

"I hope that you and your comrade will not suffer," said John. "Your friends will find you here in the morning."

Then he followed his comrades down the narrow stairway.

"What were you saying to him?" asked Carstairs. "I was apologizing for the blow I gave him from behind."

"The decent thing to do."

As they descended into the lower part of the house Wharton told them more fully what he had said over the wireless, and Carstairs patted him on the back.

"Good old chap," he said. "You Yankees do have bright ideas sometimes."

"The next bright idea is open to any one who can furnish it," said Wharton. "It's to tell us how we're to get out of the château."

"I think there's a vineyard just behind the house," said John, "and if we can reach it we're safe. And we should be able to get there as the Uhlans are watching for people who may come to the château, and not for anybody going away."

They explored the rear of the house and found a door opening upon a narrow flagged walk, lined on either side with pines, and leading straight to the vineyard about thirty yards away. They could make a dash for it, and a Uhlan might or might not see them.

"And if they should see us," said Carstairs, "we could probably get away in the garden and the darkness."

"But we don't want 'em to discover what's happened on the roof," said Wharton. "Then they might send a new wireless. If we can slip away without being seen maybe they won't know what's happened to the wireless, until morning."

"I think," said John, "that we'd better resort to the tactics, used long ago by the borderers in the American wilderness, and creep along the walk until we reach the vineyard."

"Go ahead," said Carstairs, "I'm as good a creeper as you are. But, since it's one of your Yankee tricks, you lead."

They stepped outside and instantly dropped to their hands and knees. The grass beside the walk was rather high and John led the way through it, instead of on the walk, whispering to Carstairs who was just behind him to do as he did, Carstairs in turn passing the word to Wharton.

They advanced about ten yards, and then, John lay flat. The others did the same. One of the Uhlans riding on his beat was passing near the vineyard. He was a man of good eyes and he was watchful as became his service, but it was impossible for him to see the three dark figures of his enemies lying in the grass and he rode on. Then John rose to his hands and knees again, and resumed his creeping advance with the others close behind him. He could hear Carstairs muttering against this painful mode of travel, but he would not alter it, and he knew that the Englishman would be true to his word.

Near the vineyard he flattened down a second time in the grass. The Uhlan was riding back again on his beat, and the most critical moment had come. He would certainly pass very near, and although the odds were against it, his eye might catch a glimpse of the three figures in the grass. Even then they might escape through the vineyard and across the wire fence which would impede the horses, but John recognized as fully as Wharton did the importance of the Uhlans believing until morning that all was well on the roof of the château.

The beat of the horse's hoofs came near. The Uhlan was young and blond, a handsome fellow with a kindly face. John hoped that he would never have to shoot at him. But he did not see the three prone figures. It was likely that they blended with the shadows more thoroughly than John had supposed. He passed on and the danger passed on with him.

"Let's get up now and run," whispered Carstairs.

"Not a step until we reach the bushes," replied John. "Not a step, even if your knees and elbows are worn quite away."

But it took only two or three minutes more to reach the vineyard, and they rose to a stooping position, Carstairs expelling his breath in a long sigh of relief.

"I shall never stand up straight again," he whispered.

They ran between the vines and gained the forest, where in spite of the complaint Carstairs had made all three straightened up and began to exchange rejoicings after the manner of youth. The house showed clearly in its grounds, and they saw the dusky figures of two or three of the Uhlans, but they were outside the ring and they knew they were safe from that danger at least. But the creeping had been so painful they were compelled to rest several minutes. Probably the most exultant of the three was Wharton, although he said the least. He had sent the wireless messages which would mislead at least a portion of the German army, enabling the English and French to close up the gap between them, and he carried the papers of the German prince, telling how other German armies were advancing. His hand flew once more to his coat, and when it felt of the priceless packet the blood seemed to tingle in his arm, and shoot back in a stronger flood toward his heart.

"And now Carstairs," said John, "you know this country better than we do. Lead us toward the British army. And as we've lost our horses and our automobile I suppose it's to be on foot now."

"It shouldn't be much farther," said Carstairs, "and as we're all good walkers we can make it yet."

Under his guidance they left the wood and entered a road which led north and west. Their sleep had refreshed them wonderfully, but above all they had the buoyancy that comes from success and hope. They had triumphed over every danger. Their hearts grew bolder and their muscles stronger, as they sped on their journey.

"I never knew before how good walking could be," said John.

"It's a jolly sight better than creeping and crawling," said Carstairs. "John, I don't think you'll ever get me to do that again, even to save my life."

"No, but the Germans may make you do a lot of it, if you don't get some sense through your thick British head," said Wharton.

"Is that you, Wharton, and are you still alive?" said Carstairs.

"I'm here, all right."

"Wasn't it your great president, Lincoln, who said you couldn't cross a river until you got to it?"

"He said something like that."

"Well, that's what we British are doing. But we're bound to admit that you've done great work for us tonight, old chap."

Their hands met in the darkness in a strong and friendly grasp.

"At least there's one advantage about walking," said John. "If we hear or see Uhlans it's much easier to dodge on our own feet into the woods or fields than it would be with horses or an armored car."

"I'm thinking we've seen the last of the Uhlans for the time," said Carstairs. "Another hour or two ought to take us well inside our own lines. Now, what is that?"

He was looking eastward where he saw a succession of white flashes on the horizon. The three stopped and watched. The white flashes reappeared at intervals for about ten minutes and they wondered. Then the solution came suddenly to John.

"Powerful searchlights," he said. "The Germans have everything and of course they have them too. If necessary they'll advance in the night and fight under them."

"Of course," said Carstairs. "Why didn't we think of it sooner?"

A certain awe seized the three. The reputation of the German military machine had been immense throughout the world for years, and now real war was proving it to be all that was claimed for it and more. A great and numerous nation for nearly half a century had poured its best energies into the making of an invincible army. Was it possible to stop it? The three were asking themselves that question again as they watched the searchlights flashing on the horizon.

"It must be up and away with us," said Carstairs. "We're the champion walkers of Northern France, and if we're to retain our titles we can't linger here. In another hour the day will come."

Daylight found them at a small river. The bridge was not broken down, and they inferred that it was within the lines of defense. An hour later they learned from a peasant that a British force was camped about fifteen miles north and west, and they induced him with good gold to drive them nearly the whole way in his cart. About a mile from the roadside he insisted on their getting out and drove back rapidly.

"He's afraid his cart and horse would be seized," said Carstairs. "We could have forced him to go on, but we'll not set a bad example."

The road now led over a hill and at its crest Carstairs took off his hat and waved it proudly.

"Don't you see?" he exclaimed. "Look! Look! The British flag!"

"What British flag?" said Wharton. "You've a lot of your rags."

"Never mind they're all glorious. See it, waving there by the tents!"

"Yes, I see it, but why are you English so excitable? Any way it's probably waving over valiant Scotchmen and Irishmen."

"Wharton, you grumpy old Yankee, descendant of sour Puritan ancestors, we've won our way through in face of everything!"

He seized Wharton about the waist, and the two waltzed up and down the road, while John laughed from sheer joy.

"Bill come an' look at the crazy Frenchmen dancin' in the road," said a voice that reeked of the Strand.

Bill who was from London himself came out of some bushes by the side of the road, and gazed with wonder at the whirling figures. John knew that they belonged on the first line of the British outposts and he said politely:

"You're partly wrong. My friends are crazy right enough, but they're not Frenchmen. One is an Englishman like yourselves, and the other is an American, but regularly enlisted in the Franco-British service, as I am too."

Carstairs and Wharton stopped dancing. Carstairs took off his hat, and made a deep bow to the astonished pickets.

"I'm not bowing to you, though God knows you deserve it," he said. "I'm bowing instead to the British nation which is here incarnate in your khaki clad persons."

"Touched a bit 'ere, Bill," said one of the men, putting his finger to his forehead.

"A bit off says I too, 'Arry. We used to get 'em sometimes on our 'bus in the Strand. Speak 'em gentle, and they'll stop carrying on."

Carstairs exuded joy and he extended a welcoming hand.

"I take it that you were the driver and conductor of a 'bus in the Strand."

"Right you are sir," they replied together, and then one added:

"If you'll go down to the foot of the hill you'll see the good old 'bus itself with all the signs still on it. But I'll 'ave to ask you first, sir, who you are and what do you want?"

John had never thought before that the cockney accent would be so grateful to his ear, but his pleasure at seeing the men was scarcely less than that of Carstairs. They did not come from his own land, but they came from the land of his ancestors, and that was next best.

Carstairs and Wharton quickly showed their dispatches. Bill promptly took them to a sergeant, and in a half hour they stood beside the general's tent in the center of ten thousand men, the vanguard of the British army. Dispatches have never been read more eagerly and when Wharton, in addition, told the story of the château roof and the wireless the general felt a great thrill of excitement.

"I'm bound to believe all that you say," he said looking into the three honest young faces. "Darrell, see that they have refreshment at once, because we move in an hour."

Darrell, a young aide procured them food and horses. Soon the whole detachment was marching toward the main force, and the three true to the promise of their Cockney friends saw London 'buses, still covered with their hideous signs lumbering along as transports. At noon they joined the chief British army, and the next day they were in touch with the French.

The preceding night the three received places in wagons and slept heavily. By morning their strength was fully restored and pending the arrival of the Strangers, with whom they intended to remain they served as aides.

Several days passed, but not in idleness. Incessant skirmishing went on in front, and the Uhlans were nearly always in sight. John felt the presence of vast numbers. He surmised that the British army did not number more than a hundred thousand men, but multitudes of French were on their right and still greater multitudes of Germans were in front. It was a wonderful favor of fortune or skill that the British had not been cut off and as the German hosts, fierce and determined, poured forward, there was no certainty that it would not yet happen.

John soon became at home among the English, Scotch and Irish. He found many of his own countrymen in their ranks and he continually heard his own language in more or less varied form.

The thrilling nature of the tremendous spectacle soon made him forget to some extent the awfulness of war. Riding with his comrades at night along the front he saw again the flashing of the German search-lights, and now and then came the mighty boom of the great guns.

Belgian refugees told them that the advance of the Germans was like the rolling in of the sea. Their gray hosts poured forward on every road. They would be going through a village, for hours and hours, for a day, a night and then the next day, an endless gray tide, every man perfectly equipped, every man in his place, hot food always ready for them at the appointed time, cavalry in vast masses, and cannon past counting.

The knowledge lay upon John like a weight, tremendous and appalling, and yet he would not have been elsewhere. He was glad to be on the battle front when the fate of half a billion people was being decided.

Many of the spectacular features afforded by earlier battles disappeared, but others took their place. In the clear air they sometimes saw the flashes of the giant cannon, miles away, and flying machines and captive balloons sprinkled the air. An army could no longer hide itself. Forests and hollows were of no avail. The scouts of the blue, looking down saw every move, and they brought word that the menace was growing heavier every hour.

"We'll fight on the morrow," said John as he stood with Carstairs and Wharton before a camp fire. "I feel that the Germans will surely attack in the morning."

14

THE GERMAN HOST

JOHN WAS TURNING AWAY from the camp fire with his friends, when he saw something drop out of the dark, and disappear in a little valley near them.

"Another of those aeroplanes," said Carstairs. "I can't get wholly used to the way they zigzag and spiral about at night like huge birds of prey. They always give me a chill, even when I know they're our own."

John had secured one good look at the machine as it swooped toward the earth, and he asked his friends to walk with him toward the improvised hangar, where it would surely be lying.

They saw a man of slender but very strong build step from the aeroplane, and throw back his visor, showing a tanned face, a somewhat aquiline nose, and eyes penetrating and powerful like those of some bird that soaring far up sees its prey on the earth below. It was an unusual, distinctive face, and the red firelight accentuated every salient characteristic.

"Lannes!" said John joyfully. "I thought it was the *Arrow* when I saw you descending!"

John stood in the shadow, and the young Frenchman took a step forward to see better. Then he too uttered an exclamation of gladness.

"It's Monsieur Jean the Scott, my comrade of the great battles in the air!" he said. "It was my hope rather than my expectation to find you here."

He grasped the extended hand and shook it with great warmth. Then John introduced him to his friends. Lannes and Carstairs surveyed each other a moment.

"Frenchman and Englishman have been on the same battle fields for a thousand years," said Carstairs.

"Usually the only ones there, and fighting each other," said Lannes.

"Whichever side won, the victory was never easy."

"You are a brave people. We French are the best witnesses of it."

"We are always slow to start. We are usually the last to reach the battle field."

"Also, usually the last to leave it."

"It seems fitting to me that the enemies of a thousand years should have exhausted all their enmity and should now be united against a common foe."

"Without you we could not win."

Lannes' wonderful eyes were sparkling. There is something deep and moving in the friendships of youth. Moreover it made a powerful appeal to his strongly-developed dramatic side. Foes of a thousand years were bound to acknowledge the merits of each other. Carstairs, less demonstrative, felt the same appeal. Then they too shook hands with strength and enthusiasm.

"I approve of this love-feast," said Wharton, "but don't fall to kissing each other. Man kissing man is a continental custom I can't stand."

"Don't be alarmed," said Lannes laughing. "It's passing out in France, and I certainly would not do it. I've lived a while in your country. Now will you wait here, my friends? I have a report to make, but I will return in a half hour."

When Lannes returned he handed a letter to John: "Your uncle and the worthy Mr. Anson have managed to reach Paris through Switzerland," he said. "I found them, and, on the chance that I might reach you, the distinguished Senator, your uncle, gave me the letter that I now give to you."

Making his excuses to the others John read it hastily. His uncle wrote in a resigned tone. He and Mr. Anson would remain in Paris a short time, and then if the German forces came near, as he feared they might, they would cross to London. He hoped that his nephew would leave the army and join them there, but if contrary to all good advice, he insisted on remaining he trusted that he would fight bravely and show the superiority of Americans to the decadent Europeans.

"Good old Uncle Jim," said John to himself, as he put the letter back in his pocket. "Maybe it's a faith like his that will really make us the greatest nation in the world."

He did not see any great difference at that moment between the sublime faith of Senator Pomeroy in the United States and the equally sublime faith of Carstairs in the British Empire. The only difference was in their way of expressing it. But he felt a great affection for his uncle, and he knew very well that the chances were against his ever seeing him again. A slight mist came before his eyes.

"I thank you for bringing the letter, Lannes," he said. "My uncle and Mr. Anson will remain a while in Paris, and then they will probably go to London."

He would not tell Lannes the Senator's reason for leaving Paris.

"From what place have you come after leaving Paris, if it's no army secret?" he asked.

Lannes with a dramatic gesture swept his hand over his head.

"From there. From the heavenly vault," he replied. "I have been everywhere. Over forests and many cities, over the German lines and over our own lines. I have seen the Germans coming not in thousands but in millions. I thought once that the army of our allies would be cut off, but it has joined with our own in time."

"Is it true that we fight tomorrow?"

"As surely as the rising of the sun."

"In that case it would be better for us all to go to sleep," said Carstairs phlegmatically. "We'll need our full strength in the morning."

But John was not able to close his eyes for a long time. His rather loose position as an aide enabled him to go about much with Darrell, the young officer to whom he had been introduced first, and he saw that the British army awaited the battle with eagerness, not unmixed with curiosity. In John's opinion they held the enemy far too lightly, and he did not hesitate to say so. Darrell was not offended.

"It's our national characteristic," he said, "and I suppose it can't be changed. This overweening confidence sometimes brings us defeats that we might have avoided, and again it brings us victories that we might not have won otherwise. Tommy Atkins is always convinced that he can beat two soldiers of any other nation, unless it's you Yankees. Of course he can't, but the belief helps him a lot."

"Remember how you fared in the Boer war." Darrell laughed.

"Tommy Atkins doesn't read history, and those who remember it have long since convinced themselves that the Boer successes were due to strange tricks or are merely legendary."

John was not at all sure that Darrell was not a better born and better educated Tommy Atkins himself. He, and all the other young officers whom he met, seemed to be absolutely sure of victory on the morrow, no matter how numerous the German host might be.

After a while he lay down in the grass, wrapped in a blanket, near his comrades and slept. But the August night was not quiet, and it was an uneasy sleep. He awoke far before dawn and stood up. He heard distant shots now and then from the pickets, and the powerful searchlights often played on the far horizon, casting a white, uncanny glare. Darker spots appeared in the dusky sky. The aeroplanes were already hovering above, watching for the first movement of the enemy.

He walked to the place, where the *Arrow* was lying, and saw Lannes standing beside it, fully clothed for flight.

"I'm carrying dispatches to our own army on the right," said Lannes, "and I don't think you will see me again for several days. You fight today, you know."

"And we shall win?"

Lannes was silent.

"All the English are confident of victory," continued John.

"Confidence is a sublime thing," said Lannes, "but in a great war it goes best with numbers and preparation."

John felt the gravity of his tone, but he asked no more questions, seeing that the young Frenchman was reluctant to answer them, and that he was also ready for his flight.

"You're in all senses a bird of passage, Philip," he said, "but I know that whatever happens tomorrow or rather today we're going to see each other again. Good-bye."

"Good-bye," said Lannes, extending his gloved hand. "We're comrades, John, and I hope sometimes to turn your little fraternity of three into a brotherhood of four. Tell the Englishman, Carstairs, that France and England together can't fail."

"He'll think it mostly England."

"If we only win, let him think it."

Lannes stepped into the machine, it was shoved forward, then it rose gracefully into the air and flew off in the usual spirals and zigzags toward the east, where it was soon lost in the darkness. John gazed toward the point, where he last saw it. It seemed almost a dream, that flight of his with Lannes, and the fight with the Taubes, and the Zeppelin. He was on the ground now, and the coming battle would be fought on the solid earth, as man had been fighting from time immemorial. He was about to return to his blanket when a glad voice called to him and a figure emerged from the dark.

"Mr. Scott," came a pleasant voice. "And you were not drowned after all! I thought that I alone escaped!"

It was Weber, paler than usual, but without a wound. John's surprise was lost in gladness. He liked this man, whose manners were so agreeable, and he had mourned his death.

"Mr. Weber," he said, shaking hands with him, "it's I who should say: 'and you are not dead?' We thought you were drowned under the automobile. Mr. Wharton, Mr. Carstairs and myself escaped uninjured although we had a hard time afterward with the Germans. How did you manage it?"

"I *was* under the automobile, and I *did* come near being drowned, but not quite. I'm a good swimmer, but I was caught by a strap. As soon as I could disengage myself I swam rapidly down stream under water, came up in the shadow, and crawled among some bushes on the bank. I saw the Germans ride into the river, search the opposite shore, and after a while go away. Then I emerged from the bushes, walked more hours than I can count, and you see me here. I've brought information which I think of value, and I'm on my way now to give it to high officers."

John shook hands with him again. Weber's manner, at once frank and cheerful, invited confidence.

"Providence seems to watch over all four of us," he said. "It's quite certain that none of us will ever meet his death by drowning."

"Nor by hanging either I hope," said Weber.

"Now I must hurry. If I'm not sent away immediately on another mission it's likely I'll see you tomorrow."

He disappeared almost at once. He seemed to John to have some mysterious power of melting into the air, or of re-embodying himself. It was terrifying for the moment, but John shook himself and laughed. "Lightness of foot and silence are the two great assets in his trade," he said to himself.

He wrapped himself in his blanket and again sought sleep which came readily enough despite the distant shots and the flashing white lights. But he was awakened at the first upshoot of dawn, and the whole army was soon on its feet, its front spreading a long distance across the green country. They had hot coffee and good hot food, and then turned to their duty, John at the same time telling them of the return of Weber, over which both Wharton and Carstairs rejoiced.

"It's a good omen," said Carstairs. "We'll take it that way and let it point to our success today."

"We need it," muttered Wharton, who was looking through glasses, "and a lot more just as good. If I don't make any mistake the German nation is advancing against us in a solid mass."

Carstairs had observed the same fact.

"They seem to be quite numerous," he said.

"Now's your chance," said John, "to prove not only that one Englishman is as good as any other two Europeans, but as good as four."

"Looks like it," said Carstairs coolly. "I'm bound to admit that we can get all the fighting we want. But our men are ready and willing. Listen to the bagpipes of those Highlanders."

"Sounds more like a dirge," said Wharton.

"A dirge for the other fellows."

"Do they keep their legs bare so they can run fast?"

"Yes, after the enemy."

John smiled.

"You're true blue, Carstairs, old fellow," he said. "What do you see, Wharton?"

"Germans, Germans, and then more Germans. Germans on the right, Germans on the left, and Germans in the center, always Germans. They're advancing by kingdoms, grand dukedoms, dukedoms and principalities. The whole circle of the horizon is gray with them."

The three were mounted and ready for orders. Aloft swung the aeroplanes and over the hostile front hovered those of the Germans also. John had little to do, but; as he rode slowly back and forth with the others, he heard the light talk and the jesting among these troops who spoke English. Although he knew that they underrated the danger he was proud of them, and he remembered that his transplanted blood and theirs were the same.

His eyes turned back to the gray sea, coming forward like the tide across the open fields. It's edge was yet far away, but the sunlight was so bright and the columns so deep that he saw them plainly. As in the battle with the French they made upon him the impression of irresistible strength. He saw too that their tremendous line would overlap the British on both left and right, and he was assailed by a sudden and deadly fear that they stood in the presence of the invincible. But his strong will took command of his imaginative mind, and his face seemed calm as he sat on his horse with the others and watched the advancing foe.

Rifles were already crackling in the valleys between, where the pickets were seeking the lives of one another, and now came the deep, rumbling thunder of the giant cannon as they threw their shells from a range of eight or ten miles. When a shell burst there was a crash like that of a volcano in eruption, great cavities were torn in the earth, and men fell in dozens. Vast clouds of smoke from the monster guns began to drift against the horizon, but nearer where the smaller guns were at work only light white clouds appeared.

The advancing German army was a semicircle of fire. From every point the field batteries opened, making a steady crash so frightful and

violent that it seemed to rend the earth. But above their roar the eruption of the colossal cannon in the rear could be heard now, and shells of
immense weight struck and burst in the English lines. Along the whole
British front the cannon were replying, and the roar reached incredible
proportions. Noxious fumes too filled the air. Gases seemed to be
released and the air was heavy and poisonous in the lungs. War had
taken on a new aspect, one more sinister and menacing than the old.

The shock from the great guns became so terrific that John tore little
pieces from the lining of his coat and stuffed them in his ears, in fear lest
he should be made deaf forever. He did it surreptitiously, until he saw
others doing the same, and then he put in more. Many of the troops were
lying down now. Others were kneeling, but everywhere the officers stood
up or sat their horses, reckless of death. The rifle firing had ceased,
because the pickets and skirmishers of both were driven in, and the
masses on the two sides were not yet near enough to each other for that
weapon.

But the cannon, hundreds and hundreds of them were pouring forth
two storms of death. The British position was raked through and
through by the fire of a thousand guns. Shrapnel seemed to rain from
the clouds scattering death and wounds everywhere. The air was filled
with its ferocious whine like that of a hurricane.

John, having no messages to carry, continued to watch the German
advance. He had no doubt that thousands had already fallen before the
hostile fire, but he could see no break in that living gray line. It came
steadily on, solid, tremendous and, again he felt that it was impossible to
stay it.

"The field telephone brings news that the French on our right miles
away are engaged also!" shouted Wharton.

"That doesn't concern us!" John shouted back. "Look what's coming, a
million Germans at least!"

The shrapnel whined terribly over his head and his horse fell, but he
sprang clear.

"My horse is killed!" he cried.

"So's mine," said Carstairs, as he picked himself from the grass.

Wharton's was hurt by the same deadly shower and he dismounted
to examine his wound, but the horse maddened by pain and fright broke

loose and ran toward the German lines. Before he had gone far a shell swept him away in fragments.

John thought they were safer on foot, but his fear began to leave as the madness of battle seized him. He had the curious but not uncommon feeling in a soldier that the whole hostile army was firing at him alone. His heart swelled with indignation, and his hair bristled with anger. Snatching up the rifle of a fallen man he stood, ready to use it, when the gray line came within fair range.

Carstairs and Wharton shouted something to him, but he could not hear the words. He merely saw their lips moving. The crash had become so tremendous that voices were inaudible. John was now quite certain that if he had not put the lint in his ears he would have become deaf forever. But both Wharton and Carstairs seized him and dragged him down. Wharton, through his glasses, had noticed that new German batteries were coming into action, and their fire would converge upon the place, where they stood.

As they lay almost flat behind a little ridge the shrapnel began to shriek over their heads with increased violence. Many men behind them were killed and a stream of wounded dragged themselves toward the rear. The giant shells also fell among them, spreading death over wide areas. The hideous smell of fumes and gases spread. The air seemed poisoned.

The rifles now opened fire, and the air was filled with singing steel. The little bullets flew in millions, cutting down men, bushes, grass, everything. John and his comrades using the ridge for shelter fired their own weapons as fast as they could pull the trigger. He did not know how Carstairs and Wharton had obtained their rifles, but plenty were lying about for the taking.

As the German lines drew nearer John saw the men falling in hundreds. Their ranks were swept by shell, shrapnel and the unceasing storm of bullets, but the gray hosts, a quarter of a million strong, passing over the dying and the dead, always swept on, their generals eager to cut off and destroy the English army where it stood. As they marched vast bodies of troops thundered out "The Watch on the Rhine," or "A Mighty Fortress is our God." Now and then a strain of the song came to John's ears on the roar of the battle.

The gray sea was coming nearer, ever nearer. Losses, however large, were nothing to the Germans. Their generals led them on straight into the face of the British fire, and John gasped as if all that tremendous weight were about to be hurled upon his own chest.

The British fire doubled, tripled. The German line wavered, steadied itself and came on again. Then John saw a flash extending along their own front, and he and his comrades sprang to their feet. He saw an officer give an order and then with a tremendous shout the men, their line bristling with steel, rushed forward.

John heard the shrapnel and bullets shrieking and whistling among them, but he was untouched. Whether there was any bayonet on the end of his rifle he did not know, but he was running forward with the others, and then he was in the center of a vast red whirlwind, in which the faces of men shone and steel glittered. Cannon and rifles crashed, and there was a great shouting, but the Germans at last reeled and gave back before the bayonet.

A tremendous roar of cheers came from the British line, and for a little space there was a comparative lull in the thunder of the battle. John heard a Highland brigade singing some wild song, and near him the Irish were pouring forth a fierce, wailing note. Wharton and Carstairs were still by his side, unharmed.

"The bayonet after all is the weapon for close quarters! It takes a good man to stand the cold steel!" shouted Carstairs.

"So it does!" John shouted back, "but they've stopped for only a few moments! They're gathering anew!"

"And we're here waiting for them! But I wish there were more of us!"

John echoed the wish. He saw the German army advancing again or at least enough of it to know that it could overpower the defense. The Germans were as brave as anybody and under their iron discipline they would come without ceasing. He borrowed Wharton's glasses, and also saw the vast overlapping lines to right and left. A great fear was born in his heart that the German effort would succeed, that the British army would be surrounded and destroyed. But he handed the glasses back to Wharton without a word.

The battle swelled anew. The German generals reformed their lines and the hosts poured forward again, reckless of losses. The defense

met them with a terrible fire and charged again and again with the
bayonet.

For hours the battle raged and thundered over the hills and valleys,
and the British line still held, but it was cut up, bleeding at every pore,
and to right and left the horns of the long German crescent were slowly
creeping around either flank. John from his place on a hill saw well and
he knew that their position was growing extremely dangerous. It seemed
to him that the German threat would certainly be carried out, unless
help came from the French.

[Illustration] "A vast red whirlwind in which the faces of men shone
and steel glittered."

Late in the day he was on horseback again, carrying a message from a
general to any French commander whom he could reach, urging immediate help. He had left Wharton and Carstairs on the battle line, and the
horse was that of a slain colonel.

Gaining the rear, where the weight of the fire would not reach him
John galloped toward the right, passing through a small wood, and then
emerging upon a field, in which wheat had stood.

As his blood cooled a little he slowed his speed for a moment or two,
and took a look at the battle which was spread over a vast area. He was
appalled by the spectacle of all those belching cannon, and of men
falling like grass before the mower. A continuous flash and roar came
from a front of miles, and he saw well that the German host could not be
stopped.

He galloped toward the right, but it seemed to him that distance did
not cause any decrease in the crash and roar. Either his imagination
supplied it, or the battle was increasing in violence. He rode on, and then
a new sound greeted him. It was the thunder of another battle, or rather
a link in the chain of battles. He was approaching the position of a
French army which had been assailed with a fury equal to that from
which the British suffered.

John was merely one of many messengers and the French
commander smiled grimly when he read his dispatch.

"Look!" he said, pointing a long arm.

John saw another vast gray host, rolling forward, crushing and invincible. At some points the French had already lost ground, and they were

fighting a desperate, but losing battle. No help could come from them, and he believed that the French armies farther east were in the same mortal danger.

John received his return dispatch. He knew without the telling what was in it. The French would certainly urge the British to fall back. If they did not do so they would be lost, the French line in its turn would be crumpled up, and France was conquered.

It was given to John, a youth, as he rode back in the red light of the late sun, to know that a crisis of the world was at hand. He was imaginative. He had read much and now he saw. It struck upon him like a flash of lightning. Along that vast front in face of the French armies and the British there must be a million troops, armed and trained as no other troops ever were, and driven forward by a military autocracy which unceasingly had taught the doctrine, that might is right. The kings, the princes, the dukes and the generals who believed it was their right to rule the world were out there, and it was their hour. By morning they might be masters of Europe.

He had all the clear vision of a young prophet. He saw the sword and cannon triumphant, and he saw the menace to his own land. He shuddered and turned cold, but in a minute warmth returned to his body and he galloped back with the message. Others had returned with messages like his own, and, giving up his horse, he rejoined his comrades.

Carstairs and Wharton were gloomy. The ground that had been the front line of the British was now under the German foot. The German weight, irresistible in appearance, had proved so in fact, and far to left and right those terrible horns were pushing farther and farther around the flanks, John now saw the German army as a gigantic devil fish enveloping its prey.

"What did you find, John?" shouted Carstairs.

"I found a French army pressed as hard as our own, and I heard that farther to the east other French armies were being driven with equal fury."

"Looks as if we might have to retreat."

"It will soon be a question, whether or not we can retreat. The Germans are now on both our flanks."

Carstairs' face blanched a little, but he refused to show discouragement.

"They're telling us to retire now," he said, "but we'll come again. England will never give up. John, your own transplanted British blood ought to tell you that."

"It does tell me so, but when I was riding across the hills I saw better than you can see here. If we don't get away now we never shall, and England and France cannot regain what they will have lost."

But the British army was withdrawing. Those terrible horns had not quite closed in. They were beaten back with shell, bullets and bayonets, and slowly and sullenly, giving blow for blow the British army retreated into France.

John and his comrades were with a small force on the extreme left, almost detached from the main body, serving partly as a line of defense and partly as a strong picket. They stopped at times to rest a little and eat food that was served to them, but the Germans never ceased to press them. Their searchlights flashed all through the night and their shell and shrapnel searched the woods and fields.

"It's no little war," said Carstairs.

"And I tell you again," said Wharton, "that England must wake up. A hundred thousand volunteers are nothing in this war. She must send a half million, a million and more. Germany has nearly seventy million people and nearly every able-bodied man is a trained soldier. Think of that."

"I'm thinking of it. What I saw today makes me think of it a lot. Jove, how they did come, and what numbers they have!"

A huge shell passed screaming over their heads and burst far beyond them. But they did not jump. They had heard so much sound of cannon that day that their ears were dulled by it.

"It's evident that they haven't given up hope of cutting us off," said Wharton, "since they push the pursuit in the night."

"And they'll be at it again as hard as ever in the morning," said John. "We'll see those horns of the crescent still pushing forward. They mean to get us. They mean to smash up everything here in a month, and then go back and get Russia."

The firing went on until long past midnight. Toward morning they slept a little in a field, but when day came they saw the gray masses still in pursuit. All day long the terrible retreat went on, the defense fighting fiercely, but slowly withdrawing, the Germans pressing hard, and always seeking to envelop their flanks. There was continual danger that the army would be lost, but no dismay. Cool and determined the defense never relaxed, and all the time bent to the right to get in touch with the French who were retreating also.

It was a gloomy day for John. Like most Americans his feeling for France had always been sympathetic. France had helped his own country in the crisis of her existence, and France was a free republic which for a generation had strictly minded its own business. Yet this beautiful land seemed destined to be trodden under foot again by the Germans, and the French might soon cease to exist as a great nation. French and English together had merely checked the German host for a few hours. It had swept both out of its way and was coming again, as sure and deadly as ever.

They did not hear until the next day that the French and English armies were already in touch, and while still driven back it was not probable that they could be cut apart, and then be surrounded and destroyed in detail. John felt a mighty joy. That crisis in the world's history had passed and by the breadth of a hair the military autocracy had missed its chance. Yet what the German hour had failed to bring might come with slow time, and his joy disappeared as they were driven back farther and farther into France. Thus the retreat continued for days and nights.

Carstairs was the most cheerful of the three. They had slipped from the trap, and, as he saw it, England was merely getting ready for a victory.

"You wait until our second army comes up," he said, "and then we'll give the Germans a jolly good licking."

"When is it coming up?" asked John. "In this century or the next?"

"Be patient. You Yankees are always in too much of a hurry."

"I'm not in such a hurry to get to Paris, but it seems that we'll soon be there if we keep on at the rate we're going."

"You could be in a worse place than Paris, It's had quite a reputation in its time. Full of life, gayety, color. I'll be glad to see Paris."

"So will the Germans, and if we don't do better than we've been doing they'll see it just about as soon as we do."

Carstairs refused to be discouraged, and John hoped anew that the armies would be able to turn. But he hoped against what he knew to be the facts. They were driven on mile after mile by the vast German force.

Another night came, after a day of the desperate retreat and powerful pursuit. John and his comrades by some miracle had escaped all wounds, but they were almost dead from anxiety and exhaustion. Their hearts too were sinking lower and lower. They saw the beautiful country trampled under foot, villages destroyed, everything given to ruin and the peasants in despair fleeing before the resistless rush of the enemy.

"John," said Carstairs, "you know Unter den Linden, don't you?"

"Yes, it's a fine street."

"So I've heard. Broad enough for the return of a triumphal army, isn't it?"

"Just suited to the purpose."

"Well, I don't know whether the Germans will go back to the old Roman customs, but I want to tell you right here that I won't be a captive adorning their triumphal procession."

"How are you going to keep from it?"

"I'll get myself shot first. No, I won't! I'll see that they don't have a chance for any such triumph! I and a million others."

"I feel like despairing myself sometimes," said John gravely, "and then I say to myself: 'what's the use!' I don't mean to give up, even when the Germans are in Paris."

"Well spoken," said Wharton, who was lying on his back in the grass. "All is not lost yet by a long shot. When our army drew out of their clutches their first great stroke failed. Who knows what will happen to their second?"

They were still on the extreme left of the Allied line, forming a sort of loose fringe there, but their comrades on the right were only a few hundred yards away. They heard in front the scattered firing of the pickets and skirmishers which continued day and night, while the searchlights of the pursuers winked and winked, and, at far intervals, a mighty shell crashed somewhere near.

There was a pause in the retreat and John also lay down on the grass.

At first he was flat on his back, and then he turned over on his side. His ear touched the earth, and he heard a sound that made him spring to his feet in alarm.

"Horses!" he cried. "It must be the Uhlans!"

They saw lances gleaming through the dusk, and then with a rush and a shout the Uhlans were upon them.

John sprang to one side, dodging the sweep of a sabre, and firing his rifle at the man who wielded it. He did not have time to see whether or not he fell, because the little camp, in an instant, was the scene of terrible turmoil and confusion, a wild medley of shouting men and rearing horses. Instinctively he rushed to one side, dodging the thrust of a lance, receiving a blow from the butt of another on his head, but finally coming clear of the tumult.

The lance blow had made him see stars, and he could not think or see clearly now. He had dropped his rifle, but he remembered his automatic, and drawing it he began to fire into the mass of horses and horsemen. Then a lancer rode at him with poised weapon. He fired at him, leaped aside and ran through some bushes, intending to come around on the other flank.

But the dizziness in his head increased and his sight became dimmer. The whole world suddenly turned black, and he felt himself falling through space.

15

THE GIANT GUN

WHEN JOHN CAME BACK to the world he was conscious of a painful throbbing in his head, and that he was lying in a very awkward position. He seemed to be doubled up with his feet nearly as high as his head. Around him were narrow, earthy walls, but above him was a sky full of stars.

"Well, if I'm dead," he muttered, "they certainly didn't take the trouble to bury me very well. I didn't know it was the fashion in this country to leave tombs open."

But he felt too weak and languid to "unbury" himself, and lay for a little while in this awkward position. He saw the same circle of peaceful sky, but he heard nothing. The Uhlans, whose rush he faintly remembered, evidently had passed on. He rubbed his head where the throbbing was most acute and felt a big lump there.

But his skull was not fractured. He felt of it gingerly, and it seemed to be as solid as ever.

He lay a little while longer and made an effort. Slowly and painfully he straightened himself out and stood up. His head rose considerably above the edge of the hole, in which he had lain, and he saw a country free from troops, where he stood. But he heard beyond him in the direction of Paris the flashing and roaring which had been going on for days. The German army had marched over him, and for some mysterious reason had left him there.

John looked at the hole in which he stood. It was not more than three or four feet across and at the bottom lay his automatic, which he was glad to find as he had plenty of cartridges left in his belt. But how had such a queer place happened to be there? And how had he come to be in it?

He rubbed his hand several times across his face. The throbbing in his head was becoming less acute. Evidently he had been there a long time, as he saw a faint touch of daylight in the east. He drew himself out of the hole, saw some pieces of metal lying near and then knew the truth.

One of the giant shells striking there had made the cavity and luckily for him he had fallen into it. The German cavalry riding by in the night had passed him, unseeing.

"I never expected one of those big shells to be so kind to me," murmured John.

He drew himself out of the hole, and flexed and tensed his muscles until his physical vigor returned. The throbbing in his head continued to decrease, and he felt confident and cheerful. He began to believe that a special Providence was watching over him. If a giant shell, intended to destroy his comrades and himself, merely made a safe hiding place for him while the triumphant legions stalked past then he was indeed a favorite child of fortune.

It was early dawn and the air was very crisp and fresh. He drew deep breaths of it, and continually grew stronger. Far to the southwest he saw a long, white line of smoke, and beneath it the rapid flash of many great guns. The horizon thundered. It was the pursuing German army, and John sighed. "Still on the road to Paris," he murmured.

He wondered what had become of his comrades in that wild charge of the Uhlans in the night, but his was a most hopeful nature, and since they had escaped he must have done so too. Moreover, fortune as he had observed was watching over them as well as himself. Safe therefore in supposition they slipped from his mind.

He stood for a little space watching the line of battle, as it rolled off toward the southwest and then he looked at the ground about him, the lovely country torn to pieces by the armies. He had resented sometimes that attitude of superiority assumed by Europeans, but, here was Europe gone mad. Americans were sane and sensible. No military monarchs or military autocracies could drag them into wholesale war.

It was the spectacle spread before him that caused John to condemn Europe for the moment. The armies had passed on, but all about him lay the dead. Most of them had been torn horribly by shells and shrapnel, while some had met a quick death from the bullets.

He saw the gray of the Germans and the khaki of the English often close together. Two or three shattered cannon also lay in the fields, and abandoned guns were numerous. Here and there were overturned wagons and in one of them he found food.

After eating he sat down and considered. His momentary feeling of revulsion had passed. He was heart and soul for the Franco-British cause, and he meant to rejoin the army. If he could not find his own company of the Strangers he would go with the British again. But the direction in which he must go was obvious. To Paris. Everything was going toward Paris now, because the German army was driving that way. He resolved upon a great curve to the right which would take him around the invading force, and then flight with the others to the capital.

He knew that he must act quickly, his decision once taken. German reserves or bands of cavalry might come up at any moment. He found a rifle beside one of the fallen soldiers, and cartridges in his belt. He did not hesitate to appropriate them and he walked swiftly toward a little wood on his right, where he drank at a brook and bathed his face and wound.

He was never cooler, and his mind was never more acute. He calculated that at the present rate of decrease his headache would all be gone by night, and by that time also he would pass the right flank of the German army. A man walking could not go so very fast, but at least he could go as fast as an army, impeded by another army still intact.

Choosing his course he followed it without swerving for a long time, keeping as well as he could in the shadow of woods and hedges. The day was as beautiful as any that he had seen, flecks of white on a background of blue and a pleasant coolness. The inhabitants of the villages had fled, but several times he saw small bands of Uhlans. Then he would drop down in the trampled grass, and wait until they passed out of sight.

But he feared most the watchers of the sky. He saw monoplanes, biplanes, Taubes, and every kind of flying machine soaring over the German army. Once he heard the rattle of a Zeppelin, and he saw the monstrous thing, a true dragon flying very close to the ground. Then he crept farther under the hedge and lay flat, until it was miles away in the southwest.

In the afternoon he found a cottage in the forest, still occupied by a sturdy couple who believed that France was not yet lost. They gave him food, made up more for him, putting it in a knapsack which he could carry on his back, and refused to take any pay.

"You are young, you are American, and you have come so far to fight for France," the man said. "It would be a crime for us to take your money."

They also dressed his bruise which the peasant said would disappear entirely in a day or two, and then as John was telling them adieu the woman suddenly kissed him on the forehead.

"Farewell, young stranger who fights for France. The prayers of an old woman are worth as much in the sight of God as the prayers of an emperor, and mine may protect you."

Late in the afternoon John saw the battle thicken. The earth quivered under his feet with the roll of the cannon, and the German line moved forward much more slowly. It allowed him to gain in his own great, private flanking movement. At twilight he rested a while and ate supper. Then he pushed forward all through the night, and in the morning he saw flying just above the trees an aeroplane which he recognized as the Arrow.

Shouting tremendously he attracted at last the attention of Lannes who dropped slowly to the ground. The young Frenchman was over-joyed, and, in his intense enthusiasm wanted to embrace him. But John laughingly would not allow it. Instead they shook hands violently again and again.

But after the first gladness of meeting Lannes was mournful.

"I have seen your friends Carstairs and Wharton," he said, "and they are unhurt, but the German flood moves on. Only a miracle can save Paris. My errand takes me there. Come, you shall have another flight with me, and we shall see together, for perhaps the last time, that Paris, that city of light, that crown of Europe, that fountain of civilization."

"I, an American, still hope for Paris."

"Then I do too."

John put on the coat and visor that Lannes gave him, and they took their seats.

The *Arrow* rose slowly, and John, with his visor and his clothing adjusted carefully for speed and the colder air of the upper regions, settled in his place. He felt an extraordinary sense of relief and comfort. In the air he had a wonderful trust in Lannes, the most daring of all the flying men of France, which perhaps meant the most daring in the world.

He leaned back in his seat, and watched the strong arm and shoulders and steady hand of his comrade. Again Lannes in the *Arrow* was a master musician playing on the keys of a piano. The *Arrow* responded to his slightest touch, rising swooping and darting. John, after the long and terrible tension of so many days, released his mind from all responsibility. He was no longer the leader, and he did not have any doubt that Lannes would take him, where he ought to go. His feeling of ease deepened into one of luxury.

They did not rise very high at present, and John could still catch glimpses of the world below which was now a sort of blurred green, houses and streams failing to show.

They sailed easily and John told much of what had befallen him and his comrades, Carstairs the Englishman and Wharton the American.

"The British army came within a hair's breadth of destruction," he said, "and I'm not so sure that it will escape yet."

"Oh yes it will," said Lannes, "after it once formed the junction with our own army and they were able to retreat in a solid line the great chance of the Germans to strike the most deadly blow of modern times passed. And I tell you again that the French Republic of 1914 is far different from the French Empire of 1870. We have the fire, the enthusiasm, and the strength that the First French Republic commanded. We are not prepared--that's why the Germans are rushing over us now--but we will be prepared. Nor is our nature excitable and despondent, as people have so often charged. Even though our capital be removed to Bordeaux we'll not despair. Using your own phrase, we'll 'come again.'"

"What, has Paris been abandoned?"

"They're talking of it. But John, look toward the east!"

The *Arrow* had dropped down low, toward a wood, until it almost lay against the tops of the trees, blending with their leaves. Lannes pointed with the finger of his free hand, after passing his glasses to John.

John saw puffs of flame and white smoke, and the dim outline of masses of men in gray, moving forward. From another line farther west came the blaze of many cannon.

"Our men are making a stand," said Lannes. "Perhaps it's to gain time. But whatever the reason, you and I hope it will be successful."

"And we may save our Paris," said John.

He was not conscious that he used the pronoun "our". He had become so thoroughly identified with the cause for which he fought that it seemed natural. The battle deepened in fury and volume. Although far away John felt the air quivering with the roar of the great cannonade. They rose somewhat higher and each took his turn at the glasses. John was awed by the spectacle. As far as he could see, and he could see far, men, perhaps a half million of them, were engaged in mortal struggle. The whole country seemed to roar and blaze and innumerable manikins moved over the hills and valleys.

Above the thunder of this battle rose a mighty crash that sent the air rolling in circular waves. The *Arrow* quivered and then Lannes dropped it down several hundred yards, in order that they might get a better view.

"It's one of their giant guns, a 42 centimeter," he said, "and it's posted on that hill over to our right. I didn't think they could bring so big a gun in the pursuit, but it seems that they have been able to do so."

"And it's plumping shells more than a ton in weight, right into the middle of the Franco-British army."

"It would seem so, and doubtless they're doing terrible destruction."

John was silent for a moment or two. He had felt an inspiration. It was a terrible and dangerous impulse, but he meant to act upon it.

"Philip," he said, "have you any bombs with you?"

"A good supply, John. But why?"

"I propose that you and I fly over the mammoth gun and blow it up."

Lannes turned a little in his seat, and stared at his comrade.

"I hold that against you," he said.

"Why?"

"Because I didn't think of it first. I'm considered reckless, and it's the sort of enterprise that ought to have occurred to me. Instead the idea comes to you, a reserved and conservative sort of a fellow. But John, you and I will try it. We'll either blow up that gun or die for France. Search the heavens with the glasses, and see if any of the German flyers are near."

"There are some dots far off toward the east, but I don't think they're near enough to interfere with us."

"Then we'll try for the gun at once. We've got to sink low to be sure of our aim, and for that reason, John, I'm going to ask you to drop the bombs, while I steer. But don't do it, until I say ready because I mean to go pretty close to the 'Busy Bertha.'"

"Good enough," said John, as Lannes passed him the bombs. His hand was perfectly steady and so was that of Lannes on the steering rudder, as they made a gentle curve toward the point, from which the mighty crash had come. John knew that the bombs would not make a destructive impression upon those vast tubes of steel, but he hoped to strike the caisson or ammunition supply behind, and blow up one or two of the shells themselves, involving everything in a common ruin. But to do so he knew that they must fly very low, exposing themselves to the danger of return fire from the Germans.

"I can see the gun now," said Lannes. "The gunners are all around it, and infantry with rifles are near, but I'm going to make a swoop within five hundred feet of it. Whenever we're directly over it drop two of the bombs. It may be, it's most likely in fact, that neither will hit, but I'll swoop down again and again, until we do, unless they get us first."

"I'm ready," said John, who had steeled every nerve, "and I'll do my best."

He felt the rush of air as the *Arrow* increased her speed, and shot downward in a slanting curve, and he heard also a shout from below, as the sinister shadow of the aeroplane showed black between the gunners and the sky.

He leaned over and watched. He saw hundreds of eyes turned upward, and he heard the crackle of many rifles, as they sent their bullets toward the Arrow. Some whistled near, but the darting target, high in air, was hard to hit and none touched it.

John paid no heed to the bullets, but watched the huge cannon with its monstrous mouth upturned at a sharp angle to the sky. When he thought they were directly over it he hurled two of the bombs at the caisson, but they missed. They struck among the men, and several were killed, but the gun and its equipment remained unharmed.

"Never mind," said Lannes, knowing that John felt chagrin. "You came pretty close for a first trial. Now, ready, I'm going to swoop back again."

The second attempt was not quite as good as the first, and a bullet tipped John's ear, drawing blood. Off in the east the black specks were growing larger, and they knew but little time was left to them now. The German aeroplanes were coming.

The third swoop and with an eye and hand in perfect accord John threw once and then twice. A terrific roar came from below. The giant cannon had been blown from its concrete bed and lay a vast mass of shattered steel and iron, with dead and dying men around it.

"One mighty blow for France!" exclaimed Lannes, and exultant they flew westward, dipping low, now and then behind the trees to hide their flight.

"Well consider it a good omen," said John.

"Are any of the Taubes pursuing now?" said Lannes.

"There's nothing in sight," replied John, after a long examination through the glasses.

"Then, they can't find us," exclaimed Lannes, joyfully, "and now for glorious Paris!"

THE END

16

I N PARIS

JOHN SCOTT AND PHILIP LANNES walked together down a great boulevard of Paris. The young American's heart was filled with grief and anger. The Frenchman felt the same grief, but mingled with it was a fierce, burning passion, so deep and bitter that it took a much stronger word than anger to describe it.

Both had heard that morning the mutter of cannon on the horizon, and they knew the German conquerors were advancing. They were always advancing. Nothing had stopped them. The metal and masonry of the defenses at Liège had crumbled before their huge guns like china breaking under stone. The giant shells had scooped out the forts at Maubeuge, Maubeuge the untakable, as if they had been mere eggshells, and the mighty Teutonic host came on, almost without a check.

John had read of the German march on Paris, nearly a half-century before, how everything had been made complete by the genius of Bismarck and von Moltke, how the ready had sprung upon and crushed the unready, but the present swoop of the imperial eagle seemed far more vast and terrible than the earlier rush could have been.

A month and the legions were already before the City of Light. Men with glasses could see from the top of the Eiffel Tower the gray ranks that were to hem in devoted Paris once more, and the government had fled already to Bordeaux. It seemed that everything was lost before the war was fairly begun. The coming of the English army, far too small in numbers, had availed nothing. It had been swept up with the others, escaping from capture or destruction only by a hair, and was now driven back with the French on the capital.

John had witnessed two battles, and in neither had the Germans stopped long. Disregarding their own losses they drove forward, immense, overwhelming, triumphant. He felt yet their very physical weight, pressing upon him, crushing him, giving him no time to breathe. The German war machine was magnificent, invincible, and for the fourth time in a century the Germans, the exulting Kaiser at their head, might enter Paris.

The Emperor himself might be nothing, mere sound and glitter, but back of him was the greatest army that ever trod the planet, taught for half a century to believe in the divine right of kings, and assured now that might and right were the same.

Every instinct in him revolted at the thought that Paris should be trodden under foot once more by the conqueror. The great capital had truly deserved its claim to be the city of light and leading, and if Paris and France were lost the whole world would lose. He could never forget the unpaid debt that his own America owed to France, and he felt how closely interwoven the two republics were in their beliefs and aspirations.

"Why are you so silent?" asked Lannes, half angrily, although John knew that the anger was not for him.

"I've said as much as you have," he replied with an attempt at humor.

"You notice the sunlight falling on it?" said Lannes, pointing to the Arc de Triomphe, rising before them.

"Yes, and I believe I know what you are thinking."

"You are right. I wish he was here now."

John gazed at the great arch which the sun was gilding with glory and he shared with Lannes his wish that the mighty man who had built it to commemorate his triumphs was back with Francefor a while at least. He was never able to make up his mind whether Napoleon was good or evil. Perhaps he was a mixture of both, highly magnified, but now of all times, with the German millions at the gates, he was needed most.

"I think France could afford to take him back," he said, "and risk any demands he might make or enforce."

"John," said Lannes, "you've fought with us and suffered with us, and so you're one of us. You understand what I felt this morning when on the edge of Paris I heard the German guns. They say that we can fight on, after our foes have taken the capital, and that the English will come in greater force to help us. But if victorious Germans march once through the Arc de Triomphe I shall feel that we can never again win back all that we have lost."

A note, low but deep and menacing, came from the far horizon. It might be a German gun or it might be a French gun, but the effect was the same. The threat was there. A shudder shook the frame of Lannes, but John saw a sudden flame of sunlight shoot like a glittering lance from the Arc de Triomphe.

"A sign! a sign!" he exclaimed, his imaginative mind on fire in an instant. "I saw a flash from the arch! It was the soul of the Great Captain speaking! I tell you, Philip, the Republic is not yet lost! I've read some-where, and so have you, that the Romans sold at auction at a high price the land on which Hannibal's victorious army was camped, when it lay before Rome!"

"It's so! And France has her glorious traditions, too! We won't give up until we're beatenand not then!"

The gray eyes of Lannes flamed, and his figure seemed to swell. All the wonderful French vitality was personified in him. He put his hand affectionately upon the shoulder of his comrade.

"It's odd, John," he said, "but you, a foreigner, have lighted the spark anew in me."

"Maybe it's because I *am* a foreigner, though, in reality, I'm now no foreigner at all, as you've just said. I've become one of you."

"It's true, John, and I won't forget it. I'm never going to give up hope again. Maybe somebody will arrive to save us at the last. Whatever the great one, whose greatest monument stands there, may have been, he loved France, and his spirit may descend upon Frenchmen."

"I believe it. He had the strength and courage created by a republic, and you have them again, the product of another republic. Look at the flying men, Lannes!"

Lannes glanced up where the aeroplanes hovered thick over Paris, and toward the horizon where the invisible German host with its huge guns was advancing. The look of despair came into his eyes again, but it rested there only a moment. He remembered his new courage and banished it.

"Perhaps I ought to be in the sky myself with the others," he said, "but I'd only see what I don't like to see. The *Arrow* and I can't be of any help now."

"You brought me here in the *Arrow,* Lannes," said John, seeking to assume a light tone. "Now what do you intend to do with me? As everybody is leaving Paris you ought to get me out of it."

"I hardly know what to do. There are no orders. I've lost touch with the commander of our flying corps, but you're right in concluding that we shouldn't remain in Paris. Now where are we to go?"

"We'll make no mistake if we seek the battle front. You know I'm bound to rejoin my company, the Strangers, if I can. I must report as soon as possible to Captain Colton."

"That's true, John, but I can't leave Paris until tomorrow. I may have orders to carry, I must obtain supplies for the *Arrow,* and I wish to visit once more my people on the other side of the Seine."

"Suppose you go now, and I'll meet you this afternoon in the Place de l'Opéra."

"Good. Say three o'clock. The first to arrive will await the other before the steps of the Opera House?"

John nodded assent and Lannes hurried away. Young Scott followed his figure with his eyes until it disappeared in the crowd. A back may be an index to a man's strength of mind, and he saw that Lannes, head erect and shoulders thrown back, was walking with a rapid and springy step. Courage was obviously there.

But John, despite his own strong heart, could not keep from feeling an infinite sadness and pity, not for Lannes, but for all the three million people who inhabited the City of Light, most of whom were fleeing now before the advance of the victorious invader. He could put himself in their place. France held his deepest sympathy. He felt that a great nation, sedulously minding its own business, trampled upon and robbed once before, was now about to be trampled upon and robbed again. He could not subscribe to the doctrine, that might was right.

He watched the fugitives a long time. They were crowding the railway stations, and they were departing by motor, by cart and on foot. Many of the poorer people, both men and women, carried packs on their backs. The boulevards and the streets were filled with the retreating masses.

It was an amazing and stupefying sight, the abandonment by its inhabitants of a great city, a city in many ways the first in the world, and it gave John a mighty shock. He had been there with his uncle and Mr. Anson in the spring, and he had seen nothing but peace and brightness. The sun had glittered then, as it glittered now over the Arc de Triomphe, the gleaming dome of the Invalides and the golden waters of the Seine. It was Paris, soft, beautiful and bright, the Paris that wished no harm to anybody.

But the people were going. He could see them going everywhere. The cruel, ancient times when cities were destroyed or enslaved by the conqueror had come back, and the great Paris that the world had known so long might become lost forever.

The stream of fugitives, rich and poor, mingled, poured on without ceasing. He did not know where they were going. Most of them did not know themselves. He saw a great motor, filled high with people and goods, break down in the streets, and he watched them while they worked desperately to restore the mechanism. And yet there was no panic. The sound of voices was not high. The Republic was justifying itself once more. Silent and somberly defiant, the inhabitants were leaving Paris before the giant German guns could rain shells upon the unarmed.

It was three or four hours until the time to meet Lannes, and drawn by an overwhelming curiosity and anxiety he began the climb of the Butte Montmartre. If observers on the Eiffel Tower could see the

German forces approaching, then with the powerful glasses he carried over his shoulder he might discern them from the dome of the Basilica of the Sacred Heart.

As he made his way up the ascent through the crooked and narrow little streets he saw many eyes, mostly black and quick, watching him. This by night was old Paris, dark and dangerous, where the Apache dwelled, and by day in a fleeing city, with none to restrain, he might be no less ruthless.

But John felt only friendliness for them all. He believed that common danger would knit all Frenchmen together, and he nodded and smiled at the watchers. More than one pretty Parisian, not of the upper classes, smiled back at the American with the frank and open face.

Before he reached the Basilica a little rat of a young man stepped before him and asked:

"Which way, Monsieur?"

He was three or four years older than John, wearing uncommonly tight fitting clothes of blue, a red cap with a tassel, and he was about five feet four inches tall. But small as he was he seemed to be made of steel, and he stood, poised on his little feet, ready to spring like a leopard when he chose.

The blue eyes of the tall American looked steadily into the black eyes of the short Frenchman, and the black eyes looked back as steadily. John was fast learning to read the hearts and minds of men through their eyes, and what he saw in the dark depths pleased him. Here were cunning and yet courage; impudence and yet truth; caprice and yet honor. Apache or not, he decided to like him.

"I'm going up into the lantern of the Basilica," he said, "to see if I can see the Germans, who are my enemies as well as yours."

"And will not Monsieur take me, too, and let me have look for look with him through those glasses at the Germans, some of whom I'm going to shoot?"

John smiled.

"If you're going out potting Germans," he said, "you'd better get your-self into a uniform as soon as you can. They have no mercy on *franc tireurs*."

"I'll chance that. But you'll take me with you into the dome?"

"What's your name?"

"Pierre Louis Bougainville."

"Bougainville! Bougainville! It sounds noble and also historical. I've read of it, but I don't recall where."

The little Frenchman drew himself up, and his black eyes glittered.

"There is a legend among us that it was noble once," he said, "but we don't know when. I feel within me the spirit to make it great again. There was a time when the mighty Napoleon said that every soldier carried a marshal's baton in his knapsack. Perhaps that time has come again. And the great emperor was a little man like me."

John began to laugh and then he stopped suddenly. Pierre Louis Bougainville, so small and so insignificant, was not looking at him. He was looking over and beyond him, dreaming perhaps of a glittering future. The funny little red cap with the tassel might shelter a great brain. Respect took the place of the wish to laugh.

"Monsieur Bougainville," he said in his excellent French, "my name is John Scott. I am from America, but I am serving in the allied Franco-British army. My heart like yours beats for France."

"Then, Monsieur Jean, you and I are brothers," said the little man, his eyes still gleaming. "It may be that we shall fight side by side in the hour of victory. But you will take me into the lantern will you not? Father Pelletier does not know, as you do, that I'm going to be a great man, and he will not admit me."

"If I secure entrance you will, too. Come."

They reached side by side the Basilique de Sacré-Coeur, which crowns the summit of the Butte Montmartre, and bought tickets from the porter, whose calm the proximity of untold Germans did not disturb. John saw the little Apache make the sign of the cross and bear himself with dignity. In some curious way Bougainville impressed him once more with a sense of power. Perhaps there was a spark of genius under the red cap. He knew from his reading that there was no rule about genius. It passed kings by, and chose the child of a peasant in a hovel.

"You're what they call an Apache, are you not?" he asked.

"Yes, Monsieur."

"Well, for the present, that is until you win a greater name, I'm going to call you Geronimo."

"And why Zhay-ro-nee-mo, Monsieur?"

"Because that was the name of a great Apache chief. According to our white standards he was not all that a man should be. He had perhaps a certain insensibility to the sufferings of others, but in the Apache view that was not a fault. He was wholly great to them."

"Very well then, Monsieur Scott, I shall be flattered to be called Zhay-ro-nee-mo, until I win a name yet greater."

"Where is the Father Pelletier, the priest, who you said would bar your way unless I came with you?"

"He is on the second platform where you look out over Paris before going into the lantern. It may be that he has against me what you would call the prejudice. I am young. Youth must have its day, and I have done some small deeds in the quarter which perhaps do not please Father Pelletier, a strict, a very strict man. But our country is in danger, and I am willing to forgive and forget."

He spoke with so much magnanimity that John was compelled to laugh. Geronimo laughed, too, showing splendid white teeth. The understanding between them was now perfect.

"I must talk with Father Pelletier," said John. "Until you're a great man, as you're going to be, Geronimo, I suppose I can be spokesman. After that it will be your part to befriend me."

On the second platform they found Father Pelletier, a tall young priest with a fine but severe face, who looked with curiosity at John, and with disapproval at the Apache.

"You are Father Pelletier, I believe," said John with his disarming smile. "These are unusual times, but I wish to go up into the lantern. I am an American, though, as you can see by my uniform, I am a soldier of France."

"But your companion, sir? He has a bad reputation in the quarter. When he should come to the church he does not, and now when he should not he does."

"That reputation of which you speak, Father Pelletier, will soon pass. Another, better and greater will take its place. Our friend here, and perhaps both of us will be proud to call him so some day, leaves soon to fight for France."

The priest looked again at Bougainville, and his face softened. The little Apache met his glance with a firm and open gaze, and his figure seemed to swell again, and to radiate strength. Perhaps the priest saw in his eyes the same spark that John had noticed there.

"It is a time when France needs all of her sons," he said, "and even those who have not deserved well of her before may do great deeds for her now. You can pass."

Bougainville walked close to Father Pelletier, and John heard him say in low tones:

"I feel within me the power to achieve, and when you see me again you will recognize it."

The priest nodded and his friendly hand lay for a moment on the other's shoulder.

"Come on, Geronimo," said John cheerfully. "As I remember it's nearly a hundred steps into the lantern, and that's quite a climb."

"Not for youth like ours," exclaimed Bougainville, and he ran upward so lightly that the American had some difficulty in following him. John was impressed once more by his extraordinary strength and agility, despite his smallness. He seemed to be a mass of highly wrought steel spring. But unwilling to be beaten by anybody, John raced with him and the two stood at the same time upon the utmost crest of the Basilique du Sacré-Coeur.

They paused a few moments for fresh breath and then John put the glasses to his eye, sweeping them in a slow curve. Through the powerful lenses he saw the vast circle of Paris, and all the long story of the past that it called up. Two thousand years of history rolled beneath his feet, and the spectacle was wholly magnificent.

He beheld the great green valley with its hills, green, too, the line of the Seine cutting the city apart like the flash of a sword blade, the golden dome of the Hotel des Invalides, the grinning gargoyles of Notre Dame, the arches and statues and fountains and the long green ribbons that marked the boulevards.

Although the city stood wholly in the sunlight a light haze formed on the rim of the circling horizon. He now moved the glasses slowly over a segment there and sought diligently for something. From so high a point and with such strong aid one could see many miles. He was sure that he would find what he sought and yet did not wish to see. Presently he picked out intermittent flashes which he believed were made by sunlight falling on steel. Then he drew a long and deep breath that was almost like a sigh.

"What is it?" asked Bougainville who had stood patiently by his side.

"I fear it is the glitter of lances, my friend, lances carried by German Uhlans. Will you look?"

Bougainville held out his hands eagerly for the glasses, and then drew them back a little. In his new dignity he would not show sudden emotion.

"It will give me gladness to see," he said. "I do not fear the Prussian lances."

John handed him the glasses and he looked long and intently, at times sweeping them slowly back and forth, but gazing chiefly at the point under the horizon that had drawn his companion's attention.

John meanwhile looked down at the city glittering in the sun, but from which its people were fleeing, as if its last day had come. It still seemed impossible that Europe should be wrapped in so great a war and that the German host should be at the gates of Paris.

His eyes turned back toward the point where he had seen the gleam of the lances and he fancied now that he heard the far throb of the German guns. The huge howitzers like the one Lannes and he had blown up might soon be throwing shells a ton or more in weight from a range of a dozen miles into the very heart of the French capital. An acute depression seized him. He had strengthened the heart of Lannes, and now his own heart needed strengthening. How was it possible to stop the German army which had come so far and so fast that its Uhlans could already see Paris? The unprepared French had been defeated already, and the slow English, arriving to find France under the iron heel, must go back and defend their own island.

"The Germans are there. I have not a doubt of it, and I thank you, Monsieur Scott, for the use of these," said Bougainville, handing the glasses back to him.

"Well, Geronimo," he said, "having seen, what do you say?"

"The sight is unpleasant, but it is not hopeless. They call us decadent. I read, Monsieur Scott, more than you think! Ah, it has been the bitter-ness of death for Frenchmen to hear all the world say we are a dying race, and it has been said so often that some of us ourselves had begun to believe it! But it is not so! I tell you it is not so, and we'll soon prove to the Germans who come that it isn't! I have looked for a sign. I sought for it in all the skies through your glasses, but I did not find it there. Yet I have found it."

"Where?"

"In my heart. Every beat tells me that this Paris of ours is not for the Germans. We will yet turn them back!"

He reminded John of Lannes in his dramatic intensity, real and not affected, a true part of his nature. Its effect, too, upon the American was powerful. He had given courage to Lannes, and now Bougainville, that little Apache of the Butte Montmartre, was giving new strength to his own weakening heart. Fresh life flowed back into his veins and he remembered that he, too, had beheld a sign, the flash of light on the Arc de Triomphe.

"I think we have seen enough here, Geronimo," he said lightly, "and we'll descend. I've a friend to meet later. Which way do you go from the church?"

"To the army. I shall be in a uniform tonight, and tomorrow maybe I shall meet the Germans."

John held out his hand and the Apache seized it in a firm clasp.

"I believe in you, as I hope you believe in me," said young Scott. "I belong to a company called the Strangers, made up chiefly of Americans and English, and commanded by Captain Daniel Colton. If you're on the battle line and hear of the Strangers there too I should like for you to hunt me up if you can. I'd do the same for you, but I don't yet know to what force you will belong."

Bougainville promised and they walked down to the second platform, where Father Pelletier was still standing.

"What did you see?" he asked of John, unable to hide the eagerness in his eyes.

"Uhlans, Father Pelletier, and I fancied that I heard the echo of a German forty-two centimeter. Would you care to use the glasses? The view from this floor is almost as good as it is from the lantern."

John distinctly saw the priest shudder.

"No," he replied. "I could not bear it. I shall pray today that our enemies may be confounded; tomorrow I shall throw off the gown of a priest and put on the coat of a soldier."

"Another sign," said John to himself, as they continued the descent. "Even the priests will fight."

When they were once more in the narrow streets of Montmartre, John said farewell to Bougainville.

"Geronimo," he said, "I expect to see you leading a victorious charge directly into the heart of the German army."

"If I can meet your hopes I will, Monsieur Scott," said the young Frenchman gayly, "and now, *au revoir*, I depart for my uniform and arms, which must be of the best."

John smiled as he walked down the hill. His heart had warmed toward the little Apache who might not be any Apache at all. Nevertheless the name Geronimo seemed to suit him, and he meant to think of him by it until his valor won him a better.

He saw from the slopes the same endless stream of people leaving Paris. They knew that the Germans were near, and report brought them yet nearer. The tale of the monster guns had traveled fast, and the shells might be falling among them at any moment. Aeroplanes dotted the skies, but they paid little attention to them. They still thought of war under the old conditions, and to the great mass of the people flying machines were mere toys.

But John knew better. Those journeys of his with Lannes through the heavens and their battles in the air for their lives were unforgettable. Stopping on the last slope of Montmartre he studied space with his glasses. He was sure that he saw captive balloons on the horizon where the German army lay, and one shape larger than the rest looked like a Zeppelin, but he did not believe those monsters had come so far to the south and west. They must have an available base.

His heart suddenly increased its beat. He saw a darting figure and he recognized the shape of the German Taube. Then something black shot downward from it, and there was a crash in the streets of Paris, followed by terrible cries.

He knew what had happened. He caught another glimpse of the Taube rushing away like a huge carnivorous bird that had already seized its prey, and then he ran swiftly down the street. The bomb had burst in a swarm of fugitives and a woman was killed. Several people were wounded, and a panic had threatened, but the soldiers had restored order already and ambulances soon took the wounded to hospitals.

John went on, shocked to the core. It was a new kind of war. The flying men might rain death from the air upon a helpless city, but their victims were more likely to be women and children than armed men. For the first time the clean blue sky became a sinister blanket from which dropped destruction.

The confusion created by the bomb soon disappeared. The multitude of Parisians still poured from the city, and long lines of soldiers took their place. John wondered what the French commanders would do. Surely theirs was a desperate problem. Would they try to defend Paris, or would they let it go rather than risk its destruction by bombardment? Yet its fall was bound to be a terrible blow.

Lannes was on the steps of the Opera House at the appointed time, coming with a brisk manner and a cheerful face.

"I want you to go with me to our house beyond the Seine," he said. "It is a quaint old place hidden away, as so many happy homes are in this city. You will find nobody there but my mother, my sister Julie, and a faithful old servant, Antoine Picard, and his daughter, Suzanne."

"But I will be a trespasser?"

"Not at all. There will be a warm welcome for you. I have told them of you, how you were my comrade in the air, and how you fought."

"Pshaw, Lannes, it was you who did most of the fighting. You've given me a reputation that I can't carry."

"Never mind about the reputation. What have you been doing since I left you this morning?"

"I spent a part of the time in the lantern of the Basilica on Montmartre, and I had with me a most interesting friend."

Lannes looked at him curiously.

"You did not speak of any friend in Paris at this time," he said.

"I didn't because I never heard of him until a few hours ago. I made his acquaintance while I was going up Montmartre, but I already consider him, next to you, the best friend I have in France."

"Acquaintanceship seems to grow rapidly with you, Monsieur Jean the Scott."

"It has, but you must remember that our own friendship was pretty sudden. It developed in a few minutes of flight from soldiers at the German border."

"That is so, but it was soon sealed by great common dangers. Who is your new friend, John?"

"A little Apache named Pierre Louis Bougainville, whom I have nick-named Geronimo, after a famous Indian chief of my country. He has already gone to fight for France, and, Philip, he made an extraordinary impression upon me, although I don't know just why. He is short like Napoleon, he has the same large and beautifully shaped head, and the same penetrating eyes that seem able to look you through and through. Maybe it was a spark of genius in him that impressed me."

"It may be so," said Lannes thoughtfully. "It was said, and said truly that the First Republic meant the open career to all the talents, and the Third offers the same chance. One never can tell where military genius is going to appear and God knows we need it now in whatever shape or form it may come. Did you hear of the bomb?"

"I saw it fall. But, Phil, I don't see the object in such attacks. They may kill a few people, nearly always the unarmed, but that has no real effect on a war."

"They wish to spread terror, I suppose. Lend me your glasses, John."

Lannes studied the heavens a long time, minutely examining every black speck against the blue, and John stood beside him, waiting patiently. Meanwhile the throng of fleeing people moved on as before, silent and somber, even the children saying little. John was again stirred by the deepest emotion of sympathy and pity. What a tremendous tragedy it would be if New York were being abandoned thus to a victorious foe! Lannes himself had seemed to take no notice of the flight, but John judged he had made a powerful effort of the will to hide the grief and anger that surely filled his heart.

"I don't see anything in the air but our own machines," said Lannes, as he returned the glasses. "It was evidently a dash by the Taube that threw the bomb. But we've stayed here long enough. They're waiting for us at home."

He led the way through the multitude, relapsing into silence, but casting a glance now and then at his own peculiar field, the heavens.

They reached the Place de la Concorde, and stopped there a moment or two. Lannes looked sadly at the black drapery hanging from the stone figure that typified the lost city of Strassburg, but John glanced up the great sweep of the Place to the Arc de Triomphe, where he caught again the glittering shaft of sunlight that he had accepted as a sign.

"We may be looking upon all this for the last time," said Lannes, in a voice of grief. "Oh, Paris, City of Light, City of the Heart! You may not understand me, John, but I couldn't bear to come back to Paris again, much as I love it, if it is to be despoiled and ruled by Germans."

"I do understand you, Philip," said John cheerfully, "but you mustn't count a city yours until you've taken it. The Germans are near, but they're not here. Now, lead on. It's not like you to despair!"

Lannes shook himself, as if he had laid violent hands upon his own body, and his face cleared.

"That was the last time, John," he said. "I made that promise before, but I keep it this time. You won't see me gloomy again. Henceforward it's hope only. Now, we must hurry. My mother and Julie will be growing anxious, for we are overdue."

They crossed the Seine by one of the beautiful stone bridges and entered a region of narrow and crooked streets, which John thought must be a part of old Paris. In an American city it would necessarily have been a quarter of the poor, but John knew that here wealth and distinction were often hidden behind these modest doors.

He began to feel very curious about Lannes' family, but he was careful to ask no questions. He knew that the young Frenchman was showing great trust and faith in him by taking him into his home. They stopped presently before a door, and Lannes rang a bell. The door was opened cautiously in a few moments, and a great head surmounted by thick, gray hair was thrust out. A powerful neck and a pair of immense shoulders followed the head. Sharp eyes under heavy lashes peered forth, but in an instant, when the man saw who was before him, he threw open the door and said:

"Welcome, Monsieur."

John had no doubt that this was the Antoine Picard of whom Lannes had spoken, and he knew at the first glance that he beheld a real man.

Many people have the idea that all Frenchmen are little, but John knew better.

Antoine Picard was a giant, much over six feet, and with the limbs and chest of a piano-mover. He was about sixty, but age evidently had made no impression upon his strength. John judged from his fair complexion that he was from Normandy. "Here," young Scott said to himself, "is one of those devoted European family servants of whom I've heard so often."

He regarded the man with interest, and Picard, in return, measured and weighed him with a lightning glance.

Lannes laughed.

"It's all right, Antoine," he said. "He's the young man from that far barbarian country called America, who escaped from Germany with me, only he's no barbarian, but a highly civilized being who not only likes France, but who fights for her. John, this is Antoine Picard, who rules and protects this house."

John held out his hand, American fashion, and it was engulfed in the mighty grasp of the Norseman, as he always thought of him afterward.

"Madame, your mother, and Mademoiselle, your sister, have been anxious," said Picard.

"We were delayed," said Lannes.

They stepped into a narrow hall, and Picard shut the door behind them, shooting into place a heavy bolt which sank into its socket with a click like the closing of the entrance to a fortress. In truth, the whole aspect of the house reminded John of a stronghold. The narrow hall was floored with stone, the walls were stone and the light was dim. Lannes divined John's thoughts.

"You'll find it more cheerful, presently," he said. "As for us, we're used to it, and we love it, although it's so old and cold and dark. It goes back at least five centuries."

"I suppose some king must have slept here once," said John. "In England they point out every very old house as a place where a king passed the night, and make reverence accordingly."

Lannes laughed gayly.

"No king ever slept here so far as I know," he said, "but the great Marshal Lannes, whose name I am so proud to bear, was in this house more than once, and to me, a staunch republican, that is greater than having had a king for a tenant. The Marshal, as you may know, although he took a title and served an Emperor, was always a republican and in the early days of the empire often offended Napoleon by his frankness and brusque truths. But enough of old things; we'll see my mother."

He led the way up the steps, of solid stone, between walls thick enough for a fortress, and knocked at a door. A deep, full voice responded "Enter!" and pushing open the door Lannes went in, followed by John.

It was a large room, with long, low windows, looking out over a sea of roofs toward the dome of the Invalides and Napoleon's arch of triumph. A tall woman rose from a chair, and saying "My son!" put her hands upon Lannes shoulders and kissed him on the forehead. She was fair like her son, and much less than fifty years of age. There was no stoop in her shoulders and but little gray in her hair. Her eyes were anxious, but John saw in them the Spartan determination that marked the women of France.

"My friend, John Scott, of whom I have already spoken to you, Madame my mother," said Lannes.

John bowed. He knew little of French customs, particularly in the heart of a French family, and he was afraid to extend his hand, but she gave him hers, and let it rest in his palm a moment.

"Philip has told me much of you," she said in her deep, bell-like voice, "and although I know little of your far America, I can believe the best of it, if its sons are like you."

John flushed at the compliment, which he knew to be so sincere.

"Thank you, Madame," he said. "While my country can take no part in this war, many of my countrymen will fight with you. France helped us once, and some of us, at least, will help France now."

She smiled gravely, and John knew that he was welcome in her house. Lannes would see to that anyhow, but he wished to make a good impression on his own account.

"I know that Philip risks his life daily," she said. "He has chosen the most dangerous of all paths, the air, but perhaps in that way he can serve us most."

She spoke with neither complaint nor reproach, merely as if she were stating a fact, and her son added briefly:

"You are right, mother. In the air I can work best for our people. Ah, John, here is my sister, who is quite curious about the stranger from across the sea."

A young girl came into the room. She was tall and slender, not more than seventeen, very fair, with blue eyes and hair of pure gold. John was continually observing that while many of the French were dark and small, in accordance with foreign opinion that made them all so, many more were blonde and tall. Lannes' sister was scarcely more than a lovely child, but his heart beat more quickly.

Lannes kissed her on the forehead, just as he kissed his mother.

"Julie," he said lightly and yet proudly, "this is the young American hero of whom I was telling you, my comrade in arms, or rather in the air, and adopted brother. Mr. John Scott, my sister, Mademoiselle Julie Lannes."

She made a shy curtsey and John bowed. It was the first time that he was ever in the heart of an old French home, and he did not know the rules, but he felt that he ought not to offer his hand. Young girls, he had always heard, were kept in strict seclusion in France, but the great war and the approach of the German army might make a difference. In any event, he felt bold enough to talk to her a little, and she responded, a beautiful color coming into her face.

"Dinner is ready for our guest and you," said Madame Lannes, and she led the way into another apartment, also with long, low windows, where the table was set. The curtains were drawn from the windows, and John caught through one of them a glimpse of the Seine, of marching troops in long blue coats and red trousers, and of the great city, massing up beyond like a wall.

He felt that he had never before sat down to so strange a table. The world without was shaking beneath the tread of the mightiest of all wars, but within this room was peace and quiet. Madame was like a Roman matron, and the young Julie, though shy, had ample dignity. John liked Lannes' manner toward them both, his fine subordination to his mother and his protective air toward his sister. He was glad to be there with them, a welcome guest in the family.

The dinner was served by a tall young woman. Picard's daughter Suzanne, to whom Lannes had referred, and she served in silence and with extraordinary dexterity one of the best dinners that he ever ate.

As the dinner proceeded John admired the extraordinary composure of the Lannes family. Surely a woman and a girl of only seventeen would feel consternation at the knowledge that an overwhelming enemy was almost within sight of the city they must love so much. Yet they did not refer to it, until nearly the close of the dinner, and it was Madame who introduced the subject.

"I hear, Philip," she said, "that a bomb was thrown today from a German aeroplane into the Place de l'Opéra, killing a woman and injuring several other people."

"It is true, mother."

John glanced covertly at Julie, and saw her face pale. But she did not tremble.

"Is it true also that the German army is near?" asked Madame Lannes, with just the faintest quiver in her voice.

"Yes, mother. John, standing in the lantern of the Basilique du Sacré-Coeur, saw through his glasses the flash of sunlight on the lances of their Uhlans. A shell from one of their great guns could fall in the suburbs of Paris."

John's covert glance was now for Madame Lannes. How would the matron who was cast in the antique mold of Rome take such news? But she veiled her eyes a little with her long lashes, and he could not catch the expression there.

"I believe it is not generally known in Paris that the enemy is so very near," said Philip, "and while I have not hesitated to tell you the full truth, mother, I ask you and Julie not to speak of it to others."

"Of course, Philip, we would add nothing to the general alarm, which is great enough already, and with cause. But what do you wish us to do? Shall we remain here, or go while it is yet time to our cousins, the Menards, at Lyons?"

Now it was the mother who, in this question of physical peril, was showing deference to her son, the masculine head of the family. John liked it. He remembered an old saying, and he felt it to be true, that they did many things well in France.

Lannes glanced at young Scott before replying.

"Mother," he said, "the danger is great. I do not try to conceal it from you. It was my intention this morning to see you and Julie safe on the Lyons train, but John and I have beheld signs, not military, perhaps, but of the soul, and we are firm in the belief that at the eleventh hour we shall be saved. The German host will not enter Paris."

Madame Lannes looked fixedly at John and he felt her gaze resting like a weight upon his face. But he responded. His faith had merely grown stronger with the hours.

"I cannot tell why, Madame," he said, "but I believe as surely as I am sitting here that the enemy will not enter the capital."

Then she said decisively, "Julie and I remain in our own home in Paris."

THE FOREST OF SWORDS

A STORY OF PARIS
AND THE MARNE

FOREWORD

"The Forest of Swords," while an independent story, based upon the World War, continues the fortunes of John Scott, Philip Lannes, and their friends who have appeared already in "The Guns of Europe." As was stated in the first volume, the author was in Austria and Germany for a month after the war began, and then went to England. He saw the arrival of the Emperor, Francis Joseph, in Vienna, the first striking event in the gigantic struggle, and witnessed the mobilization of their armies by three great nations.

1

THE MESSENGER

There was little more talk. The dignified quiet of the Lannes family remained unchanged, and John imitated it. If they could be so calm in the face of overwhelming disaster it should be no effort for him to remain unmoved. Yet he glanced often, though covertly, at Julie Lannes, admiring her lovely color.

When dinner was over they returned to the room in which Madame Lannes had received them. The dark had come already, and Suzanne had lighted four tall candles. There was neither gas nor electricity.

"Mr. Scott will be our guest tonight, mother," said Lannes, "and tomorrow he and I go together to the army."

John raised his hand in protest. It had not been his intention when he came to remain until morning, but Lannes would listen to no objection; nor would his mother.

"Since you fight for our country," she said, "you must let us give you shelter for at least one night."

He acquiesced, and they sat a little while, talking of the things furthest from their hearts. Julie Lannes withdrew presently, and before long her mother followed. Lannes went to the window, and looked out over Paris, where the diminished lights twinkled. John stood at the other window and saw the great blur of the capital. All sounds were fused into one steady murmur, rather soothing, like the flowing of a river.

He seemed to hear presently the distant thunder of German guns, but reason told him it was only a trick of the imagination. Nerves keyed high often created the illusion of reality.

"What are you thinking about, Lannes?" he asked.

"Of my mother and sister. Only the French know the French. The family tie is powerful with us."

"I know that, Phil."

"So you do. You're an adopted child of France. Madame Lannes is a woman of great heart, John. I am proud to be her son. I have read of your civil war. I have read how the mothers of your young soldiers suffered and yet were brave. None can know how much Madame, my mother, has suffered tonight, with the Germans at the gates of Paris, and yet she has shown no sign of it."

John was silent. He did not know what to say, but Lannes did not pursue the subject, remaining a full five minutes at the window, and not speaking again, until he turned away.

"John," he said then, "let's go outside and take a look about the quarter. It's important now to watch for everything."

John was full willing. He recognized the truth of Lannes' words and he wanted air and exercise also. A fortress was a fortress, whether one called it a home or not, Lannes led the way and they descended to the lower hall, where the gigantic porter was on watch.

"My friend and I are going to take a look in the streets, Antoine," said Lannes. "Guard the house well while we are gone."

"I will," replied the man, "but will you tell me one thing, Monsieur Philip? Do Madame Lannes and Mademoiselle Julie remain in Paris?"

"They do, Antoine, and since I leave tomorrow it will be the duty of you and Suzanne to protect them."

"I am gratified, sir, that they do not leave the capital. I have never known a Lannes to flee at the mere rumor of the enemy's coming."

"And I hope you never will, Antoine. I think we'll be back in an hour."

"I shall be here, sir."

He unbolted the door and Lannes and John stepped out, the cool night air pouring in a grateful flood upon their faces. Antoine fastened the door behind them, and John again heard the massive bolt sink into its place.

"The quarter is uncommonly quiet," said Lannes. "I suppose it has a right to be after such a day."

Then be looked up, scanning the heavens, after the manner that had become natural to him, a flying man.

"What do you see, Philip?" asked John.

"A sky of dark blue, plenty of stars, but no aeroplanes, Taubes or other machines of man's making."

"I fancy that some of them are on the horizon, but too far away to be seen by us."

"Likely as not. The Germans are daring enough and we can expect more bombs to be dropped on Paris. Our flying corps must organize to meet theirs. I feel the call of the air, John."

Young Scott laughed.

"I believe the earth has ceased to be your natural element," he said. "You're happiest when you're in the *Arrow* about a mile above our planet."

Lannes laughed also, and with appreciation. The friendship between the two young men was very strong, and it had in it all the quality of permanence. Their very unlikeness in character and temperament made them all the better comrades. What one could not do the other could.

As they walked along now they said but little. Each was striving to read what he could in that great book, the streets of Paris. John believed Lannes had not yet told him his whole mission. He knew that in their short stay in Paris Philip had spent an hour in the office of the military governor of the city, and his business must be of great importance to require an hour from a man who carried such a fearful weight of responsibility. But whatever Lannes' secret might be, it was his own and he had no right to pry into it. If the time came for his comrade to tell it he would do so.

When they reached the Seine the city did not seem so quiet. They heard the continuous sound of marching troops and people were still departing through the streets toward the country or the provincial cities. The flight went on by night as well as day, and John again felt the overwhelming pity of it.

He wondered what the French generals and their English allies would do? Did they have any possible way of averting this terrible crisis? They had met nothing but defeat, and the vast German army had crashed, unchecked, through everything from the border almost to the suburbs of Paris.

They stood in the Place Valhubert at the entrance to the Pont d'Austerlitz, and watched a regiment crossing the river, the long blue coats and red trousers of the men outlined against the white body of the bridge. The soldiers were short, they looked little to John, but they were broad of chest and they marched splendidly with a powerful swinging stride.

"From the Midi," said Lannes. "Look how dark they are! France is called a Latin nation, but I doubt whether the term is correct. These men of the Midi though are the real Latins. We of northern France, I suspect, are more Teutonic than anything else, but we are all knitted together in one race, heart and soul, which are stronger ties than blood."

"We are to go early in the morning, are we not, Philip?"

"Yes, early. The *Arrow* is at the hangar, all primed and eager for a flight, fearful of growing rusty from a long rest."

"I believe you actually look upon your plane as a human being."

"A human being, yes, and more. No human being could carry me above the clouds. No human being could obey absolutely and without question the simplest touch of my hand. The *Arrow* is not human, John, it is superhuman. You have seen its exploits."

The dark emitted a figure that advanced toward them, and took the shape of a man with black hair, a short close beard and an intelligent face. He approached John and Lannes and looked at them closely.

"Mr. Scott!" he exclaimed, with eagerness, "I did not know what had become of you. I was afraid you were lost in one of the battles!"

"Why, it's Weber!" said John, "our comrade of the flight in the automobile! And I was afraid that you too, were dead!"

The two shook hands with great heartiness and Lannes joined in the reunion. He too at once liked Weber, who always made the impression of courage and quickness. He wore a new uniform, olive in color with dark blue threads through it, and it became him, setting off his trim, compact figure.

"How did you get here, Mr. Weber?" asked John.

"I scarcely know," he replied. "My duties are to a certain extent those of a messenger, but I was caught in the last battle, wounded slightly, and separated from the main French force. The little company which I had formed tried to break through the German columns, but they were all killed or captured except myself, and maybe two or three others. I hid in a wood, slept a night there, and then reached Paris to see what is going to happen. Ah, it is terrible! terrible! my comrades! The Germans are advancing in five great armies, a million and a half strong, and no troops were ever before equipped so magnificently."

"Do you know positively that they have a million and a half?" asked Lannes.

"I did not count them," replied Weber, smiling a little, "but I have heard from many certain sources that such are their numbers. I fear, gentlemen, that Paris is doomed."

"Scott and I don't think so," said Lannes firmly. "We've gained new courage today."

Weber was silent for a few moments. Then he said, giving Lannes his title as an officer:

"I've heard of you, Lieutenant Lannes. Who does not know the name of France's most daring aviator? And doubtless you have information which is unknown to me. It is altogether likely that one who pierces the air like an eagle should bear messages between generals of the first rank."

Lannes did not answer, but looked at Weber, who smiled.

"Perhaps our trades are not so very different," said the Alsatian, "but you shoot through clouds while I crawl on the ground. You have a great advantage of me in method."

Lannes smiled back. The little tribute was pleasing to the dramatic instinct so strong in him.

"You and I, Mr. Weber," he said, "know enough never to speak of what we're going to do. Now, we'll bid you good night and wish you good luck. I'd like to be a prophet, even for a day only, and tell what the morrow would bring."

"So do I," said Weber, "and I must hurry on my own errand. It may not be of great importance, but is vital to me that I do it."

He slid away in the darkness and both John and Lannes spoke well of him as they returned to the house. Picard admitted them.

"May I ask, sir, if there is any news that favors France?" he said to Philip.

"Not yet, my good Antoine, but it is surely coming."

John heard the giant Frenchman smother a sigh, but he made no comment, and walked softly with Lannes to the little room high up that had been assigned to him. Here when he was alone with his candle he looked around curiously.

The room was quite simple, not containing much furniture, in truth, nothing of any note save on the wall a fine picture of the great Marshal Lannes, Napoleon's dauntless fighter, and stern republican, despite the ducal title that he took. It was a good portrait, painted perhaps by some great artist, and John holding up the candle, looked at it a long time.

He thought he could trace some likeness to Philip. Lannes' face was always stern, in repose, far beyond his years, although when he became animated it had all the sunniness of youth. But he noticed now that he had the same tight lips of the Marshal, and the same unfaltering eyes.

"Duke of Montebello!" said John to himself. "Well, you won that title grandly, and while the younger Lannes may do as well, if the chance comes to him, the new heroes of France will be neither dukes nor princes."

Then, after removing all the stiff pillows, inclines, foot pieces and head pieces that make European beds so uncomfortable, he slipped between the covers, and slid quickly into a long and soothing sleep, from which he was awakened apparently about a minute later by Lannes himself, who stood over him, dressed fully, tall and serious.

"Why, I just got into bed!" exclaimed John.

"You came in here a full seven hours ago. Open your window and you'll see the dawn creeping over Paris."

"Thank you, but you can open it yourself. I never fool with a European window. I haven't time to master all the mechanism, inside, outside and between, to say nothing of the various layers of curtains, full length, half length and otherwise. Nothing that I can conceive of is better fitted than the European window to keep out light and air."

Lannes smiled.

"I see that you're in fine feather this morning," he said, "I'll open it for you."

John jumped up and dressed quickly, while Lannes, with accustomed hand, laid back shutters and curtains.

"Now, shove up the window," exclaimed John as he wielded towel and brush. "A little fresh air in a house won't hurt you; it won't hurt anybody. We're a young people, we Americans, but we can teach you that. Why, in the German hotels they'd seal up the smoking-rooms and lounges in the evenings, and then boys would go around shooting clouds of perfume against the ceilings. Ugh! I can taste now that awful mixture of smoke, perfume and thrice-breathed air! Ah! that feels better! It's like a breath from heaven!"

"Ready now? We're going down to breakfast with my mother and sister."

"Yes. How do I look in this uniform, Lannes?"

"Very well. But, Oh, you Americans! we French are charged with vanity, but you have it."

John had thought little of his raiment until he came to the house of Lannes, but now there was a difference. He gave the last touch to his coat, and he and Philip went down together. Madame Lannes and Julie received them. They were dressed very simply, Julie in white and Madame Lannes in plain gray. Their good-morning to John was quiet, but he saw that it came from the heart. They recognized in him the faithful comrade in danger, of the son and brother, and he saw once more that French family affection was very powerful.

It was early, far earlier than the ordinary time for the European breakfast, and he knew that it had been served so, because he and Lannes were to depart. He sat facing a window, and he saw the dawn come over Paris in a vast silver haze that soon turned to a cloud of gold. He again stole glances at Julie Lannes. In all her beautiful fairness of hair and complexion she was like one of the blonde American girls of his own country.

When breakfast was over and the two young men rose to go John said the first farewell. He still did not know the French custom, but, bending over suddenly, he kissed the still smooth and handsome hand of Madame Lannes. As she flushed and looked pleased, he judged that he had made no mistake. Then he touched lightly the hand of the young girl, and said:

"Mademoiselle Julie, I hope to return soon to this house with your brother."

"May it be so," she said, in a voice that trembled, "and may you come back to a Paris still French!"

John bowed to them both and with tact and delicacy withdrew from the room. He felt that there should be no witness of Philip's farewell to his mother and sister, before going on a journey from which the chances were that he would never return.

He strolled down the hall, pretending to look at an old picture or two, and in a few minutes Lannes came out and joined him. John saw tears in his eyes, but his face was set and stern. Neither spoke until they reached the front door, which the giant, Picard, opened for them.

"If the worst should happen, Antoine," said Lannes, "and you must be the judge of it when it comes, take them to Lyons, to our cousins the Menards."

"I answer with my life," said the man, shutting together his great teeth, and John felt that it was well for the two women to have such a guardian. Under impulse, he said:

"I should like to shake the hand of a man who is worth two of most men."

Whether the French often shake hands or not, his fingers were enclosed in the mighty grasp of Picard, and he knew that he had a friend for life. When they went out Lannes would not look back and was silent for a long time. The day was warm and beautiful, and the stream of fugitives, the sad procession, was still flowing from the city. Troops too were moving, and it seemed to John that they passed in heavier masses than on the day before.

"I went out last night while you slept," said Lannes, when they were nearly at the hangar, "and I will tell you that I bear a message to one of our most important generals. I carry it in writing, and also in memory in case I lose the written word. That is all I feel at liberty to tell you, and in truth I know but little more. The message comes from our leader to the commander of the army at Paris, who in turn orders me to deliver it to the general whom we're going to seek. It directs him with his whole force to move forward to a certain point and hold fast there. Beyond that I know nothing. Its whole significance is hidden from me. I feel that I can tell you this, John, as we're about to start upon a journey which has a far better prospect of death than of life."

"I'm not afraid," said John, and he told the truth. "I feel, Philip, that great events are impending and that your dispatch or the effect of it will be a part in some gigantic plan."

"I feel that way, too. What an awful crisis! The Germans moved nearer in the dark. I didn't sleep a minute last night. I couldn't. If the signs that you and I saw are to be fulfilled they must be fulfilled soon, because when a thing is done it's done, and when Paris falls it falls."

"Well, here we are at the hangar, and the *Arrow* will make you feel better. You're like the born horseman whose spirits return when he's on the back of his best runner."

"I suppose I am. The air is now my proper medium, and anyway, John, my gallant Yankee, for a man like me the best tonic is always action, action, and once more action."

The *Arrow* was in beautiful condition, smooth, polished and fitted with everything that was needed. They put on their flying clothes, drew down their visors, stowed their automatics in handy pockets, and took their seats in the aeroplane. Then, as he put his hand on the steering rudder and the attendants gave the *Arrow* a mighty shove, the soul of Lannes swelled within him.

They rose slowly and then swiftly over Paris, and his troubles were left behind him on the earth. Up, up they went, in a series of graceful spirals, and although John, at first, felt the old uneasy feeling, it soon departed. He too exulted in their mounting flight and the rush of cold air.

"Use your glasses, John," said Lannes, "and tell me what you can see."

"Some captive balloons, five other planes, all our own, and on the horizon, where the German army lies, several black specks too vague and indefinite for me to make out what they are, although I've no doubt they're German flyers."

"I'd like to have a look at the Germans, but our way leads elsewhere. What else do you see, John?"

"I look downward and I see the most magnificent and glittering city in the world."

"And that's Paris, our glorious Paris, which you and I and a million others are going to save. I suppose it's hope, John, that makes me feel we'll do something. Did you know that the Germans dropped two more bombs on the city last night? One, luckily, fell in the Seine. The other struck near the Madeleine, close to a group of soldiers, killing two and wounding four more."

"Bombs from the air can't do any great damage to a city."

"No, but they can spread alarm, and it's an insult, too. We feel as the Germans would if we were dropping bombs on Berlin. I wish you'd keep those glasses to your eyes all the time, John, and watch the skies. Let me know at once, if you see anything suspicious."

John, continually turning in his seat, swept the whole curve of the world with the powerful glasses. Paris was now far below, a blur of white and gray. Above, the heavens were of the silkiest blue, beautiful in their infinite depths, with tiny clouds floating here and there like whitecaps on an ocean.

"What do you see now, John?"

"Nothing but one of the most beautiful days that ever was. It's a fine sun, that you've got over here, Philip. I can see through these glasses that it's made out of pure reddish gold."

"Never mind about that sun, John. America is a full partner in its ownership and you're used to it. I've heard that you have more sunshine than we do. Watch for our companions of the air, friend or foe."

"I see them flying; over Paris, but none is going in our direction. How far is our port of entry, Lannes?"

"We should be there in two hours, if nothing happens. Do we still have the course to ourselves or is anything coming our way now?"

"No company at all, unless you'd call a machine about three miles off and much lower down, a comrade."

"What does it look like?"

"A French aeroplane, much resembling the *Arrow*."

"Is it following us?"

"Not exactly. Yes, it is coming our way now, although it keeps much lower! A scout, I dare say."

Lannes was silent for a little while, his eyes fixed on his pathway through the blue. Then he said:

"What has become of that machine, John?"

"It has risen a little, but it's on our private course, that is, if we can claim the right of way all down to the ground."

Lannes glanced backward and downward, as well as his position would allow.

"A French plane, yes," he said thoughtfully. "There can be no doubt of it, but why should it follow us in this manner? You do think it's following us, don't you, John?"

"It begins to look like it, Phil. It's rising a little now, and is directly in our wake."

"Take a long look through those glasses of yours."

John obeyed, and the following aeroplane at once increased in size tenfold and came much nearer.

"It's French. There cannot be any doubt of it," he said, "and only one man is in it. As he's hidden by his flying-suit I can't tell anything about him."

"Watch him closely, John, and keep your hand on the butt of your automatic. I don't like that fellow's actions. Still, he may be a Frenchman on an errand like ours. We've no right to think we're the only people carrying important messages today."

"He's gaining pretty fast. Although he keeps below us, it looks as if he wanted to communicate with us."

The second aeroplane suddenly shot forward and upward at a much greater rate of speed. John, still watching through his glasses, saw the man release the steering rudder for an instant, snatch a rifle from the floor of his plane, and fire directly at Lannes.

John uttered a shout of anger, and in action, too, he was as quick as a flash. His automatic was out at once and he rained bullets upon the treacherous machine. It was hard to take aim, firing from one flying target, at another, but he saw the man flinch, turn suddenly, and then go rocketing away at a sharp angle.

Blazing with wrath John watched him, now far out of range, and then reloaded his automatic.

"Did you get him, John?" asked Lannes.

"I know one bullet found him, because I saw him shiver and shrink, but it couldn't have been mortal, as he was able to fly away."

"I'm glad that you at least hit him, because he hit me."

"What!" exclaimed John. Then he looked at his comrade and saw to his intense horror that black blood was flowing slowly down a face deadly pale.

"His bullet went through my cap and then through my head," said Lannes. "Oh, not through my skull, or I wouldn't be talking to you now. I think it glanced off the bone, as I know it's gone out on the other side. But I'm losing much blood, John, and I seem to be growing numb."

His voice trailed off in weakness and the *Arrow* began to move in an eccentric manner. John saw that Lannes' hand on the rudder was uncertain and that he had been hard hit. He was aghast, first for his friend, to whom he had become so strongly attached, and then for the *Arrow*, their mission and himself. Lannes would soon become unconscious and he, no flying man at all, would be left high in air with a terrible weight of responsibility.

"We must change seats," said Lannes, struggling against the dimness that was coming over his eyes and the weakness permeating his whole body. "Be careful, Oh, be careful as you can, and then, in your American language, a lot more. Slowly! Slowly! Yes, I can move alone. Drag yourself over me, and I can slide under you. Careful! Careful!"

The *Arrow* fluttered like a wounded bird, dropping, darting upward, and careering to one side. John was sick to his soul, both physically and mentally. His head became giddy and the wind roared in his ears, but the exchange of seats was at last, successfully accomplished.

"Now," said Lannes, "you're a close observer. Remember all that you've seen me do with the plane. Resolve to yourself that you do know how to fly the *Arrow*. Fear nothing and fly straight for our destination. Don't bother about the bleeding of my wound. My thick hair and thick cap acting together as a heavy bandage will stop it. Now, John, our fate rests with you."

The last words were almost inaudible, and John from the corner of his eye saw his comrade's head droop. He knew that Lannes had become unconscious and now, appalling though the situation was, he rose to the crisis.

He knew the immensity of their danger. A sudden movement of the rudder and the aeroplane might be wrecked. And in such a position the nerves of a novice were subject at any time to a jerk. They might be assailed by another treacherous machine, the dangers, in truth, were uncountable, but he was upborne by a tremendous desire to carry the word and to save Lannes and himself.

In the face of intense resolve all obstacles became as nothing and his hand steadied on the rudder. He knew that when it came to the air he was no Lannes and never could be. The solid earth, no matter how much it rolled around the sun or around itself, was his favorite field of action, but he felt that he must make one flight, when he carried with him perhaps the fate of a nation.

The *Arrow* was still rocking from side to side and dipping and jumping. Slowly he steadied it, handling the rudder as if it were a loaded weapon, and gradually his heart began to pound with triumph. It was no such flying as the hand of Lannes drew from the *Arrow*, but to John it seemed splendid for a first trial. He let the machine drop a little until it was only six or seven hundred yards above the earth, and took wary glances from side to side. He feared another pursuer, but the air seemed clear.

Lannes had sunk a little further forward. John saw that the bleeding from his head had ceased. There was a dark stain down either cheek, but it was drying there, and as Lannes had foreseen, his hair and the cap had acted as a bandage, at last checking the flow effectively. His breathing was heavy and jerky, but John believed that he would revive before long. It was not possible that one so vital as Lannes, so eager for great action, could die thus.

Now he looked ahead. Their landmarks as Lannes had told him before the fight, were to be a high hill, a low hill, and a small stream flowing between. Just behind it they would find a great French army marching northward and their errand would be over. He did not yet see the hills, but he was sure that he was still in the pathway of the air.

He had left Paris far behind, but when he looked down he saw a beautiful country, a fertile land upon which man had worked for two thousand years, too beautiful to be trodden to pieces by armies. He saw the cultivated fields, varying in color like a checker board, and the neat villages with trees about them. Here and there the spire of a church rose high above everything. Churches and wars were so numerous in Europe!

John checked the speed of the *Arrow*. He was afraid, despite all his high resolve, to fly fast, and then he must not go beyond the army for which he was looking. He dropped a little lower as he was passing over a wood, and then he heard the crack of rifles beneath him. Bullets whizzed and sang past his ears and he took one fearful glance downward.

He saw men, spiked helmets on their heads, galloping among the trees, and he knew that they were a daring band of Uhlans, actually scouting inside the French lines. They were shooting at the *Arrow* and firing fast.

He attempted to rise so suddenly that the plane gave a violent jerk and quivered in every fiber. He thought for a moment they were going to fall, and the sickening sensation at his heart was overpowering. But the trusty *Arrow* ceased quivering, and then rose swiftly at an angle not too great.

Bullets still whizzed around the plane, and one glanced off its polished side, but John's first nervous jerkiness in handling the machine had probably saved him. The target had been so high in air, and of such a shifting nature that the Uhlans had little chance to hit it.

He was now beyond the range of any rifle, and he drew a long breath of relief that was like a deep sigh. Then he took a single downward glance, and caught a fleeting glimpse of the Uhlans galloping away. Doubtless they were making all speed back to their own army.

He flew on for a minute or two, searching the horizon eagerly, and at last, he saw a tall hill, a low hill and a flash of water between. He felt so much joy that he uttered a cry, and an echo of it came from a point almost by his side.

"Did I hear firing, John?"

It was Lannes' voice, feeble, but showing all the signs of returning strength, and again John uttered a joyous shout.

"You did," he replied. "It was Uhlans in a grove. I was flying low and their bullets whistled around us. But the *Arrow* has taken no harm. I see, too, the hills and the stream which are our landmarks. We're about to arrive, Philip, with our message, but there's been treachery somewhere. I wish I knew who was in that French plane."

"So do I, John. It certainly came out of Paris. In my opinion it meant to destroy us and keep our message from reaching the one for whom it was intended. Who could it have been and how could he have known!"

"Feeling better now, aren't you, Phil?"

"A lot better. My head aches tremendously, but the dimness has gone from before my eyes, and I'm able to think, in a poor and feeble way, perhaps, but I'm not exactly a dumb animal. Where are the hills?"

John pointed.

"I can see them," said Lannes exultantly. "Since they did no harm I'm glad the Uhlans fired at the *Arrow*. Their shots aroused me from stupor and as we're to reach the army I want to be in possession of my five senses when I get there."

John understood perfectly.

"It's your message and you deliver it," he said.

Lannes' strength continued to increase, and his mind cleared rapidly. His head ached frightfully, but he could think with all his usual swiftness and precision. He sat erect in his seat.

"Pass me your glasses, John," he said.

"Now I see the troops," he said, after a long look. "Frenchmen, Frenchmen, Frenchmen, infantry in thousands and scores of thousands, big guns in scores and hundreds, cuirassiers, hussars, cannoneers! Ah! It's a sight to kindle a dead heart back to life! John, this is one of the great wheels in the mighty machine that is to move forward! Here come two aeroplanes, scouts sent forward to see who and what we are."

"You are sure they contain genuine Frenchmen? Remember the fellow who shot you."

"Frenchmen, good and true. I can see them for myself."

He moved his hand, and in a few moments John heard hissing and purring near, as if great birds were flying to meet him. The outlines of the hovering planes showed by his side, and Lannes called in a loud voice to shrouded and visored men.

"Philip Lannes and his comrade, John Scott, with a message from Paris to the commander!" he exclaimed.

He was his old self again, erect, intense, dramatic. He evidently expected the name Philip Lannes to be known well to them, and it was, as a cheer followed high in air.

"Now, John," said Lannes, "Be careful! Your hardest task is before you, to land. But I've noticed that with you the harder the task the better you do it. Make for that wide green space to the left of the stream and come down as slowly and gently as you can. Just slide down."

John had a fleeting glimpse of thousands of faces looking upward, but he held a true course for the grassy area, and with a multitude looking on his nerve was never steadier. Amid great cheering the *Arrow* came safely to rest at her appointed place. John and Lannes stepped forth, as an elderly man in a quiet uniform came forward to meet them.

Lannes, holding himself stiffly erect, drew a paper from his pocket and extended it to the general.

"A letter, sir, from the commander-in-chief of all our armies," he said, saluting proudly.

As the general took the letter, Lannes' knees bent beneath him, and he sank down on his face.

2

IN THE FRENCH CAMP

John rushed forward and grasped his comrade. The sympathetic hands of others seized him also, and they raised him to his feet, while an officer gave him stimulant out of a flask, John meanwhile telling who his comrade was. Lannes' eyes opened and he flushed through the tan of his face.

"Pardon," he said, "it was a momentary weakness. I am ashamed of myself, but I shall not faint again."

"You've been shot," said the officer, looking at his sanguinary cap and face.

"So I have, but I ask your pardon for it. I won't let it occur again."

Lannes was now standing stiffly erect, and his eyes shone with pride, as the general, a tall, elderly man, rapidly read the letter that Philip had delivered with his own hand. The officer who had spoken of his wound looked at him with approval.

"I've heard of you, Philip Lannes," he said, "you're the greatest flying man in the world."

Lannes' eyes flashed now.

"You do me too much honor," he said, "but it was not I who brought our aeroplane here. It was my American friend, John Scott, now standing beside me, who beat off an attack upon us and who then, although he had had no practical experience in flying, guided the machine to this spot. Born an American, he is one of us and France already owes him much."

John raised his hand in protest, but he saw that Lannes was enjoying himself. His dramatic instinct was finding full expression. He had not only achieved a great triumph, but his best friend had an important share in it. There was honor for both, and his generous soul rejoiced.

Both John and Lannes stood at attention until the general had read the letter not once but twice and thrice. Then he took off his glasses, rubbed them thoughtfully a moment or two, replaced them and looked keenly at the two. He was a quiet man and he made no gestures, but John met his gaze serenely, read his eyes and saw the tremendous weight of responsibility back of them.

"You have done well, you two, perhaps far better than you know," said the general, "and now, since you are wounded, Philip Lannes, you must have attention. De Rougemont, take care of them."

De Rougemont, a captain, was the man to whom they had been talking, and he gladly received the charge. He was a fine, well built officer, under thirty, and it was obvious that he already took a deep interest in the two young aviators. Noticing Lannes' anxious glances toward his precious machine, he promptly detailed two men to take care of the *Arrow* and then he led John and Lannes toward the group of tents.

"First I'll get a surgeon for you," he said to the Frenchman, "and after that there's food for you both."

"I hope you'll tell the surgeon to be careful how he takes off my cap," said Lannes, "because it's fastened to my head now by my own dried blood."

"Trust me for that," said de Rougemont. "I'll bring one of our best men."

Then, unable to suppress his curiosity any longer, he added:

"I suppose the message you brought was one of life or death for France."

"I think so," said Lannes, "but I know little of its nature, myself."

"I would not ask you to say any more. I know that you cannot speak of it. But you can tell me this. Are the Germans before Paris?"

"As nearly as I could tell, their vanguard was within fifteen miles of the capital."

"Then if we strike at all we must strike quickly. I think we're going to strike."

Lannes was silent, and they entered the tent, where blankets were spread for him. A surgeon, young and skillful, came promptly, carefully removed the cap and bound up his head. John stood by and handed the surgeon the bandages.

"You're not much hurt," he said to Lannes as he finished. "Your chief injury was shock, and that has passed. I can keep down the fever and you'll be ready for work very soon. The high powered bullet makes a small and clean wound. It tears scarcely at all. Nor will your beauty be spoiled in the slightest, young sir. Both orifices are under the full thickness of your hair."

"I'm grateful for all your assurances," said Lannes, his old indomitable smile appearing in his eyes, "but you'll have to cure me fast, faster than you ever cured anybody before, because I'm a flying man, and I fly again tomorrow."

"Not tomorrow. In two or three days, perhaps"

"Yes, tomorrow, I tell you! Nothing can keep me from it! This army will march tonight! I know it! and do you think such a wound as this can keep me here, when the fate of Europe is being decided? I'd rise from these blankets and go with the army even if I knew that it would make me fall dead the next day!"

He spoke with such fierce energy that the surgeon who at first sternly forbade, looked doubtful and then acquiescent.

"Go, then," he said, "if you can. The fact that we have so many heroes may save us."

He left John alone in the tent with Lannes. The Frenchman regarded his comrade with a cool, assured gaze.

"John," he said, "I shall be up in the *Arrow* tomorrow. I'm not nervous and excited now, and I'll not cause any fever in my wound. Somebody will come in five minutes with food. I shall eat a good supper, fall quietly to sleep, sleep soundly until night, then rise, refreshed and strong, and go about the work for which I'm best fitted. My mind shall rule over my body."

"I see you're what we would call at home a Christian Scientist, and in your case when a mind like yours is brought to bear there's something in it."

The food appeared within the prescribed time, and both ate heartily. John watched Lannes. He knew that he would suffer agonies of mortification if he were not able to share in the great movement which so obviously was about to take place, and, as he looked, he felt a growing admiration for Philip's immense power of self-control.

Mind had truly taken command of body. Lannes ate slowly and with evident relish. From without came many noises of a great army, but he refused to be disturbed or excited by them. He spoke lightly of his life before the war, and of a little country home that the Lannes family had in Normandy.

"We own the two places, that and the home in the city," he said. "The house in Normandy is small, but it's beautiful, hidden by flower gardens and orchards, with a tiny river just back of the last orchard. Julie has spent most of her life there. She and my mother would go there now, but it's safer at Lyons or in the Midi. A wonderful girl, Julie! I hope, John, that you'll come for a long stay with us after the war, among the Normandy orchards and roses."

"I hope so," said John. He was dreaming a little then, and he saw young Julie sitting at the table with them back in Paris. Truly, her golden hair was the purest gold he had ever seen, and there was no other blue like the blue of her blue eyes.

"Now, John," said Lannes, "I'll resume my place on the blankets and in ten minutes I'll be asleep."

He lay down, closed his eyes and three minutes short of the appointed time slept soundly. John gazed at him for a moment in wonder and admiration. The triumph of will over body had been complete. He touched Lannes' head. It was normally cool. Either the surgeon's skill had been great or the very strength of his resolve had been so immense that he had kept nerves and blood too quiet for fever to rise.

John left the tent, feeling for the time a personal detachment from everything. He had no position in this army, and no orders had been given to him by anybody. But he knew that he was among friends, and while he stood looking about in uncertainty Captain de Rougemont appeared.

"How is young Lannes?" he asked.

"Sleeping and free from fever. He will move with the army, or rather he will be hovering over it in his aeroplane. I never before saw such extraordinary power of will."

"He's a wonderful fellow. Of course, most of us have heard of him through his marvelous flying exploits, but it's the first time that I've ever seen him. What are you going to do?"

"I don't know. I seem to be left high and dry for the present, at least. My company is with one of the armies, but where that army is now is more than I can tell."

"Nor do I know either. We're all in the dark here, but any young strong man can certainly get a chance to fight in this war. I'm on the staff of General Vaugirard, a brigade commander, and he needs active young officers. You speak good French, and the fact that you came with Lannes will be a great recommendation, I'll provide you with a horse and all else necessary."

John thanked him with great sincerity. The offer was in truth most welcome. He knew that Lannes would willingly take him in the *Arrow*, but he felt that he would be in the way there and, as he had said to his friend, the rolling earth rather than the air around it was his true field of action. His first enrollment in the French army had been hurried and without due forms, but war had made it good.

"I'll not come back for you until afternoon," said de Rougemont, "because we're already making preparations to advance, and I shall have much to do meanwhile. You can watch over Lannes and see that he's not interrupted in his sleep. He'll need it."

"Yes, I have reason to know that he did not sleep at all last night, and he must be in a state of complete exhaustion. But, just as he predicted, he'll rise, his old self again."

Captain de Rougemont hurried away, and John was left alone in the midst of a great army. He stood before Lannes' tent, which was in the midst of a grassy and rather elevated opening, and he heard once more the infinite sounds made by two hundred thousand armed men, blending into one vast, fused note.

The army, too, was moving, or getting ready to move. Batteries of the splendid French artillery passed before him, squadrons of horsemen galloped by, and regiments of infantry followed. It all seemed confused, aimless to the eye, but John knew that nevertheless it was proceeding with order and method, directed by a master mind.

Often trumpets sounded and the motion of the troops seemed to quicken. Now he beheld men from the lands of the sun, the short, dark, fierce soldiers of the Midi, youths of Marseilles and youths of the first Roman province, whose native language was Provencal and not French. He remembered the men of the famous battalion who had marched from Marseilles to Paris singing Rouget de Lisle's famous song, and giving it their name, while they tore down an ancient kingdom. Doubtless, spirits no less ardent and fearless than theirs were here now.

He saw the Arabs in turbans and flowing robes, and black soldiers from Senegal, and seeing these men from far African deserts he knew that France was rallying her strength for a supreme effort. The German Empire, with the flush of unbroken victory in war after war, could command the complete devotion of its sons, but the French Republic, without such triumphs as yet, could do as well. John felt an immense pride because he, too, was republican to the core, and often there was a lot in a name.

It was about noon now, and the sun was shining with dazzling brilliancy. The tall hill and the low hill were clothed in deep green, and the waters of the little river that ran between, sparkled in the light. The air was crisp with a cool wind that blew from the west, and John felt that the omens were good for the great mysterious movement which he believed to be at hand.

He looked into the tent and saw that Lannes was sleeping soundly, with a good color in his face. A powerful constitution aided by a strong will had done its work and he was sure that on the morrow Lannes would again be the most daring French scout of the air.

John found the waiting hard work. There was so much movement and action that he wanted to be a part of it. He had thrown in his lot with this army and he wanted to share its work at once. Yet much time passed, and de Rougemont did not return. The evidences that the great French army was marching to the point designated in the note brought by Lannes multiplied. From the crest of the hill he already saw large bodies of troops marching forward steadily, their long blue coats flapping awkwardly about their legs. He wondered once more why they wore such an inharmonious and conspicuous uniform as blue frock coats and baggy red trousers.

He heard presently the martial sounds of the Marseillaise, and the regiment singing it passed very close to him. The men were nearly all short, dark, and very young. But the spring and fire with which they marched were magnificent. As they thundered out the grand old tune their feet seemed scarcely to touch the earth, and fierce eyes glowed in dark faces.

John, with a start, recognized one, a petty officer, a sergeant it seemed, who marched beside the line. He was the most eager of them all, and his face was tense and wrapt. It was Geronimo, the little Apache, in whom the spark of patriotism had lit the fire of genius. His call had come and it had drawn him from a half savage life into one of glorious deeds for his country.

"He'll be a general if he isn't killed first," murmured John, with absolute conviction.

Geronimo, at that moment, looked his way and recognized him. His hand flew to his head in a military salute, which John returned in kind, and his eyes plainly showed pleasure at sight of this new friend whom he had made in a few minutes on the Butte Montmartre.

"We meet again," he said, "and before the week is out it will be victory or death."

"I think so, too," said John.

"I know it," said Geronimo, and, saluting once more, he marched on with his regiment. John saw them pass across the valley and join the great mass of troops that filled the whole northern horizon. About an hour later a cheerful voice called to him, and he beheld Lannes standing in the door of the tent, his head well bandaged, but his eyes clear and strong and the natural color in his face.

"What has happened, John?" he asked.

"You've slept six or seven hours."

"And while I slept, the army, as I can see, has begun its march according to the order we brought. I'm sorry I had to miss any of it, but I was bound to sleep."

"You're a marvel."

"No marvel at all. I'm merely one of a million Frenchmen molded on the same model. An army can't move fast and tonight the *Arrow* and I will be hovering over its front. There's your old place for you in the plane."

"I'd only be in your way, Philip. But can't you wait until tomorrow? Don't rush yourself while you've got a new wound."

"The wound is nothing. I'm bound to go tonight with the *Arrow*. But what are you going to do if you don't go with me?"

"A new friend whom I've made while you slept has found a place for me with him, on the staff of General Vaugirard, a brigade commander. I shall serve there until I'm able to rejoin the Strangers."

"General Vaugirard! I've seen him. An able man, and a most noticeable figure. You've fared well."

"I hope so. Here comes Captain de Rougemont."

The captain showed much pleasure at seeing Lannes up and apparently well.

"What! Has our king of the air revived so soon!" he exclaimed.

"The dead themselves would rise when we're about to strike for the life of France," said Lannes, his dramatic quality again coming to the front.

"Well spoken," said de Rougemont, the color flushing into his face.

"I return to my aeroplane within two hours," said Lannes. "I hold a commission from our government which allows me to operate somewhat as a free lance, but, of course, I shall conform for the present to the wishes of the man who commands the flying corps of this army. Meanwhile, I leave with you my young Yankee friend here, John Scott. For some strange reason I've conceived for him a strong brotherly affection. Kindly see that he doesn't get killed unless it's necessary for our country, and this, I think, is a long enough speech for me to make now."

"I'll do my best for him," said de Rougemont earnestly. "I've come for you, Scott."

"Good-bye, Philip," said John, extending his hand.

"Good-bye, John," said Lannes, "and do as I tell you. Don't get your-self killed unless it's absolutely necessary."

Usually so stoical, his voice showed emotion, and he turned away after the strong pressure of the two hands. John and de Rougemont walked down the valley, where they joined General Vaugirard and the rest of his staff.

As soon as John saw the general he knew what Lannes meant by his phrase "a noticeable figure." General Vaugirard was a man of about sixty, so enormously fat that he must have weighed three hundred pounds. His face was covered with thick white beard, out of which looked small, sharp red eyes. He reminded John of a great white bear. The little red eyes bored him through for an instant, and then their owner said briefly:

"De Rougemont has vouched for you. Stay with him. An orderly has your horse."

A French soldier held for him a horse bearing all the proper equip-ment, and John, saluting the general, sprang into the saddle. He was a good horseman, and now he felt thoroughly sure of himself. If it came to the worst, and he was unseated, the earth was not far away, but if he were thrown out of the *Arrow* he would have a long and terrible time in falling.

General Vaugirard had not yet mounted, but stood beside a huge black horse, fit to carry such a weight. He was listening and looking with the deepest attention and his staff was silent around him. John saw from their manner that these men liked and respected their immense general.

More trumpets sounded, much nearer now, and a messenger galloped up, handing a note to General Vaugirard, who glanced at it hastily, uttered a deep Ah! of relief and joy and thrust it into his pocket.

Then saying to his staff, "Gentlemen, we march at once," he put one hand on his horse's shoulder, and, to John's immense surprise, leaped as lightly into the saddle as if he had been a riding master. He settled himself easily into his seat, spoke a word to his staff, and then he rode with his regiments toward that great mass of men on the horizon who were steadily marching forward.

John kept by the side of de Rougemont. There were brief introduc-tions to some of the young officers nearest him, and he felt an air of friendliness about him. As de Rougemont told them he had already given ample proof of his devotion to the cause, and he was accepted promptly as one of them.

John was now conscious how strongly he had projected himself into the life of the French. He was an American for generations back and his blood by descent was British. He had been among the Germans and he liked them personally, he had served already with the English, and their point of view was more nearly like the American than any other. But he was here with the French and he felt for them the deepest sympathy of all. He was conscious of a tie like that of blood brotherhood.

He knew it was due to the old and yet unpaid help France had given to his own country, and above all to the conviction that France, minding her own business, had been set upon by a greater power, with intent to crush and destroy. France was attacked by a dragon, and the old similes of mythology floated through his mind, but, oftenest, that of Andromeda chained to the rock. And the figure that typified France always had the golden hair and dark blue eyes of slim, young Julie Lannes.

They advanced several hours almost in silence, as far as talk was concerned, but two hundred thousand men marching made a deep and steady murmur. General Vaugirard kept well in front of his staff, riding, despite his immense bulk, like a Comanche, and occasionally putting his glasses to those fiery little red eyes. At length he turned and beckoned to John, who promptly drew up to his side.

"You speak good French?" he said in his native tongue.

"Yes, sir," replied John promptly.

"I understand that you came with the flying man, Lannes, who brought the message responsible for this march, and that it is not the only time you've done good service in our cause?"

John bowed modestly.

"Did you see any German troops on the way?"

"Only a band of Uhlans."

"A mere scouting party. It occurred to me that you might have seen masses of troops belonging to the foe, indicating perhaps what is awaiting us at the end of our march."

"I know nothing, sir. The Uhlans were all the foes we saw from the air, save the man who shot Lannes."

"I believe you. You belong to the youngest of the great nations. Your people have not yet learned to say with the accents of truth the thing that is not. I am sixty years old, and yet I have the curiosity to know where I am going and what I am expected to do when I get there. Behold how I, an old man, speak so frankly to you, so young."

"When I saw your excellency leap into the saddle you did not seem to me to be more than twenty."

John called him "your excellency" because he thought that in the absence of precise knowledge of what was fitting the term was as good as another.

A smile twinkled in the eyes of General Vaugirard. Evidently he was pleased.

"That is flattery, flattery, young man," he said, "but it pleases me. Since I've drawn from you all you know, which is but little, you may fall back with your comrades. But keep near; I fancy I shall have much for you to do before long. Meanwhile, we march on, in ignorance of what is awaiting us. Ah, well, such is life!"

He seemed to John a strange compound of age and youth, a mixture of the philosopher and the soldier. That he was a real leader John could no longer doubt. He saw the little red eyes watching everything, and he noticed that the regiments of Vaugirard had no superiors in trimness and spirit.

They marched until sundown and stopped in some woods clear of undergrowth, like most of those in Europe. The camp kitchens went to work at once, and they received good food and coffee. As far as John could see men were at rest, but he could not tell whether the whole army was doing likewise. It spread out much further to both right and left than his eyes could reach.

The members of the staff tethered their horses in the grove, and after supper stood together and talked, while the fat general paced back and forth, his brow wrinkled in deep thought.

"Good old Papa Vaugirard is studying how to make the best of us," said de Rougemont. "We're all his children. They say that he knows nearly ten thousand men under his command by face if not by name, and we trust him as no other brigade commander in the army is trusted by his troops. He's thinking hard now, and General Vaugirard does not think for nothing. As soon as he arrives at what seems to him a solution of his problem he will begin to whistle. Then he will interrupt his whistling by saying: 'Ah, well, such is life.'"

"I hope he'll begin to whistle soon," said John, "because his brow is wrinkling terribly."

He watched the huge general with a sort of fascinated gaze. Seen now in the twilight, Vaugirard's very bulk was impressive. He was immense, strong, primeval. He walked back and forth over a line about thirty feet long, and the deep wrinkles remained on his brow. Every member of his staff was asking how long it would last.

A sound, mellow and soft, but penetrating, suddenly arose. General Vaugirard was whistling, and John's heart gave a jump of joy. He did not in the least doubt de Rougemont's assertion that an answer to the problem had been found.

General Vaugirard whistled to himself softly and happily. Then he said twice, and in very clear tones: "Ah, well, such is life!" He began to whistle again, stopped in a moment or two and called to de Rougemont, with whom he talked a while.

"We're to march once more in a half-hour," said de Rougemont, when he returned to John and his comrades. "It must be a great converging movement in which time is worth everything. At least, General Vaugirard thinks so, and he has a plan to get us into the very front of the action."

"I hope so," said John. "I'm not anxious to get killed, but I'd rather be in the battle than wait. I wonder if I'll meet anywhere on the front that company to which I belong, the Strangers."

"I think I've heard of them," said de Rougemont, "a body of Americans and Englishmen, volunteers in the French service, commanded by Captain Daniel Colton."

"Right you are, and I've two particular friends in that companyI suppose they've rejoined itWharton, an American, and Carstairs, an Englishman. We went through a lot of dangers together before we reached the British army near Mons, and I'd like to see them again."

"Maybe you will, but here comes an extraordinary procession."

They heard many puffing sounds, uniting in one grand puffing chorus, and saw advancing down a white road toward them a long, ghostly train, as if a vast troop of extinct monsters had returned to earth and were marching this way. But John knew very well that it was a train of automobiles and raising the glasses that he now always carried he saw that they were empty except for the chauffeurs.

General Vaugirard began to whistle his mellowest and most musical tune, stopping only at times to mutter a few words under his breath. John surmised that he was expressing deep satisfaction, and that he had been waiting for the motor train. War was now fought under new conditions. The Germans had thousands and scores of thousands of motors, and perhaps the French were provided almost as well.

"I fancy," said de Rougemont, who was also watching the arrival of the machines, "that we'll leave our horses now and travel by motor."

De Rougemont's supposition was correct. The line of automobiles began to mass in front, many rows deep, and all the chauffeurs, their great goggles shining through the darkness, were bent over their wheels ready to be off at once with their armed freight. It filled John with elation, and he saw the same spirit shining in the eyes of the young French officers.

General Vaugirard began to puff like one of the machines. He threw out his great chest, pursed up his mouth and emitted his breath in little gusts between his lips, "Very good! Very good, my children!" he said, "Oil and electricity will carry us now, and we go forward, not backward!"

True to de Rougemont's prediction, the horses were given to orderlies, and the staff and a great portion of the troops were taken into the cars. General Vaugirard and several of the older officers occupied a huge machine, and just behind him came de Rougemont, John and a half-dozen young lieutenants and captains in another. Before them stretched a great white road. Far overhead hovered many aeroplanes. John had no doubt that the *Arrow* was among them, or rather was the farthest one forward. Lannes' eager soul, wound or no wound, would keep him in front.

They now moved rapidly, and John's spirits continued to rise. There was something wonderful in this swift march on wheels in the moonlight. As far back as he could see the machines came in a stream, and to the left and right he saw them proceeding on other roads also. All the country was strange to John. He could not remember having seen it from the aeroplane, and he was sure that the army, instead of going to Paris, was bound for some point where it would come in instant contact with the German forces.

"Do you know the road?" he asked of de Rougemont.

"Not at all. I'm from the Gironde country. I've been in Paris, but I know little of the region about it. A good way to reach the front, is it not, Mr. Scott?"

"Fine. I fancy that we're hurried forward to make a link in a chain, or at least to stop a gap."

"And those large birds overhead are scouting for us."

"Look! One of them is dropping down. I dare say it's making a report to some general higher in rank than ours."

He pointed with a long forefinger, and John watched the aeroplane come down in its slanting course like a falling star. It was a beautiful night, a light blue sky, with a fine moon and hosts of clear stars. One could see far, and soon after the plane descended John saw it rise again from the same spot, ascend high in air, and shoot off toward the east.

"That may have been Lannes," he said.

"Likely as not," said de Rougemont.

John now observed General Vaugirard, who sat erect in the front of his automobile, with a pair of glasses, relatively as huge as himself, to his eyes. Occasionally he would purse his lips, and John knew that his favorite expression was coming forth. To the young American's imaginative mind his broad back expressed rigidity and strength.

The great murmuring sound, the blended advance of so many men, made John sleepy by-and-by. In spite of himself his heavy eyelids drooped, and although he strove manfully against it, sleep took him. When he awoke he heard the same deep murmur, like the roll of the sea, and saw the army still advancing. It was yet night, though fine and clear, and there before him was the broad, powerful back of the general. Vaugirard was still using the glasses and John judged that he had not slept at all. But in his own machine everybody was asleep except the man at the wheel.

The country had grown somewhat hillier, but its characteristics were the same, fertile, cultivated fields, a small wood here and there, clear brooks, and church spires shining in the dusk. Both horse and foot advanced across the fields, but the roads were occupied by the motors, which John judged were carrying at least twenty thousand men and maybe forty thousand.

He was not sleepy now, and he watched the vast panorama wheel past. He knew without looking at his watch that the night was nearly over, because he could already smell the dawn. The wind was freshening a bit, and he heard its rustle in the leaves of a wood as they pushed through it.

Then came a hum and a whir, and a long line of men on motor cycles at the edge of the road crept up and then passed them. One checked his speed enough to run by the side of John's car, and the rider, raising his head a little, gazed intently at the young American. His cap closed over his face like a hood, but the man knew him.

"Fortune puts us on the same road again, Mr. Scott," he said.

"I don't believe I know you," said John, although there was a familiar note in the voice.

"And yet you've met me several times, and under exciting conditions. It seems to me that we're always pursuing similar things, or we wouldn't be together on the same road so often. You're acute enough. Don't you know me now?"

"I think I do. You're Fernand Weber, the Alsatian."

"And so I am. I knew your memory would not fail you. It's a great movement that we've begun, Mr. Scott. France will be saved or destroyed within the next few days."

"I think so."

"You've deserted your friend, Philip Lannes, the finest of our airmen."

"Oh, no, I haven't. He's deserted me. I couldn't afford to be a burden on his aeroplane at such a time as this."

"I suppose not. I saw an aeroplane come down to earth a little while ago, and then rise again. I'm sure it was his machine, the *Arrow*."

"So am I."

"Here's where he naturally would be. Good-bye, Mr. Scott, and good luck to you. I must go on with my company."

"Good-bye and good luck," repeated John, as the Alsatian shot forward. He liked Weber, who had a most pleasing manner, and he was glad to have seen him once more.

"Who was that?" asked de Rougemont, waking from his sleep and catching the last words of farewell.

"An Alsatian, named Fernand Weber, who has risked his life more than once for France. He belongs to the motor-cycle corps that's just passing."

"May he and his comrades soon find the enemy, because here is the day."

The leaves and grass rippled before the breeze and over the eastern hills the dawn broke.

3

THE INVISIBLE HAND

I t was a brilliant morning sun, deepening the green of the pleasant land, lighting up villages and glinting off church steeples. In a field a little distance to their right John saw two peasants at work already, bent over, their eyes upon the ground, apparently as indifferent to the troops as the troops were to them.

It was very early, but the sun was rising fast, unfolding a splendid panorama. The French army with its blues and reds was more spectacular than the German, and hence afforded a more conspicuous target. John was sure that if the war went on the French would discard these vivid uniforms and betake themselves to gray or khaki. He saw clearly that the day of gorgeous raiment for the soldier had passed.

The great puffing sound of primeval monsters which had blended into one rather harmonious note ceased, as if by signal, and the innumerable motors stopped. As far as John could see the army stretched to left and right over roads, hills and fields, but in the fields behind them the silent peasants went on with their workin fields which the Republic had made their own.

"I think we take breakfast here," said Rougemont. "War is what one of your famous American generals said it was, but for the present, at least, we are marching *de luxe*. Here comes one of those glorious camp-kitchens."

An enormous motor vehicle, equipped with all the paraphernalia of a kitchen, stopped near them, and men, trim and neatly dressed, served hot food and steaming coffee. General Vaugirard had alighted also, and John noticed that his step was much more springy and alert than that of some officers half his age. His breath came in great gusts, and the small portion of his face not covered by thick beard was ruddy and glowing with health. He drank several cups of coffee with startling rapidity, draining each at a breath, and between times he whistled softly a pleasing little refrain.

The march must be going well. Undoubtedly General Vaugirard had received satisfactory messages in the night, while his young American aide, and other Frenchmen as young, slept.

"Well, my children," he said, rubbing his hands after his last cup of coffee had gone to its fate, "the day dawns and behold the sun of France is rising. It's not the sun of Austerlitz, but a modest republican sun that can grow and grow. Behold we are at the appointed place, set forth in the message that came to us from the commander-in-chief through Paris, and then by way of the air! And, look, my children, the bird from the blue descends once more among us!"

There were flying machines of many kinds in the air, but John promptly picked out one which seemed to be coming with the flight of an eagle out of its uppermost heights. He seemed to know its slim, lithe shape, and the rapidity and decision of its approach. His heart thrilled, as it had thrilled when he saw the *Arrow* coming for the first time on that spur of the Alps near Salzburg.

"It's for me," said General Vaugirard, as he looked upward. "This flying demon, this man without fear, was told to report directly to me, and he conies at the appointed hour."

Something of the mystery that belongs to the gulf of the infinite was reflected in the general's eyes. He, too, felt that man's flight in the heavens yet had in it a touch of the supernatural. Lannes' plane had seemed to shoot from white clouds, out of unknown spaces, and the general ceased to whistle or breathe gustily. His chest rose and fell more violently than usual, but the breath came softly.

The plane descended rapidly and settled down on the grass very near them. Lannes saluted and presented a note to General Vaugirard, who started and then expelled the breath from his lungs in two or three prodigious puffs.

"Good, my son, good!" he exclaimed, patting Lannes repeatedly on the shoulder; "and now a cup of coffee for you at once! Hurry with it, some of you idle children! Can't you see that he needs it!"

John was first with the coffee, which Lannes drank eagerly, although it was steaming hot. John saw that he needed it very much indeed, as he was white and shaky. He noticed, too, that there were spots of blood on Lannes' left sleeve.

"What is it, Philip?" he whispered. "You've been attacked again?"

"Aye, truly. My movements seem to be observed by some mysterious eye. A shot was fired at me, and again it came from a French plane. That was all I could see. We were in a bank of mist at the time, and I just caught a glimpse of the plane itself. The man was a mere shapeless figure to me. I had no time to fight him, because I was due here with another message which made vengeance upon him at that time a matter of little moment."

He flecked the red drops off his sleeve, and added:

"It was but a scratch. My weary look comes from a long and hard flight and not from the mysterious bullet. I'm to rest here an hour, which will be sufficient to restore me, and then I'm off again."

"Is there any rule against your telling me what you've seen, Philip?"

De Rougemont and several other officers had approached, drawn by their curiosity, and interest in Lannes.

"None at all," he replied in a tone all could hear, "but I'm able to speak in general terms only. I can't give details, because I don't know 'em. The Germans are not many miles ahead. They're in hundreds of thousands, and I hear that this is only one of a half-dozen armies."

"And our own force?" said de Rougemont eagerly.

Lannes' chest expanded. The dramatic impulse was strong upon him again.

"There is another army on our right, and another on our left," he replied, "and although I don't know surely, I think there are others still further on the line. The English are somewhere with us, too."

John felt his face tingle as the blood rose in it. He had left a Paris apparently lost. Within a day almost a tremendous transformation had occurred. A mighty but invisible intellect, to which he was yet scarcely able to attach a name, had been at work. The French armies, the beaten and the unbeaten, had become bound together like huge links in a chain, and the same invisible and all but nameless mind was drawing the chain forward with gigantic force.

"A million Frenchmen must be advancing," he heard Lannes saying, and then he came out of his vision. General Vaugirard bustled up and gave orders to de Rougemont, who said presently to John:

"Can you ride a motor cycle?"

"I've had some experience, and I'm willing to make it more."

"Good. In this army, staff officers will no longer have horses shot under them. We're to take orders on motor cycles. They've been sent ahead for us, and here's yours waiting for you."

The cycles were leaning against trees, and the members of the staff took their places beside them. General Vaugirard walked a little distance up the road, climbed into an automobile and, standing up, looked a long time through his glasses. Lannes, who had been resting on the grass, approached the general and John saw him take a note from him. Then Lannes went away to the *Arrow* and sailed off into the heavens. Many other planes were flying over the French army and far off in front John saw through his own glasses a fleet of them which he knew must be German.

Then he heard a sound, faint but deep, which came rolling like an echo, and he recognized it as the distant note of a big gun. He quivered a little, as he leaned against his motor cycle, but quickly stiffened again to attention. The faint rolling sound came again from their right and then many times. John, using his glasses, saw nothing there, and the giant general, still standing up in the car and also using his glasses, saw nothing there either.

Yet the same quiver that affected John had gone through this whole army of two hundred thousand men, one of the huge links in the French chain. There was none among them who did not know that the far note was the herald of battle, not a mere battle of armies, but of nations face to face.

General Vaugirard did not show any excitement. He leaped lightly from the car, and then began to pace up and down slowly, as if he were awaiting orders. The men moved restlessly on the meadows, looking like a vast sea of varied colors, as the sun glimmered on the red and blue of their uniforms.

But no order came for them to advance. John thought that perhaps they were saved to be driven as a wedge into the German center and whispered his belief to de Rougemont, who agreed with him.

"They are opening on the left, too," said the Frenchman. "Can't you hear the growling of the guns there?"

John listened and soon he separated the note from other sounds. Beyond a doubt the battle had now begun on both flanks, though at distant points. He wondered where the English force was, though he had an idea that it was on the left then. Yet he was already thoroughly at home with the staff of General Vaugirard.

The growling on either side of them seemed soon to come a little closer, but John knew nevertheless that it was many miles away.

"Not an enemy in sight, not even a trace of smoke," said de Rougemont to him. "We seem to be a great army here, merely resting in the fields, and yet we know that a huge battle is going on."

"And that's about all we do know," said John. "What has impressed me in this war is the fact that high officers even know so little. When cannon throw shells ten or twelve miles, eyesight doesn't get much chance."

A wait for a full half-hour followed, a period of intense anxiety for all in the group, and for the whole army too. John used his glasses freely, and often he saw the French soldiers moving about in a restless manner, until they were checked by their officers. But most of them were lying down, their blue coats and red trousers making a vast and vivid blur against the green of the grass.

All the while the sound of the cannon grew, but, despite the power of his glasses, John could not see a sign of war. Only that roaring sound came to tell him that battle, vast, gigantic, on a scale the world had never seen before, was joined, and the volume of the cannon fire, beyond a doubt, was growing. It pulsed heavily, and either he or his fancy noticed a steady jarring motion. A faint acrid taint crept into the air and he felt it in his nose and throat. He coughed now and then, and he observed that men around him coughed also. But, on the whole, the army was singularly still, the soldiers straining eye or ear to see something or hear more of the titanic struggle that was raging on either side of them.

John again searched the horizon eagerly with his glasses, but it showed only green hills and bits of wood, bare of human activity. The French aeroplanes still hovered, but not in front of General Vaugirard. They were off to right and left, where the wings of the nations had closed in combat. He was ceasing to think of the foes as armies, but as nations in battle line. Here stood not a French army, but France, and there stood not a German army, but Germany.

As he looked toward the left he picked out a narrow road, running between hedges, and showing but a strip of white even through the glasses. He saw something coming along this road. It was far away when he first noticed it, but it was coming with great speed, and he was soon able to tell that it was a man on a motor cycle. His pulse leaped again. He felt instinctively that the rider was for them and that he bore something of great import. The figure, man and cycle, molded into one, sped along the narrow road which led to the base of the hill on which General Vaugirard and his staff stood.

The huge general saw the approaching figure too, and he began to whistle melodiously like the note of a piccolo, with the vast thunder of the guns accompanying him as an orchestra. John knew that the cyclist was a messenger, and that he was eagerly expected. An order of some kind was at hand! All the members of the staff had the same conviction.

The cyclist stopped at the bottom of the hill, leaped from the machine and ran to General Vaugirard, to whom he handed a note. The general read it, expelled his breath in a mighty gust, and turning to his staff, said:

"My children, our time has come. The whole central army of which we are a part will advance. It will perhaps be known before night whether France is to remain a great nation or become the vassal of Germany. My children, if France ever had need for you to fight with all your hearts and souls, that need is here today."

His manner was simple and majestic, and his words touched the mind and feeling of every one who heard them. John was moved as much as if he had been a Frenchman too. He felt a profound sympathy for this devoted France, which had suffered so much, to which his own country still owed that great debt, and which had a right to her own soil, fertilized with so many centuries of labor.

General Vaugirard, resting a pad on his knee, wrote rapid notes which he gave to the members of his staff in turn to be delivered. John's was to a Parisian regiment lying in a field, and expanding body and mind into instant action, he leaped upon the cycle and sped away. It was often hard for him now to separate fact from fancy. His imagination, vivid at all times, painted new pictures while such a tremendous drama passed before him.

Yet he knew afterward that the sound of the battle did increase in volume as he flew over the short distance to the regiment. Both east and west were shaking with the tremendous concussion. One crash he heard distinctly above the others and he believed it was that of a forty-two centimeter.

He reached the field, his cycle spun between the eager soldiers, and as he leaped off in the presence of the colonel he fairly thrust the note into his hand, exclaiming at the same time in his zeal, "It's an order to advance! The whole Army of the Center is about to attack."

He called it the Army of the Center at a guess, but names did not matter now. The colonel glanced at the note, waved his sword above his head and cried in a loud voice:

"My lads, up and forward!"

The regiment arose with a roar of cheering and began to advance across the fields. John caught a glimpse of a petty officer, short and small, but as compact and fierce as a panther, driving on men who needed no driving. "Geronimo is going to make good," he said to himself. "He'll do or die today."

As he raced back for new orders, if need be, he knew now that fact not fancy told him the battle was growing. The earth shook not only on right and left but in front also. A hasty look through the glasses showed little tongues of fire licking up on the horizon before them and he knew that they came from the monster cannon of the Germans who were surely advancing, while the French were advancing also to meet them.

General Vaugirard sprang into his automobile, taking only two of his senior officers with him, while the rest followed on their motor cycles. As far as John could see on either side the vast rows of French swept across hills and fields. There was little shouting now and no sound of bands, but presently a shout arose behind them: "Way for the artillery!"

Then he heard cries, the rumble of wheels and the rapid beat of hoofs. With an instinctive shudder, lest he be ground to pieces, he pulled from the road, and saw the motor of General Vaugirard turn out also. Then the great French batteries thundered past to seek positions soon in the fields behind low hills. He saw them a little later unlimbering and making ready.

The French advance changed from a walk to a trot. John saw the Parisian regiment, not far away, but at the very front and he knew that among all those ardent souls there was none more ardent than that of the little Apache, Bougainville. Meanwhile, Vaugirard in his motor kept to the road and the staff on their motor cycles followed closely.

On both flanks the thunder of massed cannon was deepening, and now John, who used his glasses occasionally, was able to see wisps and tendrils of smoke on the eastern and northern horizons. The tremor in the air was strong and continuous. It played incessantly upon the drums of his ears, and he found that he could not hear the words of the other aides so well as before. But there was no succession of crashes. The sound was more like the roaring of a distant storm.

They advanced another mile, two hundred thousand men, afire with zeal, a whole vast army moved forward as the other French armies were by the hidden hand which they could not see, of which they knew nothing, but the touch of which they could feel.

John heard a whizzing sound, he caught a glimpse of a dark object, rushing forward at frightful velocity, and then he and his wheel reeled beneath the force of a tremendous explosion. The shell coming from an invisible point, miles away, had burst some distance on his right, scattering death and wounds over a wide radius. But Vaugirard's brigades did not stop for one instant. They cheered loudly, closed up the gap in their line, and went on steadily as before. Some one began to sing the Marseillaise, and in an instant the song, like fire in dry grass, spread along a vast front. John had often wished that he could have heard the armies of the French Revolution singing their tremendous battle hymn as they marched to victory, and now he heard it on a scale far more gigantic than in the days of the First French Republic.

The vast chorus rolled for miles and for all he knew other armies, far to right and left, might be singing it, too. The immense volume of the song drowned out everything, even that tremor in the air, caused by the big guns. John's heart beat so hard that it caused actual physical pain in his side, and presently, although he was unconscious of it, he was thundering out the verses with the others.

He was riding by the side of de Rougemont, and he stopped singing long enough to shout, at the top of his voice:

"No enemy in sight yet?"

"No," de Rougemont shouted back, "but he doesn't need to be. The German guns have our range."

From a line on the distant horizon, from positions behind hills, the German shells were falling fast, cutting down men by hundreds, tearing great holes in the earth, and filling the air with an awful shrieking and hissing. It was all the more terrible because the deadly missiles seemed to come from nowhere. It was like a mortal hail rained out of heaven. John had not yet seen a German, nothing but those tongues of fire licking up on the horizon, and some little whitish clouds of smoke, lifting themselves slowly above the trees, yet the thunder was no longer a rumble. It had a deep and angry note, whose burden was death.

They must maintain their steady march directly toward the mouths of those guns. John comprehended in those awful moments that the task of the French was terrible, almost superhuman. If their nation was to live they must hurl back a victorious foe, practically numberless, armed and equipped with everything that a great race in a half-century of supreme thought and effort could prepare for war. It was spirit and patriotism against the monstrous machine of fire and steel, and he trembled lest the machine could overcome anything in the world.

He was about to shout again to de Rougemont, but his words were lost in the rending crash of the French artillery. Their batteries were posted on both sides of him, and they, too, had found the range. All along the front hundreds of guns were opening and John hastily thrust portions that he tore from his handkerchief into his ear, lest he be deafened forever.

The sight, at first magnificent, now became appalling. The shells came in showers and the French ranks were torn and mangled. Companies existed and then they were not. The explosions were like the crash of thunderbolts, but through it all the French continued to advance. Those whose knees grew weak beneath them were upborne and carried forward by the press of their comrades. The French gunners, too, were making prodigious efforts but with cannon of such long range neither side could see what its batteries were accomplishing. John was sure, though, that the great French artillery must be giving as good as it received.

He was conscious that General Vaugirard was still going forward along the long white road, sweeping his glasses from left to right and from right to left in a continuous semi-circle, apparently undisturbed, apparently now without human emotion. He was no figure of romance, but he was a man, cool and powerful, ready to die with all his men, if death for them was needed.

Still the invisible hand swept them on, the hand that a million men in action could not see, but which every one of the million, in his own way, felt. The crash of the guns on both sides had become fused together into one roar, so steady and continued so long that the sound seemed almost normal. Voices could now be heard under it and John spoke to de Rougemont.

"Can you make anything of it?" he asked. "Do we win or do we lose?"

"It's too early yet to tell anything. The cannon only are speaking, but you'll note that our army is advancing."

"Yes, I see it. Before I've only beheld it in retreat before overwhelming numbers. This is different."

General Vaugirard beckoned to his aides, and again sent them out with messages. John's note was to the commander of a battery of field guns telling him to move further forward. He started at once through the fields on his motor cycle, but he could not go fast now. The ground had been cut deep by artillery and cavalry and torn by shells and he had to pick his way, while the shower of steel, sent by men who were firing by mathematics, swept over and about him.

Shivers seized him more than once, as shrapnel and pieces of shell flew by. Now and then he covered his eyes with one hand to shut out the horror of dead and torn men lying on either side of his path, but in spite of the shells, in spite of the deadly nausea that assailed him at times, he went on. The rush of air from a shell threw him once from his motor cycle, but as he fell on soft clodded earth he was not hurt, and, springing quickly back on his wheel, he reached the battery.

The order was welcome to the commander of the guns, who was anxious to go closer, and, limbering up, he advanced as rapidly as weapons of such great weight could be dragged across the fields. John followed, that he might report the result. They were now facing toward the east and the whole horizon there was a blaze of fire. The shells were coming thicker and thicker, and the air was filled with the screaming of the shrapnel.

The commander of the battery, a short, powerful Frenchman, was as cool as ice, and John drew coolness from him. One can get used to almost anything, and his nervous tremors were passing. Despite the terrible fire of the German artillery the French army was still advancing. Many thousands had fallen already before the shells and shrapnel of the invisible foe, but there had been no check.

The cannon crossed a brook, and, unlimbering, again opened a tremendous fire. To one side and on a hill here, a man whom the commander watched closely was signaling. John knew that he was directing the aim of the battery and the French, like the Germans, were killing by mathematics.

He rode his cycle to the crest of a little elevation behind the battery and with his newfound coolness began to use his glasses again. Despite the thin, whitish smoke, he saw men on the horizon, mere manikins moving back and forth, apparently without meaning, but men nevertheless. He caught, too, the outline of giant tubes, the huge guns that were sending the ceaseless rain of death upon the French.

He also saw signs of hurry and confusion among those manikins, and he knew that the French shells were striking them. He rode down to the commander and told him. The swart Frenchman grinned.

"My children are biting," he said, glancing affectionately at his guns. "They're brave lads, and their teeth are long and sharp."

He looked at his signal man, and the guns let loose again with a force that sent the air rushing away in violent waves. Batteries farther on were firing also with great rapidity. In most of these the gunners were directed by field telephones strung hastily, but the one near John still depended upon signal men. It was composed of eight five-inch guns, and John believed that its fire was most accurate and deadly.

Using his glasses again, he saw that the disturbance among those manikins was increasing. They were running here and there, and many seemed to vanish suddenlyhe knew that they were blown away by the shells. To the right of the great French battery some lighter field guns were advancing. One drawn by eight horses had not yet unlimbered, and he saw a shell strike squarely upon it. In the following explosion pieces of steel whizzed by him and when the smoke cleared away the gun, the gunners and the horses were all gone. The monster shell had blown everything to pieces. The other guns hurried on, took up their positions and began to fire. John shuddered violently, but in a moment or two, he, too, forgot the little tragedy in the far more gigantic one that was being played before him.

He rode back to General Vaugirard and told him that his order had been obeyed. The general nodded, but did not take his glasses from the horizon, where a long gray line was beginning to appear against the green of the earth. "It goes well so far," John heard him say in the under note which was audible beneath the thunder of the battle.

In a quarter of an hour the great batteries limbered up again, and once more the French army went forward, the troops to lie down and wait again, while the artillery worked with ferocious energy. It was yet a battle of big guns, at least in the center. The armies were not near enough to each other for rifles; in truth not near enough yet to be seen. John, even with his glasses, could only discern the gray line advancing, he could make little of its form or order or of what it was trying to do.

But a light wind was now bringing smoke from one flank where the battle was far heavier than in the center, and the concussion of the artillery at that point became so frightful that the air seemed to come in waves of the utmost violence and to beat upon the drum of the ear with the force of a hammer. Owing to the wind John could not hear the battle on the other flank so well, but he believed that it was being fought there with equal fury and determination.

He was watching with such intentness that he did not hear the sweep of an aeroplane behind him, but he did see Lannes run to General Vaugirard's car and give him a note.

While the general read and pondered, Lannes turned toward the wheel on which John sat. Although he tried to preserve calm, John knew that he was tremendously excited. He had taken off his heavy glasses and his wonderful gray eyes were flashing. It was obvious to his friend, who now knew him so well, that he was moved by some tremendous emotion.

John rode up by the side of Lannes and said:

"What have you seen, Philip? You can tell a little at least, can't you?"

"More than a little! A lot! The *Arrow* and I have looked over a great area, John! Miles and miles and yet more miles! and wherever we went we gazed down upon armies locked in battle, and beyond that were other armies locked in battle, too! The nations meet in wrath! You can't see it here, nor from anywhere on the earth! It's only in the air high overhead that one can get even a partial view of its immensity! The English army is off there on the flank, a full thirty miles away, and you're not likely to see it today!"

He would have said more, but General Vaugirard beckoned to him, gave him a note which he had written hastily, and in a few more minutes Lannes was flitting like a swallow through the heavens. Then General Vaugirard's car moved forward and brigade after brigade of the French army resumed its advance also.

John felt that the great German machine had been met by a French machine as great. Perhaps the master mind that thrills through an organism of steel no less than one of human flesh was on the French side. He did not know. The invisible hand thrusting forward the French armies was still invisible to him. Yet he felt with the certainty of conviction that the eye and the brain of one man were achieving a marvel. In some mysterious manner the French defense had become an offense. The Republican troops were now attacking and the Imperial troops were seeking to hold fast.

He seemed to comprehend it all in an instant, and a mighty joy surged over him. De Rougemont saw his glistening eye and he asked curiously:

"What is it that you are feeling so strongly, Mr. Scott?"

"The thrill of the advance! The unknown plan, whatever it is, is working! Your nation is about to be saved! I feel it! I know it!"

De Rougemont gazed at him, and then the light leaped into his own eyes.

"A prophet! A prophet!" he cried. "Inspired youth speaks!"

A great crisis may call into being a great impulse, and de Rougemont's words were at once accepted as truth by all the young aides. Words of fire, words vital with life had gone forth, predicting their triumph, and as they rode among the troops carrying orders they communicated their burning zeal to the men who were already eager for closer battle.

The storm of missiles from the cannon was increasing rapidly. John now distinctly saw the huge German masses, not advancing but standing firm to receive the French attack, their front a vast line of belching guns. He knew that they would soon be within the area of rifle fire and he knew with equal truth that it would take the valor of immense numbers, wielded by the supreme skill of leaders to drive back the Germans.

The guns, some drawn by horses and others by motors, were moving forward with them. When the horses were swept away by a shell, men seized the guns and dragged them. Then they stopped again, took new positions and renewed the rain of death on the German army.

They began to hear a whistle and hiss that they knew. It was that of the bullets, and along the vast front they were coming in millions. But the French were using their rifles, too, and at intervals the deep thundering chant of the Marseillaise swept through their ranks. In spite of shell, shrapnel and bullets, in spite of everything, the French army in the center was advancing and John believed that the armies on the other parts of the line were advancing, too.

The bullets struck around them, and then among them. One aide fell from his cycle, and lay dead in the road, two more were wounded, but two hundred thousand men, their artillery blazing death over their heads, went on straight at the mouths of a thousand cannon.

Companies and regiments were swept away, but there was no check. Nor did the other French armies, the huge links in the chain, stop. A feeling of victory had swept along the whole gigantic battle front. They were fighting for Paris, for their country, for the soil which they tended, alive, and in which they slept, dead, and just at the moment when everything seemed to have been lost they were saving all. The heroic age of France had come again, and the Third Republic was justifying the First.

The battle deepened and thickened to an extraordinary degree, as the space between the two fronts narrowed. John for the first time saw the German troops without the aid of glasses. They were mere outlines against a fiery horizon, reddened by the mouths of so many belching cannon, but they seemed to him to stand there like a wall.

Another giant shell burst near them, and two more members of the staff fell from their cycles, dead before they touched the ground. That convulsive shudder seized John again, but the crash of tremendous events was so rapid that fear and horror alike passed in an instant. A piece of the same shell struck General Vaugirard's car and put it out of action at once. But the general leaped lightly to the ground, then swung his immense bulk across one of the riderless motor cycles and advanced with the surviving members of his staff. Imperturbable, he still swept the field with his glasses. Two aides were now sent to the right with messages, and a third, John himself, was despatched to the left on a similar errand.

It was John's duty to tell a regiment to bear in further to the left and close up a vacant spot in the line. He wheeled his cycle into a field, and then passed between rows of grapevines. The regiment, its ranks much thinned, was now about a hundred yards away, but shell and bullets alike were sweeping the distance between.

Nevertheless, he rode on, his wheel bumping over the rough ground, until he heard a rushing sound, and then blank darkness enveloped him. He fell one way, and the motor cycle fell another.

4

SEEN FROM ABOVE

John's period of unconsciousness was brief. The sweep of air from a gigantic shell, passing close, had taken his senses for a minute or two, but he leaped to his feet to find his motor cycle broken and puffing out its last breath, and himself among the dead and wounded in the wake of the army which was advancing rapidly. The turmoil was so vast, and so much dust and burned gunpowder was floating about that he was not able to tell where the valiant Vaugirard with the remainder of his staff marched. In front of him a regiment, cut up terribly, was advancing at a swift pace, and acting under the impulse of the moment he ran forward to join them.

When he overtook the regiment he saw that it had neither colonel, nor captains nor any other officers of high degree. A little man, scarcely more than a youth, his head bare, his eyes snapping fire, one hand holding aloft a red cap on the point of a sword, had taken command and was urging the soldiers on with every fierce shout that he knew. The men were responding. Command seemed natural to him. Here was a born leader in battle. John knew him, and he knew that his own prophecy had been fulfilled.

"Geronimo!" he gasped.

But young Bougainville did not see him. He was still shouting to the men whom he now led so well. The point of the sword, doubtless taken from the hand of some fallen officer, had pierced the red cap which was slowly sinking down the blade, but he did not notice it.

John looked again for his commander, but not seeing him, and knowing how futile it was now to seek him in all the fiery crush, he resolved to stay with the young Apache.

"Geronimo," he cried, and it was the last time he called him by that name, "I go with you!"

In all the excitement of the moment young Bougainville recognized him and something droll flashed in his eyes.

"Did I boast too much?" he shouted.

"You didn't!" John shouted back.

"Come on then! A big crowd of Germans is just over this hill, and we must smash 'em!"

John kept by his side, but Bougainville, still waving his sword, while the red cap sank lower and lower on the blade, addressed his men in terms of encouragement and affection.

"Forward, my children!" he shouted. "Men, without fear, let us be the first to make the enemy feel our bayonets! Look, a regiment on the right is ahead of you, and another also on the left leads you! Faster! Faster, my children!"

An angle of the German line was thrust forward at this point where a hill afforded a strong position. Bullets were coming from it in showers, but the Bougainville regiment broke into a run, passed ahead of the others and rushed straight at the hill.

It was the first time that men had come face to face in the battle and now John saw the French fury, the enthusiasm and fire that Napoleon had capitalized and cultivated so sedulously. Shouting fiercely, they flung themselves upon the Germans and by sheer impact drove them back. They cleared the hill in a few moments, triumphantly seized four cannon and then, still shouting, swept on.

John found himself shouting with the others. This was victory, the first real taste of it, and it was sweet to the lips. But the regiment was halted presently, lest it get too far forward and be cut off, and a general striding over to Bougainville uttered words of approval that John could not hear amid the terrific din of so many men in battlea million, a million and a half or more, he never knew.

They stood there panting, while the French line along a front of maybe fifty miles crept on and on. The French machine with the British wheels and springs coöperating, was working beautifully now. It was a match and more for their enemy. The Germans, witnessing the fire and dash of the French and feeling their tremendous impact, began to take alarm. It had not seemed possible to them in those last triumphant days that they could fail, but now Paris was receding farther and farther from their grasp.

John recovered a certain degree of coolness. The fire of the foe was turned away from them for the present, and, finding that the glasses thrown over his shoulder, had not been injured by his fall, he examined the battle front as he stood by the side of Bougainville. The country was fairly open here and along a range of miles the cannon in hundreds and hundreds were pouring forth destruction. Yet the line, save where the angle had been crushed by the rush of Bougainville's regiment, stood fast, and John shuddered at thought of the frightful slaughter, needed to drive it back, if it could be driven back at all.

Then he glanced at the fields across which they had come. For two or three miles they were sprinkled with the fallen, the red and blue of the French uniform showing vividly against the green grass. But there was little time for looking that way and again he turned his glasses in front. The regiment had taken cover behind a low ridge, and six rapid firers were sending a fierce hail on the German lines. But the men under orders from Bougainville, withheld the fire of their rifles for the present.

Bougainville himself stood up as became a leader of men, and lowered his sword for the first time. The cap had sunk all the way down the blade and picking it off he put it back on his head. He had obtained glasses also, probably from some fallen officer, and he walked back and forth seeking a weak spot in the enemy's line, into which he could charge with his men.

John admired him. His was no frenzied rage, but a courage, measured and stern. The springs of power hidden in him had been touched and he stood forth, a born leader.

"How does it happen," said John, "that you're in command?"

"Our officers were all in front," replied Bougainville, "when our regiment was swept by many shells. When they ceased bursting upon us and among us the officers were no longer there. The regiment was about to break. I could not bear to see that, and seizing the sword, I hoisted my cap upon it. The rest, perhaps, you saw. The men seem to trust me."

"They do," said John, with emphasis.

Bougainville, for the time at least, was certainly the leader of the regiment. It was an incident that John believed possible only in his own country, or France, and he remembered once more the famous old saying of Napoleon that every French peasant carried a marshal's baton in his knapsack.

Now he recalled, too, that Napoleon had fought some of his greatest defensive battles in the region they faced. Doubtless the mighty emperor and his marshals had trod the very soil on which Bougainville and he now stood. Surely the French must know it, and surely it would give them superhuman courage for battle.

"I belong to the command of General Vaugirard," he said to Bougainville. "I'm serving on his staff, but I was knocked off my motor cycle by the rush of air from a shell. The cycle was ruined and I was unconscious for a moment or two. When I revived, my general and his command were gone."

"You'd better stay with me a while," said Bougainville. "We're going to advance again soon. When night comes, if you're still alive, then you can look for General Vaugirard. The fire of the artillery is increasing. How the earth shakes!"

"So it does. I wish I knew what was happening."

"There comes one of those men in the air. He is going to drop down by us. Maybe you can learn something from him."

John felt a sudden wild hope that it was Lannes, but his luck did not hold good enough for it. The plane was of another shape than the *Arrow*, and, when it descended to the ground, a man older than Lannes stepped out upon the grass. He glanced around as if he were looking for some general of division for whom he had an order, and John, unable to restrain himself, rushed to him and exclaimed:

"News! News! For Heaven's sake, give us news! Surely you've seen from above!"

The man smiled and John knew that a bearer of bad news would not smile.

"I'm the friend and comrade of Philip Lannes," continued John, feeling that all the flying men of France knew the name of Lannes, and that it would be a password to this man's good graces.

"I know him well," said the air scout. "Who of our craft does not? My own name is Caumartin, and I have flown with Lannes more than once in the great meets at Rheims. In answer to your question I'm able to tell you that on the wings the soldiers of France are advancing. A wedge has been thrust between the German armies and the one nearest Paris is retreating, lest it be cut off."

Bougainville heard the words, and he ran among the men, telling them. A fierce shout arose and John himself quivered with feeling. It was better, far better than he had hoped. He realized now that his courage before had been the courage of despair. Lannes and he, as a last resort, had put faith in signs and omens, because there was nothing else to bear them up.

"Is it true? Is it true beyond doubt! You've really seen it with your own eyes?" he exclaimed.

Caumartin smiled again. His were deep eyes, and the smile that came from them was reassuring.

"I saw it myself," he replied. "At the point nearest Paris the gray masses are withdrawing. I looked directly down upon them. And now, can you tell me where I can find General Vaugirard?"

"I wish I could. I'm on his staff, but I've lost him. He's somewhere to the northward."

"Then I'll find him."

Caumartin resumed his place in his machine. John looked longingly at the aeroplane. He would gladly have gone with Caumartin, but feeling that he would be only a burden at such a time, he would not suggest it. Nevertheless he called to the aviator:

"If you see Philip Lannes in the heavens tell him that his friend John Scott is here behind a low ridge crested with trees!"

Caumartin nodded, and as some of the soldiers gave his plane a push he soared swiftly away in search of General Vaugirard. John watched him a moment or two and then turned his attention back to the German army in front of them.

The thudding of the heavy guns to their left had become so violent that it affected his nerves. The waves of air beat upon his ears like storm-driven rollers, and he was glad when Bougainville's regiment moved forward again. The Germans seemed to have withdrawn some of their force in the center, and, for a little while, the regiment with which John now marched was not under fire.

They heard reserves now coming up behind them, more trains of motor cars, bearing fresh troops, and batteries of field guns advancing as fast as they could. Men were busy also stringing telephone wires, and, presently, they passed a battery of guns of the largest caliber, the fire of which was directed entirely by telephone. Some distance beyond it the regiment stopped again. The huge shells were passing over their heads toward the German lines, and John believed that he could hear and count every one of them.

The remains of the regiment now lay down in a dip, as they did not know anything to do, except to wait for the remainder of the French line to advance.

Something struck near them presently and exploded with a crash. Steel splinters flew, but as they were prone only one man was injured.

"They're reaching us again with their shell fire," said John.

"Not at all," said Bougainville. "Look up."

John saw high in the heavens several black specks, which he knew at once were aeroplanes. Since the bomb had been dropped from one of them it was obvious that they were German flyers, and missiles of a like nature might be expected from the same source. Involuntarily he crouched close to the ground, and tried to press himself into it. He knew that such an effort would afford him no protection, but the body sought it nevertheless. All around him the young French soldiers too were clinging to Mother Earth. Only Bougainville stood erect.

John had felt less apprehension under the artillery fire and in the charge than he did now. He was helpless here when death fell like hail from the skies, and he quivered in every muscle as he waited. A crash came again, but the bomb had struck farther away, then a third, and a fourth, each farther and farther in its turn, and Bougainville suddenly uttered a shout that was full of vengeance and exultation.

John looked up. The group of black specks was still in the sky, but another group was hovering near, and clapping his glasses to his eyes he saw flashes of light passing between them.

"You're right, Bougainville! you're right!" he cried, although Bougainville had not said a word. "The French flyers have come and there's a fight in the air!"

He forgot all about the battle on earth, while he watched the combat in the heavens. Yet it was an affair of only a few moments. The Germans evidently feeling that they were too far away from their base, soon retreated. One of their machines turned over on its side and fell like a shot through space.

John shuddered, took the glasses down, and, by impulse, closed his eyes. He heard a shock near him, and, opening his eyes again, saw a huddled mass of wreckage, from which a foot encased in a broad German shoe protruded. The ribs of the plane were driven deep into the earth and he looked away. But a hum and swish suddenly came once more, and a sleek and graceful aeroplane, which he knew to be the *Arrow*, sank to the earth close to him. Lannes, smiling and triumphant, stepped forth and John hailed him eagerly.

"I met Caumartin in an aerial road," said Lannes, in his best dramatic manner, "and he described this place, at which you were waiting. As it was directly on my way I concluded to come by for you. I was delayed by a skirmish overhead which you may have seen."

"Yes, I saw it, or at least part of it."

"I came in at the end only. The Taubes were too presuming. They came over into our air, but we repelled the attack, and one, as I can see here, will never come again. I found General Vaugirard, although he is now two or three miles to your right, and when I deliver a message that he has given me I return. But I take you with me now."

John was overjoyed, but he would part from Bougainville with regret.

"Philip," he said, "here is Pierre Louis Bougainville, whom I met that day on Montmartre. All the officers of this regiment have been killed and by grace of courage and intuition he now leads it better than it was ever led before."

Lannes extended his hand. Bougainville's met it, and the two closed in the clasp of those who knew, each, that the other was a man. Then a drum began to beat, and Bougainville, waving his sword aloft, led his regiment forward again with a rush. But the *Arrow*, with a hard push from the last of the soldiers, was already rising, Lannes at the steering rudder and John in his old place.

"You can find your cap and coat in the locker," said Lannes without looking back, and John put them on quickly. His joy and eagerness were not due to flight from the field of battle, because the heavens themselves were not safe, but because he could look down upon this field on which the nations struggled and, to some extent, behold and measure it with his own eyes.

The *Arrow* rose slowly, and John leaned back luxuriously in his seat. He had a singular feeling that he had come back home again. The sharp, acrid odor that assailed eye and nostril departed and the atmosphere grew rapidly purer. The rolling waves of air from the concussion of the guns became much less violent, and soon ceased entirely. All the smoke floated below him, while above the heavens were a shining blue, unsullied by the dust and flame of the conflict.

"Do you go far, Philip?" John asked.

"Forty miles. I could cover the distance quickly in the *Arrow*, but on such a day as this I can't be sure of finding at once the man for whom I'm looking. Besides, we may meet German planes. You've your automatic with you?"

"I'm never without it. I'm ready to help if they come at us. I've been through so much today that I've become blunted to fear."

"I don't think we'll meet an enemy, but we must be armed and watchful."

John had not yet looked down, but he knew that the *Arrow* was rising high. The thunder of the battle died so fast that it became a mere murmur, and the air was thin, pure and cold. When he felt that the *Arrow* had reached its zenith he put the glasses to his eyes and looked over.

He saw a world spouting fire. Along a tremendous line curved and broken, thousands of cannon great and small were flashing, and for miles and miles a continuous coil of whitish smoke marked where the riflemen were at work. Near the center of the line he saw a vast mass of men advancing and he spoke of it to Lannes.

"I've seen it already," said the Frenchman. "That's where a great force of ours is cutting in between the German armies. It's the movement that has saved France, and the mind that planned it was worth a million men to us today."

"I can well believe it. Now I see running between the hills a shining ribbon which I take to be a river."

"That's the Marne. If we can, we'll drive the Germans back across it. Search the skies that way and see if you can find any of the Taubes."

"I see some black specks which I take to be the German planes, but they don't grow."

"Which indicates that they're not coming any nearer. They've had enough of us for the present and it's to their interest too to keep over their own army now. What do you see beneath us?"

"A great multitude of troops, French, as I can discern the uniform, and by Jove, Lannes, I can trace far beyond the towers and spires of Paris!"

"I knew you could. It marks how near the Germans have come to the capital, but they'll come no nearer. The great days of the French have returned, and we'll surely drive them upon the Marne."

"Suppose we fly a little lower, Lannes. Then we can get a better view of the field as we go along."

"I'll do as you say, John. I rose so high, because I thought attack here was less possible, but as no enemy is in sight we'll drop down."

The *Arrow* sank gradually, and now both could get a splendid view of a spectacle, such as no man had ever beheld until that day. The sounds of battle were still unheard, but they clearly saw the fire of the cannon, the rapid-firers, and the rifles. It was like a red streak running in curves and zigzags across fifty or maybe a hundred miles of country.

"We continue to cut in," said Lannes. "You can see how our armies off there are marching into that great open space between the Germans. Unless the extreme German army hastens it will be separated entirely from the rest. Oh, what a day! What a glorious, magnificent day! A day unlike any other in the world's story! Our heads in the dust in the morning and high in the air by night!"

"But we haven't won yet?"

"No, but we are winning enough to know that we will win."

"How many men do you think are engaged in that battle below?"

"Along all its windings two millions, maybe, or at least a million and a half anyhow. Perhaps nobody will ever know."

Then they relapsed into silence for a little while. The *Arrow* flew fast and the motor drummed steadily in their ears. Lannes let the aeroplane sink a little lower, and John became conscious of a new sound, akin nevertheless to the throb of the motor. It was the concussion of the battle. The topmost and weakest waves of air hurled off in circles by countless cannon and rifles were reaching them. But they had been softened so much by distance that the sound was not unpleasant, and the *Arrow* rocked gently as if touched by a light wind.

John never ceased to watch with his glasses, and in a few minutes he announced that men in gray were below.

"I expected that," said Lannes. "This battle line, as you know, is far from straight, and, in order to reach our destination in the quickest time possible, we must pass over a portion of the German army, an extended corner or angle as it were. What are they doing there, John?"

"Firing about fifty cannon as fast as they can. Back of the cannon is a great huddle of motors and of large automobile trucks, loaded, I should say, with ammunition."

"You're quite sure of what you say?" asked Lannes, after a silence of a moment or two.

"Absolutely sure. I fancy that it's an ammunition depot."

"Then, John, you and I must take a risk. We are to deliver a message, but we can't let go an opportunity like this. You recall how you threw the bombs on the forty-two centimeter. I have more bombs here in the *Arrow* I never fly now without 'em little fellows, but tremendously powerful. I shall dip and when we're directly over the ammunition depot drop the bombs squarely into the middle of it."

"I'm ready," said John, feeling alternate thrills of eagerness and horror, "but Philip, don't you go so near that if the depot blows up it will blow us up too."

"Never fear," said Lannes, laughing, not with amusement but with excitement, "I've no more wish to be scattered through the firmament than you have. Besides, we've that message to deliver. Do you think the Germans have noticed us?"

"No, a lot of smoke from their cannon fire has gathered above them and perhaps it veils us. Besides, their whole attention must be absorbed by the French army, and I don't think it likely that they're looking up."

"But they're bound to see us soon. We have one great advantage, however. The target is much larger than the forty-two centimeter was, and there are no Taubes or dirigibles here to drive us off. Ready now, John, and when I touch the bottom of my loop you throw the bombs. Here they are!"

Four bombs were pushed to John's side and they lay ready to his grasp. Then as the *Arrow* began its downward curve, he laid his glasses aside and watched. The most advanced German batteries were placed in a pit, into which a telephone wire ran. Evidently these guns, like the French, were fired by order from some distant point. John longed to hurl a bomb at the pit, but the chances were ten to one that he would miss it, and he held to the ammunition depot, spread over a full acre, as his target.

Now the Germans saw them. He knew it, as many of them looked up, and some began to fire at the *Arrow*, but the aeroplane was too high and swift for their bullets.

"Now!" said Lannes in sudden, sharp tones.

The aeroplane dipped with sickening velocity, but John steadied himself, and watching his chance he threw four bombs so fast that the fourth had left his hands before the first touched the ground. An awful, rending explosion followed, and for a minute the *Arrow* rocked violently, as if in a hurricane. Then, as the waves of air decreased in violence, it darted upward on an even keel.

John saw far below a vast scene of wreckage, amid which lay many dead or wounded men. Motors were blown to pieces and cannon dismounted.

"Score heavily for us," said Lannes. "I scarcely hoped for such a goodly blow as this while we were on our way!"

John would not look down again. Despite the value of the deed, he shuddered and he was glad when the *Arrow* in its swift flight had left the area of devastation far behind.

"We're flying over the French now," he said. "So I expected," said Lannes. "Can you see a hill crested with a low farm house?"

"Yes," replied John, after looking a little while. "It's straight ahead. The house is partly hidden by trees."

"Then that's the place. You wouldn't think we'd come nearly fifty miles, would you, John?"

"Fifty miles! It feels more like a thousand!"

Lannes laughed, this time with satisfaction, not excitement.

"You'll find there the general to whom we reported first," he said, "and he'll be glad to see us! I can't tell you how glad he will be. His joy will be far beyond our personal deserts. It will have little to do with the fact that you, John Scott, and I, Philip Lannes, have come back to him."

The circling *Arrow* came down in a meadow just behind the house, and officers rushed forward to meet it. Lannes and John, stepping out, left it in charge of two of the younger men. Then, proudly waving the others aside, they walked to the low stone farmhouse, in front of which the elderly, spectacled general was standing. He looked at Lannes inquiringly, but the young Frenchman, without a word, handed him a note.

John watched the general read, and he saw the transformation of the man's face. Doubting, anxious, worn, it was illumined suddenly. In a voice that trembled he said to the senior officers who clustered about him:

"We're advancing in the center, and on the other flank. Already we've driven a huge wedge between the German armies, and Paris, nay, France herself, is saved!"

The officers, mostly old men, did not cheer, but John had never before witnessed such relief expressed on human faces. It seemed to him that they had choked up, and could not speak. The commander held the note in a shaking hand and presently he turned to Lannes.

"Your fortune has been great. It's not often that one has a chance to bear such a message as this."

"My pride is so high I can't describe it," said Lannes in a dramatic but sincere tone.

"Go in the house and an orderly will give food and wine to you and your comrade. In a half hour, perhaps, I may have another message for you."

Both John and Lannes needed rest and food, and they obeyed gladly. The strain upon the two was far greater than they had realized at the time, and for a few moments they were threatened with collapse which very strong efforts of the will prevented. They were conscious, too, as they stood upon the ground, of a quivering, shaking motion. They were assailed once more by the violent waves of air coming from the concussion of cannon and rifles past counting. The thin, whitish film which was a compound of dust and burned gunpowder assailed them again and lay, bitter, in their mouths and nostrils.

"The earth shakes too much," said Lannes in a droll tone. "I think we'd better go back into the unchanging ether, where a man can be sure of himself."

"I'm seasick," said John; "who wouldn't be, with ten thousand cannon, more or less, and a million or two of rifles shaking the planet? I'm going into the house as fast as I can."

It was a building, centuries old, of gray crumbling stone, with large, low rooms, and, to John's amazement, the peasant who inhabited it and his family were present. The farmer and his wife, both strong and dark, were about forty, and there were four children, the oldest a girl of about thirteen. What fear they may have felt in the morning was gone now, and, as they knew that the French army was advancing, a joy, reserved but none the less deep, had taken its place.

John and Lannes sat down at a small table covered with a neat white cloth, and Madame, walking quickly and lightly, served them with bread, cold meat and light red wine. The smaller children hovered in the background and looked curiously at the young foreigner who wore the French uniform.

"May I ask your name, Madame?" John asked politely.

"Poiret," she said. "My man is Jules Poiret, and this farm has been in his family since the great revolution. You and your comrade came from the air, as I saw, and you can tell us, can you not, whether the Poiret farm is to become German or remain French? The enemy has been pushed back today, but will he come so near to Paris again? Tell me truly, on your soul, Monsieur!"

"I don't believe the Germans will ever again be so near to Paris," replied John with sincerity. "My friend, who is the great Philip Lannes, the flying man, and I, have looked down upon a battle line fifty, maybe a hundred miles long, and nearly everywhere the Germans are retreating."

She bent her head a little as she poured the coffee for them, but not enough to hide the glitter in her eye. "Perhaps the good God intervened at the last moment, as Father Hansard promised he would," she said calmly. "At any rate, the Germans are gone. I gathered as much from chance words of the generalsnever before have so many generals gathered under the Poiret roof, and it will never happen againbut I wished to hear it from one who had seen with his own eyes."

"We saw them withdrawing, Madame, with these two pairs of eyes of ours," said Lannes.

"And then Poiret can go back to his work with the vines. Whether it is war or peace, men must eat and drink, Monsieur."

"But certainly, Madame, and women too." "It is so. I trust that soon the Germans will be driven back much faster. The house quivers all the time. It is old and already several pieces of plaster have fallen."

Her anxiety was obvious. With the Germans driven back she thought now of the Poiret homestead. John, in the new strength that had come to him from food and drink, had forgotten for the moment that ceaseless quiver of the earth. He held the little bottle aloft and poured a thin stream of wine into his glass. The red thread swayed gently from side to side.

"You speak truly, Madame," he said. "The rocking goes on, but I'm sure that the concussion of the guns will be too far away tonight for you to feel it."

They offered her gold for the food and wine, but after one longing glance she steadfastly refused it.

"Since you have come across the sea to fight for us," she said to John, "how could I take your money?"

Lannes and John returned to the bit of grass in front of the house, where the elderly general and other generals were still standing and using their glasses.

"You are refreshed?" said the general to Lannes.

"Refreshed and ready to take your orders wherever you wish them to go."

John stepped aside, while the general talked briefly and in a low tone to his comrade. He looked upon himself merely as a passenger, or a sort of help to Lannes, and he would not pry into military secrets. But when the two rose again in the *Arrow*, the general and all his suite waved their caps to them. Beyond a doubt, Lannes had done magnificent work that day, and John was glad for his friend's sake.

The *Arrow* ascended at a sharp angle, and then hovered for a little while in curves and spirals. John saw the generals below, but they were no longer watching the aeroplane. Their glasses were turned once more to the battle front.

"Ultimately we're to reach the commander of the central army, if we can," said Lannes, "but meanwhile we're to bend in toward the German lines, in search of your immediate chief, General Vaugirard, who is one of the staunchest and most daring fighters in the whole French Army. If we find him at all it's likely that we'll find him farther forward than any other general."

"But not any farther than my friend of Montmartre, Bougainville. There's a remarkable fellow. I saw his military talent the first time I met him. Or I should better say I felt it rather than saw it. And he was making good in a wonderful manner today."

"I believe with you, John, that he's a genius. But if we find General Vaugirard and then finish our errand we must hasten. It will be night in two hours."

He increased the speed of the aeroplane and they flew eastward, searching all the hills and woods for the command of General Vaugirard.

5

IN HOSTILE HANDS

The task that lay before the two young men was one of great difficulty. The battle line was shifting continually, although the Germans were being pressed steadily back toward the east and north, but among so many generals it would be hard to find the particular one to whom they were bearing orders. The commander of the central army was of high importance, but the fact did not bring him at once before the eye.

They were to see General Vaugirard, too, but it was possible that he had fallen. John, though, could not look upon it as a probability. The general was so big, so vital, that he must be living, and he felt the same way about Bougainville. It was incredible that fate itself should snuff out in a day that spark of fire.

Lannes, uncertain of his course, bore in again toward the German lines, and dropped as low as he could, compatible with safety from any kind of shot. John meanwhile scanned every hill and valley wood and field with his powerful glasses, and he was unable to see any diminution in the fury of the struggle. The cannon thundered, with all their might, along a line of scores of miles; rapid firers sent a deadly hail upon the opposing lines; rifles flashed by the hundred thousand, and here and there masses of troops closed with the bayonet.

Seen from a height the battle was stripped of some of its horrors, but all its magnitude remained to awe those who looked down upon it. From the high, cold air John could not see pain and wounds, only the swaying back and forth of the battle lines. All the time he searched attentively for men who did not wear the red and blue of France, and at last he said:

"I've failed to find any sign of the British army."

"They're farther to the left," replied Lannes. "I caught a glimpse of their khaki lines this morning. Their regular troops are great fighters, as our Napoleon himself admitted more than once, and they've never done better than they're doing today. When I saw them they were advancing."

"I'm glad of that. It's curious how I feel about the English, Philip. They've got such a conceit that they irritate me terribly at times, yet I don't want to see them beaten by any other Europeans. That's our American privilege."

"A family feeling, perhaps," said Lannes, laughing, "but we French and English have been compelled to be allies, and after fighting each other for a thousand years we're now the best of friends. I think, John, we'll have to go down and procure information from somebody about our general. Otherwise we'll never find him."

"We must be near the center of our army, and that's where he's likely to be. Suppose we descend in the field a little to the east of us."

Lannes looked down, and, pronouncing the place suitable, began to drop in a series of spirals until they rested in a small field that had been devoted to the growth of vegetables. Here John at once felt the shaking of the earth, and tasted the bitter odor again. But woods on either side of them hid the sight of troops, although the sound of the battle was as great and violent as ever.

"We seem to have landed on a desert island," said Lannes.

"So we do," said John. "Evidently there is nobody here to tell us where we can find our dear and long lost general. I'll go down to the edge of the nearest wood and see if any of our skirmishers are there."

"All right, John, but hurry back. I'll hold the *Arrow* ready for instant flight, as we can't afford to linger here."

John ran toward the wood, but before he reached the first trees he turned back with a shout of alarm. He had caught a glimpse of horses, helmets and the glittering heads of lances. Moreover, the Uhlans were coming directly toward him.

In that moment of danger the young American showed the best that was in him. Forgetful of self and remembering the importance of Lannes' mission, he shouted:

"The Uhlans are upon us, Philip! I can't escape, but you must! Go! Go at once!"

Lannes gave one startled glance, and he understood in a flash. He too knew the vital nature of his errand, but his instant decision gave a wrench to his whole being. He saw the Uhlans breaking through the woods and John before them. He was standing beside the *Arrow*, and giving the machine a sharp push he sprang in and rose at a sharp angle.

"Up! Up, Philip!" John continued to cry, until the cold edge of a lance lay against his throat and a brusque voice bade him to surrender.

"All right, I yield," said John, "but kindly take your lance away. It's so sharp and cold it makes me feel uncomfortable."

As he spoke he continued to look upward. The *Arrow* was soaring higher and higher, and the Uhlans were firing at it, but they were not able to hit such a fleeting target. In another minute it was out of range.

John felt the cold steel come away from his throat, and satisfied that Lannes with his precious message was safe, he looked at his captors. They were about thirty in number, Prussian Uhlans.

"Well," said John to the one who seemed to be their leader, "what do you want with me?"

"To hold you prisoner," replied the man, in excellent EnglishJohn was always surprised at the number of people on the continent who spoke English"and to ask you why we find an American here in French uniform."

The man who spoke was young, blond, ruddy, and his tone was rather humorous. John had been too much in Germany to hate Germans. He liked most of them personally, but for many of their ideas, ideas which he considered deadly to the world, he had an intense dislike.

"You find me here because I didn't have time to get away," he replied, "and I'm in a French uniform because it's my fighting suit."

The young officer smiled. John rather liked him, and he saw, too, that he was no older than himself.

"It's lucky for you that you're in some kind of a uniform," the German said, "or I should have you shot immediately. But I'm sorry we didn't take the man in the aeroplane instead of you."

John looked up again. The *Arrow* had become small in the distant blue. A whimsical impulse seized him.

"You've a right to be sorry," he said. "That was the greatest flying man in the world, and all day he has carried messages, heavy with the fate of nations. If you had taken him a few moments ago you might have saved the German army from defeat today. But your chance has gone. If you were to see him again you would not know him and his plane from others of their kind."

The officer's eyes dilated at first. Then he smiled again and stroked his young mustache.

"It may be true, as you say," he replied, "but meanwhile I'll have to take you to my chief, Captain von Boehlen."

John's heart sank a little when he heard the name von Boehlen. Fortune, he thought, had played him a hard trick by bringing him face to face with the man who had least cause to like him. But he would not show it.

"Very well," he said; "which way?"

"Straight before you," said the officer. "I'd give you a mount, but it isn't far. Remember as you walk that we're just behind you, and don't try to run away. You'd have no chance on earth. My own name is Arnheim, Wilhelm von Arnheim."

"And mine's John Scott," said John, as he walked straight ahead.

They passed through a wood and into another field, where a large body of Prussian cavalry was waiting. A tall man, built heavily, stood beside a horse, watching a distant corner of the battle through glasses. John knew that uncompromising figure at once. It was von Boehlen.

"A prisoner, Captain," said von Arnheim, saluting respectfully.

Von Boehlen turned slowly, and a malicious light leaped in his eyes when he saw John on foot before him, and wholly in his power.

"And so," he said, "it's young Scott of the hotel in Dresden and of the wireless station, and you've come straight into my hands!"

The whimsical humor which sometimes seized John when he was in the most dangerous situation took hold of him again. It was not humor exactly, but it was the innate desire to make the best of a bad situation.

"I'm in your hands," he replied, "but I didn't walk willingly into 'em. Your lieutenant, von Arnheim here, and his men brought me on the points of their lances. I'm quite willing to go away again."

Von Boehlen recognized the spirit in the reply and the malice departed from his own eyes. Yet he asked sternly:

"Why do you put on a French uniform and meddle in a quarrel not your own?"

"I've made it my own. I take the chances of war."

"To the rear with him, and put him with the other prisoners," said von Boehlen to von Arnheim, and the young Prussian and two Uhlans escorted him to the edge of the field where twenty or thirty French prisoners sat on the ground.

"I take it," said von Arnheim, "that you and our captain have met before."

"Yes, and the last time it was under circumstances that did not endear me to him."

"If it was in war it will not be to your harm. Captain von Boehlen is a stern but just man, and his conduct is strictly according to our military code. You will stay here with the other prisoners under guard. I hope to see you again."

With these polite words the young officer rode back to his chief, and John's heart warmed to him because of his kindness. Then he sat down on the grass and looked at those who were prisoners with him. Most of them were wounded, but none seemed despondent. All were lying down, some propped on their elbows, and they were watching and listening with the closest attention. A half-dozen Germans, rifle in hand, stood near by.

John took his place on the grass by the side of a fair, slim young man who carried his left arm in a bandage.

"Englishman?" said the young man.

"No, American."

"But you have been fighting for us, as your uniform shows. What command?"

"General Vaugirard's, but I became separated from it earlier in the day."

"I've heard of him. Great, fat man, as cool as ice and as brave as a lion. A good general to serve under. My own name is Fleury, Albert Fleury. I was wounded and taken early this morning, and the others and I have been herded here ever since by the Germans. They will not tell us a word, but I notice they have not advanced."

"The German army is retreating everywhere. For this day, at least, we're victorious. Somebody has made a great plan and has carried it through. The cavalry of the invader came within sight of Paris this morning, but they won't be able to see it tomorrow morning. Whisper it to the others. We'll take the good news quietly. We won't let the guards see that we know."

The news was circulated in low tones and every one of the wounded forgot his wound. They spoke among themselves, but all the while the thunder of the hundred-mile battle went on with unremitting ferocity. John put his ear to the ground now, and the earth quivered incessantly like a ship shaken at sea by its machinery.

The day was now waning fast and he looked at the mass of Uhlans who stood arrayed in the open space, as if they were awaiting an order. Lieutenant von Arnheim rode back and ordered the guards to march on with them.

There was none too severely wounded to walk and they proceeded in a file through the fields, Uhlans on all sides, but the great mass behind them, where their commander, von Boehlen, himself rode.

The night was almost at hand. Twilight was already coming over the eastern hills, and one of the most momentous days in the story of man was drawing to a close. People often do not know the magnitude of an event until it has passed long since and shows in perspective, but John felt to the full the result of the event, just as the old Greeks must have known at once what Salamis or Platæa meant to them. The hosts of the world's greatest military empire were turned back, and he had all the certainty of conviction that they would be driven farther on the next day.

The little band of prisoners who walked while their Prussian captors rode, were animated by feelings like those of John. It was the captured who exulted and the captors who were depressed, though neither expressed it in words, and the twilight was too deep now for faces to show either joy or sorrow.

John and Fleury walked side by side. They were near the same age. Fleury was an Alpinist from the high mountain region of Savoy and he had arrived so recently in the main theater of conflict that he knew little of what had been passing. He and John talked in whispers and they spoke encouraging words to each other. Fleury listened in wonder to John's account of his flights with Lannes.

"It is marvelous to have looked down upon a battle a hundred miles long," he said. "Have you any idea where these Uhlans intend to take us?"

"I haven't. Doubtless they don't know themselves. The night is here now, and I imagine they'll stop somewhere soon."

The twilight died in the west as well as the east, and darkness came over the field of gigantic strife. But the earth continued to quiver with the thunder of artillery, and John felt the waves of air pulsing in his ears. Now and then searchlights burned in a white blaze across the hills. Fields, trees and houses would stand out for a moment, and then be gone absolutely.

John's vivid imagination turned the whole into a storm at night. The artillery was the thunder and the flare of the searchlights was the lightning. His mind created, for a little while, the illusion that the combat had passed out of the hands of man and that nature was at work. He and Fleury ceased to talk and he walked on, thinking little of his destination. He had no sense of weariness, nor of any physical need at all.

Von Arnheim rode up by his side and said:

"You'll not have to walk much further, Mr. Scott. A camp of ours is just beyond a brook, not more than a few hundred yards away, and the prisoners will stay there for the night. I'm sorry to find you among the French fighting against us. We Germans expected American sympathy. There is so much German blood in the United States."

"But, as I told Captain von Boehlen, we're a republic, and we're democrats. In many of the big ideas there's a gulf between us and Germany so wide that it can never be bridged. This war has made clear the enormous difference."

Von Arnheim sighed.

"And yet, as a people, we like each other personally," he said.

"That's so, but as nations we diverge absolutely."

"Perhaps, I can't dispute it. But here is our camp. You'll be treated well. We Germans are not barbarians, as our enemies allege."

John saw fires burning in an ancient wood, through which a clear brook ran. The ground was carpeted with bodies, which at first he thought were those of dead men. But they were merely sleepers. German troops in thousands had dropped in their tracks. It was scarcely sleep, but something deeper, a stupor of exhaustion so utter, both mental and physical, that it was like the effect of anesthesia. They lay in every imaginable position, and they stretched away through the forest in scores of thousands.

John and Fleury saw their own place at once. Several hundred men in French uniforms were lying or sitting on the ground in a great group near the forest. A few slept, but the others, as well as John could see by the light of the fires, were wide awake.

The sight of the brook gave John a burning thirst, and making a sign to the German guard, who nodded, he knelt and drank. He did not care whether the water was pure or not, most likely it was not, with armies treading their way across it, but as it cut through the dust and grime of his mouth and throat he felt as if a new and more vigorous life were flowing into his veins. After drinking once, twice, and thrice, he sat down on the bank with Fleury, but in a minute or two young von Arnheim came for him.

"Our commander wishes to talk with you," he said.

"I'm honored," said John, "but conversation is not one of my strong points."

"The general will make the conversation," said von Arnheim, smiling. "It will be your duty, as he sees it, to answer questions."

John's liking for von Arnheim grew. He had seldom seen a finer young man. He was frank and open in manner, and bright blue eyes shone in a face that bore every sign of honesty. Official enemies he and von Arnheim were, but real enemies they never could be.

He divined that he would be subjected to a cross-examination, but he had no objection. Moreover, he wanted to see a German general of high degree. Von Arnheim led the way through the woods to a little glade, in which about a dozen officers stood. One of them, the oldest man present, who was obviously in command, stood nearest the fire, holding his helmet in his hand.

The general was past sixty, of medium height, but extremely broad and muscular. His head, bald save for a fringe of white hair, had been reddened by the sun, and his face, with its deep heavy lines and his corded neck, was red, too. He showed age but not weakness. His eyes, small, red and uncommonly keen, gazed from under a white bushy thatch. He looked like a fierce old dragon to John.

"The American prisoner, sir," said von Arnheim in English to the general.

The old man concentrated the stare of his small red eyes upon John for many long seconds. The young American felt the weight and power of that gaze. He knew too instinctively that the man before him was a great fighter, a true representative of the German military caste and system. He longed to turn his own eyes away, but he resolutely held them steady. He would not be looked down, not even by an old Prussian general to whom the fate of a hundred thousand was nothing.

"Very well, Your Highness, you may stand aside," said the general in a deep harsh voice.

Out of the corner of his eye John saw that the man who stood aside was von Arnheim. "Your Highness!" Then this young lieutenant must be a prince. If so, some princes were likable. Wharton and Carstairs and he had outwitted a prince once, but it could not be von Arnheim. He turned his full gaze back to the general, who continued in his deep gruff voice, speaking perfect English:

"I understand that you are an American and your name is John Scott."

"And duly enrolled and uniformed in the French service," said John, "You can't shoot me as a *franc tireur*."

"We could shoot you for anything, if we wished, but such is not our purpose. I have heard from a captain of Uhlans, Rudolf von Boehlen, a most able and valuable officer, that you are brave and alert."

"I thank Captain von Boehlen for his compliment. I did not expect it from him."

"Ah, he bears you no malice. We Germans are large enough to admire skill and courage in others. He has spoken of the affair of the wireless. It cost us much, but it belongs to the past. We will achieve what we wish."

John was silent. He believed that these preliminaries on the part of the old general were intended to create an atmosphere, a belief in his mind that German power was invincible.

"We have withdrawn a portion of our force today," continued the general, "in order to rectify our line. Our army had advanced too far. Tomorrow we resume our march on Paris."

John felt that it was an extraordinary statement for an old man, one of such high rank, the commander of perhaps a quarter of a million soldiers, to be making to him, a young American, but he held his peace, awaiting what lay behind it all.

"Now you are a captive," continued the general, "you will be sent to a prison, and you will be held there until the end of the war. You will necessarily suffer much. We cannot help it. Yet you might be sent to your own country. Americans and Germans are not enemies. I know from Captain von Boehlen who took you that you have been in an aeroplane with a Frenchman. Some account of what you saw from space might help your departure for America."

And so that was it! Now the prisoner's eye steadily confronted that of the old general.

"Your Highness," he said, as he thought that the old man might be a prince as well as a general, "you have read the history of the great civil war in my country, have you not?"

"It was a part of my military duty to study it. It was a long and desperate struggle with many great battles, but what has it to do with the present?"

"Did you ever hear of any traitor on either side, North or South, in that struggle?"

The deep red veins in the old general's face stood out, but he gave no other sign.

"You prefer, then," he said, "to become a charge upon our German hospitality. But I can say that your refusal will not make terms harder for you. Lieutenant von Arnheim, take him back to the other prisoners."

"Thank you, sir," said John, and he gave the military salute. He could understand the old man's point of view, rough and gruff though he was, and he was not lacking in a certain respect for him. The general punctiliously returned the salute.

"You've made a good impression," said von Arnheim, as they walked away together.

"I gather," said John, "from a reference by the general, that you're a prince."

Von Arnheim looked embarrassed.

"In a way I am," he admitted, "but ours is a mediatized house. Perhaps it doesn't count for much. Still, if it hadn't been for this war I might have gone to your country and married an heiress."

His eyes were twinkling. Here, John thought was a fine fellow beyond question.

"Perhaps you can come after the war and marry one," he said. "Personally I hope you'll have the chance."

"Thanks," said von Arnheim, a bit wistfully, "but I'm afraid now it will be a long time, if ever. I need not seek to conceal from you that we were turned back today. You know it already."

"Yes, I know it," said John, speaking without any trace of exultation, "and I'm willing to tell you that it was one of the results I saw from the aeroplane. Can I ask what you intend to do with the prisoners you have here, including myself?"

"I do not know. You are to sleep where you are tonight. Your bed, the earth, will be as good as ours, and perhaps in the morning we'll find an answer to your question."

Von Arnheim bade him a pleasant good night and turned to duties elsewhere. John watched him as he strode away, a fine, straight young figure. He had found him a most likable man, and he was bound to admit that there was much in the German character to admire. But for the present it wasin his viewa Germany misled.

The prisoners numbered perhaps six hundred, and at least half of them were wounded. John soon learned that the hurt usually suffered in stoical silence. It was so in the great American civil war, and it was true now in the great European war.

Rough food was brought to them by German guards, and those who were able drank at the brook. Water was served to the severely wounded by their comrades in tin cups given to them by the Germans, and then all but a few lay on the grass and sought sleep.

John and his new friend, Fleury, were among those who yet sat up and listened to the sounds of battle still in progress, although it was far in the night. It was an average night of late summer or early autumn, cool, fairly bright, and with but little wind. But the dull, moaning sound made by the distant cannonade came from both sides of them, and the earth yet quivered, though but faintly. Now and then, the searchlights gleamed against the background of darkness, but John felt that the combat must soon stop, at least until the next day. The German army in which he was a prisoner had ceased already, but other German armies along the vast line fought on, failing day, by the light which man himself had devised.

Fleury was intelligent and educated. Although it was bitter to him to be a prisoner at such a time, he had some comprehension of what had occurred, and he knew that John had been in a position to see far more than he. He asked the young American many questions about his flight in the air, and about Philip Lannes, of whom he had heard.

"It was wonderful," he said, "to look down on a battle a hundred miles long."

"We didn't see all of it," said John, "but we saw it in many places, and we don't know that it was a hundred miles long, but it must have been that or near it."

"And the greatest day for France in her history! What mighty calculations must have been made and what tremendous marchings and combats must have been carried out to achieve such a result."

"One of the decisive battles of history, like Plataea, or the Metaurus or Gettysburg. There go the Uhlans with Captain von Boehlen at their head. Now I wonder what they mean to do!"

A thousand men, splendidly mounted and armed, rode through the forest. The moonlight fell on von Boehlen's face and showed it set and grim. John felt that he was bound to recognize in him a stern and resolute man, carrying out his own conceptions of duty. Nor had von Boehlen been discourteous to him, although he might have felt cause for much resentment. The Prussian glanced at him as he passed, but said nothing. Soon he and his horsemen passed out of sight in the dusk.

John, wondering how late it might be, suddenly remembered that he had a watch and found it was eleven o'clock.

"An hour of midnight," he said to Fleury.

Most all the French stretched upon the ground were now in deep slumber, wounded and unwounded alike. The sounds of cannon fire were sinking away, but they did not die wholly. The faint thunder of the distant guns never ceased to come. But the campfire, where he knew the German generals slept or planned, went out, and darkness trailed its length over all this land which by night had become a wilderness.

John was able to trace dimly the sleeping figures of Germans in the dusk, sunk down upon the ground and buried in the sleep or stupor of exhaustion. As they lay near him so they lay in the same way in hundreds of thousands along the vast line. Men and horses, strained to their last nerve and muscle, were too tired to move. It seemed as if more than a million men lay dead in the fields and woods of Northeastern France.

John, who had been wide awake, suddenly dropped on the ground where the others were stretched. He collapsed all in a moment, as if every drop of blood had been drained suddenly from his body. Keyed high throughout the day, his whole system now gave way before the accumulated impact of events so tremendous. The silence save for the distant moaning that succeeded the roar of a million men or more in battle was like a powerful drug, and he slept like one dead, never moving hand or foot.

He was roused shortly before morning by some one who shook him gently but persistently, and at last he sat up, looking around in the dim light for the person who had dragged him back from peace to a battle-mad world. He saw an unkempt, bearded man in a French uniform, one sleeve stained with blood, and he recognized Weber, the Alsatian.

"Why, Weber!" he exclaimed, "they've got you, too! This is bad! They may consider you, an Alsatian, a traitor, and execute you at once!"

Weber smiled in rather melancholy fashion, and said in a low tone:

"It's bad enough to be captured, but I won't be shot Nobody here knows that I'm an Alsatian, and consequently they will think I'm a Frenchman. If you call me anything, call me Fernand, which is my first name, but which they will take for the last."

"All right, Fernand. I'll practice on it now, so I'll make no slip. How did you happen to be taken?"

"I was in a motor car, a part of a train of about a hundred cars. There were seven in it besides myself. We were ordered to cross a field and join a line of advancing infantry. When we were in the middle of the field a masked German battery of rapid-firers opened on us at short range. It was an awful experience, like a stroke of lightning, and I don't think that more than a dozen of us escaped with our lives. I was wounded in the arm and taken before I could get out of the field. I was brought here with some other prisoners and I have been sleeping on the ground just beyond that hillock. I awoke early, and, walking the little distance our guards allow, I happened to recognize your figure lying here. I was sorry and yet glad to see you, sorry that you were a prisoner, and glad to find at least one whom I knew, a friend."

John gave Weber's hand a strong grasp.

"I can say the same about you," he said warmly. "We're both prisoners, but yesterday was a magnificent day for France and democracy."

"It was, and now it's to be seen what today will be."

"I hope and believe it will be no less magnificent."

"I learned that you were taken just after you alighted from an aeroplane, and that a man with you escaped in the plane. At least, I presume it was you, as I heard the Germans talking of such a person and I knew of your great friendship for Philip Lannes. Lannes, of course was the one who escaped."

"A good surmise, Fernand. It was no less a man than he."

Weber's eyes sparkled.

"I was sure of it," he said. "A wonderful fellow, that Lannes, perhaps the most skillful and important bearer of dispatches that France has. But he will not forget you, Mr. Scott. He knows, of course, where you were taken, and doubtless from points high in the air he has traced the course of this German army. He will find time to come for you. He will surely do so. He has a feeling for you like that of a brother, and his skill in the air gives him a wonderful advantage. In all the history of the world there have never before been any scouts like the aeroplanes."

"That's true, and that, I think, is their chief use."

Impulse made John look up. The skies were fast beginning to

brighten with the first light in the east, and large objects would be visible there. But he saw nothing against the blue save two or three captive balloons which floated not far above the trees inside the German lines. He longed for a sight of the *Arrow*. He believed that he would know its shape even high in the heavens, but they were speckless.

The Alsatian, whose eyes followed his, shook his head.

"He is not there, Mr. Scott," he said, "and you will not see him today, but I have a conviction that he will come, by night doubtless."

John lowered his eyes and his feeling of disappointment passed. It had been foolish of him to hope so soon, but it was only a momentary impulse, Lannes could not seek him now, and even if he were to come there would be no chance of rescue until circumstances changed.

"Doubtless you and he were embarked on a long errand when you were taken," said Weber.

"We were carrying a message to the commander of one of the French armies, but I don't know the name of the commander, I don't know which army it is, and I don't know where it is."

Weber laughed.

"But Lannes knew all of those things," he said. "Oh, he's a close one! He wouldn't trust such secrets not even to his brother-in-arms."

"Nor should he do so. I'd rather he'd never tell them to me unless he thought it necessary."

"I agree with you exactly, Mr. Scott. Hark! Did you hear it? The battle swells afresh, and it's not yet full day!"

The roaring had not ceased, but out of the west rose a sound, louder yet, deep, rolling and heavy with menace. It was the discharge of a great gun and it came from a point several miles away.

"We don't know who fired that," said Weber, "It may be French, English or German, but it's my opinion that we'll hear its like in our forest all day long, just as we did yesterday. However, it shall not keep me from bathing my face in this brook."

"Nor me either," said John.

The cold water refreshed and invigorated him, and as he stooped over the brook, he heard other cannon. They seemed to him fairly to spring into action, and, in a few moments, the whole earth was roaring again with the huge volume of their fire.

Other prisoners, wounded and unwounded, awakened by the cannon, strolled down to the brook and dipped into its waters.

"I'd better slip back to my place beyond the hillock," said Weber. "We're in two lots, we prisoners, and I belong in the other lot. I don't think our guards have noticed our presence here, and it will be safer for me to return. But it's likely that we'll all be gathered into one body soon, and I'll help you watch for Lannes."

"I'll be glad of your help," said John sincerely. "We must escape. In all the confusion of so huge a battle there ought to be a chance."

Weber slipped away in the crowd now hurrying down to the stream, and in a few moments John was joined by Fleury, whose attention was centered on the sounds of the distant battle. He deemed it best to say nothing to him of Weber, who did not wish to be known as an Alsatian. Fleury's heavy sleep had made him strong and fresh again, but he was in a fury at his helplessness.

"To think of our being tied here at such a time," he said. "France and England are pushing the battle again! I know it, and we're helpless, mere prisoners!"

"Still," said John, "while we can't fight we may see things worth seeing. Perhaps it's not altogether our loss to be inside the German army on such a day."

Fleury could not reconcile himself to such a view, but he sought to make the best of it, and he was cheered, too, by the vast increase in the volume of the cannon fire. Before the full day had crossed from east to west the great guns were thundering again along the long battle line. But in their immediate vicinity there was no action. All the German troops here seemed to be resting on their arms. No Uhlans were visible and John judged that the detachment under von Boehlen, having gone forth chiefly for scouting purposes, had not yet returned.

They received bread, sausage and coffee for breakfast from one of the huge kitchen automobiles, and nearly all ate with a good appetite. Their German captors did not treat them badly, but John, watching both officers and men, did not see any elation. He had no doubt that the officers were stunned by the terrible surprise of the day before, and as for the men, they would know nothing. He had seen early that the Germans were splendid troops, disciplined, brave and ingenious, but the habit of blind obedience would blind them also to the fact that fortune had turned her face away from them.

He wished that his friend von Arnheimfriend he regarded himwould appear and tell him something about the battle, but his wish did not come true for an hour and meanwhile the whole heavens resounded with the roar of the battle, while distant flashes from the guns could be seen on either flank.

The young German, glasses in hand, evidently seeking a good view, walked to the crest of the hillock behind which Weber had disappeared. John presumed enough on their brief friendship to call to him.

"Do you see anything of interest?" he asked.

Von Arnheim nodded quickly.

"I see the distant fringe of a battle," he replied amiably, "but it's too early in the morning for me to pass my judgment upon it."

"Nevertheless you can look for a day of most desperate struggle!"

Von Arnheim nodded very gravely.

"Men by tens of thousands will fall before night," he said.

As if to confirm his words, the roar of the battle took a sudden and mighty increase, like a convulsion.

6

THE TWO PRINCES

J ohn sat with the other prisoners for more than two hours listening to the thunder of the great battle or rather series of battles which were afterwards classified under the general head the Battle of the Marne. He was not a soldier, merely a civilian serving as a soldier, but he had learned already to interpret many of the signs of combat. There was an atmospheric feeling that registered on a sensitive mind the difference between victory and defeat, and he was firm in the belief that as yesterday had gone today was going. Certainly this great German army which he believed to be in the center was not advancing, and something of a character most menacing was happening to the wings of the German force. He read it in the serious, preoccupied faces of the officers who passed near. There was not a smile on the face of the youngest of them all, but deepest anxiety was written alike on young and old.

John and Fleury sat together at the edge of the brook, and for a while forgot their chagrin at not being on the battle line. The battle itself which they could not see, but which they could hear, absorbed them so thoroughly that they had no time to think of regrets.

John had thought that man's violence, his energy in destruction on the first day could not be equalled, but it seemed to him now that the second day surpassed the first. The cannon fire was distant, yet the waves of air beat heavily upon them, and the earth shook without ceasing. Wisps of smoke floated toward them and the air was tainted again with the acrid smell of burned gunpowder.

"You're a mountaineer, Fleury, you told me," said Scott, "and you should be able to judge how sound travels through gorges. I suppose you yodel, of course?"

"Yodel, what's that?"

"To make a long singing cry on a peak which is supposed to reach to somebody on another peak who sends back the same kind of a singing cry. We have a general impression in America that European mountaineers don't do much but stand in fancy costumes on crests and ridges and yodel to one another."

"It may have been so once," said the young Savoyard, "but this is a bad year for yodeling. The voice of the cannon carries so far that the voice of man doesn't amount to much. But what sound did you want me to interpret?"

"That of the cannon. Does its volume move eastward or westward? I should think it's much like your mountain storms and you know how they travel among the ridges."

"The comparison is just, but I can't yet tell any shifting of the artillery fire. The wind brings the sound toward us, and if there's any great advance or retreat I should be able to detect it. I should say that as far as the second day is concerned nothing decisive has happened yet."

"Do you know this country?"

"A little. My regiment marched through here about three weeks ago and we made two camps not far from this spot. This is the wood of Sénouart, and the brook here runs down to the river Marne."

"And we're not far from that river. Then we've pressed back the Germans farther than I thought. It's strange that the German army here does not move."

"It's waiting, and I fancy it doesn't know what to do. I've an idea that our victory yesterday was greater than the French and British have realized, but which the Germans, of course, understand. Why do they leave us here, almost neglected, and why do their officers walk about, looking so doubtful and anxious? I've heard that the Germans were approaching

Paris with five armies. It may be that we've cut off at least one of those armies and that it's in mortal danger."

"It may be so. But have you thought, Fleury, of the extraordinary difference between this morning and yesterday morning?"

"I have. In conditions they're worlds apart. Hark! Listen now, Scott, my friend!"

He lay on the grass and put his ear to the ground, just as John had often done. Listening intently for at least two minutes, he announced with conviction that the cannonade was moving eastward.

"Which means that the Germans are withdrawing again?" said John.

"Undoubtedly," said Fleury, his face glowing.

They listened a quarter of an hour longer, and John himself was then able to tell that the battle line was shifting. The Germans elsewhere must have fallen back several miles, but the army about him did not yet move. He caught a glimpse of the burly general walking back and forth in the forest, his hands clasped behind him, and a frown on his broad, fighting face. He would walk occasionally to a little telephone station, improvised under the treesJohn could see the wires stretching away through the forestand listen long and attentively. But when he put down the receiver the same moody look was invariably on his face, and John was convinced as much by his expression as by the sound of the guns that affairs were not going well with the Germans.

Another long hour passed and the sun moved on toward noon, but a German army of perhaps a quarter of a million men lay idle in the forest of Sénouart, as John now called the whole region.

Presently the general walked down the line and John lost sight of him. But Weber reappeared, coming from the other side of the hillock, and John was glad to see him, since Fleury had gone back to attend to a wounded friend.

"There doesn't seem to be as much action here as I expected," said Weber, cheerfully, sitting down on the grass beside young Scott.

"But they're shaking the world there! and there!" said John, nodding to right and to left.

"So they are. This is a most extraordinary reversal, Mr. Scott, and I can't conceive how it was brought about. Some mysterious mind has made and carried through a plan that was superbly Napoleonic. I'd give much to know how it was done."

John shook his head.

"I know nothing of it," he said.

"But doubtless your friend Lannes does. What a wonderful thing it is to carry through the heavens the dispatches which may move forward a million armed men."

"I don't know anything about Lannes' dispatches."

"Nor do I, but I can make a close guess, just as you can. He's surely hovering over the battle field today, and as I said last night he certainly has some idea where you are, and sooner or later will come for you."

John looked up, but again the heavens were bare and clear. Then he looked down and saw walking near them a heavy, middle-aged, bearded man to whom all the German officers paid great deference. The man's manner was haughty and overbearing, and John understood at once that in the monarchical sense he was a personage.

"Do you know the big fellow there?" he said to Weber. "Have you heard anyone speak of him?"

"I saw him this morning, and one of the guards told us who he is. That is Prince Karl of Auersperg. The house of Auersperg is one of the oldest in Germany, much older than the Emperor's family, the Hohenzollerns. I don't suppose the world contains any royal blood more ancient than that of Prince Karl."

"Evidently he feels that it's so. I'm getting used to princes, but our heavy friend there must be something of a specialist in the princely line. I should judge from his manner that he is not only the oldest man on earth, speaking in terms of blood, but the owner of the earth as well."

"The Auerspergs have an immense pride."

"I can see it, but a lot of pride fell before Paris yesterday, and a lot more is falling among these hills and forests today. There seems to be a lot of difference between princes, the Arnheims and the Auerspergs, for instance."

Then a sudden thought struck John. It had the vaguest sort of basis, but it came home to him with all the power of conviction.

"I wonder if Prince Karl of Auersperg once owned a magnificent armored automobile," he said.

Weber looked puzzled, and then his eyes lightened.

"Ah, I know what you mean!" he exclaimed. "The one in which we took that flight with Carstairs the Englishman and Wharton the American. It belonged to a prince, without doubt, yes. But no, it couldn't have been Prince Karl of Auersperg who owned the machine."

"I'm not so sure. I've an intuition that it is he. Besides, he looks like just the kind of prince from whom I'd like to take his best automobile, also everything else good that he might happen to have. I shall feel much disappointed if this proves not to be our prince."

"You Americans are such democrats."

"I don't go so far as to say a man is necessarily bad because of his high rank, but as I reminded you a little while ago, there are princes and princes. The ancient house of Auersperg as it walks up and down, indicating its conviction of its own superiority to everything else on earth, does not please me."

"The Uhlans are coming back!" exclaimed Weber in tones of excitement.

"And that's von Boehlen at their head! I'd know his figure as far as I could see it! And they've had a brush, too! Look at the empty saddles and the wounded men! As sure as we live they've run into the French cavalry and then they've run out again!"

The Uhlans were returning at a gallop, and the German officers of high rank were crowding forward to meet them. It was obvious to every one that they had received a terrible handling, but John knew that von Boehlen was not a man to come at a panicky gallop. Some powerful motive must send him so fast.

He saw the Prussian captain spring from his horse and rush to a little group composed of the general, the prince and several others of high rank who had drawn closely together at his coming.

Von Boehlen was wounded slightly, but he stood erect as he saluted the commander and talked with him briefly and rapidly. John's busy and imaginative mind was at work at once with surmises, and he settled upon one which he was sure must be the truth. The French advance in the center was coming, and this German army also must soon go into action.

He was confirmed in his belief by a hurried order to the guards to go eastward with the prisoners. As the captives, the wounded and the unwounded, marched off through the forest of Sénouart they heard at a distance, but behind them, the opening of a huge artillery fire. It was so tremendous that they could feel the shaking of the earth as they walked, and despite the hurrying of their guards they stopped at the crest of a low ridge to look back.

They gazed across a wide valley toward high green hills, along which they saw rapid and many flashes. John longed now for the glasses which had been taken from him when he was captured, but he was quite sure that the flashes were made by French guns. From a point perhaps a mile in front of the prisoners masked German batteries were replying. Fleury with his extraordinary power of judging sound was able to locate these guns with some degree of approximation.

"Look! the aeroplanes!" said John, pointing toward the hills which he now called to himself the French line.

Numerous dark shapes, forty or fifty at least, appeared in the sky and hovered over the western edge of the wide, shallow basin. John was sure that they were the French scouts of the blue, appearing almost in line like troops on the ground, and his heart gave a great throb. No doubt could be left now, that this German army was being attacked in force and with the greatest violence. It followed then that the entire German line was being assailed, and that the French victory was continuing its advance. The Republic had rallied grandly and was hurling back the Empire in the most magnificent manner.

All those emotions of joy and exultation that he had felt the day before returned with increased force. In daily contact he liked Germans as well as Frenchmen, but he thought that no punishment could ever be adequate for the gigantic crimes of kings. Napoleon himself had been the champion of democracy and freedom, until he became an emperor and his head swelled so much with success that he thought of God and himself together, just as the Kaiser was now thinking. It was a curious inversion that the French who were fighting then to dominate Europe were fighting now to prevent such a domination. But it was now a great French republican nation remade and reinvigorated, as any one could see.

The guards hurried them on again. Another mile and they stopped once more on the crest of a low hill, where it seemed that they would remain some time, as the Germans were too busy with a vast battle to think much about a few prisoners. It was evident that the whole army was engaged. The old general, the other generals, the princes and perhaps dukes and barons too, were in the thick of it. John's heart was filled with an intense hatred of the very name of royalty. Kings and princes could be good men personally, but as he saw its work upon the huge battle fields of Europe he felt that the institution itself was the curse of the earth.

"We shall win again today," said Fleury, rousing him from his absorption. "Look across the fields, Scott, my friend, and see how those great masses of infantry charging our army have been repulsed."

It was a far look, and at the distance the German brigades seemed to be blended together, but the great gray mass was coming back slowly. He forgot all about himself and his own fate in his desire to see every act of the gigantic drama as it passed before him. He took no thought of escape at present, nor did Fleury, who stood beside him. The fire of the guns great and small had now blended into the usual steady thunder, beneath which human voices could be heard.

"We don't have the forty-two centimeters, nor the great siege guns," said Fleury, "but the French field artillery is the best in the world. It's undoubtedly holding back the German hosts and covering the French advance."

"That's my opinion, too," said John. "I saw its wonderful work in the retreat toward Paris. I think it saved the early French armies from destruction."

The German army was made of stern material. Having planted its feet here it refused to be driven back. Its cannon was a line of flaming volcanoes, its cavalry charged again and again into the face of death, and its infantry perished in masses, but the stern old general spared nothing. Passing up and down the lines, listening at the telephone and receiving the reports of air scouts and land scouts, he always hurled in fresh troops at the critical points and Fritz and Karl and Wilhelm and August, sober and honest men, went forward willingly, sometimes singing and sometimes in silence, to die for a false and outworn system. John as a prisoner had a better view than he would have had if with the French army. In a country open now he could see a full mile to right and left, where the German hosts marched again and again to attack, and while the French troops were too far away for his eyes he beheld the continuous flare of their fire, like a broad red ribbon across the whole western horizon.

The passing of time was nothing to him. He forgot all about it in his absorption. But the sun climbed on, afternoon came, and still the battle at this point raged, the French unable to drive the Germans farther and the Germans unable to stop the French attacks. John roused himself and endeavored to dissociate the thunder on their flanks from that in front, and, after long listening, he was able to make the separation, or at least he thought so. He knew now that the struggle there was no less fierce than the one before him.

The Kaiser himself must be present with one or the other of these armies, and a man who had talked for more than twenty years of his divine right, his shining armor, his invincible sword and his mailed fist must be raging with the bitterness of death to find that he was only a mortal like other mortals, and that simple French republicans were defeating the War Lord, his Grand Army and the host of kings, princes, dukes, barons, high-born, very high-born, and all the other relics of medievalism. Dipped to the heel and beyond in the fountain of democracy, John could not keep from feeling a fierce joy as he saw with his own eyes the Germans fighting in the utmost desperation, not to take Paris and destroy France, but to save themselves from destruction.

The afternoon, slow and bright, save for the battle, dragged on. Scott and Fleury kept together. Weber appeared once more and spoke rather despondently. He believed that the Germans would hold fast, and might even resume the offensive toward Paris again, but Fleury shook his head.

"Today is like yesterday," he said.

"How can you tell?" asked Weber.

"Because the fire on both flanks is slowly moving eastward, that is, the Germans there are yielding ground. My ears, trained to note such things, tell me so. My friend, I am not mistaken."

He spoke gravely, without exultation, but John took fresh hope from his words. Toward night the fire in their front died somewhat, and after sunset it sank lower, but they still heard a prodigious volume of firing on both flanks. John remembered then that they had eaten nothing since morning, but when some of the prisoners who spoke German requested food it was served to them.

Night came over what seemed to be a drawn battle at this point, and after eating his brief supper John saw the automobiles and stretchers bringing in the wounded. They passed him in thousands and thousands, hurt in every conceivable manner. At first he could scarcely bear to look at them, but it was astonishing how soon one hardened to such sights.

The wounded were being carried to improvised hospitals in the rear, but so far as John knew the dead were left on the field. The Germans with their usual thorough system worked rapidly and smoothly, but he noticed that the fires were but very few. There was but little light in the wood of Sénouart or the hills beyond, and there was little, too, on the ridges that marked the French position.

John kept near the edges of the space allotted to the prisoners, hoping that he might again see von Arnheim. He had discovered early that the Germans were unusually kind to Americans, and the fact that he had been taken fighting against them did not prevent them from showing generous treatment. The officer in charge of the guard even wanted to talk to him about the war and prove to him how jealousy had caused the other nations to set upon Germany. But John evaded him and continued to look for the young prince who was serving as a mere lieutenant.

It was about an hour after dark when he caught his first glimpse of von Arnheim, and he was really glad to see that he was not wounded.

"I've come to tell you, Mr. Scott," said von Arnheim, "that all of you must march at once. You will cross the Marne, and then pass as prisoners into Germany. You will be well treated there and I think you can probably secure your release on condition that you return to your own country and take no further part in the war."

John shook his head.

"I don't expect any harshness from the Germans," he said, "but I'm in this war to stay, if the bullets and shells will let me. I warn you now that I'm going to escape."

Von Arnheim laughed pleasantly.

"It's fair of you to give us warning of your intentions," he said, "but I don't think you'll have much chance. You must get ready to start at once."

"I take it," said John, "that our departure means the departure of the German army also."

Von Arnheim opened his mouth to speak, but he closed it again suddenly.

"It's only a deduction of mine," said John.

Von Arnheim nodded in farewell and hurried away.

"Now I'm sure," said John to Fleury a few minutes later, "that this army is going to withdraw."

"I think so too," said Fleury. "I can yet hear the fire of the cannon on either flank and it has certainly moved to the east. In my opinion, my friend, both German wings have been defeated, and this central army is compelled to fall back because it's left without supports. But we'll soon see. They can't hide from us the evidences of retreat."

The prisoners now marched in a long file in the moonlight across the fields, and John soon recognized the proof that Fleury was right. The German army was retreating. There were innumerable dull, rumbling sounds, made by the cannon and motors of all kinds passing along the roads, and at times also he heard the heavy tramp of scores of thousands marching in a direction that did not lead to Paris.

John began to think now of Lannes. Would he come? Was Weber right when he credited to him a knowledge near to omniscience? How was it possible for him to pick out a friend in all that huge morass of battle! And yet he had a wonderful, almost an unreasoning faith in Philip, and, as always when he thought of him, he looked up at the heavens.

It was an average night, one in which large objects should be visible in the skies, and he saw several aeroplanes almost over their heads, while the rattle of a dirigible came from a point further toward the east.

The aeroplane was bound to be German, but as John looked he saw a sleek shape darting high over them all and flying eastward. Intuition, or perhaps it was something in the motion and shape of the machine, made him believe it was the *Arrow*. It must be the *Arrow!* And Lannes must be in it! High over the army and high over the German planes it darted forward like a swallow and disappeared in a cloud of white mist. His hair lifted a little, and a thrill ran down his spine.

He still looked up as he walked along, and there was the sleek shape again! It had come back out of the white mist, and was circling over the German planes, flying with the speed and certainty of an eagle. He saw three of the German machines whirl about and begin to mount as if they would examine the stranger. But the solitary plane began to rise again in a series of dazzling circles. Up, up it went, as if it would penetrate the last and thinnest layer of air, until it reached the dark and empty void beyond.

The *Arrow*—he was sure it could be no other—was quickly lost in the infinite heights, and then the German planes were lost, too, but they soon came back, although the *Arrow* did not. It had probably returned to some point over the French line or had gone eastward beyond the Germans.

John felt that he had again seen a sign. He remembered how he and Lannes had drawn hope from omens when they were looking at the Arc de Triomphe, and a similar hope sprang up now. Weber was right! Lannes would come to his rescue. Some thought or impulse yet unknown would guide him.

Light clouds now drifted up from the southwest, and all the aeroplanes were hidden, but the heavy murmur of the marching army went on. The puffing and clashing of innumerable automobiles came from the roads also, though John soon ceased to pay attention to them. As the hours passed, he felt an increased weariness. He had sat still almost the whole day, but the strain of the watching and waiting had been as great as that of the walking now was. He wondered if the guards would ever let them stop.

They waded another brook, passed through another wood and then they were ordered to halt. The guards announced that they could sleep, as they would go no farther that night. The men did not lie down. They fell, and each lay where he fell, and in whatever position he had assumed when falling.

John was conscious of hearing the order, of striking the grass full length, and he knew nothing more until the next morning when he was aroused by Fleury. He saw a whitish dawn with much mist floating over the fields, and he believed that a large river, probably the Marne, must be near.

As far as he could see the ground was covered with German soldiers.

They too had dropped at the command to stop, and had gone to sleep as they were falling. The majority of them still slept.

"What is it, Fleury? Why did you wake me up?" asked John.

"The river Marne is close by, and I'm sure that the Germans are going to retreat across it. I had an idea that possibly we might escape while there's so much mist. They can't watch us very closely while they have so much else to do, and doubtless they would care but little if some of us did escape."

"We'll certainly look for the chance. Can you see any sign of the French pursuit?"

"Not yet, but our people will surely follow. They're still at it already on the flanks!"

The distant thunder of cannon came from both right and left.

"A third day of fighting is at hand," said Fleury.

"And it will be followed by a fourth."

"And a fifth."

"But we shall continue to drive the enemy away."

Both spoke with the utmost confidence. Having seen their armies victorious for two days they had no doubt they would win again. All that morning they listened to the sounds of combat, although they saw much less than on the day before. The prisoners were in a little wood, where they lay down at times, and then, restless and anxious, would stand on tiptoe again, seeking to see at least a corner of the battle.

John and Fleury were standing near noon at the edge of the wood, when a small body of Uhlans halted close by. Being not more than fifty in number, John judged that they were scouts, and the foaming mouths of their horses showing that they had been ridden hard, confirmed him in the opinion. They were only fifty or sixty yards from him, and although they were motionless for some time, their eager faces showed that they were waiting for some movement.

It was pure chance, but John happened to be looking at a rather large man who sat his horse easily, his gloved hand resting on his thigh. He saw distinctly that his face was very ruddy and covered with beads of perspiration. Then man and horse together fell to the ground as if struck by a bolt of lightning. The man did not move at all, but the horse kicked for a few moments and lay still.

There was a shout of mingled amazement and horror from the other Uhlans, and it found its echo in John's own mind. He saw one of the men look up, and he looked up also. A dark shape hovered overhead. Something small and black, and then another and another fell from it and shot downward into the group of Uhlans. A second man was hurled from his horse and lay still upon the ground. Again John felt that thrill of horror and amazement.

"What is it? What is it?" he cried.

"I think it's the steel arrow," said Fleury, pressing a little further forward and standing on tiptoe. "As well as I can see, the first passed entirely through the head of the man and then broke the backbone of the horse beneath him."

John saw one of the Uhlans, who had dismounted, holding up a short, heavy steel weapon, a dart rather than an arrow, its weight adjusted so that it was sure to fall point downward. Coming from such a height John did not wonder that it had pierced both horse and rider, and as he looked another, falling near the Uhlan, struck deep into the earth.

"There goes the aeroplane that did it," said John to Fleury, pointing upward.

It hovered a minute or two longer and flew swiftly back toward the French lines, pursued vainly a portion of the distance by the German Taubes.

"A new weapon of death," said Fleury. "The fighters move in the air, under the water, on the earth, everywhere."

"The Uhlans are off again," said John. "Whatever their duty was the steel arrows have sent them on it in a hurry."

"And we're about to move too. See, these batteries are limbering up preparatory to a withdrawal."

Inside of fifteen minutes they were again marching eastward, though slowly and with the roar of battle going on as fiercely behind them as ever. John heard again from some of the talk of the guards that the Germans had five armies along their whole line, but whether the one with which he was now a prisoner was falling back with its whole force he had no way of knowing. Both he and Fleury were sure the prisoners themselves would soon cross the Marne, and that large detachments of the enemy would go with them.

Thoughts of escape returned. Crossing a river in battle was a perilous operation, entailing much confusion, and the chance might come at the Marne. They could see too that the Germans were now being pressed harder. The French shells were coming faster and with more deadly precision. Now and then they exploded among the masses of German infantry, and once or twice they struck close to the captives.

"It would be a pity to be killed by our own people," said Fleury.

"And at such a time as this," said John. "Do you know, Fleury, that my greatest fear about getting killed is that then I wouldn't know how this war is going to end?"

"I feel that way myself sometimes. Look, there's the Marne! See its waters shining! It's the mark of the first great stage in the German retreat."

"I wonder how we're going to cross. I suppose the bridges will be crowded with artillery and men. It might pay the Germans just to let us go."

"They won't do that. There's nothing in their rules about liberating prisoners, and they wouldn't hear of such a thing, anyhow, trouble or no trouble."

"I see some boats, and I fancy we'll cross on them. I wonder if we couldn't make what we call in my country a get-away, while we're waiting for the embarkation."

"If our gunners become much more accurate our get-away, as you call it, will be into the next life."

Two huge shells had burst near, and, although none of the flying metal struck them, their faces were stung by fine dirt. When John brushed the dust out of his eyes he saw that he was right in his surmise about the crossing in boats, but wrong about probable delays in embarkation. The German machine even in retreat worked with neatness and dispatch. There were three boats, and the first relay of prisoners, including John and Fleury, was hurried into them. A bridge farther down the stream rumbled heavily as the artillery crossed on it. But the French force was coming closer and closer. A shell struck in the river sixty or eighty feet from them and the water rose in a cataract. Some of the prisoners had been put at the oars and they, like the Germans, showed eagerness to reach the other side. John noted the landing, a narrow entrance between thick clumps of willows, and he confessed to himself that he too would feel better when they were on the farther bank.

The Marne is not a wide river, and a few powerful pulls at the oars sent them near to the landing. But at that moment a shell whistled through the air, plunged into the water and exploded practically beneath the boat.

John was hurled upward in a gush of foam and water, and then, when he dropped back, the Marne received him in its bosom.

7

THE SPORT OF KINGS

J ohn Scott, who was suffering from his second immersion in a French river, came up with mouth, eyes and nose full of water. The stream around him was crowded with men swimming or with those who had reached water shallow enough to permit of wading. As well as he could see, the shell had done no damage besides giving them a huge bath, of which every one stood in much need.

But he had a keen and active mind and it never worked quicker than it did now. He had thought his chance for escape might come in the confusion of a hurried crossing, and here it was. He dived and swam down the stream toward the willows that lined the bank. When he could hold his breath no longer he came up in one of the thickest clumps. The water reached to his waist there, and standing on the bottom in all the density of willows and bushes he was hidden thoroughly from all except watchful searchers. And who would miss him at such a time, and who, if missing, would take the trouble to look for him while the French cannon were thundering upon them and a perilous crossing was to be made?

It was all so ridiculously easy. He knew that he had nothing to do but stand close while the men pulled themselves out of the river and the remaining boats made their passage. For further protection he moved into water deep enough to reach to his neck, while he still retained the cover of the willows and bushes. Here he watched the German troops pass over, and listened to the heavy cannonade. He soon noted that the Germans, after crossing, were taking up strong positions on the other side. He could tell it from the tremendous artillery fire that came from their side of the Marne.

John now found that his position, while safe from observation, was far from comfortable. The chill of the water began to creep into his bones and more shells struck unpleasantly near. Another fell into the river and he was blinded for a moment by the violent showers of foam and spray. He began to feel uneasy. If the German and French armies were going to fight each other from the opposing sides of the Marne he would be held there indefinitely, either to be killed by a shell or bullet or to drown from cramp.

But time passed and he saw no chance of leaving his watery lair. The chill went further into his bones. He was lonesome too. He longed for the companionship of Fleury, and he wondered what had become of him. He sincerely hoped that he too had reached a covert and that they should meet again.

No rumbling came from the bridge below, and, glancing down the stream, John saw that it was empty. There must be many other bridges over the Marne, but he believed that the German armies had now crossed it, and would devote their energy to a new attack. He was squarely between the lines and he did not see any chance to escape until darkness.

He looked up and saw a bright sun and blue skies. Night was distant, and so far as he was concerned it might be a year away. If two armies were firing shells directly at a man they must hit him in an hour or two, and if not, a polar stream such as the Marne had now become would certainly freeze him to death. He had no idea French rivers could be so cold. The Marne must be fed by a whole flock of glaciers.

His teeth began to chatter violently, and then he took stern hold of himself. He felt that he was allowing his imagination to run away with him, and he rebuked John Scott sternly and often for such foolishness. He tried to get some warmth into his veins by jumping up and down in the water, but it was of little avail. Yet he stood it another hour. Then he made one more long and critical examination of the ground.

Shells were now screaming high overhead, but nobody was in sight. He judged that it was now an artillery battle, with the foes perhaps three or four miles apart, and, leaving the willows, he crept out upon the bank. It was the side held by the Germans, but he knew that if he attempted to swim the river to the other bank he would be taken with cramps and would drown.

There was a little patch of long grass about ten yards from the river, and, crawling to it, he lay down. The grass rose a foot high on either side of him, but the sun, bright and hot, shone directly down upon his face and body. It felt wonderfully good after that long submersion in the Marne. Removing all his heavy wet clothing, he wrung the water out of it as much as he could, and lay back in a state of nature, for both himself and his clothing to dry. Meanwhile, in order to avoid cold, he stretched and tensed his muscles for a quarter of an hour before he lay still again.

A wonderful warmth and restfulness flowed back into his veins. He had feared chills and a serious illness, but he knew now that they would not come. Youth, wiry and seasoned by hard campaigning, would quickly recover, but knowing that, for the present, he could neither go forward nor backward, he luxuriated in the grass, while the sun sucked the damp out of his clothing.

Meanwhile the battle was raging over his head and he scarcely noticed it. The shells whistled and shrieked incessantly, but, midway between the contending lines, he felt that they were no longer likely to drop near. So he relaxed, and a dreamy feeling crept over him. He could hear the murmur of insects in the grass, and he reflected that the smaller one was, the safer one was. A shell was not likely to take any notice of a gnat.

He felt of his clothing. It was not dry yet and he would wait a little longer. Anyhow, what was the use of hurrying? He turned over on his side and continued to luxuriate in the long grass.

The warmth and dryness had sent the blood pulsing in a strong flood through his veins once more, and the mental rebound came too. Although he lay immediately between two gigantic armies which were sending showers of metal at each other along a line of many miles, he considered his escape sure and the thought of personal danger disappeared. If one only had something to eat! It is curious how the normal instincts and wants of man assert themselves even under the most dangerous conditions. He began to think of the good German brown bread and the hot sausage that he had devoured, and the hot coffee that he had drunk. One could eat the food of an enemy without compunction.

But it was folly to move, even to seek dinner or supper, while the shells were flying in such quantities over his head. As he turned once more and lay on his back he caught glimpses as of swift shadows passing high above, and the whistling and screaming of shells and shrapnel was continuous. It was true that a missile might fall short and find him in the grass, but he considered the possibility remote and it did not give him a tremor. As he was sure now that he would suffer no bodily ill from his long bath in the Marne he might remain in the grass until night and then creep away. Blessed night! It was the kindly veil for all fugitives, and no one ever awaited it with more eagerness than John Scott.

The sun was now well beyond the zenith, and its golden darts came indirectly. His clothing was thoroughly dry at last, and he put it on again. Clad anew he was tempted to seek escape at once, but the sound of a footstep caused him to lie down in the shelter of the grass again.

His ear was now against the earth and the footsteps were much more distinct. He was sure that they were made by a horse, and he believed that a Uhlan was riding near. He remembered how long and sharp their lances were, and he was grateful that the grass was so thick and tall. He longed for the automatic revolver that had been such a trusty friend, but the Germans had taken it long since, and he was wholly unarmed.

He was afraid to raise his head high enough to see the horseman, lest he be seen, but the footsteps, as if fate had a grudge against him, were coming nearer. His blood grew hot in a kind of rebellion against chance, or the power that directed the universe. It was really a grim joke that, after having escaped so much, a mere wandering scout of a Uhlan should pick him up, so to speak, on the point of his lance.

He pressed hard against the earth. He would have pressed himself into it if he could, and imagination, the deceiver, made him think that he was doing so. The temptation to raise his head above the grass and look became more violent, but will held him firm and he still lay flat.

Then he noticed that the hoofbeats wandered about in an irregular, aimless fashion. Not even a scout hunting a good position for observation would ride in such a way, and becoming more daring he raised his head slowly, until he could peep over the grass stems. He saw a horse, fifteen or twenty feet from him, but without rider, bridle or saddle. It was a black horse of gigantic build like a Percheron, with feet as large as a half-bushel measure, and a huge rough mane.

The horse saw John and gazed at him out of great, mild, limpid eyes. The young American thought he beheld fright there and the desire for companionship. The animal, probably belonging to some farmer who had fled before the armies, had wandered into the battle area, seeking the human friends to whom he was so used, and nothing living was more harmless than he. He reminded John in some ways of those stalwart and honest peasants who were so ruthlessly made into cannon food by the gigantic and infinitely more dangerous Tammany that rules the seventy million Germans.

The horse walked nearer and the look in his eyes became so full of terror and the need of man's support that for the time he stood as a human being in John's imagination.

"Poor old horse!" he called, "I'm sorry for you, but your case is no worse than mine. Here we both are, wishing harm to nobody, but with a million men shooting over our backs."

The horse, emboldened by the friendly voice, came nearer and nuzzled at the human friend whom he had found so opportunely, and who, although so much smaller than himself, was, as he knew, so much more powerful. This human comrade would show him what to do and protect him from all harm. But John took alarm. He too found pleasure in having a comrade, even if it were only a horse, but the animal would probably attract the attention of scouts or skirmishers. He tried to shoo him away, but for a long time the horse would not move. At last he pulled a heavy bunch of grass, wadded it together and threw it in his face.

The horse, staring at him reproachfully, turned and walked away. John's lively fancy saw a tear in the huge, luminous eye, and his conscience smote him hard.

"I had to do it, Marne, old fellow," he called. "You're so big and you stick up so high that you arouse attention, and that's just what I don't want."

He had decided to call the horse Marne, after the river near by, and he noticed that he did not go far. The animal, reassured by John's friendly after-word, began to crop the grass about twenty feet away. He had a human friend after all, one on whom he could rely. Man did not want to be bothered by him just then, but that was the way of man, and he did not mind, since the grass was so plentiful and good. He would be there, close at hand, when he was needed.

John was really moved by the interlude. The loneliness, and then the friendliness of the horse appealed to him. He too needed a comrade, and here he was. He forgot, for a time, the moaning of the shells over his head, and began to think again about his escape. So thinking, the horse came once more into his mind. He showed every sign of grazing there until dark came. Then why not ride away on him? It was true that a horse was larger and made more noise than a fugitive man slipping through the grass, but there were times when strength and speed, especially speed, counted for a lot.

The last hours of the afternoon waned, trailing their slow length, minute by minute, and throughout that time the roar of the battle was as steady as the fall of Niagara. It even came to the point that John paid little attention to it, but the sport of kings, in which thousands of men were ground up, they knew not why, went merrily on. None of the shells struck near John, and with infinite joy he saw the coming of the long shadows betokening the twilight. The horse, still grazing near by, raised his head more than once and looked at him, as if it were time to go. As the sun sank and the dusk grew John stood up. He saw that the night was going to be dark and he was thankful. The Marne was merely a silver streak in the shadow, and in the wood near by the trees were fusing into a single clump of darkness.

He stood erect, stretching his muscles and feeling that it was glorious to be a man with his head in the air, instead of a creature that grovelled on the ground. Then he walked over to the horse and patted him on the shoulder.

"Marne, old boy," he said, "I think it's about time for you and me to go."

The horse rubbed his great head against John's arm, signifying that he was ready to obey any command his new master might give him. John knew from his build that he was a draught horse, but there were times in which one could not choose a particular horse for a particular need.

"Marne, old fellow," he said, stroking the animal's mane, "you're not to be a menial cart horse tonight. I am an Arabian genie and I hereby turn you into a light, smooth, beautifully built automobile for one passenger only, and I'm that passenger."

Holding fast to the thick mane he sprang upon the horse's back, and urged him down the stream, keeping close to the water where there was shelter among the willows and bushes. He had no definite idea in his head, but he felt that if he kept on going he must arrive somewhere. He was afraid to make the horse swim the river in an effort to reach the French army. Appearing on the surface of the water he felt that he would almost certainly be seen and some good rifleman or other would be sure to pick him off.

He concluded at last that if no German troops came in sight he would let the horse take him where he would. Marne must have a home and a master somewhere and habit would send him to them. So he ceased to push at his neck and try to direct him, and the horse continued a slow and peaceful progress down the stream in the shadow of small trees. The night was darker than those just before it, and the dampness of the air indicated possible flurries of rain. Cannon still rumbled on the horizon like the thunder of a summer night.

While trusting to the horse to lead him to some destination, John kept a wary watch, with eyes now growing used to the darkness. If German troops appeared and speed to escape were lacking, he would jump from Marne's back and hunt a new covert. But he saw nobody. The evidences of man's work were present continually in the cannonade, but man himself was absent.

The horse went on with ponderous and sure tread. Evidently he had wandered far under the influence of the firing, but it was equally evident that his certain instinct was guiding him back again. He crossed a brook flowing down into the Marne, passed through a wheat field, and entered a little valley, where grew a number of oaks, clear of undergrowth.

When he saw what was lying under the oaks he pulled hard at the rough mane, until the horse stopped. He had distinctly made out the figures of men, stretched upon the ground, apparently asleep, and sure to be Germans. He stared hard at them, but the horse snorted and tried to pull away. The action of the animal rather than his own eyesight made him reckon aright.

A horse would not be afraid of living men, and, slipping from the back of Marne, John approached cautiously. A few rays of wan moonlight filtered through the trees, and when he had come close he shuddered over and over again. About a dozen men lay on the ground and all were stone dead. The torn earth and their own torn figures showed that a shell had burst among them. Doubtless it had been an infantry patrol, and the survivors had hurried away.

John, still shuddering, was about to turn back to his horse, when he remembered that he needed much and that in war one must not be too scrupulous. Force of will made him return to the group and he sought for what he wanted. Evidently the firing had been hot there and the rest of the patrol had not lingered in their flight.

He took from one man a pair of blankets. He could have had his choice of two or three good rifles, but he passed them by in favor of a large automatic pistol which would not be in the way. This had been carried by a young man whom he took to be an officer, and he also found on him many cartridges for the pistol. Then he searched their knapsacks for food, finding plenty of bread and sausage and filling with it one knapsack which he put over his shoulder.

He returned hastily to his horse, guided him around the fatal spot, and when he was some distance on the other side dismounted and ate as only a half-starved man can eat. Water was obtained from a convenient brook and carefully storing the remainder of the food in the knapsack he remounted the horse.

"Now go on, my good and gallant beast," he said, "and I feel sure that your journey is nearly at an end. A draught horse like you, bulky and slow, would not wander any great distance."

The horse himself immediately justified his prediction by raising his head, neighing and advancing at a swifter pace. John saw, standing among some trees, a low and small house, built of stone and evidently very old, its humble nature indicating that it belonged to a peasant.

Behind it was a tiny vineyard, and there was a stable and another outhouse.

"Well, Marne, my lad, here's your home, beyond a doubt," said John. But no answer came to the neigh. The house remained silent and dark. It confirmed John's first belief that the horse belonged to some peasant who had fled with his family from the armies. He stroked the animal's neck, and felt real pity for him, as if he had been a child abandoned.

"I know that while I'm a friend I'm almost a stranger to you, but come, we'll examine things," he said.

He sprang off the horse, and drew his automatic. The possession of the pistol gave him an immense amount of courage and confidence, but he did not anticipate any trouble at the house as he was sure that it was abandoned.

He pushed open the door and saw a dark inside. Staring a little he made out a plainly furnished room, from which all the lighter articles had been taken. There was a hearth, but with no fire on it, and John decided that he would sleep in the house. It was in a lonely place, but he would take the risk.

The horse had already gone to the stable and was pushing the door with his nose. John let him in, and found some oat straw which he gave him. Then he left him munching in content, and as he departed he struck him a resounding blow of friendliness on the flank.

"Good old Marne," he said, "you're certainly one of the best friends I've found in Europe. In fact, you're about the only living being I've associated with that doesn't want to kill somebody."

He entered the house and closed the door. In addition to the sitting-room there was a bedroom and a kitchen, all bearing the signs of recent occupancy. He found a small petroleum lamp, but he concluded not to light it. Instead he sat on a wooden bench in the main room beside a small window, ate a little more from the knapsack, and watched a while lest friend or enemy should come.

It had grown somewhat darker and the clouds were driving across the sky. The wind was rising and the threatened flurries of rain came, beating against the cottage. John was devoutly glad that he had found the little house. Having spent many hours immersed to his neck in a river he felt that he had had enough water for one day. Moreover, his escape, his snug shelter and the abundance of food at hand, gave him an extraordinary sense of ease and rest. He noticed that in the darkness and rain one might pass within fifty feet of the cottage without seeing it.

The wind increased and moaned among the oaks that grew around the house, but above the moaning the sounds of battle, the distant thunder of the artillery yet came. The sport of kings was going merrily on. Neither night nor storm stopped it and men were still being ground by thousands into cannon food. But John had now a feeling of detachment. Three days of continuous battle had dulled his senses. They might fight on as they pleased. It did not concern him, for tonight at least. He was going to look out for himself.

He fastened the door securely, but, as he left the window open, currents of fresh cool air poured into the room. He was now fully revived in both mind and body, and he took present ease and comfort, thinking but little of the future. The flurries of rain melted into a steady pour. The cold deepened, and as he wrapped the two blankets around him his sense of comfort increased. Lightning flared at infrequent intervals and now and then real thunder mingled with that of the artillery.

He felt that he might have been back at home. It was like some snug little place in the high hills of Pennsylvania or New York. Like many other Americans, he often felt surprise that Europe should be so much like America. The trees and the grass and the rivers were just the same. Nothing was different but the ancient buildings. He knew now that history and a long literature merely created the illusion of difference.

He wondered why the artillery fire did not die, with the wind sweeping such gusts of rain before it. Then he remembered that the sound of so many great cannon could travel a long distance, and there might be no rain at the points from which the firing came. The cottage might stand in a long narrow valley up which the clouds would travel.

Not feeling sleepy yet he decided to have another look about the house. A search revealed a small box of matches near the lamp on the shelf. Then he closed the window in order to shut in the flame, and, lighting the lamp, pursued his investigation.

He found in the kitchen a jar of honey that he had overlooked, and he resolved to use a part of it for breakfast. Europeans did not seem able to live without jam or honey in the mornings, and he would follow the custom. Not much was left in the other rooms, besides some old articles of clothing, including two or three blue blouses of the kind worn by French peasants or workmen, but on one of the walls he saw an excellent engraving of the young Napoleon, conqueror of Italy.

It showed him, horseback, on a high road looking down upon troops in battle, Castiglione or Rivoli, perhaps, his face thin and gaunt, his hair long and cut squarely across his forehead, the eyes deep, burning and unfathomable. It was so thoroughly alive that he believed it must be a reproduction of some great painting. He stood a long time, fascinated by this picture of the young republican general who rose like a meteor over Europe and who changed the world.

John, like nearly all young men, viewed the Napoleonic cycle with a certain awe and wonder. A student, he had considered Napoleon the great democratic champion and mainly in the right as far as Austerlitz. Then swollen ambition had ruined everything and, in his opinion, another swollen ambition, though for far less cause, was now bringing equal disaster upon Europe. A belief in one's infallibility might come from achievement or birth, but only the former could win any respect from thinking men.

It seemed to John presently that the deep, inscrutable eyes were gazing at him, and he felt a quivering at the roots of his hair. It was young Bonaparte, the republican general, and not Napoleon, the emperor, who was looking into his heart.

"Well," said John, in a sort of defiance, "if you had stuck to your early principles we wouldn't have all this now. First Consul you might have been, but you shouldn't have gone any further."

He turned away with a sigh of regret that so great a warrior and statesman, in the end, should have misused his energies.

He returned to the room below, blew out the lamp and opened the window again. The cool fresh air once more poured into the room, and he took long deep breaths of it. It was still raining, though lightly, and the pattering of the drops on the leaves made a pleasant sound. The thunder and the lightning had ceased, though not the far rumble of artillery. John knew that the sport of kings was still going on under the searchlights, and all his intense horror of the murderous monarchies returned. He was not sleepy yet, and he listened a long time. The sound seemed to come from both sides of him, and he felt that the abandoned cottage among the trees was merely a little oasis in the sea of war.

The rain ceased and he concluded to scout about the house to see if any one was near, or if any farm animals besides the horse had been left. But Marne was alone. There was not even a fowl of any kind. He concluded that the horse had probably wandered away before the peasant left, as so valuable an animal would not have been abandoned otherwise.

His scouting—he was learning to be very cautious—took him some distance from the house and he came to a narrow road, but smooth and hard, a road which troops were almost sure to use, while such great movements were going on. He waited behind a hedge a little while, and then he heard the hum of motors.

He had grown familiar with the throbbing, grinding sound made by many military automobiles on the march, but he waited calmly, merely loosening his automatic for the sake of precaution. He felt sure that while he stood behind a hedge he would never be seen on a dark night by men traveling in haste. The automobiles came quickly into view and in those in front he saw elderly men in uniforms of high rank. Nearly all the German generals seemed to him to be old men who for forty or fifty years had studied nothing but how to conquer, men too old and hardened to think much of the rights of others or ever to give way to generous emotions.

He also saw sitting erect in one of the motors the man for whom he had felt at first sight an invincible repulsion. Prince Karl of Auersperg. Young von Arnheim had represented the good prince to him, but here was the medieval type, the believer in divine right, and in his own superiority, decreed even before birth. John noted in the moonlight his air of ownership, his insolent eyes and his heavy, arrogant face. He hoped that the present war would sweep away all such as Auersperg.

He watched nearly an hour while the automobiles, cyclists, a column of infantry, and then several batteries of heavy guns drawn by motors, passed. He judged that the Germans were executing a change of front somewhere, and that the Franco-British forces were still pressing hard. The far thunder of the guns had not ceased for an instant, although it must be nearly midnight. He wished he knew what this movement on the part of the Germans meant, but, even if he had known, he had no way of reaching his own army, and he turned back to the cottage.

Having fastened the door securely again he spread the blankets on the bench by the window and lay down to sleep. The tension was gone from his nerves now, and he felt that he could fall asleep at once, but he did not. A shift in the wind brought the sound of the artillery more plainly. His imagination again came into vivid play. He believed that the bench beneath him, the whole cottage, in fact, was quivering before the waves of the air, set in such violent motion by so many great guns.

It annoyed him intensely. He felt a sort of personal anger against everybody. It was past midnight of the third day and it was time for the killing to stop. At least they might rest until morning, and give his nerves a chance. He moved restlessly on the bench a half hour or more, but at last he sank gradually to sleep. As his eyes closed the thunder of the cannonade was as loud and steady as ever. He slept, but the murderous sport of kings went on.

8

THE PUZZLING SIGNAL

W hen John awoke a bright sun was shining in at the window, bringing with it the distant mutter of cannon, a small fire was burning on the hearth on the opposite side of the room, a man was bending over the coals, and the pleasant odor of boiling coffee came to his nostrils. He sat up in amazement and looked at the man who, not turning around, went on placidly with his work of preparing breakfast. But he recognized the figure.

"Weber!" he exclaimed.

"None other!" said the Alsatian, facing about, and showing a cheery countenance. "I was in the boat just behind you when your own was demolished by the shell. In all the spray and foam and confusion I saw my chance, and dropping overboard from ours I floated with the stream. I had an idea that you might escape, and since you must come down the river between the two armies I also, for the same reasons, chose the same path. I came upon this cottage several hours ago, picked the fastenings of the door and to my astonishment and delight found you, my friend, unharmed, but sound asleep upon the bench there. I slept a while in the corner, then I undertook to make breakfast with provisions and utensils that I found in the forest. Ah, it was easy enough last night to find almost anything one wished. The fields and forest were full of dead men."

"I provided myself in the same way, but I'm delighted to see you. I was never before in my life so lonely. How chance seems to throw us together so often!"

"And we've both profited by it. The coffee is boiling now, Mr. Scott. I've a good German coffee pot and two cups that I took from the fallen. God rest their souls, they'll need them no more, while we do."

"The battle goes on," said John, listening a moment at the window.

"Somewhere on the hundred mile line it has continued without a break of an instant, and it may go on this way for a week or a month. Ah, it's a fearful war, Mr. Scott, and we've seen only the beginning! But drink the coffee now, while it's hot. And I've warmed too, some of the cold food from the knapsacks. German sausage is good at any time."

"And just now it's heavenly. I'm glad we have such a plentiful supply of sausage and bread, even if we did have to take it from the dead. I want to tell you again how pleasant it is to see you here."

"I feel that way too. We're like comrades united. Now if we only had your English friend Carstairs, your American friend Wharton, and Lannes we'd be quite a family group."

"I fancy that we'll see Lannes before we do Carstairs and Wharton."

"I think so too. He'll certainly be hovering today somewhere over the ground between the two armieseither to observe the Germans or more likely to carry messages between the French generals. I tell you, Mr. Scott, that Philip Lannes is perhaps the most wonderful young man in Europe. In addition to his extraordinary ability in the air he has courage, coolness, perception and quickness almost without equal. There's something Napoleonic about him."

"You know he's descended from the family of the famous Marshal, Lannes, not from Lannes himself, but from a close relative, and the blood's the same. They say that blood will tell, and don't you think that the spirit of the great Lannes may have reappeared in Philip?"

"It's altogether likely."

"I've been thinking a lot about Napoleon. There's a wonderful picture of him as a young republican general in a room here. Perhaps it's the conditions around us, but at times I am sure the heroic days of the First Republic have returned to France. The spirit that animated Hoche and Marceau and Kleber and Bonaparte, before he became spoiled, seems to have descended upon the French. And there were Murat, Lannes and Lefebvre, and Berthier and the others. Think of that wonderful crowd of boys leading the republican armies to victories over all the kings! It seems to me the most marvelous thing in the history of war, since the Greeks turned back the Persians."

Weber refilled his coffee cup, drank a portion of it, and said:

"I have thought of it, Mr. Scott, I have thought of it more than once. It may be that the Gallic fury has been aroused. It has seemed so to me since the German armies were turned back from Paris. The French have burned more gunpowder than any other nation in Europe, and they're a fighting race. It would appear now that the Terrible Year, 1870, was merely an aggregation of mistakes, and did not represent either the wisdom or natural genius of the nation."

"That is, the French were then far below normal, as we would say, but have now returned to their best, and that the two Kaisers made the mistake of thinking the French in their lowest form were the French in their usual form?"

"It may be so," said Weber, thoughtfully. "Nations reckon their strength in peace, but only war itself discloses the fact. Evidently tremendous miscalculations have been made by somebody."

"By somebody? By whom? That's why I'm against the Kaisers and all the secret business of the military monarchies. War made over night by a dozen men! a third of the world's population plunged into battle! and the rest drawn into the suffering some way or other! I don't like a lot of your European ways."

Weber shook his head.

"We've inherited kings," he said. "But how did you find this place?"

"Accident. Stumbled on it, and mighty grateful I was, too. It kept me warm and dry after standing so long in the Marne I thought I was bound to turn into a fish. Isolated little place, but the Germans have been passing near. Before sleeping last night, I went out scouting and as I stood behind a hedge I saw a lot of them. I recognized in a motor the Very High Born, his High Mightiness, the owner of the earth, the Prince of Auersperg."

Weber took another drink of coffee.

"An able man and one of our most bitter enemies," he said. "A foe of democracy everywhere. I think he was to have been made governor of Paris, and then Paris would have known that it had a governor. I've seen him in Alsace, and I've heard a lot about him."

"But all that's off now. I fancy that the next governor of Paris, if it should have a governor, will be a Frenchman. But the day is advancing, Weber; what do you think we ought to do?"

"I've been thinking of your friend Lannes. I've an idea that he'll come for you, if he finds an interval in his duties."

"But how could he possibly find me? Why, it's the old needle in the haystack business."

"He couldn't unless we made some sort of signal."

"There's no signal that I can make."

"But there's one that I can. Look, Mr. Scott."

He unbuttoned his long French coat, and took from his breast a roll of red, white and blue. He opened it and disclosed a French flag about four feet long.

"If that were put in a conspicuous place," he said, "an aviator with glasses could see it a long way, and he would come to find out what it meant."

"The top of a tree is the place for it!" exclaimed John. "Now if you only had around here a real tree, or two, in place of what we call saplings in my country, we might do some fine signaling with the flag."

"We'll try it, but I think we should go a considerable distance from the cottage. If Germans instead of French should come then we'd have a better chance of escaping among the hedges and vineyards."

John agreed with him and they quickly made ready, each taking his automatic and knapsack, and leaving the fire to die of itself on the hearth.

"I'm telling that cottage good-bye with regret," said John, as they walked away. "I spent some normal and peaceful hours there last night and it's a neat little place. I hope its owners will be able to come back to it. As soon as I open the stable door, in order that the horse may go where he will, I'll be ready."

He gave the big animal a friendly pat as he left and Marne gazed after him with envious sorrowful eyes.

They walked a full mile, keeping close to the Marne, where the trees and bushes were thickest, and listened meanwhile to the fourth day's swelling roar of the battle. Its long continuance had made it even more depressing and terrifying than in its earlier stages. To John's mind, at least, it took on the form of a cataclysm, of some huge paroxysm of the earth. He ate to it, he slept to it, he woke to it, and now he was walking to it. The illusion was deepened by the fact that no human being save Weber was visible to him. The country between the two monstrous battle lines was silent and deserted.

"Apparently," said Weber, "we're in no danger of human interference as we walk here."

"Not unless a shell coming from a point fifteen miles or so beyond the hills should drop on us, or we should be pierced by an arrow from one of our Frenchmen in the clouds. But so far as I can see there's nothing above us, although I can make out one or two aeroplanes far toward the east."

"The air is heavy and cloudy and that's against them, but they'll be out before long. You'll see. I think, Mr. Scott, that we'll find a good tree in that little grove of beeches there."

"The tall one in the center. Yes, that'll suit us."

They inspected the tree and then made a long circuit about it, finding nobody near. John, full of zeal and enthusiasm, volunteered to climb the tree and fasten the flag to its topmost stem, and Weber, after some claims on his own behalf, agreed. John was a good climber, alert, agile and full of strength, and he went up the trunk like an expert. It was an uncommonly tall tree for France, much more than a sapling, and when he reached the last bough that would support him he found that he could see over all the other trees and some of the low hills. At a little distance ran the Marne, a silver sheet, and he thought he could discern faint puffs of smoke on the hills beyond. No human being was in sight, but although high in the tree he could still feel the vibrations of the air beneath the throb of so many great guns. Several aeroplanes hovered at points far distant, and he knew that others would be on the long battle line.

Reaching as high as he could he tied the flag with a piece of twine that Weber had given himthe Alsation seemed to have provided for everythingand then watched it as it unfolded and fluttered in the light breeze. He felt a certain pride, as he had done his part of the task well. The flag waved above the green leaves and any watcher of the skies could see it.

"How does it show?" he called to Weber.

"Well, indeed. You'd better climb down now. If the Germans come from the air they'll get you there, and if they come on land they'll have you in the tree. You'll be caught between air and earth."

"That being the case I'll come down at once," said John, and he descended the tree rapidly. At Weber's advice they withdrew to a cluster of vines growing near, where they would be well hidden, since their signal was as likely to draw enemies as friends.

"I think Lannes will surely see that flag," said Weber.

"Why do you have such great confidence in his coming?" asked John.

"He inspires confidence, when you see him, and there's his reputation. I've an idea that he'll be carrying dispatches between the two wings of the French army, dispatches of vast importance, since the different French forces have to cooperate now along a line of four or five score miles. Of course the telephone and the telegraph are at work, too, but the value of the aeroplane as a scout and dispatch bearer cannot be over estimated."

"One is coming now," said John, "and I think it has been attracted by our flag. I take it to be German."

"Then we'd better keep very close. Still, there's little chance of our being seen here, and the aviators, even if they suspect a presence, can't afford to descend, leave their planes and search for anybody."

"I agree with you there. One can remain here in comparative safety and watch the results of our signal. That machine is coming fast and I'm quite sure it's German."

"An armored machine with two men and a light rapid fire gun in it. Beyond a doubt it will circle about our tree."

The plane was very near now, and assuredly it was German. John could discern the Teutonic cast of their countenances, as the two men in it leaned over and looked at the flag. They dropped lower and lower and then flew in circles about the tree. John, despite his anxiety and suspense, could not fail to notice the humorous phase of it. The plane certainly could not effect a landing in the boughs, and if it descended to the ground in order that one of their number might get out, climb the tree and capture the flag, they would incur the danger of a sudden swoop from French machines. Besides, the flag would be of no value to them, unless they knew who put it there and why.

"The Germans, of course, see that it's a French flag," he said to Weber. "I wonder what they're going to do."

"I think they'll have to leave it," said Weber, "because I can now see other aeroplanes to the west, aeroplanes which may be French, and they dare not linger too long."

"And our little flag may make a big disturbance in the heavens."

"So it seems."

The German plane made circle after circle around the tree, finally drew off to some distance, and then, as it wavered back and forth, its machine gun began to spit fire. Little boughs and leaves cut from the tree fell to the ground, but the flag, untouched, fluttered defiantly in the light breeze.

"They're trying to shoot it down," said John, "and with such an unsteady gun platform they've missed every time."

"I doubt whether they'll continue firing," said Weber. "An aeroplane doesn't carry any great amount of ammunition and they can't afford to waste much."

"They're through now," said John. "See, they're flying away toward the east, and unless my imagination deceives me, their machine actually looks crestfallen, while our flag is snapping away in the wind, haughty and defiant."

"A vivid fancy yours, Mr. Scott, but it's easy to imagine that German machine looking cheap, because that's just the way the men on board it must feel. Suppose we sit down here and take our ease. No flying man can see through those vines over our heads, and we can watch in safety. We're sure to draw other scouts of the air, while for us it's an interesting and comparatively safe experience."

"Our flag is certainly an attraction," said John, making himself comfortable on the ground. "There's a bird of passage now, coming down from the north as swift as a swallow."

"It's a little monoplane," said Weber, "and it certainly resembles a swallow, as it comes like a flash toward this tree. I thought at first it might be Lannes in the *Arrow,* but the plane is too small, and it's of German make."

"I fancy it won't linger long. This is not a healthy bit of space for lone fellows in monoplanes."

The little plane slackened its speed, as it approached the tree, and then sailed by it at a moderate rate. When it was opposite the flag a spurt of flame came from the pistol of the man in it, and John actually laughed.

"That was sheer spite," he said. "Did he think he could shoot our flag away with a single bullet from a pistol when a machine gun has just failed? That's right, turn about and make off as fast as you can, you poor little mono!"

The monoplane also curved around the tree, but did not make a series of circles. Instead, when its prow was turned northward it darted off again in that direction, going even more swiftly than it had come, as if the aviator were ashamed of himself and wished to get away as soon as possible from the scene of his disgrace. Away and away it flew, dwindling to a black speck and then to nothing.

John's shoulders shook, and Weber, looking at him, was forced to smile too.

"Well, it was funny," he said. "Our flag is certainly making a stir in the heavens."

"I wonder what will come next," said John. "It's like bait drawing birds of prey."

The heavens were now beautifully clear, a vault of blue velvet, against which anything would show. Far away the cannon groaned and thundered, and the waves of air pulsed heavily, but John noticed neither now. His whole attention was centered upon the flag, and what it might call from the air.

"In such a brilliant atmosphere we can certainly see our visitors from afar," he said.

"So we can," said Weber, "and lo! another appears out of the east!"

The dark speck showed on the horizon and grew fast, coming apparently straight in their direction. John did not believe it had seen their flag at first, owing to the great distance, but was either a messenger or a scout. As it soon began to descend from its great height in the air, although still preserving a straight course for the tree, he felt sure that the flag had now come into its view. It grew very fast in size and was outlined with startling clearness against the burning blue of the sky.

The approaching machine consisted of two planes alike in shape and size, superimposed and about six feet apart, the whole with a stabilizing tail about ten feet long and six feet broad. John saw as it approached that the aviator sat before the motor and screw, but that the elevating and steering rudders were placed in front of him. There were three men besides the aviator in the machine.

"A biplane," said John.

"Yes," said Weber, "I recognize the type of the machine. It's originally a French model."

"But in this case, undoubtedly a German imitation. They've seen our flag, because I can make out one of the men with glasses to his eyes. They hover about as if in uncertainty. No wonder they can't make up their minds, because there's the tricolor floating from the top of that tall tree, and not a thing in the world to explain why it's in such a place. A man with a rifle is about to take a shot at it. Bang! There it goes! But I can't see that the bullet has damaged our flag. Look, how it whips about and snaps defiance! Now, all the men except the aviator himself have out glasses and are studying the phenomenon of our signal. They come above the tree, and I think they're going to make a swoop around the grove near the ground. Lie close, Weber! As I found out once before, a thick forest is the best defense against aeroplanes. They can't get through the screen of boughs."

They heard a whirring and drumming, and the biplane not more than fifty feet above the earth made several circles about the little wood. John saw the men in it very clearly. He could even discern the German cast of countenance where all except the one at the wheel that controlled the two rudders had thrown back their hoods and taken off their glasses. The three carried rifles which they held ready for use, in case they detected an enemy.

Whirling around like a vast primeval bird of prey the biplane began to rise, as if disappointed of a victim, and winding upward was soon above the trees. Then John heard the rapid crackle of rifles.

"Shooting at our flag again!" he exclaimed.

But the whizz of a bullet that buried itself in the earth near him told him better.

"It isn't possible that they've seen us!" he exclaimed.

"No," said Weber, "they're merely peppering the woods and vines in the hope that they'll hit a concealed enemy, if such there should be."

"That being the case," said John, "I'm going to make my body as small as possible, and push myself into the ground if I can."

He lay very close, but the rifle fire quickly passed to other portions of the wood, and then died away entirely. John straightened himself out and saw the biplane becoming smaller, as it flew off in the direction whence it had come.

"I hope you'll come to no good," he said, shaking his fist at the disappearing plane. "You've scared me half to death with your shots, and I hope that both your rudders will get out of gear and stay out of gear! I hope that the wheel controlling them will be smashed up! I hope that the top plane will crash into the bottom one! I hope that a French shell will shoot your tail off! And I hope that you'll tumble to the earth and lie there, nothing but a heap of rotting wood and rusty old metal!"

"Well done, Mr. Scott!" said Weber. "That was quite a curse, but I think it will take something more solid to disable the biplane."

"I think so too, but I've relieved my feelings, and after a man has done so he can work a lot better. What are we to look for now, Weber? We don't seem to have success in attracting anything but Germans. If Lannes is coming at all, as you think he will, he'll get a pretty late ticket of admission to our reserved section of the air."

"You must remember that the sky above us is a pretty large place, and at any rate we're a drawing power. We're always pulling something out of the ether."

"And our biggest catch is coming now! Look, Weber, look I If that isn't one of Herr Zeppelin's railroad trains of the air then I'll eat it when it gets here!"

"You're right, Mr. Scott. There the monster comes. It can't be anything but a Zeppelin! They must have one of their big sheds not far east of us."

"We'll hear its rattling soon. Like the others it will surely see our flag and make for it. But if they take a notion to shoot up the wood, as the men on that biplane did, we'd better hunt holes. A Zeppelin can carry a lot of soldiers."

The Zeppelin was not moving fast. It had none of the quick graceful movements of the aeroplanes, but came on slowly like some huge monster of the air, looking about for prey. It turned southeast for a moment or two, then some one on board saw the flag and coming back it lumbered toward the tree.

"Ugly things," said John. "Lannes and I blew up one once, and I wish I had the same chance against that fellow up there. But they're in the same puzzled state that the other fellows were. Men on both platforms are examining the flag through glasses, and the flag doesn't give a rap for them. It's standing out in the wind, now, straight and stiff. It seems to know that old Noah's ark can't make it out."

The huge Zeppelin drew its length along the grove, coming as close to the trees as it dared, then passed above, and after some circling lumbered away to the south.

"Good-bye, old Mr. Curiosity," exclaimed John. "You weren't invited here, and I don't care whether you ever come again. Besides, you're nothing but a big bluff, anyway. There's our flag, still standing straight out in the wind, so you can see every stripe on it, and yet you haven't, despite your visit, the remotest idea why it was put there!"

Weber smiled.

"They've all gone away as ignorant as they were when they came," he said, "but we must be due for a French visitor or two. After so long a run of Germans we should have Frenchmen soon."

"I begin to believe with you that Lannes will arrive some time or other. He flies fast and far and in time he must see our signal."

"I've never doubted it. Meanwhile I think I'll take a little luncheon, and I'd advise you to do the same. We haven't had such a bad time here, saving those random rifle shots from the biplane."

"Not at all. It's like watching a play, and you certainly have a clear field for observation, when you look up at the heavens. The stage is always in full view."

John was feeling uncommonly good. Their concealment while they watched the scouts and messengers from the skies coming to see the meaning of the flag had been easy and restful. Much of his long and painful tension had relaxed. The hum of distant artillery was in his ears as ever, like a moaning of the wind, but he was growing so used to it that he would now have noticed its absence rather than its presence. So he ate his share of bread and sausage with a good appetite, meanwhile keeping a watchful eye upon the heavens which burned in the same brilliant blue.

It was now about noon. The rain the night before had given fresh tints to the green of grass and foliage. The whole earth, indifferent to the puny millions that struggled on its vast bosom, seemed refreshed and revitalized. A modest little bird in brown plumage perched on a bough near them, and, indifferent too, to war, poured forth a brilliant volume of song.

"Happy little fellow," John said. "Nothing to do but eat and sleep and sing."

"Unless he's snapped up by some bigger bird," said Weber, "but having been an hour without callers we're now about to have a new one. And as this comes from the west it's likely to be French."

John felt excitement, and stood up. Yes, there was the machine coming out of the blue haze in the west, soaring beautifully and fast. It was very high, but his eye, trained now, saw that it was descending gradually. He felt an intense hope that it was Lannes, but he soon knew that it was not lie. The approaching machine could not possibly be the *Arrow*.

"It's a Bleriot monoplane," said Weber. "I can tell the type almost as far as I can see it. It's much like a gigantic bird, with powerful parchment wings mounted upon a strong body. The wings as you see now present a concave surface to the earth. They always do that. The flyer sits between the two wings and has in front of him the lever with which he controls the whole affair."

"You seem to know a good deal about flying machines, Weber."

"Oh, yes, I've observed them a lot. I've always been curious about them and I've attended the great flying meets at Rheims, but personally I'm a coward about heights. I study the types of these wonderful machines, but I don't go up in 'em. That's a little fellow coming now and he's seen the flag."

"There's only one man in the plane, but as he's undoubtedly French what do you think we ought to do? He can't carry us away with him in the machine, it's too small. Do you think we should signal him to come to the ground and have a talk?"

"Perhaps we'd better let him pass, Mr. Scott. We have no real information to give. He might suspect that we are Germans and a lot of time would be lost maneuvering. Suppose we remain in hiding, and say nothing until Lannes himself appears."

"You still feel sure that he will come?"

"It's a conviction."

"Same way with me, and I agree with you that we'd better let our friend in the Bleriot go by. He's descending fast now. The plane certainly does look like a bird. Reminds me somewhat of a German Taube, though this machine is much smaller."

"The pilot will take only a look or two at the flag. Then, if we don't hail him, he'll sail swiftly back to the west."

"For good reasons too. The air here is chiefly in the German sphere of influence, and if I were in his place I'd take to my heels too at a single glance."

"That's what he's doing now. He's flying past the flag just as one of the Germans did. He leans over to take a look at it, can't make out what it means, glances back apprehensively toward the German quarter of the heavens, and now he's sliding like a streak through the blue for French air."

"So near and yet so far! A friend in the air just over our heads, and we had to let him go. Well, he couldn't have done us any good."

"No, he couldn't, and he's gone back so fast that he's out of sight already, but another and different inhabitant of the air is coming out of the south. See, the shape off there, Mr. Scott. Wait until it comes nearer, and I think I can tell you what it is. Now it's made out the flag and is steering for it."

"What class of plane is it, Weber? Can you tell that yet?"

"Yes. It's an Esnault-Pelterie, an invention of a young Frenchman. It's a monoplane with flexible, warped wings. It's made of steel tubes, welded together, and it has two wheels, one behind the other for contact with the ground."

"I noticed something queer in its appearance. It's the wheels. I don't call this machine any great beauty, but it seems to cut the air well. I suppose we'd better treat it as we did the Bleriotlet it go as it came, none the worse and none the wiser?"

"I think so. But we have no other choice! That flyer is a suspicious fellow and he isn't taking any chances. He's come fairly close to the flag, and now he's sheering off at an angle."

"I don't blame him. He probably has something more important to do than to unravel the meaning of a flag in a tree top."

"Nor I either. But whatever comes we'll wait for Lannes, always for Lannes. The heavens here, Mr. Scott, are peopled with strange birds, but of all the lot there is one particular bird for which we are looking."

"Right again. My eyes have grown a little weary of watching the skies. For a long stare, blue isn't as soft and easy a sight as green, and I think I'll look at the grass and leaves for a little while."

"Then while you rest I'll keep an outlook and when I'm tired you can relieve me."

"Good enough."

John lay down in the grass and rested his body while he eased his worn eyes. Weber commented now and then on the new birds in the heavens, aeroplanes of all kinds, but they kept their distance.

"The air over us is not held now by either French or Germans," said Weber, "and I imagine that only the more daring make incursions into it. Perhaps, too, they are kept busy elsewhere, because, as my ears distinctly tell me, the battle is increasing in volume."

"I noticed the swelling fire when I lay down here," said John. "It seems a strange thing, but for a while I had forgotten all about the battle."

Presently Weber took his eyes from the heavens, moved about and looked uneasy.

"If I'm not mistaken," he said, "I caught a glimpse of steel down the river. I think it was a lance head glittering in the sun, and Uhlans may be near."

"How far away do you think it was."

"A half-mile or more. I must take a look in that direction. I'm a good scout, Mr. Scott, and I'll see what's up. Watch here will you, until I come back? It may be some time."

"All right, but don't get yourself captured, Weber. I'd be mighty lonesome without you."

"Don't fear for me. Of course, as I told you, I'll be gone for some time, and if I may suggest, Mr. Scott, I wouldn't move from among the vines."

"Catch me doing it! I'll say here in my green bower and as my eyes are back in form I'll watch the heavens."

"Good-bye, then, for a while."

Weber slipped away. His tread was so light that he vanished, as if he had melted into air.

"That man would certainly have made a good scout in our old Indian days," thought John, and with the thought came the conviction that Weber was too clever to let himself be caught. Then he turned his attention back to the heavens.

They were now well on into the afternoon, and the sun was at the zenith. A haze of gold shimmered against the vast blue vault. A wind perfumed with grass and green leaves, brought also the ceaseless roar of the guns, and now and then the bitter taste of burned gunpowder. The faint trembling of the earth, or rather of the air just above it, went on, and John, turning about in his little bower, surveyed the heavens from all quarters.

He saw shapes, faint, dark and floating on every horizon, but none of them came near until a full half-hour had elapsed. Then one shot out of the west, sailed toward the northeast, but curving suddenly, came back in the direction of the tree. As the shape grew larger and more defined John's heart began to throb. He had seen many aeroplanes that day, and most of them had been swift and graceful, but none was as swift and graceful as the one that was now coming.

It was a machine, beautiful in shape, and as lithe and fast as the darting swallow. There could be none other like it in the heavens, and his heart throbbed harder. Intuition, perhaps, was back of knowledge and he never for a moment doubted that it was he for whom they had looked so long.

The aeroplane seemed fairly to shoot out of space. First its outlines became visible, and then the man at the rudder. He came straight toward the tree, dropped low and circled about it, while John rushed from the vines and cried as loud as he could:

"Lannes! Lannes, it's me! John Scott! I've been waiting for you!"

The *Arrow* dropped further, barely touched the earth, and Lannes, leaning over, shouted to John in tones, tense and sharp with command:

"Give the plane a shove with all your might, and jump in. For God's sake don't linger, man! Jump!"

The impulse communicated by Lannes was so powerful that before he knew what he was doing John pushed the *Arrow* violently and sprang into the extra seat, just as it was leaving the earth.

Lannes gave the rudder a strong twist and the aeroplane shot up like a mounting bird. John got back his breath and presence of mind.

"Wait, Philip! Wait!" he cried. "We're leaving behind our friend Weber! He's down there, somewhere by the river!"

Lannes made no reply. The *Arrow* continued its rise, sharp and swift, and John heard a crackling sound below. Little missiles, steel and deadly, shot by them. One passed so close to his face that his breath went again. When he recovered it once more the *Arrow,* its inmates, unharmed, was far above the range of rifles, flying in a circle.

"Look down, John," said Lannes.

9

OLD FRIENDS

John, obeying Lannes' command, glanced down, as one looks over the side of a ship toward the sea, and he saw many horsemen galloping across the field. He recognized at once the Uhlans, and, for all he knew; they might be von Boehlen's own command.

"Hand me your glasses, will you?" he said.

When Lannes passed them to him he looked long and well, but he did not see any sign of a prisoner among the Prussians. He also searched the woods and other fields near by, but they were empty. The whole Prussian force was gathered beneath them. John breathed a deep sigh of relief.

"It's evident that Weber has escaped," he said. "Doubtless this was the very troop of Uhlans of which the Alsatian had caught a glimpse. He is clever and swift and I've no doubt he found a covert."

"I'm sorry we had to leave him," said Lannes, "but there was no other choice. I came to the tree to examine the flag, and being above I saw the Uhlans nearby before you did. Then I heard your shout and dropped down. But as I knew the Uhlans were coming for us I made you jump almost before you knew it, and we got away by a hair. The *Arrow* was struck twice, but the bullets glanced off its polished sides. There are two slight scars, but I can have them removed."

John laughed.

"Philip," he said, "I believe you love the *Arrow* as a fellow loves his best girl."

"Well spoken, Monsieur Jean the Scott, and the *Arrow* never fails me. And so you've been with Weber?"

"It's a long tale. I was in a boat crossing the Marne. It was sunk by one of the French shells, and I escaped. I reached the deserted cottage of a peasant, and Weber, who was wandering around, happened to come there, too. We've been trying to escape today, and we put that flag up in the tree as a sort of signal, while we hid among the vines below, until you should come, as he believed you would. He was right, but he was unlucky enough to be absent when you arrived." "Maybe it couldn't have happened in a better way. The *Arrow* can carry only two, and I don't know what we'd have done with him. He's a clever fellow and he'll make his way back to the army."

"I hope so, in fact I feel so. But, Philip, it's glorious to be with you again, and to be up here, where the bullets can't reach you."

"That is, so long as the German flyers don't come near enough to take shots at us."

"I don't see any in sight, and meanwhile I intend to be comfortable. Good old *Arrow!* The best little rescuer in the world! Lannes, I believe it's a large part of your business to fly about over fields of battle and rescue me."

"You certainly give me plenty of opportunities," laughed Lannes.

"What's been happening? I fancy that a lot of water has flowed under the bridges of the Marne since I left you."

"We continue to gain," replied Lannes, with quiet satisfaction. "We press the German armies back everywhere. Our supreme chief is a silent man, but he has delivered a master stroke. We've emerged from the very gulf of defeat and despair to the heights of victory. We're not only driving the Germans across the Marne, but we're driving them further. Moreover, their armies are cut apart, and one is fighting for its existence, just as the French and English were fighting for theirs in that terrible retreat from Mons and Charleroi."

"It's glorious, but we mustn't be too sanguine, Lannes. The powers that overcome the German and Austro-Hungarian Empires will not forget for a hundred years that they had a war."

"You're not telling me any news, Monsieur Jean the Scott. I've been in Germany often, and like you I've seen what they have and what they are. We're only beginning."

"Where are you going now, Philip?"

"Toward the end of our line. I've some dispatches for the commander of the British force. Your friends, Carstairs and Wharton, are there, and you may see them. But I understand that the Strangers are to remain with the French, so you, Carstairs and Wharton will have to consider yourselves Frenchmen and stay under our banner."

"That's all right. I hope we'll be under the command of General Vaugirard. Do you know anything of him?"

"Not today, but he was alive yesterday. Take the glasses now, John, will you, and be my eyes as you have been before. One needs to watch the heavens all the time."

John took Lannes' powerful glasses, and objects invisible before leaped into view.

"I see two or three rivers, a dozen villages, and troops," he said. "The troops are to the west, and although they are this side of the Marne, I should judge that they are ours."

"Ours undoubtedly," said Lannes, glancing the way John's glasses pointed. "Not less than a hundred thousand of our men have crossed the Marne at that point, and more will soon be coming. It's a part of the great wedge thrust forward by our chief. But keep your eye on the air, John. What do you see there?"

"Nothing that's near. In the east I barely catch seven or eight black dots that I take to be German aeroplanes, but they seem to be content with hovering over their own lines. They don't approach."

"Doubtless they don't, because they're beginning to watch the air over the Marne as a danger zone. That pretty little signal of yours may have scared them."

Lannes laughed. It was evident that he was in a most excellent humor.

"All right, have your fun," said John, showing his own teeth in a smile.

"If our flag didn't frighten away the German army it at least achieved what we wanted, that is, it brought you. The whole episode would be perfect if it were not for the fact that we lost sight of Weber."

"I tell you again not to worry about him. That man has shown uncommon ability to take care of himself."

"All right. I'll let him go for the present. Hello, here we are crossing the Marne again, and without getting our feet wet."

"We're a good half mile above it, but we'll cross it once more soon. I'm following the shortest road to the British army and that takes us over a loop of the river."

"Yes, here we are recrossing, and now we're coming to a region of chequered fields, green and brown and yellow. I always like these varied colors of the French country. It's a beautiful land down there, Philip."

"So it is, but see if it isn't defaced by sixty or seventy thousand sunburnt men in khaki, the khaki often stained with blood. The men, too, should be tired to death, but you can't tell that from this height."

"The British army you mean? Yes, by all that's glorious, I see them, or at least a part of them! I see thousands of men lying down in the fields as if they were dead."

"They're not dead, though. They just drop in their tracks and sleep in any position."

"I saw the Germans doing that, too. I suppose we'll land soon, Philip, won't we? They've sighted us and a plane is coming forward to meet us."

"We'll make for the meadow over there just beyond the little stream. I think I can discern the general's marquee, and I must deliver my message as soon as possible. Wave to that fellow that we're friends."

An English aeroplane was now very near them and John, leaning over, made gestures of amity. Although the aviator's head was almost completely enshrouded in a hood, he discerned a typically British face.

"Kings of the air, with dispatches for your general!" John cried. He knew that the man would not hear him, but he was so exultant that he wanted to say something, to shout to him, or in the slang of his own land, to let off steam.

But while the English aviator could not understand the words the gestures were clear to him, and he waved a hand in friendly fashion. Then, wheeling in a fine circle, he came back by their side as an escort.

The *Arrow*, like a bird, folding its wings, sank gracefully into the meadow, and Lannes, hastily jumping out, asked John to look after the aeroplane. Then he rushed toward a group of officers, among whom he recognized the chief of the army.

John himself disembarked stiffly, and stretched his limbs, while several young Englishmen looked at him curiously. He had learned long since how to deal with Englishmen, that is to take no notice of them until they made their presence known, and then to acquiesce slowly and reluctantly in their existence. So, he took short steps back and forth on the grass, flexing and tensing his muscles, as abstractedly as if he were alone on a desert island.

"I say," said a handsome fair young man at last, "would you mind telling us, old chap, where you come from?"

John continued to stretch his muscles and took several long and deep breaths. After the delay he turned to the fair young man and said:

"Beg pardon, but did you speak to me?"

The Englishman flushed a little and pulled at his yellow mustache. An older man said:

"Don't press His Highness, Lord James. Don't you see that he's an American and therefore privileged?"

"I'm privileged," said John, "because I was with you fellows from Belgium to Paris, and since then I've been away saving you from the Germans."

Lord James laughed. He had a fine face and all embarrassment disappeared from it.

"We want to be friends," he said. "Shake hands."

John shook. He also shook the hand of the older man and several others. Then he explained who he was, and told who had come with him, none less than the famous young French aviator, Philip Lannes.

"Lannes," said Mr. Yellow Mustache, who, John soon learned, was Lord James Ivor. "Why, we've all heard of him. He's come to the chief with messages a half-dozen times since this battle began, and I judge from the way he rushed to him just now that he has another, that can't be delayed."

"I think so, too," said John, "although I don't know anything about it myself. He's a close-mouthed fellow. But do any of you happen to have heard of an Englishman, Carstairs, and an American, Wharton, who belong to a company called the Strangers in the French army, but who must be at present with youthat is, if they're alive?"

John's voice dropped a little, as he added the last words, but Lord James Ivor walked to the brow of a low hill, called to somebody beyond, and then walked back.

"It's a happy chance that I can tell you what you want to know," he said. "Those two men have been serving in my own company, and they're both alive and well. But they were lying on the grass there, dead to the world, that is, sleeping, as if they were two of the original seven sleepers."

Two figures appeared on the brow of the hill, gazed at first in a puzzled manner at John and then, uttering shouts of welcome, rushed toward him. Carstairs seized him by one hand and Wharton by the other.

"Not killed, I see," said Carstairs.

"Nor is he going to be killed," said Wharton.

"Now, where have you been?" asked Carstairs.

"Yes, where have you been?" asked Wharton.

"I've been taking a couple of pleasure trips with my friend, Lannes," replied John. "Between trips I was a prisoner of the Germans, and I've seen a lot of the great battle. Has the British army suffered much?"

A shade flitted over the face of Carstairs as he replied:

"We haven't been shot up so much since Waterloo. It's been appalling. For days and nights we've been fighting and marching. Whenever we stopped even for a moment we fell on the ground and were asleep before we touched it. Half the fellows I knew have been killed. I think as long as I live I'll hear the drumming of those guns in my ears, and, confound 'em, I still hear 'em in reality now. If you turn your attention to it you can hear the confounded business quite plainly! But what I do know, Scott, is that we've been winning! I don't know where I am and I haven't a clear idea of what I've been doing all the time, but as sure as we're in France the victory is ours."

"But won by the French chiefly" John could not keep from saying.

"Quite true. Our own army is not large, but it has done as much per man."

"And the moral support," added John. "The French have felt the presence of a friend, a friend, too, who in six months will be ten times as strong as he is now."

"Where is Lannes?" asked Wharton.

"He's got your job, Wharton," replied John with a smile. "He's Envoy Extraordinary and Bearer of Messages concerning Life and Death between the armies. As soon as he landed he went directly to the British commander, and they're now conferring in a tent. That will never happen to you. You will never be closeted with the leader of a great army."

"I don't know. I may not be able to fly like the Frenchman, but he can't handle the wireless as I can, and he isn't the chain-lightning chauffeur that Carstairs is. Please to remember those facts."

"I do. But here comes Lannes, the man of mystery."

Lannes seemed preoccupied, but he greeted Carstairs and Wharton warmly.

"I'm about to take another flight," he said. "No, thank you so much, but I've time neither to eat nor to drink. I must fly at once, though it's to be a short flight. Take care of my friend, Monsieur Jean the Scott, while I'm gone, won't you? Don't let him wander into German hands again, because I won't have time to go for him once more."

"We won't!" said Carstairs and Wharton with one voice. "Having got him back we're going to keep him."

Lannes smiling sprang into the *Arrow*. The willing young Englishmen gave it a mighty push, and rising into the blue afternoon sky he sailed away toward the south.

"He'll be back all right," said Carstairs. "I've come to the conclusion that nothing can ever catch that fellow. He's a wonder, he is. One of the most difficult jobs I have, Scott, is to give the French all the credit that's due 'em. I've been trained, as all other Englishmen were, to consider 'em pretty poor stuff that we've licked regularly for a thousand years, and here we suddenly find 'em heroes and brothers-in-arms. It's all the fault of the writers. Was it Shakespeare who said: 'Methinks that five Frenchmen on one pair of English legs did walk?'"

"No," said Lord James Ivor, "It was the other way around. 'Methinks that one Englishman on five pairs of French legs did walk.'"

"I'm not so sure about the number, either," interjected Wharton. "Are you positive it was five?"

"Whatever it was," said Carstairs, "the Frenchman was slandered, and by our own great bard, too. But come and take something with us, if Lord James, our immediate chief, is willing."

"He's willing, and he'll go with you," said Lord James Ivor. "I need a bite myself and in war like this a man can't afford to neglect food and drink, when the chance is offered."

"The habits of you Europeans are strong," said John, whose spirits were still exuberant. "If you didn't have to stop now and then to work or to fight you'd eat all the time. One meal would merge into another, making a beautiful, savory chain linked together. I know the English-man's heaven perfectly well. It's made of lakes of ale, beer, porter and Scotch highballs, surrounded by high banks of cheese, mutton and roast beef."

"There could be worse heavens," said Carstairs, "and if it should happen that way it wouldn't be long before you Yankees would be trying to break out of your heaven and into ours. But here's a taste of it now, the cheese, for instance, and the beer, although it's in bottles."

A spry Tommy Atkins served them, and John, thankful at heart, ate and drank with the best of them. And while they ate the pulsing waves of air from the battle beat upon their ears. It seemed to these young men to have been beating that way for weeks.

"Lannes will be back soon," said John to Carstairs and Wharton, "and he'll tear you away from your friends here. You think, Carstairs, that you're an Englishman, and you're convinced, Wharton, that you're an American, but you're both wrong. You're Frenchmen, and you're going back to the French army, where you belong. Then Captain Daniel Colton of the Strangers will want to know from you why you haven't returned sooner."

"But how are we to go?" said Carstairs.

"And where are we to go?" said Wharton.

"I'd go in a minute," added Carstairs, "if the German army would let me."

"So would I," said Wharton, "but the Germans fight so hard that we can't get away."

"Lannes will attend to all those matters," said John. "I'll rest until he comes, if I have the chance. Is that your artillery firing?"

"It's our big guns out in front," said Lord James Ivor. "Jove, but what work they've done! A lot of our guns have been smashed, one half of our gunners maybe have been smashed with 'em, but they've never flinched. They covered our retreat from Belgium, and they've been the heralds of our advance here on the Marne! Listen to 'em! How they talk!"

The heavy crash of guns far in front and the thunder of the German guns replying came back to their ears. It was a louder note in the general and ceaseless murmur of the battle, but the young men paid it only a passing moment of attention. Carstairs presently added as an afterthought:

"Unless Lannes returns soon I don't think we'll hear from him. That blaze of the guns in front of us indicates close fighting again, and we'll probably be ordered forward soon."

"I don't think so," said Lord James Ivor. "Our guns and the German guns will talk together for quite a while before the infantry advance. You can spend a good two hours with us yet, and still have time to depart for the French army."

It was evident that Lord James Ivor knew what he was talking about, since, as far as John could see, the khaki army lay outspread on the turf. These men were too much exhausted and too much dulled to danger to stir merely because the cannon were blazing. It took the sharp orders of their officers to move them. Shells from the German guns began to fall along the fringe of the troops, but thousands slept heavily on.

John, after disposing of the excellent rations offered to him, sat down on the grass with Wharton, Carstairs and Lord James Ivor. The sun was now waning, but the western sky was full of gold, and the yellow rays slanting across the hills and fields made them vivid with light. Lord James handed his glasses to John with the remark:

"Would you like to take a look there toward the east, Scott?"

John with the help of the glasses discerned the English batteries in action. He saw the men working about them, the muzzles pointing upward, and then the flash. Some of the guns were completely hidden in foliage, and he could detect their presence only by the heavy detonations coming from such points. Yet, like many of the English soldiers about him, John's mind did not respond to so much battle. He looked at the flashes, and he listened to the reports without emotion. His senses had become dulled by it, and registered no impressions.

"We've masked our batteries as much as possible," said Lord James. "The Germans are great fellows at hiding their big guns. They use every clump of wood, hay stacks, stray stacks and anything else, behind which you could put a piece of artillery. They trained harder before the war, but we'll soon be able to match 'em."

While Lord James was talking, John turned the glasses to the south and watched the sky. He had observed two black dots, both of which grew fast into the shape of aeroplanes. One, he knew, was the *Arrow*. He had learned to recognize the plane at a vast distance. It was something in the shape or a trick of motion perhaps, almost like that of a human being, with which he had become familiar and which he could not mistake. The other plane, by the side of Lannes' machine, bothered him. It was much larger than the *Arrow*, but they seemed to be on terms of perfect friendship, each the consort of the other.

"Lannes is coming," announced John. "He's four or five miles to the south and he's about a quarter of a mile up, but he has company. Will you have a look, Lord James?"

Lord James Ivor, taking back his own glasses, studied the two approaching planes.

"The small one looks like your friend's plane," he said, "and the other, although much bigger, has only one man in it too. But they fly along like twins. We'll soon know all about them because they're coming straight to us. They're descending now into this field."

The *Arrow* slanted gently to the earth and the larger machine descended near by. Lannes stepped out of one, and an older man, whom John recognized as the aviator Caumartin, alighted from the other.

"My friends," said Lannes, cheerily, "here we are again. You see I've brought with me a friend, Monsieur Caumartin, a brave man, and a great aviator."

He paused to introduce Caumartin to Wharton and the Englishmen, and then went on:

"This flying machine in which our friend Caumartin comes is not so swift and so graceful as the *Arrow* few aeroplanes are but it is strong and it has the capacity. It is what you might call an excursion steamer of the air. It can take several people and our good Caumartin has come in it for Lieutenant Wharton and Lieutenant Carstairs. So! he has an order for them written by the brave Captain Colton of the Strangers. Produce the order, Monsieur Caumartin."

The aviator took a note from a pocket in his jacket and handed it to Lord James Ivor, who announced that it was in truth such an order.

"You're to be delivered to the Strangers F.O.B.," said John.

"What's F.O.B.?" exclaimed Carstairs.

"It's a shipping term of my country," replied John. "It means Free on Board, and you'll arrive among the Strangers without charge."

"But," said Carstairs, looking dubiously at the big, ugly machine, "automobiles are my specialty!"

"And the wireless is mine!" said Wharton in the same doubting tone.

"Oh, it's easy," said John lightly. "Easiest thing in the world. You have nothing to do but sit still and look calm and wise. If you're attacked by a Zeppelin, throw bombsno doubt Caumartin has them on boardbut if a flock of Taubes assail you use your automatics. I congratulate you both on making your first flight under such auspices, with two armies of a million men each, more or less, looking at you, and with the chance to dodge the shells from four or five thousand cannon."

"Your trouble, Scott, is talking too much," said Wharton, "because you went up in the air when you had no other way to go, you think you're a bird."

"So I am at times," laughed John. "A bird without the feathers. Come now, brace up! Remember that the solid earth is always below you, a long way below, perhaps, but it's there, and Friend Caumartin is bound to deliver you soon to your rightful master, Captain Daniel Colton, who will talk to you like an affectionate but stern parent."

"For Heaven's sake, let's start and get away from this wild Yankee," said Carstairs.

"But you won't get away from me," rejoined John. "Lannes and I in the *Arrow* will watch over you all the way, and, if we can, rescue you, should your plane break down."

Caumartin supplied Wharton and Carstairs with suitable coats and caps, and they took their places unflinchingly in the big plane. Their hearts may have been beating hard, but they would not let their hands tremble.

"I suppose the *Omnibus* starts first, Philip, doesn't it?" asked John.

"Yes," replied Lannes, smiling, "and we can overtake it. *Omnibus* is a good name for it. We'll call it that. It looks awkward, John, but it's one of the safest machines built."

Plenty of willing hands gave the *Omnibus* a lift and then did a like service for the *Arrow*. As they rose, aviators and passengers alike waved a farewell to Lord James Ivor, and he and the Englishmen about him waved back. But the thousands lying on the grass slept heavily on, while the cannon on their utmost fringe thundered and crashed and the German cannon crashed and thundered, replying.

The *Arrow* kept close to the *Omnibus*, so close that John could see the white faces of Wharton and Carstairs and their hands clenching the sides. But he remembered his own original experience, and he was not disposed to jest at them now.

"They're air-sickas I was," he said to Lannes. "Call to them to look westward at the troops," said Lannes. "Great portions of the French and English armies are now visible, and such a sight will make them forget their natural apprehensions."

Lannes was right. When they beheld the magnificent panorama spread out for them the color came back into the faces of Carstairs and Wharton, and their clenched fingers relaxed. The spectacle was indeed grand and gorgeous as they looked up at the sky, down at the earth, and at the line where they met. The sun was now low, but mighty terraces of red and gold rose in the west, making it a blaze of varied colors. In the east the terraces were silver and silver gray, and the light there was softer. The green earth beneath was mottled with the red and silver and gold from the skies.

The German army was yet invisible beyond the hills, although the cannon were flashing there, but to the west they saw vast masses of infantry, some stationary, while others moved slowly forward. Looking upon this wonderful sight, Wharton and Carstairs forgot that they were high in the air. Their hearts beat fast, and their eyes became brilliant with enthusiasm. They waved hands at the *Arrow* which flew near like a guiding friend.

"Wonderful, isn't it?" shouted John.

"I never expect to see its like again," Carstairs shouted back, and then, lest he should not be true to his faith, he added:

"But I won't desert the automobile. It's my best friend."

"British obstinacy!" shouted John.

Carstairs shouted back something, but the planes were now too far apart for him to hear. John saw that the *Omnibus*, despite her awkward look, was flying well and he also saw through Lannes' glasses four aeroplanes bearing up from the east. He did not say much until he had examined them well and had concluded that they were Taubes.

"Lannes," he said, "German machines are trespassing on our air, and unless I'm mistaken they're making for us."

"It's likely. Just under the locker there you'll find a rifle, and a belt of cartridges. It's a good weapon, and if the pinch comes you'll have to use it. Are your friends good shots?"

"I think they are, and I know they're as brave as lions."

"Then they'll have a chance to show it. The *Omnibus* carries several rifles and an abundance of ammunition. She might be called a cargo boat, as there's a lot of room on her. I'm going to bear in close, and you tell Caumartin and the others of the danger."

The *Arrow* swerved, came near to the *Omnibus*, and John shouted the warning. Carstairs and Wharton instantly seized rifles and he saw them lay two others loaded at their feet. With the prospect of a battle for life air-sickness disappeared.

"You can rely on them, Philip," said John as the *Arrow* bore away a little, "but I don't like the looks of one of those German machines."

"What's odd about it?"

"It's bigger than the others. Ah, now I see! It carries a machine gun."

"That's bad. It can send a hail of metal at us. It's lucky that aeroplanes are such unstable gun-platforms. When platforms and targets are alike swerving it's hard to hit anything. We're going to rise and dive, and rise and dive and swerve and swerve, John, so be ready. I'll signal to Caumartin to do the same, and maybe the machine gun won't get us."

John was quite sure that the *Arrow* could escape by immediate flight, but he knew that Lannes would never desert the *Omnibus*, and its passengers, and he felt the same way. The subject was not even mentioned by either.

The German machines, approaching rapidly, spread out like a fan, the heavier one with the machine gun in the center. John could see the man at the rapid firer, but he did not yet open with it. The *Arrow* and the *Omnibus* were wavering like feathers in a storm and closer range was needed. John sat with his own rifle across his knee and then looked at Wharton in the *Omnibus* scarcely a hundred yards away. The figure of Wharton was tense and rigid. His rifle was raised and his eyes never left the man at the machine gun.

"I forgot to tell you, Philip," said John, "that Wharton is a great sharp-shooter. It's natural to him, and I don't believe the shifting platform will interfere with his aim."

"Then I hope that he never has done better sharp-shooting than he will do today. Ah, there goes the machine gun!"

There was a rapid rat-a-tat, not so clear and distinct as it would have been at the same distance on ground, and a stream of bullets poured from the machine gun. But they passed between the *Arrow* and the *Omnibus*, and only cut the unoffending air. Meanwhile Wharton was watching. A wrath, cold but consuming, had taken hold of him. The fact that he was high above the earth, perched in a swaying unstable seat was forgotten. He had eyes and thought only for the murderous machine gun and the man who worked it. An instinctive marksman, he and his rifle were now as one, and of all the birds of prey in the air at that moment Wharton was the most dangerous.

The machine gun was silent for a minute. The riflemen in the Taubes on the wings of the attacking force fired a few shots, but all of them went wild. John, tense and silent, sat with his own rifle raised, but half of the time he watched Wharton.

The two forces came a little nearer. Again the machine gun poured forth its stream of bullets. Two glanced off the sides of the *Omnibus*, and then John saw Wharton's rifle leap to his shoulder. The movement and the flash of the weapon were so near together that be seemed to take no aim. Yet his bullet sped true. The man at the machine gun, who was standing in a stooped position, threw up his hands, fell backward and out of the plane. A thrill of horror shot through John, and he shut his eyes a moment to keep from seeing that falling body.

"What has happened?" asked Lannes, who had not looked around.

"Wharton has shot the man at the machine gun clean out of the aeroplane. He must be falling yet."

"Ghastly, but necessary. Has anybody taken the slain man's place?"

"Yes, another has sprung to the gun! But he's gone! Wharton has shot him too! He's fallen on the floor of the car, and he lies quite still."

"Your friend is indeed a sharpshooter. How many men are left in the plane?"

"Only one! No, good God, there's none! Wharton has shot the third man also, and now the machine goes whirling and falling through space!"

"I said that friend of yours must be a sharpshooter," said Lannes, in a tone of awe, "but he must be more! He must be the king of all riflemen. It's evident that the *Omnibus* knows how to defend herself. I'll swing in a little, and you can take a shot or two."

John fired once, without hitting anything but the air, which made no complaint, but the battle was over. Horrified by the fate that had overtaken their comrades and seeing help for their enemy at hand the Taubes withdrew.

The *Arrow* and the *Omnibus* flew on toward the French lines, whence other machines were coming to meet them.

10

THE CONTINUING BATTLE

T he *Arrow* bore in toward the *Omnibus*. Wharton had put his rifle aside and was staring downward as if he would see the wreck that he had made. Lannes called to him loudly:

"You've saved us all!"

Wharton looked rather white, but he shouted back:

"I had no other choice."

The French aeroplanes were around them now, their motors drumming steadily and the aviators shouting congratulations to Lannes and Caumartin, whom they knew well. It was a friendly group, full of pride and exultation, and the *Arrow* and the *Omnibus* had a triumphant escort. Soon they were directly over the French, and then they began their descent. As usual, when they reached the army they made it amid cheers, and the first man who greeted John was short and young but with a face of pride.

"You have come back to us out of the air, Monsieur Scott," he said, "and I salute you."

It was Pierre Louis Bougainville, made a colonel already for extraordinary, almost unprecedented, valor and ability in so young a man. John recognized his rank by his uniform, and he acknowledged it gladly.

"It's true, I have come back, Colonel Bougainville," he said, "and right glad I am to come. I see that your country has had no cause to complain of you in the last week."

"Nor of hundreds of thousands of Frenchmen," said Bougainville. "Your company, the Strangers, is close at hand, and here is your captain now."

Captain Daniel Colton, thin and ascetic, walked forward. John gave him his best salute and said:

"Captain Colton, I beg to report to you for duty."

A light smile passed swiftly over Cotton's face.

"You're a little late, Lieutenant Scott," he said.

"I know it, sir, but I've brought Lieutenant Carstairs and Lieutenant Wharton with me. There have been obstacles which prevented our speedy return. We've done our best."

"I can well believe it. You left on horseback, and you return by air. But I'm most heartily glad to see all three of you again. I feared that you were dead."

"Thank you, sir," said John. "But we don't mean to die."

"Nevertheless," said Captain Colton, gravely, "death has been all about us for days and nights. Many of the Strangers are gone. You will find the living lying in the little valley just beyond us, and you can resume your duties."

Lannes, after a word or two, left them, and Caumartin took the *Omnibus* to another part of the field. Lannes' importance was continually growing in John's eyes, nor was it the effect of imagination. He saw that under the new conditions of warfare the ability of the young Frenchman to carry messages between generals separated widely could not be overrated. He might depart that very night on another flight.

"May I ask, sir," he said to Captain Colton, "to what command or division the Strangers are now attached?"

"To that of General Vaugirard, a very able man."

"I'm glad to hear it, sir. I know him. I was with him before I was taken by the Germans."

"It seems that you're about to have a general reunion," said Carstairs to young Scott, as they walked away.

"I am, and I'm mighty happy over it. I'll admit that I was rather glad to see you, you blooming Britisher."

About one-third of the Strangers were gone forever, and the rest, except the higher officers, were prostrate in the glade. White, worn and motionless they lay in the same stupor that John had seen overtake the German troops. Some were flat upon their backs, with arms outstretched, looking like crosses, others lay on their faces, and others were curled up on their sides. Few were over twenty-five. Nearly all had mothers in America or Great Britain.

While they slept the guns yet grumbled at many points. The sound on the horizon had gone on so long now that it seemed normal to John. He knew that it would continue so throughout the night, and maybe for many more days and nights. Unless it came near and made him a direct personal menace he would pay no attention to it.

It was growing late. Night was spreading once more over the vast battle field, stretching over thirty leagues maybe. The common soldier knew nothing, majors and colonels knew little more, but the silent man whose invisible hand had swept the gigantic German army back from Paris knew much. While the fire of the artillery continued under the searchlights the exhausted infantry sank down. Then the telephones began to talk over a vast stretch of space, dazzling white lights made signals, the sputtering wireless sent messages in the air, and the flying machines shot through the heavens. Commanders talked to one another in many ways now, and they would talk all through the night.

John and his comrades ate supper, while most of the Strangers slept around them. Those who were awake recognized them, shook hands and said a few words. They were a taciturn lot. After supper Carstairs and Wharton dropped upon the grass and were soon sound asleep. Scott was inclined to be wakeful and he walked along the edge of the glade, looking anxiously at the sleeping forms.

He saw the loom of a fire just beyond the ridge and going to the crest to look at it he beheld outlined before it a gigantic figure that he recognized at once. It was General Vaugirard, and John would have been glad to speak to him, but he hesitated to approach a general. While he stood doubting a hand fell upon his shoulder and a glad voice said in his ear:

"And our young American has come back! Ah, my friend, let me shake your hand!"

It was Captain de Rougemont, trim, erect and without a wound. John gladly let him shake. Then in reply to de Rougemont's eager questions he told briefly of all that had happened since they parted.

"The general has asked twice if we had any news of you," said de Rougemont. "He does not forget. A great mind in a vast body."

"Could I speak to him?"

"Of a certainty, my friend; come."

They advanced toward the fire. General Vaugirard was walking up and down, his hands clasped behind his back, and whistling softly. His huge figure looked yet more huge outlined against the flames. He heard the tread of the two young men and looking up recognized John instantly.

"Risen from the dead!" he exclaimed with warmth, clasping the young man's hand in his own gigantic palm. "I had despaired of ever seeing you again! There are so many more gallant lads whom I will certainly never see! Ah, well, such is life! The roll of our brave young dead is long, very long!"

He reclasped his hands behind his back and walking up and down began to whistle again softly. His emotion over the holocaust had passed, and once more he was the general planning for victory. But he stopped presently and said to John:

"The Strangers, to whom you belong, have come under my command. You are one of my children now. I have my eye on all of you. You are brave lads. Go and seek rest with them while you can. You may not have another chance in a month. We have driven the German, but he will turn, and then we may fight weeks, months, no one knows how long. Ah, well, such is life!"

John saluted respectfully, and withdrew to the little open glade in which the Strangers were lying, sleeping a great sleep. Captain Colton himself, wrapped in a blanket, was now a-slumber under a tree, and Wharton and Carstairs near by, stretched on their sides, were deep in slumber too. Fires were burning on the long line, but they were not numerous, and in the distance they seemed mere pin points. At times bars of intense white light, like flashes of lightning, would sweep along the front, showing that the searchlights of either army still provided illumination for the fighting. The note of the artillery came like a distant and smothered groan, but it did not cease, and it would not cease, since the searchlights would show it a way all through the night.

John sat down, looked at the faint flashes on the far horizon and listened to that moaning which grew in volume as one paid close attention to it. Europe or a great part of it had gone mad. He was filled once more with wrath against kings and all their doings as he looked upon the murderous aftermath of feudalism, the most gigantic of all wars, made in a few hours by a few men sitting around a table. Then he laughed at himself. What was he! A mere feather in a cyclone! Certainly he had been blown about like one!

His nervous imagination now passed quickly and throwing himself upon the ground he slept like those around him. All the Strangers were awakened at early dawn by the signal of a trumpet, and when John opened his eyes he found the air still quivering beneath the throb of the guns. As he had foreseen they had never ceased in the darkness, and he could not remember how many days and nights now they had been raining steel upon human beings.

He was refreshed and strengthened by a night of good sleep, but his mind was as sensitive as ever. In the morning no less bitterly than at night he raged against the folly and ambition of the kings. But the others paid no attention to the cannon. They were light of heart and easy of tongue. They chaffed one another in the cool dawn, and cried to the cooks for breakfast, which was soon brought to them, hot and plentiful.

"I suppose it's forward again," said Carstairs between drinks of coffee.

"I fancy you're right," said Wharton. "Since we've been put in the brigade of that giant of a general, Vaugirard, we're always going forward. He seems to have an uncommon love of fighting for a fat man."

"It's an illusion," said John, "that a fat man is more peaceful than a thin one."

"How are you going to prove it?" asked Wharton.

"Look at Napoleon. When he was thin he was a great fighter, and when he became stout he was just as great a fighter as ever. Fat didn't take away his belligerency."

"I hear that the whole German army has been driven across the

Marne," said Carstairs, "and that the force we hoped to cut off has either escaped or is about to escape. If that's so they won't retreat much further. The pride of the Germans is too great, and their army is too powerful for them to yield much more ground to us."

"I think you're right, or about as near right as an Englishman can be, Carstairs," said John. "What must be the feelings of the Emperor and the kings and the princes and the grand dukes and the dukes and the martial professors to know that the German army has been turned back from Paris, just when the City of Light seemed ready to fall into their hands?"

"Pretty bitter, I think," said Carstairs, "but it's not pleasant to have the capital of a country fall into the hands of hostile armies. I don't read of such things with delight. It wouldn't give me any such overwhelming joy for us to march into Berlin. To beat the Germans is enough."

Another trumpet blew and the Strangers rose for battle again with an invisible enemy. All the officers, like the men, were on foot, their horses having been killed in the earlier fighting, and they advanced slowly across the stubble of a wheat field. The morning was still cool, although the sun was bright, and the air was full of vigor. The rumbling of the artillery grew with the day, but the Strangers said little. Battle had ceased to be a novelty. They would fight somewhere and with somebody, but they would wait patiently and without curiosity until the time came.

"I suppose Lannes didn't come back," said Carstairs. "I haven't heard anyone speak of seeing him this morning."

"He may have returned before we awoke," said John. "The *Arrow* flies very fast. Like as not he delivered his message, whatever it was, and was off again with another in a few minutes. He may be sixty or eighty miles from here now."

"Odd fellow that Lannes," said Carstairs. "Do you know anything about his people, Scott?"

"Not much except that he has a mother and sister. I spent a night with them at their house in Paris. I've heard that French family ties are strong, but they seemed to look upon him as the weak would regard a great champion, a knight, in their own phrase, without fear and without reproach."

"That speaks well for him."

John's mind traveled back to that modest house across the Seine. It had done so often during all the days and nights of fighting, and he thought of Julie Lannes in her simple white dress, Julie with the golden hair and the bluest of blue eyes. She had not seemed at all foreign to him. In her simplicity and openness she was like one of the young girls of his own country. French custom might have compelled a difference at other times, but war was a great leveler of manners. She and her mother must have suffered agonies of suspense, when the guns were thundering almost within hearing of Paris, suspense for Philip, suspense for their country, and suspense in a less degree for themselves. Maybe Lannes had gone back once in the *Arrow* to show them that he was safe, and to tell them that, for the time at least, the great German invasion had been rolled back.

"A penny for your dream!" said Carstairs.

"Not for a penny, nor for a pound, nor for anything else," said John. "This dream of mine had something brilliant and beautiful and pure at the very core of it, and I'm not selling."

Carstairs looked curiously at him, and a light smile played across his face. But the smile was sympathetic.

"I'll wager you that with two guesses I can tell the nature of your dream," he said.

John shook his head, and he, too, smiled.

"As we say at home," he said, "you may guess right the very first time, but I won't tell you whether you're right or wrong."

"I take only one guess. That coruscating core of your dream was a girl."

"I told you I wouldn't say whether you were right or wrong."

"Is she blonde or dark?"

"I repeat that I'm answering no questions."

"Does she live in one of your Northern or one of your Southern States?"

John smiled.

"I suppose you haven't heard from her in a long time, as mail from across the water isn't coming with much regularity to this battle field."

John smiled again.

"And now I'll conclude," said Carstairs, speaking very seriously. "If it is a girl, and I know it is, I hope that she'll smile when she thinks of you, as you've been smiling when you think of her. I hope, too, that you'll go through this war without getting killed, although the chances are three or four to one against it, and go back home and win her."

John smiled once more and was silent, but when Carstairs held out his hand he could not keep from shaking it. Then Paris, the modest house beyond the Seine, and the girl within it, floated away like an illusion, driven from thought in an instant by a giant shell that struck within a few hundred yards of them, exploding with a terrible crash and filling the air with deadly bits of flying shell.

There was such a whistling in his ears that John thought at first he had been hit, but when he shook himself a little he found he was unhurt, and his heart resumed its normal beat. Other shells coming out of space began to strike, but none so near, and the Strangers went calmly on. On their right was a Paris regiment made up mostly of short, but thick-chested men, all very dark. Its numbers were only one-third what they had been a week before, and its colonel was Pierre Louis Bougainville, late Apache, late of the Butte Montmartre. All the colonels, majors and captains of this regiment had been killed and he now led it, earning his promotion by the divine right of genius. He, at least, could look into his knapsack and see there the shadow of a marshal's baton, a shadow that might grow more material.

John watched him and he wondered at this transformation of a rat of Montmartre into a man. And yet there had been many such transformations in the French Revolution. What had happened once could always happen again. Napoleon himself had been the son of a poor little lawyer in a distant and half-savage island, not even French in blood, but an Italian and an alien.

Crash! Another shell burst near, and told him to quit thinking of old times and attend to the business before him. The past had nothing more mighty than the present. The speed of the Strangers was increased a little, and the French regiments on either side kept pace with them. More shells fell. They came, shrieking through the air like hideous birds of remote ages. Some passed entirely over the advancing troops, but one fell among the French on John's right, and the column opening out, passed shudderingly around the spot where death had struck.

Two or three of the Strangers were blown away presently. It seemed to John's horrified eyes that one of them entirely vanished in minute fragments. He knew now what annihilation meant.

The heavy French field guns behind them were firing over their heads, but there was still nothing in front, merely the low green hills and not even a flash of flame nor a puff of smoke. The whistling death came out of space.

The French went on, a wide shallow valley opened out before them, and they descended by the easy slope into it. Here the German shells and shrapnel ceased to fall among them, but, as the heavy thunder continued, John knew the guns had merely turned aside their fire for other points on the French line. Carstairs by his side gave an immense sigh of relief.

"I can never get used to the horrible roaring and groaning of those shells," he said. "If I get killed I'd like it to be done without the thing that does it shrieking and gloating over me."

They were well in the valley now, and John noticed that along its right ran a dense wood, fresh and green despite the lateness of the season. But as he looked he heard the shrill snarling of many trumpets, and, for a moment or two, his heart stood still, as a vast body of German cavalry burst from the screen of the wood and rushed down upon them.

It was not often in this war that cavalry had a great chance, but here it had come. The ambush was complete. The German signals, either from the sky or the hills, had told when the French were in the valley, and then the German guns had turned aside their fire for the very good reason that they did not wish to send shells among their own men.

John's feeling was one of horrified surprise. The German cavalry extending across a mile of front seemed countless. Imagination in that terrific moment magnified them into millions. He saw the foaming mouths, the white teeth and the flashing eyes of the horses, and then the tense faces and eyes of their riders. Lances and sabers were held aloft, and the earth thundered with the tread of the mounted legions.

"Good God!" cried Wharton.

"Wheel, men, wheel!" shouted Captain Colton.

As they turned to face the rushing tide of steel, the regiment of Bougainville whirled on their flank and then Bougainville was almost at his side. He saw fire leap from the little man's eye. He saw him shout commands, rapid incisive, and correct and he saw clearly that if this were Napoleon's day that marshal's baton in the knapsack would indeed become a reality.

The Paris regiment, kneeling, was the first to fire, and the next instant flame burst from the rifles of the Strangers. It was not a moment too soon. It seemed to many of the young Americans and Englishmen that they had been ridden down already, but sheet after sheet of bullets fired by men, fighting for their lives, formed a wall of death.

The Uhlans, the hussars and the cuirassiers reeled back in the very moment of triumph. Horses with their riders crashed to the ground, and others, mad with terror, rushed wildly through the French ranks.

John, Carstairs and Wharton snatched up rifles, all three, and began to fire with the men as fast as they could. A vast turmoil, frightful in its fury, followed. The German cavalry reeled back, but it did not retreat. The shrill clamor of many trumpets came again, and once more the horsemen charged. The sheet of death blazed in their faces again, and then the French met them with bayonet.

The Strangers had closed in to meet the shock. John felt rather than saw Carstairs and Wharton on either side of him, and the three of them were firing cartridge after cartridge into the light whitish smoke that hung between them and the charging horsemen. He was devoutly thankful that the Paris regiment was immediately on their right, and that it was led by such a man as Bougainville. General Vaugirard, he knew, was farther to their left, and now he began to hear the rapid firers, pouring a rain of death upon the cavalry.

"We win! we win!" cried Carstairs. "If they couldn't beat us down in the first rush they can't beat us down at all!"

Carstairs was right. The French had broken into no panic, and, when, infantry standing firm, pour forth the incessant and deadly stream of death, that modern arms make possible, no cavalry can live before them. Yet the Germans charged again and again into the hurricane of fire and steel. The tumult of the battle face to face became terrific.

John could no longer hear the words of his comrades. He saw dimly through the whitish smoke in front, but he continued to fire. Once he leaped aside to let a wounded and riderless horse gallop past, and thrice he sprang over the bodies of the dead.

The infantry were advancing now, driving the cavalry before them, and the French were able to bring their lighter field guns into action. John heard the rapid crashes, and he saw the line of cavalry drawing back. He, too, was shouting with triumph, although nobody heard him. But all the Strangers were filled with fiery zeal. Without orders they rushed forward, driving the horsemen yet further. John saw through the whitish mist a fierce face and a powerful arm swinging aloft a saber.

He recognized von Boehlen and von Boehlen recognized him. Shouting, the Prussian urged his horse at him and struck him with the saber. John, under impulse, dropped to his knees, and the heavy blade whistled above him. But something else struck him on the head and he fell senseless to the earth.

11

JULIE LANNES

John Scott came slowly out of the darkness and hovered for a while between dusk and light. It was not an unpleasant world in which he lingered. It seemed full of rest and peace. His mind and body were relaxed, and there was no urgent call for him to march and to fight. The insistent drumming of the great guns which could play upon the nervous system until it was wholly out of tune was gone. The only sound he heard was that of a voice, a fresh young voice, singing a French song in a tone low and soft. He had always liked these little love songs of the kind that were sung in a subdued way. They were pathetic and pure as a rose leaf.

He might have opened his eyes and looked for the singer, but he did not. The twilight region between sleep and consciousness was too pleasant. He had no responsibilities, nothing to do. He had a dim memory that he had belonged to an army, that it was his business to try to kill some one, and to try to keep from getting killed, but all that was gone now. He could lie there, without pain of body or anxiety of mind, and let vague but bright visions pass through his soul.

His eyes still closed, he listened to the voice. It was very low, scarcely more than a murmur, yet it was thrillingly sweet. It might not be a human voice, after all, just the distant note of a bird in the forest, or the murmur of a brave little stream, or a summer wind among green leaves.

He moved a little and became conscious that he was not going back into that winter region of dusk. His soul instead was steadily moving toward the light. The beat of his heart grew normal, and then memory in a full tide rushed upon him. He saw the great cavalry battle with all its red turmoil, the savage swing of von Boehlen's saber and himself drifting out into the darkness.

He opened his eyes, the battle vanished, and he saw himself lying upon a low, wooden platform. His head rested upon a small pillow, a blanket was under him, and another above him. Turning slowly he saw other men wrapped in blankets like himself on the platform in a row that stretched far to right and left. Above was a low roof, but both sides of the structure were open.

He understood it all in a moment. He had come back to a world of battle and wounds, and he was one of the wounded. But he listened for the soft, musical note which he believed now, in his imaginative state, had drawn him from the mid-region between life and death.

The stalwart figure of a woman in a somber dress with a red cross sewed upon it passed between him and the light, but he knew that it was not she who had been singing. He closed his eyes in disappointment, but reopened them. A man wearing a white jacket and radiating an atmosphere of drugs now walked before him. He must be a surgeon. At home, surgeons wore white jackets. Beyond doubt he was one and maybe he was going to stop at John's cot to treat some terrible wound of which he was not yet conscious. He shivered a little, but the man passed on, and his heart beat its relief.

Then a soldier took his place in the bar of light. He was a short, thick man in a ridiculous, long blue coat, and equally ridiculous, baggy, red trousers. An obscure cap was cocked in an obscure manner over his ears, and his face was covered with a beard, black, thick and untrimmed. He carried a rifle over his shoulder and nobody could mistake him for anything but a Frenchman. Then he was not a prisoner again, but was in French hands. That, at least, was a consolation.

It was amusing to lie there and see the people, one by one, pass between him and the light. He could easily imagine that he was an inspection officer and that they walked by under orders from him. Two more women in those somber dresses with the red crosses embroidered upon them, were silhouetted for a moment against the glow and then were gone. Then a man with his arm in a sling and his face very pale walked slowly by. A wounded soldier! There must be many, very many of them!

The musical murmur ceased and he was growing weary. He closed his eyes and then he opened them again because he felt for a moment on his face a fragrant breath, fleeting and very light. He looked up into the eyes of Julie Lannes. They were blue, very blue, but with infinite wistful depths in them, and he noticed that her golden hair had faint touches of the sun in it. It was a crown of glory. He remembered that he had seen something like it in the best pictures of the old masters.

"Mademoiselle Julie!" he said.

"You have come back," she said gently. "We have been anxious about you. Philip has been to see you three times."

He noticed that she, too, wore the somber dress with the red cross, and he began to comprehend.

"A nurse," he said. "Why, you are too young for such work!"

"But I am strong, and the wounded are so many, hundreds of thousands, they say. Is it not a time for the women of France to help as much as they can?"

"I suppose so. I've heard that in our civil war the women passed over the battle fields, seeking the wounded and nursed them afterward. But you didn't come here alone, did you, Mademoiselle Julie?"

"Antoine Picard—you remember him—and his daughter Suzanne, are with me. My mother would have come too, but she is ill. She will come later."

"How long have I been here?"

"Four days."

John thought a little. Many and mighty events had happened in four days before he was wounded and many and mighty events may have occurred since.

"Would you mind telling me where we are, Mademoiselle Julie?" he asked.

"I do not know exactly myself, but we are somewhere near the river,

Aisne. The German army has turned and is fortifying against us. When the wind blows this way you can hear the rumble of the guns. Ah, there it is now, Mr. Scott!"

John distinctly heard that low, sinister menace, coming from the east, and he knew what it was. Why should he not? He had listened to it for days and days. It was easy enough now to tell the thunder of the artillery from real thunder. He was quite sure that it had never ceased while he was unconscious. It had been going on so long now, as steady as the flowing of a river.

"I've been asking you a lot of questions, Mademoiselle Julie, but I want to ask you one more."

"What is it, Mr. Scott?"

"What happened to me?"

"They say that you were knocked down by a horse, and that when you were falling his knee struck your head. There was a concussion but the surgeon says that when you come out of it you will recover very fast."

"Is the man who says it a good surgeon, one upon whom a fellow can rely, one of the very best surgeons that ever worked on a hurt head?"

"Yes, Mr. Scott. But why do you ask such a question? Is it your odd American way?"

"Not at all. Mademoiselle Julie. I merely wanted to satisfy myself. He knows that I'm not likely to be insane or weak-minded or anything of the kind, because I got in the way of that horse's knee?"

"Oh, no, Mr. Scott, there is not the least danger in the world. Your mind will be as sound as your body. Don't trouble yourself."

She laughed and now John knew that it was she whom he had heard singing the chansonette in that low murmuring tone. What was that little song? Well, it did not matter about the words. The music was that of a soft breeze from the south blowing among roses. John's imaginings were growing poetical. Perhaps there were yet some lingering effects from the concussion.

"Here is the surgeon now," said Mademoiselle Julie. "He will take a look at you and he will be glad to find that what he has predicted has come true."

It was the man in the white jacket, and with that wonderful tangle of black whiskers, like a patch cut out of a scrub forest.

"Well, my young Yankee," he said, "I see that you've come around. You've raised an interesting question in my mind. Since a cavalry horse wasn't able to break it, is the American skull thicker than the skulls of other people?"

"A lot of you Europeans don't seem to think we're civilized."

"But when you fight for us we do. Isn't that so, Mademoiselle Lannes?"

"I think it is."

"War is a curious thing. While it drives people apart it also brings them together. We learn in battle, and its aftermath, that we're very much alike. And now, my young Yankee, I'll be here again in two hours to change that bandage for the last time. I'll be through with you then, and in another day you can go forward to meet the German shells."

"I prefer to run against a horse's knee," said John with spirit.

Surgeon Lucien Delorme laughed heartily.

"I'm confirmed in my opinion that you won't need me after another change of bandages," he said. "We've a couple of hundred thousand cases much worse than yours to tend, and Mademoiselle Lannes will look after you today. She has watched over you, I understand, because you're a friend of her brother, the great flying man, Philip Lannes."

"Yes," said John, "that's it, of course."

Julie herself said nothing.

Surgeon Delorme passed through the bar of brilliant light and disappeared, his place being taken by a gigantic figure with grizzled hair, and the stern face of the thoughtful peasant, the same Antoine Picard who had been left as a guardian over the little house beyond the Seine. John closed his eyes, that is nearly, and caught the glance that the big man gave to Julie. It was protecting and fatherly, and he knew that Antoine would answer for her at any time with his life. It was one remnant of feudalism to which he did not object. He opened his eyes wide and said:

"Well, my good Picard, perhaps you thought you were going to look at a dead American, but you are not. Behold me!"

He sat up and doubled up his arm to show his muscle and power. Picard smiled and offered to shake hands in the American fashion. He seemed genuinely glad that John had returned to the real world, and John ascribed it to Picard's knowledge that he was Lannes' friend.

Julie said some words to Picard, and with a little *au revoir* to John, went away. John watched her until she was out of sight. He realized again that young French girls were kept secluded from the world, immured almost. But the world had changed. Since a few men met around a table six or seven weeks before and sent a few dispatches a revolution had come. Old customs, old ideas and old barriers were going fast, and might be going faster. War, the leveler, was prodigiously at work.

These were tremendous things, but he had himself to think about too, and personality can often outweigh the universe. Julie was gone, taking a lot of the light with her, but Picard was still there, and while he was grizzled and stern he was a friend.

John sat up quite straight and Picard did not try to keep him from it.

"Picard," he said, "you see me, don't you?"

"I do, sir, with these two good eyes of mine, as good as those in the head of any young man, and fifty is behind me."

"That's because you're not intellectual, Picard, but we'll return to our lamb chops. I am here, I, a soldier of France, though an American—for which I am grateful—laid four days upon my back by a wound. And was that wound inflicted by a shell, shrapnel, bomb, lance, saber, bullet or any of the other noble weapons of warfare? No, sir, it was done by a horse, and not by a kick, either, he jostled me with his knee when he wasn't looking. Would you call that an honorable wound?"

"All wounds received in the service of one's country or adopted country are honorable, sir."

"You give me comfort, Picard. But spread the story that I was not hit by a horse's knee but by a piece of shell, a very large and wicked piece of shell. I want it to get into the histories that way. The greatest of Frenchmen, though he was an Italian, said that history was a fable agreed upon, and you and I want to make an agreement about myself and a shell."

"I don't understand you at all, sir."

"Well, never mind. Tell me how long Mademoiselle Julie is going to stay here. I'm a great friend of her brother, Lieutenant Philip Lannes. Oh, we're such wonderful friends! And we've been through such terrible dangers together!"

"Then, perhaps it's Lieutenant Lannes and not his sister, Mademoiselle Julie, that you wish to inquire about."

"Don't be ironical, Picard. I was merely digressing, which I admit is wrong, as you're apt to distract the attention of your hearer from the real subject. We'll return to Mademoiselle Julie. Do you think she's going to remain here long?"

"I would tell you if I could, sir, but no one knows. I think it depends upon many circumstances. The young lady is most brave, as becomes one of her blood, and the changes in France are great. All of us who may not fight can serve otherwise."

"Why is it that you're not fighting, Picard?"

The great peasant flung up his arms angrily.

"Because I am beyond the age. Because I am too old, they said. Think of it! I, Antoine Picard, could take two of these little officers and crush them to death at once in my arms! There is not in all this army a man who could walk farther than I can! There is not one who could lift the wheel of a cannon out of the mud more quickly than I can, and they would not take me! What do a few years mean?"

"Nothing in your case, Antoine, but they'll take you, later on. Never fear. Before this war is over every country in it will need all the men it can get, whether old or young."

"I fear that it is so," said the gigantic peasant, a shadow crossing his stern face, "but, sir, one thing is decided. France, the France of the Revolution, the France that belongs to its people, will not fall."

John looked at him with a new interest. Here was a peasant, but a thinking peasant, and there were millions like him in France. They were not really peasants in the old sense of the word, but workingmen with a stake in the country, and the mind and courage to defend it. It might be possible to beat the army of a nation, but not a nation in arms.

"No, Picard," said John, "France will not fall."

"And that being settled, sir," said Picard, with grim humor, "I think you'd better lie down again. You've talked a lot for a man who has been unconscious four days."

"You're right, my good Picard, as I've no doubt you usually are. Was I troublesome, much, when I was out in the dark?"

"But little, sir. I've lifted much heavier men, and that Dr. Delorme is strong himself, not afraid, either, to use the knife. Ah, sir, you should have seen how beautifully he worked right under the fire of the German guns! Psst! if need be he'd have taken a leg off you in five minutes, as neatly as if he had been in a hospital in Paris!"

John felt apprehensively for his legs. Both were there, and in good condition.

"If that man ever comes near me with the intention of cutting off one of my legs I'll shoot him, good fellow and good doctor though he may be," he said. "Help me up a little higher, will you, Picard? I want to see what kind of a place we're in."

Picard built up a little pyramid of saddles and knapsacks behind him and John drew himself up with his back against them. The rows and rows of wounded stretched as far as he could see, and there was a powerful odor of drugs. Around him was a forest, of the kind with which he had become familiar in Europe, that is, of small trees, free from underbrush. He saw some distance away soldiers walking up and down and beyond them the vague outline of an earthwork.

"What place is this, anyway, Picard?" he asked.

"It has no name, sir. It's a hospital. It was built in the forest in a day. More than five thousand wounded lie here. The army itself is further on. You were found and brought in by some young officers of that most singular company composed of Americans and English who are always quarreling among one another, but who unite and fight like demons against anybody else."

"A dollar to a cent it was Wharton and Carstairs who brought me here," said John, smiling to himself.

"What does Monsieur say?"

"Merely commenting on some absent friends of mine. But this isn't a bad place, Picard."

The shed was of immense length and breadth and just beyond it were some small buildings, evidently of hasty construction. John inferred that they were for the nurses and doctors, and he wondered which one sheltered Julie Lannes. The forest seemed to be largely of young pines, and the breeze that blew through it was fresh and wholesome. As he breathed it young Scott felt that he was inhaling new life and strength. But the wind also brought upon its edge that far faint murmur which he knew was the throbbing of the great guns, miles and miles away.

"Perhaps, Monsieur had better lie down again now and sleep awhile," said Picard insinuatingly.

"Sleep! I need sleep! Why, Picard, by your own account I've just awakened from a sleep four days and four nights long."

"But, sir, that was not sleep. It was the stupor of unconsciousness. Now your sleep will be easy and natural."

"Very well," said John, who had really begun to feel a little weary, "I'll go to sleep, since, in a way, you order it, but if Mademoiselle Julie Lannes should happen to pass my cot again, will you kindly wake me up?"

"If possible, sir," said Picard, the faintest smile passing over his iron features, and forced to be content with that reply, John soon slept again. Julie passed by him twice, but Picard did not awaken him, nor try. The first time she was alone. Trained and educated like most young French girls, she had seen little of the world until she was projected into the very heart of it by an immense and appalling war. But its effect upon her had been like that upon John. Old manners and customs crumbled away, an era vanished, and a new one with new ideas came to take its place. She shuddered often at what she had seen in this great hospital in the woods, but she was glad that she had come. French courage was as strong in the hearts of women as in the hearts of men, and the brusque but good Dr. Delorme had said that she learned fast. She had more courage, yes, and more skill, than many nurses older and stronger than she, and there was the stalwart Suzanne, who worked with her.

She was alone the first time and she stopped by John's cot, where he slept so peacefully. He was undeniably handsome, this young American who had come to their house in Paris with Philip. And her brother, that wonderful man of the air, who was almost a demi-god to her, had spoken so well of him, had praised so much his skill, his courage, and his honesty. And he had received his wound fighting so gallantly for France, her country. Her beautiful color deepened a little as she walked away.

John awoke again in the afternoon, and the first sound he heard was that same far rumble of the guns, now apparently a part of nature, but he did not linger in any twilight land between dark and light. All the mists of sleep cleared away at once and he sat up, healthy, strong and hungry. Demanding food from an orderly he received it, and when he had eaten it he asked for Surgeon Delorme.

The surgeon did not come for a half hour and then he demanded brusquely what John wanted.

"None of your drugs," replied happy young Scott, "but my uniform and my arms. I don't know your procedure here, but I want you to certify to the whole world that I'm entirely well and ready to return to the ranks."

Surgeon Delorme critically examined the bandage which he had changed that morning, and then felt of John's head at various points.

"A fine strong skull," he said, smiling, "and quite undamaged. When this war is over I shall go to America and make an exhaustive study of the Yankee skull. Has bone, through the influence of climate or of more plentiful food, acquired a more tenacious quality there than it has here? It is a most interesting and complicated question."

"But it's solution will have to be deferred, my good Monsieur Delorme, and so you'd better quit thumping my head so hard. Give me that certificate, because if you don't I'll get up and go without it. Don't you hear those guns out there, doctor? Why, they're calling to me all the time. They tell me, strong and well, again, to come at once and join my comrades of the Strangers, who are fighting the enemy."

"You shall go in the morning," said Surgeon Delorme, putting his broad hand upon young Scott's head. "The effects of the concussion will have vanished then."

"But I want to get up now and put on my uniform; can't I?"

"I know no reason why you shouldn't. There's a huge fellow named Picard around here who has been watching over you, and who has your uniform. I'll call him."

When John was dressed he walked with Picard into the edge of the forest. His first steps were wavering, and his head swam a little, but in a few minutes the dizziness disappeared and his walk became steady and elastic. He was his old self again, strong in every fiber. He would certainly be with the Strangers the next morning.

Many more of the wounded, thousands of them, were lying or sitting on the short grass in the forest. They were the less seriously hurt, and they were cheerful. Some of them sang.

"They'll be going back to the army fast," said Picard. "Unless they're torn by shrapnel nearly all the wounded get well again and quickly. The bullet with the great power is merciful. It goes through so fast that it does not tear either flesh or bone. If you're healthy, if your blood is good, psst! you're well again in a week."

"Do you know if Lieutenant Lannes is expected here?" asked John.

"I heard from Mademoiselle Julie that he would come at set of sun. He has been on another perilous errand. Ah, his is a strange and terrible life, sir. Up there in the sky, a half mile, maybe a mile, above the earth. All the dangers of the earth and those, too, of the air to fight! Nothing above you and nothing below you. It's a new world in which Monsieur Philip Lannes moves, but I would not go in it with him, not for all the treasures of the Louvre!"

He looked up at the calm and benevolent blue sky and shuddered.

John laughed.

"Some of us feel that way," he said. "Many men as brave as any that ever lived can't bear to look down from a height. But sunset is approaching, my gallant Picard, and Lannes should soon be here."

The rays of the sun fell in showers of red gold where they stood, but a narrow band of gray under the eastern horizon showed that twilight was not far away. The two stood side by side staring up at the heavens, where they felt with absolute certainty the black dot would appear at the appointed time. It was a singular tribute to the courage and character of Lannes that all who knew him had implicit faith in his promises, not alone in his honesty of purpose, but in his ability to carry it out in the face of difficulty and danger. The band of gray in the east broadened, but they still watched with the utmost faith.

"I see something to the eastward," said John, "or is it merely a shadow in the sky?"

"I don't think it's a shadow. It must be one of those terrible machines, and perhaps it's that of our brave Monsieur Philip."

"You're right, Picard, it's no shadow, nor is it a bit of black cloud. It's an aeroplane, flying very fast. The skies over Europe hold many aeroplanes these days, but I know all the tricks of the *Arrow*, all its pretty little ways, its manner of curving, looping and dropping, and I should say that the *Arrow*, Philip Lannes aboard, is coming."

"I pray, sir, that you are right. I always hold my breath until he is on the ground again."

"Then you'll have to make a record in holding breath, my brave Picard. He is still far, very far, from us, and it will be a good ten minutes before he arrives."

But John knew beyond a doubt, after a little more watching, that it was really the *Arrow*, and with eager eyes he watched the gallant little machine as it descended in many a graceful loop and spiral to the earth. They hurried forward to meet it, and Lannes, bright-eyed and trim, sprang out, greeting John with a welcome cry.

"Up again," he exclaimed, "and, as I see with these two eyes of mine, as well as ever! And you too, my brave Picard, here to meet me!"

He hastened away with a report, but came back to them in a few minutes.

"Now," he said, "We'll go and see my sister."

John was not at all unwilling.

They found her in one of the new houses of pine boards, and the faithful and stalwart Suzanne was with her. It was the plainest of plain places, inhabited by at least twenty other Red Cross nurses, and John stood on one side until the first greeting of brother and sister was over. Then Lannes, by a word and a gesture, included him in what was practically a family group, although he was conscious that the stalwart Suzanne was watching him with a wary eye.

"Julie and Suzanne," said Lannes, "are going tomorrow with other nurses to the little town of Ménouville, where also many wounded lie. They are less well supplied with doctors and nurses than we are here. Dr. Delorme goes also with a small detachment as escort. I have asked that you, Monsieur Jean the Scott, be sent with them. Our brave Picard goes too. Ménouville is about eight miles from here, and it's not much out of the way to the front. So you will not be kept long from your Strangers, John."

"I go willingly," said John, "and I'm glad, Philip, that you've seen fit to consider me worth while as a part of the escort."

He spoke quietly, but his glance wandered to Julie Lannes. It may have been a chance, but hers turned toward him at the same time, and the eyes, the blue and the gray, met. Again the girl's brilliant color deepened a little, and she looked quickly away. Only the watchful and grim Suzanne saw.

"Do you have to go away at once, Philip?" asked Julie.

"In one hour, my sister. There is not much rest for the *Arrow* and me these days, but they are such days as happen perhaps only once in a thousand years, and one must do his best to be worthy. I'm not preaching, little sister, don't think that, but I must answer to every call."

The twilight had spread from east to west. The heavy shadows in the east promised a dark night, but out of the shadows, as always, came that sullen mutter of the ruthless guns. Julie shivered a little, and glanced at the dim sky.

"Must you go up there in the cold dark?" she said. "It's like leaving the world. It's dangerous enough in the day, but you have a bright sky then. In the night it's terrible!"

"Don't you fear for me, little sister," said Lannes. "Why, I like the night for some reasons. You can slip by your enemies in the dark, and if you're flying low the cannon don't have half the chance at you. Besides, I've the air over these regions all mapped and graded now. I know all the roads and paths, the meeting places of the clouds, points suitable for ambush, aerial fields, meadows and forests. Oh, it's home up there! Don't you worry, and do you write, too, to Madame, my mother, in Paris, that I'm perfectly safe."

Lannes kissed her and went away abruptly. John was sure that an attempt to hide emotion caused his brusque departure.

"Believe everything he tells you, Mademoiselle Julie," he said. "I've come to the conclusion that nothing can ever trap your brother. Besides courage and skill he has luck. The stars always shine for him."

"They're not shining tonight," said Picard, looking up at the dusky sky.

"But I believe, Mr. Scott, that you are right," said Julie.

"He'll certainly come to us at Ménouville tomorrow night," said John, speaking in Englishall the conversation hitherto had been in French, "and I think we'll have a pleasant ride through the forest in the morning, Miss Lannes. You'll let me call you Miss Lannes, once or twice, in my language, won't you? I like to hear the sound of it."

"I've no objection, Mr. Scott," she replied also in English. She did not blush, but looked directly at him with bright eyes. John was conscious of something cool and strong. She was very young, she was French, and she had lived a sheltered life, but he realized once more that human beings are the same everywhere and that war, the leveler, had broken down all barriers.

"I've not heard who is to be our commander, Miss Lannes," he continued in English, "but I'll be here early in the morning. May I wish you happy dreams and a pleasant awakening, as they say at home?"

"But you have two homes now, France and America."

"That's so, and I'm beginning to love one as much as the other. Any way, to the re-seeing, Miss Lannes, which I believe is equivalent to *au revoir*."

He made a very fine bow, one that would have done credit to a trained old courtier, and withdrew. The fierce and watchful eyes of Suzanne followed him.

John was up at dawn, as strong and well as he had ever been in his life. As he was putting on his uniform an orderly arrived with a note from Lieutenant Hector Legaré, telling him to report at once for duty with a party that was going to Ménouville.

The start was made quickly. John found that the women with surgical supplies were traveling in carts. The soldiers, about twenty in number, walked. John and the doctor walked with them. All the automobiles were in use carrying troops to the front, but the carts were strong and comfortable and John did not mind. It ought to be a pleasant trip.

12

THE MIDDLE AGES

The little party moved away without attracting notice. In a time of such prodigious movement the going or coming of a few individuals was a matter of no concern. The hood that Julie Lannes had drawn over her hair and face, and her plain brown dress might have been those of a nun. She too passed before unseeing eyes.

Lieutenant Legaré was a neutral person, arousing no interest in John who walked by the side of the gigantic Picard, the stalwart Suzanne being in one of the carts beside Julie. The faint throbbing of the guns, now a distinct part of nature, came to them from a line many miles away, but John took no notice of it. He had returned to the world among pleasant people, and this was one of the finest mornings in early autumn that he had ever seen.

The country was much more heavily forested than usual. At points, the woods turned into what John would almost have called a real forest. Then they could not see very far ahead or to either side, but the road was good and the carts moved forward, though not at a pace too great for the walkers.

Picard carried a rifle over his shoulders, and John had secured an automatic. All the soldiers were well armed. John felt a singular lightness of heart, and, despite the forbidding glare of Suzanne, who was in the last cart, he spoke to Julie.

"It's too fine a morning for battle," he said in English. "Let's pretend that we're a company of troubadours, minnesingers, jongleurs, acrobats and what not, going from one great castle to another."

"I suppose Antoine there is the chief acrobat?"

"He might do a flip-flap, but if he did the earth would shake."

"Then you are the chief troubadour. Where is your harp or viol, Sir Knight of the Tuneful Road?"

"I'm merely imagining character, not action. I haven't a harp or a viol, and if I had them I couldn't play on either."

"Do you think it right to talk In English to the strange young American, Mademoiselle? Would Madame your mother approve?" said Suzanne in a fierce whisper.

"It is sometimes necessary in war, Suzanne, to talk where one would not do so in peace," replied Julie gravely, and then she said to John again in English:

"We cannot carry out the pretense, Mr. Scott. The tuneful or merry folk of the Middle Ages did not travel with arms. They had no enemies, and they were welcome everywhere. Nor did they travel as we do to the accompaniment of war. The sound of the guns grows louder."

"So it does," said John, bending an earhe had forgotten that a battle was raging somewhere, "but we're behind the French lines and it cannot touch us."

"It was a wonderful victory. Our soldiers are the bravest in the world are they not, Mr. Scott?"

John smiled. They were still talking English. He liked to hear her piquant pronunciation of it, and he surmised too that the bravest of hearts beat in the bosom of this young girl whom war had suddenly made a woman. How could the sister of such a man as Lannes be otherwise than brave? The sober brown dress, and the hood equally sober, failed to hide her youthful beauty. The strands of hair escaping from the hood showed pure gold in the sunshine, and in the same sunshine the blue of her eyes seemed deeper than ever.

John was often impressed by the weakness of generalities, and one of them was the fact that so many of the French were so fair, and so many of the English so dark. He did not remember the origin of the Lannes family, but he was sure that through her mother's line, at least, she must be largely of Norman blood.

"What are you thinking of so gravely, Mr. Scott?" she asked, still in English, to the deep dissatisfaction of Suzanne, who never relaxed her grim glare.

"I don't know. Perhaps it was the contrast of our peaceful journey to what is going on twelve or fifteen miles away."

"It is beautiful here!" she said.

Truly it was. The road, smooth and white, ran along the slopes of hills, crested with open forest, yet fresh and green. Below them were fields of chequered brown and green. Four or five clear brooks flowed down the slopes, and the sheen of a little river showed in the distance. Three small villages were in sight, and, clean white smoke rising from their chimneys, blended harmoniously into the blue of the skies. It reminded John of pictures by the great French landscape painters. It was all so beautiful and peaceful, nor was the impression marred by the distant mutter of the guns which he had forgotten again.

Julie and Suzanne, her menacing shadow, dismounted from the wagon presently and walked with John and Picard. Lieutenant Legaré was stirred enough from his customary phlegm to offer some gallant words, but war, the great leveler, had not quite leveled all barriers, so far as he was concerned, and, after her polite reply, he returned to his martial duties. John had become the friend of the Lannes family through his association with Philip in dangerous service, and his position was recognized.

The road ascended and the forest became deeper. No houses were now in sight. As the morning advanced it had grown warmer under a brilliant sun, but it was pleasant here in the shade. Julie still walked, showing no sign of a wish for the cart again. John noticed that she was very strong, or at least very enduring. Suddenly he felt a great obligation to take care of her for the sake of Lannes. The sister of his comrade-in-arms was a precious trust in his hands, and he must not fail.

The wind shifted and blew toward the east, no longer bringing the sound of guns. Instead they heard a bird now and then, chattering or singing in a tree. The illusion of the Middle Ages returned to John. They were a peaceful troupe, going upon a peaceful errand.

"Don't tell me there isn't a castle at Ménouville," he said. "I know there is, although I've never been there, and I never heard of the place before. When we arrive the drawbridge will be down and the portcullis up. All the men-at-arms will have burnished their armor brightly and will wait respectfully in parallel rows to welcome us as we pass between. His Grace, the Duke of Light Heart, in a suit of red velvet will be standing on the steps, and Her Graciousness, the Duchess, in a red brocade dress, with her hair powdered and very high on her head, will be by his side to greet our merry troupe. Behind them will be all the ducal children, and the knights and squires and pages, and ladies. I think they will all be very glad to see us, because in these Middle Ages of ours, life, even in a great ducal castle, is somewhat lonely. Visitors are too rare, and there is not the variety of interest that even the poor will have in a later time."

"You make believe well, Mr. Scott," she said.

"There is inspiration," he said, glancing at her. "We are here in the deeps of an ancient wood, and perhaps the stories and legends of these old lands move the Americans more than they do the people who live here. We're the children of Europe and when we look back to the land of our fathers we often see it through a kind of glorified mist."

"The wind is shifting again," she said. "I hear the cannon once more."

"So do I, and I hear something else too! Was that the sound of hoofs?"

John turned in sudden alarm to Legaré, who heard also and stiffened at once to attention. They were not alone on the road. The rapid beat of hoofs came, and around a corner galloped a mass of Uhlans, helmets and lances glittering. Picard with a shout of warning fired his rifle into the thick of them. Legaré snatched out his revolver and fired also.

But they had no chance. The little detachment was ridden down in an instant. Legaré and half of the men died gallantly. The rest were taken. Picard had been brought to his knees by a tremendous blow from the butt of a lance, and John, who had instinctively sprung before Julie, was overpowered. Suzanne, who endeavored to reach a weapon, fought like a tigress, but two Uhlans finally subdued her.

It was so swift and sudden that it scarcely seemed real to John, but there were the dead bodies lying ghastly in the road, and there stood

Julie, as pale as death, but not trembling. The leader of the Uhlans pushed his helmet back a little from his forehead, and looked down at John, who had been disarmed but who stood erect and defiant.

"It is odd, Mr. Scott," said Captain von Boehlen, "how often the fortunes of this war have caused us to meet."

"It is, and sometimes fortune favors one, sometimes the other. You're in favor now."

Von Boehlen looked steadily at his prisoner. John thought that the strength and heaviness of the jaw were even more pronounced than when he had first seen the Prussian in Dresden. The face was tanned deeply, and face and figure alike seemed the embodiment of strength. One might dislike him, but one could not despise him. John even found it in his heart to respect him, as he returned the steady gaze of the blue eyes with a look equally as firm.

"I hope," said John, "that you will send back Mademoiselle Lannes and the nurses with her to her people. I take it that you're not making war upon women."

Von Boehlen gave Julie a quick glance of curiosity and admiration. But the eyes flashed for only a moment and then were expressionless.

"I know of one Lannes," he said, "Philip Lannes, the aviator, a name that fame has brought to us Germans."

"I am his sister," said Julie.

"I can wish, Mademoiselle Lannes," said von Boehlen, politely in French, "that we had captured your brother instead of his sister."

"But as I said, you will send them back to their own people? You don't make war upon women?" repeated John.

"No, we do not make war upon women. We are making war upon Frenchmen, and I do not hesitate to say in the presence of Mademoiselle Lannes that this war is made upon very brave Frenchmen. Yet we cannot send the ladies back. The presence of our cavalry here within the French lines must not be known to our enemies. Moreover, I obey the orders of another, and I am compelled to hold them as prisonersfor a while at least."

Von Boehlen's tone was not lacking in the least in courtesy. It was more than respectful when he spoke directly to Julie Lannes, and John's feeling of repugnance to him underwent a further abatement he was a creation of his conditions, and he believed in his teachings.

"You will at least keep us all as prisoners together?" said John.

"I know of no reason to the contrary," replied von Boehlen briefly. Then he acted with the decision that characterized all the German officers whom John had seen. The women and the prisoners were put in the carts. Dismounted Uhlans took the place of the drivers and the little procession with an escort of about fifty cavalry turned from the road into the woods, von Boehlen and the rest, about five hundred in number, rode on down the road.

John was in the last cart with Julie, Suzanne and Picard, and his soul was full of bitter chagrin. He had just been taking mental resolutions to protect, no matter what came, Philip Lannes' sister, and, within a half hour, both she and he were prisoners. But when he saw the face of Antoine Picard he knew that one, at least, in the cart was suffering as much as he. The gigantic peasant was the only one whose arms were bound, and perhaps it was as well. His face expressed the most ferocious anger and hate, and now and then he pulled hard upon his bonds. John could see that they were cutting into the flesh. He remembered also that Picard was not in uniform. He was in German eyes only a *franc tireur*, subject to instant execution, and he wondered why von Boehlen had delayed.

"Save your strength, Antoine," he whispered soothingly. "We'll need it later. I've been a prisoner before and I escaped. What's been done once can be done again. In such a huge and confused war as this there's always a good chance."

"Ah, you're right, Monsieur," said Antoine, and he ceased to struggle.

Julie had heard the whisper, and she looked at John confidently. She was the youngest of all the women in the carts, but she was the coolest.

"They cannot do anything with us but hold us a few days," she said.

John was silent, turning away his somber face. He did not like this carrying away of the women as captives, and to him the women were embodied in Julie. They were following a little path through the woods, the German drivers and German guards seeming to know well the way. John, calculating the course by the sun, was sure that they were now going directly toward the German army and that they would pass unobserved beyond the French outposts. The path was leading into a narrow gorge and the banks and trees would hide them from all observation. He was confirmed in his opinion by the action of their guards. The leader rode beside the carts and said in very good French that any one making the least outcry would be shot instantly. No exception would be made in the case of a woman.

John knew that the threat would be kept. Julie Lannes paled a little, and the faithful Suzanne by her side was darkly menacing, but they showed no other emotion.

"Don't risk anything," said John in the lowest of whispers. "It would be useless."

Julie nodded. The carts moved on down the gorge, their wheels and the hoofs of the horses making but little noise on the soft turf. The crash of the guns was now distinctly louder and far ahead they saw wisps of smoke floating above the trees. John was sure that the German batteries were there, but he was equally sure that even had he glasses he could not have seen them. They would certainly be masked in some adroit fashion.

The roaring also grew on their right and left. That must be the French cannon, and soon they would be beyond the French lines. His bitterness increased. Nothing could be more galling than to be carried in this manner through one's own forces and into the camp of the enemy. And there was Julie, sitting quiet and pale, apparently without fear.

He reckoned that they rode at least three miles in the gorge. Then they came into a shallow stream about twenty feet wide that would have been called a creek at home. Its banks were fairly high, lined on one side by a hedge and on the other by willows. Instead of following the path any further the Germans turned into the bed of the stream and drove down it two or three miles. The roar of the artillery from both armies was now very great, and the earth shook. Once John caught the shadow of a huge shell passing high over their heads.

All the prisoners knew that they were well beyond hope of rescue for the present. The French line was far behind them and they were within the German zone. It was better to be resigned, until they saw cause for hope.

When they came to a low point in the eastern bank of the stream the carts turned out, reached a narrow road between lines of poplars and continued their journey eastward. In the fields on either side John saw detachments of German infantry, skirmishers probably, as they had not yet reached the line of cannon.

"Officer," said John to the German leader, "couldn't you unbind the arms of my friend in the cart here? Ropes around one's wrists for a long time are painful, and since we're within your lines he has no chance of escape now."

The officer looked at Picard and shrugged his shoulders.

"Giants are strong," he said.

"But a little bullet can lay low the greatest of them."

"That is so."

He leaned from his horse, inserted the point of his sword between Picard's wrists and deftly cut the rope without breaking the skin. Picard clenched and unclenched his hands and drew several mighty breaths of relief. But he was a peasant of fine manners and he did not forget them. Turning to the officer, he said:

"I did not think I'd ever thank a German for anything, but I owe you gratitude. It's unnatural and painful to remain trussed up like a fowl going to market."

The officer gave Picard a glance of pity and rode to the head of the column, which turned off at a sharp angle toward the north. The great roar and crash now came from the south and John inferred that they would soon pass beyond the zone of fire. But for a long time the thunder of the battle was undiminished.

"Do you know this country at all?" John asked Picard.

The giant shook his head.

"I was never here before, sir," he said, "and I never thought I should come into any part of France in this fashion. Ah, Mademoiselle Julie, how can I ever tell the tale of this to your mother?"

"No harm will come to me, Antoine," said Julie. "I shall be back in Paris before long. Suzanne and you are with meand Mr. Scott."

Suzanne again frowned darkly, but John gave Julie a grateful glance. Wisdom, however, told him to say nothing. The officer in command came back to the cart and said, pointing ahead:

"Behold your destination! The large house on the hill. It is the head-quarters of a person of importance, and you will find quarters there also.

I trust that the ladies will hold no ill will against me. I've done only what my orders have compelled me to do."

"We do not, sir," said Julie.

The officer bowed low and rode back to the head of the column. He was a gallant man and John liked him. But his attention was directed now to the house, an old French château standing among oaks. The German flag flew over it and sentinels rode back and forth on the lawn. John remembered the officer's words that a "person of importance" was making his headquarters there. It must be one of the five German army commanders, at least.

He looked long at the château. It was much such a place as that in which Carstairs, Wharton and he had once found refuge, and from the roof of which Wharton had worked the wireless with so much effect. But houses of this type were numerous throughout Western Europe.

It was only two stories in height, large, with long low windows, and the lawn was more like a park in size. It as now the scene of abundant life, although, as John knew instinctively, not the life of those to whom it belonged. A number of young officers sat on the grass reading, and at the edge of the grounds stood a group of horses with their riders lying on the ground near them. Not far away were a score of high powered automobiles, several of which were armored. John also saw beyond them a battery of eight field guns, idle now and with their gunners asleep beside them. He had no doubt that other troops in thousands were not far away and that, in truth, they were in the very thick of the German army.

The château and its grounds were enclosed by a high iron fence and the little procession of carts stopped at the great central gate. A group of officers who had been sitting on the grass, reading a newspaper, came forward to meet them and John, to his amazement and delight, recognized the young prince, von Arnheim. It was impossible for him to regard von Arnheim as other than a friend, and springing impulsively from the cart he said:

"I had to leave you for a while. It had become irksome to be a prisoner, but you see I've come back."

Von Arnheim stared, then recognition came.

"Ah, it's Scott, the American! I speak truth when I say that I'm sorry to see you here."

"I'm sorry to come," said John, "but I'd rather be your prisoner than anybody else's, and I wish to ask your courtesy and kindness for the young lady, sitting in the rear of the cart, Mademoiselle Julie Lannes, the sister of that great French aviator of whom everybody has heard."

"I'll do what I can, but you're mistaken in assuming that I'm in command here. There's a higher personagebut pardon me, I must speak to the lieutenant."

The officer in charge was saluting, obviously anxious to make his report and have done with an unpleasant duty. Von Arnheim gave him rapid directions in German and then asked Julie and the two Picards to dismount from the cart, while the others were carried through the gate and down a drive toward some distant out-buildings.

John saw von Arnheim's eyes gleam a little, when he noticed the beauty of young Julie, but the Prussian was a man of heart and manner. He lifted his helmet, and bowed with the greatest courtesy, saying:

"It's an unhappy chance for you, but not for us, that has made you our prisoner, Mademoiselle Lannes. In this château you must consider yourself a guest, and not a captive. It would not become us to treat otherwise the sister of one so famous as your brother."

John noticed that he paid her no direct compliment. It was indirect, coming through her brother, and he liked von Arnheim better than ever, because the young captive was, in truth, very beautiful. The brown dress and the sober hood could not hide it as she stood there, the warm red light from the setting sun glancing across her rosy face and the tendrils of golden hair that fell from beneath the hood. She was beautiful beyond compare, John repeated to himself, but scarcely more than a child, and she had come into strange places. The stalwart Suzanne also took note, and she moved a little nearer, while her grim look deepened.

"We will give you the best hospitality the house affords," continued von Arnheim. "It's scarcely equipped for ladies, although the former owners left"

He paused and reddened. John knew his embarrassment was due to the fact that the house to which he was inviting Julie belonged to one of her own countrymen. But she did not seem to notice it. The manner and appearance of von Arnheim inspired confidence.

"We'll be put with the other prisoners, of course," said John tentatively.

"I don't know," replied von Arnheim. "That rests with my superior, whom you shall soon see."

They were walking along the gravel toward a heavy bronze door, that told little of what the house contained. Officers and soldiers saluted the young prince as he passed. John saw discipline and attention everywhere. The German note was discipline and obedience, obedience and discipline. A nation, with wonderful powers of thinking, it was a nation that ceased to think when the call of the drill sergeant came. Discipline and obedience had made it terrible and unparalleled in war, to a certain point, but beyond that point the nations that did think in spite of their sergeants, could summon up reserves of strength and courage which the powers of the trained militarists could not create. At least John thought so.

The long windows of the house threw back the last rays of the setting sun, and it was twilight when von Arnheim and his four captives entered the château. A large man, middle-aged, heavy and bearded, wearing the uniform of a German general rose, and a staff of several officers rose with him. It was Auersperg, the medieval prince, and John's heart was troubled.

Von Arnheim saluted, bowing deeply. He stood not only in the presence of his general, but of royalty also. It was something in the German blood, even in one so brave and of such high rank as von Arnheim himself, that compelled humility, and John, like the fierce democrat he was, did not like it at all. The belief was too firmly imbedded in his mind ever to be removed that men like Auersperg and the mad power for which they stood had set the torch to Europe.

"Captain von Boehlen took some prisoners, Your Highness," said von Arnheim, "and as he was compelled to continue on his expedition he has sent them here under the escort of Lieutenant Puttkamer. The young lady is Mademoiselle Julie Lannes, the sister of the aviator, of whom we all know, the woman and the peasant are her servants, and the young man, whom we have seen before, is an American, John Scott in the French service."

He spoke in French, with intention, John thought, and the heavy-lidded eyes of Auersperg dwelt an instant on the fresh and beautiful face of Julie. And that momentary glance was wholly medieval. John saw it and understood it. A rage against Auersperg that would never die flamed up in his heart. He already hated everything for which the man stood. Auersperg's glance passed on, and slowly measured the gigantic figure of Picard. Then he smiled in a slow and ugly fashion.

"Ah, a peasant in civilian's dress, captured fighting our brave armies! Our orders are very strict upon that point. Von Arnheim, take this *franc tireur* behind the château and have him shot at once."

He too had spoken in French, and doubtless with intention also. John felt a thrill of horror, but Julie Lannes, turning white, sprang before Picard:

"No! No!" she cried to Auersperg. "You cannot do such a thing! He is not a soldier! They would not take him because he is too old! He is my mother's servant! It would be barbarous to have him shot!"

Auersperg looked again at Julie, and smiled, but it was the slow, cold smile of a master.

"You beg very prettily, Mademoiselle," he said.

She flushed, but stood firm.

"It would be murder," she said. "You cannot do it!"

"You know little of war. This man is a *franc tireur*, a civilian in civilian's garb, fighting against us. It is our law that all such who are caught be shot immediately."

"Your Highness," said von Arnheim, "I have reason to think that the lady's story is correct. This man's daughter is her maid, and he is obviously a servant of her house."

Auersperg turned his slow, heavy look upon the young Prussian, but John noticed that von Arnheim met it without flinching, although Picard had really fired upon the Germans. He surmised that von Arnheim was fully as high-born as Auersperg, and perhaps more so. John knew that these things counted for a lot in Germany, however ridiculous they might seem to a democratic people. Nevertheless Auersperg spoke with irony:

"Your heart is overworking, von Arnheim," he said "Sometimes I fear that it is too soft for a Prussian. Our Emperor and our Fatherland demand that we shall turn hearts of steel to our enemies, and never spare them. But it may be, my brave Wilhelm, that your sympathy is less for this hulking peasant and more for the fair face of the lady whom he serves."

John saw Julie's face flush a deep red, and his hand stole down to his belt, but no weapon was there. Von Arnheim's face reddened also, but he stood at attention before his superior officer and replied with dignity:

"I admire Mademoiselle Lannes, although I have known her only ten minutes, but I think, Your Highness, that my admiration is warranted, and also that it is not lacking in respect."

"Good for you, von Arnheim," said John, under his breath. But the medieval mind of Auersperg was not disturbed. The slow, cruel smile passed across his face again.

"You are brave my Wilhelm," he said, "but I am confirmed in my opinion that some of our princely houses have become tainted. The harm that was done when Napoleon smashed his way through Europe has never been undone. The touch of the democracy was defilement, and it does not pass. Do you think our ancestors would have wasted so much time over a miserable French peasant?"

This was a long speech, much too long for the circumstances, John thought, but von Arnheim still standing stiffly at attention, merely said:

"Your Highness I ask this man's life of you. He is not a *franc tireur* in the real sense."

"Since you make it a personal matter, my brave young Wilhelm, I yield. Let him be held a prisoner, but no more requests of the same kind. This is positively the last time I shall yield to such a weakness."

"Thank you, Your Highness," said von Arnheim. Julie gave him one flashing look of gratitude and stepped away from Picard, who had stood, his arms folded across his chest, refusing to utter a single word for mercy. "This indeed," thought John "is a man." Suzanne was near, and now both he and his daughter turned away relaxing in no wise their looks of grim resolution. "Here also is a woman as well as a man," thought John.

"I hope, Your Highness, that I may assign Mademoiselle Lannes and her maid to one of the upper rooms," said von Arnheim in tones respectful, but very firm. "Here also is another man," thought John.

"You may," said Auersperg shortly, "but let the peasant be sent to the stables, where the other prisoners are kept."

Two soldiers were called and they took Picard away. Julie and Suzanne followed von Arnheim to a stairway, and John was left alone with medievalism. The man wore no armor, but when only they two stood in the room his feeling that he was back in the Middle Ages was overpowering. Here was the baron, and here was he, untitled and unknown.

Auersperg glanced at Julie, disappearing up the stairway, and then glanced back at John. Over his heavy face passed the same slow cruel smile that set all John's nerves to jumping.

"Why have you, an American, come so far to fight against us?" he asked.

"I didn't come for that purpose. I was here, visiting, and I was caught in the whirl of the war, an accident, perhaps. But my sympathies are wholly with France. I fight in her ranks from choice."

Auersperg laughed unpleasantly.

"A republic!" he said. "Millions of the ignorant, led by demagogues! Bah! The Hohenzollerns will scatter them like chaff!"

"I can't positively say that I saw any Hohenzollern, but I did see their armies turned back from Paris by those ignorant people, led by their demagogues. I'm not even sure of the name of the French general who did it, but God gave him a better brain for war, though he may have been born a peasant for all I know, than he did to your Kaiser, or any king, prince, grand duke or duke in all the German armies!"

John had been tried beyond endurance and he knew that he had spoken with impulsive passion, but he knew also that he had spoken with truth. The face of Auersperg darkened. The medieval baron, full of power, without responsibility, believing implicitly in what he chose to call his order, but which was merely the chance of birth, was here. And while the Middle Ages in reality had passed, war could hide many a dark tale. John was unable to read the intent in the cruel eyes, but they heard the footsteps of von Arnheim on the stairs, and the clenched hand that had been raised fell back by Auersperg's side. Nevertheless medievalism did not relax its gaze.

"What to you is this girl who seems to have charmed von Arnheim?" he asked.

"Her brother has become my best friend. She has charmed me as she has charmed von Arnheim, and as she charms all others whom she meets. And I am pleased to tell Your Highness that the spell she casts is not alone her beauty, but even more her pure soul."

Auersperg laughed in an ugly fashion.

"Youth! Youth!" he exclaimed. "I see that the spell is upon you, even more than it is upon von Arnheim. But dismiss her from your thoughts. You go a prisoner into Germany, and it's not likely that you'll ever see her again."

Young Scott felt a sinking of the heart, but he was not one to show it.

"Prisoners may escape," he said boldly, "and what has been done once can always be done again."

"We shall see that it does not happen a second time in your case. Von Arnheim will dispose of you for the night, and even if you should succeed in stealing from the château there is around it a ring of German sentinels through which you could not possibly break."

Some strange kink appeared suddenly in John's brainhe was never able to account for it afterward, though Auersperg's manner rasped him terribly.

"I mean to escape," he said, "and I wager you two to one that I do."

Auersperg sat down and laughed, laughed in a way that made John's face turn red. Then he beckoned to von Arnheim.

"Take him away," he said. "He is characteristic of his frivolous democracy, frivolous and perhaps amusing, but it is a time for serious not trifling things."

John was glad enough to go with von Arnheim, who was silent and depressed. Yet the thought came to him once more that there were princes and princes. Von Arnheim led the way to a small bare room under the roof. John saw that there were soldiers in the upper halls as well as the lower, and he was sorry that he had made such a boast to Auersperg. As he now saw it his chance of escape glimmered into nothing.

"You should not have spoken so to His Highness," said von Arnheim. "I could not help but hear. He is our commander here, and it is not well to infuriate one who holds all power over you?"

"I am but human," replied John.

"And being human, you should have had complete control over your-self at such a time."

"I admit it," said John, taking the rebuke in the right spirit.

"You're to spend the night here. I've been able to secure this much lenity for you, but it's for one night only. Tomorrow you go with the other prisoners in the stables. Your door will be locked, but even if you should succeed in forcing it don't try to escape. The halls swarm with sentinels, and you would be shot instantly. I'll have food sent to you presently."

He spoke brusquely but kindly. When he went out John heard a huge key rumbling in the lock.

13

A PROMISE KEPT

The room in which John was confined contained only a bed, a chair and a table. It was lighted by a single window, from which he could see numerous soldiers below. He also heard the distant mutter of the cannon, which seemed now to have become a part of nature. There were periods of excitement or of mental detachment, when he did not notice it, but it was always there. Now the soldiers in the grounds were moving but little, and the air pulsed with the thud of the great guns.

He recalled again his promise, or rather threat, to Auersperg that he would escape. Instinctively he went to the narrow but tall window and glanced at the heavens. Then he knew that impulse had made him look for Lannes and the *Arrow*, and he laughed at his own folly. Even if Lannes knew where they were he could not slip prisoners out of a house, surrounded by watchful German troops.

He heard the heavy key turning in the lock, and a silent soldier brought him food, which he put upon the table. The man remained beside the door until John had eaten his supper, when he took the dishes and withdrew. He had not spoken a word while he was in the room, but as he was passing out John said:

"Good-bye, Pickelbaube! Let's have no ill feeling between you and me."

The German—honest peasant that he was—grinned and nodded. He could not understand the English words, but he gathered from John's tone that they were friendly, and he responded at once. But when he closed the door behind him John heard the heavy key turning in the lock again. He knew there was little natural hostility between the people of different nations. It was instilled into them from above.

Food brought back new strength and new courage. He took his place again at the window which was narrow and high, cut through a deep wall. The illusion of the Middle Ages, which Auersperg had created so completely, returned. This was the dungeon in a castle and he was a prisoner doomed to death by its lord. Some dismounted Uhlans who were walking across the grounds with their long lances over their shoulders gave another touch to this return of the past, as the first rays of the moonlight glittered on helmet and lance-head.

He was not sleepy at all, and staying by the window he kept a strange watch. He saw white flares appear often on a long line in the west. He knew it was the flashing of the searchlights, and he surmised that what he saw was meant for signals. The fighting would go on under steady light continued long, and that it would continue admitted of no doubt. He could hear the mutter of the guns, ceaseless like the flowing of a river.

He saw the battery drive out of the grounds, then turn into the road before the château and disappear. He concluded that the cannon were needed at some weak point where the Franco-British army was pressing hard.

Then a company of hussars came from the forest and rode quietly into the grounds, where they dismounted. John saw that many, obviously the wounded, were helped from their horses. In battle, he concluded, and not so far off. Perhaps not more than two or three miles. Rifle-fire, with the wind blowing the wrong way, would not be heard that distance.

The hussars, leading their horses, disappeared in a wood behind the house, and they were followed presently by a long train of automobiles, moving rather slowly. The moonlight was very bright now and John saw that they were filled with wounded who stirred but little and who made no outcry. The line of motors turned into the place and they too disappeared behind the château, following the hussars.

Two aeroplanes alighted on the grass and their drivers entered the house. Bearers of dispatches, John felt sure, and while he watched he saw both return, spring into their machines and fly away. Their departure caused him to search the heavens once more, and he knew that he was looking for Lannes, who could not come.

Now von Arnheim passed down the graveled walk that led to the great central gate, but, half way, turned from it and began to talk to some sentinels who stood on the grass. He was certainly a fine fellow, tall, well built, and yet free from the German stoutness of figure. He wore a close uniform of blue-gray which fitted him admirably, and the moonlight fell in a flood on his handsome, ruddy face.

"I hope you won't be killed," murmured John. "If there is any French shell or shrapnel that is labeled specially for a prince and that must have a prince, I pray it will take Auersperg in place of von Arnheim."

It was a serious prayer and he felt that it was without a trace of wickedness or sacrilege. Evidently von Arnheim was giving orders of importance, as two of the men, to whom he was talking, hurried to horses, mounted and galloped down the road. Then the young prince walked slowly back to the house and John could see that he was very thoughtful. He passed his hand in a troubled way two or three times across his forehead. Perhaps the medieval prince inside was putting upon the modern prince outside labors that he was far from liking.

John's unformed plan of escape included Julie Lannes. He could not go away without her. If he did he could never face Lannes again, and what was more, he could never face himself. It was in reality this thought that made his resolve to escape seem so difficult. It had been lurking continuously in the back of his head. To go away without Julie was impossible. Under ordinary circumstances her situation as a prisoner would not be alarming. Germans regarded women with respect. They had done so from the earliest times, as he had learned from the painful study of Tacitus. Von Arnheim had received a deep impression from Julie's beauty and grace. John could tell it by his looks, but those looks were honest. They came from the eyes and heart of one who could do no wrong. But the other! The man of the Middle Ages, the older prince. He was different. War re-created ancient passions and gave to them opportunities. No, he could not think of leaving without Julie!

He kept his place at the tall, narrow window, and the night was steadily growing brighter. A full, silver moon was swinging high in the heavens. The stars were out in myriads in that sky of dusky, infinite blue, and danced regardless of the tiny planet, Earth, shaken by battle. From the hills came the relentless groaning which he knew was the sound of the guns, fighting one another under the searchlights.

Then he heard the clatter of hoofs, and another company of Uhlans rode up to the château. Their leader dismounted and entered the great gate. John recognized von Boehlen, who had taken off his helmet to let the cool air blow upon his close-cropped head. He stood on the graveled walk for a few minutes directly in a flood of silver rays, every feature showing clearly. He had been arrogant and domineering, but John liked him far better than Auersperg. His cruelty would be the cruelty of battle, and there might be a streak of sentimentalism hidden under the stiff and harsh German manner, like a vein of gold in rock. As von Boehlen resumed his approach to the house he passed from John's range of vision, and then the prisoner watched the horizon for anything that he might see. Twice he beheld the far flare of searchlights, but nobody else came to the château, and the night darkened somewhat. No rattle of arms or stamp of hoofs came from the hussars in the grounds, and he judged that all but the sentinels slept. Nor was there any sound of movement in the house, and in the peaceful silence he at last began to feel sleepy. The problems of his position were too great for him to solveat least for the presentand lying down on the cot he was fast asleep before he knew it.

Youth does not always sleep soundly, and the tension of John's nerves continued long after he lapsed into unconsciousness. That, perhaps, was the reason why he awoke at once when the heavy key began to turn again in the lock. He sat up on the cothe had not undressedand his hand instinctively slipped to his belt, where there was no weapon.

The key was certainly turning in the lock, and then the door was opening! A shadow appeared in the space between door and wall, and John's first feeling was of apprehension. An atmosphere of suspicion had been created about him and he considered his life in much more danger there than it had been when he was first a prisoner.

The door closed again quickly and softly, but somebody was inside the room, somebody who had a light, feline step, and John felt the prickling of the hair at the back of his neck. He longed for a weapon, something better than only his two hands, but he was reassured when the intruder, speaking French, called in a whisper:

"Are you awake, Mr. Scott?"

It was surely not the voice and words of one who had come to do murder, and John felt a thrill of recognition.

"Weber!" he exclaimed.

"Yes, it's Weber, Mr. Scott."

"How under the sun did you get here, Weber?"

"By pretending to be a German. I'm an Alsatian, you know, and it's not difficult. I'm doing work for France. It's terribly dangerous. My life is on the turn of a hair every moment, but I'm willing to take the risk. I did not know you were here until late tonight, when I came to the château to see if I could discover anything further about the numbers and movements of the enemy. You must get away now. I think I can help you to escape."

There was a tone in Weber's voice that aroused John's curiosity.

"It's good of you, Weber," he said, "to take such a risk for me, but why is it so urgent that I escape tonight?"

"I've learned since I came to the château that the Prince of Auersperg is much inflamed against you. Perhaps you spoke to him in a way that gave offense to his dignity. Ah, sir, the members of these ancient royal houses, those of the old type, consider themselves above and beyond the other people of the earth. In Germany you cannot offend them without risk, and it may be, too, that you stand in his way in regard to something that he very much desires!"

Although Weber spoke in a whisper his voice was full of energy and earnestness. His words sank with the weight of truth into John's heart.

"Can you really help me to escape?" he asked.

"I think so. I'm sure of it. The guards in the house are relaxed at this late hour, and they would seem needless anyhow with so many sentinels outside."

"But, Weber, Julie Lannes, the sister of Philip Lannes, is here a prisoner also. She was taken when I was. She is a Red Cross nurse, and although the Germans would not harm a woman, I do not like to leave her in this château. Your Prince of Auersperg does not seem to belong to our later age."

"Perhaps not. He holds strongly for the old order, but the young von Arnheim is here also. His is a devoted German heart, but his German eyes have looked with admiration, nay more, upon a French face. He will protect that beautiful young Mademoiselle Julie with his life against anybody, against his senior in military rank, the Prince of Auersperg himself. Sir, you must come! If you wish to help Philip Lannes' sister you can be of more help to her living than dead. If you linger here you surely disappear from men tomorrow!"

"How do you know these things, Weber?"

"I have been in the house three or four hours and there is talk among the soldiers. I pray you, don't hesitate longer!"

"How can you find a way?"

"Wait a minute."

He slipped back to the door, opened it and looked into the hall.

"The path is clear," he said, when he returned. "There is no sentinel near your door, and I've found a way leading out of the château at the back. Most of these old houses have crooked, disused passages."

"But suppose we succeed in reaching the outside, Weber, what then? The place is surrounded by an army."

"A way is there, too. One man in the darkness can pass through a multitude. We can't delay, because another chance may not come!"

John was overborne. Weber was half pulling him toward the door. Moreover, there was much sense in what the Alsatian said. It was a commonplace that he could be of more service to Julie alive than dead, and the man's insistence deciding him, he crept with the Alsatian into the hall. They stood a few minutes in the dark, listening, but no sound came. Evidently the house slept well.

"This way, Mr. Scott," whispered Weber, and he led toward the rear of the house. Turning the corner of the hall he opened a small door in the wall, which John would have passed even in the daylight without noticing.

"Put a hand on my coat and follow me," said Weber.

John obeyed without hesitation, and they ascended a half dozen steps along a passage so narrow that his shoulders touched the walls. It was very dark there, but at the top they entered a room into which some moonlight came, enough for John to see barrels, boxes and bags heaped on the floor.

"A storeroom," said Weber. "The French are thrifty. The owner of this house had splendor below, and he has kept provision for it above, almost concealed by the narrowness of the door and stair. But we'll find a broader stair on the other side, and then we'll descend through the kitchen and beyond."

"This looks promising. You're a clever man, Weber, and my debt to you is too big for me."

"Don't think about it. Be careful and don't make any noise. Here's the other stair. You'd better hold to my coat again."

They stole softly down the stair, crossed an unused room, went down another narrow, unused passage, and then, when Weber opened a door, John felt the cool air of the night blowing upon his face. When the attempt at escape began, he had not been so enthusiastic, because he was leaving Julie behind, but with every step his eagerness grew and the free wind brought with it a sort of intoxication. He did not doubt now that he would make good his flight. Weber, that fast friend of his, was a wonderful man. He worked miracles. Everything came out as he predicted it would, and he would work more miracles.

"Where are we now?" asked John.

"This door is by the side of the kitchens. A little to the left is an extensive conservatory, nearly all the glass of which has been shattered by a shell, but that fact makes it all the more useful as a path for us. If we reach it unobserved we can creep through the mass of flowers and shrubbery to a large fishpond which lies just beyond it. You're a good swimmer, as I knowand you can swim along its edge until you reach the shrubbery on the other side. Then you ought to find an opening by which you can reach the French army."

"And you, Weber?"

"I? Oh, I must stay here. The Prince of Auersperg is a man of great importance. He is high in the confidence of the Kaiser. Besides his royal rank he commands one of the German armies. If I am to secure precious information for France it must be done in this house."

"Come away with me, Weber. You've risked enough already. They'll catch you and you know the fate of spies. I feel like a criminal or coward abandoning you to so much danger, after all that you've done for me."

"Thank you for your good words, Mr. Scott, but it's impossible for me to go. Keep in the shadow of the wall, and a dozen steps will take you to the conservatory."

John wrung the Alsatian's hand, stepped out, and pressed himself against the side of the house. The breeze still blew upon his face, revivifying and intoxicating. The lazy, feathery clouds were yet drifting before the moon and stars.

He saw to his right the gleam of a bayonet as a sentinel walked back and forth and he saw another to his left. His heart beat high with hope. He was merely a mote in infinite night, and surely they could not see him.

He walked swiftly along in the shadow of the house, and then sprang into the conservatory, where he crouched between two tall rose bushes. He waited there a little while, breathing hard, but he had not been observed. From his rosy shelter he could still see the sentinels on either side, walking up and down, undisturbed. Around him was a frightful litter. The shell, the history of which he would never know, had struck fairly in the center of the place, and it must have burst in a thousand fragments. Scarcely a pane of glass had been left unbroken, and the great pots, containing rare fruits and flowers, were mingled mostly in shattered heaps. It was a pitiable wreck, and it stirred John, although he had seen so many things so much worse.

He walked a little distance in a stooping position, and then stood up among some shrubs, tall enough to hide him. He noticed a slight dampness in the air, and he saw, too, that the feathery clouds were growing darker. The faint quiver in the air brought with it, as always, the rumble of the guns, but he believed that it was not a blended sound. There was real thunder on the horizon, where the French lay, and then he saw a distant flash, not white like that of a searchlight, but like yellow lightning. Rain, a storm perhaps, must be at hand. He had read that nearly all the great battles in the civil war in his own country had been followed at once by violent storms of thunder, lightning and rain. Then why not here, where immense artillery combats never ceased?

Near the end of the conservatory he paused and looked back at the house. Every window was dark. There must be light inside, but shutters were closed. His heart throbbed with intense gratitude to Weber. Without him escape would have been impossible. He would make his way to the French. He would find Lannes and together in some way they would rescue Julie, Julie so young and so beautiful, held in the castle of the medieval baron. In the lowering shadows the house became a castle and Auersperg had always been of the Middle Ages.

The wind freshened and a few drops of rain struck his face. He stood boldly erect now, unafraid of observation, and picked a way through the mass of broken glass and overturned shrubbery toward the end of the conservatory, seeing beyond it a gleam of water which must be the big fishpond.

He turned to the left and reached the edge of the pond just as four figures stepped from the dusk, their raised rifles pointing at him. The shock was so great that, driven by some unknown but saving impulse, he threw himself forward into the water just as the soldiers fired. He heard the four rifles roaring together. Then he swam below water to the far edge of the pond and came up under the shelter of its circling shrubbery, raising above its surface only enough of his face for breath.

As his eyes cleared he saw the four soldiers standing at the far edge of the pond, looking at the water. Doubtless they were waiting for his body to reappear, as his action, half fall, half spring, and the roaring of the rifles had been so close together that they seemed a blended movement.

He was trembling all over from intense nervous exertion and excitement, but his mind steadied enough for him to observe the soldiers. Undoubtedly they were talking together, as he saw them making the gestures of men who speak, but, even had he heard them, he could not have understood their German. They were watching for his body, and as it did not reappear they might make the circle of the pond looking for it. He intended, in such an event, to leap out and run, but the elements were intereceding in his favor. Thunder now preponderated greatly in that rumble on the western horizon, and a blaze of yellow lightning played across the surface of the pond. It was followed by a rush of rain and the soldiers turned back toward the house, evidently sure that they had not missed.

John drew himself out of the water and climbed up the bank. His knees gave way under him and he sank to the ground. Excitement and emotion had been so violent that he was robbed of strength, but the condition lasted only a minute or two. Then he rose and began to pick a way.

The rain was driving hard, and it had grown so dark that one could not see far. But he felt that the German sentinels now would seek a little shelter from the wrath of the skies, and keeping in the shelter of a hedge he passed by the stables, where many of the hussars and Uhlans slept, through an orchard, the far side of which was packed with automobiles, and thence into a wood, where he believed at last that he was safe.

He stopped here a little while in the lee of a great oak to protect himself from the driving rain, and he noticed then that it was but a passing shower, sent, it seemed then to him, as a providential aid. The part of the rumble that was real thunder was dying. The yellow flare of the lightning stopped and the rain swept off to the east. The moon and stars were coming out again.

John tried to see the château, but it was hidden from him by trees. They would miss him there, and then they would know that it was he whom the soldiers had fired upon at the edge of the pond. All of them would believe that he was dead, and he remembered suddenly that Julie, who was there among them, would believe it, too. Would she grieve? Or would he merely be one of the human beings passing through her life, fleeting and forgotten, like the shower that had just gone? It was true that he had escaped, but he might be killed in some battle before she was rescued from Auerspergif she was rescued.

These thoughts were hateful, and turning into the road by which they had come to the château he ran down it. He ran because he wanted motion, because he wished to reach the French army as quickly as he could, and help Lannes organize for the rescue of Julie.

He ran a long distance, because his excitement waned slowly, and because the severe exercise made the blood course rapidly through his veins, counteracting the effects of his cold and wetting. When he began to feel weary he turned out of the road, knowing that it was safer in the fields. He had the curious belief or impression now that the black shower was all arranged for his benefit. Providence was merely making things even. The soldiers had been brought upon him when the chances were a hundred to one against him, and then the shower had been sent to cover him, when the chances were a hundred to one against that, too.

He saw far to the south a sudden faint radiance and he knew that it was the last of the lightning. The little feathery clouds, which looked so friendly and pleasant against the blue of the sky, came back and the moaning on the western horizon toward which he was traveling was wholly that of the guns.

He heard a noise over his head, a mixture of a whistle and a scream, and he knew that a shell was passing high. He walked on, and heard another. But they could not be firing at him. He was still that mere mote in the infinite darkness, but, looking back for the bursting of the shells, he saw a blaze leap up near the point from which he had come.

A cold shiver seized him. The range was that of the château, and Julie was there. The French gunners could have no knowledge that their own people were prisoners in the building, and if one of those huge shells burst in it, ruin and destruction would follow. The conservatory had been a silent witness of what flying metal could do. He stopped, appalled. He had been wrong to leave without Julie, and yet he could have done nothing else. It was impossible to foresee a shelling of the château by the French themselves.

The screaming and whistling came again, but he did not see any explosion near the château. One could not tell much from such a swift and passing sound, but he concluded that it was a German shell replying. He had seen a German battery near the house and it would not remain quiet under bombardment.

He had no doubt that the French gunners, having got the range, would keep it. Somebody, perhaps an aeroplane or an officer with flags in a tree, was signaling. It was horrible, this murderous mechanism by which men fired at targets miles away, targets which they could not see, but which they hit nevertheless. Every pulse beating hard, John shook his fist at the invisible German guns and the invisible French guns alike.

Then he recovered himself with an angry shake and began to run again. He knew now that he must go forward and secure a French force for rescue. But no matter how much he urged himself on, a great power was pulling at him, and it was Julie Lannes, a prisoner of the Germans in the château. Often he stopped and looked back, always in the same direction. Twice more he saw shells burst in the neighborhood of the house, and then his heart would beat hard, but after brief hesitation he would always pursue his course once more toward the French army.

He did not know the time, but he believed it to be well past midnight. He had his watch, but his immersion in the fish pond had caused it to stop. Still, the feel of the air made him believe that he was in the morning hours. Shells continued to pass over his head, and now they came from many points. He had seen or heard so much firing in the last eight or ten days that the world, he felt, must be turned into a huge ammunition factory to feed all the guns. He laughed to himself at his own grim joke. He was overstrained and he began to see everything through a red mist.

His clothing was drying fast, but his throat was very hot from excitement and exertion. He came to a little brook, and kneeling down, drank greedily. Then he bathed his face and felt stronger and better. His nerves also grew steadier. There was not so much luminous mist in the atmosphere. Ahead of him the crash of the guns was much louder, and he knew that he had already come a long distance. It seemed that the passing of the storm had renewed the activity of the gunners. The mutter had become rolling thunder, and both to north and south the searchlights flared repeatedly.

He heard the beat of hoofs, and he hoped that they were French cavalry on patrol, but they proved to be German Hussars, Bavarians he judged by the light blue uniforms, and they were coming from the direction of the French lines. They had been scouting there, he had no doubt, but they passed in a few moments, and, leaving his hedge, he resumed his own rapid flight, continually hoping that he would meet some French force, scouting also.

But he was doomed to a long trial of patience. Twice he saw Germans and hid until they had gone by. They seemed to be scouting in the night almost to the mouths of the French guns, and he admired their energy although it stood in the way of his own plans. He came to a second brook, drank again, and then took a short cut through a small wood. He had marked the reports of guns from a hill about two miles in front of him, and he was sure that a French battery must be posted there. He reckoned that he could reach it in a half hour, if he exerted himself.

Half way through the wood and human figures rose up all about him. Strong hands seized his arms and an electric torch flashed in his face.

"Who are you?" came the fierce question in French.

But it was not necessary for John to answer. The man who held the torch was short, but very muscular and strong, his face cut in the antique mold, his eyes penetrating and eager. It was Bougainville and John gave a gasp of joy. Then he straightened up and saluted:

"Colonel Bougainville," he said, "I see that you know me! I have just escaped from the enemy for the second time. There is a house in that direction, and it is occupied by the Prince of Auersperg, one of the German generals."

He pointed where the château lay, and Bougainville uttered a shout: "Ah!"

"He holds there a prisoner, Mademoiselle Julie Lannes, the sister of the great Philip Lannes, the aviator; and other Frenchwomen."

"Ah!" said Bougainville again.

"You will help rescue them, will you not?"

Bougainville smiled slightly.

"An army can't turn aside for the rescue of women," he replied, "but it happens that this brigade, under General Vaugirard is marching forward now to find, if possible, an opening between the German armies, and you're the very man to lead it."

John's heart bounded with joy. He would be again with the general whom he admired and trusted, and he would certainly guide the brigade straight to the château.

"Is General Vaugirard near?" he asked.

"Just over the brow of this hill, down there where the dim light is visible among the trees."

"Then take me to him at once."

14

THE RESCUE

Escorted by Bougainville, John went down a little slope to a point where several officers stood talking earnestly. The central figure was that of a huge man who puffed out his cheeks as he spoke, and whose words and movements were alive with energy. Even had he seen but a dim outline, John would have recognized him with no difficulty as General Vaugirard, and beside him stood de Rougemont.

Bougainville saluted and said;

"The American, John Scott, sir. He has just escaped from the enemy and he brings important information."

Vaugirard puffed out his great cheeks and whistled with satisfaction.

"Ah, my young Yankee!" he said. "They cannot hold you!"

"No, my general," replied John, "I've come back again to fight for France."

General Vaugirard looked at him keenly.

"You're exhausted," he said. "You've been under tremendous pressure."

"But I can guide you. I want neither sleep nor rest."

"You need both, as I can see with these two old eyes of mine. Sleep you can't have now, but rest is yours. You go with me in my automobile, which this war has trained to climb mountains, jump rivers, and crash through forests. The motor has become a wonderful weapon of battle."

"May I ask one question, General?" said John.

"A dozen."

"Do you know where the aviator, Philip Lannes, is? His sister is held a prisoner by a German general in a château toward which we will march, and doubtless he would wish to go at once to her rescue."

"He is not here, but his friend, Caumartin, is only a half-mile away. I'll send a man at once with a message to him to find Lannes, who will surely follow us, if he can be found. And now, my brave young Yankee, here is my machine. Into it, and we'll lead the way."

John sprang into the automobile, and sank down upon the cushions. He had a vast sense of ease and luxury. He had not known until then, the extent of his mental and physical overstrain, but de Rougemont, who was also in the machine, observed it and gave him a drink from a flask, which revived him greatly.

Then the automobile turned into the road and moved forward at a slow gait, puffing gently like a monster trying to hold in his breath. From the wood and the fields came the tread of many thousand men, marching to the night attack. Behind their own automobile rose the hum of motors, bearing troops also, and dragging cannon.

John felt that he was going back in state, riding by the side of a general and at the head of an army. He found both pride and exultation in it. Sleep was far from his eyes. How could one think of sleep at such a moment? But youth, the restorer, was bringing fresh strength to his tired muscles and he was never more alert.

At one point they stopped while the general examined the dusky horizon through his glasses, and a company of men with faces not French marched past them. They were John's own Strangers, and despite the presence of General Vaugirard both Wharton and Carstairs reached up and shook his hand as they went by.

"Welcome home," said Wharton.

"See you again in the morning," said Carstairs.

"God bless you both," said John with some emotion.

Captain Daniel Colton nodded to him. They were not effusive, these men of the Strangers, but their feelings were strong. When the automobile in its turn passed them again and resumed its place at the head of the column, they seemed to take no notice.

No more shells passed over John's head. He knew that General Vaugirard had sent back word for the batteries to cease firing in that direction, but both to south and north of them the sullen thunder went on. The night remained light, adorned rather than obscured by the little white clouds floating against the sky. The only sound that John could hear was the great hum and murmur of a moving army, a sound in which the puffing of automobiles had introduced a new element. He wondered why they had not roused up German skirmishers, but perhaps those vigilant gentlemen, had grown weary at last.

They reached the first brook, and, as they were crossing it, the rifle fire expected so long began to crackle in front. Then the French trumpets shrilled, and the whole force marched rapidly, rifles and field guns opening in full volume. But the French had the advantage of surprise. Their infantry advanced at the double quick, a powerful force of cavalry on their right flank galloped to the charge, and Bougainville's Paris regiment and the Strangers swept over the field.

A heavy fire met them, but the general's automobile kept in front puffing along the main road. General Vaugirard puffed with it, but now and then he ceased his puffing to whistle. John knew that he was pleased and that all was going well. The battle increased in volume, and their whole front blazed with fire. The dark was thinning away in the east and dawn was coming.

"The château! The château!" cried John as a dark shape rose on the horizon. Even as he looked a shell burst over it and it leaped into flames. He cried aloud in fear, not for himself, but for those who were there. But General Vaugirard was calmly examining the field and the house through powerful glasses.

"They're pouring from the building," he said, "and it's full time. Look how the fire gains! What a pity that we should destroy the home of some good Frenchman in order to drive out the enemy."

"Faster, sir! Faster! Ah, I pray you go faster!" exclaimed John, whose heart was eaten up with anxiety as he saw the château roaring with flames. But he did not need the general's glasses now to see the people stream from it, and then rush for refuge from the fire of the French. The surprise had been so thorough that at this point the enemy was able to offer little resistance, and, in a few moments more, the automobile reached the grounds surrounding the burning château.

John, reckless of commands and of everything else, leaped out of the machine and ran forward. A gigantic man bearing a slender figure in his arms emerged from the shrubbery. Behind him came a stalwart young woman, grim of face. John shouted with joy. It was Picard, carrying Julie, and the woman who followed was the faithful Suzanne.

Picard put Julie down. She stood erect, pale as death. But the color flooded into her face when she saw John, and uttering a cry of joy she ran forward to meet him. She put her hands in his and said:

"I knew that you would save me!"

Time and place were extraordinary, and war, the great leveler, was once more at work.

"The château was set on fire by shells, Monsieur Scott," Picard said, "and when the enemy saw the French force appearing across the fields they took to flight. That dog of a prince, the Auersperg, tried to carry off Mademoiselle Julie in his automobile, but the young prince interfered and while they were quarreling I seized her and took her away. All the other women have escaped too."

"Thank God, Picard," exclaimed John, wringing the huge hand of the peasant, who was at once a peasant and a prince too.

"And look," said Carstairs, who with Wharton had approached unnoticed. "An aeroplane comes like the flight of an eagle, and my guess is poor if it is not our friend, the great Lannes."

Caumartin in truth had found Philip, and he came like the lightning, circling and swooping until he touched the ground almost at Julie's feet. Brother and sister were united in a close embrace, and Lannes turned to John.

"I have heard from Caumartin that it was you who brought the word. We can never repay you."

"We'll wait and see," said John.

Her brother did not see Julie flush rosily, as she turned her face away.

"And now," said Lannes, "we go to Paris. My duties allow me enough time for the flight. No, John, my friend, don't object. She's been up in the *Arrow* with me before. Picard, you and Suzanne can come later."

The thunder of the battle rolling toward the east still reached them, but Lannes quickly threw a coat around Julie, gave her a cap and huge glasses to put on, and exclaimed:

"Now we go."

"But I must first thank Mr. Scott himself for saving me," she said.

She put her hand, small and warm, in his, American fashion, and the two palms met in a strong clasp.

"Good-bye, Mr. Scott," she said.

"Good-bye, but not forever. I'm coming back to Paris."

"And it's my hope, too, that it's not forever."

She and her brother took their seats in the *Arrow*. Carstairs, Wharton and the others gave it a push, and it soared up into the fresh blue of the dawn. An ungloved hand, white and small, reached over the side and waved farewell, a farewell which John felt was for him.

To the east the battle still rolled, but John had forgotten its existence. Higher and higher rose the *Arrow*, flying toward Paris, until it diminished to a mere dot in the sky, and then was gone.

THE END

THE HOSTS OF THE AIR

1

THE TRENCH

A YOUNG MAN WAS SHAVING. His feet rested upon a broad plank embedded in mud, and the tiny glass in which he saw himself hung upon a wall of raw, reeking earth. A sky, somber and leaden, arched above him, and now and then flakes of snow fell in the sodden trench, but John Scott went on placidly with his task.

The face that looked back at him had been changed greatly in the last six months. The smoothness of early youth was gone--for the time-- and serious lines showed about the mouth and eyes. His cheeks were thinner and there was a slight sinking at the temples, telling of great privations, and of dangers endured. But the features were much stronger. The six months had been in effect six years. The boy of Dresden had become the man of the trenches.

He finished, rubbed his hand over his face to satisfy himself that the last trace of young beard and mustache was gone, put away his shaving materials in a little niche that he had dug with his own hands in the wall of the trench, and turned to the Englishman.

"Am I all right, Carstairs?" he asked.

"You do very well. There's mud on your boots, but I suppose you can't help it. The melting snow in our trench makes soggy footing in spite of all we can do. But you're trim, Scott. That new gray uniform with the blue threads running through it becomes you. All the Strangers are thankful for the change. It's a great improvement over those long blue coats and baggy red trousers."

"But we don't have any chance to show 'em," said Wharton, who sat upon a small stool, reading a novel. "Did I ever think that war would come to this? Buried while yet alive! A few feet of cold and muddy trench in which to pass one's life! This is an English story I'm reading. The lovely *Lady Ermentrude* and the gallant *Sir Harold* are walking in the garden among the roses, and he's about to ask her the great question. There are roses, roses, and the deep green grass and greener oaks every-where, with the soft English shadows coming and going over them. The birds are singing in the boughs. I suppose they're nightingales, but do nightingales sing in the daytime? And when I shut my book I see only walls of raw, red earth, and a floor, likewise of earth, but stickier and more hideous. Even the narrow strip of sky above our heads is the color of lead, and has nothing soft about it."

"If you'll stand up straight," said John, "maybe you'll see the rural landscape for which you're evidently longing."

"And catch a German bullet between the eyes! Not for me. While I was taking a trip down to the end of our line this morning I raised my head by chance above the edge of the trench, and quick as a wink a sharpshooter cut off one of my precious brown locks. I could have my hair trimmed that way if I were patient and careful enough. Ah, here comes a messenger!"

They heard a roar that turned to a shriek, and caught a fleeting glimpse of a black shadow passing over their heads. Then a huge shell burst behind them, and the air was filled with hissing fragments of steel. But in their five feet of earth they were untouched, although horrible fumes as of lyddite or some other hideous compound assailed them.

"This is the life," said Wharton, resuming his usual cheerfulness. "I take back what I said about our beautiful trench. Just now I appreciate it more than I would the greenest and loveliest landscape in England or all

America. Oh, it's a glorious trench! A splendid fortress for weak human flesh, finer than any castle that was ever built!"

"Don't be dithyrambic, Wharton," said Carstairs. "Besides the change is too sudden. It hasn't been a minute since you were pouring abuse upon our safe and happy little trench."

"It's time for the Germans to begin," said John, looking at his watch. "We'd better lie close for the next hour."

They heard the shrieking of more shells and soon the whole earth rocked with the fire of the great guns. The hostile trenches were only a few hundred yards in front of them, but the German batteries all masked, or placed in pits, were much further away. The French cannon were stationed in like fashion behind their own trenches.

John and his comrades, for the allotted hour, hugged the side of the trench nearest to the Germans. The shells from the heavy guns came at regular intervals. Far in the rear men were killed and others were wounded, but no fragment of steel dropped in their trench. There was not much danger unless one of the shells should burst almost directly over their heads, and they were so used to these bombardments that they paid little attention to them, except to keep close as long as they lasted.

Wharton resumed his novel, Carstairs, sitting on one end of a rude wooden bench, began a game of solitaire, and John, at the other end, gave himself over to dreaming, which the regulated thunder of many cannon did not disturb at all.

It had been months now since he had parted with Philip and Julie Lannes. He had seen Philip twice since, but Julie not at all When the German army made a successful stand near the river Aisne, and both sides went into trenches, Lannes had come in the *Arrow* and, in reply to John's restrained but none the less eager questions, had said that Julie was safe in Paris again with her mother, Antoine Picard and the faithful Suzanne. She had wanted to return to the front as a Red Cross nurse, but Madame Lannes would not let her go.

A month later he saw Lannes again and Julie was still in the capital, but he inferred from Philip's words rather than his tone that she was impatient. Thousands of French girls were at the front, attending to the wounded, and sharing hardship and danger. John knew that Julie had a will like her brother's and he believed that, in time, she would surely come again to the battle lines.

The thought made him smile, and he felt a light glow pass over his face. He knew it was due to the belief that he would see Julie once more, and yet the trenches now extended about four hundred miles across Northern France and Belgium. The chances seemed a hundred to one against her arrival in the particular trench, honored by the presence of the Strangers, but John felt that in reality they were a hundred to one in favor of it. He wished it so earnestly that it must come true.

"You're smiling, Scott," said Carstairs. "A good honest English penny for your thoughts."

"What do I care for money? What could I do with it if I had it, held here between walls of mud only four feet apart?"

"At least," interrupted Wharton, "the high cost of living is not troubling us. Next month's rent may come from where it pleases. It doesn't bother me."

A messenger turned the angle of the trench and summoned John to the presence of his commander, Captain Colton, who was about three hundred yards away. Young Scott, stooping in order to keep his head covered well, started down the trench. The artillery fire was at its height. The waves of air followed one another with great violence, and the fumes of picric acid and of other acids that he did not know became very strong. But he scarcely noticed it. The bombardment was all in the day's work, and when the Germans ceased, the French, after a decent interval, would begin their own cannonade, carried on at equal length.

John thought little of the fire of the guns, now almost a regular affair like the striking of a clock, but force of habit kept his head down and no German sharpshooter watching in the trench opposite had a chance at him. He advanced through a vast burrow. Trenches ran parallel, and other trenches cut across them. One could wander through them for miles. Most of them were uncovered, but others had roofs, partial or complete, of thatch or boards or canvas. Many had little alcoves and shelves, dug out by the patient hands of the soldiers, and these niches contained their most precious belongings.

Back of the trenches often lay great heaps of refuse like the kitchen middens of primeval man. Attempts at coziness had achieved a little success in some places, but nearly everywhere the abode of burrowing soldiers was raw, rank and fetid. Heavy and hideous odors arose from the four hundred miles of unwashed armies. Men lived amid disease, dirt and death. Civilization built up slowly through painful centuries had come to a sudden stop, and once more they were savages in caves seeking to destroy one another.

This, at least, was the external aspect of it, but the flower of civilization was still sound at the stem. When the storm was over it would grow and bloom again amid the wreckage. French and Germans, in the intervals of battle, were often friendly with each other. They listened to the songs of the foe, and sometimes at night they talked together. John recognized the feeling. He knew that man at the core had not really returned to a savage state, and a soldier, but not a believer in war, he looked forward to the time when the grass should grow again over the vast maze of trenches.

A shell bursting almost overhead put all such thoughts out of his mind for the present. A hot piece of metal shooting downward struck on the bottom of the trench and lay there hissing. John stepped over it and passed on.

The cannonade was at its height, and he noticed that it was heavier than usual. Perhaps the increase of volume was due to the presence of some great dignitary, the Kaiser himself maybe, or the Crown Prince, or the Chief of the General Staff. But it was only a flitting thought. The subject did not interest him much.

The sky was turning darker and the heavy flakes of snow fell faster. John looked up apprehensively. Snow now troubled him more than guns. It was no welcome visitor in the trenches where it flooded some of them so badly as it melted that the men were compelled to move.

As he walked along he was hailed by many friendly voices. He was well known in that part of the gigantic burrow, and the adaptable young American had become a great favorite, not only with the Strangers, but with his French comrades. Fleury, coming out of a transverse cut, greeted him. The Savoyard had escaped during the fighting on the Aisne, and had rejoined the command of General Vaugirard, wounded in the arm, but now recovered.

"Duty?" he said to John.

"Yes. Captain Colton has sent for me, but I don't know what he wants."

"Don't get yourself captured again. Twice is enough."

"I won't. There isn't much taking of prisoners while both sides keep to their holes."

Fleury disappeared in one of the earthy aisles, and John went on, turning a little later into an aisle also, and arriving at Captain Cotton's post.

Daniel Colton had for his own use a wooden bench three feet long, set in an alcove dug in the clay. Some boards and the arch of the earth formed an uncertain shelter. An extra uniform hung against the wall of earth, and he also had a tiny looking-glass and shaving materials. He was as thin and dry as ever, addicted to the use of words of one syllable, and sparing even with them.

John saluted. He had a great respect and liking for his captain.

"Sit down," said Captain Colton, making room on the bench.

John sat.

"Know well a man named Weber?"

"Yes," replied John in surprise. He had not thought of the Alsatian in days, and yet they had been together in some memorable moments.

"Thought you'd say so. Been here an hour. Asks for you. Must see you, he says."

"I'll be glad to meet him again, sir. I've a regard for him. We've shared some great dangers. You've heard that he was in the armored automobile with Carstairs, Wharton and myself that time we ran it into the river?"

Captain Colton nodded.

"Then we were captured and both escaped during the fighting along the Marne. Lannes took me away in his aeroplane, but we missed Weber. I thought, though, that he'd get back to us, and I'm glad, very glad that he's here."

"See him now," said Colton, "and find out what he wants."

He blew a whistle, and an orderly appeared, saluting.

"Bring Weber," said the captain.

The orderly returned with Weber, the two coming from one of the narrow aisles, and John rose impulsively to meet the Alsatian. But before offering his hand Weber saluted the captain.

"Go ahead. Tell all," said Colton briefly.

Weber first shook John's hand warmly. Evidently he had not been living the life of the trenches, as he looked fresh, and his cheeks were full of color. His gray uniform, with the blue threads through it, was neat and clean, and his black pointed beard was trimmed like that of a painter with money.

"We're old comrades in war, Mr. Scott," he said, "and I'm glad, very glad to find you again. You and Lannes left me rather abruptly that time near the Marne, but it was the only thing you could do. If by an effort of the mind I could have sent a wireless message to you I'd have urged you to instant flight. I hid in the bushes, in time reached one of our armies, and since then I've been a bearer of dispatches along the front. I heard some time back that you were still alive, but my duty hitherto has kept me from seeing you. Now, it sends me to you."

His tone, at first eager and joyous, as was fitting in an old friend meeting an old friend, now became very grave, and John looked at him with some apprehension. Captain Colton motioned to a small stool.

"Sit down," he said to Weber. Then he offered the Alsatian a match and a cigarette which were accepted gratefully. He made the same offer to John, who shook his head saying that he did not smoke. The captain took two or three deliberate puffs, and contemplated Weber who had made himself comfortable on the stool.

"Military duty?" he asked. "If so, Scott's concern is my concern too."

"That is quite true, Captain Colton," said Weber, respectfully. "As Mr. Scott is under your command you have a right to know what message I bring."

"Knew you'd see it," said Colton, taking another puff at his cigarette. "There! Germans have ceased firing!"

"And our men begin!" said John.

The moment the distant German thunder ceased the French reply, nearer at hand and more like a rolling crash, began. It would continue about an hour, that is until nightfall, unless the heavy clouds and falling snow brought darkness much earlier than usual. The flakes were coming faster, but the three were protected from them by the rude board shelter. John again glanced anxiously at Weber. He felt that his news was of serious import.

"I saw your friend Lieutenant Philip Lannes about three weeks ago at a village called Catreaux, lying sixty miles west of us," said Weber. "He had just made a long flight from the west, where he had observed much of the heavy fighting around Ypres, and also had been present when the Germans made their great effort to break through to Dunkirk and Calais. I hear that he had more than a messenger's share in these engagements, throwing some timely bombs."

"Was he well when you saw him?" asked John. "He had not been hurt? He had not been in any accident?"

"He was in the best of health, bard and fit. But his activities in the *Arrow* had diminished recently. Snow, rain, icy hail make difficulties and dangers for aviators. But we wander. He had not heard from his mother, Madame Lannes, or his sister, the beautiful Mademoiselle Julie, for a long time, and he seemed anxious about them."

"He himself took Mademoiselle Julie back to Paris in the *Arrow,*" said John.

"So he told me. They arrived safely, as you know, but Lannes was compelled to leave immediately for the extreme western front. The operations there were continuous and so exacting that he has been unable to return to Paris. He has not heard from his mother and sister in more than two months, and his great anxiety about them is quite natural."

"But since the retreat of the Germans there is no danger in Paris save from an occasional bomb."

"No. But a few days after seeing Lannes my own duties as a messenger carried me back to Paris, and I took it upon myself to visit Lannes' house. I had two objects, both I hope justifiable. I wanted to take to them good news of Lannes and I wanted to take to Lannes good news of them."

"You found them there?" said John, his anxiety showing in his tone.

"I did. But a letter from Lannes, by good luck, had just come through the day before. It was a noble letter. It expressed the fine spirit of that brave young man, a spirit universal now throughout France. He said the fighting had been so severe and the wounded were so many that all Frenchwomen who had the skill and strength to help must come to the hospitals, where the hurt in scores of thousands were lying."

"Did he mention any point to which she was to come?"

"A village just behind the fortress of Verdun. To say that she was willing was not enough. A great spirit, a magnificent spirit, Mr. Scott. The soul of chivalry may dwell in the heart of a young girl. She was eager to go. Madame, her mother, would have gone too, but she was ill, so she remained in the house, while the beautiful Mademoiselle Julie departed with the great peasant, Antoine Picard, and his daughter Suzanne."

"Do you know how they went?"

"By rail, I think, as far as they could go, and thence they were to travel by motor to the tiny village of Chastel, their destination. Knowing your interest in Mademoiselle Julie, I thought it would not displease you to hear this. Chastel is no vast distance from this point."

A blush would have been visible on John's face had he not been tanned so deeply, but he felt no resentment. Captain Colton took his cigarette from his lips and said tersely:

"Every man likes a pretty face. Man who doesn't--no man at all."

"I agree with you, Captain Colton," said Weber heartily. "When I no longer notice a beautiful woman I think it will be time for me to die. But I take no liberty, sir, when I say that in all the garden of flowers Mademoiselle Julie Lannes is the rarest and loveliest. She is the delicate and opening rose touched at dawn with pearly dew."

"A poet, Weber! A poet!" interjected Captain Colton.

"No, sir, I but speak the truth," said Weber seriously. "Mademoiselle Julie Lannes, though a young girl but yet, promises to become the most beautiful woman in Europe, and beauty carries with it many privileges. Men may have political equality, but women can never have an equality of looks."

"Right, Weber," said Captain Colton.

John's pulses had begun to leap. Julie was coming back to the front, and she would not be so far away. Some day he might see her again. But he felt anxiety.

"Is the journey to Chastel safe, after she leaves the railway?" he asked of Weber.

"Is anything safe now?"

"Nothing in Europe," interjected Captain Colton.

"But I don't think Mademoiselle Lannes will incur much danger," said Weber. "It's true, roving bands of Uhlans or hussars sometimes pass in our rear, but it's likely that she and other French girls going to the front march under strong escort."

His tone was reassuring, but his words left John still troubled.

"My object in telling you of Mademoiselle Lannes' movements, Mr. Scott," continued Weber, "was to enable you to notify Lieutenant Lannes of her exact location in case you should see him. Knowing your great friendship I thought it inevitable that you two should soon meet once more. If so, tell him that his sister is at Chastel. He will be glad to know of her arrival and, work permitting, will hurry to her there."

"Gladly I'll do it," said John. "I wish I could see Philip now."

But when he said "Philip" he was thinking of Julie, although the bond of friendship between him and young Lannes had not diminished one whit.

"And now," said Weber, "with Captain Colton's permission I'll go. My duties take me southward, and night is coming fast."

"And it will be dark, cold and snowy," said John, shivering a little. "These trenches are not exactly palace halls, but I'd rather be in them now than out there on such a night."

The dusk had come and the French fire was dying. In a few more minutes it would cease entirely, and then the French hour with the guns having matched the German hour, the night would be without battle.

But the silence that succeeded the thunder of the guns was somber. In all that terrible winter John had not seen a more forbidding night. The snow increased and with it came a strong wind that reached them despite their shelter. The muddy trenches began to freeze lightly, but the men's feet broke through the film of ice and they walked in an awful slush. It seemed impossible that the earth could ever have been green and warm and sunny, and that Death was not always sitting at one's elbow.

The darkness was heavy, but nevertheless as they talked they did not dare to raise their heads above the trenches. The German searchlights might blaze upon them at any moment, showing the mark for the sharp-shooters. But Captain Colton pressed his electric torch and the three in the earthy alcove saw one another well.

"Will you go to Chastel yourself?" asked John of Weber.

"Not at present. I bear a message which takes me in the Forest of Argonne, but I shall return along this line in a day or two, and it may be that I can reach the village. If so, I shall tell Mademoiselle Julie and the Picards that I have seen you here, and perhaps I can communicate also with Lannes."

"I thank you for your kindness in coming to tell me this."

"It was no more than I should have done. I knew you would be glad to hear, and now, with your permission, Captain Colton, I'll go."

"Take narrow, transverse trench, leading south. Good of you to see us," said the captain of the Strangers.

The Alsatian shook hands with John and disappeared in the cut which led a long distance from the front. Colton extinguished the torch and the two sat a little while in the darkness. Although vast armies faced one another along a front of four hundred miles, little could be heard where John and his captain sat, save the sighing of the wind and the faint sound made by the steady fall of the snow, which was heaping up at their feet.

Not a light shone in the trench. John knew that innumerable sentinels were on guard, striving to see and hear, but a million or two million men lay buried alive there, while the snow drifted down continually. The illusion that the days of primeval man had come back was strong upon him again. They had become, in effect, cave-dwellers once more, and their chief object was to kill. He listened to the light swish of the snow, and thought of the blue heights into which he had often soared with Lannes.

Captain Colton lighted another cigarette and it glowed in the dark.

"Uncanny," he said.

"I find it more so than usual tonight," said John. "Maybe it's the visit of Weber that makes me feel that way, recalling to me that I was once a man, a civilized human being who bathed regularly and who put on clean clothes at frequent intervals."

"Such days may come again--for some of us."

"So they may. But it's ghastly here, holed up like animals for the winter."

"Comparison not fair to animals. They choose snug dens. Warm leaves and brush all about 'em."

"While we lie or stand in mud or snow. After all, Captain, the animals have more sense in some ways than we. They kill one another only for food, while we kill because of hate or ignorance."

"Mostly ignorance."

"I suppose so. Hear that! It's a pleasant sound."

"So it is. Makes me think of home."

Some one further down the trench was playing a mouth organ. It was merely a thin stream of sound, but it had a soft seductive note. The tune was American, a popular air. It was glorified so far away and in such terrible places, and John suddenly grew sick for home and the pleasant people in the sane republic beyond the seas. But he crushed the emotion and listened in silence as the player played on.

"A hundred of those little mouth-organs reached our brigade this morning," said Colton. "Men in the trenches must have something to lift up their minds, and little things outside current of war will do it."

It was a long speech for him to make and John felt its truth, but he atoned for it by complete silence while they listened to many tunes, mostly American, played on the mouth-organ. John's mind continually went back to the great republic overseas, so safe and so sane. While he was listening to the thin tinkle in the dark and snowy trench his friends were going to the great opera house in New York to hear "Aida" or "Lohengrin" maybe. And yet he would not have been back there. The wish did not occur to him. Through the dark and the snow he saw the golden hair and the deep blue eyes of Julie Lannes float before him, and it pleased him too to think that he was a minute part in the huge event now shaking the world.

A sudden white light blazed through the snow, and then was gone, like a flash of lightning.

"German searchlight seeking us out," said Colton.

"I wonder what they want," said John. "They can't be thinking of a rush on such a night as this."

"Don't know, but must be on guard. Better return to your station and warn everybody as you go along. You can use your torch, but hold it low."

As John walked back he saw by the light of his little electric torch men sound asleep on the narrow shelves they had dug in the side of the trench, their feet and often a shoulder covered with the drifting snow.

Strange homes were these fitted up with the warriors' arms and clothes, and now and then with some pathetic little gift from home.

He met other men on guard like himself walking up and down the trench and also carrying similar torches. He found Carstairs and Wharton still awake, and occupied as they were when he had left them.

"What was it, Scott?" asked Carstairs. "Has the British army taken Berlin?"

"No, nor has the German army taken London."

"Good old London! I'd like to drop down on it for a while just now."

"They say that at night it's as black as this trench. Zeppelins!"

"I could find my way around it in the dark. I'd go to the Ritz or the Carlton and order the finest dinner for three that the most experienced chef ever heard of. You don't know how good a dinner I can give--if I only have the money. I invite you both to become my guests in London as soon as this war is over and share my gustatory triumph."

"I accept," said John.

"And I too," said Wharton, "though we may have to send to Berlin for our captive host."

"Never fear," said Carstairs. "I wasn't born to be taken. What did Captain Colton want with you, Scott, if it's no great military or state secret?"

"To see Fernand Weber, the Alsatian, whom you must remember."

"Of course we recall him! Didn't we take that dive in the river together? But he's an elusive chap, regular will-o'-the-wisp, messenger and spy of ours, and other things too, I suppose."

"He's done me some good turns," said John. "Been pretty handy several times when I needed a handy man most. He brought news that Mademoiselle Julie Lannes and her servants, the Picards, father and daughter, are on their way to or are at Chastel, a little village not far from here, where the French have established a huge hospital for the wounded. She left Paris in obedience to a letter from her brother, and we are to tell Philip if we should happen to see him."

"Pretty girl! Deucedly pretty!" said Carstairs.

"I don't think the somewhat petty adjective 'pretty' is at all adequate," said John with dignity.

"Maybe not," said Carstairs, noticing the earnest tone in his comrade's voice. "She's bound to become a splendid woman. Is Weber still with the captain?"

"No, he's gone on his mission, whatever it is."

"A fine night for travel," said Wharton sardonically. "A raw wind, driving snow, pitchy darkness, slush and everything objectionable underfoot. Yet I'd like to be in Weber's place. A curse upon the man who invented life in the trenches! Of all the dirty, foul, squalid monotony it is this!"

"You'll have to curse war first," said John. "War made the trench."

"Here comes a man with an electric torch," said Carstairs. "Something is going to happen in our happy lives."

They saw the faint glimmer of the torch held low, and an orderly arrived with a message from Captain Colton, commanding them to wake everybody and to stand to their arms. Then the orderly passed quickly on with similar orders for others.

"Old Never Sleep," said Carstairs, referring to Colton, "thinks we get too much rest. Why couldn't he let us tuck ourselves away in our mud on a night like this?"

"I fancy it's not restlessness," said John. "The order doubtless comes from a further and higher source. Good old Papa Vaugirard is not more than a quarter of a mile away."

"I hear they had to enlarge the trench for him," grumbled Carstairs. "He's always bound to keep us stirring."

"But he watches over us like a father. They say his troops are in the best condition of all."

The three young men traveled about the vast burrow along the main trenches, the side trenches and those connecting. The order to be on guard was given everywhere, and the men dragged themselves from their sodden beds. Then they took their rifles and were ready. But it was dark save for the glimmer of the little pocket electrics.

The task finished, the three returned to their usual position. John did not know what to expect. It might be a device of Papa Vaugirard to drag them out of a dangerous lethargy, but he did not think so. A kind heart dwelled in the body of the huge general, and he would not try them needlessly on a wild and sullen night. But whatever the emergency might be the men were ready and on the right of the Strangers was that Paris regiment under Bougainville. What a wonderful man Bougainville had proved himself to be! Fiery and yet discreet, able to read the mind of the enemy, liked by his men whom nevertheless he led where the danger was greatest. John was glad that the Paris regiment lay so close.

"Nothing is going to happen," said Carstairs. "Why can't I lay me down on my little muddy shelf and go to sleep? Nobody would send a dog out on such a night!"

"Man will often go where a dog won't," said Wharton, sententiously.

"And the night is growing worse," continued Carstairs. "Hear that wind howl! Why, it's driving the snow before it in sheets! The trenches won't dry out in a week!"

"You might be worth hearing if you'd only quit talking and say something, Carstairs," said Wharton.

"If you obeyed that rule, Wharton, you'd be known as the dumb man."

John stood up straight and looked over the trench toward the German lines, where he saw nothing. The night filled with so much driving snow had become a kind of white gloom, less penetrable than the darkness.

Only that shifting white wall met his gaze, and listen as he would, he could hear nothing. The feeling of something sinister and uncanny, something vast and mighty returned. Man had made war for ages, but never before on so huge a scale.

"Well, Sister Anna, otherwise John Scott, make your report," said Carstairs lightly. "What do you see?"

"Only a veil of snow so thick that my eyes can't penetrate it."

"And that's all you will see. Papa Vaugirard is a good man and he cares for his many children, but he's making a mistake tonight."

"I think not," said John, dropping suddenly back into the trench. A blinding white glare, cutting through the gloom of the snow, had dazzled him for a moment.

"The searchlight again!" exclaimed Wharton.

"And it means something," said John.

The blaze, whiter and more intense than usual, played for a few minutes over the French trenches, sweeping to right and left and back again and then dying away at a far distant point. After it came the same white gloom and deep silence.

"Just a way of greeting," said Carstairs.

"I think not," said John. "Papa Vaugirard makes few mistakes. To my mind the intensity of the silence is sinister. Often we hear the Germans singing in their trenches, but now we hear nothing."

Another half-hour of the long and trying waiting followed. Then the white light flared again for a moment, and powerful lights behind the French lines flared back, but did not go out. The great beams, shooting through the white gloom, disclosed masses of men in gray uniforms and spiked helmets rushing forward.

2
_____

T HE YOUNG AUSTRIAN

IT SEEMED to John that the heavy German masses were almost upon them, when they were revealed in the glare of the searchlights, sweeping forward in solid masses, and uttering a tremendous hurrah. But the French lights continued to throw an intense vivid white blaze over the advancing columns, broad German faces and stalwart German figures standing out vividly. Officers, reckless of death, waving their swords and shouting the word of command, led them on.

The French field guns behind their trenches opened, sending showers of missiles over their heads and into the charging ranks, and the trenches themselves blazed with the fire of the rifles.

"A surprise that isn't a surprise?" shouted Carstairs. "They thought to catch us napping in the night and the snow!"

The battle spread with astonishing rapidity over a front of more than a mile, and in the driving snow and white gloom it assumed a frightful character. The German guns fired for a little while over their troops at the French artillery beyond, but soon ceased lest they pour shells into their own men, and the heavy French batteries ceased also, lest they, too, mow down friend as well as foe. But the light machine guns posted in the trenches kept up a rapid and terrible crackle. The front lines of the Germans were cut down again and again, always to be replaced by fresh men, who unflinchingly exposed their bodies to the deadly hail.

"The massed attack!" exclaimed Wharton. "What courage! Nobody was ever more willing to die for victory than these Germans!"

Even in the moment of danger and utmost excitement he could not refuse tribute to the enemy. Nevertheless he snatched up a rifle and was firing as fast as he could into the gray ranks. John and Carstairs were doing the same and the trench held by the Strangers was a continuous red blaze. There was so much fire and smoke and so much whirling snow that John could not see clearly. He was a prey to illusions. Now the Germans were apparently at the very edge of the trench, and then they were further away than he had first seen them. The white gloom was shot with a red haze, and the shouts of soldiers, the commands of officers and groans of wounded were mingled in a terrible turmoil of sound. But John knew that the Germans would be driven tack. Only surprise could have enabled them to win, and the vigilance of the French scouts had put their commanders on guard.

Captain Colton walked up and down the trench, his face ghastly white, although it was the flare of the searchlight and not any retreat of the blood that made it so. Now and then under the frightful crash of the rifles and machine guns he addressed brief words of warning and encouragement to his men:

"Don't raise your heads too high! Keep cool! Aim at something! Here they come again! Fire low!"

All of John's pulses were throbbing hard with excitement. He wished the Germans would go back, and his wish was prompted--less by the desire of victory than the sickening of his soul at so much slaughter. Why would their leaders continue to hurl these simple and honest peasants upon that invincible line of rifles and machine guns? The dead and wounded were piling up fast in the driving snow, but the willing servants of an emperor came on as steadily as ever to be killed. So much slaughter for so little purpose! The height of battle, excitement and danger, could not keep him from thinking of it.

Occasionally a man fell in the trench and lay in the mud and snow, but the others never ceased for a moment to send bullets into the gray masses which fell back only to come on again. Nothing but modern weapons, machine guns from which missiles fairly flowed in an unending stream, and rifles which a man fired as fast as he could pull the trigger could check them. "Why don't they stop! Why don't they stop!" John was shouting to himself through burned lips, and again he shuddered with sick horror, when he saw a whole line of men blown away, as if they had been grain swept by a tornado.

Once they came to the very edge of the trench to be slain there, and the body of a German fell in at John's very feet. He never knew how many times they charged, but human flesh and blood must yield, in the end, before unyielding steel, and at last through the crash and confusion the notes of trumpets sounded. Then the German masses melted away and the heavy white gloom once more enveloped the ground before the trenches from which came faint cries. The wounded lay thickly there with the dead, but neither side dared to go for them. An upright human figure would draw at once a hail of bullets.

Several machine guns still purred and crackled, but no reply came. Presently they, too, ceased, and the silence in front was complete, save for the faint groans and the swish of the drifting snow. John shivered, and it was not with cold. His feeling of horror was increasing. Many men had been killed and as many maimed, and he was sure that all of them had fallen for nothing.

"It's a victory," said Carstairs, "isolated and detached, but a victory nevertheless."

"So it is," said John, "but it's just a little segment on a vast curving line of four hundred miles. Maybe the Germans have taken a trench somewhere else."

"And maybe we have, at yet another point. This isn't much like the war we've read about, is it, Scott? A great battlefield, vast batteries blazing, long lines of infantry in brilliant uniforms advancing, twenty thousand cavalry charging at the gallop the earth reeling under the hoofs of their horses!"

"No, it's just murder in the dark."

[Illustration: "Once they came to the very edge of the trench to be slain there"]

"But a black night would oppress me less than the ghastly whitish glare of the snow. I can't see a thing out there, Scott, but those low sounds I hear appall me."

The wind and the fall of snow alike were increasing in violence. The great flakes poured in a feathery storm into the trench, and, before them, all things were hidden. John knew, too, that it was covering the many dead in their front with a blanket of white and that the wounded who were unable to crawl back would probably lie frozen beneath it in the morning. Once more that shiver of horror and utter repulsion seized him. Despite himself, he could not control it, and he merely remained quiet until his nerves became steady again.

But a low moaning just beyond the trench held his attention. It did not seem to him that it was more than a dozen feet away, and he felt a great sympathy and pity. He did not doubt that some German boy hurt terribly lay almost within reach of his arm. He moved once in order that he might not hear the dreadful sound, but an irresistible attraction drew him back. Then he heard it more plainly, but the thick pouring snow covered all things.

"Carstairs," he said, "I'm going to get a wounded man out there. I just can't stand it any longer."

"Don't be foolish. They may send a volley at any time through the snow, and one of their bullets is likely to get you."

"I'll chance it."

"It's against orders."

"I'm going anyhow. Maybe I've suddenly grown squeamish, but I mean to save that wounded German from freezing to death."

"Stop, Scott! You mustn't risk your life this way. I'll report you to Captain Colton!"

But it was too late. John had climbed up the side of the trench, and, standing in the deep snow, was feeling about for the one who groaned. Guided by the sound his hands soon touched a human body.

The fallen man was lying on his side and he was already half buried in the snow. John ran his hand along his arm and shoulder, and felt cold thick blood, clotting his sleeve. But he was yet alive, because he groaned again, and John believed from the quality of his voice that he was very young. The hurt was in the shoulder and the loss of blood had been great.

He knelt beside the wounded lad and spoke to him in English and French, and in German that he had learned recently. A faint reply came; but it was too low for him to understand. Then he knelt in the snow beside him and was just barely able to see that he had a blond youth younger than himself. Shots came from the German line as he knelt there, but they were merely random bullets whistling through the snowy gloom. He was made of tenacious material, and the danger from the flying bullets merely confirmed him in his purpose. Moreover, he could not bear to return, and listen to those groans so near him. He grasped the young German under the shoulders and dragged him to the edge of the trench. Then he called softly:

"Carstairs, Wharton! I've got him! Help me down!"

Carstairs and Wharton appeared and Carstairs said:

"Well, you light-headed Yankee, you have come back!"

"Yes, and I've brought with me what I went after. Help me down with him. Easy there now! He's hit hard in the shoulder!"

The two lifted him into the trench and John slid after him, just as a half-dozen random shots whistled over his head. There they drew the rescued youth into one of the alcoves dug in the wall and Carstairs flashed his electric torch on his face, revealing features boyish, delicate, and white as death now. His gray uniform was of richer material than usual and an iron cross was pinned upon his breast.

"A brave lad as the cross shows," said Carstairs, "and I should judge too from his appearance that he's of high rank. Maybe he's a prince or the son of a prince. You've already had adventures with two of them."

"One of whom I liked."

"He looks like a good fellow," said Wharton. "I'm glad you saved him. Rub his hands while I give him a taste of this."

John and Carstairs rubbed his palms until he opened his eyes, when Wharton put a flask to his lips and made him drink. He groaned again and tried to sit up.

"Just you lie still, Herr Katzenellenbogen," said Wharton. "You're in the hands of your friends, the enemy, but we're saving your life or rather it's been done already by the man on your left; name, John Scott; nationality, American; service, French."

Captain Colton appeared and threw a white light with his own electric torch upon the little group.

"What have you there?" he asked.

"Young German who lay groaning too near the edge of our trench," replied Carstairs. "Scott couldn't stand it, so he went out and brought him in. Fancy his name is Katzenellenbogen, Kaiserslautern, Hohenfriedberg, or something else short and simple."

Captain Colton permitted himself a grim smile.

"Your act of mercy, Scott, does honor to you," he said, "though it's no part of your business to get yourself killed helping a wounded enemy. Bring him round, then send him to hospital in rear."

He walked on, continuing his inspection of the Strangers although sure that no other attack would be made that night, and the three young men applied themselves with renewed energy to the revival of their injured captive. Wharton cut the uniform away from his shoulder and, after announcing that the bullet had gone entirely through, bound up the two wounds with considerable skill. Then he gave him another but small drink out of the flask and, as they saw the color come back into his face, they felt all the pleasure of a surgeon when he sees his efforts succeed. The boy glanced at his shoulder, and then gave the three a grateful look.

"You're all right," said Carstairs cheerfully in English. "You're guest or prisoner, whichever you choose to call it and we three are your hosts or captors. My name is Carstairs and these two assistants of mine are Wharton and Scott, distant cousins, that is to say, Yankees. It was Scott who saved you."

The boy smiled faintly. He was in truth handsome with a delicate fairness one did not see often among the Germans, who were generally cast in a sterner mold.

"And I am Leopold Kratzek," he replied in good English.

"Kratzek," said John. "Ah, you're an Austrian. Now I remember there's an Austrian field-marshal of that name."

"He is my father but he is in the East. My regiment was sent with an Austrian corp to the western front. It seems that I am in great luck. My wound is not mortal, but I should certainly have frozen to death out there if one of you had not come for me."

"Scott went, of course," said Carstairs. "He's an American and naturally a tuft-hunter. He's been making a long list of princely acquaintances recently, and he was bound to bring in the son of a field-marshal and make a friend of him, too."

"Shut up, Carstairs," said John. "You talk this way to hide your own imperfections. You know that at heart every Englishman is a snob."

"Snobby is as snobby does," laughed Carstairs. "Now, Kratzek, lie back again and we'll spread these blankets over you."

The young Austrian smiled.

"I've fallen into very good company," he said.

John, whose character was serious, felt some sadness as he looked at him. He remembered those gay Viennese who had set the torch of the great war, and how merry they were over it with their visions of quick victory and glory. Poor, gay, likable, light-headed Austrians! Brave but short-sighted, they were likely to suffer more than any other nation! The fair, handsome youth, wrapped now in the blankets, seemed to him to typify all the Austrian qualities.

"You'd better go to sleep if you can," said John. "We can't move you yet, but in time you'll reach a good hospital of ours in the rear."

"I'll obey you," said Kratzek, in the most tractable manner, and closing his eyes he soon fell asleep despite his wound.

"Now, having caught your Austrian, what are you going to do with him?" said Carstairs to John.

"Nothing for the present, but later on I'll have him taken down one of the transverse trenches to a hospital. Maybe you think I'm foolish, Carstairs, but I've an idea that I've made a friend, though I didn't have that purpose in view when I went out for him. I never think that anybody hates me unless he proves it. People as a rule don't take the time and trouble to hate and plot."

"You're right, Scott. Hating is a terribly tiresome business, and I notice that you're by nature friendly."

"Which may be because I'm American."

"Oh, well, we English are friendly, too."

"But seldom polite, although I think you're unaware of the latter fact."

"If a man doesn't know he's impolite, then he isn't. It's the intention that counts."

"We'll let it go, but I've a strong premonition that this Austrian boy is going to do me a great favor some day."

"I have premonitions, too, often, but they're invariably wrong. Now, I see an orderly coming. I hope he hasn't a message from Captain Colton for us to prowl around in the snow somewhere."

Happily, the message released them from further duty that night and bade them seek rest. Young Kratzek was lying in John's bed and was sleeping. He looked so young and so pale that the heart of his captor and rescuer was moved to pity. Light-headed the Austrians might be, but no one could deny them valor.

Just beyond the niche was another and smaller one, seldom used, owing to its extreme narrowness, but John decided that he could sleep in it. At any rate, if he fell off he would land in six or eight inches of soft snow.

The flakes were still coming down heavily. It was the biggest snow that he had yet seen in Europe and he believed that it would fall all night. They had plenty of blankets and spreading two on the shelf which was no broader than himself he lay down and put two more over him.

He was in a pleasant mental glow, because he had saved young Kratzek, forgetting the rest who lay out there under the snow. All his instincts were for mercy and gentleness, but like others, he was being hardened by war, or at least he was made forgetful. Resting in the earthen side of a trench, the horrors of the battle passed out of his mind. The white gloom was so heavy there that he could not see the other wall four feet away, and the falling flakes almost grazed his face as they passed, but he had a marvelous sense of comfort and ease, even of luxury. The caveman had fared no better, often worse, because he had no blankets, and John drew a deep sigh of content.

A gun thundered somewhere far back in the German lines, and a gun also far back in the French lines thundered in reply. Then came a random and scattering fire of rifles through the falling snow from both sides, but John was not disturbed in the least by these reports. He felt as safe in his narrow trench as if he had been a hundred miles from the field of battle, and compared, with the driving storm outside, his six feet by one of an earthen bed was all he wished. The pleasant warmth from the blankets flowed through his veins, and his limbs and senses relaxed. There was firing again, faint and from a distant point, but it was soothing now like the tune played on the little mouth-organ earlier in the evening, and he fell into a deep and peaceful slumber.

When he awoke in the morning the sun was shining in the trench, the bottom of which was covered with eight inches of snow, now slushy on top from the red beams. John felt himself restored and strong, and he stepped down into the snow and slush, having first tucked his blue-gray trousers into his high boots. He was lucky in the possession of a fine pair of boots that would turn the last drop of water, and in such times as these they were worth more than gold.

A shell screaming high overhead was his morning salutation, and then came other shells, desultory but noisy. John paid no more attention to them than if they had been distant bees buzzing. He looked at his young prisoner, Kratzek, and found that he was still sleeping, with a healthy color in his face. John was impressed anew by his youth. "Why do they let such babies come to the war?" he asked himself, but he added, "They're brave babies, though."

"Well, he's pulling along all right," said Carstairs. "I was up before you and I learned that Captain Colton sent a surgeon in the night to examine him. Wharton had done a good job with his bandages, he admitted, but he cleaned and dressed the wound and said the patient was in such a healthy condition that he would be entirely well again in a short time. He's only a young boy, isn't he, Scott?"

"Yes, I suppose that's why I have such a fatherly feeling for him."

"That, or because you brought him in from sure death. We're always attached to anyone we save."

"I mean to have him exchanged and sent back to his mother in Austria. He's bound to have a mother there and she'll thank me though she may never see me. I wish these pleasant Austrians had more sense."

Kratzek opened his eyes and looked blankly at the two young men. He strove to rise, but fell back with a low sigh of pain. Then he closed his eyes, but John saw the muscles of his face working.

"He's trying to remember," whispered Carstairs.

Memory came back to Kratzek in a few moments, and he opened his eyes again.

"I was saved by somebody last night and I think it was you," he said, looking at John. "I want to say to you that I am very grateful. I do not wish to appear boastful, but I have relatives in both the Austrian and German armies who are very powerful--ours is both a North German and South German house, and East German, too."

"That is, it's *wohlgeboren* and *hochwohlgeboren*," said Wharton, who appeared at that moment.

"Yes," said the Austrian boy, smiling faintly. "I am highborn and very highborn, although it's not my fault. You, I take it, by your accent, are American and these things, of course, don't count with you."

"I don't know, they seem to count pretty heavily with some of our women, if you can judge by the newspapers."

"Who are these men of whom you speak?" asked John.

"The chief is Prince Karl of Auersperg, who is not far from your front. I betray no military secret when I say that. I shall send word to him that you have saved my life, and, if you should fall a prisoner into German hands, he will do as much for you as you have done for me."

The Austrian boy did not notice the quick glances exchanged by the three, and he went on:

"Prince Karl of Auersperg is a general of ability, and owing to that and his very high birth, he has great influence with both emperors. You have nothing to fear from our brave Germans if you should fall into their hands, but I beg you in any event, to get word to the prince and to give him my name."

"I'll do it," replied John, but he soothed his conscience by telling himself that it was a white lie. If he should be captured for the third time Prince Karl of Auersperg was the last one whom he wanted to know of it. Neither was he pleased to hear that this medieval baron was again so near, although he did not realize why until later.

"We've talked enough now," said John, "and I'll see that food is sent you. Then it's off with you to the hospital. It's a French hospital, but they'll treat a German shoulder just as they would one of their own."

The life in the vast honeycomb of trenches was awakening fast. Two million men perhaps, devoted to the task of killing one another, crept from their burrows and stood up. Along the whole line almost of twenty score miles snow had fallen, but the rifles and cannon were firing already, spasmodic sharpshooting at some points, and fierce little battles at others.

John peered over the edge of the trench. A man was allowed to put his head in the German range but not his hand. So long as he lived he must preserve a hand which could pull the trigger or wield the bayonet.

They were not firing in the immediate front, and he had a good view of fields and low hills, deep in snow. Just before him the ground was leveled, and he saw many raised places in the snow there. He knew that bodies lay beneath, and once more he shuddered violently. But the world was full of beauty that morning. The sun was a vast sheet of gold, giving a luminous tint to the snow, and two clusters of trees, covered to the last bough and twig with snow, were a delicate tracery of white, shot at times by the sun with a pale yellow glow like that of a rose. On the horizon a faint misty smoke, the color of silver, was rising, and he knew that it came from the cooking fires of the Germans.

It reminded him that he was very hungry. Cave life under fire, if it did not kill a man, gave him a ferocious appetite, and turning into one of the transverse trenches he followed a stream of the Strangers who were already on the way to their hotel.

The narrow cut led them nearly a mile, and then they came out in a valley the edges of which were fringed with beeches. But in the wide space within the valley most of the snow had been cleared away and enormous automobile kitchens stood giving forth the pleasant odors of food and drink. At one side officers were already satisfying their hunger and farther on men were doing the same. They were within easy range of the German guns, but it was not the habit of either side to send morning shells unless a direct attack was to be made.

John had no thought of danger. Youth was youth and one could get hardened to anything. He had been surprised more than once in this war to find how his spirits could go from the depths to the heights and now they were of the best. He was full of life and the world was very beautiful that morning. It was the fair land of France again, but it was under a thick robe of snow, the golden tint on the white, as the large yellow sun slowly sailed clear of the high hills on their right.

General Vaugirard stood near the first of the wagons, drinking cup after cup of hot steaming coffee, and devouring thick slices of bread and butter. He wore a long blue overcoat over his uniform, and high boots. But the dominant note was given to his appearance by the thick white beard which seemed to be touched with a light silver frost. Under the great thatch of eyebrow the keen little eyes twinkled. He made John think of a huge, white and inoffensive bear.

The general's roving eye caught sight of Scott and he exclaimed:

"Come here, you young Yankee! I hear that you distinguished yourself last night by saving the life of one of our enemies, thus enabling him perhaps to fight against us once more."

"I beg your pardon, General," said John, "but I'm no Yankee."

"What, denying your birthright! I never heard an American do that before! Everybody knows you're a Yankee."

"Pardon me. General, you and all other Europeans make a mistake about the Yankees. At home the people of the Southern States generally apply it to those living in the Northern states, but in the North it is carried still further and is properly applied to the residents of the six New England states. I don't come from one of those states, and so I'm not in a real sense a Yankee."

"What, sir, have I, a Frenchman, to do with your local distinctions? Yankees you all are and Yankee you shall remain. It's a fine name, and from what I've seen in this war you're great fighting men, worthy to stand with Frenchmen."

"Thank you for the compliment, General," said John, smiling. "Hereafter I shall always remain a Yankee."

"And now do you and your friends take your food there with de Rougemont. I've had my breakfast, and a big and good one it was. I'm going to the edge of the hill and use my glasses."

He waddled away, looking more than ever an enormous, good-natured bear. John's heart, as always, warmed to him. Truly he was the father of his children, ten thousand or more, who fought around him, and for whose welfare he had a most vigilant eye and mind.

The three joined a group of the Strangers, Captain Colton at their head, and they stood there together, eating and drinking, their appetites made wonderfully keen by the sharp morning and a hard life in the open air. Bougainville, the little colonel, came from the next valley and remained with them awhile. He was almost the color of an Indian now, but his uniform was remarkably trim and clean and he bore himself with dignity. He was distinctly a personality and John knew that no one would care to undertake liberties with him.

In the long months following the battle on the Marne Bougainville had done great deeds. Again and again he had thrown his regiment into some weak spot in the line just at the right moment. He seemed, like Napoleon and Stonewall Jackson, to have an extraordinary, intuitive power of divining the enemy's intentions, and General Vaugirard, to whose command his regiment belonged, never hesitated to consult him and often took his advice. "Ah, that child of Montmartre!" he would say. "He will go far, if he does not meet a shell too soon. He keeps a hand of steel on his regiment, there is no discipline sterner than his, and yet his men love him."

Bougainville showed pleasure at seeing John again, and gave him his hand American fashion.

"We both still live," he said briefly.

"And hope for complete victory."

"We do," said Bougainville, earnestly, "but it will take all the strength of the allied nations to achieve it. Much has happened, Monsieur Scott, since we stood that day in the lantern of Basilique du Sacré-Coeur on the Butte Montmartre and saw the Prussian cavalry riding toward Paris."

"But what has happened is much less than that which will happen before this war is over."

"You speak a great truth, Monsieur Scott. And now I must go. Hearing that the Strangers were in this valley I wished to come and see with my own eyes that you were alive and well. I have seen and I am glad."

He saluted, Captain Colton and the others saluted in return, and then he walked over the hill to his own "children."

"An antique! An old Roman! Spirit defying death," said Captain Colton looking after him.

"He has impressed me that way, too, sir," said John. But his mind quickly left Bougainville, and turned to the message that Weber had brought the night before. He was glad that Julie Lannes would be so near again, and yet he was sorry. He had not been sorry when he first heard it, but the apprehension had come later. He tried to trace the cause, and then he remembered the name of Auersperg, the prince whom his cousin, the Austrian captive, had said was near. He sought to laugh at himself for his fears. The mental connection was too vague, he said, but the relieving laughter would not come.

John hoped that a lucky chance might bring Lannes, and involuntarily he looked up at the heavens. But they were clear of aeroplanes. The heavy snow of the night before had driven in the hosts of the air, and they had not reappeared.

Then John resolved to go to Chastel himself. He did not know how he would go or what he would do when he got there, but the impulse was strong and it remained with him.

3

JULIE'S COMING

THAT DAY, the next night and the next day passed without any event save the usual desultory firing of cannon and rifles. Many men were killed and more were wounded by the sharpshooters. Little battles were fought at distant points along the lines, the Allies winning some while the Germans were victorious in others, but the result was nothing. The deadlock was unbroken.

Meanwhile the weather turned somewhat warmer and the melting snow poured fresh deluges of water into the trenches. Most of it was pumped out, but it would sink back into the ground and return. John again gave thanks for the splendid pair of high boots that he wore, and also he often searched the air for Lannes. But he saw no sign of the lithe and swift *Arrow* and his anxiety for Julie increased steadily. She must now be at Chastel, but he had not yet found any excuse that would release him from the trenches and let him go there.

He inquired for Weber, but no one had seen or heard of him again.

No doubt he was far away on some perilous mission, serving France on the ground as Lannes served her in the air.

Young Kratzek in the hospital was improving fast and John secured leave of absence long enough to see him once. He was fervent in his gratitude and renewed his promises that somehow and somewhere he would surely repay young Scott. News that he was alive, but a prisoner, had reached the German lines and already an exchange for him had been arranged, the Germans, owing to his rank, being willing to return a French brigadier in his place. The prospect filled him with happiness and he talked much. John noticed once more how very young he was, not much more than seventeen, and with manners decidedly boyish. He had the utmost confidence in the success of Germany and Austria, despite the check at the Marne, and talked freely of another advance. John led him adroitly to his cousin of Auersperg, of whom he wished to hear more. He soon discovered that Auersperg was a very great prince to Kratzek.

"I stand in some awe of him. I need scarcely tell you that Herr Scott, my captor," he said, "because he represents so much. Ah, the history and the legends clustering about our house, that goes far back into the dim ages! The Auerspergs were counts and princes of the Holy Roman Empire, and they have been grand dukes. They have decided the choice of more than one emperor at Frankfort, and they have stood with the highest when they were crowned at Augsburg. Please don't think I am boasting for myself, Herr Scott, it is only for my cousin, the august Prince Karl, *hochwohlgeboren*!"

"I understand," said John, smiling. "But I want to tell you, Leopold Kratzek, that I'm *hochwohlgeboren* myself."

"Why, how is that? You are neither German nor Austrian."

"No, I'm American, but I'm very highborn nevertheless. There are a hundred millions of us and all of us are very highborn not excepting our colored people, many of whom are descended from African princes who have a power over their people not approached by either of the kaisers."

The boy smiled.

"Now, I know you jest," he said. "You have no classes, but I've heard that all of you claim to be kings."

John saw that he had made no impression upon him. Frank, honest and brave, an Auersperg was nevertheless in the boy's mind an Auersperg, something superior, a product of untold centuries, a small and sublimated group of the human race to which nothing else could aspire, not even talent, learning, courage and honesty. To all Auerspergs, Napoleon and Shakespeare were mere men of genius, to be patronized. John smiled, too. He did not feel hurt at all. In his turn he felt a superiority, a superiority of perception, and a superiority in the sense of proportion.

"Prince Karl of Auersperg is always resolved to maintain his pride of blood, is he not?" he asked.

"He considers it his duty. The head of a house that has been princely for fifteen centuries could not do less. He could never forget or forgive an insult to his person."

"If he were insulted he would hold that all the Auerspergs who were now living and all who had lived in the last fifteen hundred years were insulted also."

"Undoubtedly!" replied Kratzek, with great emphasis.

"I merely wished to know," said John, gravely, "in order that I may know how to bear myself in case I should meet Prince Karl of Auersperg"--he had not told that he had met him already--"and now I'm going to tell you good-by, Leopold. I think it likely that I shall be sent away on a mission and before I return it is probable that you will be exchanged."

"Good-by, Mr. Scott. Don't forget my promise. If you should ever fall into our hands please try to communicate with me."

John returned to his trench. He had been very thoughtful that day, and he had evolved a plan. A considerable body of wounded soldiers were to be sent to Chastel, and as they must have a guard he had asked Captain Colton to use his influence with General Vaugirard and have him appointed a member of the guard.

Now he found Captain Colton sitting in his little alcove smoking one of his eternal cigarettes and looking very contented. He took an especially long puff when he saw John and looked at him quizzically.

"Well, Scott!" he said.

"Well, sir!" said John.

"General Vaugirard thinks your desire to guard wounded, see to their welfare, great credit to you."

"I thank him, sir, through you."

"Approve of such zeal myself."

"I thank you in person."

"Did not tell him--French girl, Mademoiselle Julie Lannes, also going to Chastel to attend to wounded. Handsome girl, wonderfully handsome girl, don't you think so, Scott?"

"I do, sir," said John, reddening.

"You and she--going to Chastel about same time. Remarkable coincidence, but nothing in it, of course, just coincidence."

"It's not a coincidence, sir. You've always been a friend to me. Captain Colton, and I'm willing to tell you that I've sought this mission to Chastel because Mademoiselle Julie Lannes is there, or is going there, and for no other reason whatever. I'm afraid she's in danger, and anyway I long for a sight of her face as we long for the sun after a storm."

Captain Colton, with his cigarette poised between his thumb and forefinger, looked John up and down.

"Good!" he said. "Frank statement of truth--I knew already. Nothing for you to be ashamed of. If girl beautiful and noble as Mademoiselle Julie Lannes looked at me as she has looked at you I'd break down walls and run gantlets to reach her. Go, John, boy. Luck to you in all the things in which you wish luck."

He held out his hand and John wrung it. And so, the terse captain himself had a soft heart which he seldom showed!

The convoy started the next morning, John with five soldiers in an armored automobile bringing up the rear. There were other men on the flank and in front, and a captain commanded. The day was wintry and gloomy. Heavy clouds obscured the sky, and the slush was deep in the roads. A desolate wind moaned through the leafless trees, and afar the cannon grumbled and groaned.

But neither the somber day nor the melancholy convoy affected John's spirits. Chastel, a village of light--light for him--would be at the end of his journey.

Despite mud, slush and snow, traveling was pleasant. The automobile had made wonderful changes. One could go almost anywhere in it, and its daring drivers whisked it gaily over fields, through forests and up hills, which in reality could be called mountains. War had merely increased their enterprise, and they took all kinds of risks, usually with success.

John was very comfortable now, as he leaned back in the armored car, driven by a young Frenchman. He wore a heavy blue overcoat over his uniform, and his only weapon was a powerful automatic revolver in his belt, but it was enough. The ambulances, filled with wounded, stretched a half-mile in front of him, but he had grown so used to such sights that they did not move him long. Moreover in this war a man was not dead until he *was* dead. The small bullets of the high-powered rifle either killed or harmed but little. It was the shrapnel that tore.

The road led across low hills, and down slopes which he knew were kissed by a warm sun in summer. It was here that the vines flourished, but the snow could not hide the fact that it was torn and trampled now. Huge armies had surged back and forth over it, and yet John, who was of a thoughtful mind, knew that in a few more summers it would be as it had been before. In this warm and watered France Nature would clothe the earth in a green robe which winter itself could not wholly drive away.

A reader of history, he knew that Europe had been torn and ravaged by war, times past counting, and yet geologically it was among the youngest and freshest of lands. Everything would pass and new youth would take the place of the youth that the shells and bullets were now carrying away.

He shook himself. Reflections like these were for men of middle years. The tide of his own youth flowed back upon him and the world, even under snow and with stray guns thundering behind him, was full of splendor. Moreover, there was the village of Chastel before him! Chastel! Chastel! He had never heard of it until two or three days ago, and yet it now loomed in his mind as large as Paris or New York. Julie must have arrived already, and he would see her again after so many months of hideous war, but deep down in his mind persisted the belief that she should not have come. Lannes must have had some reason that he could not surmise, or he would not have written the letter asking her to meet him at Chastel.

The village, he learned from one of the men in the automobile, was only ten miles away and it was built upon a broad, low hill at the base of which a little river flowed. It was very ancient. A town of the Belgæ stood there in Cæsar's time, but it contained not more than two thousand inhabitants, and its chief feature was a very beautiful Gothic cathedral.

John's automobile could have reached Chastel in less than an hour, despite the snow and the slush, but the train of the wounded was compelled to move slowly, and he must keep with it. Meanwhile he scanned the sky with powerful glasses, which he had been careful to secure after his escape from Auersperg. Nearly all officers carried strong glasses in this war, and yet even to the keenest eyes the hosts of the air were visible only in part.

John now and then saw telephone wires running through the clumps of forest and across the fields. There was a perfect web of them, reaching all the way from Alsace and the Forest of Argonne to the sea. Generals talked to one another over them, and over these wires the signal officers sent messages to the men in the batteries telling them how to fire their guns.

The telegraph, too, was at work. The wires were clicking everywhere, and the air was filled also with messages which went on no wires at all, but which took invisible wings unto themselves. The wireless, despite its constant use, remained a mystery and wonder to John. One of his most vivid memories was that night on the roof of the château, when Wharton talked through space to the German generals, and learned their plans.

He looked up now and his eyes were shut, but he almost fancied that he could see the words passing in clouds over his head, written on nothing, but there, nevertheless, the most mysterious and, in some ways, the most powerful part of the hosts of the air, the hosts that within a generation had changed the ways of armies and battles. He opened his eyes and found himself searching for aeroplanes, the most tangible portion of those hosts of the air, with which man had to fight. He saw several behind him, where the French and German lines almost met, but there was no shape resembling the *Arrow*.

The aeroplanes and Zeppelins had been much less active since winter had come in full tide. They were essentially birds of sunshine and fair weather, liking but little clouds and storms. And as the skies still looked very threatening John judged that they would not be abroad much that day. The conditions were far from promising, as a heavy massing of the clouds in the southwest indicated more snow.

"There is Chastel, sir," said Mallet, his chauffeur. "You can see the steeple of the cathedral shining through the clouds."

John's eyes followed the pointing finger, and he caught a high gleam, although all beneath was a mass of floating gray mist. But he knew it was a few beams of the sun piercing through the clouds and striking upon some solid object. He put the glasses to his eyes and then he was able to discern an old, old town, standing on a cliff above a stream that he would have called a creek at home. Some of the houses were of stone, and others were of timber and concrete, but it was evident that war had passed already over Chastel. As he rode nearer he beheld buildings ruined by shells or fire. Many of them seemed to be razed almost level with the ground. The evidences of battle were everywhere. He surmised that it had been held for a while by the Germans on their retreat from the Marne, and that the lighting there had been desperate.

In the lower ground on the near side of the stream were many small board houses arranged in a square, and these he knew were the hospital. He would remain there until the last of the wounded were discharged, and then he would enter Chastel. Mallet informed him that his surmises were correct and he saw for himself that the head of the train had already turned into the square around which the little board houses were built.

The transferring of the hurt, took nearly all the morning, and John faithfully performed his part. There was Chastel only a few hundred yards away, now clearly visible despite the massive clouds that floated persistently across the sky. Yet he made no attempt to reach it until his work was done, nor did he speak of it, not even to the chauffeur, Mallet, of whom he had made a good friend.

Near noon, the task finished, he ate luncheon and started toward Chastel. His orders from Captain Colton allowed him much liberty, and he was not compelled to account to anyone, when he chose to enter the town. He crossed the stream, muddy from the melting snow, on a small stone bridge, which he believed from its steep arch must date almost back to the time of the Romans, and pausing on the other side looked up once more at Chastel. He had no doubt that, seen in the sunshine and as it was, it had been both picturesque and beautiful. But now it lay half in ruins, under a sullen sky, and he beheld no sign of life. Just above him within its grounds stood a large château, that had been riven through and through by shells. The walls looked as if they were ready to fall apart and John shivered a little. Farther on was a public building of some kind, destroyed by fire, all save the walls which stood, blackened and desolate, and now he saw that the cathedral too had been damaged.

A flake of snow, large and damp, settled on his hand. The clouds were massing, directly over his head, and he feared another fall. It was unfortunate, but nothing could drive him back, and finding a flight of stone steps he ascended them and entered the village.

Chastel had looked somber from the plain below, where some of the effect, John had thought, might be due to distance, but here it was a silent ruin, tragic and terrible. Over this village, once so neat and trim, as he could easily see, war had swept in its most hideous fashion. Houses were riddled and the gray light showed through them from wall to wall where the great shells had passed. A bronze statue standing in a fountain in the center of the little place or square had been struck, and it lay prone and shattered in the water.

The first flakes of the new snow began to fall, and the sinister sky, heavy with clouds, took on the darkness of twilight, although night was far away. Yet the huge rents and holes in the houses and the fallen masonry seemed to grow more distinct in the gloom. The village consisted chiefly of one long street, and as John looked up and down it, he did not see a single human being. Nothing was visible to him but the iron hoof of war crushing everything under it, and he shuddered violently.

The snow began to drive, whipped by a bitter wind, and he drew the heavy blue overcoat closely about him. The shuddering which was not of the snow and the cold, passed, but his heart was ice. The abandoned town over which Germans and French had fought oppressed him like a nightmare. What had become of Julie? Why had Philip asked her to meet him at such a place? There was the hospital, but it was in the plain below, where lights now shone faintly through the heavy gray air and the driving snow.

Surely Lannes could not have made any mistake! John had learned to trust his judgment thoroughly and Philip, too, knew the country so well. If he had sent for Julie to come to Chastel he must have had a good reason for it, although the snow was bound to delay the coming of the *Arrow* to meet her. If she had reached Chastel she would remain there, and not go to the hospital in the plain below. She trusted her brother as implicitly as John did.

John, taking thought with himself, concluded that she must be now in the village. It was not possible that Chastel, silent as it was and desolate as it seemed, could be entirely deserted. Although leaving ruin behind, the fury of battle had passed and some of the people would return to their homes. Chastel lay behind the French lines, a great hospital camp was not far away, and the fear of further German invasion could not be present now.

He put one hand in his overcoat pocket over the butt of the automatic, and then, remembering how General Vaugirard whistled, he too whistled, not for want of thought but to encourage himself, to make his heart beat a little less violently, and to hear a cheerful sound where there was nothing else but the soft swish of the snow and the desolate moaning of the wind among the ruins.

He walked down the main street, and unconsciously stopped whistling. Then the awful silence and desolation brooded over him again. The storm was thickening, and the lights in the plain below were entirely gone now. He was not yet able to find any proof of human life in Chastel, and, after all, the fighting in the town might have been so recent and so fierce that not one of the inhabitants yet dared to return. The thought made his heart throb painfully. What, then, had become of Julie?

He stopped before the cathedral, and looked up at the lofty Gothic spire which seemed to tower above the whirling snow. As well as he could see some damage had been done to the roof by shells, but the beautiful stained-glass windows were uninjured. He stood there gazing, and he knew in his heart that he was looking for a sign, like that which he and Lannes had seen on the Arc de Triomphe when the fortunes of France seemed lost forever.

A stalwart figure suddenly emerged from the white gloom and heavy hands were laid upon him. John's own fingers in his overcoat pocket tightened over the automatic, but the hands on his shoulders were those of friendship.

"Ah, it is thou, Monsieur Scott!" exclaimed a deep voice. "The master has not come but thou art thrice welcome in his place!"

It was Picard, no less than Antoine Picard himself, looming white and gigantic through the storm, and John could not doubt the genuine warmth in his voice. He was in truth welcome and he knew it. As Picard's hands dropped from his shoulders he seized them in his and wrung them hard.

"Mademoiselle Julie!" he exclaimed. "What of her? Did she come? Or have you only come in her place?"

"She is here, sir! In the church with Suzanne, my daughter. We arrived two hours ago. I wanted to go on to the camp that we could see in the plain below, but Mademoiselle Lannes would not hear of it. It was here that Monsieur Philip wished her to meet him, and if she went on he would miss her. We expected to find food and rooms, but, my God, sir, the town is deserted! Most of the houses have been shot to pieces by the artillery and if people are here we cannot find them. Because of that we have taken shelter, for the present, in the church."

But John in his eagerness was already pushing open one of the huge bronze doors, and Picard, brushing some of the snow from his clothes, followed him. The door swung shut behind them both, and he stood beside one of the pews staring into the dusky interior.

But his eyes became used to the gloom, and soon it did not seem so somber as it was outside. Instead the light from the stained-glass windows made the mists and shadows luminous. A nave, the lofty pillars dividing it from the side aisles, the choir and the altar emerged slowly into view. From the walls pictures of the Madonna and the saints, unstained and untouched, looked down upon him. One of the candles near the altar had been lighted, and it burned with a steady, beckoning flame.

The cathedral, a great building for a small town, as happens so often in Europe, presented a warm and cheerful interior to John. It seemed to him soon after the huge bronze door sank into place behind him that war, cold, desolation and loneliness were shut out. The luminous glow streaming through the stained glass windows and the candle burning near the altar were beacons.

Then he saw Julie, sitting wrapped in a heavy cloak, in one of the pews before the choir, and the grim Suzanne, also shrouded in a heavy cloak, sat beside her. John's heart was in a glow. He knew now that he loved his comrade Philip's sister. Two or three of the golden curls escaping from her hood, fell down her back, and they were twined about his heart. He knew too that it was not the light from the stained windows, but Julie herself who had filled the church with splendor. She was to John a young goddess, perfect in her beauty, one who could do no wrong. His love had all the tenderness and purity of young love, the poetic love that comes only to youth.

But when he realized that Julie Lannes had become so much to him he felt a sudden shyness, and he let the gigantic Picard lead the way. They had made no noise in opening and closing the door, and their boots had been soundless on the stone floor.

"The American, Lieutenant Scott, Mademoiselle," said Picard respectfully.

John saw her little start of surprise, but when she stood up she was quite self-possessed. Her color was a little deeper than usual, but it might be the luminous glow from the stained-glass windows, or the cloak of dark red which wrapped her from chin to feet may have given that added touch.

She had been weary and anxious, and John thought he detected a gleam of welcome in her glance. At least it pleased him to think so. The stern Suzanne had given him a startled look, but the glance seemed to John less hostile than it used to be.

"I was told, Miss Lannes," said John in English, "that you had received a letter from your brother, Philip, to meet him here in Chastel. One Weber, an Alsatian, an able and trustworthy man whom I know, gave me the news."

It had often been his habit, when speaking his own language, to call her, American fashion, "Miss" instead of "Mademoiselle," and now she smiled at the little, remembered touch.

"It was Mr. Weber who brought the letter to me in Paris, Mr. Scott," she said. "You know it was my wish to serve our brave soldiers hurt in battle, and I was not surprised that the letter from Philip should come."

"In what manner did you arrive here?"

"In a small automobile. It is standing behind the cathedral now. Antoine is an excellent driver. But, Oh, Mr. Scott, it has been a strange and lonely ride! Once we thought we were going to be captured. As we passed through a forest Antoine was quite sure that he caught a gleam of German lances far away, but much too near for assurance, and he drove the motor forward at a great rate."

"And then you arrived in Chastel?"

"Yes, Mr. Scott, then we came to Chastel."

"But you did not see what you expected to see."

She shivered and the brilliant color left her face for a moment.

"No, Mr. Scott, I did not find what I thought would be here. Philip had not come, but that did not alarm me so much, and I knew that for awhile the snow had made the flight of aeroplanes impossible. No, it was not the absence of Philip that filled me with terror. Surely when he sent for me he did not anticipate such fighting as must have occurred here so recently."

"He would never have drawn you into danger."

"I know it, and that is why I am so puzzled and so full of apprehension. The sight of Chastel appalls me and it has had its influence upon Antoine and Suzanne, strong as they are. We saw ruins, Mr. Scott, the terrible path of battle, and no human being until you came."

"I had the same feeling myself, nor did I see life either until I met Antoine, Miss Julie, if I may call you so instead of Miss Lannes?"

"Yes, of course, Mr. Scott. But what does it mean? Why haven't the people come back?"

They were still talking in English, and Suzanne's customary look had returned to her face in all its grimness, but they went on, unmindful of her.

"I confess, Miss Julie, I don't understand it," replied John. "The fighting here seems to have occurred within the last two or three days. It is behind our lines and I did not hear of it, but so much has happens of which we do not hear, and there has been so much shifting of the lines in recent days that a battle could easily have occurred at Chastel without my knowledge. And the shock of cannon fire with the enormous guns now used is so tremendous that the fleeing people may not have recovered from it yet. Doubtless they will return tomorrow or the next day."

"I hope so, Mr. Scott. A ruined town with nobody in it oppresses terribly."

A sudden thought stabbed at John's heart. It was possible that the people of Chastel did not return because they were fearing another attack. If Antoine had caught the gleam of German lances in the wood then a considerable German force might be behind the French lines. Snowstorms formed a good cover for secret operations.

Julie noticed the passing shadow in his face and she knew it to be the sign of alarm.

"What is it, Mr. Scott?" she asked. "Do you know of any danger?"

"No," he replied truthfully, because he had dismissed his thought as incredible, "but you will not remain here, Miss Julie. You and your servant will go to the hospital camp, will you not? It is not much more than a mile beyond the river."

But to his surprise she shook her head.

"I must stay in Chastel," she said. "It is here that Philip wished me to come, and if I am not here when he arrives he will not know where to find me. And there is no danger. You know that, Mr. Scott. If Antoine really saw German lances as he claims, it is no proof that German horsemen will come to Chastel, running into danger. What have they to gain by raiding a ruined town?"

"There is much reason in what you say. Certainly it would avail the Germans nothing to gallop through shattered Chastel in a snowstorm. But you can't spend the night in the church. I've no doubt that we can find bed and board for all of us in some abandoned house."

The driving snow had reconciled John somewhat to the idea of Julie passing the night in Chastel. The road leading down to the river was steep and the bridge over which he had crossed was narrow with a very high arch. A motor might easily miss the way in the darkening storm, and then meet disaster.

Julie looked at him inquiringly as if she wished his indorsement of her plan, although her lips were closed tightly.

"Of course you'll stay, Miss Julie," he said, "and I'll stay too, although I'm not invited."

"You're invited now."

"Thanks. Consider me a follower, or rather a dragoman, to use the eastern term."

Then he said to Antoine in French:

"Mademoiselle Lannes is resolved to remain tonight in Chastel. She thinks that if her brother were to come her absence would upset all his plans."

Picard nodded. His was the soul of loyalty.

"It is right," he said. "It is here that Monsieur Philip expects to find her and we can guard her."

John liked the inclusive "we."

"And now to work, Antoine and Suzanne," he said. "We've agreed that we can't spend the night in the cathedral. Perhaps there is no better refuge so far as the storm is concerned, but a pew is not a good bed, except for hardened old soldiers like you and me, Antoine."

"No, Mr. Scott, it is not."

"Then I suggest that we leave Mademoiselle Lannes and Suzanne here while we look for shelter."

But Julie would not agree. They must all go out together. What was a little snow? Should a Lannes mind it? She drew her great red cloak more closely around her and led the way from the choir to the bronze doors, the others following in silence.

John felt that Julie had shown much decision and firmness. When she had declared that she would not remain in the church her tone and manner were wonderfully like those of her brother Philip. She was altogether worthy of the name of Lannes, and the fact appealed strongly to young Scott, who liked strength and courage.

When they were outside they saw that the storm had increased. The snow was driving so thickly that they could not see fifty yards ahead, and their quest of a house for the night would be difficult. But the lofty steeple of the church with its protecting cross still towered above them and John felt, if their search was vain, that the cathedral would always be there to shelter them. Doubtless the provident Picard also had provisions in the motor.

"I believe you told me your machine was behind the cathedral, Antoine," he said. "We ought first to take a look at it, and see that it's all right."

"That's very true, sir," replied Picard. "Shall we not go there and see it, Mademoiselle Julie?"

She nodded and they passed to the rear of the cathedral, where the machine stood under a shed. It was a small limousine with a powerful body, and John, although knowing little of automobiles, liked its looks.

"How about the gasoline supply?" he asked Picard.

"Enough, sir, for a long journey."

"You've brought food?"

"Food and wine both, sir, under the seats."

"That's very good, but I knew you'd be far-seeing, Picard. If we don't find a good place we can take the supplies and return to the cathedral."

"But we will find lodgings, Sir Jean the Scott," said Julie, catching the trick of the name from her brother. "I command you to lead the way and discover them."

Her dark red cloak was now white with the driven snow, and her face, rosy with the cold, looked from a dark red hood, also turned white. John saw that her eyes laughed. He realized suddenly that she felt neither fear nor apprehension. He had discovered a new quality, the same heroic soul that her brother Philip had, the unquenchable courage of the great marshal. He realized that she found a certain enjoyment in the situation, that the spirit of adventure was upon her. His own pulses leaped and his soul responded.

"Come on," he said in a strong voice. "If there's a habitation in this place fit for you I'll find it." John had resumed command, but Julie walked at his elbow, a brave and strong lieutenant. The two Picards followed close behind. Suzanne, at this moment, when the resources of Scott were needed so much, had relaxed somewhat of her grimness. She and Antoine said nothing as they bent their heads to the snow. Unconsciously they had resigned decision and leadership to the young pair who walked before them.

John glanced toward the river and the plain beyond, but he merely looked into a wall, cold, white and impenetrable. No ray of light or life came from it. The hospital camp had been blotted out completely. But from the north came a faint sullen note, and he knew that it was the throb of a great gun. Julie heard it too.

"They're still firing," she said.

"Yes, but it may not be snowing so hard a few miles away from here. I discovered when I was up in the air with Philip that the air moves in eddies and gusts and currents like the ocean, and that it has bays and straits, and this may be a narrow strait of snow that envelops us here. Hear that! Guns to the south, too! One side is shelling the other's trenches. You remember how it was in all the long fighting that we call the Battle of the Marne. Day and night, night and day the guns thundered and crashed. I seemed when I slept to hear 'em in my dreams. They never stopped."

"It makes me, too, think of that time, Mr. Scott, except that this is winter and that was summer. The cloud of battle is just the same."

"But the results are much less. It's a deadlock, and has been a deadlock for months. I don't expect anything decisive until spring, and maybe not then. Here is a good house, Miss Julie. It looks as if the mayor, or Chastel's banker might have lived here. Suppose we try it."

But the house had been stripped. All the rooms were cold and bare, and in the rear a huge shell had exploded leaving yawning gaps in the walls, through which the snow was driving fast. Julie shivered.

"Let's go away from it," she said. "I couldn't sleep in this house. It's continually talking to us in a language I don't like to hear."

"I don't hear its talk," said John, "but I see its ghosts walking, and I'm as anxious to get away from it as you are."

Nor were Antoine and Suzanne reluctant, and they hurried out to enter another house which had suffered a similar fate. They passed through a half-dozen, all torn and shattered by monster shells, and at last they came to one which had before it a stretch of grass, a pebbled walk, a fountain, now dry, and benches painted green, under their covering of snow.

"An inn!" said John. "This is surely Chastel's hotel. Either the de l'Europe, the Grand or the Hollande, because more than half the hotels in Europe bear one or the other of those names. Is it not fitting, Miss Julie, that we should enter and take our rest in an inn?"

She looked at it with sparkling eyes. Again the spirit of adventure was high within her.

"It seems to be undamaged," she said. "Perhaps we'll find someone there."

John shook his head.

"No, Miss Julie," he said, "I'm convinced that it's silent and alone. You'll observe that no smoke is rising from any of its chimneys, and every window that we can see is dark."

"What do you say, Antoine, and you Suzanne?" asked Julie.

"It is evident, since the inn has no other guests, that we have been sent here by the Supreme Power, for what purpose I know not," replied Suzanne, devoutly.

"Then there is no need to delay longer," said John, and, leading the way up the pebbled walk, he pushed open the central door.

4

THE HOTEL AT CHASTEL

JOHN WAS fast finding that in a crowded country like Europe, suddenly ravaged by war, nothing was more common than abandoned houses. People were continually fleeing at a moment's warning. He had already made use of two or three, at a time when they were needed most, and here was another awaiting him. Before he pushed open the door he had already read above it, despite the incrustations of snow, the sign, "Hôtel de l'Europe," and he felt intuitively that they were coming into good quarters. He was so confident of it that his cheerful mood deepened, turned in fact into joyousness.

As he held open the door he took off his cap, bowed low and said:

"Enter my humble hôtel, Madame la Princesse. Our guests are all too few now, but I promise you, Your Highness, that you and your entourage shall have the best the house affords. Behold, the orchestra began the moment you entered!"

As he spoke the deep thunder of guns came from invisible points along the long battle-line. The firing of the cannon was far away but the jarring of the air was distinct in Chastel, and the windows of the hotel shook in their frames. John and Julie had become so used to it that it merely heightened their fantastic mood.

"Yours is, in truth, a most welcome hotel," she said, "and I see that we shall not be annoyed by other guests."

She shook the snow from her hood and cloak and entered, and Picard and Suzanne, also divesting themselves of snow coverings, followed her. Then John too went in, and once more closed a door between them and the storm. He noticed that the great Antoine gave him a glance of strong approval, and even the somber Suzanne seemed to be thawing.

John was sorry that the European hotels did not have a big lobby after the American fashion. It would have given them a welcome now, but all was as usual in the Hôtel de l'Europe, Chastel. There was the small office for the cashier, and the smaller one for the bookkeeper. Near them was the bureau and upon it lay an open register. Through an open door beyond, the smoking-room was visible, and from where he stood John could see French and English illustrated weeklies lying upon the tables. Nothing had been taken, nothing was in disorder, the hotel was complete, save that it was as bare as *Crusoe's* deserted island. But John did not feel any loneliness. Julie and the two Picards were with him, and the aspect of the Hôtel de l'Europe changed all at once.

"We'll register first," said John. "I know it's customary to send a waiter to the rooms for the names, but as our waiters have all gone out we'll use the book now."

Pen and ink stood beside the register and he wrote in a bold hand:

Mademoiselle Julie Lannes, Paris, France. Mademoiselle Suzanne Picard, Paris, France. Monsieur Antoine Picard, Paris, France. Mr. John Scott, New York, U.S.A.

Julie looked over his shoulder.

"It is well," she said. "If Philip arrives perhaps he will come to the hotel and see our names registered here."

"And we'll reserve a good room for him," said John, "but although I don't want to appear a pessimist, Miss Julie, I don't think he'll come just now, at least not in the *Arrow*. All aeroplane, balloon and Zeppelin trains have stopped running during the blizzard. Blizzard is an American word of ours meaning a driving storm. It's expressive, and it can be used with advantage in Europe. What accommodations do you wish, Madame la Princesse?"

"A sitting-room, a bedroom and a bath for myself, and a room each for my maid, Suzanne, and my faithful retainer, her father, Antoine Picard."

"You shall have all that you wish and more," said John, and then dropping into his usual tone he said: "I think we'd better look over the rooms together. It's barely possible some looter may be prowling in the house. Of course, the electric power is cut off, but Suzanne will know where to find candles, and we can provide for all the light we need."

He thought of light, because the heavy storm outside kept the hotel in shadow, and he knew that when night came, depression and gloom would settle upon them, unless they found some way to dispel the darkness. Despite the silence of the hotel they had a sense of comfort. They had been oppressed in the cathedral by its majesty and religious gloom, but this was the haunt of men and women who used to come in cheerfully from the day's business and who laughed and talked in rooms and on the stairways.

John's imaginative mind was alive at once. He beheld pleasant specters all about him. Chastel was off the great highways, but many quiet tourists must have come here. The beautiful cathedral, the picturesque situation of the little town above the little river and the very ancient Gothic buildings must have been an attraction to the knowing. He could shut his eyes and see them now, many of them his own countrymen and countrywomen, walking in the halls after a day of sightseeing, comparing notes, or looking through the windows down at the little river that foamed below. Yes, Chastel had been a pleasant town and one could pass many days in right company in its Hôtel de l'Europe.

"What are you smiling at, Mr. John?" asked Julie.

It was the first time she had called him "Mr. John," the equivalent for his "Miss Julie," and he liked it. But he hid his pleasure and apparently took no notice of it.

"I was seeing our hotel in times of peace," he said. "It was a sort of mental transference, I suppose, but the place looked good to me. It was crowded with people, many of whom were from America, and some of whom I would like to know. I've never had a horror of tourists--in fact I think the horror of them that most people pretend to feel is a sort of affectation, a false attempt at superiority--and I always liked, when I was a sightseer myself, to come back to the hotel in the evening and meet the cheerful crowd full of chatter and gossip."

"That is what I should want to do if ever I should go to America. They say that your distances there are great and your hotels large and bright. I shouldn't want to miss seeing the people in the evenings under the blazing electric lights."

"You'll see them, Miss Julie, because I know that you're going to America some time or other."

They were speaking in English again and Suzanne, wrapped in a gray cloak and looking very large, assumed her old grim look. John glanced at her and for the moment he was just a little afraid of her. He saw her eyes saying very plainly: "You're an American and a foreigner and my mistress, Mademoiselle Julie Lannes, a very young girl, is French. You should not be talking together at all, and if you were not so necessary to us in our hour of danger I would see that she was quickly taken far away from you."

He led the way into the smoking-room, where there were many comfortable chairs, and writing-desks with pen, ink and paper at hand. Everything was ready for use, but guests and waiters were lacking.

"Let's go into the main dining-room," said John, who had opened another door. "It's a fine, big place and the windows look directly over the river. Doubtless we'd have a good view from here if it were not for the driving snow."

It was, in fact, a handsome long room, proving the truth of John's surmise that many guests came at times to Chastel, and, to their great surprise, they found several of the tables fully dressed, as if some of the people had just been sitting down to dinner, when the voice of the shells bade them go.

"You see it's waiting for us," said John. "Why, we'd have done its proprietor a wrong if we'd missed the Hôtel de l'Europe. The table is set and, hospitable Frenchman that he is, he'll be glad to know that some-body is enjoying his house in his absence. The pepper, the salt and the vinegar are there, and I actually see a small bottle of wine on one of the tables."

"Poor man!" said Julie. "It must have cost him much to go. You don't know, Mr. John, how we French love our homes and houses."

"Oh, yes, I do, and we in America, since there's no longer any Wild West in which we can seek romance and change, are settling down into the same habits."

"Would Mademoiselle and Mr. Scott wish us to serve their dinner here?" asked Antoine gravely, the duties of his position ever uppermost in his mind.

"Not now, Antoine," said Julie, "but we will later. I'm glad to see, though, that you are making the best of it. You show a spirit worthy of a Picard."

Picard bowed and smiled with gratification. John suggested that they look upstairs for rooms, and then, after putting them in order, they could return for dinner. But before ascending the grand stairway, they lighted several candles which Suzanne had found, and put them at convenient places. They were not sufficient to illuminate the interior of the hotel, but they threw a soft glow which John found warm and pleasing.

Above was the main drawing-room, and a great array of guest chambers, continued also on the third floor, which was the last. John selected the best suite, looking over the river, for Julie and also for Suzanne, who, under the circumstances, must remain with her. A running water system had not been installed in the houses of Chastel but the great pitchers were filled, and the stalwart Suzanne could easily bring more. They were good rooms, perhaps with an excess of gilt and glass after the continental fashion, but they were comfortable, and John said to Julie:

"Maybe you'd like to remain here a half-hour or so, while Antoine and I choose a place for ourselves. It's best that the members of our party remain close together in view of possible emergencies."

"Yes, Suzanne and I will stay," said Julie. "I felt no weariness a few moments ago, but I've grown suddenly tired. A short rest will restore me."

"Very well," said John. "I bid you a brief *au revoir*, and when you hear a knock on your sitting-room door don't be alarmed, because it will be

Antoine and I returning. Come, Antoine, we'll let the ladies rest while you and I look for the state apartments for ourselves."

Picard permitted a grin to pass over his broad face. His heart belonged to his daughter Suzanne and the Lannes family, and it was not moved easily by outsiders. Yet, this young John Scott from across the sea was beginning to find a favorable place in his mind. He spoke good French, he fought well for the French, he was highly esteemed by Monsieur Philip, he had done great service for Mademoiselle Julie and in the present crisis he was a tower of strength for them all. His daughter, Suzanne, regarded young Scott with a certain fear, but he, Antoine, could not share it. Henceforth John would have his distinct approval, and he felt a measure of pride in being now his comrade in danger.

When John had closed the door of the sitting-room and he knew that neither Julie nor Suzanne could hear him, he said:

"Picard, have you any weapon?"

Picard drew a heavy automatic revolver from the pocket of his jacket.

"Before I started I provided myself with this, knowing the dangers of the journey," he replied.

"Good, but don't use it, except in the last resort. Remember how near you came to execution as a *franc-tireur*."

"Does Monsieur apprehend an attack?"

"I scarcely know, Antoine. But things have come about too easily. We find here a furnished hotel waiting for us. I've no doubt that the kitchens of the Hôtel de l'Europe are well stocked, and we have all the comforts, even the luxuries sufficient for a hundred guests. So far as we know there is not a soul in all this town save our four selves. It doesn't look natural, my good Antoine. It's positively uncanny."

"But, sir, if what we want is here waiting for us, why shouldn't we take it?"

"That's true, wise Antoine. 'Take the goods the gods provide thee whilst the lovely Thaïs sits beside thee,' as Mr. Dryden said."

"Who is Mr. Dryden? Must I infer, sir, from his name, that he is one of our brave English allies?"

"Doubtless he would be if he were living, but he has been dead some time, Antoine."

"Alas, sir, the way of all flesh!"

"So it is, Antoine, but I refuse to grieve about it or get morbid over it. I like to live and living I mean to live. What do you think of this big room, Antoine? It has two beds in it, one for you and one for me, and it's near enough to hear any call from the suite, occupied by Mademoiselle Julie and your daughter."

"A wise precaution. Monsieur Scott thinks of everything."

"No, not of everything, Antoine, but the presence of Mademoiselle Lannes is bound to sharpen the wits of anyone who is trying to take care of her."

"Will you make your toilet here, sir? I will call Suzanne and we will prepare dinner. When it is ready we will serve Mademoiselle Lannes and you."

The stalwart Picard had become all at once the discreet and thoughtful servant, and John felt a sudden sense of restfulness. Intense democrat that he was, he realized in his moment of weariness that all could not be masters.

"Thank you, Picard," he said gratefully. "The afternoon is wearing on and I do need to shake myself up."

"You'll find plenty of water in the pitchers, sir, and there are clean towels on the rack. One would think, sir, that the manager of the Hôtel de l'Europe before taking his departure, made careful preparation for our coming."

"It looks like it, Picard, and it certainly will be true, if you and Suzanne find the well-filled kitchen that you predict."

"Never a doubt of it, sir. The perfect condition in which we find everything above-stairs indicates that we shall find the same below."

He went out, leaving the door open, according to John's wish, and the young American heard his firm step pass down the hall and to the stairway. He drew a deep sigh of content, and lying down on a red plush sofa rested for a little while. It was luck, most wonderful luck, that he had come into Chastel, and had found Julie and her servants, and it was luck, most marvelous luck, that this well-equipped hotel was here waiting for them.

He rose and looped back the heavy lace curtains from the windows which looked over the river. But the snow was falling so fast that he could not see far into the dense, white cataract. The stream was completely hidden, and so, of course, was the hospital camp beyond. Yet through all the driving storm came a faint moan, a light pulsing of the air, which he knew to be the far throb of the great guns.

He turned impatiently away. Why couldn't they stop at such a time? As for himself, he would think of Julie, and a very handsome, tanned young man looking into the glass over the dresser smiled, although it was not at his own reflection. Then he bathed his face and hands, straightened out his hair with the small pocket comb and brush that he, like most other young officers, carried, and felt as if he had been made over.

He hung up his hat and heavy overcoat, and, resuming his place on the sofa, waited until Julie should announce her readiness. But she took more than a half-hour. He had not expected anything else. Truly a girl in her position was entitled to at least an hour if she wanted it. So he continued to wait with great patience. Besides it was very comfortable there on the sofa, and the swish of the driving snow against the window-panes was soothing. Now and then the low mutter of the guns came, but it did not disturb him.

"I'm ready if you are, Mr. John," called a clear voice, and springing from the sofa he joined Julie in the hall. She had smoothed her hair and her Red Cross dress, and the rest had restored all her brilliant color. She was as calm, too, as if they were not alone under the cloud of war, and the hotel was full of real guests. It was her courage as much as her beauty that appealed to John. At no time in all the dangers through which they had gone had he seen her flinch. He had heard much of the courage shown by the women in the great Civil War in his own country, and this maid of France was proving anew that a girl could be as brave as a man.

"May I take you down to dinner, Mademoiselle Lannes?" he asked.

"You may, Mr. Scott," she replied, and they walked together down the hall and the stairway into the great dining-room. Antoine, a napkin on his arm, ceremoniously held open the door for them and Suzanne showed them to opposite seats at a small table by the window.

"We have found an abundance, Mademoiselle," she said, "and you shall be served as if you were real guests."

The memory of that dinner will always be vivid in the mind of John

Scott, though he live to be a hundred. Julie and he were invincible youth that always blooms anew. War and its horrors and dangers fell from them. Their sportive fancy that they were guests in the hotel and nothing ailed the world just then held true. As Antoine and his daughter served the excellent dinner that Suzanne had prepared these two found amusement in everything. The barrier of race that had been becoming more slender all the time melted quite away, and they were boy and girl looking into each other's eyes across a narrow table.

Picard and Suzanne even felt a touch of their fantastic spirits. Suzanne from the north of France, powerful in her prejudices, a Frenchwoman to the core, had viewed John from the first with a distinct hostility, softening slowly, very slowly, as time passed. It was not that she disliked his voice, his figure, his manner, or anything about him. He was a brave and true young man and he had rendered great service to the contemporary house of Lannes, but he was not a Frenchman.

But it seemed to Suzanne, as she served the courses and watched with an eye which nothing escaped, that Monsieur Jean the Scott was becoming a Frenchman--almost at least. She had seen young Frenchmen act very much as the young American was acting. The Frenchman, too, would lean forward to speak when the girl to whom he was speaking was as lovely as her Mademoiselle Julie. No, that was impossible! None other was as lovely as her Mademoiselle Julie. The glow that illumined his face was just the same, quite of the best French manner, too. She had seen people who *were* people and she knew. She admitted, too, that he was very handsome, with the slenderness of youth, but strong and muscular, and above all, his face was good.

Antoine with the napkin over his arm did most of the serving, and being a man the conventional differences did not seem to him so great as they did to his daughter.

"A handsome pair," he said to her.

But while willing to admit much to herself, Suzanne would not admit it to her father.

"Aye, handsome," she replied in a fierce whisper, "but not well matched. He comes from an uncivilized continent on the other side of the world, and soon he'll be going back there. I would that her brother, Monsieur Philip, were here where he ought to be. Perhaps he'd be foolish, too, because he likes the strange American, but it would relieve us of care."

"But America is not a barbarous continent, Suzanne, at least some of it is not. I have heard that in the eastern part of their country many of them act very much as we do, and we have seen those in Paris who appear to be quite civilized. And Suzanne, often they are rich, very rich. Before I left Paris the second time I made it a point to inquire about this young man, and I discovered that he had an immensely wealthy uncle, whose sole heir he is."

"Ah!" said Suzanne, making a long intake of the breath. It was easier than she had thought for John to become French.

"And the fortunes of the house of Lannes are moderate now, as you and I know quite well, Suzanne," continued the wise Antoine. "Surely it must have occurred to Madame her mother, when our little Mademoiselle Julie was yet but a beautiful young child, that she might make a great marriage some day. In this world of ours, Suzanne, many millions of good francs should not be allowed to escape from France."

"It is so, my father," said Suzanne. "France will need numberless millions when this war is over. Here is the vinegar for the salad. Not too much. Mademoiselle Julie likes only a little of it. What fortune it was to find a hotel furnished with everything! The faint sighing sound that still comes on the wind, is it not that of the guns, my father?"

"Aye, Suzanne, it's that of the cannon thundering far away, but Mademoiselle Julie and Mr. Scott have forgotten all about it, and it would be a pity to recall them to it."

Suzanne nodded. For a little space she, too, was compelled to relax. The salad now being complete she served it herself, and as she did so she relaxed still further, murmuring that they were just boy and girl together, but that they were very handsome. She had lifted two of the candles and put them upon the table, their light touching Julie's hair of deep gold with a ruddy tint and heightening the brilliant color of her cheeks. The heavy curtains before the window near them had been looped back a little, and the glass revealed the snow pouring down like a cataract, but they did not see it.

"It's the best dinner I ever ate," said John.

"Now you are finding what capable people Antoine and Suzanne are," said Julie.

"I give them all the credit due them," said John, as he made mental reservations.

"They're wonderfully capable, but it will always be Antoine's bitter regret that he does not serve in this war. If he could, he would be glad to represent himself fifteen years younger than he really is."

"His chance will come. Again I say to myself, Miss Julie, what luck I had in arriving at Chastel!"

"And it was lucky for us, too. We need your courage and resource, Mr. John. I know that Philip cannot come today or tonight and perhaps not tomorrow."

"In that event, what plans have you, Miss Julie?"

"To remain in Chastel. We have an excellent hotel here at our service, and as we're behind the French army we're in perfect safety."

John opened his lips to speak, but changed his intention and did not say what was in his thought. He said instead:

"Antoine is looking unusually important. He is going to serve us wine. He has mineral water, too. Will you take a little of it with your wine? It's a white wine, and the water improves it for me."

"Yes, Mr. John, I'll take mine the same way."

Any dinner, although it may have a flavor which the food and drink themselves, no matter how good, cannot give, must draw to an end, and when the dessert had been served and eaten John looped back the heavy curtain still further and looked out at the white cataract.

"The snowfall will certainly continue the rest of the day," he said, "and perhaps all through the night. Suppose we go to the smoking-room. Antoine and Suzanne must eat also. It's their hour now."

"That is true, Mr. John. The smoking-room is a good place, but I'm afraid that you have no cigarette."

"I don't smoke, but we can talk there, of your brother Philip, of your mother, safe now, of Paris, delivered as if by a miracle from the German menace, and of other good events that have happened."

He held open the door of the dining-room and when she went out he followed her, leaving Picard and Suzanne to their hour.

5

T HE REGISTER

JOHN AND JULIE in the smoking-room were not lonely. They talked of many of the events he had suggested, and of more. Two of the windows looked out upon the town instead of the river, but they could see little there save the towering spire of the cathedral and the blank and ruined walls. The snow was already very deep, but the fall was not diminishing. The gray gloom of coming twilight, however, was beginning to show through it and once more John returned silent thanks that he had come into Chastel and found Julie. He was serving vicariously for Philip who undoubtedly had been held back by the snow.

"It will be night soon," he said. "It's likely that the snow will cease in the morning, and then I'm quite sure that Philip will come for you. It must have been his intention for you to help at the hospital camp below."

"I think so, too."

"Then why not go there in the morning?"

"And he would miss me. He would be searching all Chastel for me, and perhaps would then go away, believing that I had not come."

He was about to say that Philip, missing her in the town would be sure to look for her in the hospital camp, but he forebore. It was very pleasant for them there in the hotel, and why hurry?

"At any rate, it would be unwise to leave tonight," he said. "I think Suzanne herself will agree with me in that statement. I'll ask her, as she'll be in here very soon now."

"Why so soon?"

"Because I've noticed that Suzanne, besides being your maid is also your chaperon."

"She's been that as far back as I can remember, and I believe a most excellent one. Suzanne, I know, loves me."

"I'm sure of it. I don't blame her."

"Look how the snow is leaping up against the window, Mr. John! Ah, Suzanne is ahead of your prediction! She's coming now."

Suzanne stood in the doorway. John surmised from her look that her distrust, at least in a mild form, had sent her there.

"Now that your maid can be with you," he said, "I think I'll take another look at the front of the hotel. Possibly, a new guest has arrived and registered since we last saw the bureau. Will you excuse me for a few minutes, Miss Julie?"

John was merely impelled by a sense of duty to take a look about the hotel, not that he expected to find anything, but because a good soldier should never neglect his scouting operations. He went first into the little lobby at the entrance, where the offices were. Antoine had lighted a candle and left it on the desk of the bureau. Otherwise he could have seen little in the room as the twilight was advancing fast, and the white gloom, made by the falling snow, was shading into gray.

He opened the front door. There was nothing in the street. The tower of the cathedral was almost hidden by the storm and the twilight and the gaunt ruins of the houses, covered now with snow, looked inexpressibly dreary and lonely. The dismal spectacle without heightened the bright gladness within, where he and Julie had sat face to face, only a narrow table between, and Antoine and Suzanne had served.

He stood awhile in the open door, the snow whirling now and then against him, and the faint mutter of great guns coming at almost regular intervals to his ears. He was trying to decide what to do, free from any influence, however noble, which might unconsciously turn him from his duty. His was in the nature of a roving commission, and yet he must not rove too far. He decided that if Lannes did not come in the morning he would insist upon Julie going with him to the hospital camp. It would be hard for him to go against her wishes, but he was bound to do it, and easy in little things, young John Scott had a will in greater affairs that could not be overborne.

But his heart remained singularly light. This was a good hotel, the Hôtel de l'Europe. He had not found a finer or better in Europe. Others might be larger and more magnificent, but not one of them had offered him such light and hospitality at a time when they were needed most. He went back to the bureau, where the register still lay open. He had a vague impression that it was not lying just as they had left it, that it was turned much more to one side, and he glanced at the names, which a quaint fancy had made them write on the open page. His own name had been inscribed there last, and he started when he saw another written beneath it in a bold flowing hand. But the light was so dim that he could not at first make it out, and despite all his courage and power of will an uncanny feeling seized him. A chill ran along his spine, and his hair lifted a little.

With a cry of anger at himself, he seized the candle and held it over the page. Then he read the new name:

Fernand Weber, Paris and Alsace.

With another exclamation, but this time of relief, he put the candle back upon the desk. Two beads of perspiration that had formed upon his brow rolled from it, and fell upon the register. And Weber had come, too! He was not surprised at it. Since he was Lannes' messenger, and he was free to come and go as he pleased, it was altogether likely that he would appear in Chastel to see the reunion of brother and sister, and his work well done. Moreover, he was a man who knew. John had often noticed that Weber's characteristic was knowledge and now he would help them.

He lifted the candle high above his head and looked around the lobby, but there was no sign of the Alsatian. He must have gone outside again. Saying nothing to Julie or the Picards, John resolved to seek him. He needed his heavy overcoat and he was able to secure it unobserved, because Julie had gone up to her room, and Antoine and Suzanne had disappeared in the back regions of the hotel.

He had a faint hope that when he returned to the lobby he might find Weber there, but it was still lone and silent, and drawing the collar well about his ears and throat he thrust himself out into the snow. Turning his back to the driving flakes he walked eastward, searching everywhere through the advancing twilight. Weber, of course, knew of their presence in the hotel as he had seen their names on the register, and the lighted candle on the bureau. It must have been a sudden alarm that called him away so quickly, else he would have gone in at once, and have spoken to his friends.

Unfortunately the night was coming fast. Thick gray gloom clothed the whole east, and but little light showed in the west. Looking back he saw no light in the hotel, but that was to be expected, as Picard would certainly loop the curtains heavily over the windows. Out here in the ruined town much of his extraordinary buoyancy departed. The cold and the desolation of the world made him shiver a little. He thrust his hand into the pocket of his overcoat, and closed it upon the butt of the automatic.

He thought once of calling at the top of his voice for Weber, but instinctive caution kept him from doing so. Then he caught sight of a slender moving figure far ahead and feeling sure that it must be the Alsatian he hurried forward. The figure moved on as fast as he, but, eager in pursuit, he followed. It was shadowy and slim at the distance, but he knew that it was a human being, and either it was Weber or some man of Chastel returning to see what had happened to his town. In either event he wished to overtake him.

But the figure led him a long chase. The man seemed to be moving with some definite purpose, and kept a general course toward the east. Now John called out once or twice, though not loudly, but the stranger apparently did not hear him. Then he pushed the pursuit more vigorously, breaking into a run, and just beyond the eastern rim of Chastel, feeling sure now that it was the Alsatian, he called once more:

"Weber! Weber!"

The man paused and he seemed to John to look back, but the snow drifted heavily between them just then, and when the cataract had passed he was again moving on, more slender and dim than ever. Beyond him lay a little wood, torn and mangled by shells and shrapnel, as the town had been, and John, afraid that he would lose him in it, ran as fast as he could through the deep snow, calling once more, and loudly now:

"Weber! Weber! Weber!"

The figure stopped at the edge of the wood and turned. John, holding up his hands to show that he meant no harm, continued his panting rush through the snow. The man stood upright, magnified into gigantic size by the half light and the storm, and, as John came close, he saw that in very truth it *was* Weber. His relief and joy were great. He did not know until then how anxious he was that the stranger should prove to be Weber, in whose skill and resource he had so much confidence.

"Weber! Weber!" he cried again. "It's Scott. Don't you know me, or am I so clothed in snow that nobody can recognize me?"

"I recognize you now, Mr. Scott," said Weber, "and glad am I to see that it's you. I was afraid that I was being followed by a German scout. I could have disposed of him, but it would not have saved me from his comrades."

"Comrades!" exclaimed John, as he shook his hand. "Why, are Germans about?"

"I think they are. At least, I've come out here to see. You'll forgive my jest, Mr. Scott, in writing my name under that of your party on the register, won't you? As Mademoiselle Lannes has doubtless told you, I carried the letter from her brother, directing her to join him in Chastel, and, as my duties permitted, I came here also to see that my work was effective. I'd have gone at once, but I heard suspicious sounds in front of the hotel, and I came out at once to investigate."

"What did you find?"

"Near the cathedral I saw footprints which the falling snow had covered but partially. No, it's not worth while to go back and investigate them. They're under an inch of snow now."

"Why did you think Germans had made them?"

Weber opened his gloved hand and disclosed something metallic, a spike from a German helmet.

"This," he said, "had become loosened and it fell from the cap of some careless fellow. It could have been there only a few minutes, because the snow had not yet covered it. I think a considerable party has got behind the French lines under cover of the storm and has passed through Chastel."

"But they must have gone on. Why would they remain in a ruined town like this?"

"I see no reason for their doing so, unless to seek shelter for a while in some buildings not wholly wrecked, just as you and Mademoiselle Lannes' party have done."

John felt a throb of alarm.

"Has the Hôtel de l'Europe escaped their observation?" he asked.

"I think so. I did not notice any light myself when I approached it. But I had been in Chastel before, and of course knew of the house and its location. I went there at once, hoping that it had escaped destruction, and found my hopes justified. Has Mademoiselle Lannes heard anything from her brother? I did not see his name on the register?"

"He has not come, but the weather has made it impossible. Aeroplanes can't dare such snowstorms as this."

"That's true, but he's so wonderfully skillful and bold that he might get here in some fashion. Now I think we ought to make a good search among these ruins, Mr. Scott. It's more than likely that the Germans have passed on, but there's a chance that they will linger. You're armed, of course?"

"I've an automatic handy."

"So have I. Suppose we take a look in the wood here, and then we can search among those houses on our right."

The snow and the night, now at hand, biding them, they entered the little wood with confidence that they would fall into no trap. But it was empty, and returning to the edge of the town, they scouted cautiously all the way around it, finding no sign of either a friend or an enemy.

"We alone hold Chastel," said John, "and I think we'd better go back to the Hôtel de l'Europe. I've been away a full two hours and Mademoiselle Lannes may be worried about my long absence, not about me personally, but because of what it might possibly signify."

"That's our obvious course," said Weber, "and as I've registered I'll sleep at the hotel also."

"You'll certainly be welcome," said John, as he led the way back to the Hôtel de l'Europe. But as they were on the far side of the town, and the snow had grown deeper, it took them another half-hour to reach the building.

They stood just inside the door, brushing off the snow and shaking themselves. John glanced toward the door of the smoking-room but it was dark there. He was somewhat surprised. Julie had doubtless gone to bed, but Antoine, the grim and faithful, would be on watch.

"I expected Picard to meet us," he said.

"Probably they're all worn out, and anticipating no danger, have gone to sleep," said Weber.

The candle was still burning in the bureau, and John, picking it up, hurried into the smoking-room. A sudden, terrible fear had struck like a dagger at his heart. The silence, and the absence of Picard filled him with alarm. In the smoking-room he held the candle aloft, and then he uttered a cry.

The room was in a state of utter disorder. Chairs, tables and writing-desks were overturned, and glass was smashed. It was evident to both that a mighty struggle had taken place there, but no blood was shed. John's keen mind inferred at once that Picard had been set upon without warning by many men, but they had struggled to take him alive. Nothing else could account for the wrecked furniture, and the absence of red stains.

His fears now became a horrible certainty, and without a thought of Weber, rushing up the stairway, candle in hand, he knocked at the door of Julie's room, the room that she and Suzanne were to occupy together. There was no answer. He knocked again, loud and long. Still no answer and his heart froze within him. He threw the door open and rushed in, mechanically holding his candle aloft, and, by the dim light it shed, looked about him, aghast.

This room also was in disorder. A chair had been overturned and a mirror had been broken. There had been a struggle here too, and he had no doubt that Suzanne had fought almost as well as her father. But she and Julie were gone. To John the room fairly ached with emptiness.

He put the candle upon the dresser, sat down, dropped his face in his hands and groaned.

"Be of good courage, Mr. Scott," said Weber. "No great harm can have happened to Mademoiselle Lannes."

"It was the Germans whom you saw. They must have come here while we were looking for them on the outskirts of the town."

"It would seem so. But don't be downhearted, Mr. Scott. Doubtless they've made captives of Mademoiselle Lannes and her attendants, but they have not done any bodily harm even to the big Picard. The absence of all blood shows it. And the Germans would not injure a woman like Mademoiselle Lannes. A prisoner, she is safe in their hands, she can be rescued as she was once before or more likely be sent back to her own people."

"But, Weber, we do not know what will happen in a war like this, so vast, so confused, and with passions beginning to run so high. And I was away when she was taken! I who should have been on guard every moment! How can I ever meet Philip's look! How can I ever answer my own reproaches!"

"You have nothing with which to reproach yourself, Mr. Scott. You did what anyone naturally would have done under such circumstances. It has been a chance, the one dangerous possibility out of a hundred, that has gone against us."

John stood up. His despair was gone. All his natural courage came flowing back in a torrent, and Weber saw in his eyes the glow of a resolution, stern, tenacious and singularly like that of Lannes himself.

"I mean to get her back," he said quietly. "As you said, the one dangerous chance in a hundred has gene against us, and to offset it the one favorable chance in a hundred must come our way."

"What do you mean to do?"

"I don't know yet. But we can't remain in this hotel. It's no time to be seeking our comfort when our duty lies elsewhere."

He took the candle again, holding it in a hand that was perfectly steady, and led the way down the hall and the stairway to the little lobby. He did not speak, because he was trying to think rapidly and concisely. If he followed the strict letter of command he would return that night to the hospital camp, and yet he could remain and say that he was delayed by the enemy. He was willing to be untrue to his military duty for Julie's sake, and his conscience did not reproach him.

"Is the snow diminishing, Weber?" he asked, as they came again into the little lobby.

"Somewhat, I think, Mr. Scott," replied Weber as he went to the window. "Are you thinking of pursuit?"

"Such an idea has been in my mind."

"But where and how?"

"My thought is vague yet."

"It's like an Arctic land outside. All footsteps, whether of men or horses, have been hidden by the snow. There is certainly no trail for us to follow."

"I know it, Weber, but it seems to me that Mademoiselle Lannes is calling to me. She tells me to bring her back."

The Alsatian glanced at John, but the young man's face was earnest. It was evident that he believed what he said.

"Mademoiselle Lannes may be calling to you," he said, "but how can you go, and where?"

"I don't know," repeated John obstinately, "but I mean to find her."

He walked irresolutely back and forth and his eye fell upon the register again. Certainly it had been moved once more. He had remembered just how it lay after he saw Weber's name there, and now it was turned much further to one side. He snatched up the candle and held it over the open pages. Then he saw written in a heavy hand just beneath Weber's name:

Prince Karl of Auersperg, Zillenstein, Tyrol. Luitpold Helmuth Schwenenger, " " Captain Max Sanger, Dantzig, Prussia. Suite of His Highness, twenty persons.

John understood thoroughly. He uttered a fierce cry of anger and grief, and Weber looked eagerly over his shoulder.

"We know now who has come," he said.

"Yes, we know," exclaimed John, "and I could wish that it had been anybody else! I hate this man! To me he represents all that is evil in the Old World, the concentrated wickedness of feudalism and I fear him, though not for myself! Weber, I can't bear to think of Julie Lannes in his hands! If it were von Arnheim or that young Kratzek or any normal German it would be different, but this man, Auersperg, is not of our time! He belongs to an older and worse age!"

"He is very hard and determined," said Weber. "In my secret work for France I have seen him more than once, and I know his character and family history thoroughly. An immense pride of birth and blood. Great courage and resolution and a belief that he, as a prince of the old stock, entitled to what he wishes."

"Out of place in our day."

"It may be. But war favors his beliefs, and now he holds the whip hand. The beautiful Mademoiselle Julie was his prisoner for a short time before, and you will pardon me for telling you, what you must have surmised, Mr. Scott, that her youth, her marvelous beauty and her courage and spirit, so befitting one who bears the name of Lannes, have made a great appeal to His Highness. That is why, under the cover of storm and battle, he has carried her away."

"The monster!"

"Not so bad as that, Mr. Scott. There are some things that even a prince would not dare in this comparatively mild age of ours. The Prince of Auersperg is a widower with no children. He will offer her a morganatic marriage."

"A morganatic marriage! And what is that? Neither the one nor the other. It's a disgrace for any woman! A mere halfway marriage!"

"It would be legal, and she'd have a title."

"A title! What would that amount to?"

"I've heard that you Americans are fond of titles, and that your rich women bring their daughters to Europe to marry them!"

"An infinitesimal minority, Weber. It's true that we have such foolish women, but the rest of us regard them with contempt."

"He could offer her vast wealth and even as a morganatic wife a great position."

"I think you're testing me. Weber, trying to see what I will say. Well, I will say this. I don't believe that Julie would accept Auersperg on any terms, not if he were to make her a real princess of the oldest princely house in the world, not if he were to lay the fortunes of the Rothschilds at her feet. She is of good French republican stock, and she is a thorough republican herself."

Weber smiled a little.

"Your faith in Mademoiselle Lannes is great," he said, "and I can see that it proceeds, in part at least, from a just and pure emotion."

John reddened. He saw that he had laid bare his soul, but he was not ashamed. Once more he strengthened his heart and now he resolved upon a plan.

"The snowfall is decreasing fast," he said. "Auersperg and his troop can't be far from here. The traveling is too hard for them to travel swiftly, even if they have automobiles. I shall go to the hospital camp, raise a force and search the country. The commandant will give me soldiers readily, because it would be worth while to capture such a man as Auersperg--behind our lines, too."

"I don't wish to discourage you," said Weber, "but I doubt whether you can find him."

"Maybe so and maybe not," said John, and then he remembered the automobile in which Julie and the Picards had come. Doubtless it was safe behind the cathedral where they had left it, and he could force it through the snow much faster than he could walk.

"Come!" he exclaimed to Weber. "I know of a way to save time."

He rushed through the snow to the rear of the cathedral and Weber, without question, followed him. The automobile was there, well supplied, and John sprang into the front seat. He was no skillful driver, but he had learned enough to manage a machine in some fashion, and powerful emotions were driving him on.

"Up, Weber!" he cried.

"Which way are you going?"

"To the hospital camp, of course, and we'll just touch the top of the high-arched bridge over the river! The snowfall is decreasing fast, and soon we'll be able to see a long distance."

"We can do so now, and the moon is coming out, too. Heavens, Mr. Scott, it's come too soon, because it shows us to the enemy!"

He pointed with a long and shaking finger. At the far end of the street a massive German column was emerging into view. John was startled.

"These are no raiders!" he exclaimed. "They must have broken through a portion of our lines and are attempting to flank other positions! But Chastel's hospitality for us is ended."

He put on full speed and drove the machine rapidly through the snow toward the river.

"We've another reason now why we should reach the camp!" he exclaimed. "Our people must be warned of the presence of the Germans in force in Chastel!"

There was a crash of rifle fire and bullets struck all about them. Two or three glanced off the side of the machine itself, which a moment or two later ran into a deep drift and stuck there, panting.

Weber sprang out and threw himself flat in the snow. John instinctively did the same, and the second volley fired with better aim riddled the machine. There was a heavy explosion, it turned on its side, its wheels revolving for a moment or two, and then it lay still, like a dying monster.

John sprang to his feet and rushed for the shelter of a building only a few yards away. He saw Weber's shadow flitting by his side, but when he reached cover he found that he had lost him. Doubtless in the excitement of the moment the Alsatian had found hiding elsewhere. He was sorry that they had become separated, but Weber had a great ability to take care of himself, and John was quite sure that he would escape. The task that lay upon him now was to make good his own flight.

The building, the shelter of which he had reached, was a low brick structure, already much damaged by shells and shrapnel. But the walls were thick enough to protect him for the moment from bullets, and flinging himself down in the deep snow he crouched in the shadow until he could regain sufficient breath for further flight. He heard more shots fired, but evidently random triggers only had been pulled, as no bullet struck near him.

The fall of snow ceased almost entirely, and the moon grew brighter and brighter. Chastel was a vast white ruin, tinted with silver, and as such it had an uncanny beauty of its own. But John, thankful that the snow was so deep, lay buried in it, where it had drifted against the wall. The Germans in a town so near the French lines were not likely to make a diligent search for a single man, and he felt that he was safe if he did not freeze to death.

Peeping above the snow he saw about fifty German infantrymen walk down the road toward the river, their heavy boots crunching in the snow. They were stalwart, ruddy fellows, boys of twenty-one or two--he knew now that boys did most of the world's fighting--and he liked their simple, honest faces. He felt anew that he did not hate the German people; instead he felt friendship for them, but he did hate more intensely than ever the medieval emperors and the little group of madmen about them who, almost without warning, could devote millions to slaughter. An intense democrat in the beginning and becoming more intense in the furnace of war, he believed that the young German peasants coming down the road would have much more chance before the Judgment Seat than the princes and generals who so lightly sent them there.

The soldiers went on a little distance beyond the edge of the town. The cessation of the snow and the brilliant moonlight enabled them to see far into the plain below, where the hospital camp lay. John, looking in the same direction, saw little wisps of smoke rising above the blur of the camp, but the distance was too great for him to detect anything else.

The low note of the trumpet called to the young troops, and they turned back into the town. John rose from his covert, brushed the snow from his clothing, beat his chest with his fists, and increased the circulation which would warm his body anew. Then he stood against the wall listening. He had no doubt that the Germans would go away presently-- there was nothing to keep them in Chastel--and he made a sudden shift in his plans. He would go back to the Hotel de l'Europe, and stay there until day. Lannes would surely come in the morning. He had no doubt that at daybreak he would see the lithe and sinuous figure of the *Arrow* shooting down from the blue depths, and then he and her brother would go away in search of Julie. Looking down from the air and traveling at almost unbelievable speed, their chances of finding Auersperg's party would be a hundred times better than if he merely prowled along on the ground.

The thought was a happy one to him, and again there was a great uprising of youth and hope. But the hosts of the air were already at work to defeat his plan. The invisible powers which war could now use were ready when the storm died. Far away the wireless stations sputtered and crackled, and words carried on nothing, were passing directly over him. They made no mention of John Scott, but he was vitally involved in what they were planning. Down under the horizon little black dots that were aeroplanes had begun to rise and to look cautiously over a field, where wireless had already told them that something was done. Further away telephone and telegraph wires were humming with words, and all the hosts of the air were concentrating their energies upon Chastel.

John, having left the shelter of the wall, stepped into the road, where the snow had been trodden deep by the young Germans. From that point he could not see into Chastel, but a deep solemn note came from a far point to the east. It was the voice of a great gun carrying an immense distance in the night, and it struck like a hammer upon his heart. It seemed to him a warning that the path that way, the way Auersperg had undoubtedly gone with Julie, was barred.

He walked up the newly trodden road into Chastel, and then he darted back again to cover. He saw the gleam of many gray uniforms and he heard a clank which he knew could be made only by the wheels of cannon. The new forces of the enemy were coming and evidently they were now in great strength in Chastel and beyond it. John's heart leaped in alarm. It was a powerful flank movement, a daring and successful attempt under cover of the storm, and he recognized at once all his dangers.

Keeping as well under cover as he could, he turned and raced toward the bridge. He saw the misty smoke hovering over the hospital camp, and he did not believe that any adequate force to meet the Germans could be found there, but alarms could be sent in every direction.

He expected that more than one shot would be sent after his flying figure, but none came and his swift flight took him far toward the river. Then he saw a long line of dark forms before him and the flashing tips of bayonets. Holding his arms high above his head he shouted in French over and over again that he was a friend, and then ran almost directly into the arms of a short muscular man in the uniform of a French colonel.

"Bougainville!" he cried.

"Aye, Mr. Scott, it is I! My regiment is here and many others."

"Then look out. Chastel is full of Germans."

"It is for them that we've come!"

6

JOHN'S RESOLVE

JOHN STOOD WEAKLY, and with heart palpitating, but it was only for a few moments. Strength poured back in a full tide, and he said to Bougainville:

"You'll let me go back with you?"

"Of course, but there's heavy fighting ahead. Messages warned us in the night that the Germans had broken through, and ever since the storm stopped the wireless has been talking to us, giving us the exact details. We've been marching for hours. My regiment was the first to cross the river but, as you see, others are close behind."

"And you command them all?"

The eyes of the former Apache of Montmartre glittered.

"Yes," he replied. "It was an honor that General Vaugirard assigned to me. I lead the vanguard."

Except the radiance from his eyes he showed no emotion. John noticed that his features were cast in the antique mold. The pallor and thinness of his face accentuated his powerful features, and once more John was reminded of the portraits of the young Napoleon. Could there be such a thing as reincarnation? But he remembered that while a new mind like Napoleon's might be possible a new career like Napoleon's was not. Then all thoughts of any kind upon the subject were driven from his mind by the flash of firing that came from Chastel.

The rifles were rattling fast, and with them soon came the heavy crash of artillery. Bougainville ran up and down his lines, but, to John's surprise, he was holding his men back, rather than urging them on. But he quickly saw the reason. He heard the hissing and shrieking of shells over his head and he saw them bursting in Chastel. The fire increased so fast and became so tremendous in volume that all the French lay down in the snow, and John put his fingers in his ears lest he be deafened.

He understood the purpose of the French commander. It was to hurl a continuous shower of steel upon the enemy, and then when it ceased the French were to charge. Raising his head a little he saw the ruined buildings of Chastel melting away entirely under the tremendous fire of the great French field guns. House after house was springing into flames and wall after wall was crumbling down in fragments. German guns were replying fast, but their position amid falling masonry was much worse than that of the French in the open.

John was lying in the snow near Bougainville, with the shells from both sides hissing and shrieking in a storm over their heads. He was used to being under fire and he knew that none of these missiles was intended for them, but he could not restrain a quiver of apprehension now and then, lest some piece of shrapnel, falling short, should find him. It was always the shrapnel with the hideous whine and shriek and its tearing wound that they dreaded most. The clean little rifle bullet, which if it did not kill did not hurt much, was infinitely more welcome.

"How long will this go on?" John asked of Bougainville; his voice could be heard as an undertone in the roar of the battle.

"Not long, because at present we have the advantage. The Germans know that they're worse off in the town than they would be outside. Our guns are bringing tons and tons of brick and stone about their ears. Hark to our splendid artillery, Mr. Scott! See how it sweeps Chastel!"

The French fire always increasing in volume was most accurate and deadly. The famous seventy-five-millimeter gun was again proving itself the most terrible of mobile field weapons. As walls fell, pyramids of fire shot up in many places, casting a sinister glow over the snowy earth. But above everything rose the lofty and beautiful spire of the Gothic cathedral, still untouched.

All the time the moonlight had been steadily growing more brilliant. Save where the burning houses and the flashing of the cannon cast a red glow a veil of silver mist, which brightened rather than obscured, hung over the snow. John distinctly saw Germans in the town and often, too, he saw them fall.

A man with a bugle was lying in the snow near Bougainville and the little colonel reached over and touched him. John saw the soldier put the instrument to his lips, as if he would make ready, and he knew that an important movement was at hand. He tautened his own figure that he might be ready. The artillery fire behind them ceased suddenly. The air there had been roaring with thunder, and then all at once it became as silent as the grave. The bugler leaped to his feet and blew a long and mellow note. The Bougainville regiment and other regiments both right and left sprang up and, with a short, fierce shout, rushed upon the town. John, his automatic in his hand, charged with them, keeping close to Bougainville.

A scattering fire of bullets carried away many, but John knew that he was not touched. Neither was Bougainville, who, like Bonaparte at Lodi or Arcola, was now leading his men in person, waving aloft a small sword, and continually shouting to his children to follow him. The French fell fast, but they reached the first line of the houses, and then they sent a deadly hail of their own bullets upon the defenders.

Every street and alley in Chastel was swept by the fire of the French. John heard above the crash of the rifles the incessant rattling of the machine guns, and then, as they opened out, the roar of the seventy-five-millimeters added to the terrible tumult. The Germans, withdrawing to the far edge and taking what shelter they could, replied, also with cannon, machine guns and rifles.

John saw Chastel already in ruins fairly melting away. Caught as it must have been in the former action it came tumbling, stone and brick walls and all to the ground. Detached fires were burning at many places, and a great pyramid of flame leaped up from a point where the Hôtel de l'Europe stood. The cathedral alone, as if by some singular chance, seemed to be untouched. The lofty Gothic spire shot up in the silver moonlight, and towered white and peaceful over fighting Gaul and Teuton. John looked up at it more than once, as he fired a rifle, that he had picked up, down the street at the fleeting shadows.

He was filled with an unreasoning rage. He did not hate any one of the Germans who were fighting on the other side of Chastel, but the anger that seized him when he found Julie missing was still heavy upon him. Before, whenever he had fired at an enemy he had usually felt a secret hope that the bullet would miss, but now he prayed that every one would hit. Bougainville pulled him down. "Not too fast! Not too fast!" he said. "You're worth more alive than dead. We'll soon drive them from Chastel anyhow. The seventy-fives are doing the work."

Bougainville had read the story of the battle aright. The great seventy-five-millimeter guns were too much for the German force. As the houses of Chastel were swept away the enemy on the other side was left exposed, and the Germans, despite their courage and energy, were cut down fast. Aid for the French was coming continually. New regiments rushed up the snowy slopes. John heard a shout behind him, and Captain Colton and the Strangers coming from afar rushed into the battle. As they were about to swing past John joined Wharton and Carstairs.

"We thought you were gone forever this time," shouted Carstairs. "There seems to be a special Providence for you Yankees!"

"It's skill, not luck, that counts!" exclaimed Wharton.

John joined them, and Bougainville, taking command of the whole battle, directed the charge upon the town. The spirits of the French were at the highest, and shouting tremendously they soon passed through Chastel and drove the enemy beyond it, headlong into the forest. Having superior numbers now, a better knowledge of the ground and led by a man of genius like Bougainville, they soon broke up the German force, capturing a part of it, while the rest fleeing eastward, burst through the French trenches, and, after further heavy losses, succeeded in getting back to the main German army.

The pursuit was carried on some time by the French cavalry which had appeared as the last charge was made, but Bougainville, with the clear note of trumpets, recalled the infantry. He was satisfied with the victory that had been won in Chastel, and he did not wish to exhaust his troops with vain rushes in the deep snow.

The Strangers halted with the rest, and John, coming out of the red rage that had possessed his soul, saw that Captain Colton was uninjured and that Carstairs and Wharton, who stood near him, had only scratches.

"Grazed four times," said Carstairs happily. "The bullets knew a good man when they saw him, and turned aside just in time to give him slight but honorable wounds."

"Two scratches for me, too," said Wharton.

"Which proves what I told you," said Carstairs, "that it was often luck, not skill, that saved you."

"Both count," said Captain Colton, tersely. "Napoleon had immense skill. Suppose bad luck had sent a bullet into his heart in his first battle in Italy. Would have been forgotten in a day. And if no bullet had ever touched him, wouldn't have amounted to much, without immense skill."

"Do we go back to Chastel, sir?" asked John.

"Back to what's left of it. Not much, I think. See nothing but Gothic tower!"

John looked up. The great Gothic spire hung over a scene of desolation and ruin, now complete save for the cathedral itself. Otherwise not an undamaged house remained in Chastel. Fires still smoldered, and the largest of them all, marked where the Hôtel de l'Europe had stood. The firing had ceased save for a distant murmur where the cavalry still pursued, and John choked as he gazed at ruined Chastel. He looked most often at the burning Hôtel de l'Europe where he had spent such happy hours, the happiest, in truth, of his life, hours that glowed. He could see as vividly, as if it were all real again, Julie and himself at the little table by the window, and Antoine and Suzanne serving. He choked, and for a little while he could not reply to Wharton's question:

"Why, Scott, what's struck you? You look as if you had lost your last friend!"

"Wharton," replied John at last, "I found Mademoiselle Lannes and her servants, Antoine and Suzanne Picard here, come as requested by letter, to meet her brother Philip. I found them in the cathedral waiting, and we went to the Hôtel de l'Europe, where she and I dined together."

"Good Heavens! You don't mean to say she was there under the awful fire of our guns?"

"No, else I should not have been with you. Weber, the trusty Alsatian, of whom you know, came to us in the town. It was he who had borne the letter from Philip to Mademoiselle Julie. We thought we saw Germans in the outskirts of Chastel. We did not find any, but when we came back to the Hôtel de l'Europe, where we left them, Mademoiselle Julie and her servants, the Picards, were gone."

"Perhaps they were alarmed by the German advance and have taken refuge somewhere in the woods. If so, it will be easy to find them, Scott."

"No, they're not there. They're in the hands of the enemy. I shouldn't mind it so much if she were merely a captive of the Germans, but that man Auersperg has taken her again."

"How can you possibly know that to be true, Scott?"

Then John told the story of the register, and of the successive writing of the names. Cotton heard him, too, and his face was very grave.

"It's a pity Bougainville couldn't have come earlier," he said. "We might not only have saved Mademoiselle Julie but have captured this Prince of Auersperg as well. Then we should indeed have had a prize. But the wireless could not talk through all the storm and we had no warning of the German movement until the snowfall died down."

"What are we going to do?" asked John.

"We'll stay on the site of Chastel at least until morning, which can't be far away."

John looked at his watch.

"It will be daylight in two hours," he said.

"Oh, by the way," exclaimed Carstairs, "what became of Weber?"

"We were making our escape in Mademoiselle Lannes' automobile when we ran into a detachment of Germans. Our car was riddled; we both dodged for shelter and that was the last I saw of him."

"He escaped. I wager a pound to a shilling on it. The Alsatian not only has borrowed the nine lives of a cat, but he has nine original ones of his own."

"I feel sure, like you, Carstairs, that he has escaped and I certainly hope so. He's a clever man who has the faculty of turning up at the right time."

"It promises to be a clear dawn," said Wharton. "You may not believe it, Carstairs, but I'm a fine weather prophet in my own country, and if I can do so well there I ought at least to do as well with the low-grade weather supplied by an inferior continent like Europe."

"It's no wonder they call you a mad Yankee, Wharton. Low-grade weather! Have you any fog that can equal our London variety?"

"It's quality, not quantity that counts with a superior, intellectual people such as we are."

"Intellect! It's luck! I don't remember his name, but he was a discerning Frenchman, who said that a special Providence watched over drunken men and Americans."

"A special Providence watches over only those who have superior merit."

"I think," said John, "that I'm bound to take a little rest, if Captain Colton will let me."

"Oh, he'll let you if you ask him," said Carstairs. "You're a particular favorite of his, although I can't understand why. Wharton and I are much more deserving. But you do look all played out, old fellow."

John had sustained a sudden collapse. Intense emotion and immense physical exertion, continued so long, could be endured no longer, and he felt as if he would fall in the snow. But a portion of the victorious force was to remain at Chastel, and some tents had been pitched. Captain Colton readily gave John permission to enter one of them and roll himself in the blankets.

It was still an hour of dawn, but the night was light. Fires yet burned here and there in Chastel, where not a single building now stood unharmed, save the cathedral. The mutter of the cannon came from the vast front both to east and to west.

John looked into the great misty world and his face was turned toward the east. He had no doubt that Auersperg had gone in that direction with Julie, and he meant to find her. But how? He prayed silently for the coming of Lannes with the *Arrow*. For such a search as this the swift aeroplane could serve while one might plod in vain over the ground. Lannes would come before the next night! He must come! If he had made an appointment for such a meeting nothing could delay him more than a day.

He did not have any great fear for Julie's present safety. The modern civilized world had suddenly broken loose from many of its anchors, but so conspicuous a man as Auersperg could not stain his name with a deed that would brand him throughout Europe. Weber, however, had spoken of a morganatic marriage, and fearful pressure might be brought to bear. A country so energetic and advanced as Germany had clung, nevertheless, to many repellent principles of medievalism. A nation listened with calm acceptance and complacency, while its Kaiser claimed a partnership, and not altogether a junior partnership either, with the Almighty. Much could be forgiven to an Auersperg, the head of a house that had been princely more than a thousand years. John shuddered.

He had not gone to the tent at once as he intended. His nerves were yet leaping and he knew now that they must become quiet before he could sleep. Men were moving about him, carrying the wounded or helping with the camp, but they were only misty forms in the white gloom. Looking again toward the east he saw a silver bar appear just below the horizon. He knew it was the bright vanguard that heralded the coming sun, and his imaginative, susceptible mind beheld in it once more an omen. It beckoned him toward the east, and hope rose strong in his heart.

"Wharton," he said, "I suppose we'll stay awhile in Chastel."

"So I hear. Until noon at least."

"Then you wake me three hours from now. It will be enough sleep at such a time, and I want to be up when Lannes comes. You promise?"

"Certainly, Scott, I'll do it, though you'll probably swear at me for bothering you. Still, I'm ready to do any unpleasant duty for a friend when he asks it."

John laughed, went into the tent, rolled himself in the blankets and in a minute was fast asleep. In another minute, as it seemed, Wharton was pulling vigorously at his shoulder.

"Get up, Scott!" exclaimed Wharton. "Your three hours, and a half hour's grace that I allowed you, have passed. Didn't I tell you that you'd be ungrateful and that you'd fight against me for fulfilling your request! Open your eyes, man, and stand up!"

John sprang to his feet, shook his head violently several times, and then was wide awake.

"Thanks, Wharton," he said. "You're a true friend but you're a wretched reckoner of time."

"How so?"

"You said it was three hours and a half when in reality it was only three minutes and a half."

But a clear wintry sun was shining in at the door of the tent, and he saw its gold across the snow. Beyond was a kitchen automobile at which men were obtaining coffee and food.

"Has Lannes come?" asked John.

"Not yet, but of course he'll be here soon; by noon, I fancy."

John went out and took his breakfast with his comrades of the Strangers. The morning was uncommonly bright. There was not a trace of cloud in the heavens, which had turned to the soft, velvety blue that one sometimes sees in winter, and which can make a man fancy that it is summer when he looks up, rather than winter when he looks down.

While John ate and drank, he continually scanned the skies looking for the coming of the *Arrow*. He saw aeroplanes hovering here and there over the French and German lines, but none coming toward Chastel.

He had expected, too, that Weber might return in the morning, but he did not reappear and John felt a distinct disappointment. Many had been killed, but Wharton and Carstairs had reported that no body had resembled Weber's. Then it was certain that he had not fallen. Perhaps the Germans had driven him ahead of them, and he would rejoin the French at some distant point.

The morning passed, slow and bright, but it did not bring Lannes. General Vaugirard himself came about noon, a huge purring man in a huge puffing automobile. He cast an approving eye over Bougainville's work, and puffing his cheeks still wider whistled a low, musical note.

"It could not have been done better," he said. Then he caught sight of John and exclaimed:

"Ah, here is our young American, he who has been transformed into a good Frenchman! Glad am I to see you alive and unhurt, but I bring you news which is unpleasant. Ah, well, such is life! It must be expected in a war like this."

Alarm leaped up in John's heart. He felt instinctively that it concerned Lannes! Was he dead? But he steadied his voice and said:

"May I ask what it is, General?"

"That young friend of yours and great servant of his nation, Philip Lannes, the famous aviator. He has been wounded. No, don't be alarmed, it's not mortal, but it will keep him in hospital for some time. It happened two days ago, nearly a hundred miles west of here. He had just landed from his aeroplane, and he was fired at by some German skirmishers hidden in a wood. Fortunately French cavalry were near and drove off the Germans. Lannes is so young and so healthy that his recovery will be complete, though slow."

"What a misfortune at such a time!" exclaimed John.

"What do you mean by 'at such a time'?"

Then John related the presence of Julie Lannes in Chastel and the manner of her capture by Auersperg. He told, too, why she had come there.

General Vaugirard puffed out his huge cheeks and whistled a note or two.

"I can't understand why Lannes should have wanted her to come to such an exposed place," he said. "But youth is daring and doesn't always count the risks."

Youth *was* daring and John resolved that he would help to prove it.

"General," he said, "could I ask your aid in a little matter that concerns me?"

"If it is not to betray our army to the Germans I think you can."

"I want you to help me to become a spy. I'll make the request to Captain Colton, and then, if it's indorsed, I'll go eastward and see what I can find out about the Germans."

"But I understood that she was not a German."

John reddened from brow to chin.

"I admit that much," he said, "but at the same time I intend to serve France all I can. I might be of more help that way than as a mere minor officer in the trenches."

"If you're successful, yes; if caught, all's lost. Hard trade, that of spy."

"But I want to go, sir. I never wanted to do anything so much before in my life. You'll help me, won't you?"

"But how can you go among the Germans? Your German is not the best in the world."

"It's better than you think. I've been devoting most of my leisure to the study of it in the last six months. Besides there are subjects of Germany who do not speak German at all. I shall claim to be a native of French Lorraine. I learned French in my infancy and I speak it not like an American or an Englishman but like a Frenchman."

"That helps a lot. What's to be your new name?"

It was not a matter to which John had given any thought, but as he glanced at the ruined town the question solved itself.

"Chastel, Castel," he said. "I shall drop the 'h' and call myself Jean Louis Castel, born in French Lorraine in 1893, after that region had enjoyed for more than twenty years the glorious benefits of German military rule."

"Very well," said the General. "Now go and see Captain Colton."

Captain Colton's lips twisted into a crooked smile when he heard John. His glance was a mingling of sympathy and apprehension. He knew the great dangers of the quest, but he liked John Scott and he could understand.

"John," he said, calling him by his first name, "I would not send anybody upon such an errand as yours. You recognize the fact that the chances are about ten to one you'll find a bullet at the end of your search."

"I think I'll get through."

"It's a good thing to hope. I think I can procure this commission for you from General Vaugirard. But we'll go to him at once. We'll not let the grass grow--or rather, the snow melt under our feet while we're about it."

John did not tell him that he had already spoken to the general, as he wished the whole proceeding to be in perfect order.

General Vaugirard was by a fire which had been built in the Place near the shattered fountain. Wrapped in a huge overcoat he looked truly gigantic as he walked up and down thinking.

"Let me speak with him first," said Captain Colton.

John held back and saw the two talk together earnestly a minute or two. Then the big general beckoned to him and as John approached he said:

"The request that you have made through Captain Colton is granted. In a war like this is may be the good fortune of a spy to render a very great service."

John bowed.

"Thank you, sir," he said simply.

"I understand that you wish to start at once," continued the general. "Dress like a peasant, and look with all your eyes and listen with all your ears. And don't forget while you're seeking the enemy's secrets that all France loves a lover."

John flushed a deep red, and Vaugirard and Colton laughed. The general put his hand in the most kindly fashion upon John's shoulder.

"You are one of the bravest of my children," he said, "and I have an affection for thee, thou stalwart American youth. See to it that thou comest back again. Thy hand, Monsieur Jean Castel, for such, I hear, is to be your name."

John's hand was engulfed in the huge palm. General Vaugirard gave it a great shake and turned away. Then John and Captain Colton walked back to the place that had been allotted to the Strangers, where it soon became known to Wharton and Carstairs that their comrade would depart that night upon a quest, seemingly hopeless. They drew John aside:

"Scott," said Carstairs, "are you really going? It's certain death, you know."

"A German bullet or a German rope," said Wharton, "and you'll never be seen or heard of again. It's an ignominious end."

"As surely as the night comes I'm going," replied John to both questions. "I understand the risks and I take them."

"I knew the answer before I asked you," said Carstairs. "You Americans are really our children, though sometimes you're not very respectful to your parents. They call us prosaic, but I think we're really the most romantic of the races."

"It's proved," said Wharton, "when sober fellows like Scott go away on such errands. I think you'll win through, Scott, in the way you wish."

John knew that the good wishes of these two friends, so undemonstrative and so true, would follow him all the time and he choked a little. But when the lump in his throat was gone he spoke casually, as if he were not venturing into a region that was sown thick and deep with dragon's teeth.

At the advice of Captain Colton he slept several hours more that afternoon, and in the darkest part of the night, clothed simply like a peasant, but carrying a passport that would take him through the French lines, he said good-by to his friends, and, taking his life in his hands, departed upon his mission. Lest he be taken for a *franc-tireur* he was entirely unarmed, and he wore a thick blue blouse, gray trousers equally thick, and heavy boots. He also carried, carefully concealed about his person, a supply of gold and German notes, although there would not be much use for money in that region of the dragon's teeth into which he was venturing.

He re-crossed the little river on the same high-arched bridge by which he had come, skirted the hospital camp, and then bore off toward the east. It was past midnight, the skies were free from snow, but there were many low, hovering clouds which suited his purpose. He was still back of the French lines, but his pass would take him through them at any time he wished. The problem was how to pass those of Germany, and the difficulty was very great, because for a long distance here the hostile trenches were only three or four hundred yards apart.

He discerned to the eastward a dim line of hills which, as he knew, rose farther on into mountains, and it occurred to him that he might find it easier to get through in rough country than in the region of low, rounded hills, where he now stood. He carried a knapsack, well filled with food, a blanket roll, and now he resolved to push on all night and most of the following day, before passing the French lines.

Keeping a watchful eye he pursued his steady course across the hills. The depth of the snow impeded speed, but action kept his heart strong. The terrible waiting was over, he was at least trying to do something. Fresh interests sprang up also. It was a strange, white, misty world upon which he looked. He traveled through utter desolation, but to the east, inclining to the north was a limitless double line, which now and then broke into flashes of flame, while from points further back came that mutter of the big guns like the groanings of huge, primeval monsters.

It seemed to John barbarous and savage to the last degree. He knew that he was in one of the most densely populated and highly cultivated portions of the world, but the dragon's teeth were coming up more thickly even than in the time of old Cadmus.

He walked until it was almost morning without seeing a human being, and then, the snow having dragged on him so heavily, he felt that he must take rest. Crawling into a hole in the snow that he scraped out under a ledge, he folded himself between his blankets and went to steep.

7

T HE PURSUIT

JOHN SCOTT WOULD NOT PERHAPS HAVE SLEPT so well in a hole in the snow if he had not been inured to life in a trench, reeking in turn with mud, slush, ice and water. His present quarters were a vast improvement, dry and warm with the aid of the blankets, and he had crisp fresh air in abundance to breathe. Hence in such a place in the Inn of the Hedge and the Snow he slept longer than he had intended.

His will to awake at the rising of the sun was not sufficient. The soothing influence of warmth and the first real physical relaxation that he had enjoyed in three or four days overpowered his senses, and kept him slumbering on peacefully long after the early silver of the rising sun had turned to gold on the snow.

He had dug so deep a hole and he lay so close under the hedge that even a vigilant scout looking for an enemy might have passed within a dozen feet of him without seeing him. Another drift of snow falling after he had gone to sleep had covered up his footsteps and he was as securely hidden as if he had been a hundred miles, instead of only a scant two miles, from the double French and German line.

No human being noticed his presence. A small brown bird, much like the snowbird of his own land, hopped near, detected the human presence and then hopped deliberately away. Nobody was in the snowy fields. They were within range of the great German guns, and the peasants were gone. Had John been willing to search longer he could easily have found an abandoned house for shelter. As he had made mental notes before, Europe was now full of abandoned houses. In some regions rents must be extraordinarily low.

While he slept, firing was resumed at points on the long double line. Rifles flashed, and incautious heads or hands were struck, and somewhere or other the cannon were always muttering. But it was all in the day's work. Months of it had made his whole system physical and mental so used to it that it did not awaken him now.

Nevertheless the hosts of the air were uncommonly active while he slept. The wireless, sputtering and crackling, was carrying the news from general to general that a smart little action had been fought at Chastel, where another smart little action had been fought not long before, that the Germans had been overly daring and had paid for it.

Yet it was only an incident on a gigantic battle front that extended its mighty curving line from Switzerland to the sea, and soon the wireless and its older brother the telephone, and its oldest brother the telegraph, talked of other plans which would cause a much greater slaughter than at Chastel. Chastel itself, unless its beautiful Gothic cathedral brooding unharmed over the ruins could win it a word or two, would have no place at all in history. John himself was only one among eight or ten million armed men, and not a single one of all those millions knew that he lay there in the snow under the hedge.

The aeroplanes came out in the clear frosty blue, and both German and French machines sauntered lazily up and down the air lanes, but they did not risk encounters with one another. They were scouting with powerful glasses, or directing the fire of the batteries. One French machine circled directly over John, not more than two or three hundred feet away, but the man in it, keen of eye though he was, did not dream that one of the bravest of the Strangers lay asleep under the hedge beneath him.

The fleets of flyers were larger than usual, as if they were anxious to take the fresh air, after days of storm. But the most daring and skillful of all the airmen, Philip Lannes, was not there. He still lay in a hospital a hundred miles to the west, with a bullet wound in his shoulder, and while the time was to come when the *Arrow* under his practiced hand would once more be queen of the heavens, it was yet many days away.

The sun rose higher, suffusing the frosty blue heavens with a luminous golden glow, but John slept heavily on. He had not known how near to exhaustion was his nervous system. Perhaps it was less physical exhaustion than emotion, which can make huge drains upon the system. Now he was in the keeping of nature which was restoring all his powers of both mind and body, and keeping him there until he should again have all his strength and all the keenness of his faculties, needful for the great work that lay before him.

It was halfway toward noon when he awakened, remembered dimly in the first instant, and then comprehending everything in the second. He unrolled the blankets, slipped out of his lair and knew by the height of the sun that he had slept far beyond the time appointed for himself. But he did not worry over it. Barring a little stiffness, which he removed by flexing and tensing his muscles, he felt very strong and capable. The fresh air pouring into his lungs was so different from the corruption of the trenches that he seemed to be raised upon wings.

He resumed his walk toward the hills, and ate breakfast from his knapsack as he went along. Presently he noticed a large aeroplane circling over his head, and he felt sure that it was observing him. It was bound to be French or other French machines would attack it, and, after one glance, he walked slowly on. The machine followed him. He did not look up again, but he saw a great shadow on the snow that moved with his.

The knowledge that he was being watched and followed even by one of his own army was uncomfortable, and he felt a sensation of relief when he heard a swish and a swoop and the aeroplane alighted on the snow beside him. The man in the machine stepped out and asked:

"Who are you and where are you going?"

John did not altogether like his manner, which in his own idiom he styled "fresh."

"I've a name," he replied, "but it's none of your business, and I'm going somewhere, but that's none of your business either."

"They're both my business," said the man, drawing a revolver.

"Read that," said John, producing his passport.

The document stated simply that Jean Castel was engaged upon an important mission for France, and all were commanded to give him what help they could. It was signed by the fat and famous general of brigade, Vaugirard, and therefore it was a significant document.

"I apologize for brusqueness," said the aviator handsomely, "but the times are such that we forget our politeness. What can I do for you, Monsieur Jean Castel, who I am sure has another and more rightful name at other times."

"Just now Castel is my right name, and all friends of mine will call me by it. Thank you for your offer, but you can do nothing--"

John stopped suddenly as he glanced at the aeroplane poised like a huge bird in the snow.

"Yes, you can do something," he said. "I notice that your plane is big enough for two. I want to reach the mountains to the eastward without all this tremendous toiling through the snow. You can carry me there in an hour or two, and besides this passport I give you a password."

"What's the password?"

"Lannes!"

"Lannes! Philip Lannes, do you know him?"

"I have been up with him in the *Arrow* many times. I've fought the Taubes with him. I helped him destroy both a Zeppelin and a forty-two-centimeter gun."

"Then I know you. You are his friend John Scott, the American. I thought at first that you had the accent of North America. Oh, I know of you! We flying men are a close group, and what happens to one of us is not hidden long from the others. Your password is sufficient."

"You know then that Lannes is in a hospital with a bullet wound in his shoulder?"

"I heard it two days ago. A pity! A great pity! He'll be as well as ever in a month, but France needs her king of the air every day. My own name is

Delaunois, and I'll put you down in those hills at whatever point you wish, Monsieur Jean Castel of America."

John smiled. Delaunois was a fine fellow after all.

"I can't give you an extra suit for flying," said Delaunois, "but your two blankets ought to protect you in the icy air. I'll not go very high, and an hour or a little more should put us in the heart of the hills."

"Good enough, and many thanks to you," said John.

They gave the machine the requisite push, sprang in and rose slowly above the snowy waste. It was a good aeroplane, and Delaunois was a good aviator, but John missed the *Arrow* and Philip. He knew that the heavens nowhere held such another pair. Alas! that Lannes should be laid up at such a time with a wound!

But he quickly called himself ungrateful. Delaunois had come at a most timely moment, and he was doing him a great service. It was very cold above the earth, as Delaunois had predicted, and he wrapped the blankets closely about himself, drawing one over his head and face, until he was completely covered except the eyes.

To the westward several other planes were hovering and to the eastward was another group which John knew to be German. But the flying machines did not seem disposed to enter into hostilities that morning, although John saw the double line of trenches blazing now and then with fire, and, at intervals, the heavy batteries on either side sent a stated number of shells at the enemy.

Seen from a height the opposing trenches appeared to be almost together, and the fire of the hostile marksmen blended into the same line of light. But John did not look at them long. He had seen so much of foul trenches for weary months that it was a pleasure to let the eye fill with something else.

He looked instead at the high hills which were fast coming near, and although covered with snow, with trees bare of leaves, they were a glorious sight, an intense relief to him after all that monotony of narrow mud walls. He knew that trenches or other earthworks ran among the hills also, but the nature of the ground compelled breaks, and it would be easier anyhow to pass through a forest or a ravine.

"Where do you wish me to put you down?" asked Delaunois.

"At some place in those low mountains there, where the German lines are furthest from ours."

"I think I know such a point. You won't mind my speaking of you as a spy, Mr. Jean Castel of America, will you?"

"Not at all, because that's what I am."

"Then don't take too big a risk. It hasn't been long since you were a boy, and I don't like to think of one so young being executed as a spy."

"I don't intend to be."

"It's likely that I may see Philip Lannes before long. I go westward in two or three days and I shall find a chance to visit him in the hospital. If I see him what shall I tell him about a young man whom we both know, one John Scott, an American?"

"You tell him that his sister, Mademoiselle Julie Lannes, came to the village of Chastel to meet him, in accordance with his written request, and while she was waiting for him with her servants, Antoine and Suzanne Picard, not knowing that he had been wounded since the writing of his letter, she was kidnapped and carried into Germany with the Picards by Prince Karl of Auersperg. Prince Karl is in love with her and intends to force her into a morganatic marriage. Otherwise she is safe. The American, John Scott, in addition to his duties as a spy for France, a country that he loves and admires, intends, if human endeavor can achieve it, to rescue Mademoiselle Lannes and bring her back to Paris."

Delaunois took one hand from the steering rudder and turned glistening eyes upon John.

"It's a knightly adventure," he said. "It will appeal to Frenchmen when they hear of it, and yet more to Frenchwomen. I should like to shake the hand of this American, John Scott, and since he is not here, I will, if you will let me, shake the hand of his nearest French relative, Jean Castel."

He opened his gloved palm and John's met it in a strong grasp.

"I'm glad," said Delaunois, "that I saw you, and that I am able to give you this lift. We're over the edge of the mountains now, and presently we'll cross the French lines. I think I'd better go up a considerable distance, as they won't know we're French, and they might give us a few shots."

The machine rose fast and it grew intensely cold. John looked down now upon a country, containing much forest for Europe, and sparsely inhabited. But he saw far beneath them trenches and other earthworks manned with French soldiers. Several officers were examining them through glasses, but Delaunois sailed gracefully over the line, circled around a slender peak where he was hidden completely from their view, and then dropped down in a forest of larch and pine. "So far as I know," he said, when the plane rested on the snow, "nobody has seen our descent. We're well beyond the French lines here, but you'll find German forts four or five miles ahead. As you see, this is exceedingly rough ground, not easy for men to occupy, and so the French stay on one side of this little cluster of mountains while the Germans keep to the other. And now, Monsieur Jean Castel, I leave you here, wishing you success in your quest, success in every respect."

Again the two strong hands met. A minute later the aeroplane rose in the air, carrying but one of the men, while Jean Castel, peasant of Lorraine, was left behind, standing in the snow, and feeling very grateful to Delaunois.

John watched the aeroplane disappear over the peak on its return journey, and then he walked boldly eastward toward the German lines. Modesty kept him from accepting Delaunois' tribute in full, but it had warmed his heart and strengthened his courage anew. Delaunois had considered it not a reckless quest, but high adventure with a noble impulse, and John's heart and spirit had responded quickly. Great deeds come from exaltation, and that mood was his.

He followed what seemed to be a little path under the snow, leading along the side of the mountain toward the eastward, the way he would go. Here portions of the earth were exposed, where the snow had already melted much under the heat of the high sun. Three or four hundred feet below a brook ran noisily over stones, but that was the only sound in the mountains. He felt though that the Germans must be somewhere near. Men with glasses might be watching him already.

He decided at once upon his rôle. In Europe peasants were often heavy and loutish. It was expected of them, and none would be heavier or more loutish than he. He thrust both hands in his pockets, and began to whistle familiar German songs and hymns, varying them now and then with a chanson or two that might have been sung for centuries in Lorraine.

The path led on across a little valley and then along the slope of another ridge. Under the increasing heat of the sun the snow was now melting much faster, and streams ran in every ravine. But the stalwart young peasant, Jean Castel of Lorraine, was sure of his footing, and he advanced steadily toward his goal.

Germans in rifle pits saw the figure coming their way, and several officers examined it critically with their glasses. All pronounced the stranger obviously a peasant, and they were equally sure that he could do them no harm. He was coming straight toward their pits and so they awaited him with some curiosity.

John presently caught the shimmer of sun on bayonets, and he knew now that he would soon reach the German earthworks. His first care after Delaunois left him, had been to destroy the passport that General Vaugirard had given him and there was not a scratch of writing about him to identify him as John Scott.

Whistling louder than ever, and looking vacant of countenance, he walked boldly toward the first rifle pit, and, when the sharp hail of the German sentry came, he promptly threw up his hands. An officer whom he took to be a lieutenant and four or five men came toward him. All wore heavy gray overcoats and they were really boys rather than men; not one of them, including the officers, seeming to be more than twenty. But they were large and muscular, heavily tanned by wind and snow and rain.

John had learned to read character, and as he walked carelessly toward them he nevertheless watched them keenly. And so watching he judged that they were honest youths, ready to like or hate, according to orders from the men higher up, but by nature simple and direct. He did not feel any fear of them.

"Halt!" said the officer, whom John judged to be a Saxon--he had seen his kind in Dresden and Leipsic.

John stopped obediently, and raised his hand in a clumsy military fashion, standing there while they looked him over.

"Now you can come forward, still with your hands up," said the officer, though not in any fierce manner, "and tell us who you are."

John advanced, and they quickly searched him, finding no weapon.

"You can take your hands down," said the officer. "Unarmed, I don't believe you'd be a match for our rifles. Now, who are you?"

"Jean Castel, sir, of Lorraine," replied John in German with a strong French accent.

"And what have you been doing here between our lines and those of the French?"

"I took some cattle across the mountains for the army and having sold them I was walking back home. In the storm last night I wandered through the lines into this very rough country and got lost."

"You do look battered. But you say you sold your cattle. Now what have you done with your money?"

The officer's tone had suddenly become suspicious, but John was prepared. Opening his heavy blouse he took from an inside pocket a handful of German gold and notes. The young lieutenant glanced at the money and his suspicions departed.

"It's good German," he said, "and I don't think a peasant like you could have got it unless he had something valuable to sell. Come, you shall go back with us and I'll turn you over to a higher officer. I'm Lieutenant Heinrich Schmidt, and we're part of a Saxon division."

John went with them without hesitation. In fact, he felt little fear. There was nothing to disprove his statements, and he was not one of those who looked upon Germans as barbarians. Experience had shown him that ordinary Germans had plenty of human kindness. He sniffed the pleasant odors that came from the kitchen automobiles near by, and remarked naïvely that he would be glad to share their rations until they passed him on.

"Very well, Castel," said Lieutenant Schmidt, "you shall have your share, but I must take you first to our colonel. He will have important questions to ask you."

"I'm ready," said John in an indifferent tone. But as he went with the men he noted as well as he could, without attracting attention to himself, the German position. Rifle pits and trenches appeared at irregular intervals, but the mountains themselves furnished the chief fortifications. In such country as this it would be difficult for either side to drive back the other, a fact which the enemies themselves seemed to concede, as there was no firing on this portion of the line. But at points far to the west the great guns muttered, and their faint echoes ran through the gorges.

The path led around one of the crests, and they came to a little cluster of tiny huts, which John knew to be the quarters of officers. Snug, too, they looked, with smoke coming out of stovepipes that ran through the roofs of several of them. A tall man, broad of shoulder, slender of waist, blue of eye, yellow of hair, and not more than thirty, came forward to meet them. John recognized at once a typical German officer of high birth, learned in his trade, arrogant, convinced of his own superiority, but brave and meaning to be fair.

"A peasant of Lorraine, sir," said Lieutenant Schmidt. "He says that his name is Jean Castel, and that he has been selling cattle. We found him wandering between the lines. He was unarmed and he has considerable money."

"Come closer," said the officer to John. "I'm Colonel Joachim Stratz, the commander of this regiment, and you must give a thorough account of yourself."

John advanced willingly and saluted, feeling that the glance Colonel Stratz bent upon him was heavy and piercing. Yet he awaited the result with confidence. It was true that he was American, but he had been with the French so much now that he had acquired many of their tricks of manner, and his French accent was impeccable.

"You are a seller of cattle?" said Colonel Stratz, suddenly in English.

The words of reply began to form, but John remembered himself in time. He was a French peasant who understood no English, and giving Colonel Stratz a puzzled look he shook his head. But he wondered what suspicion had caused the German to ask him a question in English. He concluded it must be a mere chance.

Colonel Stratz then addressed him in German, and John replied to all his queries, speaking with a strong French accent, repeating the tale that he had told Lieutenant Schmidt, and answering everything so readily and so convincingly that Colonel Joachim Stratz, an acute and able man, was at last satisfied.

"Where do you wish to go now, Castel?" asked the German.

"To Metz, if it please you, sir."

"Wouldn't it be better for you to stay, put on a uniform, take up a rifle and fight for our Kaiser and Fatherland?"

John shook his head and put on the preternaturally wise look of the light-witted.

"I'm no soldier," he replied.

"Why weren't you called? You're of the right age."

"A little weakness of the heart. I cannot endure the great strain, but I can drive the cattle."

"Oh, well, if that is so, you serve us better by sticking to your trade. Lieutenant Schmidt, give him food and drink, and then I'll prepare for him a pass through the lines that will take him part of the way to Metz. He'll have to get other passes as he goes along."

John saluted and thanked Colonel Stratz, and then he and Lieutenant Schmidt approached one of the great German kitchen automobiles. It was easy to play the rôle of a simple and honest peasant, and while he drank good beer and ate good cheese and sausage, he and Lieutenant Schmidt became quite friendly.

Schmidt asked him many questions. He wanted to know if he had been near the French lines, and John laughingly replied that he had been altogether too near. Three rifle bullets fired from some hidden point had whizzed very close to him, and he had run for his life.

"I shall take care never to get lost again," he said, "and I intend to keep well behind our army. The battle line is not the place for Jean Castel. Why spoil a first-class herder to make a second-class soldier?"

He winked cunningly at Schmidt, who laughed.

"You're no great hero," said the German, "but if a man wants to take care of his skin can he be blamed for doing so? Still, you're not so safe here."

"How's that?" asked John in assumed alarm.

"Now and then the French send shells over that mountain in front of us and when one is fired it's bound to hit somewhere. We haven't had any at this point yet, but our time is sure to come sooner or later."

"Then I think I'll be going," said John, willing to maintain his new reputation as a timid man.

Schmidt laughed again.

"Oh, no, not yet," he said. "Your passport isn't ready, and without it you can't move. Have another glass of this beer. It was made in Munich, and puts heart into a man."

John drank. It was really fine beer, and the food was excellent, warm and well cooked. He had not realized before how hungry and thirsty he was. It was a hunger and thirst that the cold meat and bread in his knapsack and snow water would not have assuaged. Many Germans also were refreshing themselves. He had noticed that in both armies the troops were always well fed. Distances were short, and an abundance of railways brought vast quantities of supplies from fertile regions.

While he was still eating he heard a shriek and a roar and a huge shell burst two or three hundred yards away. Much earth was torn up, four men were wounded slightly and an empty ambulance was over-turned, but the regular life of the German army went on undisturbed.

"I told you that we had French messengers now and then," said Lieutenant Schmidt, holding a glass of beer in his right hand and a sausage in his left, "but that message was delivered nearer to us than any other in three days. I don't think they'll fire again for a half-hour, and the chances are a hundred to one that it will fall much further away. So why be disturbed?"

Lieutenant Schmidt was beginning to feel happy. He had a sentimental German soul, and all the beer he wanted brought all his benevolence to the surface.

"I like you, Castel," he said. "Your blood is French, of course, or it was once, but you of Lorraine have had all the benefits of German culture and training. A German you were born, a German you have remained, and a German you will be all your life. The time is coming when we will extend the blessings of our German culture to all of France, and then to England, and then maybe to the whole world."

Lieutenant Schmidt had drunk a great deal of beer, and even beer when taken in large quantities may be heady. His tongue was loose and long.

"And to that distant and barbarous country, America, too," said John.

"Aye, and to the Americans also," said Lieutenant Schmidt. "I hear that they don't love us, although they have much of our blood in their veins. There are many people among them bearing German names who denounce us. When we finish with our enemies here in Europe we'll teach the barbarous Americans to love the Kaiser."

"A hard task," said John, with meaning.

"So it will be," said Lieutenant Schmidt, taking his meaning differently, "but the harder the task the better we Germans love it. And now, Castel, here comes your passport. Its little winged words will bear you safely to the headquarters of General Osterweiler thirty miles to the north and east, and there you'll have to get another passport, if you can. *Auf wiedersehen,* Jean Castel. Your forefathers were French, but you are German, good German, and I wish you well."

Lieutenant Schmidt's cheeks were very red just then, not altogether with the cold, and his benevolence had extended to the whole world, including the French and English, whom he must fight regretfully.

"Oh," said John, as an afterthought, although he was keenly noting his condition, "while I was wandering in the snow of the big storm, I heard from a sentinel that one of our great generals and beloved princes. Prince Karl of Auersperg, had passed this way with his train."

Perhaps if Lieutenant Schmidt had not taken so much good Munich beer after a long fast he might have become suspicious, because it was not the question that an ordinary peasant and cattle-herder would ask unless the previous conversation had led directly to it. But as it was he fairly exuded trust and kindness.

"Not here," he replied, "but at a point further toward the west and north. So great a figure as Prince Karl of Auersperg could scarcely go by without our hearing of it. Colonel Stratz himself spoke of it in my presence."

"I saw him once in Metz before the war. A grand and imposing figure. Perhaps I shall behold him there again in a few days."

"I think not. It was said that the prince was going to his estates in the east. At least, I think I heard something of the kind, but it probably means that he was on his way to the eastern frontier. Prince Karl of Auersperg is not the man to withdraw from the war."

John's heart dropped suddenly. Would he be compelled to follow the prince halfway across Europe. Oh, why had he left the Hôtel de l'Europe even for a moment? With Picard's help he might have been able to hold off Auersperg and his followers, or a lucky shot might have disposed of the prince. He felt it no crime to have wished for such a chance. But strengthening his heart anew he took up the burden that had grown heavier.

"*Auf wiedersehen,* Lieutenant Schmidt," he said, and whistling softly to himself he began his passage through the German lines, showing his passport more than a dozen times before he passed the last trench and rifle pit, and was alone among the hills behind the German lines. He might have reached the railroad and have gone by train to Metz, but he preferred, for the present at least, to cling to the country, even at the risk of much physical hardship and suffering.

He still carried his blankets, and he was traveling through a region which had been much fought over in the earlier stages of the war. Since the German lines were still in France some peasants had returned to their homes, but many houses were yet abandoned, their owners probably thinking that the tide of battle would roll back upon them, and that it was better to wait.

He turned presently from the hilly path into a good road, paved almost like a street, and breaking from a bush a stout stick, which he used peasant fashion as a cane, he walked briskly along the smooth surface, now almost clear of the snow which had fallen in much smaller quantities in the lowlands.

He met a battery of four twenty-one-centimeter guns with their numerous crews and an escort of cavalry, advancing to the front, and he stepped to one side of the road to let them pass. The leader of the cavalry hailed him and John's heart gave a sudden alarming throb as he recognized von Boehlen. But his courage came back when he saw that he would not have known the Prussian had he remained twenty feet away. Von Boehlen was deeply tanned and much thinner. There were lines in his face and he had all the appearance of a man who had been through almost unbearable hardships.

John had no doubt that a long life in the trenches and intense anxiety had made an equal change in himself. The glass had told him that he looked more mature, more like a man of thought and experience. Moreover, he was in the dress of a peasant. After the first painful heartbeat he awaited von Boehlen with confidence.

"Whence do you come?" asked the colonel of Uhlans--colonel he now was.

John pointed back over his shoulder and then produced his passport, which Colonel von Boehlen, after reading, handed carefully back to him.

"Did you see anything of the French?" he asked glancing again at John, but without a sign of recognition.

"No, sir," replied John in his new German with a French accent, "but I saw a most unpleasant messenger of theirs."

"A messenger? What kind of a messenger?"

"Long, round and made of steel. It came over a mountain and then with a loud noise divided itself into many parts near the place where I stood. One messenger turned itself into a thousand messengers, and they were all messengers of death. Honored sir, I left that vicinity as soon as I could, and I have been traveling fast, directly away from there, ever since."

Von Boehlen laughed, and then his strong jaws closed tighter. After a moment's silence, he said:

"Many such messengers have been passing in recent months. The air has been full of them. If you don't like battles, Castel, I don't blame you for traveling in the direction you take."

John, who had turned his face away for precautionary measures, looked him full in the eyes again, and he found in his heart a little liking for the Prussian. Von Boehlen seemed to have lost something of his haughtiness and confidence since those swaggering days in Dresden, and the loss had improved him. John saw some signs of a civilian's sense of justice and reason beneath the military gloss.

"May I pass on, sir?" he asked. "I wish to reach Metz, where I can obtain more horses for the army."

"Why do you walk?"

"I sold my last horse and the automobiles and trains are not for me. I know that the army needs all the space in them and I ask nothing."

"Fare on then," said von Boehlen. "Your papers are in good condition and you'll have no trouble in reaching Metz. But be sure you don't lose your passport."

The injunction was kindly and John, thanking him, took up the road. Von Boehlen and his Uhlans rode on, and John looked back once. He caught a single glimpse of the colonel's broad shoulders and then the long column of horsemen rode by. There was no military pomp about them now. Their gray uniforms were worn and stained and many of the men sagged in their saddles with weariness. Not a few showed wounds barely healed.

The cavalry were followed by infantry, and batteries of guns so heavy that often the wheels sank in the paved road. Sometimes the troops sang, pouring forth the mighty rolling choruses of the German national songs and hymns. The gay air as of sure victory just ahead that marked them in the closing months of summer the year before had departed, but in its place was a grim resolution that made them seem to John as formidable as ever. The steady beat of solid German feet made a rolling sound which the orders of officers and the creaking of wagons and artillery scarcely disturbed. The waves of the gray sea swept steadily on toward France.

John showed his passport twice more, but all that day he beheld marching troops. In the afternoon it snowed a little again and the slush was everywhere, but he trudged bravely through it. Having escaped from the trenches he felt that he could endure anything. What were snow, a gray sky and a cold wind to one who had lived for months on a floor of earth and between narrow walls of half-frozen mud? He was like a prisoner who had escaped from a steel cage.

Toward dark he turned from the road and sought refuge at a low but rather large farmhouse, standing among trees. He modestly made his way to the rear, and asked shelter for the night in the stable, saying that he would pay. He learned that the place was occupied by people bearing the German name of Gratz, which however signified little on that borderland, which at different times had been under both German and French rule.

Nor did the proprietor of the house himself, who came out to see him, enlighten him concerning his sympathies. If he liked France obviously it was no time for him to say so when he was surrounded by the German legions. But John could sleep on the hay in the stable, and have supper and breakfast for certain number of marks or francs which he must show in advance. He showed them and all was well.

John, after carefully scraping all the mud and snow from his boots was allowed to go in the big kitchen and sit on a stone bench beside the wall, while two stout women cooked at a great furnace, and trim maids came for the food which they took upstairs.

When he sank down upon the bench he realized that he was tired through and through. It was no light task even for a hardened soldier to walk all day in bad weather. One of the cooks, a stout middle-aged woman whom the others called Johanna, gave him a glance of sympathy. She saw a young man pale from great exertion, but with a singularly fine face, a face that was exceedingly strong, without being coarse or rough. Johanna thought him handsome, and so did the other cook, also stout and middle-aged, who bore the French name of Nanine.

"Poor young man!" said one and, "Poor young man!" repeated the other. Then they filled a plate with warm food and handed it to him. While he ate he talked with them and the passing maids, who were full of interest in the handsome young stranger. He told them that he was a horse-trader, and that he had been in no battle, nor would he be in any, but he saw that he was not believed, and secretly he was glad of it. These were trim young maids and a young soldier likes admiration, even if it comes from those who in the world's opinion are of a lower rank than he.

They asked him innumerable questions, and he answered as well as he could. He told of the troops that he had seen, and they informed him that German forces had been passing there at times all through the winter. Princes and great generals had stopped at the farmhouse of Herr Gratz or Monsieur Gratz, as he was indifferently called. The war had ruined many others, but it brought profit to him, because all the guests paid and paid well.

John in a pleased and restful state listened, and he was soothed by the sound of their voices. He had often heard old men at home, veterans of the Civil War, tell how grateful to them was the sight of a woman after months of marching and fighting. Now he understood. These were only cooks and housemaids, but their faces were not roughened like those of soldiers, and their voices and footsteps were light and soft. Moreover, they gave him food and drink--for which he would pay farmer Gratz, however--and made much over him.

"We had royal guests last night," said the youngest of the maids, whom they called Annette, a slender blond girl.

"Going to the battle front?"

"Oh, no. They were going the other way, toward Metz, and perhaps only one was a real prince."

"Maybe this prince had seen enough of battles?"

"I cannot say. I saw him only once. He was a large man, middle-aged, and he had a great brown beard."

John's whole body stiffened. Questions leaped to his lips, but he compelled his muscles to relax and by a great effort he assumed a tone of indifference.

"What was the prince's name?" he asked with apparent carelessness.

"I don't know, but the people around him were as respectful to him as if he were a king. There were two women with him, but the master himself served these two alone in their room."

"But you caught a glimpse of one of the women, the younger, Annette?" said Johanna.

"So I did, but it was only a glimpse."

"What did she look like?" asked John, who was trying to keep down the beating of his heart.

"It was only a second, but I saw a face that I will never forget. She was very pale, but she had beautiful blue eyes like stars, and the most lovely golden hair that ever grew in the world."

"Julie! My Julie!" groaned John under his breath.

"What did you say?"

"I was merely wondering who she was."

"I wondered, too, and so did all of us. We heard a tale that she was a princess, a niece or a daughter, perhaps, of the great prince, with whom she traveled, and we heard another that she and the woman with her were French spies of the most dangerous kind who had been captured and who were being taken into Germany. And the face of the beautiful young lady, which I saw for only a moment, was French, not German."

John felt hot and then cold from head to foot. Julie a spy! Impossible! Spies were shot or hanged, and sometimes women were no exceptions. How could such a charge be brought against her? And yet anything could happen in such a vast confused war as this. Julie, his Julie of the starry blue eyes and the deep gold hair to be condemned and executed as a spy! A cold shiver seized him again.

Then came sudden enlightenment. Auersperg was medieval. In his heart he arrogated to himself the right of justice, the upper, the middle and the low, and all other kinds, but he had ability and mingled with it an extreme order of cunning. Julie of the Red Cross, a healer of wounds and disease, would not be held a prisoner, but Julie, a spy, would be kept a close captive, and her life would be in the hands of the general commanding those who had taken her. Oh, it was cunning! So cunning that its success seemed complete, and he thrilled in every vein with pain and anger.

"Are you ill?" asked the good Johanna, who had noticed the sudden deepening of his pallor.

"Not at all, thank you," he replied, forcing himself to speak in a level tone. "I feel splendidly. All of you are too kind to me. But that was an interesting story about the prince and the girl whom he brought with him, who might be either a relative or a captive."

"I'm thinking she must have been his niece," said romantic Annette, "but I'm sure she didn't love him. Perhaps she wanted to run away with some fine young officer, and he caught her and brought her back."

"When did they leave?"

"Very early this morning. They came in automobiles, but neither when they arrived nor when they departed was the lady in the machine with the prince. She and the woman with her, who must have been her servant, were in a small machine alone, except for the chauffeur."

"It's a strange tale. Which way did they go?"

"Toward Metz. We know no more. The prince did not look like a man who would tell his intentions to everybody."

"The story has in it the elements of romance," said John. "I think with you, Annette, that the young lady who must certainly have been of high birth, was being carried away from some young man who loved her well."

A lively discussion followed. John's voice had decided the opinion of the kitchen. It had been divided hitherto, but it was not now. The beautiful young lady with the starry eyes and the golden hair had certainly been torn away, and the sympathy of cooks and maids was strongly for her. While they talked John tried to collect his thoughts. After the first shock, he was convinced that Julie's life was in no danger, but her liberty certainly was. Auersperg would use the charge that she was a spy to hold her, and he was a powerful man. The pressure upon her would grow heavier and heavier all the time. Could she resist it? He might make her think that the fate of a spy would be hers, unless she chose to marry him.

In all the world, since Philip would lie long in the hospital with a wound, there was but one man who could help her. And it was he, John Scott. Out of the depths of his misery and despair a star of hope shot up. His own strong heart and arm, and his only, would rescue her. Some minds gather most courage when things are at the worst, like steel hardening in the fire, and John's was markedly of this type. Since chance had brought him on this road, and to the very house in which Julie had slept, the same kindly chance would continue to guide him on the right way. It was a good omen.

The twilight outside, cold and gray, was deepening into night. His appetite was satisfied and he felt buoyant and strong. Had he obeyed his impulse he would have started on the road to Metz in pursuit. But he knew that it was folly to exhaust himself in such a manner for nothing. Instead he told Johanna that he would go to the stable now and sleep. Jacques, a stalwart hostler, was called to show him his quarters, and he departed with all their good wishes.

Jacques was a large brown peasant, and as he led the way to the stable he said:

"They told me your name was Jean Castel from Lorraine?"

"Yes, back of Metz."

"And the house is full of German officers."

He pointed to the windows of the dining-room, which were ruddy with light. Young men in tight-fitting uniforms, their blond hair pompadoured, were outlined vividly against the glow.

"Will they go forward or will they come back?" asked Jacques in a hoarse whisper. "Is the work of Bismarck to stand or is it to undo itself?"

John believed Jacques to be a French sympathizer, anxious for an opinion that would agree with his hopes, but one could not be sure in such times, and it behooved him above all, with Julie at the end of his journey, to be careful. So he merely shrugged his shoulders and replied:

"I know not. I'm a simple buyer and seller of horses. I'm a much better judge of a horse than of an army. I've no idea which side is the stronger. I don't love war, and I'm going away from it as fast as I can."

Jacques laughed.

"Perhaps it will follow you," he said. "There is war everywhere now, or soon will be. I hear that it's spreading all over the world."

John shrugged his shoulders, and followed Jacques up a ladder into a loft over the horses. But it was not a bad room. It had two small iron beds and it was secure from wet and cold.

"You take that," said Jacques, pointing to the bed on the right. "It belonged to Fritz who was the hostler here with me. He went to the army at the first call and was killed at Longwy. Fritz was a German, a Saxon, but he and I were friends. We had worked together here three years. I'd have been glad if the bullets had spared him. The horses miss him, too. He had a kind hand with them and they liked him. Poor Fritz! You sleep in the bed of a good man."

"My eyes are so heavy that I think I'll go to bed now."

"The bed is waiting for you. It's always welcome to one who has walked all day in the cold as you have. I have more work. I have the tasks of that poor Fritz and my own to do now. It may be an hour, two hours before I'm through, but if you sleep as soundly as I do I'll not wake you up."

John sank into deep slumber almost at once and knew nothing until the next morning.

8

INTO GERMANY

A FROSTY DAWN was just beginning to show through the single window that lighted up the little room. It opened toward the east, where the light was pink over the hills, but the upper sky was yet in dusk. John sat up in bed and rubbed the last sleep out of his eyes. A steady moaning sound made him think he was hearing again the thunder of great guns, as he had heard it days and nights at the Battle of the Marne.

The low ominous mutter came from a point toward the north, and glancing that way, although he knew his eyes would meet a blank wall, he saw that it was only Jacques, snoring, not an ordinary common snore, but the loud resounding trumpet call that can only come from a mighty chest and a powerful throat through an eagle beak. Jacques was stretched flat upon his back and John knew that he must have worked extremely hard the night before to roar with so much energy through his nose while he slept. Well, Jacques was a good fellow and a friend of France, the nation that was fighting for its existence, and if he wanted to do it he might snore until he raised the roof!

John sat up. He saw the pink on the eastern hills turning to blue and then spreading to the higher skies. The day was going to be clear and cold. He walked to the window and looked up at the skies, seeking for aeroplanes, after the habit that had now grown upon him. But the sky was speckless and no sounds came from the Gratz farmhouse. Doubtless the German officers quartered there were sleeping late, knowing that they had no need to hurry to the front, since the fighting in the hills and mountains was desultory.

But the crisp clear blue of the cold morning was wonderfully suitable to the hosts of the air and they were at work. Along a battle front of five hundred miles in the west and of seven or eight hundred in the east messages were flashing, on wires by telephone and telegraph and then on nothing but the pulsating air.

John, who had been compelled to deal so much with these invisible agencies felt them now about him. He had a highly sensitive mind like a photographic plate that registered everything, and when he opened the window that he might see better and admit the fresh air, he did not have to reach out for knowledge. It came, and registered itself upon that delicate and imaginative mind. He had thought so much and he had striven so hard to see and to divine what lay before him that he felt almost able to send messages of his own through the air, messages of hope winging their way directly to Julie.

The mind of man is a strange thing. It may be a godlike instrument, the powers of which are yet but little known. John did not believe in the least in anything supernatural, but he did believe in the immense and unfathomed power of the natural. Alone, and in the early dawn with silence all about him it seemed that he heard Julie calling to him. Her voice traveled like the wireless on the pulsating air. She needed him and she turned to him alone for aid. She had divined in some manner that only he could help her and he would come, no matter what the risk. The cry was registered again and again upon his sensitive soul, and always he sent back the answer that he was coming. His mind, like hers, had become a wireless, and both were working.

He became unconscious of time and place. He no longer saw the blue sky, but he stretched out his arms and called:

"I am coming!"

"Coming? What do you mean by coming? Who is it you're telling?"

John came out of his dream, or the misty region between here and nowhere, and turned to Jacques, who in the process of awakening at that moment had heard his words which were spoken in French.

"I was just talking to the air," replied John a little uncertainly. "Fine mornings appeal to me, and I was telling this one that I'd soon come out into it"

Jacques continued to awaken. He was a big man who worked hard and who slept heavily. Rousing from sleep was a task accomplished by degrees and it took some time. He had heard John with one ear and now he heard with the other. His right eye opened slowly and then the left. The blood became more active in his brain and in a minute or two he was awake all over.

"Telling the morning air that you're coming out into it, eh Castel?" he said as he put one foot on the floor. "You're a poet, I see. You don't look it, but being French, as you Lorrainers are, it makes you fond of poetry."

"I do believe you have it right, Jacques," said John, "but if I can get my breakfast now I mean to go upon the road at once."

"Oh, you can get it, Castel. The whole kitchen has fallen in love with you. I found that out last night after you had gone away. That little Annette told me so."

"It was to tease you," said John, who understood at once and who was willing to fib in a good cause. "I saw her watching through a window a fine big fellow, exactly your size, age and appearance, and with the same name. I said something about his being a hulking hostler and she turned upon me like a hawk."

"Now, did she?" exclaimed Jacques, a great smile spreading slowly across his face.

"She did. Told me it was a poor return for their kindness to criticize a better man."

"Ah, that Annette is bright and quick. She can see through a man at one look. Castel, I like you, and I hope you'll get to Metz without trouble. But keep a civil and a slow tongue in your mouth. Don't speak until the Germans speak to you, and then tell the truth without stammering. I'll go to the kitchen with you, as my work begins early."

John knew that he had a friend, and the two left the stable together.

But he was not thinking much then of the Gratz farm or of anybody upon it. He had sent his soul on before, and he meant that his body should catch up with it.

Johanna, Annette and the master, Gratz himself, were in the kitchen. He ate a good breakfast with Jacques, paid Gratz for food and lodging, and putting his blankets and knapsack upon his back, took once more to the road. Jacques repeated his good advice to be polite to men to whom it paid to be polite, and Annette, standing by the side of the stalwart hostler, waved him farewell.

The slush, frozen the night before, had not yet melted, and John walked rapidly along the broad firm highway, elated and bold. Julie had called to him. He would not reason with himself, and ask how or why it had been done, but he felt it. He liked to believe that wireless signals had passed between them. Anyway he was going to believe it, and hence his heart was light and his spirit strong.

He passed sentinels posted along the road, but his passport was always sufficient, and his pleasant manner bred a pleasant manner in return. Soon there was nothing but a line of smoke to mark where the Gratz farm stood, but he carried with him good memories of it. He hoped that the romance of Jacques and Annette would end happily. In truth he was quite sure that it would, and he began to whistle softly to himself, a trick that he had caught from General Vaugirard.

John had no certainty that he would enter Metz, which must now be less of a city than a great fortress with a powerful garrison. But he felt sure that he could at least penetrate to the outskirts and there find more trace of Auersperg. A prince and man of his social importance could scarcely pass through the city without being noticed, and there would be gossip among the soldiers. Fortunately he had been in Metz twice and he knew the romantic old city at the confluence of the Moselle and the Seille, dominated by its magnificent Gothic cathedral. After all he might overtake Auersperg there and in some manner achieve his task. Chance took a wide range in so great a war and nothing was impossible.

He was now approaching the line between France and Germany, and Metz lay only eleven miles beyond. The beauty of the clear cold day endured. There was snow on the hills, but the brilliant sun touched it with a luminous golden haze, and the crisp air was the breath of life.

He swung along at a great gait for one who walked. Life for months without a roof had been hard, but it had toughened wonderfully those whom it did not kill, and John with a magnificent constitution was one of those who had profited most. He felt no weariness now although he had come many miles.

About one o'clock in the afternoon he sat on a stone by the roadside and ate with the appetite of vigorous youth good food from his knapsack. While he was there a German sergeant, with about twenty men in wagons going toward Metz, stopped and spoke to him.

"Hey, you on the stone, what are you doing?" asked the sergeant.

John cut off a fresh piece of sausage with his clasp knife and answered briefly and truthfully:

"Eating."

The sergeant had a broad, red and merry face, and facing a man of good humor he was not offended.

"So I see," he said, "but that wasn't what I meant."

John, without another word, took out his passport, handed it to him and went on eating. The sergeant examined it, handed it back to him and said:

"Correct."

"I show it to everybody," said John. "When a man speaks to me I don't care who he is, or what he is, I hand it to him. I, Jean Castel, as you see by the name on the passport, don't want trouble with anybody."

"And a wise fellow you are, Castel. I'm Otto Scheller, a sergeant in the service of his Imperial Majesty and the Fatherland."

"You look as if you had seen much of war, Sergeant Scheller, but I am a dealer in horses and I am happiest where the bullets are fewest."

"It's an honest confession, but it does not bespeak a high heart."

"Perhaps not, but sometimes a horse-dealer is more useful than a soldier. For instance, the off horse of the front wagon has picked up a stone in his left hind foot, and if it's not taken out he'll go lame long before you reach Metz."

"Donnerwetter! But it's true. You do know something about horses and you have an eye in your head. Here you, Heinrich, take that stone out, quick, or it won't be good for you!"

"And the right horse of the third wagon has glanders. The swelling is just beginning to show below the jaw. It's contagious, you know. You'd better turn him loose, or all your horses will die."

"Donner und blitzen! See Fritz, if it's true. It's so, is it? Then release the poor animal as Castel says, and put in one of the extras. See, you Castel, you're a wizard, you hardly glanced at the horses, and you saw what we didn't see, although we've been with them all day."

"I've grown up with horses. It's my business to know everything about them, and maybe your trade before the war didn't bring you near them."

Scheller threw back his great head and laughed.

"If a horse had approached where I worked," he said, "much good beer would have been spilt. I was the head waiter in a restaurant on the Unter den Linden. Ah, the happy days! Oh, the glorious street! and here it's nothing but march, march, and shoot, shoot! Three of my best waiters have been killed already. And the other lads are no horsemen either. That big Fritz over there made toys, Joseph drove a taxicab, August was conductor on a train to Charlottenberg, and Eitel was porter in a hotel. We're all from Berlin, and will you tell us, Castel, how soon we can take Paris and London and go back to the Unter den Linden?"

John shook his head.

"There are about fifteen hundred million people in the world who are asking that question, Otto Scheller," he replied, "and out of all the fifteen hundred millions not one can answer it. But I will ask you a question in return."

"What is it?"

"Will you give me a ride in one of your wagons to Metz?"

"Why, certainly," replied Scheller. "Your passport is in good order, and we can take you to the first line of fortifications. There you'll meet high officers and you'll have to make more statements, because Metz, as you know, is one of the most powerful fortresses in Europe."

"I know; why shouldn't I, a Lorrainer, know? But my passport will take me in. Meanwhile, I thank you, Otto Scheller, for the kindness you're showing me."

"All right, jump in, and off we go."

It was a provision wagon, drawn by stout Percherons, which John felt sure had been bred in France, and which he also felt sure had never been paid for by German money. The wagon was empty now, evidently having delivered its burden nearer the battle lines, and John found a comfortable seat beside the sergeant, while a stout *Pickelhaube* drove.

"Looks like peace, Castel," said the sergeant, waving his hand at the landscape, "but things are not always what they seem."

"How so?"

"See the hills across there. The French hold part of them, and often the artillery goes boom! boom! They threaten an attack on Metz. We shall hear the cannon before long."

John looked long at the hills, high, white and silent, but presently they began to groan and mutter as Scheller had predicted they would. Flashes of flame appeared and giant shells were emptied like gusts of lava from a volcano. One burst in the road about three hundred yards in front of them, and tore a hole so deep that they were compelled to drive around it.

"The French are good with the guns," said Scheller, regarding the excavation meditatively, "but of course it was by mere chance that the shell struck in the road."

John felt a light and momentary chill. It would certainly be the irony of fate if on his great quest he were smitten down by a missile from his own army. But no others struck near them, although the intermittent battle of artillery in the hills continued.

Sergeant Scheller paid no attention to the distant cannon fire, to which he had grown so used long since that he regarded it as one of the ordinary accompaniments of life, like the blowing of the wind. He was in a good humor and he talked agreeably much about battle and march, although he betrayed no military secrets, chiefly because he had none to betray.

"I march here and I march there," he said, "I and my men shoot at a certain point, and from a certain point we're shot at. That's all I know."

"And that, I take it, is the cathedral in Metz," said John, pointing toward the top of a lofty spire showing against the blue.

"So it is, Castel, and here you'll have to show your passport again. We're approaching the fortifications. I couldn't tell you about them if I would. We drive along a narrow road between high earthworks and we see nothing."

Their entry into Metz was slow and long. John was compelled to show his passport again and again, and he answered innumerable questions, many searching and pointed, but again he was thrice lucky in knowing the town and something about Lorraine.

Now that he was inside, with a powerful German army all about him, he must decide soon what to do. Fortunately he had made a friend of Scheller who advised him to go to a little Inn near the Moselle, much frequented by thrifty peasants, and John concluded to take his advice.

"Good-by, Castel," said Scheller, reaching out a huge fist. "I like you and I hope we'll meet in Paris soon."

John took the fist in a hand not as large as Scheller's, but almost as powerful, and shook it.

"Here's to the meeting in Paris," he said, but he added under his breath, "may it happen, with you as my unwounded prisoner."

He left Scheller after thanks for the ride, and found his way to the Inn of the Golden Lion, which was crowded with stout farmers and peasants. It was old-fashioned, with a great room where most of the men sat on benches before a huge fire, which cast a cheerful glow over ruddy faces. Some were eating sausage and drinking beer, and there was plenty of talk, mostly in German.

John modestly found a place near the fire for which he was very grateful, and ordered beer and cheese. Apparently he was nothing but a peasant going about his own humble business, but he listened keenly to everything that was said, reckoning that someone ultimately would mention the Prince of Auersperg, or could be drawn into speaking of a man of so much consequence who might be present in Metz.

He attracted little attention, as he sat warming himself before the fire and listening. People of French sympathies might be in the crowd, but if so they were silent, because nearly all the talkers were speaking of German success. It was true that they had been turned back from Paris, but it meant a delay only, they would soon advance again, and this time they would crush France. Meantime, von Hindenburg was smashing the Russians to pieces. John smiled as he gazed into the crackling fire. After all, the Germans were not supreme. They knew a vast deal about war, but others could learn and did learn. They were splendid soldiers, but there were others just as good and they had proved it.

Men came and went through the Inn of the Golden Lion. Sometimes soldiers and officers as well as civilians sought its food and fire. The day had turned darker, full of raw cold, and a light hail was falling. John was glad to have a place in the inn. He reflected that a man's good luck and bad luck in the long run were about even, and, after so much bad luck, the good luck should be coming his way. He would certainly remain in the inn that night if he could, and a bench before the fire would be a sufficient bed for the peasant he seemed to be, at such a time, with the city full of troops, and the French batteries almost near enough to be heard.

More officers were coming in now. Some of them stood before the great fire, warming themselves and drying their uniforms, the hail having begun to drive harder. He thought he might see some one whom he knew. It was possible that von Arnheim, the young prince of whom he had such pleasant memories, was in Metz, and it was possible also that he might come to the Inn of the Golden Lion. And there was young Kratzek, who he knew had been exchanged. Some chance might make him, too, enter the inn, but John's second thought told him the fulfillment of his wish would be folly. They were his official enemies and must seize him if he made himself known to them. He was merely lonesome, longing for the sight of a familiar face.

His own appearance had been changed greatly by a stubby young beard that called aloud for a razor. Clad in a peasant's garb, and with a cap drawn down over his face Carstairs and Wharton themselves might have passed without knowing him.

Although the young Germans did not appear, one whom John expected least came. A man of medium size, built compactly, and with a short brown beard, trimmed neatly to a point, walked briskly through the room, and spread out cold hands before the flames. John was dozing in his chair, but the man's walk and manner roused him at once. They seemed familiar, and a glance at the face showed him that it was Weber.

He resisted a powerful impulse to call to him or to signal to him in some manner. The impulse was strong to recognize the appearance of a friend, but he understood the deadly danger of it. He was a spy and so was Weber. By recognition each might betray the other, and it was best that he should not attract the Alsatian's attention in any way. So he pretended to doze again, although he was really watchful.

Weber stood by the fire a little while, until he was warm. Then he sat down in one of the chairs and called for beer and sausage, which he drank and ate slowly and with evident relish. His eye roved about the room and once or twice fell upon John, but did not linger there. Evidently he did not recognize the peasant with the stubby growth of young beard. Nor did he appear to know anyone else in the room, and, after a few inquiring glances, he seemed to be busy with his own thoughts.

A half-hour or so later Weber went into the street, and John, muttering that he wished a little fresh air, rose and followed. He had in mind only a vague idea of speaking with Weber, and of finding out something about Auersperg, of whose movements the Alsatian was likely to know. But when he was outside Weber had vanished. He walked up the street, only a little distance in either direction, because the soldiers were thick everywhere, and their officers wanted explanations. Moreover, he recognized the futility of search. Weber was gone as completely as if he had been snatched up into the air by an invisible hand, and John felt that he had missed an opportunity.

He took courage, nevertheless, and dismissing Weber from his mind, he made a renewed effort. The precious passport once more came into play, and gradually, he made his way toward the finest hotel in Metz. If Auersperg was still in the city it was likely that a man of his temper and luxurious habits would be at this hotel.

There were sentinels about the building and it was crowded with guests of high degree. The assemblage here was altogether different from that of the Inn of the Golden Lion. Generals and colonels were passing, and John learned from a soldier that a prince of the empire was inside. His heart beat hard. It could be none other than Auersperg, and using every possible excuse he remained in the vicinity of the hotel.

At last while he stood there he saw a face appear at an upper window, and his heart gave a great leap. Despite the falling dusk, the strangeness of the place and the distance, the single faint glimpse was sufficient. It was Julie. He could not mistake that crown of wonderful golden hair in which slight coppery tints appeared, and the face, pale now.

John impulsively reached out his arms, but she could not see the young peasant who stood afar, watching her. He dropped his arms, caution again warning him, but he stood gazing. Perhaps it was a power-ful, mysterious current sent from his heart that drew her at last. She looked in his direction. John knew that she could not recognize him there in the gloom, but, snatching off his cap, and, reckless of risk he waved it three times about his head. It was a signal. He did not know whether she could see it, nor if, seeing, could she surmise what it meant, but he hoped vaguely that something might come of it. In any event, it was a relief to his feelings and it brought hope.

After the signal he forgot to put the cap on his head, but stood with it dangling in his hand.

"Hey, you fool!" said a rough German voice, "why do you stand there staring, with your cap in your hand, and your head bare, inviting the quick death of pneumonia that an idiot like you deserves?"

Although the voice was rough it was not unkindly, and as John came out of his dreams and wheeled about he saw again the rubicund face of Sergeant Scheller.

"I was looking at the hotel," he replied with perfect composure, as he replaced his cap, "and I saw one of our great generals pass in at the door. At least I thought him such by his uniform, and taking off my cap to honor him I forgot to put in back again."

Scheller burst into a roar.

"Why, it's our Castel once more!" he exclaimed. "Good, honest, simple, patriotic Castel! You can take off your cap when a general passes, but you needn't keep it off after he's gone."

"I thought it might be our great Kaiser himself."

"I don't think he's in Metz, although he may be near, but your act does credit to your loyalty, Castel."

John glanced up at the window. Julie was gone and the twilight was coming over city and fortress. Yet he had seen her, and he felt that he would be able to follow Auersperg wherever he might go. He had no doubt that the prince would leave in the morning, traveling swiftly by automobile, but he, plodding on foot, or in any way he could, would surely follow. It gave him courage to remember the old fable of the tortoise and the hare, a fable which doubtless has proved a vain consola-tion to many a man, far behind in the race.

"Come to the Inn of the Golden Lion," he said to Scheller, for whom he had a genuine friendly feeling, "and take a glass of beer with me. I was wandering about, and it interested me to see the great people go into the hotel or come out."

"A half-dozen of our famous generals are there," said Scheller, who seemed to be both well informed now and talkative.

"Some one told me that the great Prince Karl of Auersperg was there, too," said John at random.

"So he is," replied Scheller, seeing nothing unusual in the question, "and he has with him under close guard the two French women spies. It's quite certain that he will carry them into Austria, perhaps to Salzburg or some place near there."

It was precious information, given casually by a chance acquaintance, and John believed that it was true. It was in the region of Salzburg that his great Odyssey had begun, and now it seemed that chance, after many a curve through the smoke of battle, was taking him back there.

"I'm off duty, Castel, and I'll be glad to go with you," he heard Scheller saying. "Beer is always welcome and I think you're a good fellow. It's too bad the blood of your forefathers was French, but it's had a German stiffening under our rule."

"The German spirit is strong and the Kaiser's armies are mighty," said John sincerely. "Now we'll hurry to the inn and have our beer."

Scheller was not loath, and before the great fire John toasted his health in a huge foaming mug, and Scheller toasted back again. Then the sergeant gave him a grip of his mighty hand and told him good-by.

"I like you, Castel, lad," he said, "and whatever you want I hope you'll get it."

John, imaginative at all times, but with his nerves keyed to the highest pitch now, took it as an omen. The kindly Scheller little dreamed what he sought, but the good wishes of a sergeant might have as much effect as those of a general or a prince with the Supreme Power.

"Farewell, lad," said Scheller again, and, "Farewell," John responded.

When he was gone John sank back into his chair. He had not been able to secure for the night more than a bench in the great room, but with his blankets he could do very well. Besides, there was a certain advantage in the place, as a dozen others would be sleeping in it, making it a news center.

He bought a supper of cheese and sausage, and continued to watch the people who came to the Inn of the Golden Lion. He thought Weber might return, and if so he meant to speak with him, if a possible chance should occur, but there was no sign of the Alsatian.

The heat and the smoke made him doze, by and by, and knowing that it would be long before the room could be cleared, he resigned himself at last to sleep, a circumstance that attracted no attention as others also were sleeping in their chairs.

When he awoke it was past midnight, and only those who were to make it a bedroom remained. Then he stretched his hardy form, wrapped in his blankets, on a bench beside the wall and fell promptly into the deep slumber of the young and just.

He awoke once or twice in the night and heard healthy snores about him. German civilians and Lorrainers were asleep on the benches and they slept well. The fire in the great, ancient fireplace had burned low, but a fine bed of coals glowed there and cast quivering lights over the sleepers. John thought he beard from afar that mutter of the guns, with which he was so familiar, but he did not know whether it was fancy or reality, as he always returned quickly to his deep slumber.

9

THE GREAT CASTLE

JOHN himself the next morning saw the departure of Prince Karl of Auersperg and his suite, and it was not altogether chance that brought it about. He was aroused as the other sleepers were by the waiters who were preparing the room for the day. The Inn of the Golden Lion was doing a rushing business in a town full of German troops, who ate well and drank well and who paid.

His night's rest was refreshing to both mind and body, and, after a good breakfast, he went once more toward the hotel which was frequented by the highborn and the very highborn. He had no plan in mind, but he knew that the magnet drawing him was Julie.

The morning was clear and cold, the streets slippery, but vivid with life, mostly military. He carried his knapsack full of food, and his blankets in a pack on his back, which his passport showed to be his right as a peasant trading in horses, and returning from the front to his home for a fresh supply. But there was little danger to him at present, as there were many other peasants and farmer folk in Metz on one errand or another.

He walked about the hotel, and presently noticed signs of bustle. Several automobiles, one of much magnificence, drove up to the entrance and halted there, obviously awaiting a company of importance. John had no doubt from the first that it was the equipage of the Prince of Auersperg. No one else would travel in such state, and he would stay to see him go with his prisoners. Others drawn by curiosity joined him and they and the young peasant stood very near.

John saw the door open, and a porter of great stature, clad in a uniform, heavy with gold lace, appear, bowing profoundly. It was often difficult to tell a head porter from a field marshal, but in this case the man's deferential attitude not only indicated the difference, but the fact also that Auersperg was coming.

The prince, preceded by two young men in close-fitting blue-gray uniforms, came out. John was bound to confess once more that he was a fine-looking man, large, bearded magnificently, and imposing in appearance and manner. His effect at a state ball or a reception would be highly decorative, and many a managing American mother would have been glad to secure him as a son-in-law, provided the present war did not make such medieval survivals unfashionable.

Auersperg entered his automobile, a very dark red limousine of great size, and he was shut from John's view, save only his full beard glimmering faintly through the glass. More men came, soldiers or attendants, and among them was Antoine Picard, gigantic and sullen. His arms were unbound and he went with the others willingly. Perhaps Auersperg had divined that he would not attempt to escape, as long as Julie was in his hands.

Then came the two women, Julie first, and John heard about him the muttered exclamation: "The French spies!" He knew that this belief had taken strong hold of the soldiers and people who stood about. Women, when they chose to be, were the most dangerous of all spies and the watchers regarded them with intense curiosity.

Neither was veiled. Julie was erect, and her chin high. John saw that the girl had become a woman, matured by hardship and danger, and she looked more beautiful than ever to him that morning. Her cheeks were pale and tiny curls of the deep golden hair escaped from her hood and clustered about her temples. John's heart swam with pity. Truly, she was a bird in the hands of the fowler.

She gave a glance half appealing and half defiant at the people, but the stalwart Suzanne who followed her was wholly grim and challenging. Then something strange occurred. John had the most intense anxiety for her to look at him. He had no belief whatever in anything supernatural, but sound, intelligible words were made to travel on waves of air, and it was barely possible in this unexplored world that thought too might be propelled in the same way.

Almost unconsciously he kept his eyes upon Julie's and he poured his very soul into the gaze. It was only a little distance from the door to the automobile which she was to take, and he had time. His gaze became concentrated, burning, a thing more of the spirit than of sight, and as her eyes glanced once more about the circle of idle spectators they met his own and rested there.

John looked straight into their dark blue depths and he saw a startled flash leap up. Chance or a power yet unknown had drawn her gaze and made her vision keen. He saw that she knew him, knew him even in that peasant's dress and under the new stubble of beard. The flash became for a moment a fire, and her figure quivered, but he was not afraid. He had an instinctive confidence that she would understand, and that she would not betray him by any impulsive act.

"I am here to save you," his eyes said.

"I know it," hers replied.

"I will follow you across the world to help you."

"I know that, too."

"Don't betray the fact that you've seen a friend."

"I will not."

Thus the eyes spoke to one another and understood what was said. Julie's glance passed on, and with unfaltering step she entered an automobile, the German chauffeur standing by the side of it and respectfully holding the door. Suzanne followed, the chauffeur closed the door, sprang into his seat and the little train moved majestically through the streets of Metz. Comment was plentiful and it was not unkind to Julie.

"Too handsome to be executed as a spy," said a burly German almost in John's ear. "A girl with a face like that should never feel the touch of a bullet or a rope. It's a face to be kissed and a neck to fit into a man's arm."

The man's phrasing was rough, but both his admiration and his pity were sincere, and John felt no resentment toward him.

"Some of the French girls are wonderful for looks," said another and younger German, "but they're the most dangerous kind. If it's proved on the one the prince has caught she'll expect her blue eyes and all that hair of gold to pull her through."

Him, John hated and would have been glad to strike, but he could help neither Julie nor himself by resenting it. Instead, he watched the automobiles, four in number, disappear on the road leading from Metz toward Stuttgart, a small body of hussars following as a guard, and then, pack on back, he trudged on foot behind them.

The invaluable passport carried him through the fortifications, and along the great highway into the country. He was glad that Auersperg had not gone by train, as it would have been harder to trace him then. Now, although far behind, he could hear of him at inns and little towns by the way. Yet he was compelled to recall to himself again and again the ancient and worn fable of the hare and the tortoise.

He knew well enough that the tortoise did not often overtake the hare. Hares were cunning little animals, riot able to fight and almost wholly dependent upon speed for survival in the battle of life. Hence, they never went to sleep, and in only a single instance recorded in history had a tortoise won a footrace from a hare. Yet an old proverb, even if based upon a solitary exception, is wonderfully consoling, and John was able to use it now as comfort.

After he had passed the fortifications and was well behind the German interior lines, travel became easier. The Germans, considering their army a wall before them, were less suspicious and the interruptions were few. John, moreover, was a cheerful peasant. He had a fair voice, and he sang German hymns and war songs in a mellow baritone as he strode along. The road was really not so bad, after that long and hideous life in filthy trenches. The heat of Sahara would be autumn coolness after a return from Hades, and now John enjoyed the contrast.

There were many tracks of automobiles in the light snow and hail that covered the road, and one broader than the rest John felt sure was made by the great limousine of Auersperg. It was like a trail to lead him on, and he was a trailer who could not be shaken off.

Rejoicing in his new possession of German--thankful now that he had studied it so hard--although he spoke it with a strong accent of Lorraine, John saluted such German soldiers as he passed and wished them good day. Invariably the salute was returned in pleasant fashion. His nature was essentially friendly and therefore he bred friendliness in others. Although he was in a hostile land he was continually meeting people who seemed to have an instinctive wish to help him.

As he walked on he overtook a stout man of middle age dressed heavily in brown who appeared to be a priest, and who turned upon him a benign countenance.

"Why do you travel so fast for one on foot?" asked the man.

"Because I feel strong and my errand takes me far, Father."

"If it takes you far, my son, the less speed in the beginning the greater at the end."

"True, Father," said John, slackening his pace, and glancing at the shrewd face which was also both ruddy and kindly. "The Church can give good advice in temporal as well as spiritual matters."

"Even so, my son," said the priest, who had noted John's frank countenance, his width between the eyes. "One of my vocation cannot go through life merely looking inward. Come, walk with me. The world is mad, gone wholly mad, but let us try to be two sane beings in it for a little while."

"Thanks, Father," said John. "I can wish no better company. I agree with you that the world has gone mad. I have seen its madness at its height."

"And at such a time the Church, Protestant or Catholic, must do the best it can. But we are so few, while so many souls are leaving their bodies. And yet I tell you, young sir, that not one man in a hundred of this great European peasantry knows why he fights. I, a priest, may speak freely, and I do so because my mind is full of indignation this morning."

"I do not love war, either. You see I walk away from it. But why are you on foot, Father?"

"By preference. I might have gone in one of the automobiles with the soldiers, but they are a part of the war madness, and I wished to be alone. You will learn with years that it's well to be alone at times, when one may take the measure of himself and those about him. I have chosen to walk this morning, because it makes my blood run better, and the winds at least are pure."

"I find the case the same with me, sir. My best thoughts usually come when I'm walking and alone."

The priest threw out his hands in a wide gesture.

"We agree, I see," he said. "You appear to be a peasant, but your voice is that of another kind. No, do not protest or say anything. It is no business of mine that you're not the peasant you claim to be, nor do I ask the nature of your errand behind the German army."

"I could not tell it to you, Father, but it is an errand of peace. I think it the highest and holiest I could undertake, and, in undertaking it, I believe myself to be animated by such a spirit as the knights felt in the first flush of the Crusades."

"I believe your words. When I first looked into your eyes I said they were those of an honest young man. We of the cloth learn to know. We feel instinctively the presence of honesty or dishonesty. Young sir, I hope that your quest, although it may take you far, will take you to success."

John's heart beat hard. He knew that the man was only a village priest, but good wishes carry. They might even travel upon waves of their own, and send to a happy goal those for whom they were intended.

"Father," he said, "you and I have never met before this day, and we may never see each other after it. As I told you, mine is a long quest and it's full of danger. Will you give it your blessing without asking what it is?"

"Willingly," said the priest as he spread out his hands, and murmured rapid words in Latin. John, Protestant though he was, felt a curious lightening of the soul. The Crusaders always sought a blessing before going into battle, and a spiritual fire that would uphold him seemed to have passed from the mind of this humble village priest to his.

They went on now for a little while in silence. Uhlans, hussars, infantry and cannon passed them, but few questions were asked of them. The day remained cold, and the heavens were a brilliant blue. It was fine weather for walking and the middle-aged man and the young man kept pace with each other, stride for stride.

By and by they drank from a brook and then ate together. The priest also carried a knapsack under his heavy brown overcoat and they shared their food, finishing it with a sip or two from a flask of light wine.

"We come to a crossroad a mile further on," said the priest, "and there I think we will part. I turn into the crossroad, and you, I take it, keep the road to Stuttgart."

"I shall be sorry."

"The way of the world, my son. All through life we are meeting and parting. The number of people who travel with us all the road is very small. It may be that I have surmised somewhat of your quest. No, say nothing! I would not know more, but a far greater power than mine will help you in it."

They parted at the crossroad and John felt as if he left an old friend. When he looked back he saw the priest on a little hill gazing after him, and he felt again as if the good wish that would count was coming on a wave of air. Then his own road dipped into a valley and at nightfall he came to a village which had a little inn, humble but neat and clean. Here he procured a razor and shaved the stubble from his face. He no longer had a fear of meeting anyone whom he might know, save possibly Weber, and Weber was a friend.

John's frank face and cheerful manner again made friends for him. The stout innkeeper and his stout wife favored him with the food, and hearing that he had come from Metz they wanted to know all the gossip, which he told them as far as he knew. He had noted the broad track of the great limousine in the road before he entered the inn, and thinking it must have stopped there for a little while, he spoke casually of those who passed.

"Aye," said the innkeeper, "many go by, many of whom will never come back. They go mostly toward Metz, but a great prince traveling in the other direction came today, before noon, and we served him refreshment."

"Perhaps it was the Prince of Auersperg," said John. "He was in Metz when I was there, and I saw him leave."

"They did not tell me his name, but that must have been the man."

"He was in a great, dark red automobile."

"Then it was surely he. One could not mistake that automobile. I take it that only kings and princes travel in its like."

"He carried with him two Frenchwomen, dangerous spies, intended for imprisonment in Germany."

"So I heard, and we saw the face of one of them, very young and with the most marvelous golden hair. I never saw a fairer face. But, as all the world knows, the most beautiful women are often the most wicked. I suppose there wasn't a woman among the Philistines who could compare with Delilah in either face or figure."

"I suppose not," said John, scarcely able to restrain a smile. "Did the women come into the inn?"

"Oh, no. My wife took food to them in the automobile. She saw them much better than I did. She says that the younger one--and she was but a girl--spoke softly and did not look wicked at all. But then, my wife is fat and sentimental."

The stout hausfrau smiled.

"It is Hans who has the heart full of sentiment," she said. "When he saw that the French spy was a girl of such beauty and such youth he believed that she should not be punished, and he a good German! Ah, all men are alike!"

Hans filled his pipe and wisely made no reply. But John smiled also.

"Is it wicked in a man to have an eye for beauty?" he said. "I know that my host's heart has thrilled many a time when he caught a glimpse of the lady who is now his wife and the very competent head of his household."

It was obvious, but both smiled.

"Hans is not so bad," said the hausfrau complacently, and John's compliment won him an unusually good room that night. Hans told him also that he could probably secure him a place in an empty supply wagon the next morning, and John was grateful. Walking was good, and it had done much to maintain his strength and steady his nerves, but one could not walk all the way across Germany.

He was aware that he was surrounded by dangers but he felt that the omens remained fair. Perhaps the good wishes that had been given to him still clothed him about and protected him from harm. In abnormal times the human mind seeks more than an ordinary faith.

He would have slept well, but in the night an army passed. For hours and hours the gray legions trod by in numbers past counting, the moonlight casting gleams upon the spiked helmets. Then came masses of Uhlans and hussars and after them batteries of great guns and scores and scores of the wicked machine guns. Truly, as the priest had said, the whole world had gone mad. He remembered those days in Vienna when the gay and light-head ed Viennese had marched up and down the streets all night long, singing and dancing, and thinking only of war as a festival, in which glorious victory was sure and quick. Torrents of blood had flowed under the bridges since then, gay Austria, that had set the torch, had been shaken to its foundation, and no victory was yet in sight for anybody.

Nevertheless the German legions seemed inexhaustible. John had seen them turned back in those long days of fighting on the Marne, and more than a million had been killed or wounded since the war began, but that avalanche of men and guns still poured out of the heart of Germany. He felt more deeply than ever that the world could not afford a German victory, and the sanguinary spectacle of a Kaiser riding roughshod over civilization. The fact that so many German people were likable and that Germany had achieved so much made the case all the worse.

He took the road the next morning, not on foot this time but in an empty provision wagon, returning eastward, drawn by two powerful horses and driven by Fritz, a stout German youth. Both Hans and the hausfrau wished him well, and he soon made a friend of Fritz, who was a Bavarian from a little village near Munich. John knew Munich better than any other German city, and he and the young German soon established a common ground of conversation, because to Fritz Munich was the greatest and finest of all cities.

That was one of the pleasantest mornings he experienced on his long and solitary quest. His heavy clothing kept him warm, his seat was comfortable, the pace was good and Fritz was excellent company. Fritz was a simple peasant, though, in his belief that Germany was right in everything and omnipotent, that the other nations through jealousy had conspired to destroy her, but she, instead, would destroy them all, and rule a conquered world.

John saw readily that the poison had been instilled into him from his birth by the men higher up, and he blamed Fritz very little for his misguided beliefs. Besides, it was pleasant to have the company of one somewhat near his own age, and to listen to human talk. There was a girl, Minna, in the village near Munich whom Fritz was going to marry as soon as the war was over.

"And that won't be long now," said Fritz. "It's true that we were halted before Paris last year, but we came again more numerous and more powerful than ever. The Kaiser will make a finish of it all in the spring, and I shall marry Minna. We shall go into Munich, see the beautiful city, and then go back to our home in the village."

"A fine place, Munich," said John. "In my dealing in horses I've been there more than once. Do you remember the Wittelsbach Fountain in the Maximilienplatz?"

"Aye, and a cooling sight it is on a warm day."

"And the green Isar flowing through the Englischer Gardens!"

"And the ducks swimming down to the edge of the little falls, swimming so close that you think they're going over and then swimming away again."

"Yes, I've seen them, and once I went into the gallery and saw the strange pictures they called Futurist, which I think represent the bad dreams of painters who have gone to bed drunk."

"You're a man of sense, you Castel, even if you do have a French name. I went in there myself once, and then I hurried away to the Hofbrau and drank all the beer I could that I might forget it."

John laughed, and Fritz laughed with him.

"How far do you go?" asked John.

"Only to Stuttgart. I wish it was Munich. Then I might see Minna again before returning to the war."

But they had a placid journey to Stuttgart, sleeping by the way in the wagon. Arriving in the city John paid Fritz for his ride and parted from him with regret. He spent a night here in a humble inn, and discovered that Auersperg and his party were now two days ahead of him. The automobiles were moving with speed, and John surmised that the prince did not intend to remain long at his castle over the Austrian border. Perhaps he would have to return to the war, leaving Julie and Suzanne there. He hoped so.

Two days later John was in Munich, and he learned that Auersperg had not increased his lead. It was easy enough to trace him. He had secured an extensive suite of apartments at the large hotel, the Bayerischer Hof, although Julie and the Picards had been secluded in another part of the hotel. Auersperg had gone to the palace and had held a long conference with the old King of Bavaria, but on the second day he had left, still going eastward, escorted by hussars.

John departed again and on foot. The weather was balmier now, with touches of spring in it. Faint shades of green appeared in the grass and the foliage, and his pursuit was sanguine. Fortune had certainly favored him in a remarkable manner, so far. He had been able to answer all questions in a convincing way, and here in Bavaria the people were not so suspicious, and perhaps not so stern as they were in Prussia. Nor did he doubt for a moment that Julie knew he was following them. She had recognized him and their eyes had spoken in the language of understanding to each other. It was easy enough to re-create for himself, almost as vivid as reality, her beautiful face with the golden hair showing under the edges of the hood, and the startled look of the dark blue eyes when they first met his own. Relief and joy had been in that look too. He could read it.

John had learned in Munich the location of Auersperg's principal castle. It was Zillenstein in a spur of the Eastern Alps just inside Austria, where for centuries the Auerspergs had held great state, as princes of the Holy Roman Empire. Now when they were princes of both the German and the Austro-Hungarian empires with their greater fealty for the former, they often went there nevertheless, and John's information in Munich made him quite sure that the prince had gone directly toward the ancient stronghold.

Auersperg could cover the distance quickly in his powerful automobiles, but it would take John a long time on foot, helped by an occasional ride in a peasant's cart. Nevertheless he hung on with patience and pertinacity. He was but a single man on a quest in the heart of Germany, but in the old days men had gone alone through a world of dangers to the Holy Sepulchre and had returned. He was not far from the path taken by those from Western Europe, and he was uplifted by the knowledge. The feeling that he, too, was a crusader grew strongly upon him, and by night and day was his support.

He crossed the border at last and came to Salzburg in the mountains, where the gray-green Salzach flows down from the glaciers and divides the town. The place was thronged with soldiers, and the summit of the frowning Muenchburg was alive with activity. Here in the very heart of the Teutonic confederation, far from hostile frontiers, travelers were not subjected to such rigid scrutiny. It was deemed that everything was safely German, and John could travel at ease almost like an inhabitant of the land.

Salzburg looked familiar to him. There had been much to photo-graph it upon his mind. He remembered the uneasy night he and his uncle had passed there before his flight with Lannes, which had taken him into such a train of vast events. It had been only seven or eight months before but it seemed many times as long. He had felt himself a boy in Vienna, he felt himself a man now. He had been through great battles, he had seen the world in convulsion, his life a dozen times had hung on a hair, and since it is experience that makes a man he was older than most of those twice his age.

He was stopping after his custom at an obscure inn, and in the moon-light he strolled through the little city. In its place among the mountains on both sides of the gray-green river it was full of romance to him, romance colored all the more deeply by memory. Off there among those peaks the *Arrow* had first come for him and Lannes, while here the great Mozart had been born and lay buried. In remoter days Huns had swept through these passes, coming from Asian deserts to the pillage of Europe.

John sat down on a bench in the little square before the cathedral and looked up at the mountains. He knew the exact location in which lay Zillenstein, the ancient seat of the Auersperg race, and he calculated that in two days he could reach it on foot, the lone youth in peasant's garb, pursuing the powerful prince and general, surrounded by retainers and hussars and in the land of his ancestors.

John wondered what had become of his comrades. Was Lannes well, and had he got his message? Were Carstairs and Wharton still alive, and where was Weber? They were questions the solution of which must wait upon the success of his quest, and therefore the answer might never come. But he fiercely put away such a thought. He would succeed! He must succeed!

He was not walking in the dark. He had learned that Auersperg and his people had arrived at Salzburg two days before, and had left after a few hours for Zillenstein. The prince was in excellent health and would not remain at his castle more than a week. Then he would return to the western front, where he was one of the great generals around the Kaiser. He had brought with him two Frenchwomen, spies, who would be imprisoned in the dungeons of Zillenstein until the war was over, if, indeed, they were not shot before. One, it was said, was very young, and beautiful, but she was the more dangerous of the two.

Poor Julie! there was a conspiracy of fate against her, but John shook himself and felt his courage rising anew, powerful, indomitable, invincible. He had come so far alone, and he would rescue her with his single hand! He went back to the inn and sat for a while among peasants and listened to their talk. They knew little of what was passing beyond the Teutonic empires. As usual in Germany and Austria, they accepted what the men higher up told them. They were always winning victories everywhere, and it would be but a short time before the treacherous English, the wicked French and the ignorant Russians were crushed.

John yawned after a while and went to his room. He intended to be fresh and strong the next morning when he started on the last stage of his search, and when the dawn came he was glad to see that it was clear and bright. By noon he was deep among the hills, and so far had answered all questions without arousing any suspicion. But he knew that trouble about his identity was bound to come in time. He could not go on forever, playing the rôle of Jean Castel, a horse-buyer from Lorraine. Lorraine was far away now, and he was beyond his natural range.

And yet his frank young face and smiling eyes were continually making him friends where he expected none. Explanations that might have seemed doubtful coming from others were convincing when he spoke them, and here in this hostile land, where he would have been executed as a spy, his identity known, he was instead helped on his way.

Late in the afternoon, when he was high up on the shoulder of a mountain he came to one of the little wayside shrines that one sees in the Catholic countries of the Old World. A small stream of clear, green water ran almost at the feet of the image, and he knelt and drank. Then he sat down to eat a little bread and sausage from his knapsack, and, while he was there, a middle-aged woman with two young boys also came to the shrine, before which they knelt and prayed. When they rose John politely offered them a portion of his bread and sausage, but they declined it, thanking him, and bringing forth food of their own, ate it.

John saw that the woman's face was very sorrowful, and the boys were grave and thoughtful beyond their years. He knew that they were under the shadow of the war, and his sympathy drew him to them.

"You have other sons, perhaps," he said gently, "and they are with the armies?"

"Alas, yes," she replied. "I have two others. One went to the east to fight the Russians and the other was sent to the west to meet the French. I have not heard from either in three months. I do not know whether they are alive or dead. We go into Salzburg tomorrow to get news of them, if we can."

"I hope they may come back to you," said John simply.

"And you? You are not of Austria."

"No, I came from a land that was French before I was born but which is now German, and under the beneficent rule of the great Kaiser-- Lorraine."

"You have indeed made a great journey."

"But it's to help one who needs help. I'd go if it took me to the other side of the world. The errand is sacred."

"Then I wish you Godspeed upon it. You are young, and you have a good face. What you say must be true. I shall pray for you and the happy end of your search."

She uttered words rapidly under her breath. She was a middle-aged and uneducated Austrian woman, but as she prayed and the shadows deepened on the mountains he received an extraordinary impression. A priest had prayed, too, for his success, and the second prayer could not be a mere coincidence. It was one of a chain. His will to succeed was so powerful, and so many others were helping him with the same wish that he could not fail.

10

T HE FAIR CAPTIVE

THE WOMAN GATHERED up the remains of the food, crossed herself again before the shrine, and she and her sons prepared to resume the descent of the mountain.

"I thank you for your good wishes," said John. "They may go far."

"And so may yours," she said. "Farewell!"

"Farewell!"

He watched them, walking down the slope, until a turn in the road hid them, and then he resumed his own ascent, slow now, because he had been climbing all day, and he wished to conserve his strength. The night was coming fast, and, if it had not been for the smooth-paved road over which he was walking, he might have fancied himself in a primeval wilderness. The sun was sinking in a sea of red light and peaks and ridges were outlined against it, clear and sharp. Old and thickly inhabited Europe melted away, and the young crusader stood alone and solitary among the mountains.

The road led around a cliff, and far across a valley on the other side he saw Zillenstein, that nest from which the Auerspergs had first ruled and raided. The red light of the setting sun fell upon it, magnifying every battlement and tower, and making them all glow with color. Vast as it was, it seemed even vaster in the red light and in the fire of John's own imagination.

His mind was filled with history and old romance, and it made him think of Valhalla. Here certainly was the dusk of the gods. Auersperg was one of the last representatives of the old order that troubled Europe so much in its going, for to John, a keen and intense lover of freedom and of the career open to all the talents, the present war was in its main feature a death struggle between autocracy and democracy.

He stared at the gigantic ramparts of Zillenstein, as long as the sun endured. He would have given much then to have had a powerful pair of glasses, but no horse-buying peasant could carry such equipment without arousing suspicion.

The day sank into the night and the last tower of Zillenstein was hid by the dusk. Just before going, and, when all the red light had faded, the castle showed huge, black and sinister. But John's soul was not cast down by it. Uncommon situations bred uncommon feelings and impulses. His imaginative mind still retained the impression that all the signs and omens were in his favor, and that the prayers of the righteous availed.

He came out of his dreams, and began to think of his night's lodging. The air was turning cold on the mountain and an unpleasant wind was trying to strike through his clothing, but he still carried his pair of blankets, and he had become hardened to all kinds of weather. He had a good supply, too, of the inevitable bread and sausage, and there was water for the taking.

He turned from the road and walked through a wood higher up the side of the mountain, having caught a gleam of white through the trees and being anxious to ascertain its nature. He found the remains of a small and ancient marble temple--temple he took it to be--and he was sure that it had been erected there perhaps fifteen centuries ago by the Romans. He knew from his reading that they had marched and fought and settled throughout all this region and in almost all of Austria. Marcus Aurelius might have been here, he might even have built the temple itself, and other Roman emperors might have stood in the shadow of its shattered columns.

It was a round temple, like those to Ceres that he had seen in Italy, and while some of the columns had fallen others stood, and a portion of the roof was there. He saw for himself a place under this fragment of a roof and against a pillar.

But he devoted his attention first to supper. A small cold stream flowed from under a rock fifty feet away, and drinking from it now and then he ate his bread and sausage in comfort, and even with a sense of luxury. He was a crusader and he was upborne more strongly than ever by his faith. Alone on the mountain in the darkness everything else had melted away. America was an immeasurable distance from him and the figures of his uncle, Mr. Anson and his young friends of the army became thin shadows.

The moon, full and dominant, came out after a while and silvered the skies. Stars in myriads trooped forth and danced. John felt that they were friendly, that they were watching over him, and once more he saw happy omens. Despite his long walk he was not tired and he enjoyed the deep peace on the mountains. He might have been awed at another time, but now he was not afraid.

Zillenstein, too, came out, bathed in silver, an immense threatening mass set solidly in the shoulder of the opposite mountain, more sinister even in the moonlight than in the sunlight. He wondered how many hundreds of innocent human beings had perished in its dungeons. He had not the slightest doubt that Julie was there, but she at least was safe from everything, save a long imprisonment and a powerful pressure that might compel her to become the morganatic wife of Auersperg. It might be the old story of the drop of water wearing away the stone.

Clouds began to trail slowly up the valley, and Zillenstein faded away again. The long columns of mist and vapor seemed so near that John felt as if he could reach out his hand and touch them.

His day's exertions began to tell now, and the chill of the night deepened. He sought his chosen shelter within the old temple, and lying down on the stone floor wrapped in his blankets, sank fast into sleep. Morning dawned, sharp and clear, and the red sun came out of Asia, turning the huge pile of Zillenstein once more into a scarlet glow, a vast blood-red splotch in the side of the mountain.

He drank at the little stream, then bathed his face, ate breakfast, and, knapsack on back, returned to the road that led down the far side of the mountain. His courage was still high. The crusader of the day before was none the less the crusader this morning, and he whistled soft and happy airs as he descended. He knew that it was a trick that he had caught from General Vaugirard and he wondered where that fat old hero might be now.

But as he walked along he formed his plan. Every general who intends to attack an enemy must choose a method of approach, and the crusader's plan to assail Zillenstein was now quite clear in his mind. His decision brought him the usual relief, following the solution of a doubt, and he intended that his journey that day through the great valley should resemble somewhat a stroll of pleasure.

He whistled at times and at times he sang. He remembered the story, of the faithful troubadour, Blondel, who sought his master, Richard of the Lion Heart, imprisoned somewhere in a castle in Austria, and who, finding him, sang under his window to let him know one loyal friend was there. But Richard, under the light of history, had become merely a barbarous king, cruel to his enemies and unjust to his friends. John felt that his own quest was higher and better.

Toward noon he was in the middle of a valley down which a swift little river flowed. Old men, women and children were at work in the fields preparing for the new crop, and again John's frank eyes and hearty voice won him a welcome. He was a man of Lorraine who had been on the far western front and they welcomed Ulysses on his travels. They said that he was going to Zillenstein at a fortunate time, as the prince had just returned for a space and the great castle was full of people. When so much of the youth of the land was gone away a handy man with horses might obtain work there. The prince used automobiles chiefly, but many horses were employed also.

Once John was compelled to show the German passport. It was of no use in Austria, except as a proof of identity, and good faith, and as such it served him well.

In the afternoon he began to ascend the slope that confined the southern side of the valley, and toward night he drew near to Zillenstein. The view of the castle here was less clear than from the other side of the valley. Patches of pine on the slopes beneath hid many of the towers and battlements, but he saw lights shining from lofty windows, and about the castle were many small houses. He surmised that Zillenstein and its surroundings had not changed much since the Middle Ages. Here was the castle, and below it were the cottages and huts of the peasants and retainers who might be as loyal as ever to the prince whose lineage was more ancient than that of either Hohenzollern or Hapsburg.

Two young hussars riding down the road, their horses' hoofs ringing on the stones, brought back the modern world. They were gay young fellows, smoking cigarettes, their Austrian caps tipped back to let the cool breeze blow upon their foreheads, and they called cheerfully to the strong young peasant who walked slowly up the road. John lifted his cap and answered in a tone that was respectful but not servile.

"You look like one who has traveled far," said the younger of the two, a mere boy.

"From Lorraine," answered John. "My name is Jean Castel, which is French, but I, its owner, am not. My family became German before I was born, and has been so ever since."

"Ah, I see, made German by strength of arms."

"And growing more German every day by will and liking."

"You speak well for a peasant."

"I was a dealer in horses, which took me much over the land and everyone who travels learns. See, here is my passport."

"Why should I look at your passport?"

"Everyone else does. Then why not you?"

"No, I don't want to see it. I take your word for it You couldn't have come so deep into Germany, unless you were one of us. What do you seek at the castle?"

"My trade is gone and I want work with the horses. There must surely be a place on the estate of so great a prince."

"There is, but he wants good men, the very best."

"Let him try me."

"I'll try you now."

The hussar leaped from his horse and asked John to get into the saddle. John had noticed that it was a big brute with a red eye, and every other indication of a wicked temper, but in his earlier youth he had spent a year on a great ranch belonging to his uncle in Montana, and the cowboys had taught him everything. He was quite aware that a dramatic effect would be useful to him now, and he decided to temporize a little in order that the culmination might be greater.

"It has been my business," he said, "to try and sell horses, not to ride them."

Both officers laughed derisively.

"Prince Karl of Auersperg likes bold men around him," said the one who had dismounted, "and he would not care for a hostler who was afraid of his own horses."

John, despite the fact that he had invited it, was stung somewhat by the taunt.

"While I said it was not my business to ride horses I didn't say I couldn't ride them," he replied.

"Then up with you and prove it."

John seized the bridle, and as the great black horse, feeling the touch of an unfamiliar hand, pulled away from him, he made one leap and was in the saddle. He felt in an instant from the fierce quiver running through the mighty frame that he had a demon beneath him. The Austrians, who doubtless had not expected him to accept the challenge, were alarmed and the younger, whose name John afterward learned to be Pappenheim, shouted:

"Jump off! He'll kill you!"

John had no notion of leaving the saddle, either willingly or unwillingly. He believed that after his training by the cowboys he could ride anything, and when he felt the great frame draw itself together he was ready. He saw too that he could make capital. He would impress these volatile Austrians and at the same time he would recommend himself as an expert horsemen to Prince Karl of Auersperg.

The black horse made a series of mighty jumps, any one of which would have sent a novice flying, but the trained rider on his back knew instinctively which way he was going to leap, and swayed easily every time. Then panting, and mad with anger and fury, the horse rushed down the road. John pulled hard on the bridle to keep him from stumbling. He heard the two Austrians behind him shouting, and the one on horseback pursuing, but he did not look back.

When the horse had gone three or four hundred yards he pulled harder on the bit, and gradually turned him about in the road. Then he raced him back up the hill, a most exhausting proceeding for any animal however strong. Then the horse began to jump and kick again, but he could not shake off his incubus. A side glance by John showed that young Pappenheim was standing among the trees by the roadside well out of the way and that the mounted officer had also drawn back among the trees.

He felt that now was the time for his stroke. He knew that the horse was conquered, overcome chiefly by his own struggles, and letting him breathe a little he urged him straight forward in the road toward the castle, which was only a few hundred yards away.

As he emerged from the woods he saw that the road led through the remains of an ancient wall, and across a bridge over a moat which was partly filled up. In the cleared space in front of the wall several soldiers were standing and near them were two hussars. The hussars rode forward, as if they would prevent the flight of the horse, but John urged on his waning spirit and he dashed over the moat and through the wall into the inner precincts of the castle yard, where the animal stopped dead beat and covered with foam.

He slipped from the horse, as a man, who had been sitting in a camp chair in the shadow of a great pine, rose in surprise, and stood looking at him. It was Prince Karl of Auersperg himself, in a uniform of gray and silver, his great brown beard forked and spreading out magnificently. John took off his cap, saluted and despite the fierce beating of his heart stood calmly before him.

"What does this mean?" demanded the prince.

John was saved a reply by young Pappenheim, who came up running.

"It was my fault, Your Highness," he said. "We met him in the road coming to the castle, where he said he wished to be employed as a hostler. I told him to prove his skill by riding my horse, which hitherto has tolerated no one but myself on his back. He rode him like a Cossack, and here he is! The fault, sir, was mine, and I crave the pardon of Your Highness, but this man has proved himself a horseman."

The prince combed his great forked beard with his fingers, and looked at the young peasant with a contemplative eye. John surmised that Pappenheim stood well with him, and would be forgiven.

"The test was, perhaps, severe," he said, "but the young man seems to have endured it well. I might say that in his own little world he has achieved a triumph. Send him to the stables, and tell Walther, the head groom, to give him work."

After the one examining glance he no longer looked at John who had now disappeared from his own world. John had no fear of detection. He had let his semblance of a young beard grow again, and Prince Karl of Auersperg would not dream of his presence there in the mountains of Austria.

"Thanks, Your Highness," he said, again bowing respectfully. A groom took the horse and Pappenheim went with him to the stables, where he recommended him specially to Walther, a stalwart Tyrolean, who was evidently glad to have him, as he was short of help.

"Treat him well. Walther, because he will be of use," said Pappen-heim. "He has ridden my own horse and no one but myself has ever done that before."

The Tyrolean's eyes gleamed with wonder and approval.

"Then you must know horses," he said, and put him to work at once in the stables. John toiled with a will. All things still moved as he could wish them to go. The blessings upon his errand that he had received were not without effect. It was true that he was but a stable boy, but he was within the precincts of the castle of Auersperg, and Julie was but a few hundred yards away. He recalled an old line or two, from Walter Scott, he thought;

And he bowed his pride To ride a horse-boy in his train.

As he remembered it, the service had a motive somewhat similar to his own, and he was glad to "bow his pride," because he believed that he would have ample chance to raise it up again. As he went about his work singing and whistling softly to himself, he cast many a glance up at the huge castle.

Truly Zillenstein had been a great fortress. In the old days it must have been impregnable. Much of it was still standing in its ancient strength. John saw that the walls were many feet thick, and that in the older parts the windows were mere slits through which a human body could not pass.

A much more modern addition to the right wing had been built, and John surmised that Prince Karl and his suite lived there. Auersperg might have medieval notions of caste, but he was certain to have modern ideas of luxury.

He worked hard through all the rest of the day. What a lucky thing it was that he had always liked horses, and had spent that year on the western ranch of his uncle! Horses were the same everywhere, and as far as he could see they responded as readily to kind treatment in Europe as in America. The same friendly disposition that won him the favor of people was now winning him the favor of animals, and Walther, who had spent fifty years in the stables, complimented him on his soothing touch. John saw that he had made a new friend, and he meant to use him as a source of information.

He soon learned that Prince Karl would not stay long at Zillenstein. He had come there, partly, to meet several great officers of Austria and confer with them. His position as a Prussian general and a prince of both empires made him the most suitable person for the duty, and Zillenstein, in the heart of Austria, was the best place for the meeting.

Walther, a taciturn man, volunteered so much, but he went no farther, and John, despite his great anxiety, did not ask any questions. He knew that he was a too recent arrival at Zillenstein to be making inquiries without arousing suspicion, and it was better anyhow to go slowly. Late in the afternoon, Walther directed him to saddle and bridle a fine young horse and lead him to the front of the castle.

"One of the young noblemen who was wounded in a great battle in the west has been recovering from his wound at Zillenstein," he said, "and he has been riding every day toward evening. You will hold the horse until he comes, but he is always prompt."

John led the horse, a fine young bay, along a curving road, until he stood before the entrance of the castle. There he waited in silence, but he was using his eyes all the time. He admired the great size and strength of Zillenstein, even in its decayed state, and he was confirmed in his belief that the prince and his suite inhabited the extension of the right wing. Doubtless Julie and Suzanne should be sought there.

While he stood holding the horse one or two soldiers passing gave him scrutinizing looks, and a couple of trim Austrian maids did likewise, smiling at the same time, because John was very good looking, despite his fuzzy young beard. He smiled back at them, as became one of his lowly station who had met with approval, and whispering to each other they passed on. Now, he had two more new friends, and it occurred to him that these maids also might be of use to him in his great quest. He had formed his plan and like a good general he was marshaling every possible force for its success.

While he was thinking about it, the convalescent came, a young officer, trim, slender, in a fine uniform of blue and silver. It was none other than that same lad, Leopold Kratzek, whom he had saved in the fight at the trench. In his surprise John came very near to greeting him by name, but luckily he controlled himself in time.

He noticed that Kratzek was almost entirely recovered. The color in his face was fresh, his walk was firm and elastic, and John was glad of it. He liked the lad whose life he had saved. He recalled, too, that his presence there was not strange. Kratzek was the relative of Auersperg, and it was natural that he should be sent to Zillenstein to recover.

The young Austrian glanced at the new groom, but there was no sign of recognition on his face.

"I have not seen you before," he said.

"No, sir," replied John, "I've just come today. I've been wandering eastward from Lorraine, where I was born, and the Herr Walther has been kind enough to give me work."

"You're the man of whom I heard Pappenheim speak so well. He has been telling us all how a wandering peasant rode that black devil of his."

"I am fortunate in understanding horses."

"Well, you've made a friend in Pappenheim."

John gave him the reins and Kratzek, drawing himself a little stiffly into the saddle, cantered away. John, although not recognized, felt as if he had met a friend again, and Zillenstein seemed less lonely to him.

He watched Kratzek riding down the mountain until the firs and pines hid him, and then, as he turned to go back to the stables, he found the two maids near him, a little forward, and yet a little shy, but wholly curious about the handsome young stranger.

Bearing in mind that the news of the household, even of a huge castle, filtered most often through women, he smiled back at them and said pleasantly in his new German:

"Good morning. May I ask your names?"

One was blond and the other brunette, and the brunette answered:

"We're Ilse and Olga, maids of the household of His Highness, Prince Karl of Auersperg."

"And very pretty maids, too," said John gallantly, as he took off his cap and bowed. "When I look at Ilse I think she is the more beautiful, when I look at Olga I think she is the more beautiful, but when I see them together I think they are equally beautiful."

They giggled and nudged each other.

"You are the man who rode the young count's horse," said Ilse, who took the lead in talk as brunettes usually do, "and I hope you will pardon our forwardness in wishing to look at so wonderful a person."

There was a wicked little glint in her eye, but John only smiled again.

"I was lucky," he said.

"We saw you," said Olga. "We were standing on the edge of the lower terrace when you sprang into the saddle. We were sure you would be killed."

"But we were glad you were not," said Ilse. "We were pleased when we saw you riding the great black horse directly back to the castle. Do you mean to stay here all the time?"

"Where there is so much beauty and wit I should like to remain," replied John with increasing gallantry, still holding his cap in his hands, "but who can tell where he will be a week hence in times like these?"

Again they laughed and nudged each other. Ilse had a shrewd and observant mind.

"Your German has a French accent," she said.

"I was born in a land that was once French--Lorraine--so my blood is French by descent, although I am wholly German in loyalty and in feeling. But I'm not the first person of French blood that you ever saw, am I?"

He asked the question in a careless tone, but he awaited the answer with anxiety.

"Oh, no," replied Ilse. "Many people come to the great castle of Zillenstein. Two Frenchwomen are here now, spies, terrible spies they say, but I can scarce believe it, at least of the young one, Mademoiselle Julie, who is so beautiful, and who speaks to us so gently."

"But it may be true of the other of low degree, the surly Suzanne," said blond Olga.

"At least, they're where they can't get back to France as long as this war lasts," said John, looking up at the formidable castle. "It seems a sad thing to me that women should be spies. It isn't right."

He spoke in his most engaging manner. Again his frank look and attractive smile were winning him friends where he needed friends most. He saw, too, that he was on a subject that interested the maids. Once more fortune was favoring him who wooed her so boldly.

"But," said the blond and substantial Olga, "I think the beautiful Mademoiselle Lannes is in no danger. The prince himself loves her and would marry her. We can see it, can we not Ilse?"

"At least we think it."

"We know it. And His Highness might search Europe and not find a woman more beautiful. She has the most wonderful hair, pure gold, with little touches of copper, when the firelight or the sunlight is deep upon it, and when loosed it falls to her knees. I have seen it."

"And marvelous blue eyes," said Ilse. "A dark blue like the waters of our mountain lakes. Oh, no, the Prince of Auersperg can never punish her!"

John laughed.

"This French spy seems more dangerous as a captive than free," he said.

"That is so," said Ilse, seriously. "If Prince Karl of Auersperg, powerful as he is, were disposed to punish her, the others would not let him."

"What others?"

"The young Count Kratzek, the relative of the prince. He loves her, too, and he scarcely seeks to hide it. And Count Pappenheim, who is of kin to the emperor, worships her beauty."

"The lady must be Psyche herself," said John.

But not knowing who Psyche was, they shook their heads.

"And that is not all," continued Ilse. "A Prussian prince was here, a fine and gallant man, tall and young. He, too, is at the feet of the lovely

Mademoiselle Julie. I heard him say that he had seen her before she was brought to Zillenstein."

John's pulses suddenly beat hard. He knew instinctively the identity of the Prussian prince, but he asked quietly:

"What was the man from Prussia called?"

"Prince Wilhelm von Arnheim. I was present when he first saw here the beautiful Mademoiselle Julie. He bent before her and kissed her hand, as if she were a princess herself. The look that he gave her was full of love, and it was also most respectful. I, Ilse Brandt, know."

"I've no doubt of it, because you've received many such looks yourself, beautiful Ilse," said John.

"There she is now! At the window!" exclaimed Olga.

John looked at once, and his heart leaped within him. Julie stood framed in a window, high up in the new part of the castle. The light seemed to fall upon her, as one turns it in a flood upon a picture, and her figure was in the center of a glow that brought out the coppery touches in the wonderful golden hair, that was the marvel of everybody. She seemed to be gazing wistfully over the misty mountains, and John's heart was full of yearning.

"I can't believe," said Ilse, "that she is a spy or has ever been a spy. She has not the look, nor the manner. When the Prince von Arnheim was here they gave a great dinner, and Prince Karl bade her come to it. I took her a beautiful dress of his niece, who is away in Vienna. I thought she would refuse, but she said that she would come as Prince Karl requested. I was her maid, I dressed her and she was very beautiful. She went to the dinner, and the aged Lady Ursula, the cousin and dependent of the prince, sat with her."

"What happened?" asked John in a low voice.

"I think it was their intention at first to remind her that she was a prisoner. Prince Karl is a hard and stern man, and he would bend her to his will, but the Prince Wilhelm frowned upon them all, and the Count Kratzek was also most respectful."

"They had brought her to complete their triumph and instead the triumph was hers," John could not keep from saying.

"It is so," admitted Ilse. "They were abashed before her, and at the last when they drank a toast to the glorious victory of our German race, she withheld her glass, and then, taking a sip of the wine, she said she wished with all her heart, as long as it should beat in her body, for the triumph of France. That, too, I saw, and while I do not wish for the triumph of France it was thrilling to see but one and a girl defying so many strong men."

"I wish I had been there to see," murmured John.

"What did you say?" asked Olga.

"That only a very brave woman could have done such a thing."

"She is brave. She does not fear any of them, and the woman Suzanne with her has a tiger's temper."

"But she loves the young mademoiselle. One can see that," said Ilse, "and she will guard her."

John wished to know what had become of Antoine, but he did not dare ask pointed questions. Julie left the window presently and the light went with her. The sunlight was dying now on the eastern mountains, but a great happiness came to him. He had found her. The footsteps of the crusader had been guided aright. His star had led him on through many dangers, and his spirit was high with hope.

It was, perhaps, well that the growing twilight kept Ilse and Olga from seeing the glow in his eyes, but it was time for the two to go, and, laughing and supporting each other in what they considered a mild flirtation, they disappeared within the castle. John sent a smile after them. They were good girls and he knew that he had made two valuable friends who would tell him all that was happening to Julie in Zillenstein.

He went back to the stables and plunged anew into his work with a zeal and skill that aroused the admiration of Walther. His knowledge of horses was most useful to him now, and, as he had also learned much about automobiles in his campaigning, he volunteered to help with them too. He saw the great limousine in which the prince himself had traveled, and he helped two of the hostlers to clean it. Walther growled as he looked on.

"When I was a lad," he said, "the magnificent, living horse was king at Zillenstein. Now it's a machine that can't either think or feel."

"We can't fight the times, Herr Walther," said John, cheerfully. "The automobile like the railway has come to stay."

"I suppose so, but the noble Count Kratzek returns. Take his horse."

John went forward and held the bridle after the young Austrian had dismounted. Kratzek had a fine color from his ride, and he seemed to John to be completely well of his wound. He handed the young peasant who was holding his horse half a krone, and then walked briskly into the castle.

John put the little silver piece in his pocket, after having touched his cap, and led the horse into the stable. He did not feel humiliated. He found something humorous in receiving a tip of ten cents from the man whose life he had saved. He unsaddled the horse, put him in his stall, rubbed him down, and came forth to receive the unqualified praise of Walther.

"You, Castel," he said, "you're a fiend for work. I can see that. Most of my men look upon work as an enemy. They run from it and hide from it. Now, come you to the kitchen and you shall eat well in reward."

The great kitchen for the servants and retainers, who were many, was in the basement of the castle and John, his appetite sharp from the day's work, ate bountifully. The obvious fact that he had already won the regard of Walther, a man of importance, inspired respect for him, and once the brunette Ilse, flitting through the kitchen, gave him a glance of approval.

He slept that night in a little room above the horses, but first he saw the moon rise over Zillenstein, the valley and the mountain, a vast panorama, white and cold. He did not know what his next step was to be. He did not know how he was to communicate with Julie, but he had an implicit confidence in the Providence that had guided him so far and so well.

Three days went by and he did not yet find the way, but he saw Julie once more at the window and yet another time walking on the terrace in front of the castle accompanied by Suzanne. He was walking Pappenheim's restive horse back and forth and he was not a hundred feet from her, but he knew no sign to make. The air was cold then, and she was wrapped in the long, dark red cloak that he knew. A hood also of dark red covered her head, but tiny curls of the marvelous golden hair escaped from it, their glowing color deepening by contrast the pallor of her lovely face. Again John's heart, overflowing with pity and love, yearned for her.

The crusader worships that which he seeks. John had come to the end of his search, but apparently the way of rescue was as hard as ever. He saw her, but he could not speak to her, and there was no way to let her know that he was near. Suzanne, dark, grim and powerful, walked a step or two behind her, watching over her with a love that was ready for any sacrifice. John felt a deep respect for this faithful and taciturn woman of Normandy, and he was devoutly glad that she was there to be a comfort and support to Julie in these trying days.

As John walked the horse up and down, the maid, Ilse, passing on an errand, stopped and spoke to him.

"It's the French spy and her maid," she said. "They allow her to take the air twice a day upon the terrace. I can't think that she is merely a spy. It must be something political, too high for such as you and me to understand. Perhaps she is a great French lady who is held as a hostage. Do they do such things in war now, Jean Castel?"

"I think so."

"Prince Karl sends her flowers this morning. See, Olga comes with them, but she does not speak French, nor do I. She will not know from whom they come."

Often the great opportunity appears when it is least expected. A trifle may open the way and John, quick as lightning, saw and seized his chance. Throwing the reins of the now quiet horse over a pillar he said:

"I know French, as I come from Lorraine. Let me take them."

Without waiting for her assent he took the flowers from the hand of the willing Olga and walked boldly across the terrace to Julie, who was looking over the valley. Bending the knee he offered the flowers, saying:

"Prince Karl sends you these, Mademoiselle Lannes."

She started a little at the sound of his voice and he continued in a lower tone:

"Julie, I've come across Germany for you. Make no sign. I'm here to save you. I'm a groom in the prince's stables!"

He saw the delicate color like the first flush of dawn overspread her face, and a light that had never shone for any other spring into her eyes. All the hardships that he had endured, all the dangers that he had run were as nothing now.

"John," she exclaimed, in a voice tremulous with fear for him, not for herself, "you must leave Zillenstein at once! Your life is not safe here for a moment!"

"When I go you go with me," he said.

They had spoken rapidly in whispers and not even Suzanne had noticed. Accustomed now to the servants in the castle she had merely seen a young peasant bringing flowers from the prince to her mistress. They had been brought before and there was nothing unusual about it.

"Tell the prince that I thank him," said Julie, aloud, but in indifferent tones.

John bowed and walked back toward the horse, his heart beating hard with triumph and joy.

11

THE EFFICIENT HOSTLER

WHEN JOHN SCOTT returned to the stables his pulses were still throbbing with joy and he trod the grass of the Elysian Fields. Young love is pure and noble, a spontaneous emotion that has nothing in it of calculation, and the wild and strange setting of his romance merely served to deepen his feelings.

He was the young crusader again, a knight coming to rescue his lady from the hands of the infidels. He had made the impossible possible. He had seen her and spoken with her, and despite his peasant clothes and his position of a menial that he had willingly taken, she had known him at once. He had seen the deep color flushing into her face and the light like the first arrow of dawn spring into her eyes, and he knew that he had not come in vain.

He put so much vigor into his work, and he whistled and sang, low but so joyously that the stolid Walther took notice.

"Why are you so happy, you Castel?" he asked.

"I've seen the sun, Herr Walther."

"There is nothing uncommon about that. The sun has risen every morning for a million years and more."

"But not this sun, Herr Walther. It never rose before and it's the brightest and most glorious of them all."

Walther looked up at the sun. It was in truth bright, casting a golden glow over all the mountains, but he saw nothing new about it.

"It's a fine sun, as you say," he said, "but it's the same as ever. Ah, you're French after all--in blood, I mean, I don't question your loyalty-- and you see things that are not. Too much imagination, Castel. Quit it. It's not wholesome."

"But I'm enjoying it, Herr Walther. Imagination is a glorious thing. You see the same sun that I do in so far as our eyes are able to look upon it, but you do not see it in the same way. It appears far more splendid and glorious to me than it does to you. Our eyes are mirrors and mine reflect today with much more power and much more depth of color than yours do."

Walther stared at him, comprehending but little of what he had said, and shook his head slowly.

"Your French blood is surely on top now, Castel," he said. "I should call you a little mad if you didn't work so hard and with such a good heart."

"Ah, well, if we enjoy our madness, pray let us remain so."

Walther shook his head again, and walked away some distance where he stopped, and looked long at his new helper who toiled with uncommon diligence but who whistled and sang in a low but happy manner as he toiled. A new thought was slowly making its way into his stolid brain. A man might have a madness, and be none the worse for it. Well, every one to his own madness.

John had heard from Ilse that Julie walked on the terrace twice every day, once in the morning and once in the afternoon, and he strove so to arrange his work that he might see her again that afternoon. Knowing that he was already a favorite with Walther he made many suggestions. This horse or that needed exercise, and one that had been a favorite with the prince before he had taken to the automobile, and that even now was often ridden by him, would be all the better for sun and air. Walther agreed with him and John deftly postponed the time until about four o'clock, the warmest and brightest part of the afternoon, when he thought it most likely that Julie would come again.

He led the horse back and forth along a road that led from the stables to a forest hanging on the slope, being in sight of the terrace about half the way. But the terrace was bare and it was not until he had made three or four turns that Julie with her following shadow, Suzanne, appeared. Again John's heart beat heavily, and the hand that held the bridle trembled. He could not help it. His mind, highly sensitive and imaginative, was nevertheless powerful and tenacious to the last degree. And he was there in the heart of old romance. The vast castle, gray and sinister, loomed above him, but beyond was the golden light on the mountains.

He did not try to attract her attention, but, walking calmly on with the horse, poured all his soul into the wish that she would look his way. He had not the remotest belief in the supernatural as he told himself again, but he continued to wish it with all his power and strength, and presently her gaze turned toward the young peasant and the horse who were walking slowly up and down the road. He was too far away to read her face, but his fond fancy told him that she rejoiced again to see him there.

She looked at him a little while, but she made no sign or signal. He expected none. She would know too well that it might create suspicion and from some one of the many windows of the castle jealous eyes might be watching.

She advanced to the edge of the terrace with her faithful shadow still close behind her, and then the prince came. He was in a white and silver uniform of Austria, a magnificent figure of a man, despite his middle years, and his great brown beard gave him a majestic aspect. But John knew that his eyes were set close together and that the soul behind them was unscrupulous and cruel.

He saw Auersperg take off his gorgeous hat and bow low before the young Julie. Then they walked together on the terrace, the dark shadow of Suzanne following, but further behind now.

John's heart was filled with a fierce and consuming rage. The presence of Auersperg, magnificent, triumphant, powerful, a medieval baron here in the most medieval of all settings, a very monarch indeed, brought him back to earth. What could he do alone in the face of so much might? What could Julie herself do, helpless, before so much pressure? And, after all, from his point of view and from the point of view from his class, Auersperg was making her a great offer, one that nobles in the two empires would hold to be most honorable. For the first time he felt a tremor of doubt, and then he stilled it as base and unworthy. The very word "morganatic" was repulsive to him. It implied that the man stooped, and that the woman surrendered something no real wife could yield. Julie, whose blood was the blood of the great republican marshal, would never submit to such a wrong.

John presently saw someone standing on the steps of the terrace, and as he turned with the horse, he beheld a wild and jealous face. It was young Kratzek, and he was watching Auersperg and Julie. He was only a lad, this Austrian noble, but John's heart felt a touch of sympathy. A common love made them akin and he knew that Kratzek's love like his own was the love of youth, high and pure. He felt neither hate nor jealousy of the Austrian.

His eyes went back to Julie and Auersperg. Their faces were turned toward him now and he could see that it was the prince who talked and that Julie listened, saying but little. The thud of hoofs on the road into the valley came to him and Pappenheim, on his great black horse, galloped into view. But he pulled to a walk when he saw the two on the terrace, and John smiled to himself in grim irony. Pappenheim also loved the ground upon which the young Julie walked. Von Arnheim and von Boehlen should be there, too, and then the jealous circle would be complete.

Kratzek presently walked away, and Pappenheim rode slowly past the castle and out of sight. Julie turned from the prince and looked fixedly for a little while in John's direction. He felt that she meant it as a sign, and he was eager to reply in some way, but prudence held him. Then she went into the castle and Auersperg was left alone on the terrace.

John saw that Prince Karl of Auersperg was very thoughtful. He walked slowly back and forth, his figure magnified in the sun's glow, and now and then he thoughtfully stroked his great brown beard. He seemed to John more than ever out of place. His time was centuries ago among the robber barons. In such a group he would not have been the worst, but in his soul John wished that the hour for all such as he had come. If the great war struck that dead trunk from the living body of the human race it would not be fought wholly in vain.

He went into the castle after a while, his walk slow and thoughtful, and John returned with the horse to the stables. All the rest of the day, he worked with such diligence and effect that Walther bade him rest.

"You may go about the castle as much as you please," he said, "and you may enter the part set aside for the servants, but you must stop there. Nor can you go beyond the immediate castle grounds. If you try it you risk a shot from the sentries."

"I've no wish to be shot and so I'll not risk it," said John, with the utmost sincerity, and after bathing his face and hands, he strolled through the grounds of Zillenstein, his course soon and inevitably leading him toward the addition to the right wing from the windows of which lights were shining. Yet the grounds outside were heavy with shrubbery, and, keeping hidden in it, he advanced farther and farther, eager to see.

He was not yet twenty yards from the walls and he saw human figures passing before the windows. Then a dark form presently slipped from a small door and stood a moment or two on the graveled walk, as if undecided. John felt the pulses beating hard in his temples. He knew that stalwart figure. It was none other than the grim and faithful Suzanne and, daring all, he went to the very edge of the shrubbery, calling in a loud whisper:

"Suzanne! Suzanne!"

She stood attentive, glanced about, and, seeing that no one observed her, came to the edge of the deep shadow.

"Suzanne! Suzanne!" called John again. "It is I, John Scott! Have you any message for me from Mademoiselle Julie?"

She looked again to see that none was near, and then stepped boldly into the shrubbery, where John seized her arm half in entreaty and half to hurry her.

"O, Suzanne! Suzanne!" he repeated, with fierce insistence. "Have you any word for me?"

They were completely in the heavy shadow now, between the short clipped pines, where no one, even but a few feet away, could see, and before replying she looked at him, her grim face relaxing into a smile. She had always watched him before with a sort of angry jealousy, but John believed that he now read welcome and gladness in her eyes.

"Suzanne! Suzanne!" he repeated, his insistence ever growing stronger. "Is there no word for me?"

"Aye," she said, "my mistress bids me tell you that she is grateful, that she understands all you have risked for her sake, that she can never repay you sufficiently for your great service, and that she feels safer because you are near."

"Ah," breathed John, "it is worth every risk to hear that."

"But she fears for you. She knows that you are in great danger here. If they discover who you are, you perish at once as a spy. So she bids me tell you to go away. It is easy to escape from here to the Italian frontier. She would not have you lose your life for her."

"Is it because my life is of more value to her than that of any other man? Oh, tell me, I pray you?"

Another of her rare smiles passed over the grim face of the woman.

"It is a question that Mademoiselle Julie alone can answer," she said. "But when she went to her room she wept a little and her tears were not those of sorrow."

"Oh, then, Suzanne, she is indeed glad that I am here. Tell her that I came for her, and that I will not go away until she goes too."

"She is in no great danger here; she is a prisoner, but they treat her as a guest, one of high degree."

"Auersperg would force her to marry him."

Suzanne smiled once more, but gravely.

"The prince would marry her," she said, "and he is not the only one who wishes to do so. But fear not. Auersperg cannot force her to marry him. She is of the same tempered steel as her brother, the great Monsieur Philip. Were she a man as he is, she would dare as much as he does, and being a woman she will dare in a woman's way none the less."

"And the others, Kratzek and Pappenheim, and von Arnheim if he should come, they are young and brave and true! Might she not, as the only way of escape from the high-handed baron, marry one of them?"

For the fourth time Suzanne smiled. Never before had she permitted herself that luxury so many times in a month, but there was an odd glint in this latest smile of hers, which gave to her face a rare look of softness.

"Nor will she marry any of them," she said, "although they are brave and honest and true and love her. Mademoiselle Julie has her own reasons which she does not tell to me, but I know. She will not marry Prince Karl of Auersperg. She will not marry Prince Wilhelm von Arnheim, she will not marry Count Leopold Kratzek, she will not marry Count Maximilien Pappenheim. Do I not know her well, I who have been with her all her life?"

And once more that smile with the odd glint in it passed over her stern face. But John in the thickening dusk could not see it, although her low earnest voice carried conviction.

"Tell her for me, will you, Suzanne," he said, "that I think I can take her from the castle of Zillenstein. Tell her, too, that I am in little danger in my peasant's clothes. I have been face to face with the prince himself and he has shown no sign of recognition, nor has Count Kratzek who was my prisoner once. Tell her that I will not go. Tell her that my heart is light because she fears for my safety and, O Suzanne, tell her that I will watch over her the best I can, until all of us escape from this hateful castle."

"It is much to tell. How can I remember it alt?"

"Then tell her all you remember."

"That I promise. And now it's time for me to go back. We cannot risk too much."

She turned away, but John had another question to ask her. His heart smote him that he had not thought of Picard.

"Your father, Suzanne?" he said. "I have not heard of him. Is he here?"

"They left him a prisoner at Munich. Doubtless he will escape and he, too, will reach Zillenstein."

"Tell Mademoiselle Julie that her brother did not come to the appointed meeting at Chastel, because he was wounded. Not badly. Don't be alarmed, Suzanne. He'll be as well as ever soon."

"Then he, too, will come to Zillenstein. You are not the only one who seeks, Monsieur Scott."

"But I am the first to arrive. Nothing can take that from me."

"It is true. Now I must hasten back to the castle. If I stay longer they will suspect me."

She slipped from the shrubbery and was gone, and, John, afire with new emotions, strolled in a wide circuit back to the stables.

A week went by. Twice every day he saw Julie on the terrace, but no word passed between them, the chance never came. But the hosts of the air were at work. The invisible currents were passing between the girl on the terrace who was treated like a princess and the young peasant who walked the horses in the road.

"Be not afraid. I have a strength more than my own to save you," came on a wave of air.

"I fear not for myself, only for you lest they discover you," came the answering wave.

"I love you. You are the most beautiful woman in the world and the bravest. It's cause for pride to risk death for you."

"I know that you are here for me. I knew that you would come, when I saw you in Metz. I know that under your peasant's garb you are a prince, more of a real prince than any Auersperg that ever lived."

John was outside of himself. He felt sometimes as if he had left his body behind. The spirit of the crusader was still upon him, and in sight of his beloved, the prize that he had reached but not yet won, he cast aside all thought of danger or failure and awaited the event, whatever it might be, with the supreme confidence of youth. It is but truth to say that he was happy in those days, filled with a stolen delight, all the sweeter because it was stolen under the very eyes of the medieval baron, lord almost of life and death, who was master there.

He steadily advanced in the good graces of Walther. No other such industrious and skillful groom had appeared at Zillenstein in many a day, and he rapidly acquired dexterity also with the automobiles. None could send them spinning with more certainty along the curving mountain roads. He practiced with diligence because he had a vague premonition that all this knowledge would be of use to him some day.

Pappenheim went away, but returned after four days. John fancied that he had been in Vienna, but he knew the magnet that had brought him back. He saw the young Austrian's eyes flame more than once when Julie appeared in her favorite place on the terrace. And yet John neither hated nor feared him.

Kratzek was well enough to go back to the battle front, but he lingered. John did not know what excuses he gave, but he was there, and his eyes, too, burned when Julie passed.

Often in the evening he watched for the grim Suzanne and the word that she would bring, but she did not come. Day by day he saw her, the long black shadow behind her mistress, but she never looked toward him, however intensely he wished it.

The prince went forth occasionally, but he always used an automobile and he was never gone longer than a day. John wondered why he remained so long at Zillenstein, knowing that he was a general in the German army and a man of weight at the battle front. He concluded at last that he must be waiting there for a conference of some kind between important men of Germany and Austria. He had heard through the gossip in the castle that Italy was threatening war on Austria, and the Teutonic powers must now face also toward the southwest. Much might be decided at Zillenstein.

Ilse and Olga were still his best sources of information. Very little that passed in the castle missed their shrewd inquiring minds, and they had found in the handsome young peasant from Lorraine one with whom they liked to talk. He jested and laughed with them but there was a certain reserve on his part that they could not break down but which drew them on. He would not flirt with them. None was readier than he for light words and airy compliments, but nothing that he said permitted either of the trim young Austrian girls to think that he might become a lover.

"I think, Herr Johann," said Ilse, "that you have left behind in Lorraine a maid whom you love."

"It may be so," said John vaguely. "I saw one in Metz whom anybody could love."

"What was she like?" asked Ilse, eagerly.

"A skin the tint of the young rose, eyes like the dawn on a summer morning, hair a shower of the finest spun silk, and a walk like that of a young goddess."

"It's beautiful, but it doesn't describe; what was the color of her hair and eyes?"

"I don't know. They dazzled me so much that I merely remember their loveliness and glory."

"It can't be!" exclaimed Ilse, who did not walk in Elysian paths. "You jest with us. You recall her hair and eyes."

John shook his head impressively.

"The French prisoner, the one they call a spy, Mademoiselle Lannes, is the most beautiful woman I've ever seen," said blond Olga, "but no one could look at her without remembering the color of her hair and eyes, such a marvelous gold and such a deep, dark blue."

"His Highness, Prince Karl, remembers them well," said Ilse.

"But not better than the young Count Kratzek," said Olga.

"Nor better than Count Pappenheim."

"And yet they're going to send her away."

"It's because the generals and princes are coming for the great council and they wouldn't have more to fall in love with her."

"And it might give even Prince Karl trouble to answer questions why she is here."

John's pulses began to beat heavily despite all his efforts at calmness and he turned his face away that they might not see the eager light in his eyes. When he had mastered himself sufficiently to use a quiet voice he asked:

"When is this great council of which you speak?"

"In three or four days," replied Ilse. "We hear that many Serene High-nesses are coming from both Berlin and Vienna."

"And the French girl is to be carried away before they come?"

"She goes the day after tomorrow with the dark woman, Suzanne, to the hunting lodge of His Highness, higher in the mountains."

Then with a frightened gesture she clapped her hand upon her mouth.

"You will say nothing of it, Herr Johann?" she pleaded. "It is a secret from all but a few, and His Highness doubtless would punish us terribly if he knew that we told."

"You can trust me, Ilse," said John earnestly. "I would not bring trouble upon you or Olga. Besides, what is it to me?"

He sought by indirect questions to learn more from them, but they would not continue, seeming to be afraid that they had already said too much. Then he turned casually from the subject, lest he rouse suspicion, and spoke of his horses. But all the while he was searching his mind, as one looks for a treasure, to discover how he could follow Julie and Suzanne to their new abode.

He gathered from Walther that the hunting lodge was higher in the mountains in the depths of a great forest, about six leagues from Zillenstein where there was much big game. In times of peace the prince frequently went there, and a good automobile road led to the lodge, although in winter the snow was often so deep that the place was inaccessible.

Late that afternoon the hoofs of horses beat steadily on the road leading from the valley up to Zillenstein. John from a coign of vantage saw approaching a young man in a gray German uniform, followed by four hussars, also in German gray. Anyone who came to Zillenstein was of interest, and as John looked the leading figure became familiar. Doubt soon changed to certainty. He knew the swing of the broad shoulders and the high pose of the head. It was the young prince, von Arnheim.

"And so they all gather," said John to himself.

He was swept by the little shiver that one often feels when influenced suddenly by a powerful emotion. Fate or chance had a wonderful way of bringing about strange things. He had seen it too often not to know. He was sure in his heart now that von Boehlen too would come some time and somehow.

He looked at the terrace. Julie and Suzanne had appeared there in the last few minutes, and they were gazing at the gallant figure of young von Arnheim who was now so near. The prince himself, when he saw Julie, sprang from his horse, ran lightly up the steps, and bending low over her hand, kissed it. Nor did John feel jealousy or hate of him.

He was glad that von Arnheim had come. He was sure that Julie did not love him and never would, but he was a brave and honest man who would do no wrong. Julie was safer from insult with him near. To the rank of Prince Karl of Auersperg he could oppose a rank the equal of his own.

He was too far away to hear their words or even to note their faces, but he saw the young prince talk with her for a little space and then go into the castle, doubtless to notify Auersperg of his arrival. Julie as her eyes roved about the great panorama of mountain and valley saw John, and the wireless messages of their eyes passed and repassed again.

"I know that you are watching and risking your life for me," hers said.

"Gladly," his replied.

"I like Prince Wilhelm von Arnheim, but it's liking, not love."

"I wish to believe it and do."

Then the little waves of air were stilled, as she went back into the castle, doubtless because she feared to arouse suspicion, and John returned to his work with Walther, convinced that he must form some plan now. Von Arnheim must merely be the vanguard of the council, and Julie might be sent away earlier than Ilse had announced. He must contrive a way to follow.

That night he lurked once more in the shrubbery. He had been there nearly every night, hopeful that Suzanne would pass again, but not until tonight did she come. The tall figure, swathed almost to the eyes in a heavy cloak, came down the terrace to the walk, and John whistled low a note of a French folksong. He had merely hoped that she would stop a moment or two to listen, and the little device succeeded. She paused and looked at the black mass of the shrubbery.

"Suzanne! Suzanne!" called John, his voice showing all the intenseness of his anxiety.

"Monsieur Scott," she said in a loud whisper.

"Yes, Suzanne, here behind the bushes! I must have word with you!"

Silently she stepped into the impenetrable shadows and John eagerly seized her hand.

"Your mistress, Mademoiselle Julie," he whispered eagerly, "she does not break down with the suspense and anxiety? She still hopes?"

"You need not fear for her courage, Monsieur Scott. Did I not tell you that she had a heart of steel, even the same as that of her great brother. I should not tell it to you, but she has never despaired since you came."

John's fingers closed convulsively upon the large muscular hand of Suzanne and in the darkness the woman's grim face relaxed into a smile.

"You are holding my hand not that of Mademoiselle Julie," she said.

"Your words bring me such joy, Suzanne, that I forgot, but I must speak to your mistress."

"You cannot. It is impossible. She is watched more closely than ever."

"But there is news that she must know! Then you must tell it to her!"

"What news? You surely don't mean that they will try her on this ridiculous charge of being a spy!"

"No, not that, Suzanne, but they're preparing to send her and you away."

"And glad we both will be to leave this hateful castle of Zillenstein."

"But it's not that you will fare better. There will be no chance of freedom now. You are to be sent into the higher mountains in the wilderness to a hunting lodge belonging to Auersperg. You will be hidden from all but a few of his most trusted followers."

"Then we're not afraid. We shall even be glad to go there, anywhere from this terrible place. We do not fear the woods, my mistress and I. I can think they're more friendly than those old stone walls above us."

"But tell her this, Suzanne, I pray you, that I shall follow her there."

"How?"

"I don't yet know, but I shall find a way. Tell her, Suzanne, that I'll never leave her so long as I'm alive."

The eyes of the grim woman softened singularly, as she gazed in the dusk at the young man. A devotion such as his, a devotion so evident, would have moved a heart of stone. Her young mistress was dearer than anyone else in the world to her, dearer than her own father, and her stern spirit relaxed when she saw that another could love her in a different way, but as well.

"I'll tell her," she said, "but I tell you that 'tis needless. She knows already that wherever she goes you will follow. Does that bring any comfort to your soul, Mr. Scott?"

"Aye, Suzanne, it fills it with thankfulness. Don't forget to tell her that she will go soon. Von Arnheim, Pappenheim and Kratzek are her friends, but they can't prevent it if they would. It may be too that they will not know when or where she goes."

"She shall hear everything you say and, remember, that she has a brave heart. She has less fear for herself than for you."

She slipped away in the darkness and John went back to his own little place over the stables where he passed a night that was all but sleepless thinking over his problem and finding no good solution. He meant to follow Julie and Suzanne in any event to the hunting lodge, but it was not sufficient merely to follow. He must appear in some capacity that would permit him to be of service. And yet Providence was working for him at that moment.

Prince Karl of Auersperg in his magnificent modernized apartments in the huge castle was also troubled by an inability to sleep. Hitherto in his fifty or more years of life he had always got what he wanted. His blood was more ancient than that of either Hohenzollern or Hapsburg. The Auerspergs had been princes of the Holy Roman Empire for a thousand years and now he was a prince of both Teutonic empires and a general of the first rank in the army of Germany. His wealth was so vast that he scarcely knew the extent of his own lands and here in Zillenstein he could maintain the power and state that appertained to a baron of the Middle Ages.

A mind that has only to wish for a thing to get it becomes closed in fifty years. It mistakes desire for right. It regards opposition as sacrilege. Other minds that differ from it are wicked because they differ. The thick armor of Prince Karl's self-complacency had been pierced as it were by a tiny needle that stung, however tiny, as if its point were laden with poison.

He, the omniscient and omnipotent, had been defied and by whom? A mere slip of a girl! A child! She was not even of his own race! But perhaps it was this very defiance that made him wish for her all the more. He loved her as he had never loved that long-dead wife, a plain princess who always thought what she was told to think.

But he would take Julie in all honor as his wife. He could not make her a princess but he could make her a countess, and he would clothe her in a golden shower. There had been hundreds of morganatic marriages. They implied no disgrace. Noblewomen themselves had been glad to make them. And yet she had refused. Nothing could move her. She had not even flinched a particle when he had threatened her otherwise with death as a spy, although the threat was merely words on his lips and had no abiding place in his heart. She was most beautiful then, when the defiant fire flashed in her dark blue eyes and the sunshine coming through a tall stained glass window made deep red tints in her wonderful golden hair. It was maddening to think of her, just a child turning into a woman, and wholly in his power defying him as if he were some humble lieutenant and not the mighty Prince Karl of Auersperg.

He rose and walked angrily back and forth. Now and then he went to a window and looked out at the dusky panorama of valley, mountain and shaggy forest. As far as he could see and farther it was all his and yet he was powerless in the matter that now concerned him more than all others. She was his prisoner, and yet she was as free as air. Her soul and her heart were her own, and he could not reach either. He knew it. That knowledge like the little poisoned needle had punctured the triple-plate of his complacency and pride and left him no relief from pain, a pain that would have become intolerable had he known that of all the bars that stood between her and him the one that nothing could move was a young peasant in his employ, who watered and fed horses, and who often led them up and down the road within his plain view.

And yet knowing what he did, knowing that she would not marry him, he had no thought to give her up. Hope will often spring anew in the face of absolute knowledge itself, and deep in his heart a belief would appear now and then that he might yet break her to his wish. He knew that von Arnheim, Pappenheim and Kratzek knelt at the same shrine and he laughed harshly to himself because he was sure that they knelt in vain. They were young, handsome, attractive, men of the world, men whom any girl might love but she did not love any of them. He knew the signals, and Julie certainly hung out none for von Arnheim, nor for Kratzek nor for Pappenheim.

He ran his fingers through his great brown forked beard, just such a beard as many a robber baron might have worn, and thought deeply of what he should do with her, before the great council of princes and generals assembled in his castle. She must not be there then. Awkward questions might be asked, but if she were well hidden no trouble could befall. Von Arnheim or Kratzek or Pappenheim might speak, but any words of his would outweigh all of theirs and that term of a spy was wonderfully convenient.

But he wished only himself to know where Julie had gone. He wanted no tattle and gossip about the castle and where there were so many servants and followers it could not be prevented unless they were kept in ignorance. It would be best to use a stranger, one who was known but little at Zillenstein, and he recalled such a man. Second thought confirmed first thought and his decision was made.

12

THE HUNTING LODGE

JOHN PASSED A TROUBLED NIGHT. He could not yet see his way to follow Julie and Suzanne to the hunting lodge in the manner he wished, and the signs were multiplying that they would soon go. He had no doubt that the arrival of von Arnheim would hasten their departure. Auersperg at such a time could not tolerate the attitude of the young prince toward Julie and he would avail himself of what he considered his feudal rights to send her somewhere into the dark at the quickest possible moment.

But Providence was working for John. His courage and skill which tempted fate were winning new points in his great battle. Walther told him a little after noon that he was to take him into the presence of the august Prince Karl himself. In some manner he had fallen under the favorable eye of His Highness who was about to assign him to an important duty. It was an honor that seldom fell to one so young and ignorant and he hoped that he would conduct himself in a manner to reflect credit upon his superior and instructor, Walther.

John gave his faithful promise but he wondered what the prince could want with him personally and he did not look forward to the interview with confidence. Perhaps his identity and the nature of his errand had been discovered, and it was merely an easy method of making him walk into the lion's jaws, but he could not have refused nor did he wish to do so. His curiosity was aroused and he was willing to meet Auersperg face to face and talk with him.

Cap in hand he followed Walther, also cap in hand, into the interior of the castle. Auersperg sat in a great room overlooking the valley. His chair stood on a slightly raised portion of the floor, and he was enthroned like a sovereign. John, following Walther's example, bowed low before him.

"You may go, Walther," said Auersperg. "I wish to speak alone with this young man."

The master of the stables withdrew reluctantly, consumed by curiosity, and the young peasant in his rough brown dress stood alone before the prince. One seemed the very personification of power and pride, the other of obscurity and insignificance, and yet so strangely does fate play with the fortunes of men that the fickle goddess was inclined toward the peasant in the matter that was nearest to the hearts of both.

John, be it said once more, had not the smallest faith in the supernatural, but it often seemed to him afterward that some power greater than that of man moved the prince to do what he was about to do.

Prince Karl of Auersperg stroked his great brown beard and looked at him long and thoughtfully. John stood before him in the position of an inferior, even a menial, but his heart was far from holding any feeling of inferiority. He was awed neither by the man's rank nor his power nor his ancient blood. He knew that rank could not stop a bullet, nor turn aside a shell. He knew that inherited power could be overthrown by power acquired. There was nothing to make either sacred. He knew that old blood was usually bad blood, that in a thousand years it became a poisonous stream, for the want of fresh springs to purify it. But the head of the young peasant was lowered a little, and the last representative of ten centuries of decadence did not see the gleam of defiance, even of contempt in his eyes.

"You have not been at Zillenstein long," said the prince.

"But a week, Your Highness."

"Walther speaks well of you. The Walthers have served the Auerspergs for centuries and his judgment and loyalty are to be trusted."

John's heart, stanch republican that he was, rose in rebellion at the thought that one family should serve another for a thousand years, but of course he was silent.

"Walther tells me also," resumed the prince, "that you can handle an automobile with skill and that you understand them."

"Herr Walther is very kind to me, Your Highness."

"It was you also who rode the horse of Pappenheim. A great feat. It showed ability and courage. For these reasons I am selecting you to do a deed of trust, one of great importance to me. I am informed by Walther that you are from Lorraine and that your name is Castel."

"Yes, Your Highness, I'm Jean Castel and I was born near Metz, a subject of His Imperial Highness, the German Emperor, the Winner of Victories."

Auersperg smiled and continued to stroke his great brown beard. The young peasant pleased him. Though of humble station and ignorant of the higher world he was undoubtedly keen and intelligent. He was just the man for his task, and fortune had put this useful tool in his hand.

"Go back to the stables, Castel," he said, "and make ready for the high duty to which I am going to assign you. You are to ask no questions and to answer none. Walther will receive instructions to equip you. There is a small gate in the rear wall of the castle. Be there at nine o'clock tonight, and you will then know the work that you have to do. Now go and be silent and, if you fail to be at the gate at the appointed time, that which you like little may happen to you."

John bowed and left the illustrious presence. He was on fire with eagerness and curiosity, and there was apprehension too. Would his trust take him away from Julie at a time when he was needed most? It must not be so, and his faith was strong that it would not be so. Yet his heart was beating very hard and his impatience for the night to come was great. But he strove his utmost to preserve at least the appearance of calmness. He saw that Walther was full of curiosity and now and then asked indirect questions, but John remembering his instructions gave no answer.

Once he passed Ilse and Olga, those twin spirits of mischief and kindness, and they stopped him to speak of the great company that was coming.

"They say it's to be the mightiest array of princes and generals gathered at Zillenstein in a hundred years," said Ilse.

"So I hear," said John.

"And you may be called from the stable to serve in the castle. The man who rode the horse of Count Pappenheim may have to carry a plate and a napkin."

"One can but do his best."

"But it will be a great scene. Perhaps the Kaiser himself will be here, or the old Emperor."

"Perhaps."

"Aren't you eager to see them?" asked Ilse, piqued a little at his lack of curiosity.

"Oh yes," replied John, recalling that he must make believe, "but I've seen the Kaiser several times and once at Vienna I could almost have reached out my hand and touched the old Emperor, as he rode on his way to Schonbrunn."

He passed on and they looked after him. They liked the bearing of this young peasant who was respectful, but who certainly was never servile. But it was in John's mind that however brilliant the great council might be he would not see it. He was surely going from Zillenstein but it was for the future to say whether his absence would be short or long.

While John was at the stables young Kratzek sent for his horse, and John, after his custom, led the animal to him. He had long since ceased to fear discovery by the Austrian, and his immunity made him careless, or it may be that Kratzek's eyes were uncommonly keen that day. He stood beside John, as the young American fixed the stirrup, and some motion or gesture of the seeming peasant suddenly appeared familiar to Kratzek.

Before John had realized what he intended Kratzek suddenly seized him by both shoulders and turning him around, looked straight into his eyes.

"Scott, the American, and a spy!" he exclaimed.

John's heart missed several beats. He knew that it was useless to deny, but in a moment or two he had himself under full control.

"Yes, it's Scott, and I'm in disguise, but I'm not a spy," he said.

"The penalty anyhow is death."

"But you'll not betray me!"

"You saved my life at the great peril of your own."

John was silent. He felt that the time had come for Kratzek to repay, but he would not say so. Now his own look was straight and high, and it was Kratzek's that wavered.

"You pledge your word that you are not seeking to pry into our military secrets?" asked the Austrian at length.

"No such purpose is in my mind at all, and I leave here within twenty-four hours as ignorant of them as I was when I came."

"Then, sir, I do not know you. I never saw you before, and I believe you are the peasant you seem to be."

Kratzek gave him one look of intense curiosity, then sprang upon his horse, and rode away, never looking back.

"There goes a true man," thought John, as he returned to the stable.

Toward evening Walther gave him a heavier suit of clothes which he put on, a great overcoat like an ulster falling almost to his ankles, and an automobile cap and glasses. John could see that he longed to ask questions but he did not do so and John too was silent. A few minutes before nine o'clock Walther told him to go to the small gate in the rear wall.

"Reach it without being seen if you can," he said. "But if you are seen be sure to answer no questions. I would go with you myself, but it's forbidden. You're to be absolutely alone."

John, shrouded in the overcoat and cap and glasses, made his way in the dark to the designated gate.

As he approached the place he saw the black shadow of a heavy bulk against the dusk. No person was yet in sight and there was utter silence. The beat of his heart was so hard that it gave him actual physical pain. The shadow he knew was that of a large closed automobile, but no driver was in the seat, and he did not believe that anybody was inside. Both the silence and the loneliness became sinister.

John slipped forward boldly. It required no divination to know that he was expected to drive this machine. The gate was open and two figures hooded and cloaked came forth. But hooded and cloaked as they were John knew at once the first and slenderer one. The step disclosed the goddess. Julie and Suzanne were going somewhere and he was to take them and there was the prince himself coming through the open gate to give him his instructions.

John's first emotion was one of extraordinary wonder, qualified in a moment or two by humor. Suzanne opened the door of the machine and Julie stepped in. Then the maid followed into the darkness of the interior and closed the door. Truly that variable goddess, Fortune, had chosen to play one of her oddest tricks and for the time, at least, she had chosen him also as her favorite. But with a presence of mind bred in the terrible school of war, he stood waiting ready to receive all her gifts with a thankful heart. "These are two Frenchwomen, prisoners, whom I hold," said the prince in a whisper. "There are reasons of state why they should be taken from Zillenstein and be hidden at my hunting lodge in the mountains. Follow the road that you see there in the moonlight leading up the slope, and on the crest six leagues away you will come to the lodge. You cannot miss it because no other building is there. It lies off the road in a deep pine forest, and here is a letter to my forester Muller who lives there. You and he will hold the women at the lodge until I send for them, and let them speak with nobody, though there is little chance of such a thing on the mountain, where the winter has not yet gone. I hold you responsible for them. Do you understand?"

"Yes, Your Highness," replied John, and he meant it.

"And here is a purse of gold for you. See that you serve me well in this matter, and there is another purse at the end of it. Now go at once!"

John touched his cap, sprang into the seat and started the great automobile up the mountain road. He could not look back, but he knew instinctively that the prince had gone into the castle as silently as he had come from it. And he was alone at the wheel with Julie and Suzanne inside. In very truth chance or fortune had moved the pawns for him in a way that the most skillful player could not have equaled. For a moment, the whole world seemed to swim beneath his feet.

The night was dark and cold, and although the road up the slope showed for a long distance in the moonshine the top of the mountain was wrapped in mist. A wind began to blow and he felt raw and damp to his face. But there was nothing to check his exultation. Come wind or rain or snow they were all one to him. He was away from Zillenstein, out in the great free world and Julie was with him. Auersperg himself, unknowing, had provided the way and he was sending them not only in comfort but in luxury. John knew the big automobile. It was the prince's own and it was surely equipped in a princely way. The man who bad brought it to the gate had been forced to go away and he, John Scott, and Prince Karl of Auersperg alone knew where they were going. All the better! He laughed under his breath as he handled the wheel with hands now skilled and sent the great automobile along the smooth white road that stretched away and away up the mountain side.

At a curve a mile or more distant, he could look down almost directly upon Zillenstein. The vast castle was bathed in whitish mists floating up the valley in which it loomed gigantic and enlarged, a menacing creation that had survived far beyond its time. He shuddered at the thought that Julie and he might still be there, had not fortune been so kind, and then, pressing the accelerator, he sent the machine forward a little faster.

The road owing to the steepness of the ascent now wound a great deal, but it was smooth and safe, and the automobile, despite its size, had an organism as delicate as that of a watch. It obeyed the least pressure of his hand, and his exultation became all the greater when he fully realized that he had such a powerful mechanism at hand, subject to its lightest touch. The thought, in truth, had come to him that he might turn back into the valley, and seek escape from the mountains. But consideration showed that the idea was foolish. So large a machine by no possibility could escape from the valley. It was better to go on.

The cold increased sharply. He expected a fall in the mercury owing to the ascent, but it was greater than the height alone warranted. All the signs betokened foul weather. The castle was now wholly lost in great masses of vapor and the moon was withdrawing from the sky. The wind had an edge of ice. He knew that mountains were the breeding place of storms and he made another increase of speed in order that they might reach the hunting lodge before one broke.

He had not heard a sound from the interior of the automobile since he started. They were sitting only a few feet away, but the whistling of the wind and the crunch of the wheels on the sanded road would have drowned out all slight noises, and they did not speak, nor did he look back.

He knew that they could see only a broad back in front of them and the muffling coat and cap. He longed to say a word or two, but he deemed it wisest to wait yet a while. His full attention was concentrated upon the machine and the road and it was all the more necessary because the night was growing darker and the wind cut.

But his confidence was so high that he handled the automobile through all the dangers with a firm and sure hand. It sped on and on, climbing in a rapid series of circles up the side of the mountain. Behind him the gulf was filled with vapors and before him the clouds were growing darker on the crest, but he could yet trace the road, and it would not be long now until they reached the crest and the pine forest in which the hunting lodge stood.

He wondered what kind of man the forester Muller would prove to be. If he were suspicious, keenly alert, he might prevent their ultimate escape, but if he were merely a simple hunter John might make friends with him and use him for his purposes. Then his thoughts came quickly back to Julie. He believed that she had left the castle without resistance of any kind. She would be glad to escape from Zillenstein and Auersperg, no matter where that escape might take her.

Another half-hour and the crest was but a hundred yards or so away. How thankful he was now that he had put on extra speed despite the ascent and had driven the machine hard, because the road would soon be blotted from sight! Heavy flakes of snow had begun to fall and with the rising wind they were coming faster and faster.

He dimly made out a pine wood on his right, and, then, in the center of it the outline of a low building which he knew must be the hunting lodge. He slowed down the machine, took the last little curve, and stopped before the door of the lodge. But in that minute the snow had become a driving white storm.

He leaped out, knocked hard on the door of the lodge, and, no answer coming, threw himself heavily against it. It burst open, revealing only an interior of darkness, but he turned quickly back to the automobile, threw wide its door and beckoned with peremptory command to the two dark figures sitting within.

They stepped out, Julie first, and entered the lodge. John followed them, and there they stood, staring at one another until their eyes might grow used to the dusk and they could see their faces. It was evident that Muller was not anywhere in the building, or he would have come at the sound of the machine.

John glanced toward a window set deep in a heavy timbered wall and admitting enough light to disclose a lantern and a box of matches on a shelf. Still in his shrouding coat, cap and glasses he stepped forward, struck a match and lighted the lantern. Driven by a sudden impulse, he swept off the cap and glasses and held up the light.

He saw Julie's face turn deadly pale. Every particle of color was gone from it and her blue eyes stared at him as if he were one newly risen from the dead. Then the color flushed back in a rosy tide and such a tide of gladness as he had never seen before in human eyes came into hers.

"You! You! Is it really you?" she cried.

John was once more the knightly young crusader. No such moment had ever before come into his life. His heart was full. Triumph and joy were mingled there, and something over and beyond either. In that passing flash he had read the light in her eyes, a light that he knew was only for him, but in the instant of supreme revelation he would take no advantage. The manner as well as the spirit of the young crusader was upon him.

He knelt before her and taking one of her gloved hands in his kissed it.

"Yes, dearest Julie," he said, "by some singular fortune or chance, or rather, I should call it, the will of God, I was chosen to bring you here, and I glory because I have fulfilled the trust."

[Illustration: "'You! You! Is it really you?' she cried"]

Suzanne, tall and dark, stood looking down at them. Her grim features which relaxed so rarely relaxed now and her eyes were soft. The young stranger from beyond the seas had proved after all that he was a man among men, and no Frenchwoman could resist a romance so strong and true in the face of all that war could do.

John felt Julie's hand trembling in his, but she did not draw it away. Her lashes were lowered a little now, but her gaze still rested upon him, soft yet confident and powerful. He had believed in her courage. He had believed that she would suffer no shock when she should see that he was the strange man who had been at the wheel, and his confidence was justified.

"And it was you who brought us up the mountain?" she said.

"The Prince of Auersperg himself chose me because I was a stranger and he did not wish anyone else in the castle to know where you were sent."

He released her hand and rose. The soft but strong gaze was still upon him, as if she were yet trying to persuade herself that it was reality.

"I felt all the time that some day we should leave the castle together," she said, "but I did not dream that it was you who sat before me as we came up the mountain."

"But it was," said John, joyfully. "I think Wharton himself would have complimented me on the way I drove the machine. I have a letter in my pocket for Muller, the prince's forester who lives here, but it seems that he is absent on other duty."

"And then," said the practical Suzanne, "it becomes us to take possession of the house at once. Look forth, sir! how the storm beats!"

Through the open door they saw the snow driven past in sheets that seemed almost solid. John handed the lantern to Suzanne and said:

"Wait here a moment."

"Where are you going, Mr. Scott?" exclaimed Julie. "You will not desert us?"

"Never!"

He was out of the door in a couple of strides, and then he sprang into the automobile. He had noticed a small garage back of the lodge and he meant to save the machine, feeling sure that they would have need of it later. In a few minutes it was safely inside with the door fastened so tightly behind him that no wind could blow it loose, and he was back at the lodge with the wind and snow driving so hard that he opened the door but little, and, slipping in, slammed it shut. Then he turned the heavy key in the lock, and stared in surprise and pleasure at the room.

It was a great apartment, the heavy log walls adorned with the horns and stuffed heads of wild animals. Several bear skins and other rugs lay upon the oaken floor. There were chairs and tables with books upon them, and, at one end, the dry wood that filled a great fireplace was crackling and flashing merrily. The practical Suzanne, noticing the heap, had set a match to it at once, and already the room, great as it was, was filled with warmth and light. Julie, having taken off her heavy furs, was sitting in a chair before the fire, the leaping flames deepening the light in her eyes and the new rose in her cheeks.

John's heart swelled with thankfulness and joy. He had not dreamed that so much could be achieved. A day before he would have said that it was impossible. As the whistling of the wind rose to a fierce roar and the snow drove by, he realized, with a shudder at the danger escaped so narrowly, that they had arrived just in time. The automobile itself would have been driven from the path by the fierce Alpine storm now raging.

The stern but gifted Suzanne had found lamps and had lighted them, and like a capable soldier she was already looking over her field of battle.

"Not so bad," she said. "His Highness, Prince Karl of Auersperg, builds a little palace and calls it his hunting lodge. But his heart would turn black within him if he knew who was one of the guests in it today."

John smiled, and meeting Julie's eyes, he smiled again. He saw a flame there to which his own soul responded, and he tingled from head to foot. The omens had not been in vain. The blessings of the righteous had availed. Again it may be said that he had no faith in the supernatural, at least here on earth, but all things must have worked for him in a world that seemed wholly against him. He believed that he read such a thought too in the glowing dark blue of her own eyes.

"You are wonderfully right, Suzanne," said John. "Probably the Prince of Auersperg had the lodge especially prepared for the coming of Mademoiselle Julie. Perhaps there is a telephone."

"Truly there is, Mr. Scott," said Suzanne. "Here it is, in the corner."

"Then," said John, "it's very likely that we'll hear very soon from Zillenstein, and since he has kept your journey secret it is sure to be Prince Karl himself who will call you up. I must be the one to answer. Now will you sit here by the fire, Miss Julie, and rest while your most capable Suzanne and I look further into our new residence. There is no possibility of any caller, save the worthy Muller, to whom I bear a letter from the prince, in which I have no doubt I am highly recommended."

"Very well, Mr. John, I obey you," said Julie, sitting down again in a large armchair before the flames, where the ruddy light once more deepened the gold of her hair and the rose of her cheeks. "It seems that you intend to be master here."

"I'm master already. My rule has become supreme, nor am I any usurper. Do I not hold a commission from Prince Karl of Auersperg, the owner of this lodge, and did he not intrust you to my care? I mean to do my duty. And now come, Suzanne, you and I will see what this wilderness castle of ours contains."

The hunting lodge was worthy of a prince. It was built of massive logs, but the interior was improved and finished in modern style. There were no electric lights, but it contained almost every other luxury or convenience. Besides the great room in which Julie was now sitting, they found on the ground floor a writing-room well supplied, a small parlor, a gunroom amply equipped with a variety of arms and ammunition, a dining-room containing much princely silver, a butler's pantry, a kitchen and a storeroom holding food enough to last them a year. Above stairs were six bedrooms, any one of which the capable Suzanne could put in order in half an hour. All the house had running water drawn from some reservoir in the mountains.

John had seen such luxurious camps as this in the Adirondacks in his own country, and there were many others scattered about the mountains of Europe, but he was very grateful now to find such a refuge for Julie. Again he realized how fortunate they had been to arrive so early. As he looked from an upper window he saw that the storm was driving with tremendous fury. Even behind the huge logs he heard the wind roaring and thundering, and now and then, through the thick glass of the windows, he caught a glimpse of a young pine torn up by its roots and whirled past.

Where was Muller, the forester, who had charge of the lodge and who lived there, and what kind of a man was he? It was the only question that was troubling him now. If he did not come soon he could not come that night, nor perhaps the next day. The snowfall was immense, with every sign of heavy continuance, and by morning it certainly would lie many feet deep on the mountain. Traveling would be impossible. He heard the distant sound of a bell, and knowing that the telephone was calling, he ran down the stairway to the great room. Julie had risen and was looking at the instrument with dilated eyes, as if it sounded a note of alarm, as if their happy escape was threatened by a new danger. John believed that she had fallen asleep before the heat of the fire, and that the ring of the telephone had struck upon her dreaming ear like a shell.

"It's he! It's the terrible prince himself!" she exclaimed, her faculties not yet fully released from cloudy sleep.

"Very likely," said John, "but have no fear. Zillenstein is only six leagues away at ordinary times, but it's six hundred tonight, with the greatest storm that I've ever seen sweeping in between us."

He took down the receiver and put it to his ear.

"Who is there?" asked a deep voice, which he knew to be that of Prince Karl.

"Castel, Your Highness."

"You arrived without accident?"

"Wholly without accident, Your Highness. We reached the lodge a few minutes before the storm broke."

"The lady, Mademoiselle Lannes, is safe and comfortable?"

"Entirely so. Your Highness. The maid, Suzanne, is preparing her room for her."

"You found Muller there waiting for you according to instructions?"

Some prudential motive prompted John to reply:

"Yes, Your Highness, he had everything ready and was waiting. I presented your letter at once."

"You have done well, Castel. Keep the lady within the house, but the storm will do that anyhow. Do not under any circumstances call me up, but I will call you again when I think fit. Bear in mind that the reward of both you and Muller shall be large, if you serve me well in this most important matter."

"Yes, Your Highness. I thank you now."

"Keep it in mind, always."

"Yes, Your Highness."

His Highness, Prince Karl of Auersperg, replaced the telephone stand upon the table in his bedroom at Zillenstein, and John Scott hung up the receiver in the hunting lodge on the mountain.

"It was Prince Karl," he said to Julie, who still stood motionless looking at him. "He wanted to know if you were safe and comfortable and I said yes. He said he would call us up again but he won't."

He lifted a chair and shattered the telephone to fragments.

"It might afford a peculiar pleasure to talk with him," he said, "but it's best that we have no further communication while we're here. An incautious word or two might arouse suspicion and that's what we want most to avoid. When he fails to get an answer to his call he'll think that this huge snow has broken down the wire. Most likely it will do so anyhow. And now, Miss Julie, Suzanne has your room ready for you. If you wish to withdraw to it for a little while you'll find dinner waiting you when you return."

"And the day of the abandoned hotel in Chastel has come back?"

"But a better and a longer day. We're prisoners here together on the mountain, you and I, and your chaperon, servant and sometime ruler, Suzanne Picard, who I find is not as grim as she looks."

There was a spark in his eyes as he looked at her, and an answering fire leaped up in her own. He was in very truth a perfect and gentle knight, who would gladly come so far and through so many dangers for her and for her alone. He was her very own champion, and as her dark blue eyes looked into the gray deeps of his her soul thrilled with the knowledge of it. Deep red flushed her from brow to chin, and then slowly ebbed away.

"John," she said, putting her hand in his, "no woman has ever owed more gratitude to a man."

"And I am finding repayment now for what I was happy to do," he said, kissing her hand again in that far-off knightly fashion.

Again the red tide in her cheeks and then she swiftly left the room, but John threw himself in a chair before the great fire and gazed into the coals. Wide awake, he was dreaming. He knew they would be days in the lodge. The storm was so great that no one could come from Zillenstein in a week. Providence or fortune had been so kind that he began to fear enough had been done for them. Such good luck could not go on forever, and there, too, was the man Muller who might make trouble when he came.

Nevertheless his feeling was but momentary. The extraordinary lightness of heart returned. The storm roared without and at times it volleyed down the chimney, making the flames leap and dance, but the sense of security and safety was strong within him. The war passed by, forgotten for the time. History, it was true, repeated itself, and this was the abandoned hotel at Chastel over again, but they were in a far better position now. No one could come against them, unless the man Muller should prove to be a foe. And he resolved, too, gazing into the flames, that they should not steal Julie from him here, as they had taken her at Chastel.

Darkness, save for the gleam of the snow, came over the mountain, but the flakes were driving so thick and fast that they formed a white blanket before the window, as impervious as black night itself. It reminded him of a great storm he had seen once on his uncle's ranch on the high table land of Montana, but to him it came that night as a friend and not as an enemy, cutting them off from Zillenstein and all the dangers it held.

He lighted candles and lamps in the great room and all the smaller rooms clustering about it. He would have everything cheerful for Julie when she returned.

He had seen Suzanne take several heavy packages from the automobile and he had no doubt that they had come amply provided with clothing, that for Julie, belonging doubtless to a young cousin or niece of the prince who stayed sometimes at Zillenstein.

As for himself, if they remained long he must depend upon the spare raiment of the forester, and, remembering suddenly that he might effect his own improvement, he hunted for Muller's room and discovered it on the second floor. Here he found shaving materials, and rapidly cleared his face of the young beard that he despised. Muller's clothing was scattered about, and he judged from it that the forester was a man of about his own size. After some hesitation, he took off his own coat and put on a brilliant Tyrolean jacket which he surmised the owner reserved for occasions of state.

"If you come, Mr. Muller, I'll try to explain to you why I do this," said John aloud. "I know you'll forgive me when I tell you it's in honor of a lady."

Then he laughed at himself in a glass. It was a gorgeous jacket, but one could wear more brilliant clothes in Europe than in America, and his appearance was certainly improved. He returned to the great room and someone sitting in the chair before the fire rose to receive him.

It was Julie all in white, a semi-evening dress that heightened in a wonderful fashion her glorious, blond beauty. He had often thought how this slender maid would bloom into a woman and now he beheld her here in the lodge, his prisoner and not Auersperg's. A swift smile passed over her face as she saw him, and bowing low before him she said:

"I see, Mr. John, that you have not wasted your time. You come arrayed in purple and gold."

"But it's borrowed plumage, Miss Julie."

"And so is mine."

"It can't be. I'm sure it was made for you."

"The real owner wouldn't say so."

"You will forgive me if I tell you something, won't you?"

"It depends upon what it is."

The red in her checks deepened a little. The gray eyes of John were speaking in very plain language to Julie.

"I must say it, stern necessity compels, if I don't I'll be very unhappy."

"I wouldn't have you miserable."

"I want to tell you, Julie, that you are overwhelmingly beautiful tonight."

"I've always heard that Americans were very bold, it's true."

"But remember the provocation, Julie."

"Ah, sir, I have no protection and you take advantage of it."

"There's Suzanne."

"But she's in the kitchen."

"Where I hope she'll stay until she's wanted."

She was silent and the red in her cheeks deepened again. But the blue eyes and the gray yet talked together.

"I worship you, your beauty and your great soul, but your great soul most of all," said the gray.

"Any woman would be proud to have a lover who has followed her through so many and such great dangers, and who has rescued her at last. She could not keep from loving him," said the blue.

Suzanne appeared that moment in the doorway and stood there

unnoticed. She looked at them grimly and then came the rare smile that gave her face that wonderful softness.

"Come, Mademoiselle Julie and Mr. John," she said. "Dinner is ready and I tell you now that I've never prepared a better one. This prince has a taste in food and wine that I did not think to find in any German."

"And all that was his is ours now," said John. "Fortune of war."

Suzanne's promise was true to the last detail. The dinner was superb and they had an Austrian white wine that never finds its way into the channels of commerce.

"To you, Julie, and our happy return to Paris," said John, looking over the edge of his glass. Suzanne was in the kitchen then and he dared to drop the "Mademoiselle."

"To you, John," she said, as she touched the wine to her lips--she too dared to drop the "Mr."

And then gray depths looked into blue depths and blue into gray, speaking a language that each understood.

"We're the chosen of fortune," said John, "The hotel at Chastel presented itself to us when we needed it most, and again when we need it most this lodge gives us all hospitality."

"Fortune has been truly kind," said Julie.

After dinner they went back to the great room where the fire still blazed and Suzanne, when she had cleared everything away, joined them. She quietly took a chair next to the wall and went to work on some sewing that she had found in the lodge. But John saw that she had installed herself as a sort of guardian of them both, and she meant to watch over them as her children. Yet however often she might appear to him in her old grim guise he would always be able to see beneath it.

Now they talked but little. John saw after a while that Julie was growing sleepy, and truly a slender girl who had been through so much in one day had a right to rest. He caught Suzanne's eye and nodded. Rising, the Frenchwoman said in the tone of command which perhaps she had often used to Julie as a child:

"It's time we were off to bed, Mademoiselle. The storm will make us both sleep all the better."

"Good night, Mr. John," said Julie.

"Good night. Miss Julie."

Once more the stern face of Suzanne softened under a smile, but she and her charge marched briskly away, and left John alone before the fire. He had decided that he would not sleep upstairs, but would occupy the gunroom from which a window looked out upon the front of the house. There he made himself a bed with blankets and pillows that he brought from above and lay down amid arms.

The gunroom was certainly well stocked. It held repeating rifles and fowling-pieces, large and small, and revolvers. One big breech-loader had the weight of an elephant rifle, and there were also swords, bayonets and weapons of ancient type. But John looked longest at the big rifle. He felt that if need be he could hold the lodge against almost anything except cannon.

"It's the first time I ever had a whole armory to myself," he said, looking around proudly at the noble array.

But he was quite sure that no one could come for days except Muller, and the mystery of the forester's absence again troubled him, although not very long. Another look at the driving snow, and, wrapping himself in his blankets, he fell asleep to the music of the storm. John awoke once far in the night, and his sense of comfort, as he lay between the blankets on the sofa that he had dragged into the gunroom, was so great that he merely luxuriated there for a little while and listened to the roar of the storm, which he could yet hear, despite the thickness of the walls. But he rose at last, and went to the window.

The thick snowy blast was still driving past, and his eyes could not penetrate it more than a dozen feet. But he rejoiced. Their castle was growing stronger and stronger all the time, as nature steadily built her fortifications higher and higher around it. Mulier himself, carrying out his duties of huntsman, might have gone to some isolated point in the mountains, and would not be able to return for days. He wished no harm to Muller, but he hoped the possibility would become a fact.

He went back to his blanket and when he awoke in the morning the great Alpine storm was still raging. But he bathed and refreshed himself and found a store of clothing better than that of the forester. It did not fit him very well, nevertheless he was neatly arrayed in civilian attire and he went to the kitchen, meaning to put himself to use and cook the breakfast. But Suzanne was already there, and she saluted him with stern and rebuking words.

"I reign here," she said. "Go back and talk to Mademoiselle Julie. Since we're alone and are likely to be so, for God knows how long, it's your duty to see that she keeps up her spirits. I'd have kept you two apart if I could, but it has been willed otherwise, and maybe it's for the best."

"What has happened shows it's for the best, Suzanne. And, as you know, you've never had any real objection to me except that I'm not a Frenchman. And am I not becoming such as fast as possible?"

"You don't look very much like one, but you act like one and often you talk like one."

"Thanks, Suzanne. That's praise coming from you."

"Now be off with you. My mistress is surely in the great room, and if you care for her as much as you pretend, you will see that she is not lonely, and don't talk nonsense, either."

John, chuckling, withdrew. As Suzanne had predicted he found Julie in the large room, and she was quite composed, when she bade him good morning.

"I see that the storm goes on," she said.

"So much the better. It is raising higher the wall between us and our enemies. Our fire has burned out in the night, leaving only coals, but there is a huge store of wood in the back part of the lodge."

He brought in an armful of billets to find her fanning the coals into a blaze.

"You didn't think, sir," said she, "did you, that I mean to be a guest here, waited upon by you and Suzanne?"

"But Suzanne and I are strong and willing! Don't lean too near that blaze, Julie! You'll set your beautiful hair on fire!"

"And so you think my hair beautiful?"

"Very beautiful."

"It's not proper for you to say so. We're not in America."

"Nor are we in France, where young girls are surrounded by triple rows of brass or steel. We're in a snowstorm on top of a high mountain in Austria. There are no conventions, and Suzanne, your guardian, is in the kitchen."

"But I can call her and she'll come."

"She'd come, I know, but you won't call her. There, our fire is blazing beautifully, and we don't have to nurse it any longer. You sit here in this chair, and I'll sit there in that chair at a respectful distance. Now you realize that we are going to be here a long time, don't you Julie?"

"Miss Julie or Mademoiselle Julie would be better and perhaps Mademoiselle Lannes would be most fitting."

"No, I've said Julie several times and as it always gives me a pleasant thrill I'm sure it's best. I intend to use it continually hereafter, except when Suzanne is present."

"You're taking a high stand, Mr. John."

"John is best also."

"Well, then--John!"

"I'm taking it for your good and my pleasure."

"I wonder if Suzanne is ready with the breakfast!"

"You needn't go to see. You know it's not, and you know, too, that Suzanne will call us when it is ready. A wonderfully capable woman, that Suzanne. She didn't look upon me with favor at first, but I believe she is really beginning to like me, to view me perhaps with approval as a sort of candidate."

"Look how the snow is coming down!"

"But that's an old story. Let's go back to Suzanne."

"Oh no. She's coming for us."

It was true. The incomparable Suzanne stood in the doorway and summoned them to breakfast.

13

THE DANGEROUS FLIGHT

IT SNOWED all that day and all the next night. The lateness of the season seemed to add to the violence of the storm, as if it would make one supreme effort on these heights before yielding to the coming spring. Many of the pines were blown down, and the snow lay several feet deep everywhere. Now and then they heard thunderous sounds from the gorges telling them that great slides were taking place, and it was absolutely certain now that no one from the valley below could reach the lodge for days.

The sight from the windows of the house, when the driving snow thinned enough to permit a view, was magnificent. They saw far away peak on peak and ridge on ridge, clothed in white, and sometimes they beheld the valley filled with vast clouds of mists and vapors. Once John thought he caught a glimpse of Zillenstein, a menacing gray shadow far below, but the clouds in an instant floated between and he was not sure.

Yet it was a period of enchantment in the life of John Scott. Their very isolation on the mountain, with Suzanne there in the double rôle of servant and guardian, seemed to draw Julie and him more closely together. The world had practically melted away beneath their feet. The great war was gone for them. He was only twenty-two, but his experience had made him mentally much older, and she, too, had gained in knowledge and command of herself by all through which she had passed.

She showed to John a spirit and courage which he had never seen surpassed in any woman, and mingled with it all was a lightness and wit that filled the whole house with sunshine, despite the great storm that raged continually without. In the music-room was a piano, and she played upon it the beautiful French "little songs" that John loved. There were books and magazines in plenty, and now he read to her and then she read to him. Sometimes they sat in silence and through the thick glass of the windows watched the snow driving by.

The hours were too few for John. He served her as the crusader served his chosen lady. The spirit of the old knights of chivalry that had descended upon him still held him in a spell that he did not wish to break. Often she mocked at him and laughed at him, and then he liked her all the better. No placid, submissive woman, shrinking before the dangers, would have pleased him. In her light laughter and her banter, even at his expense, he read a noble courage and a lofty soul, and in their singular isolation it was given to him to see her spirit, so strong and yet so rarely sweet in a manner that the circumstances of ordinary life could never have brought forth. And the faithful Suzanne, still in her double rôle of servant and guardian, served and guarded them both.

John at this time began to feel a more forgiving spirit toward Auersperg. It might well be that this man of middle years, so thoroughly surrounded by old, dead things that he had never seen the world as it really was, had been bewitched. A sort of moon madness had made him commit his extraordinary deed, and John could view it with increasing tolerance because he had been bewitched himself.

He made another and more extended survey of their stores and confirmed his first opinion that the lodge was furnished in full princely style. They need not lack for any of the comforts, nor for many luxuries, no matter how long they remained.

On the morning of the third day the storm ceased and they looked out upon a white, shining world of snow, lofty and impressive, peaks and ridges outlined sharply against a steel-blue sky. John had found a pair of powerful glasses in the lodge and with them he was now able to make out Zillenstein quite clearly. Clothed in snow, a castle all in white, it was nevertheless more menacing than ever.

John believed that Muller would surely come, and many and many a time he thought over the problem how to deal with him. But the new, windless day passed and there was no sign of the forester. John himself went forth, breaking paths here and there through the snow, but he discovered nothing. He began to believe that Muller had been forced to take shelter at the start of the storm and could not now return. His hope that it was so strong that his mind turned it into a fact, and Muller disappeared from his thoughts.

The garage, besides the great automobile, contained a smaller one, but John kept the limousine in mind. He intended when the time came to escape in it with the two women, if possible. There might be a road leading down the other side of the mountain, and toward Italy. If so, he would surely try to get through when the melting of the snow permitted.

Meanwhile he devoted himself with uncommon zest to household duties. He cleared new paths about the lodge, moved in much of the wood where it would be more convenient for Suzanne, cleaned and polished the guns and revolvers in the little armory, inspected the limousine and put it in perfect order, and did everything else that he could think of to make their mountain castle luxurious and defensible.

Julie often joined him in these tasks, and John did not remonstrate, knowing that work and occupation kept a mind healthy. Wrapped in her great red cloak and wearing the smallest pair of high boots that he could find in the lodge, she often shoveled snow with him, as he increased the number of runways to the small outlying buildings, or to other parts of their domain. Thus they filled up the hours and prevented the suspense which otherwise would have been acute, despite their comfortable house.

She continually revealed herself to him now. The shell that encloses a young French girl had been broken by the hammer of war and she had stepped forth, a woman with a thinking and reasoning mind of uncommon power. It seemed often to John that the soul of the great

Lannes had descended upon this slender maid who was of his own blood. Like many another American, he had thought often of those marshals of Napoleon who had risen from obscurity to such heights, and of them all, the republican and steadfast Lannes had been his favorite. Her spirit was the same. He found in it a like simplicity and courage. They seldom talked of the war, but when they did she expressed unbounded faith in the final triumph of her nation and of those allied with it.

"I have read what the world was saying of France," she said one day when they stood together on the snowy slope. "We hear, we girls, although we are mostly behind the walls. They have told us that we were declining as a nation, and many of our own people believed it."

"The charge will never be made again against the French Republic," said John. "The French, by their patience and courage in the face of preliminary defeat and their dauntless resolution, have won the admiration of all the world."

"And many Americans are fighting for us. Tell me, John, why did you join our armies?"

"An accident first, as you know. There was that meeting with your brother at the Austrian border, and my appearance in the apparent rôle of a spy, and then my great sympathy with the French, who I thought and still think were attacked by a powerful and prepared enemy bent upon their destruction. Then I thought and still think that France and England represent democracy against absolutism, and then, although every one of these reasons is powerful enough alone, yet another has influenced me strongly."

"And what is that other, John?"

"It's intangible, Julie. It has been weighed and measured by nearly all the great philosophers, but I don't think any two of them have ever agreed about the result."

"You are a philosopher, sir, too, are you not? How do you define it?"

"I don't know that I've arrived at any conclusion."

"And yet, John, I thought that you were a man of decision."

"That's irony, Julie. But men of decision perhaps are puzzled by it more than anybody else."

"Then you can neither describe it nor give it a name?"

"It has names, several--but most of them are misleading," said John, thoughtfully.

"So you leave it to me to discover what this mysterious influence may be, or to remain forever in ignorance of it."

In her dark red cloak with tendrils of the deep golden hair showing at the edge of her hood, she seemed to John a very sprite of the snows, and the blue eyes said clearly to the gray:

"I know!"

And the gray answered back in the same language:

"I know!"

Nevertheless John would not let words betray him. He thought that the mountain and their isolation gave him an unfair advantage, and the young crusader upon whom the mantle of chivalry had descended had too knightly a soul to use it, at least in speech.

"And so, sir," she said, "you will not venture upon such an abstruse subject?"

"No, I think not. I don't believe you could call it an evasion, but perhaps it's fear."

"Fear of what, John?"

"I'm not sure about that, either. Perhaps elsewhere and under more suitable circumstances I may be able to put my thought into words, precise and understandable. It will take time, but that I shall do so some day I have no doubt."

She looked away, and then the two, the snow shovels in their hands, walked back gravely to the lodge. Suzanne stood in the doorway watching them. She knew that they were wholly oblivious of her presence, that they had not even seen her, yet the heart of the stern peasant woman was warm within her, although she felt that she now had two children instead of one under her care.

Neither was Suzanne given up wholly to the present. She spent many anxious hours thinking of the future. The deep snow could not last forever. Already there was a warmer breath in the air. When it began to melt it would go fast, and then Auersperg--if he were still at Zillenstein-- eaten up with impatience and anger because he could hear nothing from the lodge, would act, and he would show no mercy to the young man with the brown hair and the gray eyes, who was now walking by the side of her beloved Julie.

John himself took notice the next day of the signs. Spring, which already held sway in the lowlands, was creeping up the slope of the highlands. The sun was distinctly warmer and tiny rivulets of water flowed along the edges of the runways. In a few more days retainers of Auersperg or troops would come up the mountain. The prince himself might have been compelled to return to the war, but he would certainly leave orders in capable hands. John never deluded himself for a moment upon that subject. His shoveling in the snow made him quite sure now that a road led over the mountain and southward, and he had made up his mind to take the automobile and the two women and try it, as soon as the snow melted enough to permit of such an attempt. One might get through, and he had proved for himself that fortune favors the daring.

In his explorations on the southern slope he came to a deep gulch in which the tops of scrub pines showed above the snow. Following its edge for some distance his eye at length was caught by a dark shape on the rocks. He climbed slowly and painfully down to it and saw the body of a man, clothed like a German forester. His neck and many of his bones were broken, and his body was bruised frightfully.

John had no doubt that it was the missing Muller, and it was altogether likely that in the storm he had made a misstep, and had fallen into the ravine to instant death.

"What are you going to do?" asked Julie, who saw him going out, spade on shoulder.

"I've found Muller at last," he replied soberly.

"Oh! I am sorry!" she said, shuddering as she looked at the spade.

"It's all I can do for him now."

"I'm glad you thought to do as much."

When John returned he had carefully wiped all the earth from the snow shovel. The subject of Muller was never again mentioned by either of them, and while he experienced sorrow for a man whom he had never seen and who was an official enemy, he felt that a shadow was lifted from them.

The sun grew much warmer the next day, and the snow began to melt fast. The rivulets in the runways swelled rapidly. The snow sank inch by inch, and warm winds blew on the slopes. The pines were now clear and little rivers were running down every ravine and gulch. The thunder of great masses of snow, loosened by the thaw and gathering weight as they rolled down the mountain side, came to their ears. The sky was a brilliant blue, pouring down continuous warm beams, and it was obvious that it would not be long before the automobile road was clear. Then the blue eyes turned a questioning gaze upon the gray.

"Yes, I'm preparing for us to go soon," said John.

"Which way?" asked Julie.

"Toward Italy, I think."

"Is it possible for us to get through?"

"I don't know. The hardships and the dangers undoubtedly will be great."

"But one can endure them."

"You have little to fear. Prince Karl of Auersperg offers you morganatic marriage, and he thinks that he is honoring you."

"But do you, John, think that he is honoring me?"

"Although you would probably be a mere countess and not a princess, your position nevertheless would be great in most continental eyes, far grander than if you were to marry some obscure republican."

"You haven't answered me. Do you think the Prince of Auersperg would be honoring me?"

"I'm not a judge to make decisions. I'm merely stating the facts on either side."

"But suppose I should meet this simple and obscure republican and, through some singular chance, should happen to love him, would it not be better for my pride and more promising for my happiness to marry him on terms of full equality rather than to marry Prince Karl of Auersperg, a man old enough to be my father, and yet remain all my life his inferior? As we understand it in France and as you understand it in America, republicanism means equality, does it not, sir?"

"If it doesn't mean that it means nothing."

"Then, sir, being what I am, you may be sure that I shall not stay here to await Prince Karl of Auersperg, and his unsought honors."

"You are the judge, Julie, after all, and I believed it was the decision you would make. Yet, it was only fair to lay the full facts before you."

John knew that the attempt to escape southward through the mountains would be attended by great danger, not only from the Austrians, but from the risks of the road itself, when the great automobile, slipping on melting snow and ice, might go crashing at any moment into a gorge. Yet it must be done. Another day brought home the extreme necessity of it. All the mountains thundered with the sliding snow, and the prince's men would certainly come soon.

The garage contained an ample supply of gasoline and extra tires, and John saw that the machine was in perfect order. He also stored in it clothing, food for many days, two rifles and many cartridges. It was thus at once a carriage, a home and a fortress. Then he told Julie that they must start the next morning. Enough snow was gone to disclose the road leading southward, and he believed that he could drive the limousine down the mountain.

"Are you willing to trust yourself to me, Julie?" he asked.

"Through everything," she replied.

Suzanne also was eager to go, and, in her character now as a full member of the little company, she did not hesitate to say so.

"Our comfort here may cause us to linger too long, sir," she said to John, when Julie was not present. "My mistress has been twice in the hands of the Prince of Auersperg and twice through you she has escaped him. There is certain death for you if he finds you and I know not what for my mistress if she should be taken by him once more. Hardened by his years and her resistance he would seek to break her. It has seemed to me sometimes, sir, that you were sent by God to save us."

The woman's faith, which had so completely replaced her original distrust and hostility, moved John.

"Suzanne," he said, "she shall never again be in the power of that man. I don't know what the future holds for us, but I think I can promise her escape from Auersperg."

"And others will come to help us," said Suzanne, with all the intensity of a prophetess. "You left word, you have said, which way you were going, and it will reach Monsieur Philip. It will not be so hard to trace us to Zillenstein, and he will surely follow. He flies in the air like the eagle, and we will see him some day black against the sky."

The two by the same impulse looked up. But there was nothing showing in the blue vault, save feathery white clouds. Nevertheless the faith of neither was dimmed.

"I feel the certainty of it, too," said John. "Philip and the *Arrow* will answer to our call."

"And my father," said Suzanne in the same tones of unshakable faith. "He was left a prisoner in Munich, but few prisons can hold Antoine Picard. He will surely seek us through all the mountains."

John's faith was already strong, but Suzanne's made it stronger. A high nature always tries to deserve the trust it receives. Early the following morning the automobile was ready, and Julie and Suzanne, wrapped in their cloaks, took their places inside. John stood beside it, in chauffeur's garb with cap and glasses.

"It's the last look at the lodge, Julie," he said. "When the Prince of Auersperg built it he never dreamed that it would serve as a refuge for those who were escaping from him. But it hasn't been such a bad home, has it?"

"No," she replied. "It will always have a place among my pleasant memories."

"And among mine."

He sprang into his seat and grasped the wheel. The automobile began a slow and cautious descent of the mountain's southward slope. However reluctant one is to prepare for a start there is invariably a certain elation after the start is made, and John felt the uplift now. He could not yet see his way out of Austria, but he felt that he would find it. He did not even know where their present road led, except that it disappeared in a valley, filled with mists and vapors from the melting snows.

John had preserved the pass given to him by the German officer, and thinking he might be able to make use of it again, he dropped the name of John Scott once more and returned to that of Jean Castel, asking Julie and Suzanne to remember the change, whenever they should meet anyone. But it was a long before they saw a human being.

They came at last to the bottom of a narrow valley, and the strain of driving under such dangerous circumstances had been so great that John felt compelled to take a rest of a half-hour. Julie descended from the machine and walked back and forth in the road. They saw that they were in a narrow valley down which flowed a stream, much swollen by the melting snow. But the grass and foliage were heavy here and the air was warm.

"I have resolved, Julie," said John, "to say, if we are pressed closely, that you are a lady of the household of the Prince of Auersperg, accompanied by your maid, and that, wishing to get out of the war zone, I'm deputed to carry you to the port of Trieste. I can't think of anything else that seems likely to serve us better."

"We're in your hands."

"Aye, so we are, sir," said the bold Suzanne, "but we also have hands of our own and can help."

"I know it, Suzanne, and I know that you will not fail when the time comes."

Julie returned to the machine and John put his hand on the wheel again, finding it a great relief to drive on a fairly level road. Throughout the descent of the slope he had been in fear of skidding and a fatal smash. Although much snow was left on the crests and sides of the mountains, none was visible in the valley, and the great mass of green foliage was restful to the eye.

"The first inhabitant to greet us," said John.

A man driving a flock of sheep was coming toward them. He was a sturdy fellow, with a red feather in his cap, which was cocked a bit saucily on one side of his head. It was evident that he was a shepherd, whose sheep had been driven into the lowlands by the storm. John, both from prudence and natural consideration, brought his machine down to a slow pace, and spoke pleasantly to the man, who was looking at them with much curiosity.

"We're from the family of the Prince of Auersperg," said John, "and we're making our way toward the coast. The prince wishes a lady whom he esteems very highly to reach Trieste as soon as possible. Where can we find the best inn for the night?"

"The village of Tellnitz, which you should reach about dark, has a famous inn, and there is no finer landlord than Herr Leinfelder."

John thanked him, and drove on, increasing his speed, after he had passed the sheep. He looked back once, and saw the shepherd placidly driving his flock before him. He was singing, too, and the musical notes came to them, telling them very clearly that one Austrian, at least, did not suspect them.

"Our first test has been passed successfully," said John, "and I look upon it as a good omen. But don't forget that I'm Jean Castel of Lorraine, French by descent, but a devoted German subject, in the service of the Prince of Auersperg. I intend that we shall pass the night in the inn of the good Herr Leinfelder at Tellnitz, and I believe that we will go on the next day still unsuspected. I've seen no telephone wires in the valley, and doubtless there is no connection between Zillenstein and Tellnitz."

They passed more peasants, none of whom asked them any questions, but they saw no soldiers.

Toward night they beheld the usual lofty church spire, and then the huddled houses of a small village. One rather larger than the others and with a red-tiled roof John thought must be the inn of the good Herr Leinfelder, and his surmise proved to be correct.

"It's fortunate that you are blond," said John to Julie, "as most people think the French are dark. Still, both you and Suzanne look French, and I recommend that you do not take off your wraps until you go to your room, and that you also have your dinner served there. It's best for you, Mademoiselle Julie, to be seen as little as possible, and your rôle as a great lady of the semi-royal house of Auersperg permits it. Now, may I lay the injunction upon both you and Suzanne that you permit me to do all the talking?"

"I obey," said Julie, "but I'm not so sure of Suzanne."

"I never talk unless it's needful for me to speak," said Suzanne with dignity.

Many eyes watched the great limousine as it rolled into Tellnitz, and stopped before the excellent inn of Herr Johann Ignatz Leinfelder. Herr Leinfelder himself appeared upon the gravel, his round red face beaming at the sight of guests, evidently of importance, at a time when so few guests of any kind at all came. John in his rôle of chauffeur said to him with an air of importance:

"A lady of the family of Prince Karl of Auersperg, on her way to Trieste. She wishes a room, the very best room you have, to which she can retire with her maid and seek the rest she so badly needs after her long journey over bad roads."

The good Herr Leinfelder bowed low. John's manner impressed him. It was a perfect reproduction of the style affected by the flunkies of the great.

"We have a splendid chamber for the princess and a smaller one adjoining for her maid," said the host. "It's an honor to Tellnitz and to me that a lady of the house of Auersperg should stop at my inn. The prince himself, we hear, has returned to the great war."

"Ah!" said John, but there was immense satisfaction under the subdued "ah" over the important information coming to him by mere chance. He opened the door for Julie and Suzanne to alight, and still heavily muffled they were bowed into the house by Herr Leinfelder.

"I shall be on guard tonight," whispered John to Julie, as she passed. "Did you hear him say that the Prince of Auersperg had gone back to the war?"

She nodded as she disappeared into the interior of the inn, and he knew that a weight had been lifted from her heart also. The pursuit surely could not be so fierce and lasting when the one who gave it impulse was gone.

There was a small garage behind the inn, and the great automobile almost filled it, but John, clinging to his rôle of chauffeur, which was expedient in every sense, would not trust it to any of the servants of the hotel. He inspected it carefully himself, saw that everything was in proper order, and not until then did he enter the inn in search of food and fire.

"My mistress?" he asked of August, the head waiter. "Has she been properly served? His Highness, Prince Karl of Auersperg, will not forget it if a lady of his family does not receive the deference due to her."

"Dinner has just been served to the princess," said August, deferentially, as the chauffeur's tone had been peremptory. "I return in a moment myself to see that every detail is attended to properly."

"Then look to it," said John, as he slipped a five-kronen piece into his hand, "and see also that she is not disturbed afterward. Her Highness wishes a good night's rest."

August bowed low with gratitude and hurried away to do his commission. John himself, as a man who carried gold, was treated with deference, and he had an excellent dinner in a dining-room that contained but three or four other guests. Here in accordance with his plan he talked rather freely with Herr Leinfelder, and the few servants that the war had left him.

He enlarged upon the greatness of Prince Karl of Auersperg and the ancient grandeur of his Castle of Zillenstein. He referred vaguely to the young princess whom he escorted as a cousin or a niece, and spoke complacently because he had been assigned to the important duty of taking her to Trieste. There was need of haste, too. He knew his orders, and he would start in the morning at the very first breath of dawn. He was also empowered, if necessary, to fight for her safety. The rifles and pistols in the automobile were sufficient proof of it, and he had been trained to shoot by the Prince's head forester, Muller.

Herr Johann Ignatz Leinfelder was much impressed. This young chauffeur who spoke with such assurance was a fine, upstanding fellow, obviously strong and brave, the very kind of a man whom a prince like Auersperg would employ on a duty of such great importance. Hence, Herr Leinfelder bowed lower than ever, when he spoke to John.

After dinner, the waiter, August, came with word that the princess was much refreshed and bade her chauffeur come to her apartments for orders. He found her standing by a window with the watchful Suzanne hovering near, but he did not speak until the waiter withdrew and closed the door.

The paleness begat by the long weariness of the ride was gone from her face, the beautiful color flowing back in a full tide, and she stood up straight and strong. The room was lighted by two tall candles, and the glow in John's eyes was met by an answering glow in hers.

"You think it wise to spend the night here?" she asked.

"It seems to me that we should risk it. In the darkness the roads will be dangerous from the melting snows. Nor should we exhaust ourselves in the first stage of our flight. It's scarcely possible that any word from Zillenstein can reach Tellnitz tonight and tomorrow we'll be far away. What say you, Suzanne?"

"I agree, sir, with you, who are our master here," replied Suzanne with uncommon deference. "A start at dawn, and we can leave pursuit behind for the present at least."

Julie smiled a little at this proof that young Scott's conquest of her stern maid was complete.

"I'll bid Herr Leinfelder have breakfast for us at the earliest possible moment," he said, "and now, I think it would be better for you two to sleep, because tomorrow we may need all our strength. You know as well as I the dangers that lie before us."

Outside the door he was the haughty chauffeur again, the subservient servant of Auersperg, and the arrogant patron of the innkeeper and waiters. He secured a good room for himself, in which he slept until he was called by his order at the first light of dawn, and he was assured by the manner of Herr Leinfelder that no word of the fugitives had come in the night.

"Breakfast is ready for the princess," said the innkeeper, bowing.

John knocked at her door, and she came forth at once, followed by Suzanne, both fully dressed for the journey.

"No alarm has yet come to Tellnitz," whispered John, as she passed. "Remember that they think you a princess of the house of Auersperg, and that we must start in a half-hour."

He ate his own breakfast at another table, and within the appointed time the great limousine was at the door. Herr Leinfelder and his staff had no reason to change their belief that the lady of such manifest youth and beauty was a princess, as their chauffeur gave gratuities in truly royal style, and then whirled them away in a manner that was obviously ducal.

The morning was fresh and beautiful, silver as yet, since only an edge of the sun was showing over the hills, but it was fragrant with the odor of foliage and of wild flowers, blossoming in the nooks and crannies under the slopes. John felt a great surge of the spirits and he sent the machine forward at a rate that made the air rush in a swift current behind them.

"The first stage of our flight has been passed in safety," he said to Julie.

"It's an omen that we'll be as fortunate with the second."

"And with the third."

"And with all the others."

She flashed him a brilliant smile, and John felt that he could drive over any obstacle. He sent the machine forward faster than ever, and the road stretched before them, long and white.

14

T HE HAPPY ESCAPE

THEY SAID VERY LITTLE NOW. John drove on through a great happy silence. All the omens were good, and he believed that they would escape. Surely, fortune was with them when they had been able to come so far without challenge. The sun swam over the earth and threw golden beams into the valley. On their right a swift stream chattered over the stones and further away on their left rose the steep slopes, heavy with forest. They passed farmers and shepherds who had little time to take notice, as they saw the great machine but a moment, and then it was gone.

John had his mind set on escape by the way of the Adriatic. He had heard rumors that Italy might enter the war on the side of the Allies, but he knew that it had not yet taken any action and he had high hopes of finding a path to safety in that direction. Meanwhile, and whatever came of it, he must press on.

Toward noon he slackened speed, and they ate a little from the supplies they carried in the automobile. Just as they finished Suzanne held up her hand: "I think I hear another machine coming," she said.

"You are right," said John, after he had listened intently for a full minute. "It's the humming sound of tires, but it's only one automobile. Of that I'm sure, and I think it's a light one. We'll drive on at moderate speed, attending strictly to our own business."

But he loosened the revolver in his belt, and while he appeared to look straight ahead he had eye and ear also for the approaching machine, which obviously was coming at a great pace.

"It's a small automobile with only one person in it," said Julie.

"Then we have nothing to fear," said John. "But the figure of the man at the wheel looks familiar."

"Ah!" said John, drawing a deep breath. In that region a familiar face could scarcely be the face of a friend. He stiffened a little, and cast another look at the revolver in his belt to see that it was convenient to his hand. Then, to indicate that he was not running away and to prevent suspicion, he slackened the speed of the machine. As he did so the humming behind them rapidly grew louder and a light runabout drew up by their side. John uttered a cry of amazement as he saw the man at the wheel.

It was Weber, the Alsatian, in civilian clothing, his black beard trimmed nicely to a point, his eyes flashing a smile of welcome, as he took off his cap and bowed low to John and Mademoiselle Julie Lannes, but lower to Julie. John brought his machine down to a slow pace, and there was room for Weber's by their side in the road.

"You never dreamed of being overtaken by me here," said the Alsatian, smiling again, and showing his white teeth.

"No," replied John. "It never occurred to me that it was you behind us."

"After all, I am, I think, your good angel. In your flight with Mademoiselle Lannes you need advice and guidance, and I can give both."

"You do appear at the most opportune times. It has become a habit for which I am grateful."

"It's not chance that I'm here. It's pursuit and design. You know my duties as a spy, an ugly name, perhaps, but one that calls for daring and patriotism. Hearing of the council held at Zillenstein by Prince Karl of

Auersperg I went there to learn what I could of it. The information that I was able to secure is in the hands of a confederate now on his way to Paris, and I remained to probe into the mystery of Mademoiselle Lannes' disappearance."

"Then you learned of the hunting lodge on the mountain?"

"Very quickly. I discovered, too, that Mademoiselle Lannes and her maid had been taken away by a young chauffeur, coming from somewhere in Lorraine, who had been only a short time at the castle. Knowing you for what you are, Mr. Scott, and understanding your devotion, I leaped at once to the conclusion that it was you. I slipped away as soon as the snow melted sufficiently, and was the first from the outside world to reach the lodge. The absence of the limousine, the tire tracks leading toward Tellnitz and other evidence at the lodge showed without doubt that my conclusions were right."

"And you followed immediately?"

"Without delay. I reached Tellnitz, where you stopped, obtained this light machine and came on at speed. It will be my pleasure to help as much as I can you and the sister of the great Philip Lannes, the first aviator of France."

"You left France after we did, Monsieur Weber," said Julie. "Did you hear anything of Philip?"

"That he had recovered fully of his wound, Mademoiselle, and that he and the *Arrow* were once more in the service of his country. He knows of your abduction by Prince Karl of Auersperg. A friend, an aviator, Delaunois, furnished him with many facts, and I cannot doubt that he will come over Austria in the *Arrow* to seek your rescue."

The eyes of Julie, John and Suzanne, as with one impulse, turned upward. It seemed to John, for a moment or two, that his vivid imagination could fairly create the slender and graceful shape of Philip's aeroplane, outlined against the sky. But the heavens were flawless, a pure, unbroken blue, without speck or stain, and he suppressed a little sigh of disappointment.

"Do you know the country at all?" he asked of Weber.

"Somewhat. It was a part of my work before the war to pass through all the regions of Germany and Austria, and learn as much of them as I could. At the end of this valley is a small village called Obenstein, where perhaps it would be wise for us to spend the next night. After that we must devise some method of getting out of Austria--and I do not seek to conceal from you that it will be a most difficult task. Perhaps it would be better to change your plan and enter Switzerland, a neutral country. It, of course, would end your service as a soldier, but that, I take it, would be no great hardship to you now."

The color came into John's face, but he was bound to admit that Weber was right. His interest in the war had become far less than his interest in Julie Lannes.

"Perhaps we can tell better after we spend the night at Obenstein," he said.

"Nothing can be hurt by reserving our verdict until tomorrow," said Weber. "Obenstein is very secluded. I believe that it has neither telephone nor telegraph, and we'll surely be able to leave it tomorrow before any pursuit can reach us."

"Do you think the plan a good one?" said John to Julie.

"I know of no better," she replied in English. "I trust to you and Mr. Weber."

"Then it's agreed," said John to Weber.

"It's agreed."

The Alsatian now led the way in his light machine, and the limousine followed at an interval of fifty or sixty yards. One hour, then two and three passed, and nothing came in the way of their easy and rapid progress. It all seemed too smooth and fortunate to John. It was incredible that they could travel thus great distances through Austria, the land of the enemy. He knew that chance had a way of finding a balance, and violent and fierce events might be before them.

But as he drove on he scanned the heavens now and then with a questing eye. It had not occurred to him until Weber spoke that all of them might escape through the air. Lannes would trail them, not on the earth, but through mists and clouds. He would come, too, with friends almost as daring and skillful as himself, perhaps with Caumartin and the two, Castelneau and Méry, who had responded to the thrilling signal near Salzburg, when he took his first flight. His blood leaped and danced, and once more his eyes roved over the blue in search of the *Arrow*.

They came to Obenstein a little before dusk. It was a tiny village, almost hidden in a recess of the mountain, with a shaggy pine forest rising above it and casting its shadow over the houses. But there was a small, neat inn, and a garage for the machines, and the guests were received with the same hospitality that had been shown at Tellnitz. John again spread the rumor that it was a princess of the house of Auersperg who came, and he added Weber to the list of those who were attending her in her flight to a safer region. Julie withdrew as before to her room with her maid, but giving John, before she went, the brilliant smile of faith and confidence that would have sent him, sword in hand, against dragons.

He and Weber sat awhile in the little smoking-room talking in low tones of their journey. Most of the time they were alone, a waiter merely passing through now and then, and they had no fear of being overheard.

"Weber," he said, "I've learned from the innkeeper that a mountain road leads from here toward Switzerland and I feel sure already that your suggestion about our escaping into that country is good. You, of course, when you reach the border will do as you choose, as you will want to continue the dangerous work upon which you're engaged. But you may be sure that if we do get through, Mademoiselle Lannes and I will never forget the help that you have given us."

"All that I do I do gladly," said Weber. "You may not have spoken to each other but it is easy for me to tell how matters stand between Mademoiselle Lannes and you."

John was silent but his color deepened.

"You must not mind my saying these things," said Weber, speaking easily. "I'm older than you and the times are unusual. When you reach Paris you and Mademoiselle Lannes will be married."

John was still silent.

"And you will take her to America for the present, or at least Until the war is over. Ah, well! You're a happy man! Youth and the springtime! Beauty and love! Kings can procure no more and seldom as much! I think I'll walk in the air a little and have a smoke."

"And I," said John, "will go to sleep. I've a tiny room on the ground floor, but it's big enough to hold me. Good night."

"Good night, Mr. Scott."

There was only a single window in John's little room, but before undressing he opened it and stood there to breathe the cool night air for a while. It looked upon the forest that ran up the slope of the mountain, and the odor of the pines was very pleasant. Looking idly at the trunks and the foliage he saw a shadow pass into the depths of the forest and something, a pulse in his temple, perhaps, struck a warning note.

A shiver ran down his back and his hair lifted, as if touched with electric sparks. Acting at once under impulse he touched the pistol inside the pocket of his jacket to see that it was all right, and slipped out of the room.

He had marked the point at which the shadow disappeared in the forest and he followed it on light foot. He had been awakened as if a stroke of lightning had blazed suddenly before his eyes, and now his brain was seething with fierce thoughts, called up by a long chain of incidents, all at once made complete.

His hand slipped again to the revolver and he drew it forth, holding it ready for instant use. Then he went forward swiftly again on noiseless steps, and once more he caught a glimpse of the flitting shadow straight ahead. He increased his speed and the shadow resolved itself into the figure of a man, a figure that seemed familiar to him.

Two or three times the man stopped and looked back, but John had shrunk behind a tree and no pursuit was visible. Then he resumed his rapid flight up the steep slope, and young Scott persistently followed, never once losing sight of the active figure.

The way led to the crest of the mountain which hung about two thousand feet above the village and it was a climb requiring some time and endurance, but though John's pulse beat fast it was with excitement and not with exhaustion. At the summit he saw the figure emerge upon an open space upon which stood a slender round tower of considerable height.

John stopped at the edge of the pines and saw the figure disappear within the tower, upon the summit of which something presently began to flash and crackle. He caught his breath and the blood leaped fiercely through his veins. He knew that the tower was a wireless signal station and that it was talking to another somewhere. It sent, too, as he well knew, through the velvety blue of the night the message that Mademoiselle Julie Lannes, Suzanne, her maid, and John Scott, the American, were in the village of Obenstein where they could be taken.

He cursed himself for a fool, thrice a fool! Why had he not understood long before? Why had he not seen that so many coincidences could not be the result of chance? Only design and skill could have brought them about! Who had disabled the automobile in that flight with Carstairs and Wharton from the Germans? Who had sought to delay Lannes until he could be caught by the enemy? Who was the mysterious man in the aeroplane who had wounded Philip, who had led John from the château under the very rifles of the waiting marksmen, and who had been responsible for Julie's capture at Chastel? That letter, purporting to be from Philip, and directing her to come to Chastel, was surely a forgery!

These and all the other details crashed upon him with cumulative force, and he was so mad with fury that he thought his heart would burst with the surging blood. Why had the man worked with such energy and such cruel persistence against him? But his wonder quickly passed, because the reason did not matter now. Instead he put his finger on the trigger of the automatic and waited.

The wireless flashed and crackled for five minutes, then five minutes of silence and the figure of Weber reappeared at the base of the tower. He lingered there for a little space looking warily about him, before he began the descent of the mountain, and John quietly withdrew further into the pines. Weber presently crossed the open space, entering the forest, and John, noiseless, retreated before him.

Thus they proceeded down the mountain until the wireless tower was left several hundred yards behind and they were buried deep in the pine forest. Then John stepped suddenly into the road not twenty yards before the Alsatian and leveling his automatic said sharply:

"Hands up, Weber!"

Weber started violently and slowly raised his hands. But he said with composure:

"Why this sudden violence, Mr. Scott?"

"Because you have been upon the wireless tower signaling to our enemies. I've just understood everything, Weber. You're a German and not a French spy, and you've played the traitor to Julie and Philip Lannes and me all along."

There was enough moonlight for John to see that Weber's face was distorted by an evil smile.

"You've been a trifle slow in discovering just what I am," he said, calmly. "I've wondered that a young man of your perception didn't find me out earlier."

John flushed. The Alsatian's effrontery, in truth, had been amazing and in that perhaps lay his success--so far.

"It's true," he said, "I should have suspected you sooner, but it did not occur to me that human nature could be so vile. To undertake such risks and to use so much trickery and guile there must be a powerful motive, and in your case I can't guess it. Now, Weber, why did you do it?"

"Let me drop my hands, Mr. Scott, and I'll answer you," said Weber. "It's difficult to argue a case in such a strained and awkward position."

"Put them down, then, but remember that I'm watching you, and that I'm willing to shoot. Now, go ahead. Why have you been such a persistent enemy of Mademoiselle Lannes, her brother and myself? Why have you been such a triple traitor?"

"Don't call me a traitor, because a traitor I am not. On the contrary I am loyal with a loyalty of which you, John Scott, an American, know nothing. I've called myself an Alsatian, but really I am not. I am an Austrian. I was born on the Zillenstein estate of Prince Karl of Auersperg. My family has served his for a thousand years. Great as I hold Hapsburg and Hohenzollern, Auersperg means even more to me. The Auerspergs are the very essence and spirit of that aristocracy and rule of the very highborn, in which I believe and to which your country and later the French have stood in the exact opposite. Every time that my pulse beats within me it beats with the wish that you and all that you stand for should fail."

John did not feel the slightest doubt of Weber's sincerity. The increasing moonlight, falling in a silver flood across his face, showed too clearly his earnestness. Yet that earnestness was not good to look upon. It was sinister, tinged strongly with the beliefs of an old and wicked past. He too, like his master, was of the Middle Ages.

"And so in all these deeds you were serving Prince Karl of Auersperg?" said John.

"To the death. It was a false escape that I planned for you at the château. You were to have been shot down, but by an unlucky chance you escaped in the water."

"I've surmised that already."

"I'm an aviator, not so great as your friend Lannes, but no mean one nevertheless. It was I who pursued him, when you were with him in the *Arrow* near Paris, and wounded him."

"I've surmised that, too."

"And when Prince Karl coveted Mademoiselle Julie Lannes--and I do not blame him--I was of the most help to him in that matter so near to his heart. Do you understand that it was a great honor he offered Mademoiselle Lannes, to make her his morganatic wife? He need not have offered her so much."

The great pulse in John's throat beat heavily and his hand pressed the automatic, but he compressed his lips and said nothing.

"I see that my words anger you," continued Weber, "but from my point of view I am right. I serve my overlord!"

"What message were you sending by the wireless from the tower?"

"Doubtless you have guessed it. I was sending word to the detachment now on the road from Zillenstein to come here for Mademoiselle Lannes, her maid and you. They're ahorse, and they should arrive in three hours and you can't possibly escape. Before Prince Karl was compelled to leave for the theater of war he put this most important affair in my charge. He has not yet yielded all hope of Mademoiselle Lannes."

"It may be true that we can't escape, but what of yourself, Weber? We're alone in the forest and I hold the whip hand. The score that I owe you is large. You may have wrecked the life of Mademoiselle Julie and perhaps you will destroy my own, but you said it would be three hours before the detachment arrived, and I need only a few seconds."

"But I don't think you'll fire, Mr. Scott."

"Why, Weber?"

"Because I fire first!"

Absorbed in the talk John had unconsciously lowered the automatic, and, as agile as a panther, Weber suddenly leaped to one side, snatched a revolver from his own pocket and pulled the trigger. But the bullet flew wild. A huge shadow hovered over him and a weight crashed upon his head, smiting him down as if he had been struck by a giant shell. He sank in the path and lay motionless, dead ere he fell.

John stared, stricken with horror. The great shadow bent down a moment over the fallen man, then straightened itself up again, and two eyes in which the vengeful fire had not yet died gazed at John. Then as his dazed mind cleared he saw and knew. It was Antoine Picard, the gigantic and faithful servitor of the Lannes family.

"Antoine! Antoine!" cried John. "How did you come here? I thought you were in Munich!"

"It seems, your honor, that I'm here at the right moment. His bullet would certainly have found your heart had not my club descended upon his head at the very instant that his finger touched the trigger. He'll never stir again."

"But Antoine, it's you, yourself! It doesn't seem real that you should be here at such a time!"

"It's none other than Antoine Picard, your honor, and he never struck a truer or more timely blow. They were to hold me a prisoner in Munich, but I escaped. I did not return to France. I could never desert Mademoiselle Julie, and I followed. My size drew their attention, but in one way or another I kept down suspicion or escaped them. I traced Mademoiselle Julie and my daughter to the great castle and then to the lodge on the mountain. I saw the traitor who lies so justly dead here talking with German troops, and I knew that there was need for me to hasten. In the night I stole the horse of a Uhlan and galloped to Obenstein.

"I approached the inn just in time to see the traitor come forth, and knowing that he was bent upon some devil's work I followed him to the signal tower. I did not see you until he started back and then I bided my time. I was in the bush not ten feet from him while you talked."

"Lucky for your mistress and lucky for us all that you were, Picard!"

"We must leave Obenstein, your honor, at once!"

"Of course, Picard. We must take flight in the machine."

"As it would be hard to explain my presence, your honor, suppose I wait down the road for you. I've already turned the horse loose in the forest. First I'll move this from the path lest someone see it and give the alarm too soon."

He lifted the body of Weber and hid it among the bushes. Then they separated, John returning quickly to the inn. He saw a light in Julie's window and inferring that she had not yet retired he went hastily to her room and knocked on the door.

"Who's there?" came the brave voice of his beloved.

"It's John!" he replied, guardedly. "Open at once, Julie! We're in great danger and must act quickly!"

He heard the bolt shoot back, the door was opened, and Julie stood before him, pale but erect and courageous. Behind her, as usual, hovered the protecting shadow of Suzanne. John stepped inside and closed the door.

"Julie," he said, in a whisper, sharp with anxiety, "we must leave Obenstein in fifteen minutes! Weber is a traitor in the service of Prince Karl of Auersperg! He followed us to get you back to him! He has been signaling from a wireless station on the mountain! A detachment of hussars will be here in three hours!"

Her pallor deepened, but the courage that he loved still glowed in her eyes.

"But Weber?" she said. "He will stop our flight?"

"He will never harm us more, Julie. He is dead."

"You--"

"No, Julie, I did not kill him. It was a stronger arm than mine that struck the blow. Suzanne, your father is waiting for us in the forest. He has followed us all the way from Munich to Zillenstein, to the lodge, and here to Obenstein. It was he who sent Weber to the doom that he deserved."

"Ah!" said Suzanne, and John saw her stern eyes shining. She was the worthy daughter of her father.

"Put on your cloaks and hoods at once," said John, "and I'll have the automobile out in a few minutes! It doesn't matter what they think at the inn. We disregard it and fly."

Suzanne, quick and capable, began to prepare her mistress and John went down to the innkeeper. He was so swift and emphatic that the worthy Austrian was dazed, and, after all a princess of the house of

Auersperg had a right to her whims. It was not for him to question the minds of the great, and the heavy gold piece that John dropped into his hands was potent to allay undue curiosity.

The automobile properly equipped was before the main door of the inn within ten minutes. John helped into it the hooded and cloaked figure of the great lady, and her maid, also hooded and cloaked, followed. Then he sprang into his own seat, turned the wheel, and the huge machine shot down the road. But at the first curve it slackened speed, then stopped for an instant beside a dark figure, and when it went on again four instead of three rode.

Picard sat beside his daughter and in those two faithful hearts was no doubt of their escape.

"Antoine," said Julie, "I know that we owe our lives to you."

She offered him a small gloved hand. It rested in his giant grasp a moment, then he raised it to his lips and kissed it.

"I'd have followed you across the world, my lady," he said.

"I know it, Antoine."

John, watching intently, sent the machine forward at fair speed. The road again stretched before him lone and white in the moonlight, which fell in a heavy silver shower. He did not know where they were going, but there was the road, and the hussars could not ride hard enough to overtake them. Now and then he stole a glance at Julie, and the same indomitable courage was always shining in her eyes. She was not weary and she was as wide awake as he. By and by both Antoine and Suzanne slept, sitting upright, but Julie, wrapped almost to the eyes in cloak and hood, was still quiet, watching everything with wide fearless eyes. John brought the machine down to a slow pace and guided it for the moment with one hand.

"Julie," he said softly, "I don't know where we're going, but I know that we'll escape, and knowing it I now have something to ask you."

"What is it, John?"

"When we reach Paris, you'll marry me, Julie?"

"Yes, John, I'll marry you."

The other hand came from the wheel and as he leaned back, they kissed in the moonlight. The great machine ran on, unguided but true.

They kissed again in the moonlight, and for a splendid moment or two her arms were about his neck.

"Julie," whispered John, "will your mother consent?"

"Yes, when I tell her to do so."

"And Philip?"

"Yes, without telling."

The automobile, still unguided, ran on straight and true as if it were alive, and knew that it carried the precious freight of two young and faithful hearts, and that nothing else in all the world was so tender and true as young love.

Far in the night, when the road had climbed up the hills, John saw a light flashing and winking in the valley, and from a more distant point another light winked and flashed in reply. He read the fiery signals and he knew that the alarm was abroad. The hussars had come to Obenstein, only to find that the birds had flown, and doubtless, too, to find among the bushes the dead body of Weber, Prince Karl's most trusted and unscrupulous agent. Julie had gone to sleep at last and Antoine and Suzanne slumbered on.

He alone watched and worked, and for a few moments he felt a chill of dread. The hussars would spread the alarm and the whole country would now be seeking them. He saw a road turning from the main one, and leading deeper into the mountains. Instinctively he followed it, like an animal seeking hiding in the wilderness, and now the machine rose fast on the slopes, dense forest lining the way on either side. Far below in the valley the lights and the wireless signals talked incessantly to one another and the hounds were hot on the chase.

It was about halfway between midnight and morning when John stopped the machine among dense pines on the very crest of a mountain, where the road, without any reason, seemed to end. Antoine awoke with a start and, springing out, began to curse himself under his breath for having gone to sleep.

"Take no blame, Antoine," said John. "You could have done nothing then, and it was much better for you to have slept. You now have back all your strength and we may need it."

Julie awoke with a start and after a moment or two of bewilderment understood. Then she gave John that old brilliant, flashing look, softened now by the memory of a kiss when no hand was at the wheel.

"Julie," said John, trusting as ever in her courage, "we seem to have come to the end of things. Our enemies are in the valley following us, and it's not hard to trace the path of our automobile. I don't know how many will come, but Antoine and I can make a stand with the rifles."

"All hope is not yet lost!" said Suzanne, in a voice as deep as that of a man. "Remember that when the earth cannot hide us the air may open to receive us. Remember, too, Mademoiselle Julie, that your brother seeks you, and when the time comes we are to look aloft."

Driven again by that extraordinary impulse, John and Julie gazed up. But they saw only the dancing stars in the blue velvet of the sky.

"He may come! He may come in time!" said Suzanne, speaking like an inspired prophet of old, and her manner carried conviction. John, clinging to the last desperate hope, recalled how Lannes and he had summoned Castelneau and Méry from the sky to save them, and though it was a wild hope he resolved to send up the same signal.

It was a quick task to gather dry wood and build a little heap, Julie and Suzanne helping with energy and enthusiasm. There were plenty of matches in the car, and presently John lighted the heap, which crackled and sent up leaping tongues of flame.

"It may serve also as a signal to those who follow us," he said, "but we must take the chance. Cavalry can't reach us except by the road that we came and with our rifles we can hold it a long time."

The mention of the word "rifle," put a thought in the head of Antoine Picard, in whose veins the blood of Vikings flowed, and who that night was a veritable Viking of the land. Leaving John and the two women to feed the signal fire, he secured one of the powerful breech-loading rifles from the automobile, and quietly stole down the path.

Antoine, although he held a modern weapon in his hand, had shed centuries of civilization. As still as death as he trod lightly in the dark road, he was, nevertheless, consumed with the wild Berserk rage against those who followed him. He knew that hussars would soon appear on the slope, but he intended that a lion should be in their path and he stroked lovingly the barrel of the powerful breech-loader. Behind him the flames were shooting higher and higher, pouring red streaks against the velvet blue of the sky. But all of Picard's attention was concentrated now on what lay before him.

He heard soon the distant beat of hoofs and he drew a little to the side of the road, down which he could see a long distance, as it stretched straight before him, narrow and steep. He made out clearly a half dozen figures, hussars struggling forward on tired horses, and he chuckled a little to himself. It was a splendid weapon that he held in his hand, and he was a great marksman. Armed as he was, he felt that he had little to fear on that lone mountain road from six or seven horsemen.

He pushed the rifle forward a little and waited in the shadow of the pines. The hoofbeats rang louder, and the shadows became the distinct figures of horses and men. Picard uttered a deep "Ah!" because he recognized the one who led them, a powerful, erect man, the Prussian Rudolf von Boehlen, now in the very center of the moonlight.

When they were yet two hundred yards away, Picard stepped into the middle of the road and called to them in a loud voice to halt. He saw von Boehlen throw up his head, say something to his troop, and then try to urge his horse to a faster gait.

Picard sighed. He knew that von Boehlen was a brave man and he respected brave men. A disagreeable task lay before him, one that must be done, but he would give him another chance. He called again and louder than before for them to halt, but von Boehlen came on steadily. Then Picard promptly raised his rifle and shot him through the heart.

When von Boehlen fell dead in the road his hussars halted and while they were hesitating Picard shot the horses of two under them, while a third received a bullet in the shoulder. Then all of them fled on horse or on foot into the valley while Picard went calmly back to the fire which was now sending its signal across the whole heavens. He told John in a whisper of what had befallen, and soon he returned to his place in the road to watch.

John and Julie by and by left Suzanne to feed the fire and they stood hand in hand gazing now at the heavens and now at the dark pine forests. The velvet blue of the sky faded into the dark hour and then the dawn came, edged with silver, turning to pink and then to gold, like a robe of many colors, drawn slowly out of the infinite. Suzanne suddenly uttered a great cry.

"Look up! Look up, my children!" she cried.

Coming out of the west which was yet in dusk was a black dot and then three others behind it in Indian file.

"We're saved," cried Suzanne. "It's Monsieur Philip and his friends'"

"How do you know? You can't see yet," said John, almost afraid to hope.

"I don't need to see it! I feel it, and I know!" replied Suzanne. "Look, how they come!"

John trembled and the hand of Julie in his own trembled too, but it was not fear, it was the feeling that a miracle, a miracle to save them, was coming to pass.

The four black dots moved on out of the west and John knew that they were aeroplanes coming swiftly and directly toward their mountain. The dawn reaching the zenith spread also to the west and the flying machines were outlined clearly in the luminous golden haze. Then John, too, uttered a great cry.

He knew the slender sinuous shape that led. As far as eye could reach he would recognize the *Arrow*. The miracle was done. They had called to Philip in their desperate need and he had come.

"Philip and the *Arrow*!" he exclaimed. "We're saved!"

"I knew that he would come!" Julie said, as she stared wide-eyed into the blue and gold of the heavens.

Now the aeroplanes flew at almost incredible speed, the *Arrow* always at their head, poised for a few moments directly over their heads, and then came down in a dazzling series of spirals, landing almost at their feet.

"Philip, my brother!" exclaimed Julie, as the slender compact figure that they knew so well stepped gracefully from the *Arrow*.

He took off his heavy glasses and gazed at them as they stood, forgetting that they were still hand in hand. Then he smiled and lifting his cap in his old dramatic way he said:

"It seems that for several reasons I didn't come too soon."

"No," replied John, calmly, and holding firmly the little hand in his, "you have arrived just in time to give your consent to my marriage with your sister."

"And what does Mademoiselle Julie Lannes say?"

The rising sun clothed Julie in a shower of gold. Never before had the wonderful golden hair seemed more wonderful. Never before had she seemed to the youthful eyes of her lover more nearly divine.

"Julie Lannes says," she replied bravely, "that if John Scott wishes her to be his wife and her mother and brother consent she will gladly marry him."

[Illustration: "Now the aeroplanes flew at almost incredible speed, the *Arrow* always at their head"]

"Then we must hurry away, or it will be a wedding; without either a bride or a bridegroom. Are not those Austrian hussars at the bottom of the slope, Picard?"

"Yes, monsieur."

"Then it's up and away with us. Here are Caumartin, Méry and Castelneau, old friends of yours, John, but it was Delaunois who brought me the last news of you. Caumartin has the *Omnibus*, and in it the bridal pair must travel. I can't take you with me in the *Arrow* now, John, as it admits of only a single passenger. But do you, Picard, take the rifles and come with me. We'll cover the rear of our flight. Now, hasten! Hasten!"

John and Julie in an instant were side by side in the *Omnibus*, Picard, forgetting all fear of aeroplanes, was with Philip, and the four machines rose, circling above the mountain, Caumartin's big plane leading. John and Julie sat very close together and her hand was again in his.

"Fear not, dearest," he said. "When all seemed lost Philip came for us."

"But you came for me first and you risked your life many times. To give myself to you seems but a small reward for all that you've done."

"It's a reward that kings and princes in their power cannot win."

Then they fell silent, their emotion too deep for speech. Philip had spoken in jest, but it was almost like a wedding trip. The hussars below had reached the abandoned automobile, and fired vain shots at the disappearing aeroplanes, but John and Julie heeded them not. War and brute passions were left behind, and they were sailing through the calm blue ether.

Caumartin, the stalwart, was wholly absorbed in steering his great machine and they sat behind him, very close together, still hand in hand, watching the great panorama of the heavens, unrolled before them. It was the most beautiful sky that they had ever seen, dyed that day into intensely vivid colors by the master hand. Far away were great pink terraces of color, changing to blue or gold or silver, while below them revolved the earth, clad in deepest green, save where far peaks were crested with snow.

Both John and Julie breathed an infinite peace. The war sank farther and farther away, as they sailed on through peaceful heavens, surcharged with infinite color. Both felt, with the certainty of truth, that their troubles and dangers were over, and they now left the journey and its needs to Philip and his able comrades.

"After we're married, Julie, you'll go to America with me for awhile," said John, "but we'll come back to France. We shall divide our time between two homes, your country and mine, now the countries of both."

The hand within his own returned his pressure. Caumartin turned his machine toward the north, avoiding neutral Switzerland, and sailing at great speed they passed beyond the German lines and over the fair land of France that all of them loved so well.

Caumartin kept his place in front. Suzanne was in the machine just behind and Philip and Picard in the *Arrow* always hovered in the rear. That night they descended within the French lines, and John heard the next day that Prince Karl of Auersperg had been killed in battle. It was singular, perhaps, but John felt a touch of pity for him. He had wanted something very greatly and, powerful prince though he was, his power had not been great enough to win it for him.

THEY WERE MARRIED in Notre Dame by the Archbishop of Paris. The influence of John's uncle, the senator and great mining millionaire, was sufficient to procure John's release from the army. In truth, General Vaugirard, although he was fat and sixty, had a strong vein of sentiment, and he was one of the most distinguished guests in Notre Dame, where he puffed mightily and kept himself with great difficulty from whistling his approval. He and Senator Pomeroy stood together and he nodded emphatically when the senator told him, with a certain pride in his whisper, that while John, his sole heir, was not a prince, he could buy and sell many who were.

General Vaugirard was not the only distinguished officer at the marriage. There was a lull in the operations and all of John's friends came to Paris to see him wed the beautiful Julie Lannes. A little man, with the brow of a Napoleon, the famous general, Bougainville, whose rise had been so astonishing, stood beside General Vaugirard.

Daniel Colton, now a colonel, his arm in a sling, was not far away. Carstairs was there, a bandage about his head, and Wharton was with him, his shoulder yet sore from the path that a bullet had made through it. It was decreed that while these friends of John's should receive many wounds, all of them were to survive the great war.

They were to spend three days at the little house beyond the Seine before sailing, and as the twilight came on they sat together and looked out over the City of Light, melting into the dusk after a golden day. The subdued hum of Paris came to them in a note of infinite sweetness and peace.

John was stirred to the depths, but his emotion, like that of most deep natures, was quiet. He felt Julie's hand tremble a little in his own, as the voice of Paris grew fainter but sweeter. The twilight faded into the night and the buildings grew misty.

"We have passed through many dangers, Julie," said John, "but for me at least the reward is greater than them all. When did you begin to love me?"

"You were my gallant knight from the first, but, if it had not been so, how could I have kept from loving the fearless crusader who dared all and who risked his life every day in the country of the enemy to save me?"

"I'd have been a poor and worthless creature if I hadn't done so, Julie."

"Few men have done so, though, even for love."

Stirred by an emotion deeper than ever, and wholly pure, he put his arms around her, and their lips met in a long kiss of young love.

The first dusk thinned away, the sky turned to a vault of burnished silver, and, the infinite stars coming out, danced their approval.

THE END

Printed in Great Britain
by Amazon